WITHOUT REMORSE

ALSO BY TOM CLANCY

WITHOUT REMORSE

Tom Clancy

HarperCollins*Publishers*

This is a work of fiction. The events described here are imaginary:
the settings and characters are fictitious and not intended to represent
specific places or living persons.

HarperCollins*Publishers*
77-85 Fulham Palace Road,
Hammersmith, London W6 8JB

Published by HarperCollins*Publishers* 1993
1 3 5 7 9 8 6 4 2

A catalogue record for this book
is available from the British Library

ISBN 0 00 224205 2

Printed in Australia by
Griffin Paperbacks, South Australia

It never happens without help:
Bill, Darrell, and Pat, for "professional" advice;
C.J., Craig, Curt, Gerry, and Steve, for more of the same;
Russell for unexpected expertise

And for some *ex post facto* help of the highest magnitude:
G.R. and Wayne, for finding it;
Shelly, for doing the work;
Craig, Curt, Gerry, Steve P., Steve R.,
and Victor, for helping me to understand:

Think where man's glory most begins and ends.
And say my glory was I had such friends.
—William Butler Yeats

And if I go,
while you're still here . . .
Know that I live on,
vibrating to a different measure
—behind a veil you cannot see through.
You will not see me,
so you must have faith.
I wait for the time when we can soar together again
—both aware of each other.
Until then, live your life to its fullest and when you need me,
Just whisper my name in your heart
. . . I will be there.

he is

in loving memory of Kyle Haydock,
July 5, 1983–August 1, 1991

Arma virumque cano
—*Publius Vergilius Maro*

Beware the fury of a patient man
—*John Dryden*

Meeting Places

NOVEMBER

Camille had either been the world's most powerful hurricane or the largest tornado in history. Certainly it had done the job to this oil rig, Kelly thought, donning his tanks for his last dive into the Gulf. The superstructure was wrecked, and all four of the massive legs weakened—twisted like the ruined toy of a gigantic child. Everything that could safely be removed had already been torched off and lowered by crane onto the barge they were using as their dive base. What remained was a skeletal platform which would soon make a fine home for local game fish, he thought, entering the launch that would take him alongside. Two other divers would be working with him, but Kelly was in charge. They went over procedures on the way over while a safety boat circled nervously to keep the local fishermen away. It was foolish of them to be here—the fishing wouldn't be very good for the next few hours—but events like this attracted the curious. And it would be quite a show, Kelly thought with a grin as he rolled backwards off the dive boat.

It was eerie underneath. It always was, but comfortable, too. The sunlight wavered under the rippled surface, making variable curtains of light that trained across the legs of the platform. It also made for good visibility. The C4 charges were already in place, each one a block about six inches square and three inches deep, wired tight against the steel and fused to blow inward. Kelly took his time, checking each one, starting with the first rank ten feet above the bottom. He did it quickly because he didn't want to be down here that long, and neither did the others. The men behind him ran the prima-cord, wrapping it tight around the blocks. Both were local, experienced UDT men, trained almost as well as Kelly. He checked their work, and they checked his, for caution and thoroughness was the mark of such men. They finished the lower level in twenty minutes, and came up slowly to the upper rank, just ten feet below the surface, where the process was repeated, slowly and carefully. When you dealt with explosives, you didn't rush and you didn't take chances.

Colonel Robin Zacharias concentrated on the task at hand. There was an SA-2 site just over the next ridge. Already it had volleyed off three missiles, searching for the fighter-bombers he was here to protect. In the back seat of his F-105G Thunderchief was Jack Tait, his "bear," a lieutenant colonel and an expert in the field of defense-suppression. The two men had helped invent the doctrine which they were now implementing. He drove the Wild Weasel fighter, showing himself, trying to draw a shot, then ducking under it, closing in on the rocket site. It was a deadly, vicious game, not of hunter and prey, but of hunter and hunter—one small, swift, and delicate, and the other massive, fixed, and fortified. This site had given fits to the men of his wing. The commander was just too good with his radar, knowing when to switch it on and when to switch it off. Whoever the little bastard was, he'd killed two Weasels under Robin's command in the previous week, and so the colonel had drawn the mission for himself as soon as the frag order had gone up to hit this area again. It was his specialty: diagnosing, penetrating, and destroying air defenses—a vast, rapid, three-dimensional game in which the prize of winning was survival.

He was roaring low, never higher than five hundred feet, his fingers controlling the stick semiautomatically while Zacharias's eyes watched the karsk hilltops and his ears listened to the talk from the back seat.

"He's at our nine, Robin," Jack told him. "Still sweeping, but he doesn't have us. Spiraling in nicely."

We're not going to give him a Shrike, Zacharias thought. *They tried that the last time and he spoofed it somehow.* That error had cost him a major, a captain, and an aircraft . . . a fellow native of Salt Lake City, Al Wallace . . . friends for years. . . . damn it! he shook the thought off, not even reproving himself for the lower-case profanity.

"Giving him another taste," Zacharias said, pulling back on the stick. The Thud leaped upwards into the radar coverage of the site, hovering there, waiting. This site commander was probably Russian-trained. They weren't sure how many aircraft the man had killed—only that it had been more than enough—but he had to be a proud one because of it, and pride was deadly in this business.

"Launch . . . two, two valid launches, Robin," Tait warned from the back.

"Only two?" the pilot asked.

"Maybe he has to pay for them," Tait suggested coolly. "I have them at nine. Time to do some pilot magic, Rob."

"Like this?" Zacharias rolled left to keep them in view, pulling into them, and split-S-ing back down. He'd planned it well, ducking behind a ridge. He pulled out at a dangerous low altitude, but the SA-2 Guideline missiles went wild and dumb four thousand feet over his head.

"I think it's time," Tait said.

"I think you're right." Zacharias turned hard left, arming his cluster munitions. The F-105 skimmed over the ridge, dropping back down again while his eyes checked the next ridge, six miles and fifty seconds away.

"His radar is still up," Tait reported. "He knows we're coming."

"But he's only got one left." *Unless his reload crews are really hot today. Well, you can't allow for everything.*

"Some light flak at ten o'clock." It was too far to be a matter of concern, though it did tell him which way out not to take. "There's the plateau."

Maybe they could see him, maybe not. Possibly he was just one moving blip amid a screen full of clutter that some radar operator was striving to understand. The Thud moved faster at low level than anything ever made, and the camouflage motif on the upper surfaces was effective. They were probably looking up. There was a wall of jamming there now, part of the plan he'd laid out for the other Weasel bird, and normal American tactics were for a medium-altitude approach and steep dive. But they'd done that twice and failed, and so Zacharias decided to change the technique. Low level, he'd Rockeye the place, then the other Weasel would finish things off. His job was killing the command van and the commander within. He jinked the Thud left and right, up and down, to deny a good shooting track to anybody on the ground. You still had to worry about guns, too.

"Got the star!" Robin said. The SA-6 manual, written in Russian, called for six launchers around a central control point. With all the connective paths, the typical Guideline site looked just like a Star of David, which seemed rather blasphemous to the Colonel, but the thought only hovered at the edge of his mind as he centered the command van on his bombsight pipper.

"Selecting Rockeye," he said aloud, confirming the action to himself. For the last ten seconds, he held the aircraft rock steady. "Looking good . . . release . . . now!"

Four of the decidedly un-aerodynamic canisters fell free of the fighter's ejector racks, splitting open in midair, scattering thousands of submunitions over the area. He was well beyond the site before the bomblets landed. He didn't see people running for slit trenches, but he stayed low, reefing the Thud into a tight left turn, looking up to make sure he'd gotten the place once and for all. From three miles out his eyes caught an immense cloud of smoke in the center of the Star.

That's for Al, he allowed himself to think. No victory roll, just a thought, as he leveled out and picked a likely spot to egress the area. The strike force could come in now, and that SAM battery was out of business. Okay. He selected a notch in the ridge, racing for it just under Mach-1, straight and level now that the threat was behind him. *Home for Christmas.*

The red tracers that erupted from the small pass startled him. That wasn't supposed to be there. No deflection on them, just coming right in. He jinked up, as the gunner had thought he would, and the body of the aircraft passed right through the stream of fire. It shook violently and in the passage of a second good changed to evil.

"Robin!" a voice gasped over the intercom, but the main noise was from wailing alarms, and Zacharias knew in a fatal instant that his aircraft was doomed. It got worse almost before he could react. The engine died in flames, and then the Thud started a roll-yaw that told him the controls were gone. His reaction was automatic, a shout for ejection, but another gasp from the back made him turn just as he yanked the handles even though he knew the gesture was useless. His last sight of Jack Tait was blood that hung below the seat like a vapor trail, but by then his own back was wrenched with more pain than he'd ever known.

"Okay," Kelly said and fired off a flare. Another boat started tossing small explosive charges into the water to drive the fish away from the area. He watched and waited for five minutes, then looked at the safety man.

"Area's clear."

"Fire in the hole," Kelly said, repeating the mantra three times more. Then he twisted the handle on the detonator. The results were gratifying. The water around the legs turned to foam as the rig's legs were chopped off bottom and top. The fall was surprisingly slow. The entire structure slid off in one direction. There was an immense splash as the platform hit, and for one incongruous moment it appeared as though steel might float. But it couldn't. The see-through collection of light I-beams sank below sight, to rest right on the bottom, and another job was done.

Kelly disconnected the wires from the generator and tossed them over the side.

"Two weeks early. I guess you really wanted that bonus," the executive said. A former Navy fighter pilot, he admired a job well and quickly done. The oil wasn't going anywhere, after all. "Dutch was right about you."

"The Admiral is a good guy. He's done a lot for Tish and me."

"Well, we flew together for two years. Bad-ass fighter jock. Good to know those nice things he said were true." The executive liked working with people who'd had experiences like his own. He'd forgotten the terror of combat somehow. "What's with that? I've been meaning to ask." He pointed to the tattoo on Kelly's arm, a red seal, sitting up on his hind flippers and grinning impudently.

"Something we all did in my unit," Kelly explained as offhandedly as he could.

"What unit was that?"

"Can't say." Kelly added a grin to mute the refusal.

"I bet it's something to do with how Sonny got out—but okay." A former naval officer had to respect the rules. "Well, the check'll be in your account by the end of the business day, Mr. Kelly. I'll radio in so your wife can pick you up."

Tish Kelly was glowing her me-too look at the women in The Stork Shop. Not even three months yet, she could wear anything she wanted—well, almost. Too soon to shop for anything special, but she had the free time and wanted to see what the options were. She thanked the clerk, deciding that she'd bring John here in the evening and help him pick something out for her because he liked doing that. Now it was time to pick him up. The Plymouth wagon they'd driven down from Maryland was parked right outside, and she'd learned to navigate the streets of the coastal town. It was a nice break from the cold autumn rain of their home, to be here on the Gulf Coast where the summer was never really gone for more than a few days. She brought the wagon onto the street, heading south for the oil company's huge support yard. Even the traffic lights were in her favor. One changed to green in such a timely fashion that her foot didn't even have to touch the brakes.

The truck driver frowned as the light changed to amber. He was late, and running a little too fast, but the end of his six-hundred-mile run from Oklahoma was in sight. He stepped on the clutch and brake pedals with a sigh that abruptly changed to a gasp of surprise as both pedals went all the way to the floor at the same speed. The road ahead was clear, and he kept going straight, downshifting to cut speed, and frantically blowing his diesel horn. *Oh God, oh God, please don't—*

She never saw it coming. Her head never turned. The station wagon just jumped right through the intersection, and the driver's lingering memory would be of the young woman's profile disappearing under the hood of his diesel tractor, and then the awful lurch and shuddering surge upwards as the truck crushed the wagon under his front wheels.

The worst part of all was not feeling. Helen was her friend. Helen was dying, and Pam knew she should feel something, but she couldn't. The body was gagged, but that didn't stop all the sounds as Billy and Rick did what they were doing. Breath found its way out, and though her mouth couldn't move, the sounds were those of a woman soon to leave her life behind, but the trip had a price which had to be paid first, and Rick and Billy and Burt and Henry were doing the collecting. She tried to tell herself that she was really in another place, but the awful choking sounds kept bringing her eyes and her consciousness back to what reality had become. Helen was bad. Helen had tried to run away, and they couldn't have that. It had been explained to them all more than once, and was now being explained again in a way, Henry said, that they would be sure to remember. Pam felt where her ribs had once been broken, remembering her lesson. She knew there was nothing she could do as Helen's eyes fixed on her face. She tried to convey sympathy with her eyes. She didn't dare do more than that, and presently Helen stopped making noise, and it was over, for now. Now she could close her eyes and wonder when it would be her turn.

The crew thought it was pretty funny. They had the American pilot tied up right outside their sandbagged emplacement so he could see the guns that had shot him down. Less funny was what their prisoner had done, and they'd expressed their displeasure for it with fists and boots. They had the other body, too, and they set it right next to him, enjoying the look of sorrow and despair on his face as he looked at his fellow bandit. The intelligence officer from Hanoi was here now, checking the man's name against a list he'd brought along, bending down again to read off the name. It must have been something special, the gunners all thought, from the way he reacted to it, and the urgent phone call he'd made. After the prisoner passed out from his pain, the intelligence officer had swabbed some blood from the dead body and covered the live one's face with it. Then he'd snapped a few photos. That puzzled the gun crew. It was almost as though he wanted the live one to look as dead as the body next to him. How very odd.

It wasn't the first body he'd had to identify, but Kelly had thought that aspect of his life was a thing left far behind. Other people were there to support him, but not falling down wasn't the same thing as surviving, and there was no consolation at a moment such as this. He walked out of the emergency room, people's eyes on him, doctors and nurses. A priest had been called to perform his last duty, and had said a few things that he knew were unheard. A police officer explained that it hadn't been the driver's fault. The brakes had failed. Mechanical defect. Nobody's fault, really. Just one of those things. All the things he'd said before, on other such occasions, trying to explain to some innocent person why the main part of his world had just ended, as though it mattered. This Mr. Kelly was a tough one, the officer saw, and all the more vulnerable because of it. His wife and unborn child, whom he might have protected against any hazard, were dead by an accident. Nobody to blame. The trucker, a family man himself, was in the hospital, under sedation after having gone under his rig in the hope of finding her alive. People Kelly had been working with sat with him, and would help him make arrangements. There was nothing else to be done for a man who would have accepted hell rather than this; because he'd seen hell. But there was more than one hell, and he hadn't seen them all quite yet.

1

Enfant perdu

MAY

He'd never know why he stopped. Kelly pulled his Scout over to the shoulder without a conscious thought. She hadn't had her hand out soliciting a ride. She'd just been standing at the side of the road, watching the cars speed past in a spray of highway grit and a wake of fumes. Her posture was that of a hitchhiker, one knee locked, the other bent. Her clothes were clearly well used and a backpack was loosely slung over one shoulder. Her tawny, shoulder-length hair moved about in the rush of air from the traffic. Her face showed nothing, but Kelly didn't see that until he was already pressing his right foot on the brake pedal and angling onto the loose rock of the shoulder. He wondered if he should go back into the traffic, then decided that he was already committed, though to what he didn't know, exactly. The girl's eyes followed the car and, as he looked in his rearview mirror, she shrugged without any particular enthusiasm and walked towards him. The passenger window was down already, and in a few seconds she was there.

"Where you goin'?" she asked.

That surprised Kelly. He thought the first question—*Need a ride?*—was supposed to be his. He hesitated for a second or two, looking at her. Twenty-one, perhaps, but old for her years. Her face wasn't dirty, but neither was it clean, perhaps from the wind and dust on the interstate. She wore a man's cotton shirt that hadn't been ironed in months, and her hair was knotted. But what surprised him most of all were her eyes. Fetchingly gray-green, they stared past Kelly into . . . what? He'd seen the look before often enough, but only on weary men. He'd had the look himself, Kelly remembered, but even then he'd never known what his eyes saw. It didn't occur to him that he wore a look not so different now.

"Back to my boat," he answered finally, not knowing what else to say. And that quickly, her eyes changed.

"You have a boat?" she asked. Her eyes lit up like a child's, a smile started there and radiated down the remainder of her face, as though he'd just answered an important question. She had a cute gap between her front teeth, Kelly noticed.

"Forty-footer—she's a diesel cruiser." He waved to the back of the Scout, whose cargo area was completely filled with cartons of groceries. "You want to come along?" he asked, also without thinking.

"Sure!" Without hesitation she yanked open the door and tossed her backpack on the floor in front of the passenger seat.

Pulling back into traffic was dangerous. Short of wheelbase and short of power, the Scout wasn't built for interstate-highway driving, and Kelly had to concentrate. The car wasn't fast enough to go in any other lane than the right, and with people coming on and off at every interchange, he had to pay attention because the Scout wasn't nimble enough to avoid all the idiots who were heading out to the ocean or wherever the hell people went on a three-day weekend.

You want to come along? he'd asked, and she'd said *Sure,* his mind reported to him. *What the hell?* Kelly frowned in frustration at the traffic because he didn't know the answer, but then there were a lot of questions to which he hadn't known the answers in the last six months. He told his mind to be quiet and watched the traffic, even though it kept up its inquiries in a nagging sort of background noise. One's mind, after all, rarely obeys its own commands.

Memorial Day weekend, he thought. The cars around him were filled with people rushing home from work, or those who'd already made that trip and picked up their families. The faces of children stared out of the rear-seat windows. One or two waved at him, but Kelly pretended not to notice. It was hard not having a soul, most especially when you could remember having had one.

Kelly ran a hand across his jaw, feeling the sandpaper texture. The hand itself was dirty. No wonder they'd acted that way at the grocery warehouse. *Letting yourself go, Kelly.*

Well, who the hell cares?

He turned to look at his guest and realized that he didn't know her name. He was taking her to his boat, and he didn't know her name. Amazing. She was staring forward, her face serene. It was a pretty face in profile. She was thin—perhaps willowy was the right word, her hair halfway between blonde and brown. Her jeans were worn and torn in a few places, and had begun life at one of those stores where they charged you extra to sell jeans that were pre-faded—or whatever they did with them. Kelly didn't know and cared less. One more thing not to care about.

Christ, how did you ever get this screwed up? his mind demanded of him. He knew the answer, but even that was not a full explanation. Different segments of the organism called John Terrence Kelly knew different parts of the whole story, but somehow they'd never all come together, leaving the separate fragments of what had once been a tough, smart, decisive man to blunder about in confusion—and despair? There was a happy thought.

He remembered what he'd once been. He remembered all the things that he had survived, amazed that he had done so. And perhaps the worst torment of all was that he didn't understand what had gone wrong. Sure, he knew what had *happened,* but those things had all been on the outside, and somehow his understanding had gotten lost, leaving him alive and confused and without purpose. He was on autopilot. He knew that, but not where fate was taking him.

She didn't try to talk, whoever she was, and that was just as well, Kelly told himself, though he sensed that there was something he ought to know. The realization came as a surprise. It was instinctual, and he'd always trusted his instincts, the warning chill on his neck and forearms. He looked around at the traffic and Kelly saw no particular danger other than cars with too much engine under the hood and not enough brains behind the wheel. His eyes scanned carefully and found nothing. But the warning didn't go away, and Kelly found himself checking the mirror for no good reason, while his left hand wandered down between his legs and found the checkered grips of the Colt automatic that hung hidden under the seat. His hand was stroking the weapon before he realized it.

Now what the hell did you do that for? Kelly pulled his hand back and shook his head with a grimace of frustration. But he did keep checking the mirror—just the normal watch on traffic, he lied to himself for the next twenty minutes.

The boatyard was a swarm of activity. The three-day weekend, of course. Cars were zipping about too fast for the small and badly paved parking lot, each driver trying to evade the Friday rush that each was, of course, helping to create. At least here the Scout came into its own. The high ground clearance and visibility gave Kelly an advantage as he maneuvered to *Springer*'s transom, and he looped around to back up to the slip he'd left six hours before. It was a relief, to crank up the windows and lock the car. His adventure on the highways was over, and the safety of the trackless water beckoned.

Springer was a diesel-powered motor yacht, forty-one feet long, custom built but similar in her lines and internal arrangements to a Pacemaker Coho. She was not especially pretty, but she had two sizable cabins, and the midships salon could be converted easily into a third. Her diesels were large but not supercharged, because Kelly preferred a large comfortable engine to a small straining one. He had a high-quality marine radar, every sort of communications gear that he could legally use, and navigation aids normally reserved for offshore fishermen. The fiberglass hull was immaculate, and there was not a speck of rust on the chromed rails, though he had deliberately done without the topside varnish that most yacht-owners cherished because it wasn't worth the maintenance time. *Springer* was a workboat, or was supposed to be.

Kelly and his guest alighted from the car. He opened the cargo door and started carrying the cartons aboard. The young lady, he saw, had the good sense to stay out of the way.

"Yo, Kelly!" a voice called from the flying bridge.

"Yeah, Ed, what was it?"

"Bad gauge. The generator brushes were a little worn, and I replaced them, but I think it was the gauge. Replaced that, too." Ed Murdock, the yard's chief mechanic, started down, and spotted the girl as he began to step off the ladder. Murdock tripped on the last step and nearly landed flat on his face in surprise. The mechanic's face evaluated the girl quickly and approvingly.

"Anything else?" Kelly asked pointedly.

"Topped off the tanks. The engines are warm," Murdock said, turning back to his customer. "It's all on your bill."

"Okay, thanks, Ed."

"Oh, Chip told me to tell you, somebody else made an offer in case you ever want to sell—"

Kelly cut him off. "No chance, Ed."

"She's a jewel, Kelly," Murdock said as he gathered his tools and walked away smiling, pleased with himself for the double entendre.

It took several seconds for Kelly to catch that one. It evoked a belated grunt of semi-amusement as he loaded the last of the groceries into the salon.

"What do I do?" the girl asked. She'd just been standing there, and Kelly had the impression that she was trembling a little and trying to hide it.

"Just take a seat topside," Kelly said, pointing to the flying bridge. "It'll take me a few minutes to get things started."

"Okay." She beamed a smile at him guaranteed to melt ice, as though she knew exactly what one of his needs was.

Kelly walked aft to his cabin, pleased at least that he kept his boat tidy. The master-cabin head was also neat, and he found himself staring into the mirror and asking, "Okay, now what the fuck are you going to do?"

There was no immediate answer, but common decency told him to wash up. Two minutes later he entered the salon. He checked to see that the grocery cartons were secure, then went topside.

"I, uh, forgot to ask you something—" he began.

"Pam," she said, extending her hand. "What's yours?"

"Kelly," he replied, nonplussed yet again.

"Where we going, Mr. Kelly?"

"Just Kelly," he corrected her, keeping his distance for the moment. Pam just nodded and smiled again.

"Okay, Kelly, where to?"

"I own a little island about thirty—"

"You own an *island?*" Her eyes went wide.

"That's right." Actually, he just leased it, and that had been a fact long enough that Kelly didn't find it the least bit remarkable.

"Let's go!" she said with enthusiasm, looking back at the shore.

Kelly laughed out loud. "Okay, let's do that!"

He flipped on the bilge blowers. *Springer* had diesel engines, and he didn't really have to worry about fumes building up, but for all his recently acquired slovenliness, Kelly was a seaman, and his life on the water followed a strict routine, which meant observing all the safety rules that had been written in the blood of less careful men. After the prescribed two minutes, he punched the button to start the portside, then the starboard-side diesel. Both of the big Detroit Diesel engines caught at once, rumbling to impressive life as Kelly checked the gauges. Everything looked fine.

He left the flying bridge to slip his mooring lines, then came back and eased the throttles forward to take his boat out of the slip, checking tide and wind—there was not much of either at the moment—and looking for other boats. Kelly advanced the port throttle a notch farther as he turned the wheel, allowing *Springer* to pivot all the more quickly in the narrow channel, and then he was pointed straight out. He advanced the starboard throttle next, bringing his cruiser to a mannerly five knots as he headed past the ranks of motor and sail yachts. Pam was looking around at the boats, too, mainly aft, and her eyes fixed on the parking lot for a long couple of seconds before she looked forward again, her body relaxing more as she did so.

"You know anything about boats?" Kelly asked.

"Not much," she admitted, and for the first time he noticed her accent.

"Where you from?"

"Texas. How about you?"

"Indianapolis, originally, but it's been a while."

"What's this?" she asked. Her hands reached out to touch the tattoo on his forearm.

"It's from one of the places I've been," he said. "Not a very nice place."

"Oh, over there." She understood.

"That's the place." Kelly nodded matter-of-factly. They were out of the yacht basin now, and he advanced the throttles yet again.

"What did you do there?"

"Nothing to talk to a lady about," Kelly replied, looking around from a half-standing position.

"What makes you think I'm a lady?" she asked.

It caught him short, but he was getting used to it by now. He'd also found that talking to a girl, no matter what the subject, was something that he needed to do. For the first time he answered her smile with one of his own.

"Well, it wouldn't be very nice of me if I assumed that you weren't."

"I wondered how long it would be before you smiled." *You have a very nice smile,* her tone told him.

How's six months grab you? he almost said. Instead he laughed, mainly at himself. That was something else he needed to do.

"I'm sorry. Guess I haven't been very good company." He turned to look at her again and saw understanding in her eyes. Just a quiet look, very human and feminine, but it shook Kelly. He could feel it happen, and ignored the part of his consciousness that told him that it was something he'd needed badly for months. That was something he didn't need to hear, especially from himself. Loneliness was bad enough without reflection on its misery. Her hand reached out yet again, ostensibly to stroke the tattoo, but that wasn't what it was all about. It was amazing how warm her touch was, even under a hot afternoon sun. Perhaps it was a measure of just how cold his life had become.

But he had a boat to navigate. There was a freighter about a thousand yards ahead. Kelly was now at full cruising power, and the trim tabs at the stern had automatically engaged, bringing the boat to an efficient planing angle as her speed came to eighteen knots. The ride was smooth until they got into the merchant ship's wake. Then *Springer* started pitching, up and down three or four feet at the bow as Kelly maneuvered left to get around the worst of it. The freighter grew before them like a cliff as they overtook her.

"Is there someplace I can change?"

"My cabin is aft. You can move in forward if you want."

"Oh, really?" She giggled. "Why would I do that?"

"Huh?" She'd done it to him again.

Pam went below, careful to hold on to the rails as she carried her backpack. She hadn't been wearing much. She reappeared in a few minutes wearing even less, short-shorts and a halter, no shoes, and perceptibly more relaxed. She had dancer's legs, Kelly noticed, slim and very feminine. Also very pale, which surprised him. The halter was loose on her, and frayed at the edges. Perhaps she'd recently lost weight, or maybe she'd deliberately bought it overlarge. Whatever the reason, it showed quite a bit of her chest. Kelly caught himself shifting his eyes, and chastised himself for ogling the girl. But Pam made it hard not to. Now she grasped his upper arm and sat up against him. Looking over, he could see right down the halter just as far as he wanted.

"You like them?" she asked.

Kelly's brain and mouth went into lock. He made a few embarrassed sounds, and before he could decide to say anything she was laughing. But not at him. She was waving at the crew of the freighter, who waved back. It was an Italian ship, and one of the half dozen or so men hanging over the rail at the stern blew Pam a kiss. She did the same in return.

It made Kelly jealous.

He turned the wheel to port again, taking his boat across the bow wave of the freighter, and as he passed the vessel's bridge he tooted his horn. It was the correct thing to do, though few small boaters ever bothered. By this time, a watch officer had his glasses on Kelly—actually Pam, of course. He turned and shouted something to the wheelhouse. A moment later the freighter's enormous "whistle" sounded its own bass note, nearly causing the girl to leap from her seat.

Kelly laughed, and so did she, and then she wrapped her arms tightly around his bicep. He could feel a finger tracing its way around the tattoo.

"It doesn't feel like—"

Kelly nodded. "I know. Most people expect it to feel like paint or something."

"Why did—"

"—I get it? Everybody in the outfit did. Even the officers. It was something to do, I guess. Pretty dumb, really."

"I think it's cute."

"Well, I think you're pretty cute."

"You say the nicest things." She moved slightly, rubbing her breast against his upper arm.

Kelly settled down to a steady cruising speed of eighteen knots as he worked his way out of Baltimore harbor. The Italian freighter was the only merchant ship in view, and the seas were flat, with one-foot ripples. He kept to the main shipping channel all the way out into the Chesapeake Bay.

"You thirsty?" she asked as they turned south.

"Yeah. There's a fridge in the kitchenette—it's in the—"

"I saw it. What do you want?"

"Get two of anything."

"Okay," she replied brightly. When she stood, the soft feeling worked its way straight up his arm, finally departing at the shoulder.

"What's that?" she asked on returning. Kelly turned and winced. He'd been so content with the girl on his arm that he'd neglected to pay attention to the weather. "That" was a thunderstorm, a towering mass of cumulonimbus clouds that reached eight or ten miles skyward.

"Looks like we're going to get some rain," he told her as he took the beer from her hand.

"When I was a little girl, that meant a tornado."

"Well, not here, it doesn't," Kelly replied, looking around the boat to make sure that there was no loose gear. Below, he knew, everything was in its proper place, because it always was, ennui or not. Then he switched on his marine radio. He caught a weather forecast at once, one that ended with the usual warning.

"Is this a small craft?" Pam asked.

"Technically it is, but you can relax. I know what I'm doing. I used to be a chief bosun's mate."

"What's that?"

"A sailor. In the Navy, that is. Besides, this is a pretty big boat. The ride might get a little bumpy, is all. If you're worried, there are life jackets under the seat you're on."

"Are you worried?" Pam asked. Kelly smiled and shook his head. "Okay." She resumed her previous position, her chest against his arm, her head on his shoulder, a dreamy expression in her eyes, as though anticipating something that was to be, storm or no storm.

Kelly wasn't worried—at least not about the storm—but he wasn't casual about things either. Passing Bodkin Point, he continued east across the shipping channel. He didn't turn south until he was in water he knew to be too shallow for anything large enough to run him down. Every few minutes he turned to keep an eye on the storm, which was charging right in at twenty knots or so. It had already blotted out the sun. A fast-moving storm most often meant a violent one, and his new southerly course meant that he wasn't outrunning it any longer. Kelly finished off his beer and decided against another. Visibility would drop fast. He pulled out a plastic-coated chart and fixed it in place on the table to the right of the instrument panel, marked his position with a grease pencil, and then checked to make sure that his course didn't take him into shallows—*Springer* drew four and a half feet of water, and for Kelly anything less than eight feet constituted shallow water. Satisfied, he set his compass course and relaxed again. His training was his buffer against both danger and complacency.

"Won't be long now," Pam observed, just a trace of unease in her voice as she held on to him.

"You can head below if you want," Kelly said. "It's gonna get rainy and windy. And bumpy."

"But not dangerous."

"No, unless I do something really dumb. I'll try not to," he promised.

"Can I stay here and see what it's like?" she asked, clearly unwilling to leave his side, though Kelly did not know why.

"It's going to get wet," he warned her again.

"That's okay." She smiled brightly, fixing even more tightly to his arm.

Kelly throttled back some, taking the boat down off plane. There was no reason to hurry. With the throttles eased back, there was no longer a need for two hands on the controls either. He wrapped his arm around the girl, her head came automatically down on his shoulder again, and despite the approaching storm everything was suddenly right with the world. Or that's what Kelly's emotions told him. His reason said something else, and the two views would not reconcile themselves. His reason reminded him that the girl at his side was—what? He didn't know. His emotions told him that it didn't matter a damn. She was what he needed. But Kelly was not a man ruled by emotions, and the conflict made him glower at the horizon.

"Something wrong?" Pam asked.

Kelly started to say something, then stopped, and reminded himself that he was alone on his yacht with a pretty girl. He let emotion win this round for a change.

"I'm a little confused, but, no, nothing is wrong that I know about."

"I can tell that you—"

Kelly shook his head. "Don't bother. Whatever it is, it can wait. Just relax and enjoy the ride."

The first gust of wind arrived a moment later, heeling the boat a few degrees to port. Kelly adjusted his rudder to compensate. The rain arrived quickly. The first few warning sprinkles were rapidly followed by solid sheets that marched like curtains across the surface of the Chesapeake Bay. Within a minute visibility was down to only a few hundred yards, and the sky was as dark as late twilight. Kelly made sure his running lights were on. The waves started kicking up in earnest, driven by what felt like thirty knots of wind. Weather and seas were directly on the beam. He decided that he could keep going, but he was in a good anchoring place now, and wouldn't be in another for five hours. Kelly took another look at the chart, then switched on his radar to verify his position. Ten feet of water, a sand bottom that the chart called HRD and was therefore good holding ground. He brought *Springer* into the wind and eased the throttles until the propellers were providing just enough thrust to overcome the driving force of the wind.

"Take the wheel," he told Pam.

"But I don't know what to do!"

"It's all right. Just hold her steady and steer the way I tell you to. I have to go forward to set the anchors. 'Kay?"

"You be careful!" she shouted over the gusting wind. The waves were about five feet now, and the bow of the boat was leaping up and down. Kelly gave her shoulder a squeeze and went forward.

He had to watch himself, of course, but his shoes had no-skid soles, and Kelly knew his business. He kept his hands on the grab rail all the way around the superstructure, and in a minute he was on the foredeck. Two anchors were clipped to the deck, a Danforth and a CQR plow-type, both slightly oversized. He tossed the Danforth over first, then signaled for Pam to ease the wheel to port. When the boat had moved perhaps fifty feet south, he dropped the CQR over the side as well. Both ropes were already set to the proper lengths, and after checking that all was secure, Kelly made his way back to the flying bridge.

Pam looked nervous until the moment that he sat back down on the vinyl bench—everything was covered with water now, and their clothes were soaked through. Kelly eased the throttles to idle, allowing the wind to push *Springer* back nearly a hundred feet. By that time both anchors had dug into the bottom. Kelly frowned at their placement. He ought to have set them farther apart. But only one anchor was really necessary. The second was just insurance. Satisfied, he switched off the diesels.

"I could fight the storm all the way down, but I'd prefer not to," he explained.

"So we park here for the night?"

"That's right. You can go down to your cabin and—"

"You want me to go away?"

"No—I mean, if you don't like it here—" Her hand came up to his face. He barely caught her words through the wind and rain.

"I like it here." Somehow it didn't seem like a contradiction at all.

A moment later Kelly asked himself why it had taken so long. All the signals had been there. There was another brief discussion between emotion and reason, and reason lost again. There was nothing to be afraid of here, just a person as lonely as he. It was so easy to forget. Loneliness didn't tell you what you had lost, only that something was missing. It took something like this to define that emptiness. Her skin was soft, dripping with rain, but warm. It was so different from the rented passion that he'd tried twice in the past month, each time coming away disgusted with himself.

But this was something else. This was real. Reason cried out one last time that it couldn't be, that he'd picked her up at the side of the road and had known her for only a brief span of hours. Emotion said that it didn't matter. As though observing the conflict in his mind, Pam pulled the halter over her head. Emotion won.

"They look just fine to me," Kelly said. His hand moved to them, touching delicately. They felt just fine, too. Pam hung the halter on the steering wheel and pressed her face against his, her hands pulling him forward, taking charge in a very feminine way. Somehow her passion wasn't animalistic. Something made it different. Kelly didn't know what it was, but didn't search for the reason, not now.

Both rose to their feet. Pam nearly slipped, but Kelly caught her, dropping to his knees to help remove her shorts. Then it was her turn to unbutton his shirt after placing his hands on her breasts. His shirt remained in place for a long moment because neither wanted his hands to move, but then it was done, one arm at a time, and his jeans went next. Kelly slipped out of his shoes as the rest came off. Both stood for the next embrace, weaving as the boat pitched and rocked beneath then, the rain and wind pelting them. Pam took his hand and led him just aft of the driver's console, guiding him down to a supine position on the deck. She mounted him at once. Kelly tried to sit up, but she didn't let him, instead leaning forward while her hips moved with gentle violence. Kelly was as unready for that as he'd been for everything else this afternoon, and his shout seemed to outscream the thunder. When his eyes opened, her face was inches from him, and the smile was like that on a stone angel in a church.

"I'm sorry, Pam, I—"

She stopped his apology with a giggle. "Are you always this good?"

Long minutes later, Kelly's arms were wrapped around her thin form, and so they stayed until the storm passed. Kelly was afraid to let go, afraid of the possibility that this was as unreal as it had to be. Then the wind acquired a chill, and they went below. Kelly got some towels and they dried each other off. He tried to smile at her, but the hurt was back, all the more powerful from the joy of the previous hour, and it was Pam's turn to be surprised. She sat beside him on the deck of the salon, and when she pulled his face down to her chest, he was the one who wept, until her chest was wet again. She didn't ask. She was smart enough for that. Instead she held him tightly until he was done and his breathing came back to normal.

"I'm sorry," he said after a while. Kelly tried to move but she wouldn't let him.

"You don't have to explain. But I'd like to help," she said, knowing that she already had. She'd seen it from almost the first moment in the car: a strong man, badly hurt. So different from the others she had known. When he finally spoke, she could feel his words on her breast.

"It's been nearly seven months. Down in Mississippi on a job. She was pregnant, we just found out. She went to the store, and—it was a truck, a big tractor-trailer rig. The linkage broke." He couldn't make himself say more, and he didn't have to.

"What was her name?"

"Tish—Patricia."

"How long were you—"

"Year and a half. Then she was just . . . gone. I never expected it. I mean, I put my time in, did some dangerous stuff, but that's all over, and that was me, not her. I never thought—" His voice cracked again. Pam looked down at him in the muted light of the salon, seeing the scars she'd missed before and wondering what their story was. It didn't matter. She brought her cheek down to the top of his head. *He should have been a father right about now. Should have been a lot of things.*

"You never let it out, did you?"

"No."

"And why now?"

"I don't know," he whispered.

"Thank you." Kelly looked up in surprise. "That's the nicest thing a man has ever done to me."

"I don't understand."

"Yes, you do," Pam replied. "And Tish understands, too. You let me take her place. Or maybe she did. She loved you, John. She must have loved you a lot. And she still does. Thank you for letting me help."

He started crying again, and Pam brought his head back down, cradling him like a small child. It lasted ten minutes, though neither looked at a clock. When he was done, he kissed her in gratitude that rapidly turned to renewed passion. Pam lay back, letting him take charge as he needed to do now that he was again a man in spirit. Her reward was in keeping with the magnitude of what she had done for him, and this time it was her cries that canceled out the thunder. Later, he fell asleep at her side, and she kissed his unshaven cheek. That was when her own tears began at the wonder of what the day had brought after the terror with which it had begun.

2

Encounters

Kelly awoke at his accustomed time, thirty minutes before sunrise, to the mewing of gulls and saw the first dull glow on the eastern horizon. At first he was confused to find a slender arm across his chest, but other feelings and memories explained things in a few seconds. He extricated himself from her side and moved the blanket to cover her from the morning chill. It was time for ship's business.

Kelly got the drip coffee machine going, then he pulled on a pair of swim trunks and headed topside. He hadn't forgotten to set the anchor light, he was gratified to see. The sky had cleared off, and the air was cool after the thunderstorms of the previous night. He went forward and was surprised to see that one of his anchors had dragged somewhat. Kelly reproached himself for that, even though nothing had actually gone wrong. The water was a flat, oily calm and the breeze gentle. The pink-orange glow of first light decorated the tree-spotted coastline to the east. All in all, it seemed as fine a morning as he could remember. Then he remembered that what had changed had nothing at all to do with the weather.

''Damn,'' he whispered to the dawn not yet broken. Kelly was stiff, and did some stretching exercises to get the kinks out, slow to realize how fine he felt without the usual hangover. Slower still to recall how long it had been. Nine hours of sleep? he wondered. That much? No wonder he felt so good. The next part of the morning routine was to get a squeegee to dispose of the water that had pooled on the fiberglass deck.

His head turned at the low, muted rumble of marine diesels. Kelly looked west to spot it, but there was a little mist that way, being pushed his way by the breeze, and he couldn't make anything out. He went to the control station on the flying bridge and got out his glasses, just in time to have a twelve-inch spotlight blaze through the marine 7 × 50s. Kelly was dazzled by the lights, which just as suddenly switched off, and a loud-hailer called across the water.

"Sorry, Kelly. Didn't know it was you." Two minutes later the familiar shape of a Coast Guard forty-one-foot patrol boat eased alongside *Springer.* Kelly scrambled along the portside to deploy his rubber fenders.

"You trying to kill me or something?" Kelly said in a conversational voice.

"Sorry." Quartermaster First Class Manuel "Portagee" Oreza stepped from one gun'l to the other with practiced ease. He gestured to the fenders. "Wanna hurt my feelings?"

"Bad sea manners, too," Kelly went on as he walked towards his visitor.

"I spoke to the young lad about that already," Oreza assured him. He held out his hand. "Morning, Kelly."

The outstretched hand had a Styrofoam cup filled with coffee. Kelly took it and laughed.

"Apology accepted, sir." Oreza was famous for his coffee.

"Long night. We're all tired, and it's a young crew," the coastguardsman explained wearily. Oreza was nearly twenty-eight himself, and by far the oldest man of his boat crew.

"Trouble?" Kelly asked.

Oreza nodded, looking around at the water. "Kinda. Some damned fool in a little day-sailer turned up missing after that little rainstorm we had last night, and we've been looking all over bejazzus for him."

"Forty knots of wind. Fair blow, Portagee," Kelly pointed out. "Came in right fast, too."

"Yeah, well, we rescued six boats already, just this one still missing. You see anything unusual last night?"

"No. Came outa Baltimore around . . . oh, sixteen hundred, I suppose. Two and a half hours to get here. Anchored right after the storm hit. Visibility was pretty bad, didn't see much of anything before we went below."

"We," Oreza observed, stretching. He walked over to the wheel, picked up the rain-soaked halter, and tossed it to Kelly. The look on his face was neutral, but there was interest behind the eyes. He hoped his friend had found someone. Life hadn't been especially fair to the man.

Kelly handed the cup back with a similarly neutral expression.

"There was one freighter coming out behind us," he went on. "Italian flag, container boat about half full, must have been knocking down fifteen knots. Anybody else clear the harbor?''

"Yeah." Oreza nodded and spoke with professional irritation. "I'm worried about that. Fuckin' merchies plowing out at full speed, not paying attention.''

"Well, hell, you stand outside the wheelhouse, you might get wet. Besides, sea-and-anchor detail might violate some union rule, right? Maybe your guy got run down," Kelly noted darkly. It wouldn't have been the first time, even on a body of water as civilized as the Chesapeake.

"Maybe," Oreza said, surveying the horizon. He frowned, not believing the suggestion and too tired to hide it. "Anyway, you see a little day-sailer with an orange-and-white candystripe sail, you want to give me a call?''

"No problem.''

Oreza looked forward and turned back. "Two anchors for that little puff o' wind we had? They're not far enough apart. Thought you knew better.''

"Chief Bosun's Mate," Kelly reminded him. "Since when does a bookkeeper get that snotty with a real seaman?" It was only a joke. Kelly knew Portagee was the better man in a small boat. Though not by much of a margin, and both knew that, too.

Oreza grinned on his way back to the cutter. After jumping back aboard, he pointed to the halter in Kelly's hand. "Don't forget to put your shirt on, *Boats!* Looks like it oughta fit just fine.'' A laughing Oreza disappeared inside the wheelhouse before Kelly could come up with a rejoinder. There appeared to be someone inside who was not in uniform, which surprised Kelly. A moment later, the cutter's engines rumbled anew and the forty-one-boat moved northwest.

"Good mornin'.'' It was Pam. "What was that?''

Kelly turned. She wasn't wearing any more now than when he'd put the blanket on her, but Kelly instantly decided that the only time she'd surprise him again would be when she did something predictable. Her hair was a medusalike mass of tangles, and her eyes were unfocused, as though she'd not slept well at all.

"Coast Guard. They're looking for a missing boat. How'd you sleep?''

"Just fine." She came over to him. Her eyes had a soft, dreamlike quality that seemed strange so early in the morning, but could not have been more attractive to the wide-awake sailor.

"Good morning.'' A kiss. A hug. Pam held her arms aloft and executed something like a pirouette. Kelly grabbed her slender waist and hoisted her aloft.

"What do you want for breakfast?" he asked.

"I don't eat breakfast," Pam replied, reaching down for him.

"Oh." Kelly smiled. "Okay."

She changed her mind about an hour later. Kelly fixed eggs and bacon on the galley stove, and Pam wolfed it down so speedily that he fixed seconds despite her protests. On further inspection, the girl wasn't merely thin, some of her ribs were visible. She was undernourished, an observation that prompted yet another unasked question. But whatever the cause, he could remedy it. Once she'd consumed four eggs, eight slices of bacon, and five pieces of toast, roughly double Kelly's normal morning intake, it was time for the day to begin properly. He showed her how to work the galley appliances while he saw to recovering the anchors.

They got back under way just shy of a lazy eight o'clock. It promised to be a hot, sunny Saturday. Kelly donned his sunglasses and relaxed in his chair, keeping himself alert with the odd sip from his mug. He maneuvered west, tracing down the edge of the main ship channel to avoid the hundreds of fishing boats he fully expected to sortie from their various harbors today in pursuit of rockfish.

"What are those things?" Pam asked, pointing to the floats decorating the water to port.

"Floats for crab pots. They're really more like cages. Crabs get in and can't get out. You leave floats so you know where they are." Kelly handed Pam his glasses and pointed to a bay-build workboat about three miles to the east.

"They trap the poor things?" Kelly laughed.

"Pam, the bacon you had for breakfast? The hog didn't commit suicide, did he?"

She gave him an impish look. "Well, no."

"Don't get too excited. A crab is just a big aquatic spider, even though it tastes good."

Kelly altered course to starboard to clear a red nun-buoy.

"Seems kinda cruel, though."

"Life can be that way," Kelly said too quickly and then regretted it.

Pam's response was as heartfelt as Kelly's. "Yeah, I know."

Kelly didn't turn to look at her, only because he stopped himself. There'd been emotional content in her reply, something to remind him that she, too, had demons. The moment passed quickly, however. She leaned back into the capacious conning chair, leaning against him and making things right again. One last time Kelly's senses warned him that something was not right at all. But there were no demons out here, were there?

"You'd better go below."

"Why?"

"Sun's going to be hot today. There's some lotion in the medicine cabinet, main head."

"Head?"

"Bathroom!"

"Why is everything different on a boat?"

Kelly laughed. "That's so sailors can be the boss out here. Now, shoo! Go get that stuff and put a lot on or you'll look like a french fry before lunch."

Pam made a face. "I need a shower, too. Is that okay?"

"Good idea," Kelly answered without looking. "No sense scaring the fish away."

"You!" She swatted him on the arm and headed below.

"Vanished, just plain vanished," Oreza growled. He was hunched over a chart table at the Thomas Point Coast Guard Station.

"We shoulda got some air cover, helicopter or something," the civilian observed.

"Wouldn't have mattered, not last night. Hell, the gulls rode that blow out."

"But where'd he go?"

"Beats me, maybe the storm sank his ass." Oreza glowered at the chart. "You said he was northbound. We covered all these ports and Max took the western shore. You sure the description of the boat was correct?"

"Sure? Hell, we did everything but buy the goddamned boat for 'em!" The civilian was as short-tempered as twenty-eight hours of caffeine-induced wakefulness could explain, even worse for having been ill on the patrol boat, much to the amusement of the enlisted crew. His stomach felt like it was coated with steel wool. "Maybe it did sink," he concluded gruffly, not believing it for a moment.

"Wouldn't that solve your problem?" His attempt at levity earned him a growl, and Quartermaster First Class Manuel Oreza caught a warning look from the Station commander, a gray-haired warrant officer named Paul English.

"You know," the man said in a state of exhaustion, "I don't think anything is going to solve this problem, but it's my job to try."

"Sir, we've all had a long night. My crew is racked out, and unless you have a really good reason to stay up, I suggest you find a bunk and get a few Zs, sir.''

The civilian looked up with a tired smile to mute his earlier words. "Petty Officer Oreza, smart as you are, you ought to be an officer.''

"If I'm so smart, how come we missed our friend last night?''

"That guy we saw around dawn?''

"Kelly? Ex–Navy chief, solid guy.''

"Kinda young for a chief, isn't he?'' English asked, looking at a not very good photo the spotlight had made possible. He was new at the station.

"It came along with a Navy Cross,'' Oreza explained.

The civilian looked up. "So, you wouldn't think—''

"Not a chance in hell.''

The civilian shook his head. He paused for a moment, then headed off to the bunk room. They'd be going out again before sunset, and he'd need the sack time.

"So how was it?'' English asked after the man left the room.

"That guy is shipping a lot of gear, Cap'n.'' As a station commander, English was entitled to the title, all the more so that he let Portagee run his boat his way. "Sure as hell he doesn't sleep much.''

"He's going to be with us for a while, on and off, and I want you to handle it.''

Oreza tapped the chart with a pencil. "I still say this would be a perfect place to keep watch from, and I know we can trust the guy.''

"The man says no.''

"The man ain't no seaman, Mr. English. I don't mind when the guy tells me what to do, but he don't know enough to tell me how to do it.'' Oreza circled the spot on the chart.

"I don't like this.''

"You don't have to like it,'' the taller man said. He unfolded his pocket knife and slit the heavy paper to reveal a plastic container of white powder. "A few hours' work and we turn three hundred thousand. Something wrong with that, or am I missin' something?''

"And this is just the start,'' the third man said.

"What do we do with the boat?'' asked the man with the scruples.

The tall one looked up from what he was doing. "You get rid of that sail?''

"Yeah.''

"Well, we can stash the boat . . . but probably smarter to scuttle. Yeah, that's what we'll do."

"And Angelo?" All three looked over to where the man was lying, unconscious still, and bleeding.

"I guess we scuttle him, too," the tall one observed without much in the way of emotion. "Right here ought to be fine."

"Maybe two weeks, there won't be nothin' left. Lots of critters out there." The third one waved outside at the tidal wetlands.

"See how easy it is? No boat, no Angelo, no risk, and three hundred thousand bucks. I mean, how much more do you expect, Eddie?"

"His friends still ain't gonna like it." The comment came more from a contrarian disposition than moral conviction.

"What friends?" Tony asked without looking. "He ratted, didn't he? How many friends does a rat have?"

Eddie bent to the logic of the situation and walked over to Angelo's unconscious form. The blood was still pumping out of the many abrasions, and the chest was moving slowly as he tried to breathe. It was time to put an end to that. Eddie knew it; he'd merely been trying to delay the inevitable. He pulled a small .22 automatic from his pocket, placed it to the back of Angelo's skull, and fired once. The body spasmed, then went slack. Eddie set his gun aside and dragged the body outside, leaving Henry and his friend to do the important stuff. They'd brought some fish netting, which he wrapped around the body before dumping it in the water behind their small motorboat. A cautious man, Eddie looked around, but there wasn't much danger of intruders here. He motored off until he found a likely spot a few hundred yards off, then stopped and drifted while he lifted a few concrete blocks from the boat and tied them to the netting. Six were enough to sink Angelo about eight feet to the bottom. The water was pretty clear here, and that worried Eddie a little until he saw all the crabs. Angelo would be gone in less than two weeks. It was a great improvement over the way they usually did business, something to remember for the future. Disposing of the little sailboat would be harder. He'd have to find a deeper spot, but he had all day to think about it.

Kelly altered course to starboard to avoid a gaggle of sports craft. The island was visible now, about five miles ahead. Not much to look at, just a low bump on the horizon, not even a tree, but it was his and it was as private as a man could wish. About the only bad news was the miserable TV reception.

Battery Island had a long and undistinguished history. Its current name, more ironic than appropriate, had come in the early nineteenth century, when some enterprising militiaman had decided to place a small gun battery there to guard a narrow spot in the Chesapeake Bay against the British, who were sailing towards Washington, D.C., to punish the new nation that had been so ill-advised as to challenge the power of the world's foremost navy. One British squadron commander had taken note of a few harmless puffs of smoke on the island, and, probably with more amusement than malice, had taken one ship within gun range and let loose a few salvos from the long guns on his lower deck. The citizen soldiers manning the battery hadn't needed much encouragement to make a run for their rowboats and hustle to the mainland, and shortly thereafter a landing party of Jack Tars and a few Royal Marines had rowed ashore in a pinnace to drive nails into the touch holes, which was what "spiking guns" meant. After this brief diversion, the British had continued their leisurely sail up the Patuxent River, from which their army had walked to Washington and back, having forced Dolly Madison to evacuate the White House. The British campaign had next headed to Baltimore, where a somewhat different outcome resulted.

Battery Island, under reluctant federal ownership, became an embarrassing footnote to a singularly useless war. Without so much as a caretaker to look after the earthen emplacements, weeds overtook the island, and so things had remained for nearly a hundred years.

With 1917 came America's first real foreign war, and America's navy, suddenly faced with the U-boat menace, needed a sheltered place to test its guns. Battery Island seemed ideal, only a few steaming hours from Norfolk, and so for several months in the fall of that year, 12- and 14-inch battleship rifles had crashed and thundered, blasting nearly a third of the island below mean low water and greatly annoying the migratory birds, who'd long since realized that no hunters ever shot at them from the place. About the only new thing that happened was the scuttling of over a hundred World War I–built cargo ships a few miles to the south, and these, soon overgrown with weeds, rapidly took on the appearance of islands themselves.

A new war and new weapons had brought the sleepy island back to life. The nearby naval air station needed a place for pilots to test weapons. The happy coincidence of the location of Battery Island and the scuttled ships from World War I had made for an instant bombing range. As a result, three massive concrete observation bunkers were built, from which officers could observe TBFs and SB2C bombers practicing runs on targets that looked like ship-shaped islands—and pulverizing quite a few of them until one bomb hung on the rack just long enough to obliterate one of the bunkers, thankfully empty. The site of the destroyed bunker had been cleared in the name of tidiness, and the island converted to a rescue station, from which a crashboat might respond to an aircraft accident. *That* had required building a concrete quay and boathouse and refurbishment of the two remaining bunkers. All in all, the island had served the local economy, if not the federal budget, well, until the advent of helicopters made crashboats unnecessary, and the island had been declared surplus. And so the island remained unnoticed on a register of unwanted federal property until Kelly had managed to acquire a lease.

Pam leaned back on her blanket as they approached, basting in the warm sun beneath a thick coating of suntan lotion. She didn't have a swimsuit, and wore only a bra and panties. It didn't offend Kelly, but the impropriety of it was vaguely disturbing for no reason that stood up to logical analysis. In any case, his current job was driving his boat. Further contemplation of her body could wait, he told himself about every minute, when his eyes darted that way to make sure she was still there.

He eased the wheel farther to the right to pass well clear of a large fishing yacht. He gave Pam another look. She'd slipped the straps of her bra down off her shoulders for a more even tan. Kelly approved.

The sound startled both of them, rapid short blasts on the fishing boat's diesel horns. Kelly's head scanned all the way around, then centered on the boat that lay two hundred yards to port. It was the only thing close enough to be of concern, and also seemed to be the source of the noise. On the flying bridge a man was waving at him. Kelly turned to port to approach. He took his time bringing *Springer* alongside. Whoever this guy was, he wasn't much of a boat handler, and when he brought his craft to a halt, twenty feet away, he kept his hand on the throttles.

"What's the problem?" Kelly called over the loud-hailer.

"Lost our props!" a swarthy man hollered back. "What do we do?"

Row, Kelly almost replied, but that wasn't very neighborly. He brought his boat closer in to survey the situation. It was a medium-sized fishing cruiser, a fairly recent Hatteras. The man on the bridge was about five-eight, fiftyish, and bare-chested except for a mat of dark hair. A woman was also visible, also rather downcast.

"No screws at all?" Kelly asked when they were closer.

"I think we hit a sandbar," the man explained. "About half a mile that way." He pointed to a place Kelly kept clear of.

"Sure enough, there's one that way. I can give you a tow if you want. You have good enough line for it?"

"Yes!" the man replied immediately. He went forward to his rope locker. The woman aboard continued to look embarrassed.

Kelly maneuvered clear for a moment, observing the other "captain," a term his mind applied ironically. He couldn't read charts. He didn't know the proper way of attracting another boat's attention. He didn't even know how to call the Coast Guard. All he'd managed to do was buy a Hatteras yacht, and while that spoke well of his judgment, Kelly figured it had more likely come from a smart salesman. But then the man surprised Kelly. He handled his lines with skill and waved *Springer* in.

Kelly maneuvered his stern in close, then went aft to his well deck to take the towing line, which he secured to the big cleat on the transom. Pam was up and watching now. Kelly hustled back to the fly bridge and coaxed his throttle a crack.

"Get on your radio," he told the Hatteras owner. "Leave your rudder amidships till I tell you different. Okay?"

"Got it."

"Hope so," Kelly whispered to himself, pushing the throttle levers until the towing line came taut.

"What happened to him?" Pam asked.

"People forget there's a bottom under this water. You hit it hard enough and you break things." He paused. "You might want to put some more clothes on."

Pam giggled and went below. Kelly increased speed carefully to about four knots before starting the turn south. He'd done this all before, and grumbled that if he did it one more time he'd have special stationery printed up for the bills.

Kelly brought *Springer* alongside very slowly, mindful of the boat he was towing. He scurried off the bridge to drop his fenders, then jumped ashore to tie off a pair of spring lines before heading towards the Hatteras. The owner already had his mooring lines set up, and tossed them to Kelly on the quay while he set his fenders. Hauling the boat in a few feet was a good chance to show his muscles to Pam. It only took five minutes to get her snugged in, after which Kelly did the same with *Springer*.

"This is yours?"

"Sure enough," Kelly replied. "Welcome to my sandbar."

"Sam Rosen," the man said, holding his hand out. He'd pulled a shirt on, and while he had a strong grip, Kelly noted that his hands were so soft as to be dainty.

"John Kelly."

"My wife, Sarah."

Kelly laughed. "You must be the navigator."

Sarah was short, overweight, and her brown eyes wavered between amusement and embarrassment. "Somebody needs to thank you for your help," she observed in a New York accent.

"A law of the sea, ma'am. What went wrong?"

"The chart shows six feet where we struck. This boat only takes four! And low tide was five hours ago!" the lady snapped. She wasn't angry at Kelly, but he was the closest target, and her husband had already heard what she thought.

"Sandbar, it's been building there from the storms we had last winter, but my charts show less than that. Besides, it's a soft bottom."

Pam came up just then, wearing clothing that was nearly respectable, and Kelly realized he didn't know her last name.

"Hi, I'm Pam."

"Y'all want to freshen up? We have all day to look at the problem." There was general agreement on that point, and Kelly led them off to his home.

"What the hell is that?" Sam Rosen asked. "That" was one of the bunkers that had been built in 1943, two thousand square feet, with a roof fully three feet thick. The entire structure was reinforced concrete and was almost as sturdy as it looked. A second, smaller bunker lay beside it.

"This place used to belong to the Navy," Kelly explained, "but I lease it now."

"Nice dock they built for you," Rosen noted.

"Not bad at all," Kelly agreed. "Mind if I ask what you do?"

"Surgeon," Rosen replied.

"Oh, yeah?" That explained the hands.

"Professor of surgery," Sarah corrected. "But he can't drive a boat worth a damn!"

"The goddamned charts were off!" the professor grumbled as Kelly led them inside. "Didn't you hear?"

"People, that's history now, and lunch and a beer will allow us to consider it in comfort." Kelly surprised himself with his words. Just then his ears caught a sharp *crack* coming across the water from somewhere to the south. It was funny how sound carried across the water.

"What was that?" Sam Rosen had sharp ears, too.

"Probably some kid taking a muskrat with his .22," Kelly judged. "It's a pretty quiet neighborhood, except for that. In the fall it can get a little noisy around dawn—ducks and geese."

"I can see the blinds. You hunt?"

"Not anymore," Kelly replied.

Rosen looked at him with understanding, and Kelly decided to reevaluate him for a second time.

"How long?"

"Long enough. How'd you know?"

"Right after I finished residency, I made it to Iwo and Okinawa. Hospital ship."

"Hmm, kamikaze time?"

Rosen nodded. "Yeah, lots of fun. What were you on?"

"Usually my belly," Kelly answered with a grin.

"UDT? You look like a frogman," Rosen said. "I had to fix a few of those."

"Pretty much the same thing, but dumber." Kelly dialed the combination lock and pulled the heavy steel door open.

The inside of the bunker surprised the visitors. When Kelly had taken possession of the place, it had been divided into three large, bare rooms by stout concrete walls, but now it looked almost like a house, with painted drywall and rugs. Even the ceiling was covered. The narrow view-slits were the only reminder of what it had once been. The furniture and rugs showed the influence of Patricia, but the current state of semiarray was evidence that only a man lived here now. Everything was neatly arranged, but not as a woman would do things. The Rosens also noted that it was the man of the house who led them to the "galley" and got things out of the old-fashioned refrigerator box while Pam wandered around a little wide-eyed.

"Nice and cool," Sarah observed. "Damp in the winter, I bet."

"Not as bad as you think." Kelly pointed to the radiators around the perimeter of the room. "Steam heat. This place was built to government specifications. Everything works and everything cost too much."

"How do you get a place like this?" Sam asked.

"A friend helped me get the lease. Surplus government property."

"He must be some friend," Sarah said, admiring the built-in refrigerator.

"Yes, he is."

Vice Admiral Winslow Holland Maxwell, USN, had his office on the E-Ring of the Pentagon. It was an outside office, allowing him a fine view of Washington—and the demonstrators, he noted angrily to himself. *Baby Killers!* one placard read. There was even a North Vietnamese flag. The chanting, this Saturday morning, was distorted by the thick window glass.

He could hear the cadence but not the words, and the former fighter pilot couldn't decide which was more enraging.

"That isn't good for you, Dutch."

"Don't I know it!" Maxwell grumbled.

"The freedom to do that is one of the things we defend," Rear Admiral Casimir Podulski pointed out, not quite making that leap of faith despite his words. It was just a little too much. His son had died over Haiphong in an A-4 strike-fighter. The event had made the papers because of the young aviator's parentage, and fully eleven anonymous telephone calls had come in the following week, some just laughing, some asking his tormented wife where the blotter was supposed to be shipped. "All those nice, peaceful, sensitive young people."

"So why are you in such a great mood, Cas?"

"This one goes in the wall safe, Dutch." Podulski handed over a heavy folder. Its edges were bordered in red-and-white striped tape, and it bore the coded designator BOXWOOD GREEN.

"They're going to let us play with it?" *That* was a surprise.

"It took me till oh-three-thirty, but yes. Just a few of us, though. We have authorization for a complete feasibility study." Admiral Podulski settled into a deep leather chair and lit up a cigarette. His face was thinner since the death of his son, but the crystal-blue eyes burned as bright as ever.

"They're going to let *us* go ahead and do the planning?" Maxwell and Podulski had worked towards that end for several months, never in any real expectation that they'd be allowed to pursue it.

"Who'd ever suspect us?" the Polish-born Admiral asked with an ironic look. "They want us to keep it off the books."

"Jim Greer, too?" Dutch asked.

"Best intel guy I know, unless you're hiding one somewhere."

"He just started at CIA, I heard last week," Maxwell warned.

"Good. We need a good spy, and his suit's still blue, last time I checked."

"We're going to make enemies doing this, lots of 'em."

Podulski gestured at the window and the noise. He hadn't changed all that much since 1944 and USS *Essex*. "With all those a hundred feet away from us, what'll a few more matter?"

"How long have you had the boat?" Kelly asked about halfway through his second beer. Lunch was rudimentary, cold cuts and bread supplemented by bottled beer.

"We bought it last October, but we've only been running it two months,'' the doctor admitted. ''But I took the Power Squadron courses, finished top in my class.'' He was the sort who finished number one in nearly everything, Kelly figured.

''You're a pretty good line-handler,'' he observed, mainly to make the man feel better.

''Surgeons are pretty good with knots, too.''

''You a doc, too, ma'am?'' Kelly asked Sarah.

''Pharmacologist. I also teach at Hopkins.''

''How long have you and your wife lived here?'' Sam asked, and the conversation ground to an awkward halt.

''Oh, we just met,'' Pam told them artlessly. Naturally enough it was Kelly who was the most embarrassed. The two physicians merely accepted the news as a matter of course, but Kelly worried that they'd see him as a man taking advantage of a young girl. The thoughts associated with his behavior seemed to race in circles around the inside of his skull until he realized that no one else seemed to care all that much.

''Let's take a look at that propeller.'' Kelly stood. ''Come on.''

Rosen followed him out the door. The heat was building outside, and it was best to get things done quickly. The secondary bunker on the island housed Kelly's workshop. He selected a couple of wrenches and wheeled a portable air compressor towards the door.

Two minutes later he had it sitting next to the doctor's Hatteras and buckled a pair of weight belts around his waist.

''Anything I have to do?'' Rosen asked.

Kelly shook his head as he stripped off his shirt. ''Not really. If the compressor quits, I'll know pretty quick, and I'll only be down five feet or so.''

''I've never done that.'' Rosen turned his surgeon's eyes to Kelly's torso, spotting three separate scars that a really good surgeon might have been skillful enough to conceal. Then he remembered that a combat surgeon didn't always have the time for cosmetic work.

''I have, here and there,'' Kelly told him on the way to the ladder.

''I believe it,'' Rosen said quietly to himself.

Four minutes later, by Rosen's watch, Kelly was climbing back up the ladder.

''Found your problem.'' He set the remains of both props on the concrete dock.

''God! What did we hit?''

Kelly sat down for a moment to strip off the weights. It was all he could do not to laugh. ''Water, doc, just water.''

"What?"

"Did you have the boat surveyed before you bought it?"

"Sure, the insurance company made me do that. I got the best buy around, he charged me a hundred bucks."

"Oh, yeah? What deficiencies did he give you?" Kelly stood back up and switched the compressor off.

"Practically nothing. He said there was something wrong with the sinks, and I had a plumber check it, but they were fine. I guess he had to say something for his money, right?"

"Sinks?"

"That's what he told me over the phone. I have the written survey somewhere, but I took the information over the phone."

"Zincs," Kelly said, laughing. "Not sinks."

"What?" Rosen was angry at not getting the joke.

"What destroyed your props was electrolysis. Galvanic reaction. It's caused by having more than one kind of metal in saltwater, corrodes the metal. All the sandbar did was to scuff them off. They were already wrecked. Didn't the Power Squadron tell you about that?"

"Well, yes, but—"

"*But*—you just learned something, Doctor Rosen." Kelly held up the remains of the screw. The metal had the flaked consistency of a soda cracker. "This used to be bronze."

"Damn!" The surgeon took the wreckage in his hand and picked off a waferlike fragment.

"The surveyor meant for you to replace the zinc anodes on the strut. What they do is to absorb the galvanic energy. You replace them every couple of years, and that protects the screws and rudder by remote control, like. I don't know all the science of it, but I do know the effects, okay? Your rudder needs replacement, too, but it's not an emergency. Sure as hell, you need two new screws."

Rosen looked out at the water and swore. "Idiot."

Kelly allowed himself a sympathetic laugh. "Doc, if that's the biggest mistake you make this year, you're a lucky man."

"So what do I do now?"

"I make a phone call and order you a couple of props. I'll call a guy I know over in Solomons, and he'll have somebody run them down here, probably tomorrow." Kelly gestured. "It's not that big a deal, okay? I want to see your charts, too."

Sure enough, when he checked their dates, they were five years old. "You need new ones every year, doc."

"Damn!" Rosen said.

"Helpful hint?" Kelly asked with another smile. "Don't take it so seriously. Best kind of lesson. It hurts a little but not much. You learn and you get on with it."

The doctor relaxed, finally, allowing himself a smile. "I suppose you're right, but Sarah'll never let me forget it."

"Blame the charts," Kelly suggested.

"Will you back me up?"

Kelly grinned. "Men have to stick together at times like this."

"I think I'm going to like you, Mr. Kelly."

"So where the fuck is she?" Billy demanded.

"How the hell should I know?" Rick replied, equally angry—and fearful of what Henry would say when he got back. Both their eyes turned to the woman in the room.

"You're her friend," Billy said.

Doris was trembling already, wishing she could run from the room, but there was no safety in that. Her hands were shaking as Billy took the three steps to her, and she flinched but didn't evade the slap that landed her on the floor.

"*Bitch.* You better tell me what you know!"

"I don't know anything!" she screamed up at him, feeling the burning spot on her face where she'd been hit. She looked over to Rick for sympathy, but saw no emotion at all on his face.

"You know something—and you better tell me right now," Billy said. He reached down to unbutton her shorts, then removed the belt from his pants. "Get the rest in here," he told Rick.

Doris stood without waiting for the order, nude from the waist down, crying silently, her body shaking with sobs for the pain soon to come, afraid even to cower, knowing she couldn't run. There was no safety for her. The other girls came in slowly, not looking in her direction. She'd known that Pam was going to run, but that was all, and her only satisfaction as she heard the belt whistle through the air was that she would reveal nothing that could hurt her friend. As searing as the pain was, Pam had escaped.

3
Captivity

A fter replacing all the diving gear in the machine shop, Kelly took a two-wheel hand truck out onto the quay to handle the groceries. Rosen insisted on helping. His new screws would arrive by boat the next day, and the surgeon didn't seem in any hurry to take his boat back out.

"So," Kelly said, "you teach surgery?"

"Eight years now, yeah." Rosen evened up the boxes on the two-wheeler.

"You don't look like a surgeon."

Rosen took the compliment with grace. "We're not all violinists. My father was a bricklayer."

"Mine was a fireman." Kelly started wheeling the groceries towards the bunker.

"Speaking of surgeons . . ." Rosen pointed at Kelly's chest. "Some good ones worked on you. That one looks like it was nasty."

Kelly nearly stopped. "Yeah, I got real careless that time. Not as bad as it looks, though, just grazed the lung."

Rosen grunted. "So I see. Must have missed your heart by nearly two inches. No big deal."

Kelly moved the boxes into the pantry. "Nice to talk to somebody who understands, doc," he noted, wincing inwardly at the thought, remembering the feel of the bullet when it had spun him around. "Like I said—careless."

"How long were you over there?"

"Total? Maybe eighteen months. Depends on if you count the hospital time."

"That's a Navy Cross you have hanging on the wall. Is that what it's for?"

Kelly shook his head. "That was something else. I had to go up north to retrieve somebody, A-6 pilot. I didn't get hurt, but I got sicker 'n' hell. I had some scratches—you know—from thorns and stuff. They got infected as hell from the river water, would you believe? Three weeks in the hospital from that. It was worse'n being shot."

"Not a very nice place is it?" Rosen asked as they came back for the last load.

"They say there's a hundred different kinds of snake there. Ninety-nine are poisonous."

"And the other one?"

Kelly handed a carton over to the doctor. "That one eats your ass whole." He laughed. "No, I didn't like it there much. But that was the job, and I got that pilot out, and the Admiral made me a chief and got me a medal. Come on, I'll show you my baby." Kelly waved Rosen aboard. The tour took five minutes, with the doctor taking note of all the differences. The amenities were there, but not glitzed up. This guy, he saw, was all business, and his charts were all brand new. Kelly fished out another beer from his cooler for the doctor and another for himself.

"What was Okinawa like?" Kelly asked with a smile, each man sizing up the other, each liking what he saw.

Rosen shrugged and grunted eloquently. "Tense. We had a lot of work, and the kamikazes seemed to think the red cross on the ship made a hell of a nice target."

"You were working while they were coming in at you?"

"Injured people can't wait, Kelly."

Kelly finished his beer. "I'd rather be shooting back. Let me get Pam's stuff and we can get back in the air conditioning." He headed aft and picked up her backpack. Rosen was already on the quay, and Kelly tossed the backpack across. Rosen looked too late, missed the catch, and the pack landed on the concrete. Some contents spilled out, and from twenty feet away, Kelly immediately saw what was wrong even before the doctor's head turned to look at him.

There was a large brown plastic prescription bottle, but without a label. The top had been loose, and from it had spilled a couple of capsules.

Some things are instantly clear. Kelly stepped slowly off the boat to the quay. Rosen picked up the container and placed the spilled capsules back in it before snapping down the white plastic top. Then he handed it to Kelly.

"I know they're not yours, John."

"What are they, Sam?"

His voice could not have been more dispassionate. "The trade name is Quaalude. Methaqualone. It's a barbiturate, a sedative. A sleeping pill. We use it to get people off into dreamland. Pretty powerful. A little too powerful, in fact. A lot of people think it ought to be taken off the market. No label. It's not a prescription."

Kelly suddenly felt tired and old. And betrayed somehow. "Yeah."

"You didn't know?"

"Sam, we only met—not even twenty-four hours ago. I don't know anything about her."

Rosen stretched and looked around the horizon for a moment. "Okay, now I'm going to start being a doctor, okay? Have you ever done drugs?"

"No! I *hate* the goddamned stuff. People die because of it!" Kelly's anger was immediate and vicious, but it wasn't aimed at Sam Rosen.

The professor took the outburst calmly. It was his turn to be business-like. "Settle down. People get hooked on these things. How doesn't matter. Getting excited doesn't help. Take a deep breath, let it out slow."

Kelly did, and managed a smile at the incongruity of the moment. "You sound just like my dad."

"Firemen are smart." He paused. "Okay, your lady friend may have a problem. But she seems like a nice girl, and you seem like a *mensch*. So do we try and solve the problem or not?"

"I guess that's up to her," Kelly observed, bitterness creeping into his voice. He felt betrayed. He'd started giving his heart away again, and now he had to face the fact that he might have been giving it to drugs, or what drugs had made of what ought to have been a person. It might all have been a waste of time.

Rosen became a little stern. "That's right, it is up to her, but it might be up to you, too, a little, and if you act like an idiot, you won't help her very much."

Kelly was amazed by how rational the man sounded under the circum-stances. "You must be a pretty good doc."

"I'm one hell of a good doc," Rosen announced. "This isn't my field, but Sarah is damned good. It may be you're both lucky. She's not a bad girl, John. Something's bothering her. She's nervous about something, in case you didn't notice."

"Well, yes, but—" And some part of Kelly's brain said, *See!*

"But you mainly noticed she's pretty. I was in my twenties once my-self, John. Come on, we may have a little work ahead." He stopped and peered at Kelly. "I'm missing something here. What is it?"

"I lost a wife less than a year ago." Kelly explained on for a minute or two.

"And you thought that maybe she—"

"Yeah, I guess so. Stupid, isn't it?" Kelly wondered why he was opening up this way. Why not just let Pam do whatever she wanted? But that wasn't an answer. If he did that, he would just be using her for his selfish needs, discarding her when the bloom came off the rose. For all the reverses his life had taken in the past year, he knew that he couldn't do that, couldn't be one of those men. He caught Rosen looking fixedly at him.

Rosen shook his head judiciously. "We all have vulnerabilities. You have training and experience to deal with your problems. She doesn't. Come on, we have work to do." Rosen took the hand truck in his large, soft hands and wheeled it towards the bunker.

The cool air inside was a surprisingly harsh blast of reality. Pam was trying to entertain Sarah, but not succeeding. Perhaps Sarah had written it off to the awkward social situation, but physicians' minds are always at work, and she was starting to apply a professional eye to the person in front of her. When Sam entered the living room, Sarah turned and gave him a look that Kelly was able to understand.

"And so, well, I left home when I was sixteen," Pam was saying, rattling on in a monotonal voice that exposed more than she knew. Her eyes turned, too, and focused on the backpack Kelly held in his hands. Her voice had a surprisingly brittle character that he'd not noticed before.

"Oh, great. I need some of that stuff." She came over and took the pack from his hands, then headed towards the master bedroom. Kelly and Rosen watched her leave, then Sam handed his wife the plastic container. She needed only one look.

"I didn't know," Kelly said, feeling the need to defend himself. "I didn't see her take anything." He thought back, trying to remember times when she had not been in his sight, and concluded that she might have taken pills two or perhaps three times, then realizing what her dreamy eyes had really been after all.

"Sarah?" Sam asked.

"Three-hundred-milligram. It ought not to be a severe case, but she does need assistance."

Pam came back into the room a few seconds later, telling Kelly that she'd left something on the boat. Her hands weren't trembling, but only because she was holding them together to keep them still. It was so clear, once you knew what to look for. She was trying to control herself, and almost succeeding, but Pam wasn't an actress.

"Is this it?" Kelly asked. He held the bottle in his hands. His reward for the harsh question was like a well-earned knife in the heart.

Pam didn't reply for a few seconds. Her eyes fixed on the brown plastic container, and the first thing Kelly saw was a sudden, hungry expression as though her thoughts were already reaching for the bottle, already picking one or more of the tablets out, already anticipating whatever it was that she got from the damned things, not caring, not even noting that there were others in the room. Then the shame hit her, the realization that whatever image she had tried to convey to the others was rapidly diminishing. But worst of all, after her eyes swept over Sam and Sarah, they settled on Kelly again, oscillating between his hand and his face. At first hunger vied with shame, but shame won, and when her eyes locked on his, the expression on her face began as that of a child caught misbehaving, but it and she matured into something else, as she saw that something which might have grown into love was changing over an interval of heartbeats into contempt and disgust. Her breathing changed in a moment, becoming rapid, then irregular as the sobs began, and she realized that the greatest disgust was within her own mind, for even a drug addict must look inward, and doing so through the eyes of others merely added a cruel edge.

"I'm s–s–s-orry, Kel–el–y. I di–didn't tel–el . . ." she tried to say, her body collapsing into itself. Pam seemed to shrink before their eyes as she saw what might have been a chance evaporate, and beyond that dissipating cloud was only despair. Pam turned away, sobbing, unable to face the man she'd begun to love.

It was decision time for John Terrence Kelly. He could feel betrayed, or he could show the same compassion to her that she had shown to him less than twenty hours before. More than anything else, what decided it was her look to him, the shame so manifest on her face. He could not just stand there. He had to do something, else his own very proud image of himself would dissolve as surely and rapidly as hers.

Kelly's eyes filled with tears as well. He went to her and wrapped his arms around her to keep her from falling, cradling her like a child, pulling her head back against his chest, because it was now his time to be strong for her, to set whatever thoughts he had aside for a while, and even the dissonant part of his mind refused to cackle its *I told you so* at this moment, because there was someone hurt in his arms, and this wasn't the time for that. They stood together for a few minutes while the others watched with a mixture of personal unease and professional detachment.

"I've been trying," she said presently, "I really have—but I was so scared."

"It's okay," Kelly told her, not quite catching what she had just said. "You were there for me, and now it's my turn to be here for you."

"But—" She started sobbing again, and it took a minute or so before she got it out. "I'm not what you think I am."

Kelly let a smile creep into his voice as he missed the second warning. "You don't know what I think, Pammy. It's okay. Really." He'd concentrated so hard on the girl in his arms that he hadn't noticed Sarah Rosen at his side.

"Pam, how about we take a little walk?" Pam nodded agreement, and Sarah led her outside, leaving Kelly to look at Sam.

"You are a *mensch,*" Rosen announced with satisfaction at his earlier diagnosis of the man's character. "Kelly, how close is the nearest town with a pharmacy?"

"Solomons, I guess. Shouldn't she be in a hospital?"

"I'll let Sarah make the call on that, but I suspect it's not necessary."

Kelly looked at the bottle still in his hand. "Well, I'm going to deep-six these damned things."

"No!" Rosen snapped. "I'll take them. They all carry lot numbers. The police can identify the shipment that was diverted. I'll lock them up on my boat."

"So what do we do now?"

"We wait a little while."

Sarah and Pam came back in twenty minutes later, holding hands like mother and daughter. Pam's head was up now, though her eyes were still watery.

"We got a winner here, folks," Sarah told them. "She's been trying for a month all by herself."

"She says it isn't hard," Pam said.

"We can make it a lot easier," Sarah assured her. She handed a list to her husband. "Find a drugstore. John, get your boat moving. Now."

"What happens?" Kelly asked thirty minutes and five miles later. Solomons was already a tan-green line on the northwestern horizon.

"The treatment regime is pretty simple, really. We support her with barbiturates and ease her off."

"You give her drugs to get her off drugs?"

"Yep." Rosen nodded. "That's how it's done. It takes time for the body to flush out all the residual material in her tissues. The body becomes dependent on the stuff, and if you try to wean them off too rapidly, you can get some adverse effects, convulsions, that sort of thing. Occasionally people die from it."

"What?" said Kelly, alarmed. "I don't know anything about this, Sam."

"Why should you? That's our job, Kelly. Sarah doesn't think that's a problem in this case. Relax, John. You give"— Rosen took the list from his pocket—"yeah, I thought so, phenobarb, you give that to attenuate the withdrawal symptoms. Look, you know how to drive a boat, right?"

"Yep," Kelly said, turning, knowing what came next.

"Let us do our job. Okay?"

The man didn't feel much like sleep, the coastguardsmen saw, much to their own displeasure. Before they'd had the chance to recover from the previous day's adventures, he was up again, drinking coffee in the operations room, looking over the charts yet again, using his hand to make circles, which he compared with the memorized course track of the forty-one-boat.

"How fast is a sailboat?" he asked an annoyed and irritable Quartermaster First Class Manuel Oreza.

"That one? Not very, with a fair breeze and calm seas, maybe five knots, a little more if the skipper is smart and experienced. Rule of thumb is, one point three times the square root waterline length is your hull speed, so for that one, five or six knots." And he hoped the civilian was duly impressed with that bit of nautical trivia.

"It was windy last night," the official noted crossly.

"A small boat doesn't go faster on choppy seas, it goes slower. That's because it spends a lot of time going up and down instead of forward."

"So how did he get away from you?"

"He didn't get away from *me*, okay?" Oreza wasn't clear on who this guy was or how senior a position he actually held, but he wouldn't have taken this sort of abuse from a real officer—but a real officer would not have harassed him this way; a real officer would have listened and understood. The petty officer took a deep breath, wishing for once that there was an officer here to explain things. Civilians listened to officers, which said a lot about the intelligence of civilians. "Look, sir, you told me to lay back, didn't you? I *told* you that we'd lose him in the clutter from the storm, and we did. Those old radars we use aren't worth a damn in bad weather, least not for a dinky little target like a day-sailer."

"You already said that."

And I'll keep saying it until you figure it out, Oreza managed not to say, catching a warning look from Mr. English. Portagee took a deep breath and looked down at the chart.

"So where do you think he is?"

"Hell, the Bay ain't that wide, so's you have two coastlines to worry about. Most houses have their own little docks, you have all these creeks. If it was me, I'd head up a creek. Better place to hide than a dock, right?"

"You're telling me he's gone," the civilian observed darkly.

"Sure as hell," Oreza agreed.

"Three *months* of work went into that!"

"I can't help that, sir." The coastguardsman paused. "Look, he probably went east rather than west, okay? Better to run before the wind than tack into it. That's the good news. Problem is, a little boat like that you can haul it out, put it on a trailer. Hell, it could be in Massachusetts by now."

He looked up from the chart. "Oh, that's just what I wanted to hear!"

"Sir, you want me to lie to you?"

"Three months!"

He just couldn't let go, Oreza and English thought at the same time. You had to learn how to do that. Sometimes the sea took something, and you did your best looking and searching, and mostly you found it, but not always, and when you failed, the time came when you had to let the sea claim the prize. Neither man had ever grown to like it, but that was the way things were.

"Maybe you can whistle up some helicopter support. The Navy has a bunch of stuff at Pax River," Warrant Officer English pointed out. It would also get the guy out of his station, an objective worthy of considerable effort for all the disruption he was causing to English and his men.

"Trying to get rid of me?" the man asked with an odd smile.

"Excuse me, sir?" English responded innocently. A pity, the warrant officer thought, that the man wasn't a total fool.

Kelly tied back up at his quay after seven. He let Sam take the medications ashore while he snapped various covers over his instrument panels and settled his boat down for the night. It had been a quiet return trip from Solomons. Sam Rosen was a good man at explaining things, and Kelly a good questioner. What he'd needed to learn he'd picked up on the way out, and for most of the return trip he'd been alone with his thoughts, wondering what he would do, how he should act. Those were questions without easy answers, and attending to ship's business didn't help, much as he'd hoped that it would. He took even more time than was necessary checking the mooring lines, doing the same for the surgeon's boat as well before heading inside.

*   *   *

The Lockheed DC-130E Hercules cruised well above the low cloud deck, riding smoothly and solidly as it had done for 2,354 hours of logged flight time since leaving the Lockheed plant at Marietta, Georgia, several years earlier. Everything had the appearance of a pleasant flying day. In the roomy front office, the flight crew of four watched the clear air and various instruments, as their duties required. The four turboprop engines hummed along with their accustomed reliability, giving the aircraft a steady high-pitched vibration that transmitted itself through the comfortable high-backed seats and created standing circular ripples in their Styrofoam coffee cups. All in all, the atmosphere was one of total normality. But anyone seeing the exterior of the aircraft could tell different. This aircraft belonged to the 99th Strategic Reconnaissance Squadron.

Beyond the outer engines on each wing of the Hercules hung additional aircraft. Each of these was a Model-147SC drone. Originally designed to be high-speed targets with the designation Firebee-II, now they bore the informal name "Buffalo Hunter." In the rear cargo area of the DC-130E was a second crew which was now powering up both of the miniature aircraft, having already programmed them for a mission sufficiently secret that none of them actually knew what it was all about. They didn't have to. It was merely a matter of telling the drones what to do and when to do it. The chief technician, a thirty-year-old sergeant, was working a bird code-named Cody-193. His crew station allowed him to turn and look out a small port-hole to inspect his bird visually, which he did even though there was no real reason to do so. The sergeant loved the things as a child will love a particularly entertaining toy. He'd worked with the drone program for ten years, and this particular one he had flown sixty-one times. That was a record for the area.

Cody-193 had a distinguished ancestry. Its manufacturers, Teledyne-Ryan of San Diego, California, had built Charles Lindbergh's *Spirit of St. Louis,* but the company had never quite managed to cash in on that bit of aviation history. Struggling from one small contract to another, it had finally achieved financial stability by making targets. Fighter aircraft had to practice shooting at something. The Firebee drone had begun life as just that, a miniature jet aircraft whose mission was to die gloriously at the hands of a fighter pilot—except that the sergeant had never quite seen things that way. He was a drone controller, and his job, he thought, was to teach those strutting eagles a lesson by flying "his" bird in such a way as to make their missiles hit nothing more substantial than air. In fact, fighter pilots had learned to curse his name, though Air Force etiquette also required them to buy him a bottle of booze for every miss. Then a few years earlier someone had noted that if a Firebee drone was hard for our people to hit, the same might be true of others who fired at aircraft for more serious purposes than the annual William Tell competition. It was also a hell of a lot easier on the crews of low-level reconnaissance aircraft.

Cody-193's engine was turning at full power, hanging from its pylon and actually giving the mother aircraft a few knots of free airspeed. The sergeant gave it a final look before turning back to his instruments. Sixty-one small parachute symbols were painted on the left side just forward of the wing, and with luck, in a few days he would paint a sixty-second. Though he was not clear on the precise nature of this mission, merely beating the competition was reason enough to take the utmost care in preparing his personal toy for the current game.

"Be careful, baby," the sergeant breathed as it dropped free. Cody-193 was on its own.

Sarah had a light dinner cooking. Kelly smelled it even before opening the door. Kelly came inside to see Rosen sitting in the living room.

"Where's Pam?"

"We gave her some medication," Sam answered. "She ought to be sleeping now."

"She is," Sarah confirmed, passing through the room on the way to the kitchen. "I just checked. Poor thing, she's exhausted, she's been doing without sleep for some time. It's catching up with her."

"But if she's been taking sleeping pills—"

"John, your body reacts strangely to the things," Sam explained. "It fights them off, or tries to, at the same time it becomes dependent on them. Sleep will be her big problem for a while."

"There's something else," Sarah reported. "She's very frightened of something, but she wouldn't say what it was." She paused, then decided that Kelly ought to know. "She's been abused, John. I didn't ask about it—one thing at a time—but somebody's given her a rough time."

"Oh?" Kelly looked up from the sofa. "What do you mean?"

"I mean she's been sexually assaulted," Sarah said in a calm, professional voice that belied her personal feelings.

"You mean raped?" Kelly asked in a low voice while the muscles of his arms tensed.

Sarah nodded, unable now to hide her distaste. "Almost certainly. Probably more than once. There is also evidence of physical abuse on her back and buttocks."

"I didn't notice."

"You're not a doctor," Sarah pointed out. "How did you meet?"

Kelly told her, remembering the look in Pam's eyes and knowing now what it must have been from. Why hadn't he noticed it? Why hadn't he noticed a lot of things? Kelly raged.

"So she was trying to escape. . . . I wonder if the same man got her on the barbiturates?" Sarah asked. "Nice guy, whoever it was."

"You mean that somebody's been working her over, and got her on drugs?" Kelly said. "But why?"

"Kelly, please don't take this wrong . . . but she might have been a prostitute. Pimps control girls that way." Sarah Rosen hated herself for saying that, but this was business and Kelly had to know. "She's young, pretty, a runaway from a dysfunctional family. The physical abuse, the undernourishment, it all fits the pattern."

Kelly was looking down at the floor. "But she's not like that. I don't understand." But in some ways he did, he told himself, thinking back. The ways in which she'd clung to him and drawn him to her. How much was simply skill, and how much real human feelings? It was a question he had no desire to face. What was the right thing to do? Follow your mind? Follow your heart? And where might they lead?

"She's fighting back, John. She's got guts." Sarah sat across from Kelly. "She's been on the road for over four years, doing God knows what, but something in her won't quit. But she can't do it alone. She needs you. Now I have a question." Sarah looked hard at him. "Will you be there to help her?"

Kelly looked up, his blue eyes the color of ice as he searched for what he really felt. "You guys are really worked up about this, aren't you?"

Sarah sipped from a drink she'd made for herself. She was rather a dumpy woman, short and overweight. Her black hair hadn't seen a stylist in months. All in all she looked like the sort of woman who, behind the wheel of a car, attracts the hatred of male drivers. But she spoke with focused passion, and her intelligence was already very clear to her host. "Do you have any idea how bad it's getting? Ten years ago, drug abuse was so rare that I hardly had to bother with it. Oh, sure, I *knew* about it, read the articles from Lexington, and every so often we'd get a heroin case. Not very many. Just a black problem, people thought. Nobody really gave much of a damn. We're paying for that mistake now. In case you didn't notice, that's all changed—and it happened practically overnight. Except for the project I'm working on, I'm nearly full-time on kids with drug problems. I wasn't *trained* for this. I'm a *scientist,* an expert on adverse interactions, chemical structures, how we can design new drugs to do special things—but now I have to spend nearly all of my time in clinical work, trying to keep children alive who should be just learning how to drink a beer but instead have their systems full of chemical *shit* that never should have made it outside a goddamned laboratory!''

"And it's going to get worse," Sam noted gloomily.

Sarah nodded. "Oh yeah, the next big one is cocaine. She needs you, John," Sarah said again, leaning forward. It was as though she had surrounded herself with her own storm cloud of electrical energy. "You'd damned well better be there for her, boy. You be there for her! Somebody dealt her a really shitty hand, but she's *fighting*. There's a *person* in there."

"Yes, ma'am," Kelly said humbly. He looked up and smiled, no longer confused. "In case you were worried, I decided that a while back."

"Good." Sarah nodded curtly.

"What do I do first?"

"More than anything else, she needs rest, she needs good food, and she needs time to flush the barbiturates out of her system. We'll support her with phenobarb, just in case we have withdrawal problems—I don't expect that. I examined her while you two were gone. Her physical problem is not so much addiction as exhaustion and undernourishment. She ought to be ten pounds heavier than she is. She ought to tolerate withdrawal rather well if we support her in other ways."

"Me, you mean?" Kelly asked.

"That's a lot of it." She looked over towards the open bedroom door and sighed, the tension going out of her. "Well, given her underlying condition, that phenobarb will probably have her out for the rest of the night. Tomorrow we start feeding her and exercising her. For now," Sarah announced, "we can feed ourselves."

Dinner talk focused deliberately on other subjects, and Kelly found himself delivering a lengthy discourse on the bottom contours of the Chesapeake Bay, segueing into what he knew about good fishing spots. It was soon decided that his visitors would stay until Monday evening. Time over the dinner table lengthened, and it was nearly ten before they rose. Kelly cleaned up, then quietly entered his bedroom to hear Pam's quiet breathing.

Only thirteen feet long, and a scant three thousand sixty-five pounds of mass—nearly half of that fuel—the Buffalo Hunter angled towards the ground as it accelerated to an initial cruising speed of over five hundred knots. Already its navigational computer, made by Lear-Siegler, was monitoring time and altitude in a very limited way. The drone was programmed to follow a specific flight path and altitude, all painstakingly predetermined for systems that were by later standards absurdly primitive. For all that, Cody-193 was a sporty-looking beast. Its profile was remarkably like that of a blue shark with a protruding nose and underslung air intake for a mouth—stateside it was often painted with aggressive rows of teeth. In this particular case, an experimental paint scheme—flat white beneath and mottled brown and green atop—was supposed to make it harder to spot from the ground—and the air. It was also stealthy—a term not yet invented. Blankets of RAM—radar-absorbing material—were integral with the wing surfaces, and the air intake was screened to attenuate the radar return off the whirling engine blades.

Cody-193 crossed the border between Laos and North Vietnam at 11:-41:38 local time. Still descending, it leveled out for the first time at five hundred feet above ground level, turning northeast, somewhat slower now in the thicker air this close to the ground. The low altitude and small size of the speeding drone made it a difficult target, but by no means an impossible one, and outlying gun positions of the dense and sophisticated North Vietnamese air-defense network spotted it. The drone flew directly towards a recently sited 37mm twin gun mount whose alert crew got their mount slued around quickly enough to loose twenty quick rounds, three of which passed within feet of the diminutive shape but missed. Cody-193 took no note of this, and neither jinked nor evaded the fire. Without a brain, without eyes, it continued along on its flight path rather like a toy train around a Christmas tree while its new owner ate breakfast in the kitchen. In fact it was being watched. A distant EC-121 Warning Star tracked -193 by means of a coded radar transponder located atop the drone's vertical fin.

"Keep going, baby," a major whispered to himself, watching his scope. He knew of the mission, how important it was, and why nobody else could be allowed to know. Next to him was a small segment from a topographical map. The drone turned north at the right place, dropping down to three hundred feet as it found the right valley, following a small tributary river. At least the guys who programmed it knew their stuff, the major thought.

-193 had burned a third of its fuel by now and was consuming the remaining amount very rapidly at low level, flying below the crests of the unseen hills to the left and right. The programmers had done their best, but there was one chillingly close call when a puff of wind forced it to the right before the autopilot could correct, and -193 missed an unusually tall tree by a scant seventy feet. Two militiamen were on that crest and fired off their rifles at it, and again the rounds missed. One of them started down the hill towards a telephone, but his companion called for him to stop as -193 flew blindly on. By the time a call was made and received, the enemy aircraft would be long gone, and besides, they'd done their duty in shooting at it. He worried about where their bullets had landed, but it was too late for that.

Colonel Robin Zacharias, USAF, was walking across the dirt of what might in other times and circumstances be called a parade ground, but there were no parades here. A prisoner for over six months, he faced every day as a struggle, contemplating misery more deep and dark than anything he'd been able to imagine. Shot down on his eighty-ninth mission, within sight of rotation home, a completely successful mission brought to a bloody end by nothing more significant than bad luck. Worse, his "bear" was dead. And he was probably the lucky one, the Colonel thought as he was led across the compound by two small, unfriendly men with rifles. His arms were tied behind him, and his ankles were hobbled because they were afraid of him despite their guns, and even with all that he was also being watched by men in the guard towers. *I must really look scary to the little bastards,* the fighter pilot told himself.

Zacharias didn't feel very dangerous. His back was still injured from the ejection. He'd hit the ground severely crippled, and his effort to evade capture had been little more than a token gesture, a whole hundred yards of movement over a period of five minutes, right into the arms of the gun crew which had shredded his aircraft.

The abuse had begun there. Paraded through three separate villages, stoned and spat upon, he'd finally ended up here. Wherever here was. There were sea birds. Perhaps he was close to the sea, the Colonel speculated. But the memorial in Salt Lake City, several blocks from his boyhood home, reminded him that gulls were not merely creatures of the sea. In the preceding months he had been subjected to all sorts of physical abuse, but it had strangely slackened off in the past few weeks. Perhaps they'd become tired of hurting him, Zacharias told himself. And maybe there really was a Santa Claus, too, he thought, his head looking down at the dirt. There was little consolation to be had here. There were other prisoners, but his attempts at communicating with them had all failed. His cell had no windows. He'd seen two faces, neither of which he had recognized. On both occasions he'd started to call out a greeting only to be clubbed to the ground by one of his guards. Both men had seen him but made no sound. In both cases he'd seen a smile and a nod, the best that they could do. Both men were of his age, and, he supposed, about his rank, but that was all he knew. What was most frightening to a man who had much to be frightened about was that this was not what he had been briefed to expect. It wasn't the Hanoi Hilton, where all the POWs were supposed to have been congregated. Beyond that he knew virtually nothing, and the unknown can be the most frightening thing of all, especially to a man accustomed over a period of twenty years to being absolute master of his fate. His only consolation, he thought, was that things were as bad as they could be. On that, he was wrong.

"Good morning, Colonel Zacharias," a voice called across the compound. He looked up to see a man taller than himself, Caucasian, and wearing a uniform very different from that of his guards. He strode towards the prisoner with a smile. "Very different from Omaha, isn't it?"

That was when he heard a noise, a thin screeching whine, approaching from the southwest. He turned on instinct—an aviator must always look to see an aircraft, no matter where he might be. It appeared in an instant, before the guards had a chance to react.

Buffalo Hunter, Zacharias thought, standing erect, turning to watch it pass, staring at it, holding his head up, seeing the black rectangle of the camera window, whispering a prayer that the device was operating. When the guards realized what he was doing, a gun butt in the kidneys dropped the colonel to the ground. Suppressing a curse, he tried to deal with the pain as a pair of boots came into his restricted field of vision.

"Do not get overly excited," the other man said. "It's heading to Haiphong to count the ships. Now, my friend, we need to become acquainted."

Cody-193 continued northeast, holding a nearly constant speed and altitude as it entered the dense air-defense belt surrounding North Vietnam's only major port. The cameras in the Buffalo Hunter recorded several triple-A batteries, observation points, and more than a few people with AK-47s, all of whom made at least a token shot at the drone. The only thing -193 had going for it was its small size. Otherwise it flew on a straight and level course while its cameras snapped away, recording the images on 2.25-inch film. About the only thing not shot at it were surface-to-air missiles: -193 was too low for that.

"Go, baby, go!" the Major said, two hundred miles away. Outside, the four piston engines of the Warning Star were straining to maintain the altitude necessary for him to watch the drone's progress. His eyes were locked on the flat glass screen, following the blinking blip of the radar transponder. Other controllers monitored the location of other American aircraft also visiting the enemy country, in constant communication with RED CROWN, the Navy ship that managed air operations from the seaward side. "Turn east, baby—now!"

Right on schedule, Cody-193 banked hard to the right, coming a touch lower and screaming over the Haiphong docks at 500 knots, a hundred tracer rounds in its wake. Longshoremen and sailors from various ships looked up in curiosity and irritation, and not a little fear for all the steel flying in the sky over their heads.

"Yes!" the Major shouted, loudly enough that the sergeant-controller to his left looked up in irritation. You were supposed to keep things quiet here. He keyed his mike to speak to RED CROWN. "Cody-one-niner-three is bingo."

"Roger, copy bingo on one-niner-three," the acknowledgment came back. It was a false use of the "bingo" code word, which ordinarily meant an aircraft with a low fuel state, but it was a term so commonly used that it made a more than adequate disguise. The Navy enlisted man on the other end of the circuit then told an orbiting helicopter crew to wake up.

The drone cleared the coast right on schedule, keeping low for a few more miles before going into its final climb, down to its last hundred pounds of fuel as it reached its pre-programmed point thirty miles offshore and began circling. Now another transponder came on, one tuned to the search radars of U.S. Navy picket ships. One of these, the destroyer *Henry B. Wilson*, took note of the expected target at the expected time and place. Her missile technicians used the opportunity to run a practice intercept problem, but had to switch off their illumination radars after a few seconds. It made the airedales nervous.

Circling at five thousand feet, Cody-193 finally ran out of fuel and became a glider. When the airspeed fell to the right number, explosive bolts blew a hatch cover off the top, deploying a parachute. The Navy helicopter was already on station, and the white 'chute made for a fine target. The drone's weight was a scant fifteen hundred pounds now, barely that of eight men. Wind and visibility cooperated this day. The 'chute was snagged on their first attempt, and the helicopter turned at once, heading for the carrier USS *Constellation*, where the drone was carefully lowered into a cradle, ending its sixty-second combat mission. Before the helicopter could find its own spot on the flight deck, a technician was already unfastening the cover plate on the photo compartment and yanking the heavy film cassette from its slot. He took it below at once, and handed it over to another technician in the ship's elaborate photo lab. Processing required a brief six minutes, and the still-damp film was wiped clean and handed over yet again to an intelligence officer. It was better than good. The film was run from one spool to another over a flat glass plate under which was a pair of fluorescent lights.

"Well, Lieutenant?" a captain asked tensely.

"Okay, sir, wait one . . ." Turning the spool, he pointed to the third image. "There's our first reference point . . . there's number two, she was right on course . . . okay, here's the IP . . . down the valley, over the hill— there, sir! We have two, three frames! Good ones, the sun was just right, clear day—you know why they call these babies Buffalo Hunters? It's—"

"Let me see!" The Captain nearly shoved the junior officer out of the way. There was a man there, an American, with two guards, and a fourth man—but it was the American he wanted to see.

"Here, sir." The Lieutenant handed over a magnifying glass. "We might get a good face off of this, and we can play with the negative some more if you give us a little time. Like I said, the cameras can tell the difference between a male and a female—"

"Mmmmm." The face was black, meaning a white man on the negative. But— "Damn, I can't tell."

"Cap'n, that's our job, okay?" He was an intelligence officer. The Captain was not. "Let us do our job, sir."

"He's one of ours!"

"Sure as hell, sir, and this guy isn't. Let me take these back to the lab for positive prints and blowups. The air wing will want a look at the port shots, too."

"They can wait."

"No, sir, they can't," the Lieutenant pointed out. But he took a pair of scissors and removed the relevant shots. The remainder of the roll was handed to a chief petty officer, while the Lieutenant and the Captain went back to the photo lab. Fully two months of work had gone into the flight of Cody-193, and the Captain lusted for the information he knew to be on those three two-and-a-quarter-inch frames.

An hour later he had it. An hour after that, he boarded a flight to Danang. Another hour and he was on a flight to Cubi Point Naval Air Station in the Philippines, followed by a puddle-jumper to Clark Air Force Base, and a KC-135 that would fly directly to California. Despite the time and rigors of the next twenty hours of flying, the Captain slept briefly and fitfully, having solved a mystery whose answer just might change the policy of his government.

4

First Light

Kelly slept nearly eight hours, again arising at the sound of the gulls to find that Pam wasn't there. He went outside and saw her standing on the quay, looking out over the water, still weary, still robbed of the ability to get the rest she needed. The Bay had its usual morning calm, the glassy surface punctuated by the circular ripples of bluefish chasing after insects. Conditions like this seemed so fitting to the start of a day, a gentle westerly breeze in his face, and the odd silence that allowed one to hear the rumble of a boat's motor from so far away that the boat could not be seen. It was the sort of time that allowed you to be alone with nature, but he knew that Pam merely felt alone. Kelly walked out to her as quietly as he could and touched her waist with both his hands.

"Good morning." She didn't answer for a long time, and Kelly stood still, holding her lightly, just enough that she could feel his touch. She was wearing one of his shirts, and he didn't want his touch to be sexual, only protective. He was afraid to press himself on a woman who'd suffered that kind of abuse, and could not predict where the invisible line might be.

"So now you know," she said, just loudly enough to be heard over the silence, unable to turn and face him.

"Yes," Kelly answered, equally quiet.

"What do you think?" Her voice was a painful whisper.

"I'm not sure what you mean, Pam." Kelly felt the trembling start, and he had to resist the urge to hold her tighter.

"About me."

"About you?" He allowed himself to get a little closer, altering his hold until his arms wrapped around her waist, but not tightly. "I think you're beautiful. I think I'm real glad we met."

"I do drugs."

"The docs say you're trying to quit. That's good enough for me."

"It's worse than that, I've done things—" Kelly cut her off.

"I don't care about that, Pam. I've done things, too. And one thing you did, for me was very nice. You gave me something to care about, and I didn't ever expect that to happen." Kelly pulled her tighter. "The things you did before we met don't matter. You're not alone, Pam. I'm here to help if you want me to."

"When you find out . . ." she warned.

"I'll take my chances. I think I know the important parts already. I love you, Pam." Kelly surprised himself with those words. He'd been too afraid to voice the thought even to himself. It was too irrational, but again emotion won out over reason, and reason, for once, found itself approving.

"How can you say that?" Pam asked. Kelly gently turned her around and smiled.

"Damned if I know! Maybe it's your tangled hair—or your runny nose." He touched her chest through the shirt. "No, I think it's your heart. No matter what's behind you, your heart is just fine."

"You mean that, don't you?" she asked, looking at his chest. There was a long moment, then Pam smiled up at him, and that, too, was like a dawn. The orange-yellow glow of the rising sun lit up her face and highlighted her fair hair.

Kelly wiped the tears from her face, and the wet feel of her cheeks eliminated whatever doubts he might have had. "We're going to have to get you some clothes. This is no way for a lady to dress."

"Who says I'm a lady?"

"I do."

"I'm so scared!"

Kelly pulled her against his chest. "It's okay to be scared. I was scared all the time. The important part is to know that you're going to do it." His hands rubbed up and down her back. He hadn't intended to make this a sexual encounter, but he found himself becoming aroused until he realized that his hands were rubbing over scars made by men with whips or ropes or belts or other odious things. Then his eyes looked straight out over the water, and it was just as well that she couldn't see his face.

"You must be hungry," he said, stepping away from her, holding on to her hands.

She nodded. "Starving."

"That I can fix." Kelly led her by the hand back to the bunker. Already he loved her touch. They met Sam and Sarah coming from the other side of the island after a morning's walk and stretch.

"How are our two lovebirds?" Sarah asked with a beaming smile, because she'd already seen the answer, watching from two hundred yards away.

"Hungry!" Pam replied.

"And we're getting a couple of screws today," Kelly added with a wink.

"What?" Pam asked.

"Propellers," Kelly explained. "For Sam's boat."

"Screws?"

"Sailor talk, trust me." He grinned at her, and she wasn't sure if she could believe it or not.

"That took long enough," Tony observed, sipping coffee from a paper cup.

"Where's mine?" Eddie demanded, irritable from lack of sleep.

"You told me to put the fucking heater outside, remember? Get your own."

"You think I want all that smoke and shit in here? You can die from that monoxide shit," Eddie Morello said irritably.

Tony was tired as well. Too tired to argue with this loudmouth. "Okay, man, well, the coffeepot's outside. Cups are there too."

Eddie grumbled and went outside. Henry, the third man, was bagging the product and kept out of the argument. It had actually worked out a little better than he'd planned. They'd even bought his story about Angelo, thus eliminating one potential partner and problem. There was at least three hundred thousand dollars' worth of finished drugs now being weighed and sealed in plastic bags for sale to dealers. Things hadn't gone quite as planned. The expected "few hours" of work had lingered into an all-night marathon as the three had discovered that what they paid for others to do wasn't quite as easy as it looked. The three bottles of bourbon they'd brought along hadn't helped either. Still and all, over three hundred thousand dollars of profit from sixteen hours of work wasn't all that bad. And this was just the beginning. Tucker was just giving them a taste.

Eddie was still worried about the repercussions of Angelo's demise. But there was no turning back, not after the killing, and he'd been forced into backing Tony's play. He grimaced as he looked out of a vacant port-hole towards an island north of what had once been a ship. Sunlight was reflecting off the windows of what was probably a nice, large power cruiser. Wouldn't it be nice to get one of those? Eddie Morello liked to fish, and maybe he could take his kids out sometime. It would be a good cover activity, wouldn't it?

Or maybe crab, he told himself. After all, he knew what crabs ate. The thought evoked a quiet bark of a laugh, followed by a brief shudder. Was he safe, linked up with these men? They—he—had just killed Angelo Vorano, not twenty-four hours earlier. But Angelo wasn't part of the outfit, and Tony Piaggi was. He was their legitimacy, their pipeline to the street, and that made him safe—for a while. As long as Eddie stayed smart and alert.

"What room do you suppose this was?" Tucker asked Piaggi, just to make conversation.

"What do you mean?"

"When this was a ship, looks like it was a cabin or something," he said, sealing the last envelope and placing it inside the beer cooler. "I never thought about that." Which was actually true.

"Captain's cabin, you think?" Tony wondered. It was something to pass the time, and he was thoroughly sick of what they'd done all night.

"Could be, I suppose. It's close to the bridge." The man stood, stretching, wondering why it was that he had to do all the hard work. The answer came easily enough. Tony was a "made" man. Eddie wanted to become one. He would never be, and neither would Angelo, Henry Tucker reflected, glad for it. He'd never trusted Angelo, and now he was no longer a problem. One thing about these people, they seemed to keep their word—and they would continue to, as long as he was their connection to the raw material, and not one minute longer. Tucker had no illusions about that. It had been good of Angelo to make his connection with Tony and Eddie, and Angelo's death had had exactly the effect on Henry that his own death would have on the other two: none. All men have their uses, Tucker told himself, closing the beer cooler. And the crabs had to eat too.

With luck that would be the last killing for a while. Tucker didn't shrink from it, but he disliked complications that often came from killing. A good business ran smoothly, without fuss, and made money for everyone, which kept everyone happy, even the customers at the far end of the process. Certainly this load would keep them happy. It was good Asian heroin, scientifically processed and moderately cut with nontoxic elements that would give the users a rocketship high and a calm, gentle descent back to whatever reality they were trying to escape. The sort of rush they would want to experience again, and so they'd return to their pushers, who could charge a little extra for this very good stuff. "Asian Sweet" was already the trade name.

There was danger, having a street name. It gave the police something to target, a name to chase after, specific questions to ask, but that was the risk in having a hot product, and for that reason he'd selected his associates for their experience, connections, and security. His processing site had also been selected with an eye to security. They had a good five miles of visibility, and a fast boat with which to make their escape. Yeah, there was danger, to be sure, but all life was danger, and you measured risk against reward. Henry Tucker's reward for less than a single day's work was one hundred thousand dollars in untaxed cash, and he was willing to risk a lot for that. He was willing to risk far more for what Piaggi's connections could do, and now he had them interested. Soon they'd become as ambitious as he was.

The boat from Solomons arrived a few minutes early, with the propellers. The doctors hadn't told Kelly to keep Pam busy, but it was a simple enough prescription for her problems. Kelly wheeled the portable compressor back onto the dock and started it up, telling her how to regulate the airflow by keeping an eye on a gauge. Next he got the wrenches he needed and set them on the dock also.

"One finger, this one, two fingers, that one, and three fingers, this one here, okay?"

"Right," Pam replied, impressed with Kelly's expertise. He was hamming things up a little, the rest of them knew, but that was okay with everyone.

Kelly climbed down the ladder into the water, and his first job was to check the threads on the prop shafts, which appeared to be in decent shape. He reached his hand out of the water with one finger up and was rewarded with the right wrench, which he used to remove the retaining nuts, then handed them up one at a time. The whole operation took only fifteen minutes, and the shiny new screws were fully attached, and new protective anodes set in place. He took his time giving the rudders a look, and decided that they'd be okay for the rest of the year, though Sam should keep an eye on them. It was a relief, as usual, to climb out of the water and breathe air that didn't taste like rubber.

"What do I owe you?" Rosen asked.

"For what?" Kelly took off his gear and switched off the compressor.

"I always pay a man for his work," the surgeon said somewhat self-righteously.

Kelly had to laugh. "Tell you what, if I ever need a back operation, you can make it a freebie. What is it you docs call this sort of thing?"

"Professional courtesy—but you're not a physician," Rosen objected.

"And you're not a diver. You're not a seaman yet, either, but we're going to fix that today, Sam."

"I was at the top of my power-squadron class!" Rosen boomed.

"Doc, when we got kids from training school, we used to say, 'That's fine, sonny, but this here's the fleet.' Let me get the gear stowed and we'll see how well you can really drive this thing."

"I bet I'm a better fisherman than you are," Rosen proclaimed.

"Next they're going to see who can pee the farthest," Sarah observed acidly to Pam.

"That, too." Kelly laughed on his way back inside. Ten minutes later he'd cleaned off and changed into a T-shirt and cutoffs.

He took a place on the flying bridge and watched Rosen prepare his boat for getting under way. The surgeon actually impressed Kelly, particularly with his line handling.

"Next time let your blowers work for a while before you light off the engines," Kelly said after Rosen started up.

"But it's a diesel."

"Number one, 'it' is a 'she,' okay? Number two, it's a good habit to get into. The next boat you drive might be gas. Safety, doc. You ever take a vacation and rent a boat?"

"Well, yes."

"In surgery you do the same thing the same way, every time?" Kelly asked. "Even when you don't really have to?"

Rosen nodded thoughtfully. "I hear you."

"Take her out." Kelly waved. This Rosen did, and rather smartly, the surgeon thought. Kelly didn't: "Less rudder, more screws. You won't always have a breeze helping you away from alongside. Propellers push water; rudders just direct it a little. You can always depend on your engines, especially at low speed. And steering breaks sometimes. Learn how to do without it."

"Yes, Captain," Rosen growled. It was like being an intern again, and Sam Rosen was used to having those people snap to his orders. Forty-eight, he thought, was a little old to be a student.

"You're the captain. I'm just the pilot. These are my waters, Sam." Kelly turned to look down at the well deck. "Don't laugh, ladies, it'll be your turn next. Pay attention!" Quietly: "You're being a good sport, Sam."

Fifteen minutes later they were drifting lazily on the tide, fishing lines out under a warm holiday sun. Kelly had little interest in fishing, and instead assigned himself lookout duty on the flying bridge while Sam taught Pam how to bait her line. Her enthusiasm surprised all of them. Sarah made sure that she was liberally covered with Coppertone to protect her pale skin, and Kelly wondered if a little tan would highlight her scars. Alone with his thoughts on the flying bridge, Kelly asked himself what sort of man would abuse a woman. He stared out through squinted eyes at a gently rolling surface dotted with boats. How many people like that were within his sight? Why was it that you couldn't tell from looking at them?

Packing the boat was simple enough. They'd stocked in a good supply of chemicals, which they would have to replenish periodically, but Eddie and Tony had access through a chemical-supply business whose owner had casual ties to their organization.

"I want to see," Tony said as they cast off. It wasn't as easy as he'd imagined, snaking their eighteen-footer through the tidal swamps, but Eddie remembered the spot well enough, and the water was still clear.

"Sweet Jesus!" Tony gasped.

"Gonna be a good year for crabs," Eddie noted, glad that Tony was shocked. A fitting kind of revenge, Eddie thought, but it was not a pleasant sight for any of them. Half a bushel's worth of crabs were already on the body. The face was fully covered, as was one arm, and they could see more of the creatures coming in, drawn by the smell of decay that drifted through the water as efficiently as through the air: nature's own form of advertising. On land, Eddie knew, it would be buzzards and crows.

"What do you figure? Two weeks, maybe three, and then no more Angelo."

"What if somebody—"

"Not much chance of that," Tucker said, not bothering to look. "Too shallow for a sailboat to risk coming in, and motorboats don't bother much. There's a nice wide channel half a mile south, fishing's better there, they say. I guess the crabbers don't like it here either."

Piaggi had trouble looking away, though his stomach had already turned over once. The Chesapeake Bay blue crabs, with their claws, were dismantling the body already softened by warm water and bacteria, one little pinch at a time, tearing with their claws, picking up the pieces with smaller pincers, feeding them into their strangely alien mouths. He'd wondered if there would still be a face there, eyes to stare up at a world left behind, but crabs covered it, and somehow it seemed likely that the eyes had been the first things to go. The frightening part, of course, was that if one man could die this way, so could another, and even though Angelo had already been dead, somehow Piaggi was sure that being disposed of this way was worse than mere death. He would have regretted Angelo's death, except that it was business, and . . . Angelo had deserved it. It was a shame, in a way, that his gruesome fate had to be kept a secret, but that was business, too. That was how you kept the cops from finding out. Hard to prove murder without a body, and here they had accidentally found a way to conceal a number of murders. The only problem was getting the bodies here—and not letting others know of the method of disposal, because people talk, Tony Piaggi told himself, as Angelo had talked. A good thing that Henry had found out about that.

"How 'bout crab cakes when we get back to town?" Eddie Morello asked with a laugh, just to see if he could make Tony puke.

"Let's get the fuck outa here," Piaggi replied quietly, settling into his seat. Tucker took the engine out of idle and picked his way out of the tidal marsh, back into the Bay.

Piaggi took a minute or two to get the sight out of his mind, hoping that he could forget the horror of it and remember only the efficiency of their disposal method. After all, they might be using it again. Maybe after a few hours he'd see humor in it, Tony thought, looking at the cooler. Under the fifteen or so cans of National Bohemian was a layer of ice, under which were twenty sealed bags of heroin. In the unlikely event that anyone stopped them, it was unlikely that they'd look farther than the beer, the real fuel for Bay boaters. Tucker drove the boat north, and the others laid out their fishing rods as though they were trying to find a good place to harvest a few rockfish from the Chesapeake.

"Fishing in reverse," Morello said after a moment, then he laughed loudly enough that Piaggi joined in.

"Toss me a beer!" Tony commanded between laughs. He was a "made man," after all, and deserved respect.

"Idiots," Kelly said quietly to himself. That eighteen-footer was going too fast, too close to other fishing boats. It could catch a few lines, and certainly would throw a wake sure to disturb other craft. That was bad sea manners, something Kelly was always careful to observe. It was just too easy to—hell, it wasn't even hard enough to be "easy." All you had to do was buy a boat and you had the right to sail her around. No tests, no nothing. Kelly found Rosen's 7 × 50 binoculars and focused them on the boat that was coming close aboard. Three assholes, one of them holding up a can of beer in mock salute.

"Bear off, dickhead," he whispered to himself. The jerks in a boat, drinking beer, probably half-potted already, not even eleven o'clock yet. He gave them a good look, and was vaguely grateful that they passed no closer than fifty yards. He caught the name: *Henry's Eighth.* If he saw that name again, Kelly told himself, he'd remember to keep clear.

"I got one!" Sarah called.

"Heads up, we got a big wake coming in from starboard!" It arrived a minute later, causing the big Hatteras to rock twenty degrees left and right of vertical.

"That," Kelly said, looking down at the other three, "is what I mean by bad sea manners!"

"Aye aye!" Sam called back.

"I've still got him," Sarah said. She worked the fish in, Kelly saw, with consummate skill. "Pretty big, too!"

Sam got the net and leaned over the side. A moment later he stood back up. The net contained a struggling rockfish, maybe twelve or fourteen pounds. He dumped the net in a water-filled box in which the fish could wait to die. It seemed cruel to Kelly, but it was only a fish, and he'd seen worse things than that.

Pam started squealing a moment later as her line went taut. Sarah put her rod in its holder and started coaching her. Kelly watched. The friendship between Pam and Sarah was as remarkable as that between himself and the girl. Perhaps Sarah was taking the place of the mother who had been lacking in affection, or whatever Pam's mother had lacked. Regardless, Pam was responding well to the advice and counsel of her new friend. Kelly watched with a smile that Sam caught and returned. Pam was new at this, tripping twice as she walked the fish around. Again Sam did the honors with the net, this time recovering an eight-pound blue.

"Toss it back," Kelly advised. "They don't taste worth a damn!"

Sarah looked up. "Throw back her first fish? What are you, a Nazi? You have any lemon at your place, John?"

"Yeah, why?"

"I'll show you what you can do with a bluefish, that's why." She whispered something to Pam that evoked a laugh. The blue went into the same tank, and Kelly wondered how it and the rock would get along.

Memorial Day, Dutch Maxwell thought, alighting from his official car at Arlington National Cemetery. To many just a time for a five-hundred-mile auto race in Indianapolis, or a day off, or the traditional start of the summer beach season, as testified to by the relative lack of auto traffic in

Washington. But not to him, and not to his fellows. This was their day, a time to remember fallen comrades while others attended to other things both more and less personal. Admiral Podulski got out with him, and the two walked slowly and out of step, as admirals do. Casimir's son, Lieutenant (junior grade) Stanislas Podulski, was not here, and probably never would be. His A-4 had been blotted from the sky by a surface-to-air missile, the reports had told them, nearly a direct hit. The young pilot had been too distracted to notice until perhaps the last second, when his voice had spoken its last epithet of disgust over the "guard" channel. Perhaps one of the bombs he'd been carrying had gone off sympathetically. In any case, the small attack-bomber had dissolved into a greasy cloud of black and yellow, leaving little behind; and besides, the enemy wasn't all that fastidious about respecting the remains of fallen aviators. And so the son of a brave man had been denied his resting place with comrades. It wasn't something that Cas spoke about. Podulski kept such feelings inside.

Rear Admiral James Greer was at his place, as he'd been for the previous two years, about fifty yards from the paved driveway, setting flowers next to the flag at the headstone of his son.

"James?" Maxwell said. The younger man turned and saluted, wanting to smile in gratitude for their friendship on a day like this, but not quite doing so. All three wore their navy-blue uniforms because they carried with them a proper sort of solemnity. Their gold-braided sleeves glistened in the sun. Without a spoken word, all three men lined up to face the headstone of Robert White Greer, First Lieutenant, United States Marine Corps. They saluted smartly, each remembering a young man whom they had bounced on their knees, who had ridden his bike at Naval Station Norfolk and Naval Air Station Jacksonville with Cas's son, and Dutch's. Who had grown strong and proud, meeting his father's ships when they'd returned to port, and talked only about following in his father's footsteps, but not too closely, and whose luck had proven insufficient to the moment, fifty miles southwest of Danang. It was the curse of their profession, each knew but never said, that their sons were drawn to it also, partly from reverence for what their fathers were, partly from a love of country imparted by each to each, most of all from a love of their fellow man. As each of the men standing there had taken his chances, so had Bobby Greer and Stas Podulski taken theirs. It was just that luck had not smiled on two of the three sons.

Greer and Podulski told themselves at this moment that it *had* mattered, that freedom had a price, that some men must pay that price else there would be no flag, no Constitution, no holiday whose meaning people had the right to ignore. But in both cases, those unspoken words rang hollow. Greer's marriage had ended, largely from the grief of Bobby's death. Podulski's wife would never be the same. Though each man had other children, the void created by the loss of one was like a chasm never to be bridged, and as much as each might tell himself that, yes, it was worth the price, no man who could rationalize the death of a child could truly be called a man at all, and their real feelings were reinforced by the same humanity that compelled them to a life of sacrifice. This was all the more true because each had feelings about the war that the more polite called "doubts," and which they called something else, but only among themselves.

"Remember the time Bobby went into the pool to get Mike Goodwin's little girl—saved her life?" Podulski asked. "I just got a note from Mike. Little Amy had twins last week, two little girls. She married an engineer down in Houston, works for NASA."

"I didn't even know she was married. How old is she now?" James asked.

"Oh, she must be twenty . . . twenty-five? Remember her freckles, how the sun used to breed them down at Jax?"

"Little Amy," Greer said quietly. "How they grow." Maybe she wouldn't have drowned that hot July day, but it was one more thing to remember about his son. *One life saved, maybe three?* That was something, wasn't it? Greer asked himself.

The three men turned and left the grave without a word, heading slowly back to the driveway. They had to stop there. A funeral procession was coming up the hill, soldiers of the Third Infantry Regiment, "The Old Guard," doing their somber duty, laying another man to rest. The admirals lined up again, saluting the flag draped on the casket and the man within. The young Lieutenant commanding the detail did the same. He saw that one of the flag officers wore the pale blue ribbon denoting the Medal of Honor, and the severity of his gesture conveyed the depth of his respect.

"Well, there goes another one," Greer said with quiet bitterness after they had passed by. "Dear God, what are we burying these kids for?"

" 'Pay any price, bear any burden, meet any hardship, support any friend, oppose any foe . . .' " Cas quoted. "Wasn't all that long ago, was it? But when it came time to put the chips on the table, where were the bastards?"

"We *are* the chips, Cas," Dutch Maxwell replied. "This *is* the table."

Normal men might have wept, but these were not normal men. Each surveyed the land dotted with white stones. This had been the front lawn of Robert E. Lee once—the house was still atop the hill—and the placement of the cemetery had been the cruel gesture of a government that had felt itself betrayed by the officer. And yet Lee had in the end given his ancestral home to the service of those men whom he had most loved. That was the kindest irony of this day, Maxwell reflected.

"How do things look up the river, James?"

"Could be better, Dutch. I have orders to clean house. I need a pretty big broom."

"Have you been briefed in on Boxwood Green?"

"No." Greer turned and cracked his first smile of the day. It wasn't much, but it was something, the others told themselves. "Do I want to be?"

"We'll probably need your help."

"Under the table?"

"You know what happened with Kingpin," Casimir Podulski noted.

"They were damned lucky to get out," Greer agreed. "Keeping this one tight, eh?"

"You bet we are."

"Let me know what you need. You'll get everything I can find. You doing the 'three' work, Cas?"

"That's right." Any designator with a -3 at the end denoted the operations and planning department, and Podulski had a gift for that. His eyes glittered as brightly as his Wings of Gold in the morning sun.

"Good," Greer observed. "How's little Dutch doing?"

"Flying for Delta now. Copilot, he'll make captain in due course, and I'll be a grandfather in another month or so."

"Really? Congratulations, my friend."

"I don't blame him for getting out. I used to, but not now."

"What's the name of the SEAL who went in to get him?"

"Kelly. He's out, too," Maxwell said.

"You should have gotten the Medal for him, Dutch," Podulski said. "I read the citation. That was as hairy as they come."

"I made him a chief. I couldn't get the Medal for him." Maxwell shook his head. "Not for rescuing the son of an admiral, Cas. You know the politics."

"Yeah." Podulski looked up the hill. The funeral procession had stopped, and the casket was being moved off the gun carriage. A young widow was watching her husband's time on earth end. "Yeah, I know about politics."

Tucker eased the boat into the slip. The inboard-outboard drive made that easy. He cut the engine and grabbed the mooring lines, which he tied off quickly. Tony and Eddie lifted the beer cooler out while Tucker collected the loose gear and snapped a few covers into place before joining his companions on the parking lot.

"Well, that was pretty easy," Tony noted. The cooler was already in the back of his Ford Country Squire station wagon.

"Who do you suppose won the race today?" Eddie asked. They'd neglected to take a radio with them for the trip.

"I had a yard bet on Foyt, just to make it interesting."

"Not Andretti?" Tucker asked.

"He's a paisan, but he ain't lucky. Betting is business," Piaggi pointed out. Angelo was a thing of the past now, and the manner of his disposal was, after all, a little amusing, though the man might never eat crab cakes again.

"Well," Tucker said, "you know where to find me."

"You'll get your money," Eddie said, speaking out of place. "End of the week, the usual place." He paused. "What if demand goes up?"

"I can handle it," Tucker assured him. "I can get all you want."

"What the hell kind of pipeline do you have?" Eddie asked, pushing further.

"Angelo wanted to know that, too, remember? Gentlemen, if I told you that, you wouldn't need me, would you?"

Tony Piaggi smiled. "Don't trust us?"

"Sure." Tucker smiled. "I trust you to sell the stuff and share the money with me."

Piaggi nodded approval. "I like smart partners. Stay that way. It's good for all of us. You have a banker?"

"Not yet, haven't thought about it much," Tucker lied.

"Start thinking, Henry. We can help set you up, overseas bank. It's secure, numbered account, all that stuff. You can have somebody you know check it out. Remember, they can track money if you're not careful. Don't live it up too much. We've lost a lot of friends that way."

"I don't take chances, Tony."

Piaggi nodded. "Good way to think. You have to be careful in this business. The cops are getting smart."

"Not smart enough." Neither were his partners, when it came to that, but one thing at a time.

5
Commitments

The package arrived with a very jet-lagged Captain at the Navy's intelligence headquarters in Suitland, Maryland. On-staff photo-interpretation experts were supplemented by specialists from the Air Force's 1127th Field Activities Group at Fort Belvoir. It took twenty hours to go through the entire process, but the frames from the Buffalo Hunter were unusually good, and the American on the ground had done what he was supposed to do: look up and stare at the passing reconnaissance drone.

"Poor bastard paid the price for it," a Navy chief observed to his Air Force counterpart. Just behind him the photo caught an NVA soldier with his rifle up and reversed. "I'd like to meet you in a dark alley, you little fuck."

"What do you think?" The Air Force senior master sergeant slid an ID photo over.

"Close enough I'd bet money on it." Both intelligence specialists thought it odd that they had such a thin collection of files to compare with these photographs, but whoever had guessed had guessed well. They had a match. They didn't know that what they had was a series of photographs of a dead man.

Kelly let her sleep, glad that she was able to without any chemical help. He got himself dressed, went outside, and ran around his island twice—the circumference was about three quarters of a mile—to work up a sweat in the still morning air. Sam and Sarah, early risers also, bumped into him while he was cooling down on the dock.

"The change in you is remarkable, too," she observed. She paused for a moment. "How was Pam last night?"

The question jarred Kelly into a brief silence, followed by: *"What?"*

"Oh, shit, Sarah . . ." Sam looked away and nearly laughed. His wife flushed almost as crimson as the dawn.

"She persuaded me not to medicate her last night," Sarah explained. "She was a little nervous, but she wanted to try and I let her talk me out of it. That's what I meant, John. Sorry."

How to explain last night? First he'd been afraid to touch her, afraid to seem to be pressing himself on her, and then she'd taken that as a sign that he didn't like her anymore, and then . . . things had worked out.

"Mainly she has some damned-fool idea—" Kelly stopped himself. Pam could talk to her about this, but it wasn't proper for him to do so, was it? "She slept fine, Sarah. She really wore herself out yesterday."

"I don't know that I've ever had a more determined patient." She stabbed a hard finger into Kelly's chest. "You've helped a lot, young man."

Kelly looked away, not knowing what he was supposed to say. *The pleasure was all mine*? Part of him still believed that he was taking advantage of her. He'd stumbled upon a troubled girl and . . . exploited her? No, that wasn't true. He loved her. Amazing as that seemed. His life was changing into something recognizably normal—probably. He was healing her, but she was healing him as well.

"She's—she's worried that I won't—the stuff in her past, I mean. I really don't care much about that. You're right, she's a very strong girl. Hell, I have a somewhat checkered past, too, y'know? I ain't no priest, guys."

"Let her talk it out," Sam said. "She needs that. You have to let things in the open before you start dealing with them."

"You're sure it won't affect you? It might be some pretty ugly stuff," Sarah observed, watching his eyes.

"Uglier than war?" Kelly shook his head. Then he changed the subject. "What about the . . . medications?"

The question relieved everyone, and Sarah was talking work again. "She's been through the most crucial period. If there were going to be a serious withdrawal reaction, it would have happened already. She may still have periods of agitation, brought on by external stress, for example. In that case you have the phenobarb, and I've already written out instructions for you, but she's gutting it out. Her personality is far stronger than she appreciates. You're smart enough to see if she's having a bad time. If so, make her—*make her*—take one of the tablets."

The idea of forcing her to do anything bridled Kelly. "Look, doc, I can't—"

''Shut up, John. I don't mean jamming it down her throat. If you tell her that she really needs it, she's going to listen to you, okay?''

''How long?''

''For another week, maybe ten days,'' Sarah said after a moment's reflection.

''And then?''

''Then you can think about the future you two might have together,'' Sarah told him.

Sam felt uneasy getting this personal. ''I want her fully checked out, Kelly. When's the next time you're due into Baltimore?''

''A couple of weeks, maybe sooner. Why?''

Sarah handled that: ''I wasn't able to do a very thorough exam. She hasn't seen a physician in a long time, and I'll feel better if she has a CPX— complete history and physical. Who do you think, Sam?''

''You know Madge North?''

''She'll do,'' Sarah thought. ''You know, Kelly, it wouldn't hurt for you to get checked out, too.''

''Do I look sick?'' Kelly held his arms out, allowing them to survey the magnificence of his body.

''Don't give me that crap,'' Sarah snapped back. ''When she shows up, you show up. I want to make sure you're both completely healthy—period. Got it?''

''Yes, ma'am.''

''One more thing, and I want you to hear me through,'' Sarah went on. ''She needs to see a psychiatrist.''

''Why?''

''John, life isn't a movie. People don't put their problems behind and ride into a sunset in real life, okay? She's been sexually abused. She's been on drugs. Her self-esteem isn't very high right now. People in her position blame *themselves* for being victims. The right kind of therapy can help to fix that. What you're doing is important, but she needs professional help, too. Okay?''

Kelly nodded. ''Okay.''

''Good,'' Sarah said, looking up at him. ''I like you. You listen well.''

''Do I have a choice, ma'am?'' Kelly inquired with a twisted grin.

She laughed. ''No, not really.''

''She's always this pushy,'' Sam told Kelly. ''She really ought to be a nurse. Docs are supposed to be more civilized. Nurses are the ones who push us around.'' Sarah kicked her husband playfully.

"Then I better never run into a nurse," Kelly said, leading them back off the dock.

Pam ended up sleeping just over ten hours, and without benefit of barbiturates, though she did awaken with a crushing headache which Kelly treated with aspirin.

"Get Tylenol," Sarah told him. "Easier on the stomach." The pharmacologist made a show of checking Pam again while Sam packed up their gear. On the whole she liked what she saw. "I want you to gain five pounds before I see you again."

"But—"

"And John's going to bring you in to see us so that we can get you completely checked out—two weeks, say?"

"Yes, ma'am." Kelly nodded surrender again.

"But—"

"Pam, they ganged up on me. I have to go in, too," Kelly reported in a remarkably docile voice.

"You have to leave so early?"

Sarah nodded. "We really should have left last night, but what the hell." She looked at Kelly. "If you don't show up like I said, I'll call you and scream."

"Sarah. Jesus, you're a pushy broad!"

"You should hear what Sam says."

Kelly walked her out to the dock, where Sam's boat was already rumbling with life. She and Pam hugged. Kelly tried just to shake hands, but had to submit to a kiss. Sam jumped down to shake their hands.

"New charts!" Kelly told the surgeon.

"Aye, Cap'n."

"I'll get the lines."

Rosen was anxious to show him what he'd learned. He backed out, drawing mainly on his starboard shaft and turning his Hatteras within her own length. The man didn't forget. A moment later Sam increased power on both engines and drove straight out, heading directly for water he knew to be deep. Pam just stood there, holding Kelly's hand, until the boat was a white speck on the horizon.

"I forgot to thank her," Pam said finally.

"No, you didn't. You just didn't say it, that's all. So how are you today?"

"My headache's gone." She looked up at him. Her hair needed washing, but her eyes were clear and there was a spring in her step. Kelly felt the need to kiss her, which he did. "So what do we do now?"

"We need to talk," Pam said quietly. "It's time."

"Wait here." Kelly went back into the shop and returned with a pair of folding lounge chairs. He gestured her into one. "Now tell me how terrible you are."

Pamela Starr Madden was three weeks shy of her twenty-first birthday, Kelly learned, finally discovering her surname as well. Born to a lower-working-class family in the Panhandle region of northern Texas, she'd grown up under the firm hand of a father who was the sort of man to make a Baptist minister despair. Donald Madden was a man who understood the form of religion, but not the substance, who was strict because he didn't know how to love, who drank from frustration with life—and was angry at himself for that, too—yet never managed to come to terms with it. When his children misbehaved, he beat them, usually with a belt or a switch of wood until his conscience kicked in, something which did not always happen sooner than fatigue. Never a happy child, the final straw for Pam had come on the day after her sixteenth birthday, when she'd stayed late at a church function and ended up going on what was almost a date with friends, feeling that she finally had the right to do so. There hadn't even been a kiss at the end of it from the boy whose household was almost as restrictive as her own. But that hadn't mattered to Donald Madden. Arriving home at ten-twenty on a Friday evening, Pam came into a house whose lights blazed with anger, there to face an enraged father and a thoroughly cowed mother.

"The things he said . . ." Pam was looking down at the grass as she spoke. "I didn't do any of that. I didn't even *think* of doing it, and Albert was so innocent . . . but so was I, then."

Kelly squeezed her hand. "You don't have to tell me any of this, Pam." But she did have to, and Kelly knew that, and so he continued to listen.

After sustaining the worst beating of her sixteen years, Pamela Madden had slipped out her first-floor bedroom window and walked the four miles to the center of the bleak, dusty town. She'd caught a Greyhound bus for Houston before dawn, only because it had been the first bus, and it hadn't occurred to her to get off anywhere in between. So far as she could determine, her parents had never even reported her as missing. A series of menial jobs and even worse housing in Houston had merely given emphasis to her misery, and in short order she'd decided to head elsewhere. With what little money she'd saved, she'd caught yet another bus—this one Continental Trailways—and stopped in New Orleans. Scared, thin, and young, Pam had never learned that there were men who preyed on young runaways. Spotted almost at once by a well-dressed and smooth-talking twenty-five-year-old named Pierre Lamarck, she'd taken his offer of shelter and assistance after he had sprung for dinner and sympathy. Three days later he had become her first lover. A week after that, a firm slap across the face had coerced the sixteen-year-old girl into her second sexual adventure, this one with a salesman from Springfield, Illinois, whom Pam had reminded of his own daughter—so much so that he'd engaged her for the entire evening, paying Lamarck two hundred fifty dollars for the experience. The day after that, Pam had emptied one of her pimp's pill containers down her throat, but only managed to make herself vomit, earning a savage beating for the defiance.

Kelly listened to the story with a serene lack of reaction, his eyes steady, his breathing regular. Inwardly it was another story entirely. The girls he'd had in Vietnam, the little childlike ones, and the few he'd taken since Tish's death. It had never occurred to him that those young women might not have enjoyed their life and work. He'd never even thought about it, accepting their feigned reactions as genuine human feelings—for wasn't he a decent, honorable man? But he had paid for the services of young women whose collective story might not have been the least bit different from Pam's, and the shame of it burned inside him like a torch.

By nineteen, she'd escaped Lamarck and three more pimps, always finding herself caught with another. One in Atlanta had enjoyed whipping his girls in front of his peers, usually using light cords. Another in Chicago had started Pam on heroin, the better to control a girl he deemed a little too independent, but she'd left him the next day, proving him right. She'd watched another girl die in front of her eyes from a hot-shot of uncut drugs, and that frightened her more than the threat of a beating. Unable to go home—she'd called once and had the phone slammed down by her mother even before she could beg for help—and not trusting the social services which might have helped her along a different path, she finally found herself in Washington, D.C., an experienced street prostitute with a drug habit that helped her to hide from what she thought of herself. But not enough. And that, Kelly thought, was probably what had saved her. Along the way she'd had two abortions, three cases of venereal disease, and four arrests, none of which had ever come to trial. Pam was crying now, and Kelly moved to sit beside her.

"You see what I really am?"

"Yes, Pam. What I see is one very courageous lady." He wrapped his arm tightly around her. "Honey, it's okay. Anybody can mess up. It takes guts to change, and it really takes guts to talk about it."

The final chapter had begun in Washington with someone named Roscoe Fleming. By this time Pam was hooked solidly on barbiturates, but still fresh and pretty-looking when someone took the time to make her so, enough to command a good price from those who liked young faces. One such man had come up with an idea, a sideline. This man, whose name was Henry, had wanted to broaden his drug business, and being a careful chap who was used to having others do his bidding, he'd set up a stable of girls to run drugs from his operation to his distributors. The girls he bought from established pimps in other cities, in each case a straight cash transaction, which each of the girls found ominous. This time Pam tried to run almost at once, but she'd been caught and beaten severely enough to break three ribs, only later to learn of her good fortune that the first lesson hadn't gone further. Henry had also used the opportunity to cram barbiturates into her, which both attenuated the pain and increased her dependence. He'd augmented the treatment by making her available to any of his associates who wanted her. In this, Henry had achieved what all the others had failed to do. He had finally cowed her spirit.

Over a period of five months, the combination of beatings, sexual abuse, and drugs had depressed her to a nearly catatonic state until she'd been jarred back to reality only four weeks earlier by tripping over the body of a twelve-year-old boy in a doorway, a needle still in his arm. Remaining outwardly docile, Pam had struggled to cut her drug use. Henry's other friends hadn't complained. She was a much better lay this way, they thought, and their male egos had attributed it to their prowess rather than her increased level of consciousness. She'd waited for her chance, waiting for a time when Henry was away somewhere, because the others got looser when he wasn't around. Only five days earlier she'd packed what little she had and bolted. Penniless—Henry had never let them have money—she'd hitched her way out of town.

"Tell me about Henry," Kelly said softly when she'd finished.

"Thirty, black, about your height."

"Did any other girls get away?"

Pam's voice went cold as ice. "I only know of one who tried. It was around November. He . . . killed her. He thought she was going to the cops, and"—she looked up—"he made us all watch. It was terrible."

Kelly said quietly, "So why did you try, Pam?"

"I'd rather die than do that again," she whispered, the thought now out in the open. "I wanted to die. That little boy. Do you know what happens? You just *stop*. Everything stops. And I was helping. I helped kill him."

"How did you get out?"

"Night before . . . I . . . fucked them all . . . so they'd like me, let me . . . let me out of their sight. You understand now?"

"You did what was necessary to escape," Kelly replied. It required every bit of his strength to keep his voice even. "Thank God."

"I wouldn't blame you if you took me back and set me on my way. Maybe Daddy was right, what he said about me."

"Pam, do you remember going to church?"

"Yes."

"Do you remember the story that ends, 'Go forth and sin no more'? You think that I've never done something wrong? Never been ashamed? Never been scared? You're not alone, Pam. Do you have any idea how brave you've been to tell me all this?"

Her voice by now was entirely devoid of emotion. "You have a right to know."

"And now I do, and it doesn't change anything." He paused for a second. "Yes, it does. You're even gutsier than I thought you were, honey."

"Are you sure? What about later?"

"The only 'later' thing I'm worried about is those people you left behind," Kelly said.

"If they ever find me . . ." Emotion was coming back now. Fear. "Every time we go back to the city, they might see me."

"We'll be careful about that," Kelly said.

"I'll never be safe. Never."

"Yeah, well, there's two ways to handle that. You can just keep running and hiding. Or you can help put them away."

She shook her head emphatically. "The girl they killed. They knew. They knew she was going to the cops. That's why I can't trust the police. Besides, you don't know how scary these people are."

Sarah had been right about something else, Kelly saw. Pam was wearing her halter again, and the sun had given definition to the marks on her back. There were places which the sun didn't darken as it did the others. Echoes of the welts and bloody marks that others had made for their pleasure. It had all started with Pierre Lamarck, or more correctly, Donald Madden, small, cowardly men who managed their relations with women through force.

Men? Kelly asked himself.

No.

Kelly told her to stay in place for a minute and headed off into the machinery bunker. He returned with eight empty soda and beer cans, which he set on the ground perhaps thirty feet from their chairs.

"Put your fingers in your ears," Kelly told her.

"Why?"

"Please," he replied. When she did, Kelly's right hand moved in a blur, pulling a .45 Colt automatic from under his shirt. He brought it up into a two-hand hold, going left to right. One at a time, perhaps half a second apart, the cans alternatively fell over or flew a foot or two in the air to the crashing report of the pistol. Before the last was back on the ground from its brief flight, Kelly had ejected the spent magazine and was inserting another, and seven of the cans moved a little more. He checked to be sure the weapon was clear, dropped the hammer, and replaced it in his belt before sitting down next to her.

"It doesn't take all that much to be scary to a young girl without friends. It takes a little more to scare me. Pam, if anybody even *thinks* about hurting you, he has to talk to me first."

She looked over at the cans, then up at Kelly, who was pleased with himself and his marksmanship. The demonstration had been a useful release for him, and in the brief flurry of activity, he'd assigned a name or a face to each of the cans. But he could see she still was not convinced. It would take a little time.

"Anyway." He sat down with Pam again. "Okay, you told me your story, right?"

"Yes."

"Do you still think it makes a difference to me?"

"No. You say it doesn't. I guess I believe you."

"Pam, not all the men in the world are like that—not very many, as a matter of fact. You've been unlucky, that's all. There isn't anything wrong with you. Some people get hurt in accidents or get sick. Over in Vietnam I saw men get killed from bad luck. It almost happened to me. It wasn't because there was something wrong with them. It was just bad luck, being in the wrong place, turning left instead of right, looking the wrong way. Sarah wants you to meet some docs and talk it through. I think she's right. We're going to get you all fixed up."

"And then?" Pam Madden asked. He took a very deep breath, but it was too late to stop now.

"Will you . . . stay with me, Pam?"

She looked as though she'd been slapped. Kelly was stunned by her reaction. "You can't, you're just doing it because—"

Kelly stood and lifted her by the arms. "Listen to me, okay? You've been sick. You're getting better. You've taken everything that goddamned world could toss at you, and you didn't quit. I *believe* in you! It's going to take time. Everything does. But at the end of it, you will be one goddamned fine person.'' He set her down on her feet and stepped back. He was shaking with rage, not only at what had happened to her, but at himself for starting to impose his will on her. "I'm sorry. I shouldn't have done that. Please, Pam . . . just believe in yourself a little.''

"It's hard. I've done terrible things.''

Sarah was right. She did need professional help. He was angry at himself for not knowing exactly what to say.

The next few days settled into a surprisingly easy routine. Whatever her other qualities, Pam was a horrible cook, which failing made her cry twice with frustration, though Kelly managed to choke down everything she prepared with a smile and a kind word. But she learned quickly, too, and by Friday she'd figured out how to make hamburger into something tastier than a piece of charcoal. Through it all, Kelly was there, encouraging her, trying hard not to be overpowering and mainly succeeding. A quiet word, a gentle touch, and a smile were his tools. She was soon aping his habit of rising before dawn. He started getting her to exercise. This came very hard indeed. Though basically healthy, she hadn't run more than half a block in years, and so he made her walk around the island, starting with two laps, by the end of the week up to five. She spent her afternoons in the sun, and without much to wear she most often did so in her panties and bra. She acquired the beginnings of a tan, and never seemed to notice the thin, pale marks on her back that made Kelly's blood chill with anger. She began to pay more serious attention to her appearance, showering and washing her hair at least once per day, brushing it out to a silky gloss, and Kelly was always there to comment on it. Not once did she appear to need the phenobarbital Sarah had left behind. Perhaps she struggled once or twice, but by using exercise instead of chemicals, she worked herself onto a normal wake-sleep routine. Her smiles acquired more confidence, and twice he caught her looking into the mirror with something other than pain in her eyes.

"Pretty nice, isn't it?'' he asked Saturday evening, just after her shower.

"Maybe,'' she allowed.

Kelly lifted a comb from the sink and started going through her wet hair. "The sun has really lightened it up for you.''

"It took a while to get all the dirt out,'' she said, relaxing to his touch.

Kelly struggled with a tangle, careful not to pull too hard. "But it did come out, Pammy, didn't it?''

"Yeah, I guess so, maybe,'' she told the face in the mirror.

"How hard was that to say, honey?"

"Pretty hard." A smile, a real one with warmth and conviction.

Kelly set the comb down and kissed the base of her neck, letting her watch in the mirror. Kelly got the comb back and continued his work. It struck him as very unmanly, but he loved doing this. "There, all straight, no tangles."

"You really ought to buy a hair-dryer."

Kelly shrugged. "I've never needed one."

Pam turned around and took his hands. "You will, if you still want to."

He was quiet for perhaps ten seconds, and when he spoke, the words didn't quite come out as they should, for now the fear was his. "You sure?"

"Do you still—"

"Yes!" It was hard lifting her with wet hair, still nude and damp from the shower, but a man had to hold his woman at a time like this. She was changing. Her ribs were less pronounced. She'd gained weight on a regular, healthy diet. But it was the person inside who had changed the most. Kelly wondered what miracle had taken place, afraid to believe that he was part of it, but knowing that it was so. He set her down after a moment, looking at the mirth in her eyes, proud that he'd helped to put it there.

"I have my rough edges, too," Kelly warned her, unaware of the look in his eyes.

"I've seen most of them," she assured him. Her hands started rubbing over his chest, tanned and matted with dark hair, marked with scars from combat operations in a faraway place. Her scars were inside, but so were some of his, and together each would heal the other. Pam was sure of that now. She'd begun to look at the future as more than a dark place where she could hide and forget. It was now a place of hope.

6
Ambush

The rest was easy. They made a quick boat trip to Solomons, where Pam was able to buy a few simple things. A beauty shop trimmed her hair. By the end of her second week with Kelly, she'd started to run and had gained weight. Already she could wear a two-piece swimsuit without an overt display of her rib cage. Her leg muscles were toning up; what had been slack was now taut, as it ought to be on a girl her age. She still had her demons. Twice Kelly woke to find her trembling, sweating, and murmuring sounds that never quite turned into words but were easily understood. Both times his touch calmed her, but not him. Soon he was teaching her to run *Springer,* and whatever the defects in her schooling, she was smart enough. She quickly grasped how to do the things that most boaters never learned. He even took her swimming, surprised somehow that she'd learned the skill in the middle of Texas.

Mainly he loved her, the sight, the sound, the smell, and most of all the feel of Pam Madden. Kelly found himself slightly anxious if he failed to see her every few minutes, as though she might somehow disappear. But she was always there, catching his eye, smiling back playfully. Most of the time. Sometimes he'd catch her with a different expression, allowing herself to look back into the darkness of her past or forward into an alternate future different from that which he had already planned. He found himself wishing that he could reach into her mind and remove the bad parts, knowing that he would have to trust others to do that. At those times, and the others, for the most part, he'd find an excuse to head her way, and let his fingertips glide over her shoulder, just to be sure she knew that he was there.

Ten days after Sam and Sarah had left, they had a little ceremony. He let her take the boat out, tie the bottle of phenobarbital to a large rock, and dump it over the side. The splash it made seemed a fitting and final end to one of her problems. Kelly stood behind her, his strong arms about her waist, watching the other boats traveling the Bay, and he looked into a future bright with promise.

"You were right," she said, stroking his forearms.

"That happens sometimes," Kelly replied with a distant smile, only to be stunned by her next statement.

"There are others, John, other women Henry has . . . like Helen, the one he killed."

"What do you mean?"

"I have to go back. I have to help them . . . before Henry—before he kills more of them."

"There's danger involved, Pammy," Kelly said slowly.

"I know . . . but what about them?"

It was a symptom of her recovery, Kelly knew. She had become a normal person again, and normal people worried about others.

"I can't hide forever, can I?" Kelly could feel her fear, but her words defied it and he held her a little tighter.

"No, you can't, not really. That's the problem. It's too hard to hide."

"Are you sure you can trust your friend on the police?" she asked.

"Yes: he knows me. He's a lieutenant I did a job for a year ago. A gun got tossed, and I helped find it. So he owes me one. Besides, I ended up helping to train their divers, and I made some friends." Kelly paused. "You don't have to do it, Pam. If you just want to walk away from it, that's okay with me. I don't *have* to go back to Baltimore ever, except for the doctor stuff."

"All the things they did to me, they're doing to the others. If I don't do something, then it'll never really be gone, will it?"

Kelly thought about that, and his own demons. You simply could not run away from some things. He knew. He'd tried. Pam's collection was in its way more horrible than his own, and if their relationship were to go further, those demons had to find their resting place.

"Let me make a phone call."

"Lieutenant Allen," the man said into his phone in Western District. The air conditioning wasn't working well today, and his desk was piled with work as yet undone.

"Frank? John Kelly," the detective heard, bringing a smile.

"How's life in the middle of the Bay, fella?" *Wouldn't I like to be there.*

"Quiet and lazy. How about you?" the voice asked.

"I wish," Allen answered, leaning back in his swivel chair. A large man, and like most cops of his generation, a World War II veteran—in his case a Marine artilleryman—Allen had risen from foot patrol on East Monument Street to homicide. For all that, the work was not as demanding as most thought, though it did carry the burden associated with the untimely end of human life. Allen immediately noted the change in Kelly's voice. "What can I do for you?"

"I, uh, met somebody who might need to talk with you."

"How so?" the cop asked, fishing around in his shirt pocket for a cigarette and matches.

"It's business, Frank. Information regarding a killing."

The cop's eyes narrowed a bit, while his brain changed gears. "When and where?"

"I don't know yet, and I don't like doing this over a phone line."

"How serious?"

"Just between us for now?"

Allen nodded, staring out the window. "That's fine, okay."

"Drug people."

Allen's mind went *click*. Kelly had said his informant was "somebody," not a "man." That made the person a female, Allen figured. Kelly was smart, but not all that sophisticated in this line of work. Allen had heard the shadowy reports of a drug ring using women for something or other. Nothing more than that. It wasn't his case. It was being handled by Emmet Ryan and Tom Douglas downtown, and Allen wasn't even supposed to know that much.

"There's at least three drug organizations up and running now. None of them are very nice folks," Allen said evenly. "Tell me more."

"My friend doesn't want much involvement. Just some information for you, that's it, Frank. If it goes further, we can reevaluate then. We're talking some scary people if this story is true."

Allen considered that. He'd never dwelt upon Kelly's background, but he knew enough. Kelly was a trained diver, he knew, a bosun's mate who'd fought in the brown-water Navy in the Mekong Delta, supporting the 9th Infantry; a squid, but a very competent, careful squid whose services had come highly recommended to the force from somebody in the Pentagon and who'd done a nice job retraining the force's divers, and, by the way, earning a nice check for it, Allen reminded himself. The ''person'' had to be female. Kelly would never worry about guarding a man that tightly. Men just didn't think that way about other men. If nothing else, it sure sounded interesting.

''You're not screwing me around, are you?'' he had to ask.

''That's not my way, man,'' Kelly assured him. ''My rules: it's for information purposes only, and it's a quiet meet. Okay?''

''You know, anybody else, I'd probably say come right in here and that would be it, but I'll play along with you. You did break the Gooding case open for me. We got him, you know. Life plus thirty. I owe you for that. Okay, I'll play along for now. Fair enough?''

''Thanks. What's your schedule like?''

''Working late shift this week.'' It was just after four in the afternoon, and Allen had just come on duty. He didn't know that Kelly had called three times that day already without leaving a message. ''I get off around midnight, one o'clock, like that. It depends on the night,'' he explained. ''Some are busier than others.''

''Tomorrow night. I'll pick you up at the front door. We can have a little supper together.''

Allen frowned. This was like a James Bond movie, secret agent crap. But he did know Kelly to be a serious man, even if he didn't know squat about police work.

''See you then, sport.''

''Thanks, Frank. 'Bye.'' The line clicked off and Allen went back to work, making a note on his desk calendar.

''Are you scared?'' he asked.

''A little,'' she admitted.

He smiled. ''That's normal. But you heard what I said. He doesn't know anything about you. You can always back out if you want. I'll be carrying a gun all the time. And it's just a talk. You can get in and get out. We'll do it in one day—one night, really. And I'll be with you all the time.''

''Every minute?''

''Except when you're in the ladies' room, honey. There you have to look out for yourself.'' She smiled and relaxed.

''I have to fix dinner,'' she said, heading off to the kitchen.

Kelly went outside. Something in him called for more weapons practice, but he'd done that already. Instead he walked into the equipment bunker and took the .45 down from the rack. First he depressed the stud and action spring. Next he swiveled the bushing. That allowed the spring to go free. Kelly dismounted the slide assembly, removing the barrel, and now the pistol was field-stripped. He held the barrel up to a light, and, as expected, it was dirty from firing. He cleaned every surface, using rags, Hoppe's cleaning solvent, and a toothbrush until there was no trace of dirt on any metal surface. Next he lightly oiled the weapon. Not too much oil, for that would attract dirt and grit, which could foul and jam the pistol at an inconvenient moment. Finished cleaning, he reassembled the Colt quickly and expertly— it was something he could and did do with his eyes closed. It had a nice feel in his hand as he jacked the slide back a few times to make sure it was properly assembled. A final visual inspection confirmed it.

Kelly took two loaded magazines from a drawer, along with a single loose round. He inserted one loaded clip into the piece, working the slide to load the first round in the chamber. He carefully lowered the hammer before ejecting the magazine and sliding another round into place. With eight cartridges in the weapon, and a backup clip, he now had a total of fifteen rounds with which to face danger. Not nearly enough for a walk in the jungles of Vietnam, but he figured it was plenty for the dark environs of a city. He could hit a human head with a single aimed shot from ten yards, day or night. He'd never once rattled under fire, and he'd killed men before. Whatever the dangers might be, Kelly was ready for them. Besides, he wasn't going after the Vietcong. He was going in at night, and the night was his friend. There would be fewer people around for him to worry about, and unless the other side knew he was there—which they wouldn't—he didn't have to worry about an ambush. He just had to stay alert, which came easily to him.

Dinner was chicken, something Pam knew how to fix. Kelly almost got out a bottle of wine but thought better of it. Why tempt her with alcohol? Maybe he'd stop drinking himself. It would be no great loss, and the sacrifice would validate his commitment to her. Their conversation avoided serious matters. He'd already shut the dangers from his mind. There was no need to dwell on them. Too much imagination made things worse, not better.

"You really think we need new curtains?" he said.

"They don't match the furniture very well."

Kelly grunted. "For a boat?"

"It's kinda dull there, you know?"

"Dull," he observed, clearing the table. "Next thing, you'll say that men are all alike—" Kelly stopped dead in his tracks. It was the first time he'd slipped up that way. "Sorry . . ."

She gave him an impish smile. "Well, in some ways you are. And stop being so nervous about talking to me about things, okay?"

Kelly relaxed. "Okay." He grabbed her and pulled her close. "If that's the way you feel . . . well . . ."

"Mmm." She smiled and accepted his kiss. Kelly's hands wandered across her back, and there was no feel of a bra under the cotton blouse. She giggled at him. "I wondered how long it would take you to notice."

"The candles were in the way," he explained.

"The candles were nice, but smelly." And she was right. The bunker was not well ventilated. Something else to fix. Kelly looked forward into a very busy future as he moved his hands to a nicer place.

"Have I gained enough weight?"

"Is it my imagination, or . . . ?"

"Well, maybe just a little," Pam admitted, holding his hands on her.

"We need to get you some new clothes," he said, watching her face, the new confidence. He had her on the wheel, steering the proper compass course past Sharp's Island Light, well east of the shipping channel, which was busy today.

"Good idea," she agreed. "But I don't know any good places." She checked the compass like a good helmsman.

"They're easy to find. You just look at the parking lot."

"Huh?"

"Lincolns and Caddys, honey. Always means good clothes," Kelly noted. "Never fails."

She laughed as intended. Kelly marveled at how much more in control she seemed, though there was still a long ways to go.

"Where will we stay tonight?"

"On board," Kelly answered. "We'll be secure here." Pam merely nodded, but he explained anyway.

"You look different now, and they don't know me from Adam. They don't know my car or my boat. Frank Allen doesn't know your name or even that you're a girl. That's operational security. We ought to be safe."

"I'm sure you're right," Pam said, turning to smile at him. The confidence in her face warmed his blood and fed his already capacious ego.

"Going to rain tonight," Kelly noted, pointing at distant clouds. "That's good, too. Cuts down visibility. We used to do a lot of stuff in the rain. People just aren't alert when they're wet."

"You really know about this stuff, don't you?"

A manly smile. "I learned in a really tough school, honey."

They made port three hours later. Kelly made a great show of being alert, checking out the parking lot, noting that his Scout was in its accustomed place. He sent her below while he tied up, then left her there while he drove the car right to the dock. Pam, as instructed, walked straight from the boat to the Scout without looking left or right, and he drove off the property at once. It was still early in the day, and they drove immediately out of the city, finding a suburban shopping center in Timonium, where Pam over a period of two—to Kelly, interminable—hours selected three nice outfits, for which he paid cash. She dressed in the one he liked best, an understated skirt and blouse that went well with his jacket and no tie. For once Kelly was dressing in accordance with his own net worth, which was comfortable.

Dinner was eaten in the same area, an upscale restaurant with a dark corner booth. Kelly didn't say so, but he'd needed a good meal, and while Pam was okay with chicken, she still had a lot to learn about cooking.

"You look pretty good—relaxed, I mean," he said, sipping his after-dinner coffee.

"I never thought I'd feel this way. I mean, it's only been . . . not even three weeks?"

"That's right." Kelly set his coffee down. "Tomorrow we'll see Sarah and her friends. In a couple of months everything will be different, Pam." He took her left hand, hoping that it would someday bear a gold ring on the third finger.

"I believe that now. I really do."

"Good."

"What do we do now?" she asked. Dinner was over and there were hours until the clandestine meeting with Lieutenant Allen.

"Just drive around some?" Kelly left cash on the table and led her out to the car.

It was dark now. The sun was nearly set, and rain was starting to fall. Kelly headed south on York Road towards the city, well fed and relaxed himself, feeling confident and ready for the night's travail. Entering Towson, he saw the recently abandoned streetcar tracks that announced his proximity to the city and its supposed dangers. His senses perked up at once. Kelly's eyes darted left and right, scanning the streets and sidewalks, checking his three rearview mirrors every five seconds. On getting in the car, he'd put his .45 Colt automatic in its accustomed place, a holster just under the front seat that he could reach faster than one in his belt—and besides, it was a lot more comfortable that way.

"Pam?" he asked, watching traffic, making sure the doors were locked—a safety provision that seemed outrageously paranoid when he was so alert.

"Yes?"

"How much do you trust me?"

"I do trust you, John."

"Where did you—work, I mean?"

"What do you mean?"

"I mean, it's dark and rainy, and I'd like to see what it's like down there." Without looking, he could feel her body tense. "Look, I'll be careful. If you see anything that worries you, I'll make tracks like you won't believe."

"I'm scared of that," Pam said immediately, but then she stopped herself. She *was* confident in her man, wasn't she? He'd done so much for her. He'd saved her. She had to trust him—no, he had to know that she did. She had to show him that she did. And so she asked: "You promise you'll be careful?"

"Believe it, Pam," he assured her. "You see one single thing that worries you and we're gone."

"Okay, then."

It was amazing, Kelly thought, fifty minutes later. The things that are there but which you never see. How many times had he driven through this part of town, never stopping, never noticing. And for years his survival had depended on his noting everything, every bent branch, every sudden bird-call, every footprint in the dirt? But he'd driven through this area a hundred times and never noticed what was happening because it was a different sort of jungle filled with very different game. Part of him just shrugged and said, *Well, what did you expect?* Another part noted that there had always been danger here, and he'd failed to take note of it, but the warning was not as loud and clear as it should have been.

The environment was ideal. Dark, under a cloudy, moonless sky. The only illumination came from sparse streetlights that created lonely globes of light along sidewalks both deserted and active. Showers came and went, some fairly heavy, mostly moderate, enough to keep heads down and limit visibility, enough to reduce a person's normal curiosity. That suited Kelly fine, since he was circulating around and around the blocks, noting changes from the second to the third pass by a particular spot. He noted that not even all the streetlights were functioning. Was that just the sloth of city workers or creative maintenance on the part of the local "businessmen"? Perhaps a little of both, Kelly thought. The guys who changed the bulbs couldn't make all that much, and a twenty-dollar bill would probably persuade them to be a little slow, or maybe not screw the bulb in all the way. In any case, it set the mood. The streets were dark, and the dark had always been Kelly's trusted friend.

The neighborhoods were so . . . sad, he thought. Shabby storefronts of what had been mom-and-pop grocery stores, probably run out of business by

supermarkets which had themselves been wrecked in the '68 rioting, opening a hole in the economic fabric of the area, but one not yet filled. The
cracked cement of the sidewalks was littered with all manner of debris. Were
there people who lived here? Who were they? What did they do? What were
their dreams? Surely not all could be criminals. Did they hide at night? And
if then, what about the daylight? Kelly had learned it in Asia: give the enemy
one part of the day and he would secure it for himself, and then expand it, for
the day had twenty-four hours, and he would want them all for himself and
his activities. No, you couldn't give the other side anything, not a time, not
a place, nothing that they could reliably use. That's how people lost a war,
and there *was* a war going on here. And the winners were not the forces of
good. That realization struck him hard. Kelly had already seen what he knew
to be a losing war.

The dealers were a diverse group, Kelly saw as he cruised past their
sales area. Their posture told him of their confidence. They owned the streets
at this hour. There might be competition from one to the other, a nasty
Darwinian process that determined who owned what segment of what sidewalk, who had territorial rights in front of this or that broken window, but as
with all such competition, things would soon attain some sort of stability,
and business would be conducted, because the purpose of the competition
was business, after all.

He turned right onto a new street. The thought evoked a grunt and a
thin, ironic smile. New street? No, these streets were old ones, so old that
"good" people had left them years ago to move out of the city into greener
places, allowing other people, deemed less valuable than themselves, to
move in, and then they too had moved away, and the cycle had continued for
another few generations until something had gone very badly wrong to create what he saw now in this place. It had taken an hour or so for him to grasp
the fact that there were people here, not just trash-laden sidewalks and criminals. He saw a woman leading a child by the hand away from a bus stop. He
wondered where they were returning from. A visit with an aunt? The public
library? Some place whose attractions were worth the uncomfortable passage between the bus stop and home, past sights and sounds and people
whose very existence could damage that little child.

Kelly's back got straighter and his eyes narrower. He'd seen that
before. Even in Vietnam, a country at war since before his birth, there were
still parents, and children, and, even in war, a desperate quest for something
like normality. Children needed to play some of the time, to be held and
loved, protected from the harsher aspects of reality for as long as the courage
and talents of their parents could make that possible. And it was true here,

too. Everywhere there were victims, all innocent to some greater or lesser degree, and the children the most innocent of all. He could see it there, fifty yards away, as the young mother led her child across the street, short of the corner where a dealer stood, making a transaction. Kelly slowed his car to allow her safe passage, hoping that the care and love she showed that night would make a difference to her child. Did the dealers notice her? Were the ordinary citizens worthy of note at all? Were they cover? Potential customers? Nuisances? Prey? And what of the child? Did they care at all? Probably not.

"Shit," he whispered quietly to himself, too detached to show his anger openly.

"What?" Pam asked. She was sitting quietly, leaning away from the window.

"Nothing. Sorry." Kelly shook his head and continued his observation. He was actually beginning to enjoy himself. It was like a reconnaissance mission. Reconnaissance was learning, and learning had always been a passion for Kelly. Here was something completely new. Sure, it was evil, destructive, ugly, but it was also different, which made it exciting. His hands tingled on the wheel.

The customers were diverse, too. Some were obviously local, you could tell from their color and shabby clothing. Some were more addicted than others, and Kelly wondered what that meant. Were the apparently functional ones the newly enslaved? Were the shambling ones the veterans of self-destruction, heading irrevocably towards their own deaths? How could a normal person look at them and not be frightened that it was possible to destroy yourself one dose at a time? What drove people to do this? Kelly nearly stopped the car with that thought. That was something beyond his experience.

Then there were the others, the ones with medium-expensive cars so clean that they had to come from the suburbs, where standards had to be observed. He pulled past one and gave the driver a quick look. *Even wears a tie!* Loose in the collar to allow for his nervousness in a neighborhood such as this one, using one hand to roll down the window while the other perched at the top of the wheel, his right foot doubtless resting lightly on the gas pedal, ready to jolt the car forward if danger should threaten. The driver's nerves must be on edge, Kelly thought, watching him in the mirror. He could not be comfortable here, but he had come anyway. Yes, there it was. Money was passed out the window, and something received for it, and the car moved off as quickly as the traffic-laden street would allow. On a whim, Kelly followed the Buick for a few blocks, turning right, then left onto a main artery, where the car got into the left lane and stayed there, driving as rapidly as was prudent to get the hell out of this dreary part of the city, but without drawing the unwanted attention of a police officer with a citation book.

Yeah, the police, Kelly thought as he gave up the pursuit. *Where the hell are they?* The law was being violated with all the apparent drama of a block party, but they were nowhere to be seen. He shook his head as he turned back into the trading area. The disconnect from his own neighborhood in Indianapolis, merely ten years before, was vast. How had things changed so rapidly? How had he missed it? His time in the Navy, his life on the island, had insulated him from everything. He was a rube, an innocent, a tourist in his own country.

He looked over at Pam. She seemed all right, though a little tense. Those people were dangerous, but not to the two of them. He'd been careful to remain invisible, to drive like everyone else, meandering around the few blocks of the "business" area in an irregular pattern. He was not blind to the dangers, Kelly told himself. In searching for patterns of activity, he hadn't made any of his own. If anyone had eyeballed him and his vehicle especially hard, he would have noticed. And besides, he still had his Colt .45 between his legs. However formidable these thugs might appear, they were nothing compared to the North Vietnamese and Vietcong he'd faced. They'd been good. He'd been better. There was danger on these streets, but far less than he had survived already.

Fifty yards away was a dealer dressed in a silk shirt that might have been brown or maroon. It was hard to tell the color in the poor illumination, but it had to be silk from the way it reflected light. Probably real silk, Kelly was willing to bet. There was a flashiness to these vermin. It wasn't enough for them merely to violate the law, was it? Oh, no, they had to let people know how bold and daring they were.

Dumb, Kelly thought. *Very dumb to draw attention to yourself that way. When you do dangerous things, you conceal your identity, conceal your very presence, and always leave yourself with at least one route of escape.*

"It's amazing they can get away with this," Kelly whispered to himself.

"Huh?" Pam's head turned.

"They're so stupid." Kelly waved at the dealer near the corner. "Even if the cops don't do anything, what if somebody decides to—I mean, he's holding a lot of money, right?"

"Probably a thousand, maybe two thousand," Pam replied.

"So what if somebody tries to rob him?"

"It happens, but he's carrying a gun, too, and if anyone tries—"

"Oh—the guy in the doorway?"

"He's the real dealer, Kelly. Didn't you know that? The guy in the shirt is his lieutenant. He's the guy who does the actual—what do you call it?"

"Transaction," Kelly replied dryly, reminding himself that he'd failed to spot something, knowing that he'd allowed his pride to overcome his caution. *Not a good habit,* he told himself.

Pam nodded. "That's right. Watch—watch him now."

Sure enough, Kelly saw what he now realized was the full transaction. Someone in a car—another visitor from the suburbs, Kelly thought—handed over his money (an assumption, since Kelly couldn't really see, but surely it wasn't a BankAmericard). The lieutenant reached inside the shirt and handed something back. As the car pulled off, the one in the flamboyant shirt moved across the sidewalk, and in shadows that Kelly's eyes could not quite penetrate there was another exchange.

"Oh, I get it. The lieutenant holds the drugs and makes the exchange, but he gives the money to his boss. The boss holds the earnings, but he also has a gun to make sure nothing goes wrong. They're not as dumb as I thought they were."

"They're smart enough."

Kelly nodded and made a mental note, chastising himself for having made at least two wrong assumptions. But that's why you did reconnaissance, after all.

Let's not get too comfortable, Kelly, he told himself. *Now you know that there's two bad guys up there, one armed and well concealed in that doorway.* He settled in his seat and locked his eyes on the potential threat, watching for patterns of activity. The one in the doorway would be the real target. The misnamed "lieutenant" was just a hireling, maybe an apprentice, undoubtedly expendable, living on crumbs or commission. The one he could just barely see was the real enemy. And that fit the time-honored pattern, didn't it? He smiled, remembering a regional political officer for the NVA. That job had even carried a code name. ERMINE COAT. Four days they'd stalked that bastard, *after* they'd positively identified him, just to make sure he was the one, then to learn his habits, and determine the best possible way to punch his ticket. Kelly would never forget the look on the man's face when the bullet entered his chest. Then their three-mile run to the LZ, while the NVA's reaction team headed in the wrong direction because of the misleading pyro-charge he'd set up.

What if that man in the shadows was his target? How would he do it?

It was an interesting mental game. The feeling was surprisingly godlike. He felt like an eagle, watching, cataloging, but above it all, a predator at the top of the food chain, not hungry now, riding the thermals over them.

He smiled, ignoring the warnings that the combat-experienced part of his brain was beginning to generate.

Hmm. He hadn't seen that car before. It was a muscle car, a Plymouth Roadrunner, red as a candy apple, half a block away. There was something odd about the way it—

"Kelly . . ." Pam suddenly tensed in her seat.

"What is it?" His hand found the .45 and loosened it in the holster just a millimeter or so, taking comfort from the worn wooden grips. But the fact that he'd reached for it, and the fact that he'd felt a sudden need for that comfort, were a message that his mind could not ignore. The cautious part of his brain began to assert itself, his combat instincts began to speak more loudly. Even that brought a surge of reflective pride. *It's so nice,* he reflected in the blink of an eye, *that I still have it when I need it.*

"I know that car—it's—"

Kelly's voice was calm. "Okay, I'll get us out of here. You're right, it's time to leave." He increased speed, maneuvering left to get past the Road-runner. He thought to tell Pam to get down, but that really wasn't necessary. In less than a minute he'd be gone, and—*damn!*

It was one of the gentry customers, someone in a black Karmann-Ghia convertible who'd just made his transaction, and, eager to have this area behind him, shot left from beyond the Roadrunner only to stop suddenly for yet another car doing much the same thing. Kelly stood on his brakes to avoid a collision, didn't want that to happen right now, did he? But the timing worked out badly, and he stopped almost right next to the Roadrun-ner, whose driver picked that moment to get out. Instead of going forward, he opted to walk around the back of the car, and in the course of turning, his eyes ended up not three feet from Pam's cringing face. Kelly was looking that way also, knowing that the man was a potential danger, and he saw the look in the man's eyes. He recognized Pam.

"Okay, I see it," his voice announced with an eerie calm, his combat voice. He turned the wheel farther to the left and stepped on the gas, bypass-ing the little sports car and its invisible driver. Kelly reached the corner a few seconds later, and after the briefest pause to check traffic, executed a hard left turn to evacuate the area.

"He saw me!" Her voice hovered on the edge of a scream.

"It's okay, Pam," Kelly replied, watching the road and his mirror. "We are leaving the area. You're with me and you're safe."

Idiot, his instincts swore at the rest of his consciousness. *You'd better hope they don't follow. That car has triple your horsepower and—*

"Okay." Bright, low-slung headlights made the same turn Kelly'd executed twenty seconds earlier. He saw them wiggle left and right. The car was accelerating hard and fishtailing on the wet asphalt. Double headlights. It wasn't the Karmann-Ghia.

You are now in danger, his instincts told him calmly. *We don't know how much yet, but it's time to wake up.*

Roger that.

Kelly put both hands on the wheel. The gun could wait. He started evaluating the situation, and not much of it was good. His Scout was not made for this sort of thing. It wasn't a sports car, wasn't a muscle car. He had four puny cylinders under the hood. The Plymouth Roadrunner had eight, each one of them bigger than what Kelly was now calling on. Even worse, the Roadrunner was made for low-end acceleration and cornering, while the Scout had been designed for plodding across unpaved ground at a hot fifteen miles per hour. This was not good.

Kelly's eyes divided their time equally between the windshield and the rearview mirror. There wasn't much of a gap, and the Roadrunner was closing it rapidly.

Assets, his brain started cataloging. *The car isn't completely useless, she's a rugged little bitch. You have big, mean bumpers, and that high ground-clearance means you can ram effectively. So what about the coachwork? That Plymouth might be a status symbol for jerks, but this little baby can be—is—a weapon, and you know how to use weapons.* The cobwebs fell completely from his mind.

"Pam," Kelly said as quietly as he could manage, "you want to get down on the floor, honey?"

"Are they—" She started to turn, the fear still manifest in her voice, but Kelly's right hand pushed her down towards the floor.

"Looks like they're following us, yes. Now, you let me handle this, okay?" The last unengaged part of his consciousness was proud of Kelly's calm and confidence. Yes, there was danger, but Kelly knew about danger, knew a hell of a lot more than the people in the Roadrunner. If they wanted a lesson in what danger really was, they'd come to the right fucking place.

Kelly's hands tingled on the wheel as he eased left, then braked and turned hard right. He couldn't corner as well as the Roadrunner, but these streets were wide—and being in front gave him the choice of path and timing. Losing them would be hard, but he knew where the police station was. It was just a matter of leading them there. They'd break contact at that point.

They might shoot, might find a way to disable the car, but if that happened, he had the .45, and a spare clip, and a box of ammo in the glove compartment. They might be armed, but they sure as hell weren't trained. He'd let them get close . . . how many? Two? Maybe three? He ought to have checked, Kelly told himself, remembering that there hadn't been time.

Kelly looked in the mirror. A moment later he was rewarded. The headlights of another, uninvolved car a block away shone straight through the Roadrunner. Three of them. He wondered what they might be armed with. Worst-case was a shotgun. The real worst-case was a rapid-fire rifle, but street hoods weren't soldiers, and that was unlikely.

Probably not, but let's not make any assumptions, his brain replied.

His .45 Colt, at close range, was as lethal as a rifle. He quietly blessed his weekly practice as he turned left. *If it comes to that, let them get close and go for a quick ambush.* Kelly knew all there was to know about ambushes. Suck 'em in and blow 'em away.

The Roadrunner was ten yards behind now, and its driver was wondering what to do next.

That's the hard part, isn't it? Kelly thought for his pursuer. *You can get close as you want, but the other guy is still surrounded by a ton of metal. What are you going to do now? Ram me, maybe?*

No, the other driver wasn't a total fool. Sitting on the rear bumper was the trailer hitch, and ramming would have driven it right through the Roadrunner's radiator. Too bad.

The Roadrunner made a move to the right. Kelly saw its headlights rock backwards as the driver floored his big V-8, but being in front helped. Kelly snapped the wheel to the right to block. He immediately learned that the other driver didn't have the stomach to hurt his car. He heard tires squeal as the Roadrunner braked down to avoid a collision. *Don't want to scratch that red paint, do we? Good news for a change!* Then the Roadrunner snapped left, but Kelly covered that move also. It was like sailboats in a tacking duel, he realized.

"Kelly, what's happening?" Pam asked, her voice cracking on every word.

His reply was in the same calm voice he'd used for the past few minutes. "What's happening is that they're not very smart."

"That's Billy's car—he loves to race."

"Billy, eh? Well, Billy likes his car a little too much. If you want to hurt somebody, you ought to be willing to—" Just to surprise them, Kelly stomped on his brakes. The Scout nose-dived, giving Billy a really good look at the chromed trailer hitch. Then Kelly accelerated again, watching the

Roadrunner's reaction. *Yeah, he wants to follow close, but I can intimidate him real easy, and he won't like that. He's probably a proud little fuck.*

There, that's how I do it.

Kelly decided to go for a soft kill. No sense getting things complicated. Still, he knew that he had to play this one very carefully and very smart. His brain started measuring angles and distances.

Kelly hit his accelerator too hard taking a corner. It almost made him spin out, but he'd planned for that and only botched the recovery enough to make his driving look sloppy to Billy, who was doubtless impressed with his own abilities. The Roadrunner used its cornering and wide tires to close the distance and hold formation on Kelly's starboard-quarter. A deliberate collision now could throw the Scout completely out of control. The Roadrunner held the better hand now, or so its driver thought.

Okay . . .

Kelly couldn't turn right now. Billy had blocked that. So he turned hard left, taking a street through a wide strip of vacant lots. Some highway would be built here. The houses had been cleared off, and the basements filled in with dirt, and the night's rain had turned that to mud.

Kelly turned to look at the Roadrunner. *Uh-oh.* The right-side passenger window was coming down. That meant a gun, sure as hell. *Cutting this a little close, Kelly . . .* But that, he realized instantly, could be made to help. He let them see his face, staring at the Roadrunner, mouth open now, fear clearly visible. He stood on the brakes and turned hard right. The Scout bounded over the half-destroyed curb, obviously a maneuver of panic. Pam screamed with the sudden jolt.

The Roadrunner had better power, its driver knew, better tires, and better brakes, and the driver had excellent reflexes, all of which Kelly had noted and was now counting on. His braking maneuver was covered and nearly matched by the Roadrunner, which then mimicked his turn, also bouncing over the crumbling cement of an eradicated neighborhood, following the Scout across what had recently been a block of homes, falling right into the trap Kelly had sprung. The Roadrunner made it about seventy feet.

Kelly had already downshifted. The mud was a good eight inches deep, and there was the off-chance that the Scout might get stuck momentarily, but the odds were heavily against that. He felt his car slow, felt the tires sink a few inches into the gooey surface, but then the big, coarsely treaded tires bit and started pulling again. *Yeah.* Only then did he turn around.

The headlights told the story. The Roadrunner, already low-slung for cornering paved city streets, yawed wildly to the left as its tires spun on the gelatinous surface, and when the vehicle slowed, their spinning merely dug wet holes. The headlights sank rapidly as the car's powerful engine merely excavated its own grave. Steam rose instantly when the hot engine block boiled off some standing water.

The race was over.

Three men got out of the car and just stood there, uncomfortable to have mud on their shiny punk shoes, looking at the way their once-clean car sat in the mud like a weary sow hog. Whatever nasty plans they'd had, had been done in by a little rain and dirt. *Nice to know I haven't lost it yet,* Kelly thought.

Then they looked up to where he was, thirty yards away.

"You dummies!" he called through the light rain. "See ya 'round, assholes!" He started moving again, careful, of course, to keep his eyes on them. That's what had won him the race, Kelly told himself. Caution, brains, experience. Guts, too, but Kelly dismissed that thought after allowing himself just the tiniest peek at it. Just a little one. He nursed the Scout back onto a strip of pavement, upshifted, and drove off, listening to the little clods of mud thrown by his tires into the wheel wells.

"You can get up now, Pam. We won't be seeing them for a while."

Pam did that, looking back to see Billy and his Roadrunner. The sight of him so close made her face go pale again. "What did you do?"

"I just let them chase me into a place that I selected," Kelly explained. "That's a nice car for running the street, but not so good for dirt."

Pam smiled for him, showing bravery she didn't feel at the moment, but completing the story just as Kelly would have told it to a friend. He checked his watch. Another hour or so until shift change at the police station. Billy and his friends would be stuck there for a long time. The smart move was to find a quiet place to wait. Besides, Pam looked like she needed a little calming down. He drove for a little while, then, finding an area with no major street activity, he parked.

"How are you feeling?" he asked.

"That was scary," she replied, looking down and shaking badly.

"Look, we can go right back to the boat and—"

"No! Billy raped me . . . and killed Helen. If I don't stop him, he'll just keep doing it to people I know." The words were as much to persuade herself as him, Kelly knew. He'd seen it before. It was courage, and it went part and parcel with fear. It was the thing that drove people to accomplish missions, and also the thing that selected those missions for them. She'd seen the darkness, and finding the light, she had to extend its glow to others.

"Okay, but after we tell Frank about it, we get you the hell out of Dodge City."

"I'm okay," Pam said, lying, knowing he saw the lie, and ashamed of it because she didn't grasp his intimate understanding for her feelings of the moment.

You really are, he wanted to tell her, but she hadn't learned about those things yet. And so he asked a question: "How many other girls?"

"Doris, Xantha, Paula, Maria, and Roberta . . . they're all like me, John. And Helen . . . when they killed her, they made us watch."

"Well, with a little luck you can do something about that, honey." He put his arm around her, and after a time the shaking stopped.

"I'm thirsty," she said.

"There's a cooler on the backseat."

Pam smiled. "That's right." She turned in the seat to reach for a Coke—and her body suddenly went rigid. She gasped, and Kelly's skin got that all-too-familiar unwelcome feeling, like an electric charge running along its surface. The danger feeling.

"Kelly!" Pam screamed. She was looking towards the car's left rear. Kelly was already reaching for his gun, turning his body as he did so, but it was too late, and part of him already knew it. The outraged thought went through his mind that he'd erred badly, fatally, but he didn't know how, and there was no time to figure it out because before he could reach his gun, there was a flash of light and an impact on his head, followed by darkness.

7
Recovery

It was a routine police patrol that spotted the Scout. Officer Chuck Monroe, sixteen months on the force, just old enough to have his own solo radio car, made it a habit to patrol his part of the District after taking to the street. There wasn't much he could do about the dealers—that was the job of the Narcotics Division—but he could show the flag, a phrase he'd learned in the Marine Corps. Twenty-five, newly married, young enough to be dedicated and angry at what was happening in his city and his old neighborhood, the officer noted that the Scout was an unusual vehicle for this area. He decided to check it out, record its tag number, and then came the heart-stopping realization that the car's left side had taken at least two shotgun blasts. Officer Monroe stopped his car, flipped on his rotating lights, and made the first, preliminary call of possible trouble, please stand by. He stepped out of the car, switching his police baton into his left hand, leaving his right at the grip of his service revolver. Only then did he approach the car. A well-trained officer, Chuck Monroe moved in slowly and carefully, his eyes scanning everything in sight.

"Oh, shit!" The return to his radio car was rapid. First Monroe called for backup and then for an ambulance, and then he notified his District desk of the license number of the subject automobile. Then, grabbing his first-aid kit, he returned to the Scout. The door was locked, but the window was blown out, and he reached inside to unlock it. What he saw then froze him in his tracks.

The head rested on the steering wheel, along with the left hand, while the right rested in his lap. Blood had sprayed all over the inside. The man was still breathing, which surprised the officer. Clearly a shotgun blast, it had

111

obliterated the metal and fiberglass of the Scout's body and hit the victim's head, neck, and upper back. There were several small holes in the exposed skin, and these were oozing blood. The wound looked as horrible as any he had seen on the street or in the Marine Corps, and yet the man was alive. That was sufficiently amazing that Monroe decided to leave his first-aid kit closed. There would be an ambulance here in minutes, and he decided that any action he took was as likely to make things worse as better. Monroe held the kit under his right hand like a book, looking at the victim with the frustration of a man of action to whom action was denied. At least the poor bastard was unconscious.

Who was he? Monroe looked at the slumped form and decided that he could extricate the wallet. The officer switched the first-aid kit to his left hand and reached in for the wallet pocket with his right. Unsurprisingly, it was empty, but his touch had elicited a reaction. The body moved a little, and that wasn't good. He moved his hand to steady it, but then the head moved, too, and he knew that the head had better stay still, and so his hand automatically and wrongly touched it. Something rubbed against something else, and a cry of pain echoed across the dark, wet street before the body went slack again.

"Shit!" Monroe looked at the blood on his fingertips and unconsciously rubbed it off on his blue uniform trousers. Just then he heard the banshee-wail of a Fire Department ambulance approaching from the east, and the officer whispered a quiet prayer of thanks that people who knew what they were doing would shortly relieve him of this problem.

The ambulance turned the corner a few seconds later. The large, boxy, red-and-white vehicle halted just past the radio car, and its two occupants came at once to the officer.

"What d'we got." Strangely, it didn't come out like a question. The senior fireman-paramedic hardly needed to ask in any case. In this part of town at this time of night, it wouldn't be a traffic accident. It would be "penetrating trauma," in the dry lexicon of his profession. "Jesus!"

The other crewman was already moving back to the ambulance when another police car arrived on the scene.

"What gives?" the watch supervisor asked.

"Shotgun, close range, and the guy's still alive!" Monroe reported.

"I don't like the neck hits," the first ambulance guy observed tersely.

"Collar?" the other paramedic called from an equipment bay.

"Yeah, if he moves his head . . . damn." The senior firefighter placed his hands on the victim's head to secure it in place.

"ID?" the sergeant asked.

"No wallet. I haven't had a chance to look around yet."

"Did you run the tags?"

Monroe nodded. "Called 'em in; it takes a little while."

The sergeant played his flashlight on the inside of the car to help the firemen. A lot of blood, otherwise empty. Some kind of cooler in the backseat. "What else?" he asked Monroe.

"The block was empty when I got here." Monroe checked his watch. "Eleven minutes ago." Both officers stood back to give the paramedics room to work.

"You ever seen him before?"

"No, Sarge."

"Check the sidewalks."

"Right." Monroe started quartering the area around the car.

"I wonder what this was all about," the sergeant asked nobody in particular. Looking at the body and all the blood, his next thought was that they might never find out. So many crimes committed in this area were never really solved. That was not something pleasing to the sergeant. He looked at the paramedics. "How is he, Mike?"

"Damned near bled out, Bert. Definite shotgun," the man answered, affixing the cervical collar. "A bunch of pellets in the neck, some near the spine. I don't like this at all."

"Where you taking him?" the police sergeant asked.

"University's full up," the junior paramedic advised. "Bus accident on the Beltway. We have to take him to Hopkins."

"That's an extra ten minutes." Mike swore. "You drive, Phil, tell them we have a major trauma and we need a neurosurgeon standing by."

"You got it." Both men lifted him onto the gurney. The body reacted to the movement, and the two police officers—three more radio cars had just arrived—helped hold him in place while the firefighters applied restraints.

"You're a real sick puppy, my friend, but we'll have you in the hospital real quick now," Phil told the body, which might or might not still be alive enough to hear the words. "Time to roll, Mike."

They loaded the body in the back of the ambulance. Mike Eaton, the senior paramedic, was already setting up an IV bottle of blood-expanders. Getting the intravenous line was difficult with the man facedown, but he managed it just as the ambulance started moving. The sixteen-minute trip to Johns Hopkins Hospital was occupied with taking vital signs—the blood pressure was perilously low—and doing some preliminary paperwork.

Who are you? Eaton asked silently. Good physical shape, he noted, twenty-six or -seven. Odd for a probable drug user. This guy would have looked pretty tough standing up, but not now. Now he was more like a large, sleeping child, mouth open, drawing oxygen from the clear plastic mask, breathing shallowly and too slowly for Eaton's comfort.

"Speed it up," he called to the driver, Phil Marconi.

"Roads are pretty wet, Mike, doing my best."

"Come on, Phil, you wops are supposed to drive crazy!"

"But we don't drink like you guys," came the laughing reply. "I just called ahead, they got a neck-cutter standing by. Quiet night at Hopkins, they're all ready for us."

"Good," Eaton responded quietly. He looked at his shooting victim. It often got lonely and a little spooky in the back of an ambulance, and that made him glad for the otherwise nerve-grating wail of the electronic siren. Blood dripped off the gurney down to the floor of the vehicle; the drops traveled around on the metal floor, as though they had a life entirely of their own. It was something you never got used to.

"Two minutes," Marconi said over his shoulder. Eaton moved to the back of the compartment, ready to open the door. Presently he felt the ambulance turn, stop, then back up quickly before stopping again. The rear doors were yanked open before Eaton could reach for them.

"Yeow!" the ER resident observed. "Okay, folks, we're taking him into Three." Two burly orderlies pulled the gurney out while Eaton disconnected the IV bottle from the overhead hook and carried it beside the moving cart.

"Trouble at University?" the resident asked.

"Bus accident," Marconi reported, arriving at his side.

"Better off here anyway. Jesus, what did he back into?" The doctor bent down to inspect the wound as they moved. "Must be a hundred pellets in there!"

"Wait till you see the neck," Eaton told him.

"Shit . . ." the resident breathed.

They wheeled him into the capacious emergency room, selecting a cubicle in the corner. The five men moved the victim from the gurney to a treatment table, and the medical team went to work. Another physician was standing by, along with a pair of nurses.

The resident, Cliff Severn, reached around delicately to remove the cervical collar after making sure the head was secured by sandbags. It took only one look.

"Possible spine," he announced at once. "But first we have to replace blood volume." He rattled off a series of orders. While the nurses got two more IVs started, Severn took the patient's shoes off and ran a sharp metal instrument across the sole of his left foot. The foot moved. Okay, there was no immediate nerve damage. Good news. A few more sticks on the legs also got reactions. Remarkable. While that was happening, a nurse took blood for the usual battery of tests. Severn scarcely had to look as his well-trained crew did their separate jobs. What appeared to be a flurry of activity was more like the movement of a football backfield, the end product of months of diligent practice.

"Where the hell's neuro?" Severn asked the ceiling.

"Right here!" a voice answered.

Severn looked up. "Oh—Professor Rosen."

The greeting stopped there. Sam Rosen was not in a good mood, as the resident saw at once. It had been a twenty-hour day for the professor already. What ought to have been a six-hour procedure had only begun a marathon effort to save the life of an elderly woman who'd fallen down a flight of stairs, an effort that had ended unsuccessfully less than an hour before. He ought to have saved her, Sam was telling himself, still not sure what had gone wrong. He was grateful rather than angry about this extension to a hellish day. Maybe he could win this one.

"Tell me what we have," the professor ordered curtly.

"Shotgun wound, several pellets very close to the cord, sir."

"Okay." Rosen bent down, his hands behind his back. "What's with the glass?"

"He was in a car," Eaton called from the other side of the cubicle.

"We need to get rid of that, need to shave the head, too," Rosen said, surveying the damage. "What's his pressure?"

"BP fifty over thirty," a nurse-practitioner reported. "Pulse is one-forty and thready."

"We're going to be busy," Rosen observed. "This guy is very shocky. Hmm." He paused. "Overall condition of the patient looks good, good muscle tone. Let's get that blood volume back up." Rosen saw two units being started even as he spoke. The ER nurses were especially good and he nodded approval at them.

"How's your son doing, Margaret?" he asked the senior one.

"Starting at Carnegie in September," she answered, adjusting the drip-rate on the blood bottle.

"Let's get the neck cleaned off next, Margaret. I need to take a look."

"Yes, doctor."

The nurse selected a pair of forceps, grabbed a large cotton ball, which she dipped in distilled water, then wiped across the patient's neck with care, clearing away the blood and exposing the actual wounds. It looked worse than it might really be, she saw at once. While she swabbed the patient off, Rosen looked for and got sterile garb. By the time he got back to the bedside, Margaret Wilson had a sterile kit in place and uncovered. Eaton and Marconi stayed in the corner, watching it all.

"Nice job, Margaret," Rosen said, putting his glasses on. "What's he going to major in?"

"Engineering."

"That's good." Rosen held his hand up. "Tweezers." Nurse Wilson set a pair in his hand. "Always room for a bright young engineer."

Rosen picked a small, round hole on the patient's shoulder, well away from anything really vital. With a delicacy that his large hands made almost comical to watch, he probed for and retrieved a single lead ball which he held up to the light. "Number seven shot, I believe. Somebody mistook this guy for a pigeon. That's good news," he told the paramedics. Now that he knew the shot size and probable penetration, he bent down low over the neck. "Hmm . . . what's the BP now?"

"Checking," another nurse said from the far side of the table. "Fifty-five over forty. Coming up."

"Thank you," Rosen said, still bent over the patient. "Who started the first IV?"

"I did," Eaton replied.

"Good work, fireman." Rosen looked up and winked. "Sometimes I think you people save more lives than we do. You saved this one, that's for damned sure."

"Thank you, doctor." Eaton didn't know Rosen well, but he made a note that the man's reputation was deserved. It wasn't every day that a fireman-paramedic got that sort of praise from a full professor. "How's he going to—I mean, the neck injury?"

Rosen was down again, examining it. "Responses, doctor?" he asked the senior resident.

"Positive. Good Babinsky. No gross indications of peripheral impairment," Severn replied. This was like an exam, which always made the young resident nervous.

"This may not be as bad as it looks, but we're going to have to clean it up in a hurry before these pellets migrate. Two hours?" he asked Severn. Rosen knew the ER resident was better on trauma than he was.

"Maybe three."

"I'll get a nap out of it anyway." Rosen checked his watch. "I'll take him at, oh, six."

"You want to handle this one personally?"

"Why not? I'm here. This one is straightforward, just takes a little touch." Rosen figured he was entitled to an easy case, maybe once a month. As a full professor, he drew a lot of the hard ones.

"Fine with me, sir."

"Do we have an ID on the patient?"

"No, sir," Marconi replied. "The police ought to be here in a few."

"Good." Rosen stood and stretched. "You know, Margaret, people like us shouldn't work these kind of hours."

"I need the shift-differential," Nurse Wilson replied. Besides which, she was the nursing-team leader for this shift. "What's this, I wonder?" she said after a moment.

"Hmph?" Rosen walked around to her side of the table while the rest of the team did its work.

"A tattoo on his arm," she reported. Nurse Wilson was surprised by the reaction it drew from Professor Rosen.

The transition from sleep to wakefulness was usually easy for Kelly, but not this time. His first coherent thought was to be surprised, but he didn't know why. Next came pain, but not so much pain as the distant warning that there would be pain, and lots of it. When he realized that he could open his eyes, he did, only to find himself staring at a gray linoleum floor. A few scattered drops of liquid reflected the bright overhead fluorescents. He felt needles in his eyes, and only then did he realize that the real stabs were in his arms.

I'm alive.

Why does that surprise me?

He could hear the sound of people moving around, muted conversations, distant chimes. The sound of rushing air was explained by air-conditioning vents, one of which had to be nearby, since he could feel the moving chill on the skin of his back. Something told him that he ought to move, that being still made him vulnerable, but even after he managed a command to his limbs to do something, nothing happened. That's when the pain announced its presence. Like the ripple on a pond from the fall of an insect, it started somewhere on his shoulder and expanded. It took a moment to classify. The nearest approximation was a bad sunburn, because everything from the left side of his neck on down to his left elbow felt scorched. He knew he was forgetting something, probably something important.

Where the fuck am I?

Kelly thought he felt the distant vibration of—what? Ship's engines? No, that wasn't right somehow, and after a few more seconds he realized it was the faraway sound of a city bus pulling away from a stop. Not a ship. A city. Why am I in a city?

A shadow crossed his face. He opened his eyes to see the bottom half of a figure dressed all over in light-green cotton. The hands held a clipboard of some sort. Kelly couldn't even focus his eyes well enough to tell if the figure was male or female before it went away, and it didn't occur to him to say anything before he drifted back to sleep.

"The shoulder wound was extensive but superficial," Rosen told the neurosurgical resident, thirty feet away.

"Bloody enough. Four units," she noted.

"Shotgun wounds are like that. There was only one real threat to the spine. Took me a little while to figure how to remove it without endangering anything."

"Two hundred thirty-seven pellets, but"—she held the X ray up to the light—"looks like you got them all. This fellow just got a nice collection of freckles, though."

"Took long enough," Sam said tiredly, knowing that he ought to have let someone else handle it, but he'd volunteered, after all.

"You know this patient, don't you?" Sandy O'Toole said, arriving from the recovery room.

"Yeah."

"He's coming out, but it'll be a while." She handed over the chart which showed his current vitals. "Looking good, doctor."

Professor Rosen nodded and explained further to the resident, "Great physical shape. The firemen did a nice job holding up his BP. He did almost bleed out, but the wounds looked worse than they really were. Sandy?"

She turned back. "Yes, doctor?"

"This one is a friend of mine. Would you mind terribly if I asked you to take—"

"A special interest?"

"You're our best, Sandy."

"Anything I need to know?" she asked, appreciating the compliment.

"He's a good man, Sandy." Sam said it in a way that carried real meaning. "Sarah likes him, too."

"Then he must be all right." She headed back into recovery, wondering if the professor was playing matchmaker again.

"What do I tell the police?"

"Four hours, minimum. I want to be there." Rosen looked over at the coffeepot and decided against it. Any more and his stomach might rupture from all the acid.

"So who is he?"

"I don't know all that much, but I ran into trouble on the Bay in my boat and he helped me out. We ended up staying at his place for the weekend." Sam didn't go any further. He didn't really know that much, but he had inferred a lot, and that scared him very much indeed. He'd done his part. While he hadn't saved Kelly's life—luck and the firemen had probably done that—he had performed an exceedingly skillful procedure, though he had also annoyed the resident, Dr. Ann Pretlow, by not allowing her to do much of anything except watch. "I need a little sleep. I don't have much scheduled for today. Can you do the follow-up on Mrs. Baker?"

"Certainly."

"Have someone wake me up in three hours," Rosen said on the way to his office, where a nice comfortable couch awaited.

"Nice tan," Billy observed with a smirk. "I wonder where she got it." There was general amusement. "What do we do with her?"

He thought about that. He'd just discovered a fine way to deal with bodies, much cleaner, in its way, and far safer than what they'd been doing. But it also involved a lengthy boat trip, and he just didn't have the time to be bothered. He also didn't want to have anyone else use that particular method. It was too good to share with anyone. He knew that one of them would talk. That was one of his problems.

"Find a spot," he said after a moment's consideration. "If she's found, it doesn't matter much." Then he looked around the room, cataloging the expressions he saw. The lesson had been learned. Nobody else would try this again, not anytime soon. He didn't even have to say anything.

"Tonight? Better at night."

"That's fine. No hurry." Everyone else could learn even more from looking at her for the rest of the day, lying there in the middle of the floor. He took only a little pleasure from it, and people had to learn their lessons, and even when it was too late for one of them, others could learn from that one's mistakes. Especially when the lessons were clear and hard. Even the drugs wouldn't block this one out.

"What about the guy?" he asked Billy.

Billy smirked again. It was his favorite expression. "Blew him away. Both barrels, ten feet. We won't be seeing him no more."

"Okay." He left. There was work to be done and money to collect. This little problem was behind him. It was a pity, he thought on the way to his car, that they couldn't all be solved this easily.

The body remained in place. Doris and the others sat in the same room, unable to look away from what had once been a friend, learning their lesson as Henry wished.

Kelly vaguely noted that he was being moved. The floor moved under him. He watched the lines between the floor tiles travel like movie credits until they backed him into another room, a small one. This time he tried to raise his head, and indeed it moved a few inches, enough to see the legs of a woman. The green surgical slacks ended above her ankles, and they were definitely a woman's. There was a whirring sound, and his horizon moved downwards. After a moment he realized that he was on a powered bed, hanging between two hoops of stainless steel. His body was attached to the bed somehow, and as the platform rotated he could feel the pressure of the restraints that held him in place, not uncomfortable, but there. Presently he saw a woman. His age, perhaps a year or two younger, with brown hair stuffed under a green cap and light eyes that sparkled in a friendly way.

"Hello," she said from behind her mask. "I'm your nurse."

"Where am I?" Kelly asked in a raspy voice.

"Johns Hopkins Hospital."

"What—"

"Somebody shot you." She reached out to touch his hand.

The softness of her hand ignited something in his drug-suppressed consciousness. For a minute or so, Kelly couldn't figure out what it was. Like a cloud of smoke, it shifted and revolved, forming a picture before his eyes. The missing pieces began to come together, and even though he understood it was horror that awaited him, his mind struggled to hurry them along. In the end it was the nurse who did it for him.

Sandy O'Toole had left her mask on for a reason. An attractive woman, like many nurses she felt that male patients responded well to the idea of someone like her taking a personal interest in them. Now that Patient Kelly, John, was more or less alert, she reached up and untied the mask to give him her beaming feminine smile, the first good thing of the day for him. Men liked Sandra O'Toole, from her tall, athletic frame to the gap between her front teeth. She had no idea why they considered the gap sexy—food got caught there, after all—but as long as it worked, it was one more tool for her business of helping to make sick people well. And so she smiled at him, just for business. The result was like no other she had encountered.

Her patient went ghostly pale, not the white of snow or fresh linen, but the mottled, sickly look and texture of Styrofoam. Her first thought was that something had gone gravely wrong, a massive internal bleed, perhaps, or even a clot-driven thrombosis. He might have screamed, but couldn't catch his breath, and his hands fell limp. His eyes never left her, and after a moment O'Toole realized that she had somehow caused whatever it was. O'Toole's first instinct was to take his hand and say that everything was all right, but she knew instantly that it wasn't true.

"Oh, God . . . oh, God . . . Pam." The look on what ought to have been a ruggedly handsome face was one of black despair.

"She was with me," Kelly told Rosen a few minutes later. "Do you know anything, doc?"

"The police will be here in a few minutes, John, but, no, I don't know anything. Maybe they took her to another hospital." He tried to hope. But Sam knew that it was a lie, and he hated himself for lying. He made a show of taking Kelly's vital signs, something Sandy could have done just as well, before examining his patient's back. "You're going to be okay. How's the shoulder?"

"Not real great, Sam," Kelly replied, still groggy. "How bad?"

"Shotgun—you took quite a bit, but—was the window on the car rolled up?"

"Yeah," Kelly said, remembering the rain.

"That's one of the things that saved you. The shoulder muscles are pretty beaten up, and you damned near bled to death, but there won't be any permanent damage except for some scarring. I did the job myself."

Kelly looked up. "Thanks, Sam. Pain isn't so bad . . . worse the last time I—"

"Quiet down, John," Rosen ordered gently, giving the neck a close look. He made a mental note to order a complete new set of X rays just to make sure there wasn't something he had missed, maybe close to the spine. "The pain medication will kick in pretty fast. Save the heroics. We don't award points for that here. 'Kay?"

"Aye aye. Please—check the other hospitals for Pam, okay?" Kelly asked, hope yet in his voice though he knew better, too.

Two uniformed officers had been waiting the whole time for Kelly to come out from under. Rosen brought in the older of the two a few minutes later. The questioning was brief, on doctor's orders. After confirming his identity, they asked about Pam; they already had a physical description from Rosen, but not a surname, which Kelly had to provide. The officers made note of his appointment with Lieutenant Allen and left after a few minutes as the victim started to fade out. The shock of the shooting and surgery, added to the pain medications, would diminish the value of what he said anyway, Rosen pointed out.

"So who's the girl?" the senior officer asked.

"I didn't even know her last name until a couple minutes ago," Rosen said, seated in his office. He was dopey from lack of sleep, and his commentary suffered as well. "She was addicted to barbiturates when we met them—she and Kelly were living together, I suppose. We helped her clean up."

"Who's 'we'?"

"My wife, Sarah. She's a pharmacologist here. You can talk to her if you want."

"We will," the officer assured him. "What about Mr. Kelly?"

"Ex-Navy, Vietnam vet."

"Do you have any reason to believe that he's a drug user, sir?"

"Not a chance," Rosen answered, a slight edge on his voice. "His physical condition is too good for that, and I saw his reaction when we found out that Pam was using pills. I had to calm him down. Definitely not an addict. I'm a physician, I would have noticed."

The policeman was not overly impressed, but accepted it at face value. The detectives would have a lot of fun with this one, he thought. What had appeared to be a simple robbery was now at least a kidnapping as well. Wonderful news. "So what was he doing in that part of town?"

"I don't know," Sam admitted. "Who's this Lieutenant Allen?"

"Homicide, Western District," the cop explained.

"I wonder why they had an appointment."

"That's something we'll get from the Lieutenant, sir."

"Was this a robbery?"

"Probably. It sure looks that way. We found his wallet a block away, no cash, no credit cards, just his driver's license. He also had a handgun in his car. Whoever robbed him must have missed that. That's against the law, by the way," the cop noted. Another officer came in.

"I checked the name again—I *knew* I heard it before. He did a job for Allen. Remember last year, the Gooding case?"

The senior man looked up from his notes. "Oh, yeah! He's the guy who found the gun?"

"Right, and he ended up training our divers."

"It still doesn't explain what the hell he was doing over there," the cop pointed out.

"True," his partner admitted. "But it makes it hard to believe he's a player."

The senior officer shook his head. "There was a girl with him. She's missing."

"Kidnapping, too? What do we have on her?"

"Just a name. Pamela Madden. Twenty, recovering doper, missing. We have Mr. Kelly, his car, his gun, and that's it. No shells from the shotgun. No witnesses at all. A missing girl, probably, but a description that could fit ten thousand local girls. Robbery-kidnapping." All in all, not that atypical a case. They often started off knowing damned little. In any case, the two uniformed officers had mainly determined that the detectives would take this one over almost immediately.

"She wasn't from around here. She had an accent, Texas, somewhere out there."

"What else?" the senior officer asked. "Come on, doc, anything you know, okay?"

Sam grimaced. "She had been the victim of sexual abuse. She might have been a hooker. My wife said—hell, I saw it, evidence of scars on her back. She'd been whipped, some permanent scarring from welts, that sort of thing. We didn't press, but she might have been a prostitute."

"Mr. Kelly has strange habits and acquaintances, doesn't he?" the officer observed while making notes.

"From what you just said, he helps cops, too, doesn't he?" Professor Rosen was getting angry. "Anything else? I have rounds to make."

"Doctor, what we have here is a definite attempted murder, probably as part of a robbery, and maybe a kidnapping also. Those are serious crimes. I have procedures to follow, just like you do. When will Kelly be up for a real interview?"

"Tomorrow, probably, but he's going to be very rocky for a couple of days."

"Is ten in the morning okay, sir?"

"Yes."

The cops rose. "Somebody will be back then, sir."

Rosen watched them leave. This, strangely enough, had been his first real experience with a major criminal investigation. His work more often dealt with traffic and industrial accidents. He found himself unable to believe that Kelly could be a criminal, yet that had seemed to be the thrust of their questions, wasn't it? That's when Dr. Pretlow came in.

"We finished the blood work on Kelly." She handed the data over.

"Gonorrhea. He should be more careful. I recommend penicillin. Any known allergies?"

"No." Rosen closed his eyes and swore. What the hell else would happen today?

"Not that big a deal, sir. It looks like a very early case. When he's feeling better I'll have Social Services talk to him about—"

"No, you won't," Rosen said in a low growl.

"But—"

"But the girl he got it from is probably dead, and we will *not* force him to remember her that way." It was the first time Sam had admitted the probable facts to himself, and that made it all the worse, declaring her dead. He had little to base it on, but his instincts told him it must be so.

"Doctor, the law requires—"

It was just too much. Rosen was on the point of exploding. "That's a good *man* in there. I watched him fall in love with a girl who's probably been murdered, and his last memory of her will *not* be that she gave him venereal disease. Is that clear, doctor? As far as the patient is concerned, the medication is for a post-op infection. Mark the chart accordingly."

"No, doctor, I will not do that."

Professor Rosen made the proper notations. "Done." He looked up. "Doctor Pretlow, you have the makings of an excellent technical surgeon. Try to remember that the patients upon whom we perform our procedures are human beings, with feelings, will you? If you do so, I think you will find that the job is somewhat easier in the long run. It will also make you a much better physician."

And what was he so worked up about? Pretlow asked herself on the way out.

8

Concealment

I t was a combination of things. June 20 was a hot day, and a dull one. A photographer for the *Baltimore Sun* had a new camera, a Nikon to replace his venerable Honeywell Pentax, and while he mourned for his old one, the new camera, like a new love, had all sorts of new features to explore and enjoy. One of them was a whole collection of telephoto lenses that the distributor had thrown in. The Nikon was a new model, and the company had wanted it accepted within the news-photo community quickly, and so twenty photographers at various papers around the country had gotten free sets. Bob Preis had gotten his because of a Pulitzer Prize earned three years before. He was sitting in his car on Druid Lake Drive now, listening to his police radio, hoping for something interesting to happen, but nothing was. And so he was playing with his new camera, practicing his lens-switching skills. The Nikon was beautifully machined, and as an infantryman will learn to strip and clean his rifle in total darkness, Preis was changing from one lens to another by feel, forcing himself to scan the area just as a means of keeping his eyes off a procedure that had to become as natural and automatic as zipping his pants.

It was the crows that caught his attention. Located off-center in the irregularly shaped lake was a fountain. No example of architectural prowess, it was a plain concrete cylinder sticking six or eight feet up from the water's surface, and in it were a few jets that shot water more or less straight up, though today shifting winds were scattering the water haphazardly in all directions. Crows were circling the water, trying occasionally to get in, but defeated by the swirling sheets of clear white spray, which appeared to frighten them. What were the crows interested in? His hands searched the camera case for the 200mm lens, which he attached to the camera body, bringing it up to his eyes smoothly.

"Sweet Jesus!" Preis instantly shot ten rapid frames. Only then did he get on his car radio, telling his base office to notify the police at once. He switched lenses again, this time selecting a 300mm, his longest. After finishing one roll, he threaded another, this one 100-speed color. He steadied the camera on the windowsill of the tired old Chevy and fired off another roll. One crow, he saw, got through the water, settling on—

"Oh, God, no . . ." Because it was, after all, a human body there, a young woman, white as alabaster, and in the through-the-lens optics, he could see the crow right there, its clawed feet strutting around the body, its pitiless black eyes surveying what to the bird was nothing more than a large and diverse meal. Preis sat his camera down and shifted his car into gear. He violated two separate traffic laws getting as close to the fountain as he could, and in what was for him a rare case of humanity overcoming professionalism, slammed his hand down on the horn, hoping to startle the bird away. The bird looked up, but saw that whatever the noise came from, there was no immediate threat here, and it went back to selecting the first morsel for its iron-hard beak. It was then that Preis made a random but effective guess. He blinked his lights on and off, and to the bird that was unusual enough that it thought better of things and flew away. It might have been an owl, after all, and the meal wasn't going anywhere. The bird would just wait for the threat to go away before returning to eat.

"What gives?" a cop asked, pulling alongside.

"There's a body on the fountain. Look." He handed the camera over.

"God," the policeman breathed, handing it back after a long quiet moment. He made the radio call while Preis shot another roll. Police cars arrived, rather like the crows, one at a time, until eight were parked within sight of the fountain. A fire truck arrived in ten minutes, along with someone from the Department of Recreation and Parks, trailering a boat behind his pickup. This was quickly put into the water. Then came the forensics people with a lab truck, and it was time to go out to the fountain. Preis asked to go along—he was a better photographer than the one the cops used—but was rebuffed, and so he continued to record the event from the lake's edge. There wouldn't be another Pulitzer in this. There could have been, he thought. But the price of that would have involved immortalizing the instinctive act of a carrion bird, defiling the body of a girl in the midst of a major city. And that wasn't worth the nightmares. He had enough of those already.

A crowd had already gathered. The police officers congregated in small knots, trading quiet comments and barbed attempts at grim humor. A TV news truck arrived from its studio on Television Hill just north of the park, which held the city zoo. It was a place Bob Preis often took his young children, and they especially liked the lion, not so originally named Leo, and the polar bears, and all the other predators that were safely confined behind steel bars and stone walls. *Unlike some people,* he thought, watching them lift the body and place it in a rubber bag. At least her torment was over. Preis changed rolls one more time to record the process of loading the body into the coroner's station wagon. A *Sun* reporter was here now. He'd ask the questions while Preis determined how good his new camera really was back at his darkroom on Calvert Street.

"John, they found her," Rosen said.

"Dead?" Kelly couldn't look up. The tone of Sam's voice had already told him the real news. It wasn't a surprise, but the end of hope never comes easily to anyone.

Sam nodded. "Yeah."

"How?"

"I don't know yet. The police called me a few minutes ago, and I came over as quick as I could."

"Thanks, pal." If a human voice could sound dead, Sam told himself, Kelly's did.

"I'm sorry, John. I—you know how I felt about her."

"Yes, sir, I do. It's not your fault, Sam."

"You're not eating." Rosen gestured to the food tray.

"I'm not real hungry."

"If you want to recover, you have to get your strength back."

"Why?" Kelly asked, staring at the floor.

Rosen came over and grasped Kelly's right hand. There wasn't much to say. The surgeon didn't have the stomach to look at Kelly's face. He'd pieced enough together to know that his friend was blaming himself, and he didn't know enough to talk to him about it, at least not yet. Death was a companion for Sam Rosen, M.D., F.A.C.S. Neurosurgeons dealt with major injuries to that most delicate part of the human anatomy, and the injuries to which they most often responded were frequently beyond anyone's power to repair. But the unexpected death of a person one knows can be too much for anyone.

"Is there anything I can do?" he asked after a minute or two.

"Not right now, Sam. Thanks."

"Maybe a priest?"

"No, not now."

"It wasn't your fault, John."

"Whose, then? She trusted me, Sam. I blew it."

"The police want to talk to you some more. I told them tomorrow morning."

He'd been through his second interview in the morning. Kelly had already told them much of what he knew. Her full name, her hometown, how they'd met. Yes, they had been intimate. Yes, she had been a prostitute, a runaway. Yes, her body had shown signs of abuse. But not everything. Somehow he'd been unable to volunteer information because to have done so would have entailed admitting to other men the dimensions of his failure. And so he had avoided some of their inquiries, claiming pain, which was quite real, but not real enough. He already sensed that the police didn't like him, but that was okay. He didn't much like himself at the moment.

"Okay."

"I can—I should do some things with your medications. I've tried to go easy, I don't like overdoing the things, but they'll help you relax, John."

"Dope me up more?" Kelly's head lifted, and the expression was not something that Rosen ever wanted to see again. "You think that's really going to make a difference, Sam?"

Rosen looked away, unable to meet his eyes now that it was possible to do so. "You're ready for a regular bed. I'll have you moved into one in a few minutes."

"Okay."

The surgeon wanted to say more, but couldn't find the right words. He left without any others.

It took Sandy O'Toole and two orderlies to move him, as carefully as they could, onto a standard hospital bed. She cranked up the head portion to relieve the pressure on his injured shoulder.

"I heard," she told him. It bothered her that his grief wasn't right. He was a tough man, but not a fool. Perhaps he was one of those men who did his weeping alone, but she was sure he hadn't done it yet. And that was necessary, she knew. Tears released poisons from inside, poisons which if not released could be as deadly as the real kind. The nurse sat beside his bed. "I'm a widow," she told him.

"Vietnam?"

"Yes, Tim was a captain in the First Cavalry."

"I'm sorry," Kelly said without turning his head. "They saved my butt once."

"It's hard. I know."

"Last November I lost Tish, and now—"

"Sarah told me. Mr. Kelly—"

"John," he said softly. He couldn't find it in himself to be gruff to her.

"Thank you, John. My name is Sandy. Bad luck does not make a bad person," she told him in a voice that meant what it said, though it didn't quite sound that way.

"It wasn't luck. She told me it was a dangerous place and I took her there anyway because I wanted to see for myself."

"You almost got yourself killed trying to protect her."

"I didn't protect her, Sandy. I killed her." Kelly's eyes were wide open now, looking at the ceiling. "I was careless and stupid and I killed her."

"Other people killed her, and other people tried to kill you. You're a victim."

"Not a victim. Just a fool."

We'll save that for later, Nurse O'Toole told herself. "What sort of girl was she, John?"

"Unlucky." Kelly made an effort to look at her face, but that just made it worse. He gave the nurse a brief synopsis of the life of Pamela Starr Madden, deceased.

"So after all the men who hurt her or used her, you gave her something that nobody else did." O'Toole paused, waiting for a reply and getting none. "You gave her love, didn't you?"

"Yes." Kelly's body shuddered for a moment. "Yes, I did love her."

"Let it out," the nurse told him. "You have to."

First he closed his eyes. Then he shook his head. "I can't."

This would be a difficult patient, she told herself. The cult of manhood was a mystery to her. She'd seen it in her husband, who had served a tour in Vietnam as a lieutenant, then rotated back again as a company commander. He hadn't relished it, hadn't looked forward to it, but he hadn't shrunk from it. It was part of the job, he'd told her on their wedding night, two months before he'd left. A stupid, wasteful job that had cost her a husband and, she feared, her life. Who really cared what happened in a place so far away? And yet it had been important to Tim. Whatever that force had been, its legacy to her was emptiness, and it had no more real meaning than the grim pain she saw on the face of her patient. O'Toole would have known more about that pain if she'd been able to take her thought one step further.

"That was really stupid."

"That's one way of looking at it," Tucker agreed. "But I can't have my girls leaving without permission, can I?"

"You ever hear of burying them?"

"Anybody can do that." The man smiled in the darkness, watching the movie. They were in the back row of a downtown theater, a 1930s film palace that was gradually falling to ruin, and had started running films at 9 A.M. just to keep up with the painting bill. It was still a good place for a covert meeting with a confidential informant, which was how this meeting would go on the officer's time sheet.

"Sloppy not killing the guy, too."

"Will he be a problem?" Tucker asked.

"No. He didn't see anything, did he?"

"You tell me, man."

"I can't get that close to the case, remember?" The man paused for a handful of popcorn and munched away his irritation. "He's known to the department. Ex-Navy guy, skin diver, lives over on the Eastern Shore somewhere, sort of a rich beach bum from what I gather. The first interview didn't develop anything at all. Ryan and Douglas are going to be working the case now, but it doesn't look like they have much of anything to work with."

"That's about what she said when we . . . 'talked' to her. He picked her up, and it looks like they had a mighty good time together, but her supply of pills ran out, she said, and she had him bring her in town to score some 'ludes. So, no harm done?"

"Probably not, but let's try to control loose ends, okay?"

"You want me to get him in the hospital?" Tucker asked lightly. "I can probably arrange that."

"No! You damned fool, this is going on the books as a robbery. If anything else happens, it just gets bigger. We don't want that. Leave him be. He doesn't know anything."

"So he's not a problem?" Tucker wanted to be clear on that.

"No. But try to remember that you can't open a murder investigation without a body."

"I have to keep my people in line."

"From what I hear you did to her—"

"Just keeping them in line," Tucker reemphasized. "Making an example, like. You do that right and you don't have any more problems for a while. You're not a part of that. Why does it bother you?"

Another handful of popcorn helped him bend to the logic of the moment. "What do you have for me?"

Tucker smiled in the darkness. "Mr. Piaggi is starting to like doing business with me."

A grunt in the darkness. "I wouldn't trust him."

"It does get complicated, doesn't it?" Tucker paused. "But I need his connections. We're about to hit the big time."

"How long?"

"Soon," Tucker said judiciously. "Next step, I think, we start feeding stuff north. Tony is up there talking to some people today, matter of fact."

"What about now? I could use something juicy."

"Three guys with a ton of grass good enough?" Tucker asked.

"Do they know about you?"

"No, but I know about them." That was the point, after all—his organization was tight. Only a handful of people knew who he was, and those people knew what would happen if they got a little loose. You just had to have the stones to enforce discipline.

"Take it easy on him," Rosen said outside the private room. "He's recovering from a major injury and he's still on several medications. He's really not capable of talking to you with a full deck."

"I have my job, too, doctor." It was a new officer on the case now, a detective sergeant named Tom Douglas. He was about forty, and looked every bit as tired as Kelly, Rosen thought, and every bit as angry.

"I understand that. But he's been badly hurt, plus the shock of what happened to his girlfriend."

"The quicker we get the information we need, the better our chances are to find the bastards. Your duty is to the living, sir. Mine is to the dead."

"If you want my medical opinion, he's not really capable of helping you right now. He's been through too much. He's clinically depressed, and that has implications for his physical recovery."

"Are you telling me that you want to sit in?" Douglas asked. *Just what I need—an amateur Sherlock to watch over us.* But that was a battle he couldn't win and wouldn't bother to fight.

"I'll feel better if I can keep an eye on things. Go easy on him," Sam repeated, opening the door.

"Mr. Kelly, we're sorry," the detective said after introducing himself. Douglas opened his notebook. The case had been booted up the ladder to his office because of its high profile. The first-page color photo on the *Evening Sun* had come as close to the pornographic as anything the media could publish, and the mayor had personally called for action on this one. Because of that, Douglas had taken the case, wondering how long the mayor's interest would last. *Not very,* the detective thought. The only thing that occupied a politician's mind for more than a week was getting and holding votes. This case had more spin on it than one of Mike Cuellar's screwballs, but it was his case, and what was always the worst part was about to take place. "Two nights ago you were in the company of a young lady named Pamela Madden?"

"Yes." Kelly's eyes were closed when Nurse O'Toole came in with his morning antibiotic dose. She was surprised to see the two other men there and stopped in the doorway, not knowing if she should interrupt or not.

"Mr. Kelly, yesterday afternoon we discovered the body of a young woman who fits the physical description of Miss Madden." Douglas reached into his coat pocket.

"No!" Rosen said, getting out of his chair.

"Is this she?" Douglas asked, holding the photo before Kelly's face, hoping that his proper grammar would somehow lessen the impact.

"God *damn* it!" The surgeon turned the cop around and pushed him against the wall. In the process the photo dropped on the patient's chest.

Kelly's eyes went wide in horror. His body sprang upwards, fighting the restraints. Then he collapsed, his skin pasty white. All in the room turned away but for the nurse, whose eyes were locked on her patient.

"Look, doc, I—" Douglas tried to say.

"Get the hell out of my hospital!" Rosen fairly screamed. "You can *kill* somebody with that kind of shock! Why didn't you tell me—"

"He has to identify—"

"*I* could have done that!"

O'Toole heard the noise as the two grown men scuffled like children in a playground, but John Kelly was her concern, the antibiotic medication still in her hand. She tried to remove the photograph from Kelly's view, but her own eyes were first drawn to the image and then repulsed by it as Kelly's hand seized the print and held it a scant twelve inches from his own wide-open eyes. It was his expression now that occupied her consciousness. Sandy recoiled briefly at what she saw there, but then Kelly's face composed itself and he spoke.

"It's okay, Sam. He has his job to do, too." Kelly looked down at the photo one last time. Then he closed his eyes and held it up for the nurse to take.

And things settled down for everyone except Nurse O'Toole. She watched Kelly swallow the oversized pill and left the room for the calm of the corridor.

Sandra O'Toole walked back to the nurses' station, remembering what she alone had seen. Kelly's face turning so pale that her first reaction to it was that he must be in shock, then the tumult behind her as she reached for her patient—but then what? It wasn't like the first time at all. Kelly's face had transformed itself. Only an instant, like opening a door into some other place, and she'd seen something she had never imagined. Something very old and feral and ugly. The eyes not wide, but focused on something she could not see. The pallor of his face not that of shock, but of rage. His hands balled briefly into fists of quivering stone. And then his face had changed again. There had been comprehension to replace the blind, killing rage, and what she'd seen next was the most dangerous sight she had ever beheld, though she knew not why. Then the door closed. Kelly's eyes shut, and when he opened them, his face was unnaturally serene. The complete sequence had not taken four seconds, she realized, all of it while Rosen and Douglas had been scuffling against the wall. He'd passed from horror to rage to understanding—then to concealment, but what had come in between comprehension and disguise was the most frightening thing of all.

What had she seen in the face of this man? It took her a moment to answer the question. Death was what she'd seen. Controlled. Planned. Disciplined.

But it was still Death, living in the mind of a man.

"I don't like doing this sort of thing, Mr. Kelly," Douglas said back in the room as he adjusted his coat. The detective and the surgeon traded a look of mutual embarrassment.

"John, are you all right?" Rosen looked him over and took his pulse quickly, surprised to find it nearly normal.

"Yeah." Kelly nodded. He looked at the detective. "That's her. That's Pam."

"I'm sorry. I really am," Douglas said with genuine sincerity, "but there's no easy way to do this. There never is. Whatever happened, it's over now, and now it's our job to try and identify the people who did it. We need your help to do that."

"Okay," Kelly said neutrally. "Where's Frank? How come he's not here?"

"He can't have a hand in this," Sergeant Douglas answered, with a look to the surgeon. "He knows you. Personal involvement in a criminal case isn't terribly professional." It wasn't entirely true—in fact, was hardly true at all—but it served the purpose. "Did you see the people who—"

Kelly shook his head, looking down at the bed, and he spoke just above a whisper. "No. I was looking the wrong way. She said something, but I didn't get around. Pam saw them, I turned right, then started turning left. I never made it."

"What were you doing at the time?"

"Observing. Look, you talked to Lieutenant Allen, right?"

"That's correct." Douglas nodded.

"Pam witnessed a murder. I was bringing her in to talk to Frank about it."

"Go on."

"She was linked up with people who deal drugs. She saw them kill somebody, a girl. I told her she had to do something about it. I was curious about what it was like," Kelly said in a flat monotone, still bathing in his guilt while his mind replayed the image.

"Names?"

"None that I remember," Kelly answered.

"Come on," Douglas said, leaning forward. "She must have told you something!"

"I didn't ask much. I figured that was your job—Frank's job, I mean. We were supposed to meet with Frank that night. All I know is it's a bunch of people who deal drugs and who use women for something."

"That's all you know?"

Kelly looked him straight in the eyes. "Yes. Not very helpful, is it?"

Douglas waited a few seconds before going on. What might have been an important break in an important case was not going to happen, and so it was his turn to lie again, beginning with some truth to make it easier. "There's a pair of robbers working the west side of town. Two black males, medium size, and that's all we have for a description. Their MO is a sawed-off shotgun. They specialize in taking down people coming in for a drug buy, and they particularly like the gentry customers. Probably most of their robberies don't even get reported. We have them linked to two killings. This might be number three."

"That's all?" Rosen asked.

"Robbery and murder are major crimes, doctor."

"But that's just an accident!"

"That's one way of looking at it," Douglas agreed, turning back to his witness. "Mr. Kelly, you must have seen something. What the hell were you doing around there? Was Miss Madden trying to buy something—"

"No!"

"Look, it's over. She's dead. You can tell me. I have to know."

"Like I said, she was linked up with this bunch, and I—dumb as it sounds, I don't know shit about drugs." *I'll be finding out, though.*

* * *

Alone in his bed, alone with his mind, Kelly's eyes calmly surveyed the ceiling, scanning the white surface like a movie screen.

First, the police are wrong, Kelly told himself. He didn't know how he knew, but he did, and that was enough. *It wasn't robbers, it was* them, *the people Pam were afraid of.*

What had happened fit what Pam had told him. It was something they had done before. He had allowed himself to be spotted—twice. His guilt was still quite real, but that was history now and he couldn't change it. Whatever he had done wrong, it was done. Whoever had done this to Pam, they were still out there, and if they'd done this twice already, they would do it again. But that was not really what occupied his mind behind the blank staring mask.

Okay, he thought. *Okay. They've never met anyone like me before.*

I need to get back into shape, Chief Bosun's Mate John Terrence Kelly told himself.

The injuries were severe, but he'd survive them. He knew every step of the process. Recovery would be painful, but he'd do what they told him, he'd push the envelope a little bit, enough to make them proud of their patient. Then the really hard part would start. The running, the swimming, the weights. Then the weapons training. Then the mental preparation—but that was already underway, he realized . . .

Oh, no. Not in their wildest nightmares have they ever met anyone like me.

The name they had given him in Vietnam boiled up from the past.

Snake.

Kelly pushed the call button pinned to his pillow. Nurse O'Toole appeared within two minutes.

"I'm hungry," he told her.

"I hope I never have to do that again," Douglas told his lieutenant, not for the first time.

"How did it go?"

"Well, that professor might make a formal complaint. I think I calmed him down enough, but you never know with people like that."

"Does Kelly know anything?"

"Nothing we can use," Douglas replied. "He's still too messed up from being shot and all to be coherent, but he didn't see any faces, didn't— hell, if he had seen anything, he would probably have done something. I even showed him the picture, trying to shake him a little. I thought the poor bastard would have a heart attack. The doctor went crazy. I'm not real proud of that, Em. Nobody should have to see something like that.''

"Including us, Tom, including us." Lieutenant Emmet Ryan looked up from a large collection of photos, half taken at the scene, half at the coroner's office. What he saw there sickened him despite all his years of police work, especially because this wasn't a crime of madness or passion. No, this event had been done for a purpose by coldly rational men. "I talked to Frank. This Kelly guy is a good scout, helped him clear the Gooding case. He's not linked up with anything. The doctors all say that he's clean, not a user.''

"Anything on the girl?" Douglas didn't need to say that this could have been the break they'd needed. If only Kelly had called them instead of Allen, who didn't know about their investigation. But he hadn't, and their best potential source of information was dead.

"The prints came back. Pamela Madden. She was picked up in Chicago, Atlanta, and New Orleans for prostitution. Never came to trial, never did any time. The judges just kept letting her go. Victimless crime, right?''

The sergeant suppressed a curse at the many idiots on the bench. "Sure, Em, no victims at all. So we're not any closer to these people than we were six months ago, are we? We need more manpower," Douglas said, stating the obvious.

"To chase down the murder of a street hooker?" the Lieutenant asked. "The mayor didn't like the picture, but they've already told him what she was, and after a week, things go back to normal. You think we'll break something loose in a week, Tom?''

"You could let him know—"

"No." Ryan shook his head. "He'd talk. Ever know a politician who didn't? They've got somebody inside this building, Tom. You want more manpower? Tell me, where do we get it, the kind we can trust?''

"I know, Em." Douglas conceded the point. "But we're not getting anywhere.''

"Maybe Narcotics will shake something loose.''

"Sure." Douglas snorted.

"Can Kelly help us?''

"No. Damned fool was just looking the wrong way.''

"Then do the usual follow-up, just to make sure everything looks okay and leave it at that. Forensics isn't in yet. Maybe they'll turn something.''

"Yes, sir," Douglas replied. As so often happened in police work, you played for breaks, for mistakes the other side made. These people didn't make many, but sooner or later they all did, both officers told themselves. It was just that they never seemed to come soon enough.

Lieutenant Ryan looked back down at the photos. "They sure had their fun with her. Just like the other one."

"Good to see you're eating."

Kelly looked up from a mostly empty plate. "The cop was right, Sam. It's over. I have to get better, have to focus on something, right?"

"What are you going to do?"

"I don't know. Hell, I could always go back in the Navy or something."

"You have to deal with your grief, John," Sam said, sitting down next to the bed.

"I know how. I've had to do that before, remember?" He looked up. "Oh—what did you tell the police about me?"

"How we met, that sort of thing. Why?"

"What I did over there. It's secret, Sam." Kelly managed to look embarrassed. "The unit I belonged to, it doesn't officially exist. The things we did, well, they never really happened, if you know what I mean."

"They didn't ask. Besides, you never really told me," the surgeon said, puzzled—even more so by the relief on his patient's face.

"I got recommended to them by a pal in the Navy, mainly to help train their divers. What they know is what I'm allowed to tell. It's not what I really did, exactly, but it sounds good."

"Okay."

"I haven't thanked you for taking such good care of me."

Rosen stood and walked to the door, but he stopped dead three feet short of it and turned.

"You think you can fool me?"

"I guess not, Sam," Kelly answered guardedly.

"John, I have spent my whole damned *life* using these hands to fix people. You have to stay aloof, you can't get too involved, because if you do you can lose it, lose the edge, lose the concentration. I've never hurt anyone in my life. You understand me?"

"Yes, sir, I do."

"What are you going to do?"

"You don't want to know, Sam."

"I want to help. I really do," Rosen said, genuine wonder in his voice. "I liked her, too, John."

"I know that."

"So what can I do?" the surgeon asked. He was afraid that Kelly might ask for something he was unfitted to do; more afraid still that he might agree.

"Get me better."

9
Labor

It was almost grim to watch, Sandy thought. The strange thing was that he was being a good patient. He didn't whine. He didn't bitch. He did just what they told him to do. There was a streak of the sadist in all physical therapists. There had to be, since the job meant pushing people a little further than they wanted to go—just as an athletic coach would do—and the ultimate aim was to help, after all. Even so, a good therapist had to push the patient, encourage the weak, and browbeat the strong; to cajole and to shame, all in the name of health; that meant taking satisfaction from the exertion and pain of others, and O'Toole could not have done that. But Kelly, she saw, would have none of it. He did what was expected, and when the therapist asked for more, more was delivered, and on, and on, until the therapist was pushed beyond the point of pride in the result of his efforts and began to worry.

"You can ease off now," he advised.

"Why?" Kelly asked somewhat breathlessly.

"Your heart rate is one-ninety-five." And had been there for five minutes.

"What's the record?"

"Zero," the therapist replied without a smile. That earned him a laugh, and a look, and Kelly slowed his pace on the stationary bike, easing himself down over a period of two minutes to a reluctant stop.

"I've come to take him back," O'Toole announced.

"Good, do that before he breaks something."

Kelly got off and toweled his face, glad to see that she hadn't brought a wheelchair or something similarly insulting. "To what do I owe this honor, ma'am?"

"I'm supposed to keep an eye on you," Sandy replied. "Trying to show us how tough you are?"

Kelly had been a touch lighthearted, but turned serious. "Mrs. O'Toole, I'm supposed to get my mind off my troubles, right? Exercise does that for me. I can't run with one arm tied up, I can't do push-ups, and I can't lift weights. I *can* ride a bike. Okay?"

"You have me there. Okay." She pointed to the door. Out in the bustling anonymity of the corridor, she said, "I'm very sorry about your friend."

"Thank you, ma'am." He turned his head, slightly dizzy from the exertion, as they walked along in the crowd. "We have rituals in uniform. The bugle, the flag, the guys with rifles. It works fairly well for the men. It helps you to believe that it all meant something. It still hurts, but it's a formal way to say goodbye. We learned to deal with it. But what happened to you is different, and what just happened to me is different. So what did you do? Get more involved in work?"

"I finished my masters. I'm a nurse-practitioner. I teach. I worry about patients." And that was her whole life now.

"Well, you don't have to worry about me, okay? I know my limits."

"Where are the limits?"

"A long way off," Kelly said with the beginnings of a smile that he quickly extinguished. "How am I doing?"

"Very well."

It hadn't gone all that smoothly, and both knew it. Donald Madden had flown to Baltimore to claim the body of his daughter from the coroner's office, leaving his wife home, never meeting with anyone despite pleas from Sarah Rosen. He wasn't interested in talking to a fornicator, the man had said over the phone, a remark that Sandy knew about but which neither medic had passed on. The surgeon had filled her in on the background of the girl, and it was merely a final sad chapter to a brief and sad life, something the patient didn't need to know. Kelly had asked about funeral arrangements, and both had told him that he would be unable to leave the hospital in any case. Kelly had accepted that in silence, surprising the nurse.

His left shoulder was still immobilized, and there had to be pain, the nurse knew. She and others could see the occasional wince, especially close to the time for a new pain medication, but Kelly wasn't the type to complain. Even now, still breathing hard from a murderous thirty minutes on the bike, he was making quite a point of walking as rapidly as he could, cooling himself down like a trained athlete.

"Why the big show?" she asked.

"I don't know. Does there have to be a reason for everything? It's the way I am, Sandy."

"Well, your legs are longer than mine. Slow down, okay?"

"Sure." Kelly eased off his pace as they reached the elevator. "How many girls are there—like Pam I mean?"

"Too many." She didn't know the numbers. There were enough that they were noticed as a class of patient, enough that you knew they were there.

"Who helps them?"

The nurse pushed the elevator button. "Nobody. They're starting up programs for dealing with the drug habits, but the real problems, the abusive backgrounds and what comes from it—there's a new term now, 'behavioral disorder.' If you're a thief, there are programs. If you abuse kids, there's a program, but girls like that are outcasts. Nobody does much of anything. The only people who deal with that are church groups. If somebody said it was a disease, maybe people would pay attention."

"Is it a disease?"

"John, I'm not a doctor, just a nurse-practitioner, and it's outside my field anyway. I do post-op care for surgical patients. Okay, we talk over lunch, and I know a little. It's surprising how many of them show up dead. Drug overdoses, accidental or deliberate, who can say? Or they meet the wrong person or their pimp gets a little too rough, and they show up here, and their underlying medical problems don't help very much, and a lot of them just don't make it. Hepatitis from bad needles, pneumonia, add that to a major injury and it's a deadly combination. But is anybody going to do anything about it?" O'Toole looked down as the elevator arrived. "Young people aren't supposed to die that way."

"Yeah." Kelly gestured for her to get in the elevator first.

"You're the patient," she objected.

"You're the lady," he insisted. "Sorry, it's the way I was raised."

Who is this guy? Sandy asked herself. She was managing the care of more than one patient, of course, but the professor had ordered her—well, not exactly, she told herself, but a "suggestion" from Dr. Rosen carried a lot of weight, especially since she had great respect for him as a friend and counselor—to keep a special eye on him. It wasn't matchmaking, as she'd initially suspected. He was still too hurt—and so was she, though she would not admit it. Such a strange man. So like Tim in many ways, but much more guarded. A strange mixture of the gentle and the rough. She hadn't forgotten what she had seen the previous week, but it was gone now, and never a hint of it had returned. He treated her with respect and good humor, never once commenting on her figure, as many patients did (and to which she pretended to object). He was so unlucky and yet so purposeful. His furious effort in rehab. His outward toughness. How to reconcile that with his incongruous good manners?

"When will I get out?" Kelly asked in a voice that was light but not light enough.

"Another week," O'Toole replied, leading him off the elevator. "Tomorrow we unwrap your arm."

"Really? Sam didn't tell me. Then I can start using the arm again?"

"It's going to hurt when you do," the nurse warned.

"Hell, Sandy, it hurts already." Kelly grinned. "I might as well get some use out of the pain."

"Lay down," the nurse ordered. Before he could object, she had a thermometer in his mouth and was taking his pulse. Then she checked his blood pressure. The numbers she put on the chart were 98.4, 64, and 105/60. The last two were especially surprising, she thought. Whatever else she might say about the patient, he was rapidly getting himself back into shape. She wondered what the urgency was.

One more week, Kelly thought after she left. *Got to get this damned arm working.*

"So what have you found out for us?" Maxwell asked.

"Good news and bad news," Greer replied. "The good news is that the opposition has very little in the way of regular ground forces within response distance of the objective. We have ID'd three battalions. Two are training to go south. One just returned from Eye Corps. It's pretty beat-up, in the process of reconstituting. The usual TO and E. Not much in the way of heavy weapons. What mechanized formations they have are well away from here."

"And the bad news?" Admiral Podulski asked.

"Do I have to tell you? Enough triple-A along the coast to turn the sky black. SA-2 batteries here, here, and probably here, too. It's dangerous there for fast-movers, Cas. For helicopters? One or two rescue birds, sure, it's doable, but a large lift will be real dicey. We went all over this when we scoped out KINGPIN, remember?"

"It's only thirty miles from the beach."

"Fifteen or twenty minutes in a helo, flying in a straight line, which they will *not* be able to do, Cas. I went over the threat maps myself. The best route I can identify—it's your area, Cas, but I do know a little, okay?—is twenty-five minutes, and I wouldn't want to fly it in daylight."

"We can use -52s to blast a corridor through," Podulski suggested. He'd never been the most subtle man in the world.

"I thought you wanted to keep this small," Greer observed. "Look, the real bad news is that there isn't much enthusiasm for this kind of mission anywhere. KINGPIN failed—"

"That wasn't our fault!" Podulski objected.

"I know that, Cas," Greer said patiently. Podulski had always been a passionate advocate.

"It ought to be doable," Cas growled.

All three men hovered over the reconnaisance photos. It was a good collection, two from satellites, two from SR-71 Blackbirds, and three very recent low-obliques from Buffalo Hunter drones. The camp was two hundred meters square, an exact square in fact, undoubtedly fitting exactly the diagram in some East Bloc manual for building secure facilities. Each corner had a guard tower, each of which was exactly ten meters in height. Each tower had a tin roof to keep the rain off the NVA-standard-issue RPD light machine gun, an obsolete Russian design. Inside the wire were three large buildings and two small ones. Inside one of the large buildings were, they believed, twenty American officers, all lieutenant-colonel/commander rank or higher, for this was a special camp.

It was the Buffalo Hunter photos that had first come to Greer's attention. One was good enough to have identified a face, Colonel Robin Zacharias, USAF. His F-105G Wild Weasel had been shot down eight months earlier; he and his weapons-systems operator had been reported killed by the North Vietnamese. Even a picture of his body had been published. This camp, whose code name, SENDER GREEN, was known to fewer than fifty men and women, was separate from the better-known Hanoi Hilton, which had been visited by American citizens and where, since the spectacular but unsuccessful Operation KINGPIN raid on the camp at Song Tay, nearly all American POWs had been concentrated. Out of the way, located in the most unlikely of places, not acknowledged in any way, SENDER GREEN was ominous. However the war would turn out, America wanted her pilots back. Here was a place whose very existence suggested that some would never be returned. A statistical study of losses had shown an ominous irregularity: flight officers of relatively high rank were reported killed at a higher rate than those of lower rank. It was known that the enemy had good intelligence sources, many of them within the American "peace" movement, that they had dossiers on senior American officers, who they were, what they knew, what other jobs they had held. It was possible that those officers were being held in a special place, that their knowledge was being used by North Vietnam as a bargaining chip for dealing with their Russian sponsors. The prisoners' knowledge in areas of special strategic interest was being traded—maybe—for continuing support from a sponsor nation that was losing interest in this lengthy war, with the new atmosphere of detente. So many games were going on.

"Gutsy," Maxwell breathed. The three blowups showed the man's face, each one staring straight at the camera. The last of the three caught one of his guards in the act of swinging a rifle butt into his back. The face was clear. It was Zacharias.

"This guy is Russian," Casimir Podulski said, tapping the drone photos. The uniform was unmistakable.

They knew what Cas was thinking. The son of Poland's one-time ambassador to Washington, by heredity a count and scion of a family that had once fought at the side of King John Sobieski, his family had been extinguished on one side of the demarcation line by the Nazis along with the rest of the Polish nobility and on the other by the Russians in Katyn Forest, where two brothers had been murdered after fighting a brief and futile two-front war. In 1941, the day after graduating Princeton University, Podulski had joined the U.S. Navy as an aviator, adopting a new country and a new profession, both of which he had served with pride and skill. And rage. That was now all the more intense because soon he would be forced to retire. Greer could see the reason. His surprisingly delicate hands were gnarled with arthritis. Try as he might to conceal it, his next physical would down-check him for good, and Cas would face retirement with memories of a dead son and a wife on antidepressant medications, after a career he would probably deem a failure despite his medals and personal flag.

"We've got to find a way," Podulski said. "If we don't, we'll never see these men again. You know who might be there, Dutch? Pete Francis, Hank Osborne."

"Pete worked for me when I had *Enterprise*," Maxwell acknowledged. Both men looked at Greer.

"I concur in the nature of the camp. I had my doubts. Zacharias, Francis, and Osborne are all names they'd be interested in." The Air Force officer had spent a tour at Omaha, part of the joint-targeting staff that selected the destinations for strategic weapons, and his knowledge of America's most secret war plans was encyclopedic. The two naval officers had similarly important information, and while each might be brave, and dedicated, and obstinately determined to deny, conceal, and disguise, they were merely men, and men had limits; and the enemy had time. "Look, if you want, I can try to sell the idea to some people, but I'm not very hopeful."

"If we don't, we're breaking faith with our people!" Podulski slammed his fist on the desk. But Cas had an agenda, too. Discovery of this camp, rescue of its prisoners, would make it explicitly clear that North Vietnam had publicly lied. That might poison the peace talks enough to force Nixon to adopt yet another optional plan being drawn up by a larger Pentagon working group: the invasion of the North. It would be that most American of military operations, a combined-arms assault, without precedent for its daring, scope, and potential dangers: an airborne drop directly into Hanoi, a division of marines hitting the beaches on both sides of Haiphong, airmobile assaults in the middle, supported by everything America could bring to bear in one, massive, crushing, attempt to break the North by capture of its political leadership. That plan, whose cover name changed on a monthly basis—currently it was CERTAIN CORNET—was the Holy Grail of vengeance for all the professionals who had for six years watched their country blunder about in indecision and the profligate waste of America's children.

"Don't you think I know that? Osborne worked for me at Suitland. I went with the chaplain when he delivered the fucking telegram, okay? I'm on your side, remember?" Unlike Cas and Dutch, Greer knew that CERTAIN CORNET would never be more than a staff study. It just couldn't happen, not without briefing Congress, and Congress had too many leaks. A possibility in 1966 or '67, maybe even as late as 1968, such an operation was unthinkable now. But SENDER GREEN was still there, and this mission was possible, just.

"Cool down, Cas," Maxwell suggested.

"Yes, sir."

Greer shifted his gaze to the relief map. "You know, you airedales kind of limit your thinking."

"What do you mean?" Maxwell asked.

Greer pointed to a red line that ran from a coastal town nearly to the camp's main gate. On the overhead photos it looked like a good road, blacktopped and all. "The reaction forces are here, here, and here. The road's here, follows the river most of the way up. There are flak batteries all over the place, the road supports them, but, you know, triple-A isn't dangerous to the right sort of equipment."

"That's an invasion," Podulski observed.

"And sending in two companies of air-mobile troops isn't?"

"I've always said you were smart, James," Maxwell said. "You know, this is right where my son was shot down. That SEAL went in and recovered him right about here," the Admiral said, tapping the map.

"Somebody who knows the area from ground level?" Greer asked. "That's a help. Where is he?"

"Hi, Sarah." Kelly waved her to the chair. She looked older, he thought.

"This is my third time, John. You were asleep the other two."

"I've been doing a lot of that. It's okay," he assured her. "Sam's in here a couple times a day." He was already uncomfortable. The hardest part was facing friends, Kelly told himself.

"Well, we've been busy in the lab." Sarah spoke rapidly. "John, I needed to tell you how sorry I am that I asked you to come into town. I could have sent you somewhere else. She didn't need to see Madge. There's a guy I know in Annapolis, perfectly good practitioner . . ." Her voice stumbled on.

So much guilt, Kelly thought. "None of this was your fault, Sarah," he said when she stopped talking. "You were a good friend to Pam. If her mom had been like you, maybe—"

It was almost as though she hadn't heard him. "I should have given you a later date. If the timing had been a little different—"

She was right on that part, Kelly thought. The variables. What if? What if he'd selected a different block to be parked on? What if Billy had never spotted him? *What if I hadn't moved at all and let the bastard just go on his way?* A different day, a different week? What if a lot of things. The past happened because a hundred little random things had to fall exactly into place in exactly the right way, in exactly the proper sequence, and while it was easy to accept the good results, one could only rage at the bad ones. What if he'd taken a different route from the food warehouse? What if he'd not spotted Pam at the side of the road and never picked her up? What if he'd never spotted the pills? What if he hadn't cared, or what if he'd been so outraged that he had abandoned her? Would she be alive now? If her father had been a little more understanding, and she'd never run away, they would never have met. Was that good or bad?

And if all that were true, then what *did* matter? Was *everything* a random accident? The problem was that you couldn't tell. Maybe if he were God looking down on everything from above, maybe then it would fit some pattern, but from the inside it merely *was,* Kelly thought, and you did the best you could, and tried to learn from your mistakes for when the next random event happened to you. But did that make sense? Hell, did anything really make sense? That was far too complex a question for a former Navy chief lying in a hospital bed.

"Sarah, none of this is your fault. You helped her in the best way you could. How could you change that?"

"Damn it, Kelly, we had her saved!"

"I know. And I brought her here, and I got careless, not you. Sarah, everyone tells me it's not my fault, and then you come in here and tell me it's yours." The grimace was almost a smile. "This can be very confusing, except for one thing."

"It wasn't an accident, was it?" Sarah noted.

"No, it wasn't."

"There he is," Oreza said quietly, keeping his binoculars on the distant speck. "Just like you said."

"Come to papa," the policeman breathed in the darkness.

It was just a happy coincidence, the officer told himself. The people in question owned a corn farm in Dorchester County, but between the corn-rows were marijuana plants. Simple, as the saying went, but effective. With a farm came barns and outbuildings, and privacy. Being clever people, they didn't want to drive their product across the Bay Bridge in their pickup truck, where the summer traffic was unpredictably interrupted, and besides, a sharp-eyed toll taker had helped the State Police make a bust only a month before. They were careful enough to become a potential threat to his friend. That had to be stopped.

So they used a boat. This heaven-sent coincidence gave the Coast Guard the chance to participate in a bust and thus to raise his stature in their eyes. It couldn't hurt, after he'd used them as the stalking horse to help get Angelo Vorano killed, Lieutenant Charon thought, smiling in the wheel-house.

"Take 'em now?" Oreza asked.

"Yes. The people they're delivering to are under our control. Don't tell anybody that," he added. "We don't want to compromise them."

"You got it." The quartermaster advanced his throttles and turned the wheel to starboard. "Let's wake up, people," he told his crew.

The forty-one-boat squatted at the stern with the increased power. The rumble of the diesels was intoxicating to the boat's commander. The small steel wheel vibrated in his hands as he steadied up on his new course. The funny part was that it would come as a surprise to them. Although the Coast Guard was the principal law-enforcement agency on the water, their main activity had always been search and rescue, and the word hadn't quite gotten out yet. Which, Oreza told himself, was just too goddamned bad. He'd found a few coastguardsmen smoking pot in the past couple of years, and his wrath was something still talked about by those who'd seen it.

The target was easily seen now, a thirty-foot Bay-built fishing boat of the sort that dotted the Chesapeake, probably with an old Chevy engine, and that meant she couldn't possibly outrun his cutter. It was a perfectly good thing to have a good disguise, Oreza thought with a smile, but not so clever to bet your life and your freedom on one card, however good it might be.

"Just let everything look normal," the policeman said quietly.

"Look around, sir," the quartermaster replied. The boat crew was alert but not obviously so, and their weapons were holstered. The boat's course was almost a direct one toward their Thomas Point station, and if the other boat even took note of them—and nobody was looking aft at the moment—they could easily assume that the forty-one-footer was just heading back to the barn. Five hundred yards now. Oreza jammed the throttles to the stops to get the extra knot or two of overtake speed.

"There's Mr. English," another crewman said. The other forty-one-boat from Thomas Point was on a reciprocal course, outbound from the station, holding steady on a straight line, roughly towards the lighthouse that the station also supported.

"Not real smart, are they?" Oreza asked.

"Well, if they were smart, why break the law?"

"Roger that, sir." Three hundred yards now, and a head turned aft to see the gleaming white shape of the small cutter. Three people aboard the target craft, and the one who had looked at them leaned forward to say something to the guy at the wheel. It was almost comical to watch. Oreza could imagine every word they were saying. There's a Coast Guard boat back there. So just play it cool, maybe they're just changing the duty boat or something, see the one there . . . Uh-oh, I don't like this . . . Just be cool, damn it! I really don't like this. Settle down, their lights aren't on and their station is right down there, for Christ's sake.

Just about time, Oreza smiled to himself, *just about time for: oh, shit!*

He grinned when it happened. The guy at the wheel turned, and his mouth opened and shut, having said just that. One of the younger crewmen read the man's lips and laughed.

"I think they just figured it out, skipper."

"Hit the lights!" the quartermaster ordered, and the cop lights atop the wheelhouse started blinking, somewhat to Oreza's displeasure.

"Aye aye!"

The Bay boat turned rapidly south, but the outbound cutter turned to cover the maneuver, and it was instantly clear that neither could outrun the twin-screw forty-one-boats.

"Should have used the money to buy something sportier, boys," Oreza said to himself, knowing that criminals learned from their mistakes, too, and buying something to outrun a forty-one-foot patrol boat was not exactly a taxing problem. This one was easy. Chasing another little sailboat would be easy, if this damned fool of a cop would let them do it right, but the easy ones wouldn't last forever.

The Bay boat cut power, trapped between two cutters. Warrant Officer English kept station a few hundred yards out while Oreza drove in close.

"Howdy," the quartermaster said over his loud-hailer. "This is the U.S. Coast Guard, and we are exercising our right to board and conduct a safety inspection. Let's everybody stay where we can see you, please."

It was remarkably like watching people who'd just lost a pro-football game. They knew they couldn't change anything no matter what they did. They knew that resistance was futile, and so they just stood there in dejection and acceptance of their fate. Oreza wondered how long that would last. How long before somebody would be dumb enough to fight it out?

Two of his sailors jumped aboard, covered by two more on the forty-one's fantail. Mr. English brought his boat in closer. A good boat-handler, Oreza saw, like a warrant was supposed to be, and he had his people out to offer cover, too, just in case the bad guys got a crazy idea. While the three men stood in plain view, mostly looking down at the deck and hoping that it might really be a safety inspection, Oreza's two men went into the forward cabin. Both came out in less than a minute. One tipped the bill of his cap, signaling all-clear, then patted his belly. Yes, there were drugs aboard. Five pats—a lot of drugs aboard.

"We have a bust, sir," Oreza observed calmly.

Lieutenant Mark Charon of the Narcotics Division, Baltimore City Police Department, leaned against the doorframe—hatch, whatever these sailors called the thing—and smiled. He was dressed in casual clothes, and might have easily been mistaken for a coastie with the required orange life jacket.

"You handle it, then. How does it go in the books?"

"Routine safety inspection, and, golly, they had drugs aboard," Oreza said in mock surprise.

"Exactly right, Mr. Oreza."

"Thank you, sir."

"My pleasure, Captain."

He'd already explained the procedure to Oreza and English. In order to protect his informants, credit for the arrest would go to the coasties, which didn't exactly displease the quartermaster or the warrant officer. Oreza would get to paint a victory symbol on his mast, or whatever they called the thing the radar was attached to, a representation of the five-leafed marijuana plant, and the crewmen would have something to brag about. They might even have the adventure of testifying before a federal district court—probably not, since these small-timers would undoubtedly cop to the smallest offense their attorney could negotiate. They would get word out that the people to whom they were making the delivery had probably informed on them. With luck those people might even disappear, and that would really make his task easy. There would be an opening in the drug ecostructure—another new buzzword Charon had picked up on. At the very least, a potential rival in that ecostructure was now out of business for good. Lieutenant Charon would get a pat on the back from his captain, probably a flowery thank-you letter from the United States Coast Guard and the U.S. Attorney's office, not to mention congratulations for running such a quiet and effective operation that had not compromised his informants. One of our best men, his captain would affirm again. How do you get informants like that? Cap'n, you know how that works, I have to protect these people. Sure, Mark, I understand. You just keep up the good work.

I'll do my best, sir, Charon thought to himself, staring off at the setting sun. He didn't even watch the coasties cuffing the suspects, reading them their constitutional rights from the plastic-coated card, smiling as they did so, since for them this was a very entertaining game. But then, that's what it was for Charon, too.

Where were the damned helicopters? Kelly asked himself.

Everything about the damned mission had been wrong from the first moment. Pickett, his usual companion, had come down with violent dysentery, too bad for him to go out, and Kelly had gone out alone. Not a good thing, but the mission was too important, and they had to cover every little hamlet or *ville*. So he'd come in alone, very, very carefully moving up the stinking water of this—well, the map called it a river, but it wasn't quite large enough for Kelly to think of it that way.

And, of course, this is the *ville* they'd come to, the fuckers.

PLASTIC FLOWER, he thought, watching and listening. *Who the hell came up with* that *name?*

PLASTIC FLOWER was the code name for an NVA political-action team or whatever they called it. His team had several other names, none of them complimentary. Certainly they weren't the precinct workers he'd seen on election day in Indianapolis. Not these people, schooled in Hanoi on how to win hearts and minds.

The *ville*'s headman, chief, mayor, whatever the hell he was, was just a little too courageous to be called anything but a fool. He was paying for that foolishness before the distant eyes of Bosun's Mate 1/c J.T. Kelly. The team had arrived at oh-one-thirty, and in a very orderly and almost civilized way, entered every little hooch, awakening the whole population of farmers, bringing them into the common area to see the misguided hero, and his wife, and his three daughters, all waiting for them, sitting in the dirt, their arms cruelly tied behind their backs. The NVA major who led PLASTIC FLOWER invited them all to sit in a mannerly voice that reached Kelly's observation point, less than two hundred meters away. The *ville* needed a lesson in the foolishness of resistance to the people's liberation movement. It was not that they were bad people, just misguided, and he hoped that this simple lesson would make clear to them the error of their ways.

They started with the man's wife. That took twenty minutes.

I have to do something! he told himself.

There's eleven of them, idiot. And while the Major might be a sadistic motherfucker, the ten soldiers with him had not been selected exclusively for their political correctness. They would be reliable, experienced, and dedicated soldiers. How a man could be dedicated to such things as this, Kelly didn't have the imagination to understand. That they were was a fact that he could not afford to ignore.

Where was the fucking reaction team? He'd called in forty minutes earlier, and the support base was only twenty minutes off by chopper. They wanted this Major. His team might also be useful, but they wanted the Major alive. He knew the location of the local political leaders, those the Marines hadn't swept up in a superb raid six weeks earlier. This mission was probably a reaction to that, a deliberate response so close to the American base, to say that, no, you hadn't gotten us all yet, and you never will.

And they were probably right, Kelly thought, but that question went far beyond the mission for tonight.

The oldest daughter was maybe fifteen. It was hard to tell with the small, deceptively delicate Vietnamese women. She'd lasted all of twenty-five minutes and was not yet dead. Her screams carried clearly across the flat, open ground to Kelly's watery post, and his hands squeezed the plastic of his CAR-15 so hard that had he thought or noticed, he might have worried about breaking something.

The ten soldiers with the Major were deployed as they should be. Two men were with the Major, and they rotated duty with the perimeter guards so that all of them could partake in the evening's festivities. One of them finished the girl with a knife. The next daughter was perhaps twelve.

Kelly's ears scanned the cloudy sky, praying to hear the distinctive mutter of a Huey's two-bladed rotor. There were other sounds. The rumble of 155s from the marine fire base to the east. Some jets screaming overhead. None were loud enough to mask the high-pitched screech of a child, but there were still eleven of them, and only one of him, and even if Pickett had been here, the odds would not have been remotely close enough to try a play. Kelly had his CAR-15 carbine, a thirty-round magazine securely fixed in its place, another taped, inverted, to the end of that one, and two more similar sets. He had four fragmentation grenades, two willie-petes, and two smokes. His deadliest appliance was his radio, but he'd already called out twice and gotten an acknowledgment both times, along with orders to sit tight.

Easy thing to say back at the base, wasn't it?

Twelve years old, maybe. Too young for this. There was no age for this, he told himself, but he'd never be able to change things alone, and there was no good for anyone in adding his death to those of this family.

How could they do it? Were they not men, soldiers, professional warriors like himself? Could anything be so important that they could cast aside their humanity? What he saw was impossible. It could not be. But it was. The rumbles of the distant artillery continued, dropping planned fire-missions on a suspected supply route. A continuous stream of aircraft overhead, maybe Marine intruders doing a Mini-Arc Light strike at something or other, probably empty woods, because most of those targets were just that. Not here, where the enemy was, but that wouldn't help anything, would it? These villagers had bet their lives and their families on something that wasn't working, and maybe that Major thought he was being merciful in just eliminating one family in the most graphic method possible instead of ending all their lives in a more efficient way. Besides, dead men told no tales, and this was a tale he would want repeated. Terror was something they could use, and use well.

Time crept on, slowly and rapidly, and presently the twelve-year-old stopped making noise and was cast aside. The third and final daughter was eight, he saw through his binoculars. The *arrogance* of the fuckers, building a large fire. They couldn't have anyone miss this, could they?

Eight years old, not even old enough, not a throat large enough for a proper scream. He watched the changing of the guard. Two more men moved from the perimeter into the center of the *ville*. R&R for the political-action group, who couldn't go to Taiwan as Kelly had. The man nearest to

Kelly hadn't had his chance yet, probably wouldn't. The headman didn't have enough daughters, or maybe this one was on the Major's shit list. Whatever the real reason, he wasn't getting any, and it must have frustrated him. The soldier's eyes were looking in now, watching his squadmates partake in something that he would miss tonight. Maybe next time . . . but at least he could watch . . . and he did, Kelly saw, forgetting his duty for the first time tonight.

Kelly was halfway there before his mind remarked on the fact, crawling as rapidly as he could in silence, helped by the moist ground. A low crawl, his body as flat as he could manage, closer, closer, both driven and drawn by the whine that emanated from near the fire.

Should have done it sooner, Johnnie-boy.

It wasn't possible then.

Well, fuck, it isn't possible now*!*

It was then that fate intervened in the sound of a Huey, probably more than one, off to the southeast. Kelly heard it first, rising carefully behind the soldier, his knife drawn. They still hadn't heard it when he struck, driving his knife into the base of the man's skull, where the spinal cord meets the base of the brain—the medulla, someone had told him in a lecture. He twisted it, almost like a screwdriver, his other hand across the soldier's mouth, and, sure enough, it worked. The body went instantly limp, and he lowered it gently, not from any feelings of humanity, but to limit noise.

But there was noise. The choppers were too close now. The Major's head went up, turning southeast, recognizing the danger. He shouted an order for his men to assemble, then turned and shot the child in the head just as soon as one of his privates moved off of her and out of the way.

It only took a few seconds for the squad to assemble. The Major did a quick and automatic head count, coming up one short, and he looked in Kelly's direction, but his eyes and his vision had been long since compromised by the fire, and the only thing he did see was some spectral movement in the air.

"One, two, three," Kelly whispered to himself after pulling the cotter pin out of one of his frags. The boys in 3rd SOG cut their own fuses. You never knew what the little old lady in the factory might do. Theirs burned for exactly five seconds, and on "three," the grenade left his hand. It was just metallic enough to glint with the orange firelight. A nearly perfect toss, it landed in the exact center of the ring of soldiers. Kelly was already prone in the dirt when it landed. He heard the shout of alarm that was just a second too late to help anyone.

The grenade killed or wounded seven of the ten men. He stood with his carbine and dropped the first one with three rounds to the head. His eyes didn't even pause to see the flying red cloud, for this was his profession, and not a hobby. The Major was still alive, lying on the ground but trying to aim his pistol until his chest took five more. His death made the night a success. Now all Kelly had to do was survive. He had committed himself to a foolish act, and caution was his enemy.

Kelly ran to the right, his carbine held high. There were at least two NVA moving, armed and angry and confused enough that they weren't running away as they should. The first chopper overhead was an illum bird, dropping flares that Kelly cursed, because the darkness was his best friend right now. He spotted and hosed down one of the NVA, emptying his magazine into the running figure. Moving right still, he switched magazines, circling around, hoping to find the other one, but his eyes lingered on the center of the *ville*. People scurrying around, some of them probably hurt by his grenade, but he couldn't worry himself about that. His eyes froze on the victims—worse, they stayed too long on the fire, and when he turned away, the shape of it stayed in his eyes, alternating between orange and blue ghost images that wrecked his night vision. He could hear the roar of a Huey flared for landing close to the *ville,* and that was loud enough to mask even the screams of the villagers. Kelly hid behind the wall of a hooch, eyes looking outward, away from the fire as he tried to blink them clear. At least one more unhurt NVA was moving, and he wouldn't be running toward the sound of the chopper. Kelly kept heading right, more slowly now. There was a ten-meter gap from this hooch to the next, like a corridor of light in the glow of the fire. He looked around the corner before making the run, then took off fast, his head low for once. His eyes caught a moving shadow, and when he turned to look, he stumbled over something and went down.

Dust flew up around him, but he couldn't find the source of the noise quickly enough. Kelly rolled left to avoid the shots, but that took him towards the light. He half stood and pushed himself backwards, hitting the wall of a hooch, eyes scanning frantically for the muzzle flashes. There! He brought his CAR-15 to bear and fired just as two 7.62 rounds caught him in the chest. The impact spun him around, and two more hits destroyed the carbine in his hands. When next he looked up he was on his back, and it was quiet in the *ville.* His first attempt to move achieved nothing but pain. Then the muzzle of a rifle pressed to his chest.

"Over here, Lieutenant!" Followed by: "Medic!"

The world moved as they dragged him closer to the fire. Kelly's head hung limply to the left, watching the soldiers sweep through the *ville,* two of them disarming and examining the NVA.

"This fucker's alive," one of them said.

"Oh, yeah?" The other walked over from the body of the eight-year-old, touched his muzzle to the NVA's forehead, and fired once.

"Fuck, Harry!"

"Knock that shit off!" the Lieutenant screamed.

"Look at what they done, sir!" Harry screamed back, falling to his knees to vomit.

"What's your problem?" the medical corpsman asked Kelly, who was quite unable to reply. "Oh, shit," he observed further. "Ell-Tee, this must be the guy who called in!"

One more face appeared, probably the Lieutenant commanding the Blue Team, and the oversized patch on his shoulder was that of the 1st Cavalry Division.

"Lieutenant, looks all clear, sweeping the perimeter again now!" an older voice called.

"All dead?"

"That's affirm, sir!"

"Who the hell are you?" the Lieutenant said, looking back down. "Crazy fucking Marines!"

"Navy!" Kelly gasped, spraying a little blood on the medic.

"What?" Nurse O'Toole asked.

Kelly's eyes opened wide. His right arm moved rapidly across his chest as his head swiveled to survey the room. Sandy O'Toole was in the corner, reading a book under a single light.

"What are you doing here?"

"Listening to your nightmare," she answered. "Second time. You know, you really ought to—"

"Yeah, I know."

10
Pathology

"Your gun's in the back of the car," Sergeant Douglas told him. "Unloaded. Keep it that way from now on."

"What about Pam?" Kelly asked from his wheelchair.

"We've got some leads," Douglas replied, not troubling himself to conceal the lie.

And that said it all, Kelly thought. Someone had leaked it to the papers that Pam had an arrest record for prostitution, and with that revelation, the case had lost its immediacy.

Sam brought the Scout up to the Wolfe Street entrance himself. The bodywork was all fixed, and there was a new window on the driver's side. Kelly got out of the wheelchair and gave the Scout a long look. The door-frame and adjacent pillar had broken up the incoming shot column and saved his life. Bad aim on someone's part, really, after a careful and effective stalk—helped by the fact that he hadn't troubled himself to check his mirrors, Kelly told himself behind a blank expression. How had he managed to forget that? he asked himself for the thousandth time. Such a simple thing, something he'd stressed for every new arrival in 3rd SOG: always check your back, because there might be somebody hunting you. Simple thing to remember, wasn't it?

But that was history. And history could not be changed.

"Back to your island, John?" Rosen asked.

Kelly nodded. "Yeah. I have work waiting, and I have to get myself back into shape."

"I want to see you back here in, oh, two weeks, for a follow-up."

"Yes, sir. I'll be back," Kelly promised. He thanked Sandy O'Toole for her care, and was rewarded with a smile. She'd almost become a friend in the preceding eighteen days. Almost? Perhaps she already was, if only he would allow himself to think in such terms. Kelly got into his car and fixed the seat belt in place. Goodbyes had never been his strong suit. He nodded and smiled at them and drove off, turning right towards Mulberry Street, alone for the first time since his arrival at the hospital.

Finally. Next to him, on the passenger seat where he'd last seen Pam alive, was a manila envelope marked *Patient Records/Bills* in Sam Rosen's coarse handwriting.

"God," Kelly breathed, heading west. He wasn't just watching traffic now. The cityscape was forever transformed for John Kelly. The streets were a curious mixture of activity and vacancy, and his eyes swept around in a habit he'd allowed himself to forget, zeroing in on people whose inactivity seemed to display a purpose. It would take time, he told himself, to distinguish the sheep from the goats. The city traffic was light, and in any case, people didn't linger on these streets. Kelly looked left and right to see that the other drivers' eyes were locked forward, shutting out what lay around them, just as he had once done, stopping uneasily for red lights they couldn't comfortably run and hitting the gas hard when the lights changed. Hoping that they could leave it all behind, that the problems here would stay here and never move outward to where the good people lived. In that sense it was a reversal of Vietnam, wasn't it? There the bad things were out in the boonies, and you wanted to keep them from moving in. Kelly realized that he'd come home to see the same kind of lunacy and the same kind of failure in a very different kind of place. And he'd been as guilty and as foolish as everyone else.

The Scout turned left, heading south past another hospital, a large white one. Business district, banks and offices, courthouse, city hall, a good part of town where good people came in daylight, leaving quickly at night, all together because there was safety in their hurried numbers. Well-policed, because without these people and their commerce, the city would surely die. Or something like that. Maybe it wasn't a question of life or death at all, but merely of speed.

Only a mile and a half, Kelly wondered. *That much?* He'd have to check a map. A dangerously short distance in any case between these people and what they feared. Stopped at an intersection, he could see a long way, because city streets, like firebreaks, offered long and narrow views. The light changed and he moved on.

Springer was in her accustomed place, twenty minutes later. Kelly assembled his things and went aboard. Ten minutes after that, the diesels were chugging away, the air conditioning was on, and he was back in his little white bubble of civilization, ready to cast off. Off of pain medications and feeling the need for a beer and some relaxation—just the symbolic return to normality—he nevertheless left the alcohol alone. His left shoulder was distressingly stiff despite his having been able to use it, after a fashion, for almost a week. He walked around the main salon, swinging his arms in wide circles, and wincing from the pain on the left side, before heading topside to cast off. Murdock came out to watch, but said nothing from the door into his office. Kelly's experience had made the papers, though not the involvement with Pam, which somehow the reporters had failed to connect. The fuel tanks were topped off, and all the boat's systems appeared to be operating, but there was no bill for whatever the yard had done.

Kelly's line-handling was awkward as his left arm refused to do the things his mind commanded in the usual timely fashion. Finally, the lines were slipped, and *Springer* headed out. After clearing the yacht basin, Kelly settled into the salon control station, steering a straight course out to the Bay in the comfort of the air conditioning and the security of the enclosed cabin. Only after clearing the shipping channel an hour later did he look away from the water. A soft drink chased two Tylenol down his throat. That was the only drug he'd allowed himself for the last three days. He leaned back in the captain's chair and opened the envelope Sam had left him, while the autopilot drove the boat south.

Only the photos had been left out. He'd seen one of them, and that one had been enough. A handwritten cover note—every page in the envelope was a photocopy, not an original—showed that the professor of pathology had gotten the copies from his friend, the state medical examiner, and could Sam please be careful how he handled this. Kelly couldn't read the signature.

The ''wrongful death'' and ''homicide'' blocks on the cover sheet were both checked. The cause of death, the report said, was manual strangulation, with a deep, narrow set of ligature marks about the victim's neck. The severity and depth of the ligature marks suggested that brain death had occurred from oxygen deprivation even before the crushed larynx terminated airflow to the lungs. Striations on the skin suggested that the instrument used was probably a shoestring, and from bruises that appeared to come from the knuckles of a large-handed man about the throat, that the killer had faced the supine victim while performing the act. Beyond that, the report went on for five single-spaced pages, the victim had been subjected to violent and extensive traumatic insult prior to death, all of which was cataloged at length in dry medical prose. A separate form noted that she had been raped, further that the genital area showed definite signs of bruising and other abuse. An unusually large quantity of semen was still evident in her vagina upon her discovery and autopsy, indicating that the killer had not been alone in raping the victim. (''Blood types O+, O– and AB–, per attached serology report.'') Extensive cuts and bruises about the hands and forearms were termed ''defensive-classical.'' Pam had fought for her life. Her jaw had been broken, along with three other bones, one of them a compound fracture of the left ulna. Kelly had to set the report down, staring at the horizon before reading on. His hands didn't shake, and he didn't utter a word, but he needed to look away from the cold medical terminology.

''As you can see from the photos, Sam,'' the handwritten page at the back said, ''this was something from a couple of really sick folks. It was deliberate torture. It must have taken hours to do all this. One thing the report leaves out. Check Photo #6. Her hair was combed or brushed out, probably, almost certainly postmortem. The pathologist who handled the case missed it somehow. He's a youngster. (Alan was out of town when she came in, or I'm sure he would have handled it himself.) It seems a little odd, but it's clear from the photo. Funny how you can miss the obvious things. It was probably his first case like this, and probably he was too focused on listing the major insults to notice something so minor. I gather you knew the girl. I'm sorry, my friend. Brent,'' the page was signed, more legibly than the cover sheet. Kelly slid the package back into the envelope.

He opened a drawer in the console and removed a box of .45 ACP ammunition, loading the two magazines for his automatic, which went back into the drawer. There were few things more useless than an unloaded pistol. Next he went into the galley and found the largest can on the shelves. Sitting back down at the control station, he held the can in his left hand, and continued what he'd been doing for almost a week, working the can like a dumbbell, up and down, in and out, welcoming the pain, savoring it while his eyes swept the surface of the water.

''Never again, Johnnie-boy,'' he said aloud in a conversational tone. ''We're not going to make any more mistakes. Not ever.''

The C-141 landed at Pope Air Force Base, adjacent to Fort Bragg, North Carolina, soon after lunch, ending a routine flight that had originated over eight thousand miles away. The four-engine jet transport touched down rather hard. The crew was tired despite their rest stops along the way, and their passengers required no particular care. On flights such as this, there was rarely any live cargo. Troops returning from the theater of operations rode ''Freedom Birds,'' almost invariably chartered commercial airliners whose stewardesses passed out smiles and free booze for the duration of the lengthy return trip to the real world. No such amenities were required on the flights into Pope. The flight crew ate USAF-standard box lunches, and for the most part flew without the usual banter of young airmen.

The roll-out slowed the aircraft, which turned at the end of the runway onto a taxiway, while the crew stretched at their seats. The pilot, a captain, knew the routine by heart, but there was a brightly painted jeep in case he forgot, and he followed it to the receiving center. He and his crew had long since stopped dwelling on the nature of their mission. It was a job, a necessary one, and that was that, they all thought as they left the aircraft for their mandated crew-rest period, which meant, after a short debrief and notification of whatever shortcomings the aircraft had exhibited in the past thirty hours, heading off to the O-Club for drinks, followed by showers and sleep in the Q. None of them looked back at the aircraft. They'd see it again soon enough.

The routine nature of the mission was a contradiction. In most previous wars, Americans had lain close to where they fell, as testified to by American cemeteries in France and elsewhere. Not so for Vietnam. It was as though people understood that no American wanted to remain there, living or dead, and every recovered body came home, and having passed through one processing facility outside Saigon, each body would now be processed again prior to transshipment to whatever hometown had sent the mainly young men off to die in a distant place. The families would have had time by now to decide where burial would take place, and instructions for those arrangements waited for each body identified by name on the aircraft's manifest.

Awaiting the bodies in the receiving center were civilian morticians. That was one occupational specialty that the military did not carry in its multiplicity of training regimens. A uniformed officer was always present to verify identification, for that *was* a responsibility of the service, to make sure that the right body went off to the right family, even though the caskets that left this place were in almost all cases sealed. The physical insult of combat death, plus the ravages of often late recovery in a tropical climate, were not things families wanted or needed to see on the bodies of their loved ones. As a result, positive identification of remains wasn't really something that anyone could check, and for that very reason, it was something the military took as seriously as it could.

It was a large room where many bodies could be processed at once, though the room was not as busy as it had been in the past. The men who worked here were not above grim jokes, and some even watched weather reports from that part of the world to predict what the next week's work load would be like. The smell alone was enough to keep the casual observer away, and one rarely saw a senior officer here, much less a civilian Defense Department official, for whose equilibrium the sights here might be a little too much to bear. But one becomes accustomed to smells, and that of the preserving agents was much preferred over the other odors associated with death. One such body, that of Specialist Fourth Class Duane Kendall, bore numerous wounds to the torso. He'd made it as far as a field hospital, the mortician saw. Some of the scarring was clearly the desperate work of a combat surgeon—incisions that would have earned the wrath of a chief of service in a civilian hospital were far less graphic than the marks made by fragments from an explosive booby-trap device. The surgeon had spent maybe twenty minutes trying to save this one, the mortician thought, wondering why he had failed—probably the liver, he decided from the location and size of the incisions. You can't live without one of those no matter how good the doctor was. Of more interest to the man was a white tag located between the right arm and the chest which confirmed an apparently random mark on the card on the outside of the container in which the body had arrived.

"Good ID," the mortician said to the Captain who was making his rounds with a clipboard and a sergeant. The officer checked the required data against his own records and moved on with a nod, leaving the mortician to his work.

There was the usual number of tasks to be performed, and the mortician went about them with neither haste nor indolence, lifting his head to make sure the Captain was at the other end of the room. Then he pulled a thread from the stitches made by another mortician at the other end of the pipeline. The stitches came completely undone almost instantly, allowing him to reach into the body cavity and remove four clear-plastic envelopes of white powder, which he quickly put into his bag before reclosing the gaping hole in Duane Kendall's body. It was his third and last such recovery of the day. After spending half an hour on one more body, it was the end of his working day. The mortician walked off to his car, a Mercury Cougar, and drove off post. He stopped off at a Winn-Dixie supermarket to pick up a loaf of bread, and on the way out dropped some coins into a public phone.

"Yeah?" Henry Tucker said, picking it up on the first ring.

"Eight." The phone clicked off.

"Good," Tucker said, really to himself, putting the receiver down. Eight kilos from this one. Seven from his other man; neither man knew that the other was there, and the pickups from each were done on different days of the week. Things could pick up rapidly now that he was getting his distribution problems in hand.

The arithmetic was simple enough. Each kilo was one thousand grams. Each kilo would be diluted with nontoxic agents like milk sugar, which his friends obtained from a grocery-supply warehouse. After careful mixing to ensure uniformity throughout the entire batch, others would divide the bulk powder into smaller "hits" of the drugs that could be sold in smaller batches. The quality and burgeoning reputation of his product guaranteed a slightly higher than normal price which was anticipated by the wholesale cost he received from his white friends.

The problem would soon become one of scale. He'd started his operation small, since Tucker was a careful man, and size made for greed. That would soon become impossible. His supply of pure refined heroin was far more extensive than his partners knew. They were, for now, happy that its quality was so high, and he would gradually reveal to them the magnitude of his supply, while never giving them a hint of his method of shipment, for which he regularly congratulated himself. The sheer elegance of it was striking, even to him. The best government estimates—he kept track of such things—of heroin imports from Europe, the "French" or "Sicilian" connection, since they could never seem to get the terminology right, amounted to roughly one metric ton of pure drugs per year. That, Tucker judged, would have to grow, because drugs were the coming thing in American vice. If he could bring in a mere twenty kilos of drugs per week—and his shipment modality was capable of more than that—he had that number beaten, and he didn't have to worry about customs inspectors. Tucker had set up his organization with a careful eye on the security issue. For starters, none of the important people on his team touched drugs. To do so was death, a fact that he had made clear early on in the simplest and clearest possible way. The distant end of the operation required only six people. Two procured the drugs from local sources whose security was guaranteed by the usual means—large sums of cash paid to the right people. The four on-site morticians were also very well paid and had been selected for their businesslike stability. The United States Air Force handled transportation, reducing his costs and headaches for what was usually the most complicated and dangerous part of the import process. The two at the receiving station were similarly careful men. More than once, they'd reported, circumstances had compelled them to leave the heroin in the bodies, which had been duly buried. That was too bad, of course, but a good business was a careful business, and the street markup easily compensated for the loss. Besides, those two knew what would happen if they even thought about diverting a few kilos for their own enterprises.

From there it was merely a matter of transport by automobile to a convenient place, and that was handled by a trusted and well-paid man who never once exceeded a speed limit. Doing things on the Bay, Tucker thought, sipping on his beer and watching a baseball game, was his masterstroke. In addition to all the other advantages that the location gave him, he'd given his new partners reason to believe that the drugs were dropped off ships heading up the Chesapeake Bay to the Port of Baltimore—which they thought wonderfully clever—when in fact he transported them himself from a covert pickup point. Angelo Vorano had proven that by buying his dumb little sailboat and offering to make a pickup. Convincing Eddie and Tony that he'd burned them to the police had been so easy.

With a little luck he could take over the entire East Cost heroin market for as long as Americans continued to die in Vietnam. It was also time, he told himself, to plan for the peace that would probably break out someday. In the meantime he needed to think about finding a way to expand his distribution network. What he had, while it had worked, and while it had brought him to the attention of his new partners, was rapidly becoming outdated. It was too small for his ambitions, and soon it would have to be restructured. But one thing at a time.

"Okay, it's official." Douglas dropped the case file on the desk and looked at his boss.

"What's that?" Lieutenant Ryan asked.

"First, nobody saw anything. Second, nobody knew what pimp she worked for. Third, nobody even knows who she was. Her father hung up on me after he said he hasn't talked to his daughter in four years. That boyfriend didn't see shit before or after he was shot." The detective sat down.

"And the mayor's not interested anymore," Ryan finished the case summary.

"You know, Em, I don't mind running a covert investigation, but it is hurting my success rate. What if I don't get promoted next board?"

"Funny, Tom."

Douglas shook his head and stared out the window. "Hell, what if it really was the Dynamic Duo?" the sergeant asked in frustration. The pair of shotgun robbers had killed again two nights before, this time murdering an attorney from Essex. There had been a witness in a car fifty yards away, who had confirmed that there were two of them, which wasn't exactly news.

There was also a generally held belief in police work that the murder of a lawyer ought not to be a crime at all, but neither man joked about this investigation.

"Let me know when you start believing that," Ryan said quietly. Both knew better, of course. These two were only robbers. They'd killed several times, and had twice driven their victim's car a few blocks, but in both cases it had been a sporty car, and probably they'd wanted no more than to have a brief fling with a nice set of wheels. The police knew size, color, and little else. But the Duo were businesslike crooks, and whoever had murdered Pamela Madden had wanted to make a very personal impression; or there was a new and very sick killer about, which possibility added merely one more complication to their already busy lives.

"We were close, weren't we?" Douglas asked. "This girl had names and faces, and she was an eyewitness."

"But we never knew she was there until after that bonehead lost her for us," Ryan said.

"Well, he's back to wherever the hell he goes to, and we're back to where we were before, too." Douglas picked up the file and walked back to his desk.

It was after dark when Kelly tied *Springer* up. He looked up to note that a helicopter was overhead, probably doing something or other from the nearby naval air station. In any case it didn't circle or linger. The outside air was heavy and moist and sultry. Inside the bunker was even worse, and it took an hour to get the air conditioning up to speed. The "house" seemed emptier than before, for the second time in a year, the rooms automatically larger without a second person to help occupy the space. Kelly wandered about for fifteen minutes or so. His movements were aimless until he found himself staring at Pam's clothes. Then his brain clicked in to tell him that he was looking for someone no longer there. He took the articles of clothing and set them in a neat pile on what had once been Tish's dresser, and might have become Pam's. Perhaps the saddest thing of all was that there was so little of it. The cutoffs, the halter, a few more intimate things, the flannel shirt she'd worn at night, her well-worn shoes on top of the pile. So little to remember her by.

Kelly sat on the edge of his bed, staring at them. How long had it all lasted? Three weeks? Was that all? It wasn't a matter of checking the days on a calendar, because time wasn't really measured in that way. Time was something that filled the empty spaces in your life, and his three weeks with Pam had been longer and deeper than all the time since Tish's death. But all that was now a long time ago. His hospital stay seemed like a mere blink of an eye, but it was as though it had become a wall between that most precious part of his life and where he was now. He could walk up to the wall and look over it at what had been, but he could never more reach out and touch it. Life could be so cruel and memory could be a curse, the taunting reminder of what had been and what might have developed from it if only he'd acted differently. Worst of all, the wall between where he was and where he might have gone was one of his own construction, just as he had moments earlier piled up Pam's clothes because they no longer had a use. He could close his eyes and see her. In the silence he could hear her, but the smells were gone, and her feel was gone.

Kelly reached over from the bed and touched the flannel shirt, remembering what it had once covered, remembering how his large strong hands had clumsily undone the buttons to find his love inside, but now it was merely a piece of cloth whose shape contained nothing but air, and little enough of that. It was then that Kelly began sobbing for the first time since he'd learned of her death. His body shook with the reality of it, and alone inside the walls of rebarred concrete he called out her name, hoping that somewhere she might hear, and somehow she might forgive him for killing her with his stupidity. Perhaps she was at rest now. Kelly prayed that God would understand that she'd never really had a chance, would recognize the goodness of her character and judge her with mercy, but that was one mystery whose solutions were well beyond his ability to solve. His eyes were limited by the confines of this room, and they kept returning to the pile of clothing.

The bastards hadn't even given her body the dignity of being covered from the elements and the searching eyes of men. They'd wanted everybody to know how they'd punished her and enjoyed her and tossed her aside like a piece of rubbish, something for a bird to pick at. Pam Madden had been of no consequence to them, except perhaps a convenience to be used in life, and even in death, as a demonstration of their prowess. As central as she had been to his life, that was how unimportant she had been to them. Just like the headman's family, Kelly realized. A demonstration: defy us and suffer. And if others found out, so much the better. Such was their pride.

Kelly lay back in the bed, exhausted by weeks of bed rest followed by a long day of exertion. He stared at the ceiling, the light still on, hoping to sleep, hoping more to find dreams of Pam, but his last conscious thought was something else entirely.

If his pride could kill, then so could theirs.

* * *

Dutch Maxwell arrived at his office at six-fifteen, as was his custom. Although as Assistant Chief of Naval Operations (Air) he was no longer part of any operational command hierarchy, he was still a Vice Admiral, and his current job required him to think of every single aircraft in the U.S. Navy as his own. And so the top item on his pile of daily paperwork was a summary of the previous day's air operations over Vietnam—actually it was today's, but had happened yesterday due to the vagaries of the International Dateline, something that had always seemed outrageous even though he'd fought one battle practically astride the invisible line on the Pacific Ocean.

He remembered it well: less than thirty years earlier, flying an F4F-4 Wildcat fighter off USS *Enterprise,* an ensign, with all his hair—cut very short—and a brand-new wife, all piss-and-vinegar and three hundred hours under his belt. On the fourth of June, 1942, in the early afternoon, he'd spotted three Japanese "Val" dive bombers that ought to have followed the rest of the Hiryu air group to attack *Yorktown* but had gotten lost and headed towards his carrier by mistake. He'd killed two of them on his first surprise pass out of a cloud. The third had taken longer, but he could remember every glint of the sun off his target's wings and the tracers from the gunner's futile efforts to drive him off. Landing on his carrier forty minutes later, he'd claimed three kills before the incredulous eyes of his squadron commander—then had all three confirmed by gunsight cameras. Overnight, his "official" squadron coffee mug had changed from "Winny"—a nickname he'd despised—to "Dutch," engraved into the porcelain with blood-red letters, a call sign he'd borne for the remainder of his career.

Four more combat cruises had added twelve additional kills to the side of his aircraft, and in due course he'd commanded a fighter squadron, then a carrier air wing, then a carrier, then a group, and then been Commander, Air Forces, U.S. Pacific Fleet, before assuming his current job. With luck a fleet command lay in his future, and that was as far as he'd ever been able to see. Maxwell's office was in keeping with his station and experience. On the wall to the left of his large mahogany desk was the side plate from the F6F Hellcat he'd flown at Philippine Sea and off the coast of Japan. Fifteen rising-sun flags were painted on the deep blue background lest anyone forget that the Navy's elder statesman of aviators had really done it once, and done it better than most. His old mug from the old *Enterprise* sat on his desk as well, no longer used for something so trivial as drinking coffee, and certainly not for pencils.

This near-culmination of his career should have been a matter of the utmost satisfaction to Maxwell, but instead his eyes fell upon the daily loss report from Yankee Station. Two A-7A Corsair light-attack bombers had been lost, and the notation said they were from the same ship and the same squadron.

"What's the story on this?" Maxwell asked Rear Admiral Podulski.

"I checked," Casimir replied. "Probably a midair. Anders was the element leader, his wingman, Robertson, was a new kid. Something went wrong but nobody saw what it was. No SAM call, and they were too high for flak."

" 'Chutes?"

"No." Podulski shook his head. "The division leader saw the fireball. Just bits and pieces came out."

"What were they in after?"

Cas's face said it all. "A suspected truck park. The rest of the strike went in, hit the target, good bomb patterns, but no secondaries."

"So the whole thing was a waste of time." Maxwell closed his eyes, wondering what had gone wrong with the two aircraft, with the mission assignment, with his career, with his Navy, with his whole country.

"Not at all, Dutch. *Somebody* thought it was an important target."

"Cas, it's too early in the morning for that, okay?"

"Yes, sir. The CAG is investigating the incident and will probably take some token action. If you want an explanation, it's probably that Robertson was a new kid, and he was nervous—second combat mission—and probably he thought he saw something, and probably he jinked too hard, but they were the trail element and nobody saw it. Hell, Dutch, we saw that sort of thing happen, too."

Maxwell nodded. "What else?"

"An A-6 got shredded north of Haiphong—SAM—but they got it back to the boat all right. Pilot and B/N both get DFCs for that," Podulski reported. "Otherwise a quiet day in the South China Sea. Nothing much in the Atlantic. Eastern Med, picking up some signs the Syrians are getting frisky with their new MiGs, but that's not our problem yet. We have that meeting with Grumman tomorrow, and then it's off to The Hill to talk with our worthy public servants about the F-14 program."

"How do you like the numbers on the new fighter?"

"Part of me wishes we were young enough to qualify, Dutch." Cas managed a smile. "But, Jesus, we used to build carriers for what one of these things is going to cost."

"Progress, Cas."

"Yeah, we have so much of that." Podulski grunted. "One other thing. Got a call from Pax River. Your friend may be back home. His boat's at the dock, anyway."

"You made me wait this long for it?"

"No sense rushing it. He's a civilian, right? Probably sleeps till nine or ten."

Maxwell grunted. "That must be nice. I'll have to try it sometime."

11
Fabrication

ive miles can be a long walk. It is always a long swim. It is a particularly long swim alone. It was an especially long swim alone and for the first time in weeks. That fact became clear to Kelly before the halfway point, but even though the water east of his island was shallow enough that he could stand in many places, he didn't stop, didn't allow himself to slacken off. He altered his stroke to punish his left side all the more, welcoming the pain as the messenger of progress. The water temperature was just about right, he told himself, cool enough that he didn't overheat, and warm enough that it didn't drain the energy from his body. Half a mile out from the island his pace began to slow, but he summoned the inner reservoir of whatever it was that a man drew on and gutted it out, building the pace up again until, when he touched the mud that marked the eastern side of Battery Island, he could barely move. Instantly his muscles began to tighten up, and Kelly had to force himself to stand and walk. It was then that he saw the helicopter. He'd heard one twice during his swim, but made no note of it. He had long experience with helicopters, and hearing them was as natural as the buzz of an insect. But having one land on his sandbar was not all that common, and he walked over towards it until a voice called him back towards the bunkers.

"Over here, Chief!"

Kelly turned. The voice was familiar, and on rubbing his eyes he saw the undress whites of a very senior naval officer—that fact made clear by the golden shoulder boards that sparkled in the late-morning sun.

"Admiral Maxwell!" Kelly was glad for the company, especially this man, but his lower legs were covered in mud from the walk out of the water. "I wish you'd called ahead, sir."

"I tried, Kelly." Maxwell came up to him and took his hand. "We've been calling here for a couple of days. Where the hell were you? Out on a job?" The Admiral was surprised at the instant change in the boy's face.

"Not exactly."

"Why don't you go get washed off? I'll go looking for a soda." It was then that Maxwell saw the recent scars on Kelly's back and neck. *Jesus!*

Their first meeting had been aboard USS *Kitty Hawk,* three years earlier, he as AirPac, Kelly as a very sick Bosun's Mate First Class. It wasn't the sort of thing a man in Maxwell's position could forget. Kelly had gone in to rescue the flight crew of Nova One One, whose pilot had been Lieutenant, junior grade, Winslow Holland Maxwell III, USN. Two days of crawling about in an area that was just too hot for a rescue helicopter to go trolling, and he'd come out with Dutch 3rd, injured but alive, but Kelly had caught a vicious infection from the putrid water. And how, Maxwell still asked himself, how did you thank a man for saving your only son? So young he'd looked in the hospital bed, so much like his son, the same sort of defiant pride and shy intelligence. In a just world Kelly would have received the Medal of Honor for his solo mission up that brown river, but Maxwell hadn't even wasted the paper. Sorry, Dutch, CINCPAC would have said, I'd like to go to bat for you on this, but it's a waste of effort, just would look too, well, suspicious. And so he'd done what he could.

"Tell me about yourself."

"Kelly, sir, John T., bosun's mate first—"

"No." Maxwell had interrupted him with a shake of the head. "No, I think you look more like a *Chief* Bosun's Mate to me."

Maxwell had stayed on *Kitty Hawk* for three more days, ostensibly to conduct a personal inspection of flight operations, but really to keep an eye on his wounded son and the young SEAL who'd rescued him. He'd been with Kelly for the telegram announcing the death of his father, a firefighter who'd had a heart attack on the job. And now, he realized, he'd arrived just after something else.

Kelly returned from his shower in a T-shirt and shorts, dragging a little physically, but with something tough and strong in his eyes.

"How far was that swim, John?"

"Just under five miles, sir."

"Good workout," Maxwell observed, handing over a Coca-Cola for his host. "You better cool down some."

"Thank you, sir."

"What happened to you? That mess on your shoulder is new." Kelly told his story briefly, in the way of one warrior to another, for despite the difference in age and station they were of a kind, and for the second time Dutch Maxwell sat and listened like the surrogate father he had become.

"That's a hard hit, John," the Admiral observed quietly.

"Yes, sir." Kelly didn't know what else he was supposed to say, and looked down for a moment. "I never thanked you for the card . . . when Tish died. That was good of you, sir. How's your son doing?"

"Flying a 727 for Delta. I'm going to be a grandfather any day now," the Admiral said with satisfaction, then he realized how cruel the addition might have seemed to this young, lonely man.

"Great!" Kelly managed a smile, grateful to hear something good, that something he'd done had come to a successful conclusion. "So what brings you out here, sir?"

"I want to go over something with you." Maxwell opened his portfolio and unfolded the first of several maps on Kelly's coffee table.

The younger man grunted. "Oh, yeah, I remember this place." His eyes lingered on some symbols that were hand-sketched in. "Classified information here, sir."

"Chief, what we're going to talk about is very sensitive."

Kelly turned to look around. Admirals always traveled around with aides, usually a shiny young lieutenant who would carry the official briefcase, show his boss where the head was, fuss over where the car was parked, and generally do the things beneath the dignity of a hardworking chief petty officer. Suddenly he realized that although the helicopter had its flight crew, now wandering around outside, Vice Admiral Maxwell was otherwise alone, and that was most unusual.

"Why me, sir?"

"You're the only person in the country who's seen this area from ground level."

"And if we're smart, we'll keep it that way." Kelly's memories of the place were anything but pleasant. Looking at the two-dimensional map instantly brought bad three-dimensional recollections.

"How far did you go up the river, John?"

"About to here." Kelly's hand wandered across the map. "I missed your son on the first sweep so I doubled back and found him right about here."

And that wasn't bad, Maxwell thought, tantalizingly close to the objective. "This highway bridge is gone. Only took us sixteen missions, but it's *in* the river now."

"You know what that means, don't you? They build a ford, probably, or a couple underwater bridges. You want advice on taking those out?"

"Waste of time. The objective is here." Maxwell's finger tapped a spot marked with red pen.

"That's a long way to swim, sir. What is it?"

"Chief, when you retired you checked the box for being in the Fleet Reserve," Maxwell said benignly.

"Hold on, sir!"

"Relax, son, I'm not recalling you." *Yet,* Maxwell thought. "You had a top-secret clearance."

"Yeah, we all did, because of—"

"This stuff is higher than TS, John." And Maxwell explained why, pulling additional items from his portfolio.

"Those motherfuckers . . ." Kelly looked up from the recon photo. "You want to go in and get them out, like Song Tay?"

"What do you know about that?"

"Just what was in the open," Kelly explained. "We talked it around the group. It sounded like a pretty slick job. Those Special Forces guys can be real clever when they work at it. But—"

"Yeah, *but* there was nobody home. This guy"—Maxwell tapped the photo—"is positively ID'd as an Air Force colonel. Kelly, you can never repeat this."

"I understand that, sir. How do you plan to do it?"

"We're not sure yet. You know something about the area, and we want your information to help look at alternatives."

Kelly thought back. He'd spent fifty sleepless hours in the area. "It would be real hairy for a helo insertion. There's a lot of triple-A there. The nice thing about Song Tay, it wasn't close to anything, but this place is close enough to Haiphong, and you have these roads and stuff. This is a tough one, sir."

"Nobody ever said it was going to be easy."

"If you loop around here, you can use this ridgeline to mask your approach, but you have to hop the river somewhere . . . here, and you run into that flak trap . . . and that one's even worse, 'cording to these notations."

"Did SEALs plan air missions over there, Chief?" Maxwell asked, somewhat amused, only to be surprised at the reply.

"Sir, 3rd SOG was always short of officers. They kept getting shot up. I was the group operations officer for two months, and we *all* knew how to plan insertions. We had to, that was the most dangerous part of most missions. Don't take this wrong, sir, but even enlisted men know how to think."

Maxwell bristled a little. "I never said they didn't."

Kelly managed a grin. "Not all officers are as enlightened as you are, sir." He looked back down at the map. "You plan this sort of thing backwards. You start with what do you need on the objective, then you backtrack to find out how you get it all there."

"Save that for later. Tell me about the river valley," Maxwell ordered.

Fifty hours, Kelly remembered, picked up from Danang by helo, deposited aboard the submarine USS *Skate,* which then had moved Kelly right into the surprisingly deep estuary of that damned stinking river, fighting his way up against the current behind an electrically powered sea-scooter, which was still there, probably, unless some fisherman had snagged a line on it, staying underwater until his air tanks gave out, and he remembered how frightening it was not to be able to hide under the rippled surface. When he couldn't do that, when it had been too dangerous to move, hiding under weeds on the bank, watching traffic move on the river road, hearing the ripping thunder of the flak batteries on the hilltops, wondering what some 37mm fire could do to him if some North Vietnamese boy scout stumbled across him and let his father know. And now this flag officer was asking him how to risk the lives of other men in the same place, trusting him, much as Pam had, to know what to do. That sudden thought chilled the retired chief bosun's mate.

"It's not a really nice place, sir. I mean, your son saw a lot of it, too."

"Not from your perspective," Maxwell pointed out.

And that was true, Kelly remembered. Little Dutch had bellied up in a nice thick place, using his radio only on alternate hours, waiting for Snake to come and fetch him while he nursed a broken leg in silent agony, and listened to the same triple-A batteries that had splashed his A-6 hammer the sky at other men trying to take out the same bridge that his own bombs had missed. *Fifty hours,* Kelly remembered, no rest, no sleep, just fear and the mission.

"How much time, sir?"

"We're not sure. Honestly, I'm not sure if we can get the mission green-lighted. When we have a plan, then we can present it. When it's approved, we can assemble assets, and train, and execute."

"Weather considerations?" Kelly asked.

"The mission has to go in the fall, this fall, or maybe it'll never go."

"You say these guys will never come back unless we get them?"

"No other reason for them to set this place up in the way they did," Maxwell replied.

"Admiral, I'm pretty good, but I'm just an enlisted guy, remember?"

"You're the only person who's been close to the place." The Admiral collected the photographs and the maps. He handed Kelly a fresh set of the latter. "You turned down OCS three times. I'd like to know why, John."

"You want the truth? It would have meant going back. I pushed my luck enough."

Maxwell accepted that at face value, silently wishing that his best source of local information had accumulated the rank to match his expertise, but Maxwell also remembered flying combat missions off the old *Enterprise* with enlisted pilots, at least one of whom had displayed enough savvy to be an air-group commander, and he knew that the best helicopter pilots around were probably the instant Warrant Officers the Army ran through Fort Rucker. This wasn't the time for a wardroom mentality.

"One mistake from Song Tay," Kelly said after a moment.

"What's that?"

"They probably overtrained. After a certain period of time, you're just dulling the edge. Pick the right people, and a couple of weeks, max, will handle it. Go further than that and you're just doing embroidery."

"You're not the first person to say that," Maxwell assured him.

"Will this be a SEAL job?"

"We're not sure yet. Kelly, I can give you two weeks while we work on other aspects of the mission."

"How do I get in touch, sir?"

Maxwell dropped a Pentagon pass on the table. "No phones, no mail, it's all face-to-face contact."

Kelly stood and walked him out to the helicopter. As soon as the Admiral came into view, the flight crew started lighting up the turbine engines on the SH-2 SeaSprite. He grabbed the Admiral's arm as the rotor started turning.

"Was the Song Tay job burned?"

That stopped Maxwell in his tracks. "Why do you ask?"

Kelly nodded. "You just answered my question, Admiral."

"We're not sure, Chief." Maxwell ducked his head under the rotor and got into the back of the helicopter. As it lifted off, he found himself wishing again that Kelly had taken the invitation to officer-candidate school. The lad was smarter than he'd realized, and the Admiral made a note to look up his former commander for a fuller evaluation. He also wondered what Kelly would do on his formal recall to active duty. It seemed a shame to betray the boy's trust—it might be seen that way to him, Maxwell thought as the Sea-Sprite turned and headed northeast—but his mind and soul lingered with the twenty men believed to be SENDER GREEN, and his first loyalty had to be to them. Besides, maybe Kelly needed the distraction from his personal troubles. The Admiral consoled himself with that thought.

* * *

Kelly watched the helo disappear into the forenoon haze. Then he walked towards his machine shop. He'd expected that by this time today his body would be hurting and his mind relaxed. Strangely, the reverse was now true. The exercise at the hospital had paid off more handsomely than he'd dared to hope. There was still a problem with stamina, but his shoulder, after the usual start-up pain, had accepted the abuse with surprising good grace, and now having passed through the customary post-exercise agony, the secondary period of euphoria had set in. He'd feel good all day, Kelly expected, though he'd hit the bed early tonight in anticipation of yet another day's punishing exercise, and tomorrow he'd take a watch and start exercising in earnest by rating himself against the clock. The Admiral had given him two weeks. That was about the time he'd given to himself for his physical preparation. Now it was time for another sort.

Naval stations, whatever their size and purpose, were all alike. There were some things they all had to have. One of these was a machine shop. For six years there had been crashboats stationed at Battery Island, and to support them, there had to be machine tools to repair and fabricate broken machine parts. Kelly's collection of tools was the rough equivalent of what would be found on a destroyer, and had probably been purchased that way, the Navy Standard Mark One Mod Zero machine shop selected straight out of some service catalog. Maybe even the Air Force had the same thing for all he knew. He switched on a South Bend milling machine and began checking its various parts and oil reservoirs to make sure it would do what he wanted.

Attendant to the machine were numerous hand tools and gauges and drawers full of various steel blanks, just roughly machined metal shapes intended for further manufacturing into whatever specific purpose a technician might need. Kelly sat in a stool to decide exactly what he needed, then decided that he needed something else first. He took down the .45 automatic from its place on the wall, unloaded and disassembled it before giving the slide and barrel a very careful look inside and out.

"You're going to need two of everything," Kelly said to himself. But first things first. He set the slide on a sturdy jig and used the milling machine first of all to drill two small holes in the top of the slide. The South Bend machine made an admirably efficient drill, not even a tenth of a turn on the four-handled wheel and the tiny cutting bit lanced through the ordnance steel of the automatic. Kelly repeated the exercise, making a second hole 1.25 inches from the first. Tapping the holes for threads was just as easy, and a screwdriver completed the exercise. That ended the easy part of the day's work and got him used to operating the machine, something he hadn't done in over a year. A final examination of the modified gun slide assured Kelly that he hadn't hurt anything. It was now time for the tricky part.

He didn't have the time or equipment to do a really proper job. He knew how to use a welding set well enough, but lacked the gear to fabricate the special parts needed for the sort of instrument he would have liked to have. To do that would mean going to a small foundry whose artisans might have guessed what he was up to, and that was something he could not risk. He consoled himself with the thought that good enough was good enough, while perfect was always a pain in the ass and often not worth the effort anyway.

First he got a sturdy steel blank, rather like a can, but narrower and with thicker walls. Again he drilled and tapped a hole, this time in the center of the bottom plate, axial with the body of the "can," as he already thought of it. The hole was .60 inches in diameter, something he had already checked with a pair of calipers. There were seven similar blanks, but of lesser outside diameter. These he cut off to a length of three quarters of an inch before drilling holes in their bottoms. These new holes were .24 inches, and the shapes he ended up with were like small cups with holes in the bottom, or maybe diminutive flowerpots with vertical sides, he thought with a smile. Each of these was a "baffle." He tried to slide the baffles into the "can," but they were too wide. That earned Kelly a grumble at himself. Each baffle had to go on his lathe. This he did, trimming down the outside of each to a shiny, uniform diameter exactly one millimeter less than that of the inside of the can, a lengthy operation that had him swearing at himself for the fifty minutes it required. Finished, finally, he rewarded himself with a cold Coke before sliding the baffles inside the can. Agreeably, they all fit snugly enough that they didn't rattle, but loosely enough that they slid out with only a shake or two. Good. He dumped them out and next machined a cover cap for the can, which had to be threaded as well. Finished with that task, he first screwed it into place with the baffles out, and then with the baffles in, congratulating himself for the tight fit of all the parts—before he realized that he hadn't cut a hole in the cover plate, which he had to do next, again with the milling machine. This hole was a scant .23 inches in diameter, but when he was done he could see straight through the entire assembly. At least he'd managed to drill everything straight.

Next came the important part. Kelly took his time setting up the machine, checking the arrangements no less than five times before doing the last tapping operation with one pull on the operating handle—that after a long breath. This was something he'd observed a few times but never actually done himself, and though he was pretty good with tools, he was a retired bosun, not a machinist's mate. Finished, he dismounted the barrel and reassembled the pistol, heading outside with a box of .22 Long Rifle ammunition.

Kelly had never been intimidated by the large, heavy Colt automatic, but the cost of .45 ACP was far higher than that of .22 rimfire cartridges, and so the previous year he'd purchased a conversion kit allowing the lighter rounds to be fired through the pistol. He tossed the Coke can about fifteen feet before loading three rounds in the magazine. He didn't bother with ear protection. He stood as he always did, relaxed, hands at his sides, then brought the gun up fast, dropping into a crouching two-hand stance. Kelly stopped cold, realizing that the can screwed onto the barrel blanked out his sights. That would be a problem. The gun went back down, then came up again, and Kelly squeezed off the first round without actually seeing the target. With the predictable results: when he looked, the can was untouched. That was the bad news. The good news was that the suppressor had functioned well. Often misrepresented by TV and movie sound editors into an almost musical *zing,* the noise radiated by a really good silencer is much like that made by swiping a metal brush along a piece of finished lumber. The expanding gas from the cartridge was trapped in the baffles as the bullet passed through the holes, largely plugging them and forcing the gas to expand in the enclosed spaces inside the can. With five internal baffles—the cover plate made for number six—the noise of the firing was muted to a whisper.

All of which was fine, Kelly thought, but if you missed the target, he would probably hear the even louder sound of the pistol's slide racking back and forth, and the mechanical sounds of a firearm were impossible to mistake for anything harmless. Missing a soda can at fifteen feet did not speak well of his marksmanship. The human head was bigger, of course, but his target area inside the human head was not. Kelly relaxed and tried again, bringing the gun up from his side in a smooth and quick arc. This time he started pulling the trigger just as the silencer can began to occult the target. It worked, after a fashion. The can went down with a .22-inch hole an inch from the bottom. Kelly's timing wasn't quite right. His next shot was roughly in the center of the can, however, evoking a smile. He ejected the magazine, loading five hollow-point rounds, and a minute later, the can was no longer usable as a target, with seven holes, six of them roughly grouped in the center.

"Still have the old touch, Johnnie-boy," Kelly said to himself, safing the pistol. But this was in daylight against a stationary piece of red metal, and Kelly knew that. He walked back to his shop and stripped the pistol down again. The suppressor had tolerated the use without any apparent damage, but he cleaned it anyway, lightly oiling the internal parts. One more thing, he thought. With a small brush and white enamel he painted a straight white line down the top of the slide. Now it was two in the afternoon. Kelly allowed himself a light lunch before starting his afternoon exercises.

"Wow, that much?"

"You complaining?" Tucker demanded. "What's the matter, can't you handle it?"

"Henry, I can handle whatever you deliver," Piaggi replied, more than a little miffed at first by the man's arrogance, then wondering what might come next.

"We're going to be here three days!" Eddie Morello whined for his part.

"Don't trust your old lady that long?" Tucker grinned at the man. Eddie would have to be next, he had already decided. Morello didn't have much sense of humor anyway. His face flushed red.

"Look, Henry—"

"Settle down, everybody." Piaggi looked at the eight kilos of material on the table before turning back to Tucker. "I'd love to know where you get this stuff."

"I'm sure you would, Tony, but we already talked about that. Can you handle it?"

"You gotta remember, once you start this sort of thing, it's kinda hard to stop it. People depend on you, kinda like what do you tell the bear when you're outa cookies, y'know?" Piaggi was already thinking. He had contacts in Philadelphia and New York, young men—like himself, tired of working for a mustache with old-fashioned rules. The money potential here was stunning. Henry had access to—what? he wondered. They had started only two months before, with two kilograms that had assayed out to a degree of purity that only the best Sicilian White matched, but at half the delivery price. And the problems associated with delivery were Henry's, not his, which made the deal doubly attractive. Finally, the physical security arrangements were what most impressed Piaggi. Henry was no dummy, not some upstart with big ideas and small brains. He was, in fact, a businessman, calm and professional, someone who might make a serious ally and associate, Piaggi thought now.

"My supply is pretty solid. Let me worry about that, paisan."

"Okay." Piaggi nodded. "There is one problem, Henry. It'll take me a while to get the cash together for something this big. You should have warned me, man."

Tucker allowed himself a laugh. "I didn't want to scare you off, Anthony."

"Trust me on the money?"

A nod and a look. "I know you're a serious guy." Which was the smart play. Piaggi wouldn't walk away from the chance to establish a regular supply to his associates. The long-term money was just too good. Angelo Vorano might not have grasped that, but he had served as the means to meet Piaggi, and that was enough. Besides, Angelo was now crab shit.

"This is pure stuff, same as before?" Morello asked, annoying both of the others.

"Eddie, the man isn't going to trust us on the cash and fuck us at the same time, is he?" Piaggi asked.

"Gentlemen, let me tell you what's happening here, okay? I got a big supply of good stuff. Where I get it, how I get it, that's my business. I even got a territory I don't want you fooling with, but we ain't bumped heads yet on the street and we'll keep it that way." Both of the Italians nodded, Tucker saw. Eddie dumbly, but Tony with understanding and respect. Piaggi spoke the same way:

"You need distribution. We can handle that. You have your own territory, and we can respect that, too."

It was time for the next play. "I didn't get this far by being stupid. After today, you guys are out of this part of the business."

"What do you mean?"

"I mean, no more boat rides. I mean you guys don't handle the material anymore."

Piaggi smiled. He'd done this four times now, and the novelty had already worn off. "You have no argument from me on that. If you want, I can have my people take deliveries whenever you want."

"We separate the stuff from the money. We handle it like a business," Tucker said. "Line of credit, like."

"The stuff comes over first."

"Fair enough, Tony. You pick good people, okay? The idea is we separate you and me from the drugs as much as possible."

"People get caught, they talk," Morello pointed out. He felt excluded from the conversation, but wasn't quite bright enough to grasp the significance of that.

"Mine don't," Tucker said evenly. "My people know better."

"That was you, wasn't it?" Piaggi asked, making the connection and getting a nod. "I like your style, Henry. Try to be more careful next time, okay?"

"I spent two years getting this all set up, cost me a lot of money. I want this operation to run for a long time, and I'm not taking any more chances than I have to anymore. Now, when can you pay me off for this load?"

"I brought an even hundred with me." Tony waved towards the duffel bag on the deck. This little operation had grown with surprising rapidity as it was, but the first three loads had sold off for fine prices, and Tucker, Piaggi thought, was a man you could trust, insofar as you could trust anyone in this line of work. But, he figured, a rip would have happened already if that was what Tucker wanted, and this much drugs was too much for a guy running that kind of setup. "It's yours to take, Henry. Looks like we're going to owe you another . . . five hundred? I'll need some time, like a week or so. Sorry, man, but you kinda sandbagged me this way. Takes time to front up that much cash, y'know?"

"Call it four, Tony. No sense squeezing your friends first time out. Let's generate a little goodwill at first, okay?"

"Special introductory offer?" Piaggi laughed at that and tossed Henry a beer. "You gotta have some Italian blood in you, boy. Okay! We'll do it like you say, man." *Just how good is that supply of yours, Henry?* Piaggi couldn't ask.

"And now there's work to do." Tucker slit open the first plastic bag and dumped it into a stainless-steel mixing bowl, glad that he wouldn't have to trouble himself with this mess again. The seventh step in his marketing plan was now complete. From now on he'd have others do this kitchen stuff, under his supervision at first, of course, but starting today Henry Tucker would start acting like the executive he had become. Mixing the inert material into the bowl, he congratulated himself on his intelligence. He'd started the business in exactly the right way, taking risks, but carefully considered ones, building his organization from the bottom up, doing things himself, getting his hands dirty. Perhaps Piaggi's antecedents had started the same way, Tucker thought. Probably Tony had forgotten that, and forgotten also its implications. But that wasn't Tucker's problem.

"Look, Colonel, I was just an aide, okay? How many times do I have to tell you that? I did the same thing your generals' aides do, all the littler dumb stuff."

"Then why take such a job?" It was sad, Colonel Nikolay Yevgeniyevich Grishanov thought, that a man had to go through this, but Colonel Zacharias wasn't a man. He was an enemy, the Russian reminded himself with some reluctance, and he wanted to get the man talking again.

"Isn't it the same in your air force? You get noticed by a general and you get promoted a lot faster.'' The American paused for a moment. ''I wrote speeches, too.'' That couldn't get him into any trouble, could it?

''That's the job of a political officer in my air force.'' Grishanov dismissed that frivolity with a wave.

It was their sixth session. Grishanov was the only Soviet officer allowed to interview these Americans, the Vietnamese were playing their cards so carefully. Twenty of them, all the same, all different. Zacharias was as much an intelligence officer as fighter pilot, his dossier said. He'd spent his twenty-odd-year career studying air-defense systems. A master's degree from the University of California, Berkeley, in electrical engineering. The dossier even included a recently acquired copy of his master's thesis, ''Aspects of Microwave Propagation and Diffusion over Angular Terrain,'' photocopied from the university archives by some helpful soul, one of the unknown three who had contributed to his knowledge of the Colonel. The thesis ought to have been classified immediately upon its completion—as would have happened in the Soviet Union, Grishanov knew. It was a very clever examination of what happened to low-frequency search-radar energy—and how, incidentally, an aircraft could use mountains and hills to mask itself from it. Three years after that, following a tour of duty in a fighter squadron, he'd been assigned to a tour of duty at Offutt Air Force Base, just outside Omaha, Nebraska. Part of the Strategic Air Command's war-plans staff, he'd worked on flight profiles which might allow American B-52 bombers to penetrate Soviet air defenses, applying his theoretical knowledge of physics to the practical world of strategic-nuclear war.

Grishanov could not bring himself to hate this man. A fighter pilot himself, having just completed a regimental command in PVO-Strany, the Soviet air-defense command, and already selected for another, the Russian colonel was in a curious way Zacharias's exact counterpart. His job, in the event of war, was to stop those bombers from ravaging his country, and in peace to plan methods of making their penetration of Soviet air space as difficult as possible. That identity made his current job both difficult and necessary. Not a KGB officer, certainly not one of these little brown savages, he took no pleasure at all in hurting people—shooting them down was something else entirely—even Americans who plotted the destruction of his country. But those who knew how to extract information did not know how to analyze what he was looking for, nor even what questions to ask—and writing the questions down would be no help; you had to see the man's eyes when he spoke. A man clever enough to formulate such plans was also clever enough to lie with enough conviction and authority to fool almost anyone.

Grishanov didn't like what he saw now. This was a skillful man, and a courageous one, who had fought to establish missile-hunting specialists the Americans called Wild Weasels. It was a term a Russian might have used for the mission, named for vicious little predators who chased their prey into their very dens. This prisoner had flown eighty-nine such missions, if the Vietnamese had recovered the right pieces from the right aircraft—like Russians, Americans kept a record of their accomplishments on their aircraft— this was exactly the man he needed to talk to. Perhaps that was a lesson he would write about, Grishanov thought. Such pride told your enemies whom they had captured, and much of what he knew. But that was the way of fighter pilots, and Grishanov would himself have balked at the concealment of his deeds against his country's enemies. The Russian also tried to tell himself that he was sparing harm to the man across the table. Probably Zacharias had killed many Vietnamese—and not simple peasants, but skilled, Russian-trained missile technicians—and this country's government would want to punish him for that. But that was not his concern, and he didn't want to allow political feelings to get in the way of his professional obligations. His was one of the most scientific and certainly the most complex aspects of national defense. It was his duty to plan for an attack of hundreds of aircraft, each of which had a crew of highly trained specialists. The way they thought, their tactical doctrine, was as important as their plans. And as far as he was concerned, the Americans could kill all of the bastards they wanted. The nasty little fascists had as much to do with his country's political philosophy as cannibals did with gourmet cooking.

"Colonel, I do know better than that," Grishanov said patiently. He laid the most recently arrived document on the table. "I read this last night. It's excellent work."

The Russian's eyes never left Colonel Zacharias. The American's physical reaction was remarkable. Though something of an intelligence officer himself, he had never dreamed that someone in Vietnam could get word to Moscow, then to have Americans under their control find something like this. His face proclaimed what he was thinking: *How could they know so much about me?* How could they have reached that far back into his past? Who possibly could have done it? Was anyone that good, that professional? The Vietnamese were such fools! Like many Russian officers, Grishanov was a serious and thorough student of military history. He'd read all manner of arcane documents while sitting in regimental ready rooms. From one he'd never forget, he learned how the Luftwaffe had interrogated captured airmen, and that lesson was one he would try to apply here. While physical abuse had only hardened this man's resolve, he had just been shaken to his soul by a mere sheaf of paper. Every man had strengths and every man had weaknesses. It took a person of intelligence to recognize the differences.

"How is it that this was never classified?" Grishanov asked, lighting a cigarette.

"It's just theoretical physics," Zacharias said, shrugging his thin shoulders, recovering enough that he tried to conceal his despair. "The telephone company was more interested than anybody else."

Grishanov tapped the thesis with his finger. "Well, I tell you, I learned several things from that last night. Predicting false echoes from topographical maps, modeling the blind spots mathematically! You can plan an approach route that way, plot maneuvers from one such point to another. Brilliant! Tell me, what sort of place is Berkeley?"

"Just a school, California style," Zacharias replied before catching himself. He was talking. He wasn't supposed to talk. He was trained not to talk. He was trained on what to expect, and what he could safely do, how to evade and disguise. But that training never quite anticipated this. And, dear God, was he tired, and scared, and sick of living up to a code of conduct that didn't count for beans to anyone else.

"I know little of your country—except professional matters, of course. Are there great regional differences? You come from Utah. What sort of place is it?"

"Zacharias, Robin G. Colonel—"

Grishanov raised his hands. "Please, Colonel. I know all that. I also know your place of birth in addition to the date. There is no base of your air force near Salt Lake City. All I know is from maps. I will probably never visit this part—any part of your country. In this Berkeley part of California, it is green, yes? I was told once they grow wine grapes there. But I know nothing of Utah. There is a large lake there, but it's called Salt Lake, yes? It's salty?"

"Yes, that's why—"

"How can it be salty? The ocean is a thousand kilometers away, with mountains in between, yes?" He didn't give the American time to reply. "I know the Caspian Sea quite well. I was stationed at a base there once. It isn't salty. But this place is? How strange." He stubbed out his cigarette.

The man's head jerked up a little. "Not sure, I'm not a geologist. Something left over from another time, I suppose."

"Perhaps so. There are mountains there, too, yes?"

"Wasatch Mountains," Zacharias confirmed somewhat drunkenly.

One clever thing about the Vietnamese, Grishanov thought, the way they fed their prisoners, food a hog would eat only from necessity. He wondered if it were a deliberate and thought-out diet or something fortuitously resulting from mere barbarity. Political prisoners in the Gulag ate better, but the diet of these Americans lowered their resistance to disease, debilitated them to the point that the act of escape would be doomed by inadequate stamina. Rather like what the *fascisti* did to Soviet prisoners, distasteful or not, it was useful to Grishanov. Resistance, physical and mental, required energy, and you could watch these men lose their strength during the hours of interrogation, watch their courage wane as their physical needs drew more and more upon their supply of psychological resolve. He was learning how to do this. It was time-consuming, but it was a diverting process, learning to pick apart the brains of men not unlike himself.

"The skiing, is it good?"

Zacharias's eyes blinked, as though the question took him away to a different time and place. "Yeah, it is."

"That is something one will never do here, Colonel. I like cross-country skiing for exercise, and to get away from things. I had wooden skis, but in my last regiment my maintenance officer made me steel skis from aircraft parts."

"Steel?"

"Stainless steel, heavier than aluminum but more flexible. I prefer it. From a wing panel on our new interceptor, project E-266."

"What's that?" Zacharias knew nothing of the new MiG-25.

"Your people now call it Foxbat. Very fast, designed to catch one of your B-70 bombers."

"But we stopped that project," Zacharias objected.

"Yes, I know that. But your project got me a wonderfully fast fighter to fly. When I return home, I will command the first regiment of them."

"Fighter planes made of steel? Why?"

"It resists aerodynamic heating much better than aluminum," Grishanov explained. "And you can make good skis from discarded parts." Zacharias was very confused now. "So how well do you think we would do with my steel fighters and your aluminum bombers?"

"I guess that depends on—" Zacharias started to say, then stopped himself cold. His eyes looked across the table, first with confusion at what he'd almost said, then with resolve.

Too soon, Grishanov told himself with disappointment. He'd pushed a little too soon. This one had courage. Enough to take his Wild Weasel "downtown," the phrase the Americans used, over eighty times. Enough to resist for a long time. But Grishanov had plenty of time.

12

Outfitters

63 Vw, LOW MLGE, RAD, HTR. . . .

Kelly dropped a dime in the pay phone and called the number. It was a blazing hot Saturday, temperature and humidity in a neck-and-neck race for triple digits while Kelly fumed at his own stupidity. Some things were so blatantly obvious that you didn't see them until your nose split open and started bleeding.

"Hello? I'm calling about the ad for the car . . . that's right," Kelly said. "Right now if you want . . . Okay, say about fifteen minutes? Fine, thank you, ma'am. I'll be right there. 'Bye." He hung up. At least something had gone right. Kelly grimaced at the inside of the phone booth. *Springer* was tied up in a guest slip at one of the marinas on the Potomac. He had to buy a new car, but how did you get to where the new car was? If you drove there, then you could drive the new car back, but what about the one you took? It was funny enough that he started laughing at himself. Then fate intervened, and an empty cab went driving past the marina's entrance, allowing him to keep his promise to a little old lady.

"The 4500 block, Essex Avenue," he told the driver.

"Where's that, man?"

"Bethesda."

"Gonna cost extra, man," the driver pointed out, turning north.

Kelly handed a ten-dollar bill across. "Another one if you get me there in fifteen minutes."

"Cool." And the acceleration dropped Kelly back in his seat. The taxi avoided Wisconsin Avenue most of the way. At a red light the driver found Essex Avenue on his map, and he ended up collecting the extra ten with about twenty seconds to spare.

It was an upscale residential neighborhood, and the house was easy to spot. There it was, a VW Beetle, an awful peanut-butter color speckled with a little body rust. It could not have been much better. Kelly hopped up the four wooden front steps and knocked on the door.

"Hello?" It was a face to match the voice. She had to be eighty or so, small and frail, but with fey green eyes that hinted at what had been, enlarged by the thick glasses she wore. Her hair still had some yellow in the gray.

"Mrs. Boyd? I called a little while ago about the car."

"What's your name?"

"Bill Murphy, ma'am." Kelly smiled benignly. "Awful hot, isn't it?"

"T'rble," she said, meaning *terrible*. "Wait a minute." Gloria Boyd disappeared and then came back a moment later with the keys. She even came out to walk him to the car. Kelly took her arm to help her down the steps.

"Thank you, young man."

"My pleasure, ma'am," he replied gallantly.

"We got the car for my granddaughter. When she went to college, then Ken used it," she said, expecting Kelly to know who Ken was.

"Excuse me?"

"My husband," Gloria said without turning. "He died a month ago."

"I'm very sorry to hear that, ma'am."

"He was sick a long time," said the woman, not yet recovered from the shock of her loss but accepting the fact of it. She handed him the keys. "Here, take a look."

Kelly unlocked the door. It looked like the car used by a college student and then by an elderly man. The seats were well worn, and one had a long slash in it, probably by a packing box of clothes or books. He turned the key in the lock and the engine started immediately. There was even a full tank of gas. The ad hadn't lied about the mileage, only 52,000 miles on the odometer. He asked for and got permission to take it around the block. The car was mechanically sound, he decided, bringing it back to the waiting owner.

"Where did all the rust come from?" he asked her, giving the keys back.

"She went to school in Chicago, at Northwestern, all that terrible snow and salt."

"That's a good school. Let's get you back inside." Kelly took her arm and directed her back to the house. It smelled like an old person's house, the air heavy with dust that she was too tired to wipe, and stale food, for the meals she still fixed were for two, not one.

"Are you thirsty?"

"Yes, ma'am, thank you. Water will be just fine." Kelly looked around while she went to the kitchen. There was a photo on the wall, a man in a high-necked uniform and Sam Browne belt, holding the arm of a young woman in a very tight, almost cylindrical, white wedding dress. Other photos cataloged the married life of Kenneth and Gloria Boyd. Two daughters and a son, a trip to the ocean, an old car, grandchildren, all the things earned in a full and useful life.

"Here you go." She handed over a glass.

"Thank you. What did your husband do?"

"He worked for the Commerce Department for forty-two years. We were going to move to Florida, but then he got sick so now I'm going alone. My sister lives in Fort Pierce, she's a widow too, her husband was a policeman . . ." Her voice trailed off as the cat came in to examine the new visitor. That seemed to invigorate Mrs. Boyd. "I'm moving down there next week. The house is already sold, have to get out next Thursday. I sold it to a nice young doctor."

"I hope you like it down there, ma'am. How much do you want for the car?"

"I can't drive anymore because of my eyes, cataracts. People have to drive me everywhere I go. My grandson says it's worth one thousand five hundred dollars."

Your grandson must be a lawyer to be that greedy, Kelly thought. "How about twelve hundred? I can pay cash."

"Cash?" Her eyes became fey again.

"Yes, ma'am."

"Then you can have the car." She held out her hand and Kelly took it carefully.

"Do you have the paperwork?" It made Kelly feel guilty that she had to get up again, this time heading upstairs, slowly, holding on to the banister while Kelly took out his wallet and counted off twelve crisp bills.

It should have taken only another ten minutes, but instead it was thirty. Kelly had already checked up on how to do the mechanics of a title transfer, and besides, he wasn't going to do all of that. The auto-insurance policy was tucked into the same cardboard envelope as the title, in the name of Kenneth W. Boyd. Kelly promised to take care of that for her, and the tags, too, of course. But it turned out that all the cash made Mrs. Boyd nervous, and so Kelly helped her fill out a deposit ticket, and then drove her to her bank, where she could drop it into the night depository. Then he stopped off at the supermarket for milk and cat food before bringing her home and walking her to the door again.

"Thank you for the car, Mrs. Boyd," he said in parting.

"What are you going to use it for?"

"Business." Kelly smiled and left.

At quarter of nine that night, two cars pulled into the service area on Interstate 95. The one in front was a Dodge Dart and the one behind it a red Plymouth Roadrunner. Roughly fifty feet apart, they picked a half-full area north of Maryland House, a rest stop set in the median of the John F. Kennedy Highway, offering full restaurant services along with gas and oil—good coffee, but, understandably, no alcoholic beverages. The Dart took a few meandering turns in the parking lot, finally stopping three spaces from a white Oldsmobile with Pennsylvania tags and a brown vinyl top. The Roadrunner took a space in the next row. A woman got out and walked towards the brick restaurant, a path that took her past the Olds.

"Hey, baby," a man said. The woman stopped and took a few steps towards the vinyl-topped automobile. The man was Caucasian, with long but neatly combed black hair and an open-necked white shirt.

"Henry sent me," she said.

"I know." He reached out to stroke her face, a gesture which she did not resist. He looked around a little before moving his hand downwards. "You have what I want, baby?"

"Yes." She smiled. It was a forced, uneasy smile, frightened but not embarrassed. Doris was months beyond embarrassment.

"Nice tits," the man said with no emotional content at all in his voice. "Get the stuff."

Doris walked back to her car, as though she'd forgotten something. She returned with a large purse, almost a small duffel, really. As she walked past the Olds, the man's hand reached out and took it. Doris proceeded into the building, returning a minute later holding a can of soda, her eyes on the Roadrunner, hoping that she'd done everything right. The Olds had its motor running, and the driver blew her a kiss, to which she responded with a wan smile.

"That was easy enough," Henry Tucker said, fifty yards away, at the outdoor eating area on the other side of the building.

"Good stuff?" another man asked Tony Piaggi. The three of them sat at the same table, "enjoying" the sultry evening while the majority of the patrons were inside with the air conditioning.

"The best. Same as the sample we gave you two weeks ago. Same shipment and everything," Piaggi assured him.

"And if the mule gets burned?" the man from Philadelphia asked.

"She won't talk," Tucker assured him. "They've all seen what happens to bad girls." As they watched, a man got out of the Roadrunner and got into the Dart's driver's seat.

"Very good," Rick told Doris.

"Can we go now?" she asked him, shaking now that the job was over, sipping nervously at her soda.

"Sure, baby, I know what you want." Rick smiled and started the car. "Be nice, now. Show me something."

"There's people around," Doris said.

"So?"

Without another word, Doris unbuttoned her shirt—it was a man's shirt—leaving it tucked into her faded shorts. Rick reached in and smiled, turning the wheel with his left hand. *It could have been worse,* Doris told herself, closing her eyes, pretending that she was someone else in some other place, wondering how long before her life would end too, hoping it wouldn't be long.

"The money?" Piaggi asked.

"I need a cup of coffee." The other man got up and walked inside, leaving his briefcase, which Piaggi took in his hand. He and Tucker walked off to his car, a blue Cadillac, without waiting for the other man to come back.

"Not going to count it?" Tucker asked halfway across the parking lot.

"If he stiffs us, he knows what happens. This is business, Henry."

"That's right," Tucker agreed.

"Bill Murphy," Kelly said. "I understand you have some vacant apartments." He held up the Sunday paper.

"What are you looking for?"

"A one-bedroom would be fine. I really just need a place to hang my clothes," Kelly told the man. "I travel a lot."

"Salesman?" the manager asked.

"That's right. Machine tools. I'm new here—new territory, I mean."

It was an old garden-apartment complex, built soon after the Second World War for returning veterans, composed exclusively of three-story brick structures. The trees looked about right for that time period. They'd been planted then and grown well, tall enough now to support a good population of squirrels, wide enough to give shade to the parking areas. Kelly looked around approvingly as the manager took him to a first-floor furnished unit.

"This is just fine," Kelly announced. He looked around, testing the kitchen sink and other plumbing fixtures. The furniture was obviously used, but in decent shape. There were even air conditioners in the windows of every room.

"I have other ones—"

"This is just what I need. How much?"

"One seventy-five a month, one month security deposit."

"Utilities?"

"You can pay them yourself or we can bill it. Some of our renters prefer that. They'll average about forty-five dollars a month."

"Easier to pay one bill than two or three. Let's see. One seventy-five, plus forty-five . . ."

"Two-twenty," the manager said helpfully.

"Four-forty," Kelly corrected. "Two months, right? I can pay you with a check, but it's an out-of-town bank. I don't have a local account yet. Is cash okay?"

"Cash is always okay with me," the manager assured him.

"Fine." Kelly took out his wallet, handing over the bills. He stopped. "No, six-sixty, we'll make it three months, if that's okay. And I need a receipt." The helpful manager pulled a pad from his pocket and wrote one up on the spot. "How about a phone?" Kelly asked.

"I can have that done by Tuesday if you want. There's another deposit for that."

"Please take care of that, if you would." Kelly handed over some more money. "My stuff won't be here for a while. Where can I get sheets and stuff?"

"Nothing much open today. Tomorrow, lots of 'em."

Kelly looked through the bedroom door at the bare mattress. He could see the lumps from this distance. He shrugged. "Well, I've slept on worse."

"Veteran?"

"Marine," Kelly said.

"So was I once," the manager replied, surprising Kelly. "You don't do anything wild, do you?" He didn't expect so, but the owner insisted that he ask, even ex-Marines. The answer was a sheepish, reassuring grin.

"I snore pretty bad, they tell me."

Twenty minutes later Kelly was in a cab heading downtown. He got out at Penn Station and caught the next train to D.C., where another taxi delivered him to his boat. By nightfall, *Springer* was headed down the Potomac. It would have been so much easier, Kelly told himself, if there were just one person to help him. So much of his time was tied up with useless commuting. But was it really useless? Maybe not. He was getting a lot of thinking done, and that was as important as his physical preparations. Kelly arrived at his home just before midnight after six continuous hours of thinking and planning.

Despite a weekend of almost nonstop motion, there was no time to dawdle. Kelly packed clothing, most of it purchased in the suburbs of Washington. Linens he would buy in Baltimore. Food the same. His .45 automatic, plus the .22–.45 conversion kit, was packed in with old clothing, along with two boxes of ammunition. He shouldn't need more than that, Kelly thought, and ammo was heavy. While he fabricated one more silencer, this one for the Woodsman, he thought through his preparations. His physical condition was excellent, nearly as good as it had been in 3rd SOG, and he'd been shooting every day. His aim was probably better than it had ever been, he told himself, going through what were now almost mindless mechanical operations on the machine tools. By three in the morning the new suppressor was fitted to the Woodsman and tested. Thirty minutes after that he was back aboard *Springer,* headed north, looking forward to a few hours' sleep once he got past Annapolis.

It was a lonely night, with scattered clouds, and his mind drifted somewhat before he commanded himself to concentrate. He was not a lazy civilian anymore, but Kelly allowed himself his first beer in weeks while his mind churned over variables. What had he forgotten? The reassuring answer was that he could think of nothing. The less-than-satisfactory thought was that he still knew little. Billy with his red Plymouth muscle car. A black guy named Henry. He knew their area of operation. And that was all.

But.

But he'd fought armed and trained enemies with less knowledge than that, and though he would force himself to be just as careful now as he had been there, deep down he knew that he would accomplish this mission. Partly it was because he was more formidable than they, and far more highly motivated. The other part, Kelly realized with surprise, was because he didn't care about the consequences, only the results. He remembered something from his Catholic prep school, a passage from Virgil's *Aeneid* that had defined his mission almost two thousand years before: *Una salus victus nullam sperare salutem.* The one hope of the doomed is not to hope for safety. The very grimness of the thought made him smile as he sailed under the stars, light dispatched from distances so vast that it had begun its journey long before Kelly, or even Virgil, had been born.

The pills helped shut out reality, but not all the way. Doris didn't so much think the thought as listen to it, sense it, like recognizing something that she didn't wish to face but refused to go away. She was too dependent on the barbiturates now. Sleep came hard to her, and in the emptiness of the room she was unable to avoid herself. She would have taken more pills if she could, but they didn't allow her what she wanted, not that she wanted much. Just brief oblivion, a short-term liberation from her fear, that was all—and that was something they had no interest in granting her. She could see more than they knew or would have expected, she could peer into the future, but that was little consolation. Sooner or later she would be caught by the police. She'd been arrested before, but not for something of this magnitude, and she'd go away for a long time for this. The police would try to get her to talk, promise her protection. She knew better. Twice now she'd seen friends die. Friends? As close to that as was possible, someone to talk to, someone who shared her life, such as it was, and even in this captivity there were little jokes, small victories against the forces that ruled her existence, like distant lights in a gloomy sky. Someone to cry with. But two of them were dead, and she'd watched them die, sitting there, drugged but unable to sleep and blot it out, the horror so vast that it became numbing, watching their eyes, seeing and feeling the pain, knowing that she could do nothing, knowing even that they knew it as well. A nightmare was bad enough, but one of those couldn't reach out and touch you. You could wake up and flee from one of those. Not this. She could watch herself from outside, as though she were a robot outside her own command but not that of others. Her body would not move unless others commanded it, and she even had to conceal her thoughts, was even afraid to voice them within her own mind lest they hear them or see them on her face, but now, try as she might, she could not force them away.

Rick lay next to her, breathing slowly in the darkness. Part of her liked Rick. He was the gentlest of them, and sometimes she allowed herself to think that he liked her, maybe a little, because he didn't beat her badly. She had to stay in line, of course, because his anger was every bit as bad as Billy's, and so around Rick she tried very hard to be good. Part of her knew that it was foolish, but her reality was defined by other people now. And she'd seen the results of real resistance. After one especially bad night Pam had held her, and whispered her desires to escape. Later, Doris had prayed that she had gotten away, that there might be hope after all, only to see her dragged in and to watch her die, sitting helplessly fifteen feet away while they did everything to her that they could imagine. Watching her life end, her body convulsing from lack of oxygen with the man's face staring at her, laughing at her from an inch away. Her only act of resistance, thankfully unnoticed by the men, had been to brush out her friend's hair, crying all the while, hoping somehow that Pam would know there was someone who cared, even in death. But the gesture had seemed empty even as she'd done it, making her tears all the more bitter.

What had she done wrong? Doris wondered, how badly had she offended God that her life should be this way? How could anyone possibly deserve such a bleak and hopeless existence?

"I'm impressed, John," Rosen said, staring at his patient. Kelly sat on the examining table, his shirt off. "What have you been doing?"

"Five-mile swim for the shoulders. Better than weights, but a little of that, too, in the evening. A little running. About what I used to do back in the old days."

"I wish I had your blood pressure," the surgeon observed, removing the cuff. He'd done a major procedure that morning, but he made time for his friend.

"Exercise, Sam," Kelly advised.

"I don't have the time, John," the surgeon said—rather weakly, both thought.

"A doc should know better."

"True," Rosen conceded. "How are you otherwise?"

The reply was just a look, neither a smile nor a grimace, just a neutral expression that told Rosen all he needed to know. One more try: "There's an old saying: Before setting out on revenge, dig two graves."

"Only two?" Kelly asked lightly.

Rosen nodded. "I read the post report, too. I can't talk you out of it?"

"How's Sarah?"

Rosen accepted the deflection with good grace. "Deep into her project. She's excited enough that she's telling me about it. It's pretty interesting stuff."

Just then Sandy O'Toole came in. Kelly startled both of them by lifting his T-shirt and covering his chest. "Please!"

The nurse was so startled that she laughed, and so did Sam until he realized that Kelly was indeed ready for whatever he was planning. The conditioning, the looseness, the steady, serious eyes that changed to mirth when he wanted them to. *Like a surgeon,* Rosen thought, and what a strange thought that was, but the more he looked at this man, the more intelligence he saw.

"You're looking healthy for a guy who got shot a few weeks ago," O'Toole said with a friendly look.

"Clean living, ma'am. Only one beer in thirty-some days."

"Mrs. Lott is conscious now, Doctor Rosen," the nurse reported. "Nothing unusual, she appears to be doing fine. Her husband's been in to see her. I think he'll be okay, too. I had my doubts."

"Thanks, Sandy."

"Well, John, you're healthy, too. Put your shirt on before Sandy starts blushing," Rosen added with a chuckle.

"Where do you get lunch around here?" Kelly asked.

"I'd show you myself, but I have a conference in about ten minutes. Sandy?"

She checked her watch. "About time for mine. You want to risk hospital food or something outside?"

"You're the tour guide, ma'am."

She guided him to the cafeteria, where the food was hospital-bland, but you could add salt and other spices if you wanted. Kelly selected something that might be filling, even healthy, to compensate for the lack of taste.

"Have you been keeping busy?" he asked after they selected a table.

"Always," Sandy assured him.

"Where do you live?"

"Off Loch Raven Boulevard, just in the County." She hadn't changed, Kelly saw. Sandy O'Toole was functioning, quite well in fact, but the emptiness in her life wasn't qualitatively different from his. The real difference was that he could do something; she could not. She was reaching out, she had a capacity for good humor, but her grief overcame it at every turn. A powerful force, grief. There were advantages in having enemies you could seek out and eliminate. Fighting a shadow was far more difficult.

"Row house, like they have around here?"

"No, it's an old bungalow, whatever you call it, big square two-story house. Half an acre. That reminds me," she added. "I have to cut the grass this weekend." Then she remembered that Tim had liked cutting grass, had decided to leave the Army after his second Vietnam tour and get his law degree and live a normal kind of life, all of that taken away from her by little people in a distant place.

Kelly didn't know what she was thinking, exactly, but he didn't have to. The change in her expression, the way her voice trailed off, said it all. How to cheer her up? It was a strange question for him, considering his plans for the next few weeks.

"You were very kind to me while I was upstairs. Thanks."

"We try to take care of our patients," she said with a friendly and unaccustomed expression.

"A face as pretty as yours should do that more," Kelly told her.

"Do what?"

"Smile."

"It's hard," she said, serious again.

"I know, ma'am. But I did have you laughing before," Kelly told her.

"You surprised me."

"It's Tim, isn't it?" he asked, jolting her. People weren't supposed to talk about that, were they?

She stared into Kelly's eyes for perhaps five seconds. "I just don't understand."

"In some ways it's easy. In some ways it's hard. The hard part," Kelly said, thinking it through himself as he did so, "is understanding why people make it necessary, why people do things like that. What it comes down to is, there are bad people out there, and somebody has to deal with them, 'cuz if you don't, then someday they'll deal with you. You can try ignoring them, but that doesn't ever work, really. And sometimes you see things you just can't ignore." Kelly leaned back, searching for more words. "You see lots of bad things here, Sandy. I've seen worse. I've watched people doing things—"

"Your nightmare?"

Kelly nodded. "That's right. I almost got myself killed that night."

"What was—"

"You don't want to know, honest. I mean, I don't understand that part either, how people can do things like that. Maybe they believe in something so much that they stop remembering that it's important to be human. Maybe they want something so much that they don't care. Maybe there's just something wrong with them, how they think, how they feel. I don't know. But what they do is real. Somebody has to try and stop it." *Even when you know it's not going to work,* Kelly didn't have the heart to add. How could he tell her that her husband had died for a failure?

"My husband was a knight in shiny armor on a white horse? Is that what you're telling me?"

"You're the one wearing white, Sandy. You fight against one kind of enemy. There's other kinds. Somebody has to fight against them, too."

"I'll never understand why Tim had to die."

It really came down to that, Kelly thought. It wasn't about great political or social issues. Everyone had a life, which was supposed to have a natural end after an amount of time determined by God or Fate or something men weren't supposed to control. He'd seen young men die, and caused his share of deaths, each life something of value to its owner and others, and how did you explain to the others what it was all about? For that matter, how did you explain it to yourself? But that was from the outside. From the inside it was something else. Maybe that was the answer.

"You do some pretty hard work, right?"

"Yes," Sandy said, nodding a little.

"Why not do something easier? I mean, work a department where it's different, I don't know—the nursery, maybe? That's a happy place, right?"

"Pretty much," the nurse admitted.

"It's still important, too, right? Taking care of little babies, it's routine, yeah, but it still has to be done the right way, doesn't it?"

"Of course."

"But you don't do that. You work Neuro. You do the hard stuff."

"Somebody has to—" *Bingo!* Kelly thought, cutting her off.

"It's hard—hard to do the work, hard on you—it hurts you some, right?"

"Sometimes."

"But you do it anyway," Kelly pointed out.

"Yes," Sandy said, not as an admission, but something stronger.

"That's why Tim did what he did." He saw the understanding there, or perhaps the beginnings of it, just for a moment before her lingering grief pushed the argument aside.

"It still doesn't make sense."

"Maybe the *thing* doesn't make sense, but the *people* do," Kelly suggested. That was about as far as his mind stretched. "Sorry, I'm not a priest, just a broken-down Navy chief."

"Not too broken down," O'Toole said, finishing her lunch.

"And part of that is your doing, ma'am. Thank you." That earned him another smile.

"Not all our patients get better. We're kind of proud of those who do."

"Maybe we're all trying to save the world, Sandy, one little bit at a time," Kelly said. He rose and insisted on walking her back to the unit. It took the whole five minutes to say what he wanted to say.

"You know, I'd like to have dinner with you, maybe? Not now, but, well—"

"I'll think about it," she allowed, half dismissing the idea, half wondering about it, knowing as Kelly did that it was too soon for both of them, though probably not as much for her. What sort of man was this? she asked herself. What were the dangers of knowing him?

13
Agendas

It was his first-ever visit to the Pentagon. Kelly felt ill at ease, wondering if he should have worn his khaki chief's uniform, but his time for wearing that had passed. Instead he wore a blue lightweight suit, with a miniature of the Navy Cross ribbon on the lapel. Arriving in the bus and car tunnel, he walked up a ramp and searched for a map of the vast building, which he quickly scanned and memorized. Five minutes later he entered the proper office.

"Yes?" a petty officer asked.

"John Kelly, I have an appointment with Admiral Maxwell." He was invited to take a seat. On the coffee table was a copy of *Navy Times,* which he hadn't read since leaving the service. But Kelly was able to control his nostalgia. The bitches and gripes he read about hadn't changed very much.

"Mr. Kelly?" a voice called. He rose and walked through the open door. After it closed, a red do-not-disturb light blinked on to warn people off.

"How are you feeling, John?" Maxwell asked first of all.

"Fine, sir, thank you." Civilian now or not, Kelly could not help feeling uneasy in the presence of a flag officer. That got worse at once when another door opened to admit two more men, one in civilian clothes, the other a rear admiral—another aviator, Kelly saw, with the medal of honor, which was even more intimidating. Maxwell did the introductions.

"I've heard a lot about you," Podulski said, shaking the younger man's hand.

"Thank you, sir." Kelly didn't know what else to say.

"Cas and I go back a ways," Maxwell observed, handling the introduc-

tions. "I got fifteen"—he pointed to the aircraft panel hanging on the wall—
"Cas got eighteen."

"All on film, too," Podulski assured him.

"I didn't get any," Greer said, "but I didn't let the oxygen rot my brain
either." In addition to wearing soft clothes, this admiral had the map case.
He took one out, the same panel he had back at his home, but more marked
up. Then came the photographs, and Kelly got another look at the face of
Colonel Zacharias, this time enhanced somehow or other, and recognizably
similar to the ID photo Greer put next to it.

"I was within three miles of the place," Kelly noted. "Nobody ever
told me about—"

"It wasn't there yet. This place is new, less than two years old," Greer
explained.

"Any more pictures, James?" Maxwell asked.

"Just some SR-71 overheads, high-obliques, nothing new in them. I
have a guy checking every frame of this place, a good guy, ex–Air Force. He
reports to me only."

"You're going to be a good spy," Podulski noted with a chuckle.

"They need me there," Greer replied in a lighthearted voice bordered
with serious meaning. Kelly just looked at the other three. The banter wasn't
unlike that in a chief's mess, but the language was cleaner. He looked over
at Kelly again. "Tell me about the valley."

"A good place to stay away from—"

"First, tell me how you got little Dutch back. Every step of the way,"
Greer ordered.

Kelly needed fifteen minutes for that, from the time he left USS *Skate*
to the moment the helicopter had lifted him and Lieutenant Maxwell from
the river's estuary for the flight to *Kitty Hawk*. It was an easy story to tell.
What surprised him were the looks the admirals passed back and forth.

Kelly wasn't equipped to understand the looks yet. He didn't really
think of the admirals as old or even as totally human. They were *admirals*,
godlike, ageless beings who made important decisions and looked as they
should look, even the one out of uniform. Nor did Kelly think of himself as
young. He'd seen combat, after which every man is forever changed. But
their perspective was different. To Maxwell, Podulski, and Greer, this young
man was not terribly unlike what they had been thirty years earlier. It was
instantly clear that Kelly was a warrior, and in seeing him they saw themselves. The furtive looks they traded were not unlike those of a grandfather
watching his grandson take his first tentative step on the living-room rug.
But these were larger and more serious steps.

"That was some job," Greer said when Kelly finished. "So this area is densely populated?"

"Yes and no, sir. I mean, it's not a city or like that, but some farms and stuff. I heard and saw traffic on this road. Only a few trucks, but lots of bicycles, oxcarts, that sort of thing."

"Not much military traffic?" Podulski asked.

"Admiral, that stuff would be on this road here." Kelly tapped the map. He saw the notations for the NVA units. "How are you planning to get in here?"

"There's nothing easy, John. We've looked at a helicopter insertion, maybe even trying an amphibious assault and racing up this road."

Kelly shook his head. "Too far. That road is too easy to defend. Gentlemen, you have to understand, Vietnam is a real nation in arms, okay? Practically everybody there has been in uniform, and giving people guns makes them feel like part of the team. There are enough people with guns there to give you a real pain coming up this way. You'd never make it."

"The people really support the communist government?" Podulski asked. It was just too much for him to believe. But not for Kelly.

"Jesus, Admiral, why do you think we've been fighting there so long? Why do you think nobody helps pilots who get shot down? They're not *like* us over there. That's something we've never understood. Anyway, if you put Marines on the beach, nobody's going to welcome them. Forget racing up this road, sir. I've been there. It ain't much of a road, not even as good as it looks on these pictures. Drop a few trees and it's closed." Kelly looked up. "Has to be choppers."

He could see the news was not welcome, and it wasn't hard to understand why. This part of the country was dotted with antiaircraft batteries. Getting a strike force in wasn't going to be easy. At least two of these men were pilots, and if a ground assault had looked promising to them, then the triple-A problem must have been worse than Kelly appreciated.

"We can suppress the flak," Maxwell thought.

"You're not talking about -52s again, are you?" Greer asked.

"*Newport News* goes back on the gunline in a few weeks. John, ever see her shoot?"

Kelly nodded. "Sure did. She supported us twice when we were working close to the coast. It's impressive what those eight-inchers can do. Sir, the problem is, how many things do you need to go right for the mission to succeed? The more complicated things get, the easier it is for things to go wrong, and even one thing can be real complicated." Kelly leaned back on the couch, and reminded himself that what he had just said wasn't only for the admirals to consider.

"Dutch, we have a meeting in five minutes," Podulski said reluctantly. This meeting had not been a successful one, he thought. Greer and Maxwell weren't so sure of that. They had learned a few things. That counted for something.

"Can I ask why you're keeping this so tight?" Kelly asked.

"You guessed it before." Maxwell looked over at the junior flag officer and nodded.

"The Song Tay job was compromised," Greer said. "We don't know how, but we found out later through one of our sources that they knew—at least suspected—something was coming. They expected it later, and we ended up hitting the place right after they evacuated the prisoners, but before they had their ambush set up. Good luck, bad luck. They didn't expect Operation KINGPIN for another month."

"Dear God," Kelly breathed. "Somebody over here deliberately betrayed them?"

"Welcome to the real world of intelligence operations, Chief," Greer said with a grim smile.

"But *why?*"

"If I ever meet the gentleman, I will be sure to ask." Greer looked at the others. "That's a good hook for us to use. Check the records of the operation, real low-key like?"

"Where are they?"

"Eglin Air Force base, where the KINGPIN people trained."

"Whom do we send?" Podulski asked.

Kelly could feel the eyes turn in his direction. "Gentlemen, I was just a chief, remember?"

"Mr. Kelly, where's your car parked?"

"In the city, sir. I took the bus over here."

"Come with me. There's a shuttle bus you can take back later."

They walked out of the building in silence. Greer's car, a Mercury, was parked in a visitor slot by the river entrance. He waved for Kelly to get in and headed towards the George Washington Parkway.

"Dutch pulled your package. I got to read it. I'm impressed, son." What Greer didn't say was that on his battery of enlistment tests, Kelly had scored an average of 147 on three separately formatted IQ tests. "Every commander you had sang your praises."

"I worked for some good ones, sir."

"So it appears, and three of them tried to get you into OCS, but Dutch asked you about that. I also want to know why you didn't take the college scholarship.''

"I was tired of schools. And the scholarship was for swimming, Admiral.''

"That's a big deal at Indiana, I know, but your marks were plenty good to get an academic scholarship. You attended a pretty nice prep school—''

"That was a scholarship, too.'' Kelly shrugged. "Nobody in my family ever went to college. Dad served a hitch in the Navy during the war. I guess it just seemed like something to do.'' That it had been a major disappointment to his father was something he'd never told anyone.

Greer pondered that. It still didn't answer things. "The last ship I commanded was a submarine, *Daniel Webster.* My chief of the boat, senior chief sonarman, the guy had a doctorate in physics. Good man, knew his job better than I knew mine, but not a leader, shied away from it some. You didn't, Kelly. You tried to, but you didn't.''

"Look, sir, when you're out there and things happen, somebody has to get it done.''

"Not everybody sees things that way. Kelly, there's two kinds of people in the world, the ones who need to be told and the ones who figure it out all by themselves,'' Greer pronounced.

The highway sign said something that Kelly didn't catch, but it wasn't anything about CIA. He didn't tumble to it until he saw the oversized guardhouse.

"Did you ever interact with Agency people while you were over there?''

Kelly nodded. "Some. We were—well, you know about it, Project PHOENIX, right? We were part of that, a small part.''

"What did you think of them?''

"Two or three of them were pretty good. The rest—you want it straight?''

"That's exactly what I want,'' Greer assured him.

"The rest are probably real good mixing martinis, shaken not stirred,'' Kelly said evenly. That earned him a rueful laugh.

"Yeah, people here do like to watch the movies!'' Greer found his parking place and popped his door open. "Come with me, Chief.'' The out-of-uniform admiral led Kelly in the front door and got him a special visitor's pass, the kind that required an escort.

For his part, Kelly felt like a tourist in a strange and foreign land. The very normality of the building gave it a sinister edge. Though an ordinary, and rather new, government office building, CIA headquarters had some sort of aura. It wasn't like the real world somehow. Greer caught the look and chuckled, leading Kelly to an elevator, then to his sixth-floor office. Only when they were behind the closed wooden door did he speak.

"How's your schedule for the next week?"

"Flexible. I don't have anything tying me down," Kelly answered cautiously.

James Greer nodded soberly. "Dutch told me about that, too. I'm very sorry, Chief, but my job right now concerns twenty good men who probably won't see their families again unless we do something." He reached into his desk drawer.

"Sir, I'm real confused right now."

"Well, we can do it hard or easy. The hard way is that Dutch makes a phone call and you get recalled to active duty," Greer said sternly. "The easy way is, you come to work for me as a civilian consultant. We pay you a per-diem that's a whole lot more than chief's pay."

"Doing what?"

"You fly down to Eglin Air Force Base, via New Orleans and Avis, I suppose. This"—Greer tossed a billfold-like ID in Kelly's lap—"gives you access to their records. I want you to go over the operations plans as a model for what we want to do." Kelly looked at the photo-ID. It even had his old Navy photograph, which showed only his head, as in a passport.

"Wait a minute, sir. I am not qualified—"

"As a matter of fact I think you are, but from the outside it will look like you're not. No, you're just a very junior consultant gathering information for a low-level report that nobody important will ever read. Half the money we spend in this damned agency goes out the door that way, in case nobody ever told you," Greer said, his irritation with the Agency giving flight to mild exaggeration. "That's how routine and pointless we want it to look."

"Are you really serious about this?"

"Chief, Dutch Maxwell is willing to sacrifice his career for those men. So am I. If there's a way to get them out—"

"What about the peace talks?"

How do I explain that to this kid? Greer asked himself. "Colonel Zacharias is officially dead. The other side said so, even published a photo of a body. Somebody went to visit his wife, along with the base chaplain and another Air Force wife to make things easier. Then they gave her a week to vacate the official quarters, just to make things official," Greer added. "He's *officially* dead. I've had some very careful talks with some people, and we"— this part came very hard—"our country will not screw up the peace talks over something like this. The photo we have, enhancement and all, isn't good enough for a court of law, and that's the standard that is being used. That's a standard of proof that we can't possibly meet, and the people who made the decision know it. They don't want the peace talks sidetracked, and if the lives of twenty more men are necessary to end the goddamned war, then that's what it takes. Those men are being written off.''

It was almost too much for Kelly to believe. How many people did America write off every year? And not all were in uniform, were they? Some were right at home, in American cities.

''It's really that bad?''

The fatigue on Greer's face was unmistakable. ''You know why I took this job? I was ready to retire. I've served my time, commanded my ships, done my work. I'm ready for a nice house and playing golf twice a week and doing a little consulting on the side, okay? Chief, too many people come to places like this, and reality to them is a memo. They focus in on 'process' and forget that there's a human being at the far end of the paper chain. That's why I re-upped. Somebody has to try and put a little reality back into the process. We're handling this as a 'black' project. Do you know what that means?''

''No, sir, I don't.''

''It's a new term that's cropped up. That means it doesn't exist. It's crazy. It shouldn't be that way, but it is. Are you on the team or not?''

New Orleans... Kelly's eyes narrowed for a moment that lingered into fifteen seconds and a slow nod. ''If you think I can help, sir, then I will. How much time do I have?''

Greer managed a smile and tossed a ticket folder into Kelly's lap. ''Your ID is in the name of John Clark; should be easy to remember. You fly down tomorrow afternoon. The return ticket is open, but I want to see you next Friday. I expect good work out of you. My card and private line are in there. Get packed, son.''

''Aye aye, sir.''

Greer rose and walked Kelly to the door. ''And get receipts for everything. When you work for Uncle Sam you have to make sure everyone gets paid off properly.''

''I will do that, sir.'' Kelly smiled.

''You can catch the blue bus back to the Pentagon outside.'' Greer went back to work as Kelly left the office.

The blue shuttle bus arrived moments after he walked up to the covered pickup point. It was a curious ride. About half the people who boarded were uniformed, and the other half civilians. Nobody talked to anyone, as though merely exchanging a pleasantry or a comment on the Washington Senators' continuing residency at the bottom of the American League would violate security. He smiled and shook his head until he reflected on his own secrets and intentions. And yet—Greer had given him an opportunity that he'd not considered. Kelly leaned back in his seat and looked out the window while the other passengers on the bus stared fixedly forward.

"They're real happy," Piaggi said.

"I told you all along, man. It helps to have the best product on the street."

"Not everybody's happy. Some people are sitting on a couple hundred keys of French stuff, and we've knocked the price down with our special introductory offer."

Tucker allowed himself a good laugh. The "old guard" had been over-charging for years. That was monopoly pricing for you. Anyone would have taken the two of them for businessmen, or perhaps lawyers, since there were lots of both in this restaurant two blocks from the new Garmatz courthouse. Piaggi was somewhat better dressed, in Italian silk, and he made a mental note to introduce Henry to his tailor. At least the guy had learned how to groom himself. Next he had to learn not to dress too flashy. Respectable was the word. Just enough that people treated you with deference. The flashy ones, like the pimps, were playing a dangerous game that they were too dumb to understand.

"Next shipment, twice as much. Can your friends handle it?"

"Easy. The people in Philly are especially happy. Their main supplier had a little accident."

"Yeah, I saw the paper yesterday. Sloppy. Too many people in the crew, right?"

"Henry, you just keep getting smarter and smarter. Don't get too smart, okay? Good advice," Piaggi said with quiet emphasis.

"That's cool, Tony. What I'm saying is, let's not make that kind of mistake ourselves, okay?"

Piaggi relaxed, sipping his beer. "That's right, Henry. And I don't mind saying that it's nice to do business with somebody who knows how to organize. There's a lot of curiosity about where your stuff comes from. I'm covering that for you. Later on, though, if you need more financing . . ."

Tucker's eyes blazed briefly across the table. "No, Tony. No now, no forever."

"Okay for now. Something to think about for later."

Tucker nodded, apparently letting it go at that, but wondering what sort of move his "partner" might be planning. Trust, in this sort of enterprise, was a variable quantity. He trusted Tony to pay on time. He'd offered Piaggi

favorable terms, which had been honored, and the eggs this goose laid were
his real life insurance. He was already at the point that a missed payment
wouldn't harm his operation, and as long as he had a steady supply of good
heroin, they'd do business like a business, which was why he'd approached
them in the first place. But there was no real loyalty here. Trust stopped at his
usefulness. Henry had never expected any more than that, but if his associate
ever started pressing on his pipeline . . .

Piaggi wondered if he'd pressed too far, wondering if Tucker knew the
potential of what they were doing. To control distribution on the entire East
Coast, and do so from within a careful and secure organization, that was like
a dream come true. Surely he would soon need more capital, and his contacts
were already asking how they might help. But he could see that Tucker did
not recognize the innocence of the inquiry, and if he discussed it further,
protesting his goodwill, that would only make things worse. And so Piaggi
went back to his lunch and decided to leave things be for a while. It was too
bad. Tucker was a very smart small-timer, but still a small-timer at heart.
Perhaps he'd learn to grow. Henry could never be "made," but he could still
become an important part of the organization.

"Next Friday okay?" Tucker asked.

"Fine. Keep it secure. Keep it smart."

"You got it, man."

It was an uneventful flight, a Piedmont 737 out of Friendship International Airport. Kelly rode coach, and the stewardess brought him a light
lunch. Flying over America was so different from his other adventures aloft.
It surprised him how many swimming pools there were. Everywhere you
flew, lifting off from the airport, even over the rolling hills of Tennessee, the
overhead sun would sparkle off little square patches of chlorine-blue water
surrounded by green grass. His country appeared to be so benign a place, so
comfortable, until you got closer. But at least you didn't have to watch for
tracer fire.

The Avis counter had a car waiting, along with a map. It turned out that
he could have flown into Panama City, Florida, but New Orleans, he decided, would suit him just fine. Kelly tossed both his suitcases into the trunk
and headed east. It was rather like driving his boat, though somewhat more
hectic, dead time in which he could let his mind work, examining possibilities and procedures, his eyes sweeping the traffic while his mind saw something else entirely. That was when he started to smile, a thin, composed
expression that he never thought about while his imagination took a careful
and measured look at the next few weeks.

Four hours after landing, having passed through the lower ends of Mississippi and Alabama, he stopped his car at the main gate of Eglin AFB. A fitting place for the KINGPIN troopers to have trained, the heat and humidity were an exact match with the country they'd ultimately invaded, hot and moist. Kelly waited outside the guard post for a blue Air Force sedan to meet him. When it did, an officer got out.

"Mr. Clark?"

"Yes." He handed over his ID folder. The officer actually saluted him, which was a novel experience. Clearly someone was overly impressed with CIA. This young officer had probably never interacted with anybody from there. Of course, Kelly had actually bothered to wear a tie in the hope of looking as respectable as possible.

"If you'll follow me, please, sir." The officer, Captain Griffin, led him to a first-floor room at the Bachelor Officers Quarters, which was somewhat like a medium-quality motel and agreeably close to the beach. After helping Kelly get unpacked, Griffin walked him to the Officers' Club, where, he said, Kelly had visitor's privileges. All he had to do was show his room key.

"I can't knock the hospitality, Captain." Kelly felt obligated to buy the first beer. "You know why I'm here?"

"I work intelligence," Griffin replied.

"KINGPIN?" As though in a movie, the officer looked around before replying.

"Yes, sir. We have all the documents you need ready for you. I hear you worked special ops over there, too."

"Correct."

"I have one question, sir," the Captain said.

"Shoot," Kelly invited between sips. He'd dried out on the drive from New Orleans.

"Do they know who burned the mission?"

"No," Kelly replied, and on a whim added, "Maybe I can pick up something on that."

"My big brother was in that camp, we think. He'd be home now except for whatever . . ."

"Motherfucker," Kelly said helpfully. The Captain actually blushed.

"If you identify him, then what?"

"Not my department," Kelly replied, regretting his earlier comment. "When do I start?"

"Supposed to be tomorrow morning, Mr. Clark, but the documents are all in my office."

"I need a quiet room, a pot of coffee, maybe some sandwiches."

"I think we can handle that, sir."

"Then let me get started."

Ten minutes later, Kelly got his wish. Captain Griffin had supplied him with a yellow legal pad and a battery of pencils. Kelly started off with the first set of reconnaissance photographs, these taken by an RF-101 Voodoo, and as with SENDER GREEN, the discovery of Song Tay had been a complete accident, the random discovery of an unexpected thing in a place expected to have been a minor military training installation. But in the yard of the camp had been letters stomped in the dirt, or arranged with stones or hanging laundry: "K" for "come and get us out of here," and other such marks that had been made under the eyes of the guards. The list of people who had become involved was a genuine who's who of the special operations community, names that he knew only by reputation.

The configuration of the camp was not terribly different from the one in which he was interested now, he saw, making appropriate notes. One document surprised him greatly. It was a memo from a three-star to a two-star, indicating that the Song Tay mission, though important in and of itself, was also a means to an end. The three-star had wanted to validate his ability to get special-ops teams into North Vietnam. That, he said, would open all sorts of possibilities, one of which was a certain dam with a generator room . . . oh, yeah, Kelly realized. The three-star wanted a hunting license, to insert several teams in-country and play the same games OSS had behind German lines in the Second World War. The memo concluded with a note that political factors made the latter aspect of POLAR CIRCLE—one of the first cover names for what became Operation KINGPIN—extremely sensitive. Some would see it as a widening of the war. Kelly looked up, finishing his second cup of coffee. What was it about politicians? he wondered. The enemy could do anything he wanted, but our side was always trembling at the possibility of being seen to widen the war. He'd even seen some of that at his level. The PHOENIX project, the deliberate targeting of the enemy's political infrastructure, was a matter of the greatest sensitivity. Hell, they wore uniforms, didn't they? A man in a combat zone wearing a uniform was fair game in anyone's book of rules, wasn't he? The other side took out local mayors and school-teachers with savage abandon. There was a blatant double standard to the way the war had been conducted. It was a troubling thought, but Kelly set it aside as he turned back to the second pile of documents.

Assembling the team and planning the operation had taken half of for-ever. Good men all, however. Colonel Bull Simons, another man he knew only by his reputation as one of the toughest sharp-end combat commanders any Army had ever produced. Dick Meadows, a younger man in the same mold. Their only waking thought was to bring harm and distraction to the enemy, and they were skilled in doing so with small forces and minimum exposure. How they must have lusted for this mission, Kelly thought. But the oversight they'd had to deal with . . . Kelly counted ten separate documents to higher authority, promising success—as though a memo could make such a claim in the harsh world of combat operations—before he stopped bothering to count them. So many of them used the same language until he suspected that a form letter had been ginned up by some unit clerk. Probably someone who'd run out of fresh words for his colonel, and then expressed a sergeant's contempt for the interlocutors by giving them the same words every time, in the expectation that the repeats would never be noticed—and they hadn't been. Kelly spent three hours going through reams of paper between Eglin and CIA, concerns of deskbound bean-counters distracting the men in green suits, ''helpful'' suggestions from people who probably wore ties to bed, all of which had required answers from the operators who carried guns . . . and so KINGPIN had grown from a relatively minor and dramatic insertion mission to a Cecil B. DeMille epic which had more than once gone to the White House, there becoming known to the President's National Security Council staff—

And that's where Kelly stopped, at two-thirty in the morning, defeated by the next pile of paper. He locked everything up in the receptacles provided and jogged back to his room at the Q, leaving notice for a seven-o'clock wake-up call.

It was surprising how little sleep you needed when there was important work to be done. When the phone rang at seven, Kelly bounced from the bed, and fifteen minutes later was running along the beach barefoot, in a pair of shorts. He was not alone. He didn't know how many people were based at Eglin, but they were not terribly different from himself. Some had to be special operations types, doing things that he could only guess at. You could tell them from the somewhat wider shoulders. Running was only part of their fitness game. Eyes met and evaluated others, and expressions were exchanged as each man knew what the other was thinking—*How tough is* he, *really?*—as an automatic mental exercise, and Kelly smiled to himself that he was enough a part of the community that he merited that kind of competitive respect. A large breakfast and shower left him fully refreshed, enough to get him back to his clerk's work, and on the walk back to the office building, he asked himself, surprisingly, why he'd ever left this community of men. It was, after all, the only real home he'd known after leaving Indianapolis.

And so the days continued. He allowed himself two days of six-hours' sleep, but never more than twenty minutes for a meal, and not a single drink after that first beer, though his exercise periods grew to several hours per day, mainly, he told himself, to firm up. The real reason was one that he never quite admitted. He wanted to be the toughest man on that early-morning beach, not just an associate part of the small, elite community. Kelly was a SEAL again, more than that, a bullfrog, and more still, he was again becoming *Snake*. By the third or fourth morning, he could see the change. His face and form were now an expected part of the morning routine for the others. The anonymity only made it better, that and the scars of battle, and some would wonder what he'd done wrong, what mistakes he'd made. Then they would remind themselves that he was still in the business, scars and all, not knowing that he'd left it—*quit*, Kelly's mind corrected, with not a little guilt.

The paperwork was surprisingly stimulating. He'd never before tried to figure things out in quite this way, and he was surprised to find he had a talent for it. The operational planning, he saw, had been a thing of beauty flawed by time and repetition, like a beautiful girl kept too long in her house by a jealous father. Every day the mockup of the Song Tay camp had been erected by the players, and each day, sometimes more than once, taken down lest Soviet reconnaissance satellites take note of what was there. How debilitating that must have been to the soldiers. And it had all taken so long, the soldiers practicing while the higher-ups had dithered, pondering the intelligence information so long that . . . the prisoners had been moved.

"Damn," Kelly whispered to himself. It wasn't so much that the operation might have been betrayed. It had just taken too long . . . and that meant that *if* it had been betrayed, the leaker had probably been one of the last people to discover what was afoot. He set that thought aside with a penciled question.

The operation itself had been meticulously planned, everything done just right, a primary plan and a number of alternates, with each segment of the team so fully briefed and trained that every man could do every function in his sleep. *Crashing* a huge Sikorsky helicopter right in the camp itself so that the strike team would not have to wait to get to the objective. Using miniguns to take down the guard towers like chainsaws against saplings. No finesse, no pussyfooting, no movie-type bullshit, just brutally direct force. The after-action debriefs showed that the camp guards had been immolated in moments. How elated the troopers must have felt as the first minute or two of the operation had run more smoothly than their simulations, and then the stunning, bitter frustration when the "negative Item" calls had come again and again over their radio circuits. "Item" was the simple code word for an

American POW, and none were home that night. The soldiers had assaulted and liberated an empty camp. It wasn't hard to imagine how quiet the choppers must have been for the ride back to Thailand, the bleak emptiness of failure after having done everything better than right.

There was, nonetheless, much to learn here. Kelly made his notes, cramping fingers and wearing out numerous pencils. Whatever else it had been, KINGPIN was a supremely valuable lesson. So much had gone right, he saw, and all of that could be shamelessly copied. All that had gone wrong, really, was the time factor. Troops of that quality could have gone in much sooner. The quest for perfection hadn't been demanded at the operational level, but higher, from men who had grown older and lost contact with the enthusiasm and intelligence of youth. And a consequence had been the failure of the mission, not because of Bull Simons, or Dick Meadows, or the Green Berets who'd gladly placed their lives at risk for men they'd never met, but because of others too afraid to risk their careers and their offices—matters of far greater importance, of course, than the blood of the guys at the sharp end. Song Tay was the whole story of Vietnam, told in the few minutes it had taken for a superbly-trained team to fail, betrayed as much by process as by some misguided or traitorous person hidden in the federal bureaucracy.

SENDER GREEN would be different, Kelly told himself. If for no other reason than that it was being run as a private game. If the real hazard to the operation was oversight, then why not eliminate the oversight?

"Captain, you've been very helpful," Kelly said.

"Find what you wanted, Mr. Clark?" Griffin asked.

"Yes, Mr. Griffin," he said, dropping unconsciously back into naval terminology for the young officer. "The analysis you did on the secondary camp was first-rate. In case nobody ever told you, that might have saved a few lives. Let me say something for myself: I wish we'd had an intel-weenie like you working for us when I was out in the weeds."

"I can't fly, sir. I have to do something useful," Griffin replied, embarrassed by the praise.

"You do." Kelly handed over his notes. Under his eyes they were placed in an envelope that was then sealed with red wax. "Courier the package to this address."

"Yes, sir. You're due some time off. Did you get any sleep at all?" Captain Griffin asked.

"Well, I think I'll depressurize in New Orleans before I fly back."

"Not a bad place for it, sir." Griffin walked Kelly to his car, already loaded.

One other bit of intelligence had been stunningly easy, Kelly thought, driving out. His room in the Q had contained a New Orleans telephone directory in which, to his amazement, had been the name he'd decided to look up while sitting in James Greer's office in CIA.

This was the shipment that would make his reputation, Tucker thought, watching Rick and Billy finish loading things up. Part of it would find its way to New York. Up until now he'd been an interloper, an outsider with ambition. He'd provided enough heroin to get people interested in himself and his partners—the fact that he had partners had attracted interest of its own, in addition to the access. But now was different. Now he was making his move to be part of the crew. He would be seen as a serious businessman because this shipment would handle all the needs of Baltimore and Philadelphia for . . . maybe a month, he estimated. Maybe less if their distribution network was as good as they said. The leftovers would start meeting the growing needs in the Big Apple, which needed the help after a major bust. After so long a time of making small steps, here was the giant one. Billy turned on a radio to get the sports news, and got a weather forecast instead.

"I'm glad we're going now. Storms coming in later."

Tucker looked outside. The sky was still clear and untroubled. "Nothing for us to worry about," he told them.

He loved New Orleans, a city in the European tradition, which mixed Old World charm with American zest. Rich in history, owned by Frenchmen and Spaniards in their turn, it had never lost its traditions, even to its maintenance of a legal code that was nearly incomprehensible to the other forty-nine states, and was often a matter of some befuddlement to federal authorities. So was the local patois, for many mixed French into their conversations, or what they called French. Pierre Lamarck's antecedents had been Acadians, and some of his more distant relatives were still residents in the local bayous. But customs that were eccentric and entertaining to tourists, and a comfortable life rich in tradition to others, had little interest to Lamarck except as a point of reference, a personal signature to distinguish him from his peers. That was hard enough to do, as his profession demanded a certain flash, a personal flair. He accentuated his uniqueness with a white linen suit complete with vest, a white, long-sleeved shirt, and a red, solid-color tie, which fitted his own image as a respectable, if ostentatious, local businessman. That went along well with his personal automobile, an egg-shell-white Cadillac. He eschewed the ornamental excesses that some other pimps placed on their automobiles, nonfunctional exhaust pipes. One supposed Texan even had the horns of a longhorn steer on his Lincoln, but that one was really poor white trash from lower Alabama, and a boy who didn't know how to treat his ladies.

This latter quality was Lamarck's greatest talent, he told himself with great satisfaction, opening the door of his car for his newest acquisition, fifteen years old and recently broken in, possessed of an innocent look and demure movement that made her a noteworthy and enticing member of his eight-girl stable. She'd earned the pimp's unaccustomed courtesy with a special service of her own earlier in the day. The luxury car started on the first turn of the key, and at seven-thirty, Pierre Lamarck set off on another night's work, for the nightlife in his city started early and lasted late. There was a convention in town, distributors for something or other. New Orleans attracted a lot of conventions, and he could track the cash flow of his business by their comings and goings. It promised to be a warm and lucrative night.

It had to be him, Kelly thought, half a block away, behind the wheel of his still-rented car. Who else would wear a three-piece suit and be accompanied by a young girl dressed in a tight mini? Certainly not an insurance agent. The girl's jewelry looked cheap-showy even from this distance. Kelly slipped the car into gear, following. He was able to lay back. How many white Caddies could there be? he wondered, crossing the river, three cars back, eyes locked on his target while peripheral parts of his mind dealt with the other traffic. Once he had to risk a ticket at a traffic light, but otherwise the tracking was simple. The Caddy stopped at the entrance to an upscale hotel, and he saw the girl get out, and walk towards the door, her stride a mixture of the businesslike and the resigned. He didn't want to see her face all that closely, afraid of what memories might result from it. This was not a night for emotion. Emotion was what had given him the mission. How he accomplished it had to come from something else. That would be a constant struggle, Kelly told himself, but one he would have to contend with successfully. That was, after all, why he'd come to this place, on this night.

The Cadillac moved on a few more blocks, finding a parking place by a seedy, flashy bar close enough to the nice hotels and businesses that a person could walk there quickly, yet never be far from the safety and comfort of civilized safety. A fairly constant stream of taxicabs told him that this aspect of local life had a firm, institutional foundation. He identified the bar in question and found himself a place to park three blocks away.

There was a dual purpose in parking so far from his objective. The walk in along Decatur Street gave him both a feel for the territory and a look at likely places for his action. Surely it would be a long night. Some short-skirted girls smiled at him as mechanically as the changing of the traffic lights, but he walked on, his eyes sweeping left and right while a distant voice reminded him of what he had once thought of such gestures. He silenced that voice with another, more current thought. His clothes were casual, what a moderately comfortable man might wear in this humid heat and heavy atmosphere, dark and anonymous, loose and baggy. They proclaimed money, but not too much, and his stride told people that he was not one to be trifled with. A man of understated substance having a discreet night on the wild side.

He walked into Chats Sauvages at eight-seventeen. His initial impression of the bar was smoke and noise. A small but enthusiastic rock band played at the far end. There was a dance floor, perhaps twenty-five feet square, where people his age and younger moved with the music; and there was Pierre Lamarck, sitting at a table in the corner with a few acquaintances, or so they seemed from their demeanor. Kelly walked to the men's room, both an immediate necessity and an opportunity to look the place over. There was another entrance on the side, but no closer to Lamarck's table than the one through which both he and Kelly had entered. The nearest path to the white Caddy led past Kelly's place at the bar, and that told him where his perch had to be. Kelly ordered a beer and turned conveniently to watch the band.

At nine-ten two young women came to Lamarck. One sat on his lap while the other nibbled at his ear. The other two men at the table watched with neutral interest while both women handed over something to him. Kelly couldn't tell what it was because he was looking towards the band, careful not to stare too often in Lamarck's direction. The pimp solved that problem immediately: it turned out, unsurprisingly, to be cash, and the man somewhat ostentatiously wrapped the bills around a roll removed from his pocket. Flash money, Kelly had troubled himself to learn, an important part of a pimp's public image. The first two women left, and Lamarck was soon joined by another, in what became an intermittent stream that didn't stop. His table mates enjoyed the same sort of traffic, Kelly saw, sipping their drinks, paying cash, joshing with and occasionally fondling the waitress who served them, then tipping her heavily by way of apology. Kelly moved from time to time. He removed his jacket, rolling up his sleeves, to present a different image to the bar's patrons, and limiting himself to two beers, which he nursed as carefully as he could. Tedious as it was, he disregarded the unpleasant nature of the evening, instead noticing things. Who went where. Who came and left. Who stayed. Who lingered in one place. Kelly soon started recognizing patterns and identifying individuals to whom he assigned names of his own creation. Most of all he observed everything there was to see about Lamarck. He never took off his suit jacket, kept his back to the wall. He talked amiably with his two companions, but their familiarity was not that of friends. Their joking was too affected. There was too much emphasis on their interactive gestures, not the casual comfort that you saw among people whose company was shared for some purpose other than money. Even pimps got lonely, Kelly thought, and though they sought out their own kind, theirs was not friendship but mere association. The philosophical observations he put aside. If Lamarck never took off his coat, he had to be carrying a weapon.

Just after midnight, Kelly put his coat back on and made yet another trip to the men's room. In the toilet stall he took the automatic he'd hidden inside his slacks and moved it to the waistband. Two beers in four hours, he thought. His liver ought to have eliminated the alcohol from his system, and even if it hadn't, two beers should not have had much effect on one as bulky as he. It was an important statement which, he hoped, wasn't a lie.

His timing was good. Washing his hands for the fifth time, Kelly saw the door open in the mirror. Only the back of the man's head, but under the dark hair was a white suit, and so Kelly waited, taking his time until he heard the urinal flush. A sanitary sort of fellow, the man turned, and their eyes met in the mirror.

"Excuse me," Pierre Lamarck said. Kelly stepped away from the sink, still drying his hands with a paper towel.

"I like the ladies," he said quietly.

"Hmph?" Lamarck had no less than six drinks in him, and his liver had not been up to the task, which didn't prevent his self-admiration in the dirty mirror.

"The ones that come up to you." Kelly lowered his voice. "They, uh, work for you, like?"

"You might say that, my man." Lamarck took out a black plastic comb to readjust his coiffeur. "Why do you ask?"

"I might need a few," Kelly said with embarrassment.

"A few? You sure you can handle that, my man?" Lamarck asked with a sly grin.

"Some friends in town with me. One's having a birthday, and—"

"A party," the pimp observed pleasantly.

"That's right." Kelly tried to be shy, but mainly came off as being awkward. The error worked in his favor.

"Well, why didn't you say so? How many ladies do you require, sir?"

"Three, maybe four. Talk about it outside? I could use some air."

"Sure thing. Just let me wash my hands, okay?"

"I'll be outside the front door."

The street was quiet. Busy city though New Orleans might be, it was still the middle of the week, and the sidewalks, while not empty, weren't crowded either. Kelly waited, looking away from the bar's entrance until he felt a friendly hand on his back.

"It's nothing to be embarrassed about. We all like to have a little fun, especially when we're away from home, right?"

"I'll pay top dollar," Kelly promised with an uneasy smile.

Lamarck grinned, like the man of the world he was, to put this chicken farmer at ease. "With my ladies, you have to. Anything else you might need?"

Kelly coughed and took a few steps, willing Lamarck to follow, which he did. "Maybe some, well, something to help us party, like?"

"I can handle that, too," Lamarck said as they approached an alley.

"I think I met you before, couple years back. I remember the girl, really, her name was . . . Pam? Yeah, Pam. Thin, tawny hair."

"Oh, yeah, she was fun. She's not with me anymore," Lamarck said lightly. "But I have lots more. I cater to the men who like 'em young and fresh."

"I'm sure you do," Kelly said, reaching behind his back. "They're all on—I mean they all use things that make it—"

"Happy stuff, man. So they're always in the mood to party. A lady has to have the proper attitude." Lamarck stopped at the entrance to the alley, looking outward, maybe worried about cops, which suited Kelly just fine. Behind him, he had not troubled to see, was a dark, scarcely lit corridor of blank brick walls, inhabited by nothing more than trash cans and stray cats, and open at the far end. "Let's see. Four girls, rest of the evening, shall we say, and something to help get the party started . . . five hundred should do it. My girls aren't cheap, but you will get your money's—"

"Both hands in the open," Kelly said, the Colt automatic leveled twelve inches from the man's chest.

Lamarck's first response was a disbelieving bluster: "My man, that is a very foolish—"

Kelly's voice was all business. "Arguing with a gun is even more foolish, my man. Turn, walk down the alley, and you might even make it back to the bar for a nightcap."

"You must need money real bad to try something this dumb," the pimp said, trying an implied threat.

"Your roll worth dying for?" Kelly asked reasonably. Lamarck measured the odds and turned, moving into the shadows.

"Stop," Kelly told him after fifty yards, still behind the blank wall of the bar, or perhaps another just like it. His left arm grabbed the man's neck and pushed him against the bricks. His eyes looked up and down the alley three times. His ears searched for sounds separate from traffic noise and distorted music. For the moment it was a safe and quiet place. "Hand me your gun—real careful."

"I don't—" The sound of a hammer being cocked sounded awfully loud, that close to his ear.

"Do I look stupid?"

"Okay, okay," Lamarck said, his voice losing its smooth edge now. "Let's be real cool. It's only money."

"That's smart," Kelly said approvingly. A small automatic appeared. Kelly put his right index finger into the trigger guard. There was no sense in putting fingerprints on the weapon. He was taking enough chances, and as careful as he'd been to this point, the dangers of his action were suddenly very real and very large. The pistol fit nicely into his coat pocket.

"Let's see the roll next."

"Right here, man." Lamarck was starting to lose it. That was both good and bad, Kelly thought. Good because it was pleasing to see. Bad because a panicked man might do something foolish. Instead of relaxing, Kelly actually became more tense.

"Thank you, Mr. Lamarck," Kelly said politely, to calm the man.

Just then he wavered, and his head turned a few inches or so, as his consciousness asserted itself through the six drinks he'd had this evening. "Wait a minute—you said you knew Pam."

"I did," Kelly said.

"But why—" He turned farther to see a face that was bathed in darkness, only eyes showing with light glistening off their moisture, and the rest of the face a shadow white.

"You're one of the guys who ruined her life."

Outrage: "Hey, man, she came to *me!*"

"And you got her on pills so she could party real good, right?" the disembodied voice asked. Lamarck could hardly remember what the man looked like now.

"That was *business,* so you met her, so she was a good fuck, right?"

"She certainly was."

"I shoulda trained her better an' you coulda had her again insteada— was, you say?"

"She's dead," Kelly told him, reaching in his pocket. "Somebody killed her."

"So? I didn't do it!" It seemed to Lamarck that he was facing a final exam, a test he didn't understand, based on rules he didn't know.

"Yes, I know that," Kelly said, screwing the silencer onto the pistol. Lamarck saw that somehow, his eyes making the adjustment to the darkness. His voice became a shrill rasp.

"Then what are you doing this for?" the man said, too puzzled even to scream, too paralyzed by the incongruity of the past few minutes, by the passage of his life from the normality of his hangout bar to its end only forty feet away in front of a windowless brick wall, and he had to have an answer. Somehow it was more important than the escape, whose attempt he knew to be futile.

Kelly thought about that for a second or two. He could have said many things, but it was only fair, he decided, to tell the man the truth as the gun came up quickly and finally.

"Practice."

14
Lessons Learned

T he early flight back from New Orleans to Washington National was too short for a movie, and Kelly had already eaten breakfast. He settled on a glass of juice at his window seat and was thankful that the flight was only about a third full as, after every combat action of his life, he went over every detail. It was a habit that had begun in the SEALs. Following every training exercise there had been an event called various things by his various commanders. "Performance Critique" seemed most appropriate at the moment.

His first mistake had been the product of something desired and something forgotten. In wanting to see Lamarck die in the darkness, he'd stood too close, simultaneously forgetting that head wounds often bleed explosively. He'd jumped out of the way of the spouting blood like a child avoiding a wasp in his backyard, but had still not escaped it entirely. The good news was that he'd made only that one mistake; and his selection of dark clothing had mitigated the danger there. Lamarck's wounds had been immediately and definitively fatal. The pimp had fallen to the ground as limp as a rag doll. The two screws that Kelly had drilled in the top of his pistol held a small cloth bag he'd sewn himself, and the bag had caught the two ejected cartridge cases, leaving the police who'd investigate the scene without that valuable bit of evidence. His stalk had been effectively carried out, just one more anonymous face in a large and anonymous bar.

His hastily selected site for the elimination had also worked well enough. He remembered walking down the alley and blending back into the sidewalk traffic, walking the distance to his car and driving back to the motel. There, he'd changed clothes, bundling the blood-splattered slacks, shirt, and, just to be sure, the underwear as well, into a plastic cleaner bag, which he'd walked across the street and deposited in a supermarket Dumpster. If the clothing was discovered, it might well be taken as something soiled by a sloppy meatcutter. He hadn't met with Lamarck in the open. The only lighted place in which they'd spoken was the bar's men's room, and there fortune—and planning—had smiled on him. The sidewalk they'd walked on was too dark and too anonymous. Perhaps a casual observer who might have known Lamarck could give an investigator a rough idea of Kelly's size, but little else, and that was a reasonable gamble to have taken, Kelly judged, looking down at the wooded hills of northern Alabama. It had been an apparent robbery, the pimp's one thousand, four hundred seventy dollars of flash money tucked away in his bag. Cash was cash, after all, and not to have taken it would have shown the police that there had been a real motive in the elimination aside from something easily understandable and agreeably random. The physical side of the event—he could not think of it as a crime—was, he thought, as clean as he could have done it.

Psychological? Kelly asked himself. More than anything else Kelly had tested his nerve, the elimination of Pierre Lamarck having been a kind of field experiment, and in that he'd surprised himself. It had been some years since Kelly had entered combat, and he'd halfway expected a case of the shakes after the event. Such things had happened to him more than once before, but though his stride away from Lamarck's body had been slightly uneasy, he'd handled the escape with the sort of tense aplomb that had marked many of his operations in Vietnam. So much had come back to him. He could catalog the familiar sensations that had returned as though he'd been watching a training film of his own production: the increased sensory awareness, as though his skin had been sandblasted, exposing every nerve; hearing, sight, smell all amplified. *I was so fucking alive at that moment,* he thought. It was vaguely sad that such a thing had happened due to the ending of a human life, but Lamarck had long since forfeited his right to life. In any just universe, a person—Kelly simply could not think of him as a *man*—who exploited helpless girls simply did not deserve the privilege of breathing the same air used by other human beings. Perhaps he'd taken the wrong turn, been unloved by his mother or beaten by his father. Perhaps he'd been socially deprived, raised in poverty, or exposed to inadequate schooling. But those were matters for psychiatrists or social workers. Lamarck had acted normally enough to function as a person in his community, and the only question that mattered to Kelly was whether or not he had lived his life in accordance with his own free will. That had clearly been the case, and those who took improper actions, he had long since decided, ought to have considered the possible consequences of those actions. Every girl they exploited might have had a father or mother or sister or brother or lover to be outraged at her victimization. In knowing that and in taking the risk, Lamarck had knowingly gambled his life to some greater or lesser degree. *And gambling means that sometimes you lose,* Kelly told himself. If he hadn't weighed the hazards accurately enough, that was not Kelly's problem, was it?

No, he told the ground, thirty-seven thousand feet below.

And what did Kelly feel about it? He pondered that question for a while, leaning back and closing his eyes as though napping. A quiet voice, perhaps conscience, told him that he ought to feel *something,* and he searched for a genuine emotion. After several minutes of consideration, he could find none. There was no loss, no grief, no remorse. Lamarck had meant nothing to him and probably would be no loss to anyone else. Perhaps his girls— Kelly had counted five of them in the bar—would be without a pimp, but then maybe one of them would seize the opportunity to correct her life. Unlikely, perhaps, but possible. It was realism that told Kelly he couldn't fix all the problems of the world; it was idealism that told him his inability to do so did not preclude him from addressing individual imperfections.

But all that took him away from the initial question: What did he *feel* about the elimination of Pierre Lamarck? The only answer he could find was, Nothing. The professional elation of having done something difficult was different from satisfaction, from the nature of the task. In ending the life of Pierre Lamarck he had removed something harmful from the surface of the planet. It had enriched him not at all—taking the money had been a tactic, a camouflage measure, certainly not an objective. It had not avenged Pam's life. It had not changed very much. It had been like stepping on an offensive insect—you did it and moved on. He would not try to tell himself different, but neither would his conscience trouble him, and that was sufficient to the moment. His little experiment had been a success. After all the mental and physical preparation, he had proven himself worthy of the task before him. Kelly's mind focused behind closed eyes on the mission before him. Having killed many men better than Pierre Lamarck, he could now think with confidence about killing men worse than the New Orleans pimp.

This time they visited him, Greer saw with satisfaction. On the whole, CIA's hospitality was better. James Greer had arranged parking in the VIP Visitors' area—the equivalent at the Pentagon was always haphazard and difficult to use—and a secure conference room. Cas Podulski thoughtfully selected a seat at the far end, close to the air-conditioning vent, where his smoking wouldn't bother anyone.

"Dutch, you were right about this kid," Greer said, handing out typed copies of the handwritten notes which had arrived two days earlier.

"Somebody ought to have put a gun to his head and walked him into OCS. He would have been the kind of junior officer we used to be."

Podulski chuckled at his end of the table. "No wonder he got out," he said with lighthearted bitterness.

"I'd be careful putting a gun to his head," Greer observed with a chuckle of his own. "I spent a whole night last week going through his package. This guy's a wild one in the field."

"Wild?" Maxwell asked with a hint of disapproval in his voice. "Spirited, you mean, James?"

Perhaps a compromise, Greer thought: "A self-starter. He had three commanders and they backed him on every play he made except one."

"PLASTIC FLOWER? The political-action major he killed?"

"Correct. His lieutenant was furious about that, but if it's true about what he had to watch, the only thing you can fault was his judgment, rushing in the way he did."

"I read through that, James. I doubt I could have held back," Cas said, looking up from the notes. Once a fighter pilot, always a fighter pilot. "Look at this, even his grammar is good!" Despite his accent, Podulski had been assiduous in learning his adopted language.

"Jesuit high school," Greer pointed out. "I've gone over our in-house assessment of KINGPIN. Kelly's analysis tracks on every major point except where he calls a few spades."

"Who did the CIA assessment?" Maxwell asked.

"Robert Ritter. He's a European specialist they brought in. Good man, a little terse, knows how to work the field, though."

"Operations guy?" Maxwell asked.

"Right." Greer nodded. "Did some very nice work working Station Budapest."

"And why," Podulski asked, "did they bring in a guy from that side of the house to look over the KINGPIN operation?"

"I think you know the answer, Cas," Maxwell pointed out.

"If BOXWOOD GREEN goes, we need an Operations guy from this house. We have to have it. I don't have the juice to do everything. Are we agreed on that?" Greer looked around the table, seeing the reluctant nods. Podulski looked back down at his documents before saying what they all thought.

"Can we trust him?"

"He's not the one who burned KINGPIN. Cas, we have Jim Angleton looking at that. It was his idea to bring Ritter onboard. I'm new here, people. Ritter knows the bureaucracy here better than I do. He's an operator; I'm just an analyst-type. And his heart's in the right place. He damned near lost his job protecting a guy—he had an agent working inside GRU, and it was time to get him out. The decision-weenies upstairs didn't like the timing, with the arms talks going on, and they told him no. Ritter brought the guy out anyway. It turned out his man had something State needed, and that saved Ritter's career.'' It hadn't done much for the martini-mixer upstairs, Greer didn't add, but that was a person CIA was doing rather well without.

"Swashbuckler?'' Maxwell asked.

"He was loyal to his agent. Sometimes people here forget about that,'' Greer said.

Admiral Podulski looked up the table. "Sounds like our kind of guy.''

"Brief him in,'' Maxwell ordered. "But you tell him that if I ever find out some civilian in the building fucked up our chance to get these men out, I will *personally* drive down to Pax River, *personally* check out an A-4, and *personally* napalm his house.''

"You should let me do that, Dutch,'' Cas added with a smile. "I've always had a better hand for dropping things. Besides, I have six hundred hours in the Scooter.''

Greer wondered how much of that was humor.

"What about Kelly?'' Maxwell asked.

"His CIA identity is 'Clark' now. If we want him in, we can utilize him better as a civilian. He'd never get over being a chief, but a civilian doesn't have to worry about rank.''

"Make it so,'' Maxwell said. It was convenient, he thought, to have a naval officer seconded to CIA, wearing civilian clothes but still subject to military discipline.

"Aye aye, sir. If we get to training, where will it be done?''

"Quantico Marine Base,'' Maxwell replied. "General Young is a pal from the old days. Aviator. He understands.''

"Marty and I went through test-pilot school together,'' Podulski explained. "From what Kelly says, we don't need that many troops. I always figured KINGPIN was overmanned. You know, if we bring this off, we have to get Kelly his Medal.''

"One thing at a time, Cas.'' Maxwell set that aside, looking back to Greer as he stood. "You will let us know if Angleton finds out anything?''

"Depend on it,'' Greer promised. "If there's a bad guy inside, we'll get his ass. I've fished with the guy. He can pull a brook trout out of thin air.''

After they left he set an afternoon meeting with Robert Ritter. It meant putting Kelly off, but Ritter was more important now, and while there was a rush on the mission, it wasn't all that great a rush.

Airports were useful places, with their bustling anonymity and telephones. Kelly placed his call, as he waited for his baggage to appear—he hoped—in the proper place.

"Greer," the voice said.

"Clark," Kelly replied, smiling at himself. It seemed so James Bond to have a cover name. "I'm at the airport, sir. Do you still want me in this afternoon?"

"No. I'm tied up." Greer flipped through his daybook. "Tuesday . . . three-thirty. You can drive in. Give me your car type and license number."

Kelly did that, surprised that he'd been bumped. "You get my notes, sir?"

"Yes, and you did a fine job, Mr. Clark. We'll be going over them Tuesday. We are very pleased with your work."

"Thank you, sir," Kelly said into the phone.

"See you Tuesday." The line clicked off.

"And thanks for that, too," Kelly said after he hung up. Twenty minutes later he had his bags and was walking off to his car. About an hour after that he was in his Baltimore apartment. It was lunchtime, and he fixed a couple of sandwiches, chasing both down with Coca-Cola. He hadn't shaved today, and his heavy beard made a shadow on his face, he saw in the mirror. He'd leave it. Kelly headed into the bedroom for a lengthy nap.

The civilian contractors didn't really understand what they were up to, but they were being paid. That was all they really required, since they had families to feed and house payments to make. The buildings they had just erected were well to the right of spartan: bare concrete block, nothing in the way of utilities, built to odd proportions, not like American construction at all except for the building materials. It was as though their size and shape had been taken from some foreign construction manual. All the dimensions were metric, one worker noted, though the actual plans were noted in odd numbers of inches and feet, as American building plans had to be. The job itself had been simple enough, the site already cleared when they'd first arrived. A number of the construction workers were former servicemen, most ex-Army, but a few Marines as well, and they were at turns pleased and uncomfortable to be at this sprawling Marine base in the wooded hills of northern

Virginia. On the drive into the construction site they could see the morning
formations of officer candidates jogging along the roads. All those bright
young kids with shaved heads, one former corporal of the 1st Marines had
thought this very morning. How many would get their commissions? How
many would deploy *there?* How many would come home early, shipped in
steel boxes? It was nothing he could foresee or control, of course. He'd
served his time in hell and returned unscratched, which was still remarkable
to the former grunt who'd heard all too often the supersonic *crack* of rifle
bullets. To have survived at all was amazing enough.

The roofs were finished. Soon it would be time to leave the site for
good, after a mere three weeks of well-paid work. Seven-day weeks. Plenty
of overtime on every working day he'd been here. Somebody had wanted
this place built in a hurry. Some very odd things about it, too. The parking
lot, for one. A hundred-slot blacktopped lot. Someone was even painting the
lines. For buildings with no utilities? But strangest of all was the current job
that he'd drawn because the site foreman liked him. Playground equipment.
A large swing set. A huge jungle gym. A sandbox, complete with half a
dump truck's load of sand. All the things that his two-year-old son would
someday cavort on when he was old enough for kindergarten in the Fairfax
County Schools. But it was structural work, and it required assembly, and
the former Marine and two others fumbled through the plans like fathers in
a backyard, figuring which bolts went where. Theirs was not to reason why,
not as union construction workers on a government contract. Besides, he
thought, there was no understanding the Green Machine. The Corps operated according to a plan that no man really figured out, and if they wanted to
pay him overtime for this, then that was another monthly house payment
earned for every three days he came here. Jobs like this might be crazy, but
he sure liked the money. About the only thing he didn't like was the length
of the commute. Maybe they'd have to do something equally crazy at Fort
Belvoir, he hoped, finishing the last item on the jungle gym. He could drive
from his house to that place in twenty minutes or so. But the Army was a little
more rational than the Corps. It had to be.

"So what's new?" Peter Henderson asked. They were dining just off
The Hill, two acquaintances from New England, one a Harvard graduate, the
other from Brown, one a junior aide to a senator, the other a junior member
of the White House staff.

"It never changes, Peter," Wally Hicks said resignedly. "The peace
talks are going nowhere. We keep killing their people. They keep killing
ours. I don't think there's ever going to be peace in our time, you know?"

"It has to, Wally," Henderson said, reaching for his second beer.

"If it doesn't—" Hicks started to say gloomily.

Both had been seniors at the Andover Academy in October 1962, close friends and roommates who had shared class notes and girlfriends. Their real political majority had come one Tuesday night, however, when they'd watched their country's president give a tense national address on the black-and-white television in the dormitory lounge. There were missiles in Cuba, they'd learned, something that had been hinted at in the papers for several days, but these were children of the TV generation, and contemporary reality came in horizontal lines on a glass tube. For both of them it had been a stunning if somewhat belated entrée into the real world for which their expensive boarding school ought to have prepared them more speedily. But theirs was the fat and lazy time for American youth, all the more so that their wealthy families had further insulated them from reality with the privilege that money could buy without imparting the wisdom required for its proper use.

The sudden and shocking thought had arrived in both minds at the same instant: it could all be *over*. Nervous chatter in the room told them more. They were *surrounded* by Targets. Boston to the southeast, Westover Air Force Base to the southwest, two other SAC bases, Pease and Loring, within a hundred-mile radius. Portsmouth Naval Base, which housed nuclear submarines. If the missiles flew, they would not survive; either the blast or the fallout would get them. And neither of them had even gotten *laid* yet. Other boys in the dorm had made their claims—some of them, perhaps, might even have been true—but Peter and Wally didn't lie to each other, and neither had scored, despite repeated and earnest efforts. How was it possible that the world didn't take their personal needs into account? Weren't they the elite? Didn't their lives *matter?*

It was a sleepless night, that Tuesday in October, Henderson and Hicks sitting up, whispering their conversation, trying to come to terms with a world that had transformed itself from comfort to danger without the proper warning. Clearly, they had to find a way to change things. After graduation, though each went a separate way, Brown and Harvard were separated by only a brief drive, and both their friendship and their mission in life continued and grew. Both majored in political science because that was the proper major for entering into the process which really mattered in the world. Both got master's degrees, and most important of all, both were noticed by people who mattered—their parents helped there, and in finding a form of government service that did not expose them to uniformed servitude. The time of their vulnerability to the draft was early enough that a quiet telephone call to the right bureaucrat was sufficient.

And so, now, both young men had achieved their own entry-level positions in sensitive posts, both as aides to important men. Their heady expectations of landing policymaking roles while still short of thirty had run hard into the blank wall of reality, but in fact they were closer to it than they fully appreciated. In screening information for their bosses and deciding what appeared on the master's desk in what order, they had a real effect on the decision process; and they also had access to data that was wide, diverse, and sensitive. As a result in many ways both knew more than their bosses did. And that, Hicks and Henderson thought, was fitting, because they often *understood* the important things better than their bosses did. It was all so clear. War was a *bad thing* and had to be avoided entirely, or when that wasn't possible, ended as rapidly as one could bring it about; because war ended lives, and that was a *very bad thing,* and with war out of the way, people could learn to solve their disagreements peacefully. It was so obvious both stood in wonder that so many people failed to grasp the simple clarity of the Truth that both men had discovered in high school.

There was only one difference between the two, really. As a White House staffer, Hicks worked inside the system. But he shared everything with his classmate, which was okay because both had Special Access security clearances—and besides, he needed the feedback of a trained mind he both understood and trusted.

Hicks didn't know that Henderson had taken one step beyond him. If he couldn't change government policy from the inside, Henderson had decided during the Days of Rage following the Cambodia incursion, he had to get help from the outside—some outside agency that could assist him in blocking government actions that endangered the world. There were others around the world who shared his aversion to war, people who saw that you couldn't force people to accept a form of government they really didn't want. The first contact had come at Harvard, a friend in the peace movement. Now he communicated with someone else. He ought to have shared this fact with his friend, Henderson told himself, but the timing just wasn't right. Wally might not understand yet.

"—it has to, and it will," Henderson said, waving to the waitress for another round. "The war will end. We will get out. Vietnam will have the government it wants. We will have lost a war, and that will be a good thing for our country. We'll learn from that. We'll learn the limits of our power. We'll learn to live and let live, and then we can give peace a chance."

*   *   *

Kelly arose after five. The events of the previous day had left him more fatigued than he had appreciated, and besides, traveling had always tired him out. But he was not tired now. A total of eleven hours' sleep in the last twenty-four had left him fully rested and alert. Looking in the mirror, he saw the heavy beard from almost two days' worth of growth. Good. Then he selected his clothing. Dark, baggy, and old. He'd taken the whole bundle down to the laundry room and washed everything with hot water and extra bleach to abuse the fabric and mute the colors, making already shabby clothing look all the more unsightly. Old white gym socks and sneakers completed the picture, though both were more serviceable than their appearance suggested. The shirt was too large for him, and long, which suited his purposes. A wig completed the picture he wanted, made of coarse black Asian hair, none too long. He held it under a hot-water faucet and soaked it, then brushed it out in a deliberately sloppy way. He'd have to find a way to make it smell, too, Kelly thought.

Nature again provided some additional cover. Evening storms were rolling in, bringing with them leaf-swirling wind and rain that covered him on the way to his Volkswagen. Ten minutes later he parked near a neighborhood liquor store, where he purchased a bottle of cheap yellow wine and a paper bag to semiconceal it. He took off the twist cap and poured about half of it into a gutter. Then it was time to go.

It all looked different now, Kelly thought. It was no longer an area he could pass through, seeing the dangers or not. Now it was a place of sought danger. He drove past the spot where he'd led Billy and his Roadrunner, turning to see if the tire marks were still there—they weren't. He shook his head. That was in the past, and the future occupied his thoughts.

In Vietnam there always seemed to be the treeline, a spot where you passed from the openness of a field or farmed area into the jungle, and in your mind that was the place where safety ended and danger began because Charlie lived in the woods. It was just a thing of the mind, a boundary imaginary rather than real, but in looking around this area he saw the same thing. Only this time he wasn't walking in with five or ten comrades in striped jungle fatigues. He was driving through the barrier in a rust-speckled car. He accelerated, and just like that, Kelly was in the jungle, and again at war.

He found a parking place among autos as decrepit as his own, and quickly got out, as he once would have run away from a helicopter LZ the enemy might see and approach, and headed into an alley dotted with trash and several discarded appliances. His senses were alert now. Kelly was already sweating, and that was good. He wanted to sweat and smell. He took a mouthful of the cheap wine and sloshed it around his mouth before letting it dribble out onto his face, neck, and clothing. Bending down briefly, he got a handful of dirt, which he rubbed onto his hands and forearms, and a little onto his face. An afterthought added some to the hair of his wig, and by the time Kelly had passed through the city-block-length of the alley, he was just one more wino, a street bum like those who dotted the area even more than the drug pushers. Kelly adjusted his gait, slowing down and becoming deliberately sloppy in his movements while his eyes searched for a good perch. It wasn't all that difficult. Several of the houses in the area were vacant, and it was just a matter of finding one with a good view. That required half an hour. He settled for a corner house with upstairs bay windows. Kelly entered it from the back door. He nearly jumped out of his skin when he saw two rats in the wreckage of what a few years before had been a kitchen. *Fuckin' rats!* It was foolish to fear them, but he loathed their small black eyes and leprous hair and naked tails.

"Shit!" he whispered to himself. Why hadn't he thought about that? Everybody got a creeping chill from something: spiders, snakes, or tall buildings. For Kelly, it was rats. He walked towards the doorway, careful to keep his distance. The rats merely looked at him, edging away but less afraid of him than he was of them. "Fuck!" they heard him whisper, leaving them to their meal.

What followed was anger. Kelly made his way up the unbanistered stairs and found the corner bedroom with the bay windows, furious with himself for allowing such a dumb and cowardly distraction. Didn't he have a perfectly good weapon for dealing with rats? What were they going to do, assemble into a battalion for a rat-wave attack? That thought finally caused an embarrassed smile in the darkness of the room. Kelly crouched at the windows, evaluating his field of view and his own visibility. The windows were dirty and cracked. Some glass panels were missing entirely, but each window had a comfortable sill on which he could sit, and the house's location at the corner of two streets gave him a long view along each of the four main points of the compass, since this part of the city streets was laid out along precisely surveyed north-south, east-west lines. There wasn't enough illumination on the streets for those below him to see into the house. With his dark, shabby clothing, in this unfit and derelict house, Kelly was invisible. He took out a small pair of binoculars and began his reconnaissance.

His first task was to learn the environment. The rain showers passed, leaving moisture in the air that made for little globes of light punctuated by the flying insects attracted to their eventual doom by streetlights. The air was still warm, perhaps mid-eighties, falling slowly, and Kelly was perspiring a little. His first analytical thought was that he should have brought water to drink. Well, he could correct that in the future, and he didn't really need a drink for some hours. He had thought to bring chewing gum, and that made things easier. The sounds of the streets were curious. In the jungle he'd heard the tittering of insects, the calls of birds, and the flapping of bats. Here it was automotive sounds near or distant, the occasional squeal of brakes, conversations loud or muted, barking dogs, and rattling trash cans, all of which he analyzed while watching through his binoculars and considering his actions for the evening.

Friday night, the start of the weekend, and people were making their purchases. It seemed this was a busy night for the gentry business. He identified one probable dealer a block and a half away. Early twenties. Twenty minutes of observation gave him a good physical picture of both the dealer and his assistant-"lieutenant." Both moved with the ease that came both with experience and security in their place, and Kelly wondered if they had fought either to take this place or to defend it. Perhaps both. They had a thriving trade, perhaps regular customers, he thought, watching both men approach an imported car, joshing with the driver and passenger before the exchange was made, shaking hands and waving afterwards. The two were of roughly the same height and build, and he assigned them the names Archie and Jughead.

Jesus, what an innocent I was, Kelly told himself, looking down another street. He remembered that one asshole they'd caught smoking grass in 3rd SOG—right before going out on a job. It had been Kelly's team, and Kelly's man, and though he was an FNK right from SEAL school, that was no excuse at all. Confronting the man, he'd explained reasonably but positively that going into the field in anything less that a hundred-percent-alert state could mean death for the entire team. "Hey, man, it's cool, I know what I'm doing" had not been a particularly intelligent response, and thirty seconds later another team member had found it necessary to pull Kelly off the instantly ex-member of the team, who was gone the next day, never to return.

And that had been the only instance of drug use in the entire unit as far as Kelly knew. Sure, off-duty they'd had their beer bashes, and when Kelly and two others had flown to Taiwan for R&R, their collective vacation had not been terribly unlike a mobile earthquake of drunken excesses. Kelly truly believed that was different, blind to the explicit double standard. But they didn't drink beer before heading into the boonies either. It was a matter of common sense. It had also been one of unit morale. Kelly knew of no really elite unit that had developed a drug problem. The problem—a very serious one indeed, he'd heard—was mainly in the REMFs and the draftee units composed of young men whose presence in Vietnam was even less willing than was his own, and whose officers hadn't been able to overcome the problem either because of their own failings or their not dissimilar feelings.

Whatever the cause, the fact that Kelly had hardly considered the problem of drug use was both logical and absurd. He set all of that aside. However late he had learned about it, it was here before his eyes.

Down another street was a solo dealer who didn't want, need, or have a lieutenant. He wore a striped shirt and had his own clientele. Kelly thought of him as Charlie Brown. Over the next five hours, he identified and classified three other operations within his field of view. Then the selection process began. Archie and Jughead seemed to be doing the most business, but they were in line of sight to two others. Charlie Brown seemed to have his block entirely to himself, but there was a bus stop only a few yards away. Dagwood was right across the street from the Wizard. Both had lieutenants, and that took care of that. Big Bob was even larger than Kelly, and his lieutenant was larger still. That was a challenge. Kelly wasn't really looking for challenges—yet.

I need to get a good map of the area and memorize it. Divide it into discrete areas, Kelly thought. *I need to plot bus lines, police stations. Learn police shift times. Patrol patterns. I have to learn this area, a ten-block radius ought to be enough. I can't ever park the car in the same place twice, no one parking place even visible from another.*

You can hunt a specific area only once. That means you have to be careful whom you select. No movement on the street except in darkness. Get a backup weapon . . . not a gun . . . a knife, a good one. A couple lengths of rope or wire. Gloves, rubber ones like women use to wash dishes. Another thing to wear, like a bush jacket, something with pockets—no, something with pockets on the inside. A water bottle. Something to eat, candy bars for energy. More chewing gum . . . maybe bubble gum? Kelly thought, allowing himself some levity. He checked his watch: three-twenty.

Things were slowing down out there. Wizard and his number-two walked away from their piece of sidewalk, disappearing around a corner. Dagwood soon did the same, getting right into his car while his lieutenant drove. Charlie was gone the next time he looked. That left Archie and Jughead to his south, and Big Bob to the west, both still making sporadic sales, many of them still to upscale clients. Kelly continued to watch for another hour, until Arch and Jug were the last to call it quits for the night . . . and they disappeared rather fast, Kelly thought, not sure how they'd done it. Something else to check. He was stiff when he rose, and made another note on that. He shouldn't sit still so much. His dark-accustomed eyes watched the stairs as he descended, as quietly as he could, for there was activity in the house next door. Fortunately, the rats were gone, too. Kelly looked out the back door, and finding the alley empty, walked away from the house, keeping his pace to that of a drunk. Ten minutes later his car was in sight. Fifty yards away, Kelly realized that he'd unthinkingly parked the car close to a streetlight. That was a mistake not to be repeated, he reproached himself, approaching slowly and drunkenly until he was within a car length. Then, first checking up and down the now-vacant street, he got in quickly, started the engine, and pulled away. He didn't flip on the headlights until he was two blocks away, turning left and reentering the wide vacant corridor, leaving the not-so-imaginary jungle and heading north towards his apartment.

In the renewed comfort and safety of his car he went over everything he'd seen in the past nine hours. The dealers were all smokers, igniting their cigarettes with what seemed to be Zippo lighters whose bright flames would injure their night vision. The longer the night got, the less business there was and the sloppier they seemed to become. They were human. They got tired. Some stayed out longer than others. Everything he'd seen was useful and important. In their operating characteristics, and especially in their differences, were their vulnerabilities.

It had been a fine night, Kelly thought, passing the city's baseball stadium and turning left onto Loch Raven Boulevard, relaxing finally. He even considered a sip of the wine, but this wasn't the time to indulge in any bad habits. He removed his wig, wiping away the sweat it had caused. Jesus, he was thirsty.

He addressed that need ten minutes later, having parked his car in the proper place and made his way quietly into the apartment. He looked longingly at the shower, needing the clean feeling after being surrounded by dust and squalor and . . . rats. That final thought made him shudder. *Fucking rats,* he thought, filling a large glass with ice, then adding tap water. He followed it with several more, using his free hand to strip off his clothing. The air conditioning felt wonderful, and he stood in front of the wall unit, letting the chilled air wash over his body. All this time, and he didn't need to urinate. Had to take water with him from now on. Kelly took a package of lunch meat from the refrigerator and made two thick sandwiches, chased down by another pint of ice water.

Need a shower bad, he told himself. But he couldn't allow himself one. He'd have to get used to the feeling of a sticky, plasticlike coating all over his body. He'd have to like it, cultivate it, for in that was a part of his personal safety. His grime and odor were part of his disguise. His looks and smell had to make people look away from him, to avoid coming too close. He couldn't be a person now. He had to be a street creature, shunned. Invisible. The beard was even darker now, he saw in the mirror before heading to the bedroom, and his last decision of the day was to sleep on the floor. He couldn't dirty up new sheets.

15

Lessons Applied

Hell began promptly at eleven that morning, though Colonel Zacharias had no way of knowing the time. The tropical sun seemed always to be overhead, beating mercilessly down. Even in his windowless cell there was no escaping it, any more than he could escape the insects that seemed to thrive on the heat. He wondered how anything could thrive here, but everything that did seemed to be something that hurt or offended him, and that was as concise a definition of hell as anything he'd learned in the temples of his youth. Zacharias had been trained for possible capture. He'd been through the survival, evasion, resistance, and escape course, called SERE School. It was something you had to do if you flew airplanes for a living, and it was purposefully the most hated thing in the military because it did things to otherwise pampered Air Force and Navy officers that Marine drill instructors would have quailed at—things which were, in any other context, deeds worthy of a general court-martial followed by a lengthy term at Leavenworth or Portsmouth. The experience for Zacharias, as for most others, had been one he would never willingly repeat. But his current situation was not of his own volition either, was it? And he *was* repeating SERE School.

He'd considered capture in a distant sort of way. It wasn't the sort of thing you could really ignore once you'd heard the awful, despairing electronic *rawwwww* of the emergency radios, and seen the 'chutes, and tried to organize a RESCAP, hoping the Jolly Green Giant helicopter could swoop in from its base in Laos or maybe a Navy "Big Mutha"—as the squids called the rescue birds—would race in from the sea. Zacharias had seen that work, but more often he'd seen it fail. He'd heard the panicked and tragically unmanly cries of airmen about to be captured: "Get me out of here," one major had screamed before another voice had come on the radio, speaking spiteful words none of them could understand, but which they had understood even so, with bitterness and killing rage. The Jolly crews and their Navy counterparts did their best, and though Zacharias was a Mormon and had never touched alcohol in his life, he had bought those chopper crews enough drinks to lay low a squad of Marines, in gratitude and awe at their bravery, for that was how you expressed your admiration within the community of warriors.

But like every other member of that community, he'd never really thought capture would happen to him. Death, that was the chance and the likelihood he'd thought about. Zacharias had been King Weasel. He'd helped invent that branch of his profession. With his intellect and superb flying skills he'd created the doctrine and validated it in the air. He'd driven his F-105 into the most concentrated antiair network anyone had yet built, actually seeking out the most dangerous weapons for his special attention, and using his training and intelligence to duel with them, matching tactic for tactic, skill for skill, teasing them, defying them, baiting them in what had become the most exhilarating contest any man had ever experienced, a chess game played in three dimensions over and under Mach-1, with him driving his two-seater Thud and with them manning Russian-built radars and missile launchers. Like mongoose and cobra, theirs was a very private vendetta played for keeps every day, and in his pride and his skill, he'd thought he would win, or, at worst, meet his end in the form of a yellow-black cloud that would mark a proper airman's death: immediate, dramatic, and ethereal.

He'd never thought himself a particularly brave man. He had his faith. Were he to meet death in the air, then he could look forward to staring God in the face, standing with humility at his lowly station and pride at the life he had lived, for Robin Zacharias was a righteous man, hardly ever straying from the path of virtue. He was a good friend to his comrades, a conscientious leader mindful of his men's needs; an upright family man with strong, bright, proud children; most of all, he was an Elder in his church who tithed his Air Force salary, as his station in the Church of Jesus Christ of Latter-Day Saints required. For all of those reasons he had never feared death. What lay beyond the grave was something whose reality he viewed with confidence. It was life that was uncertain, and his current life was the most uncertain of all, and faith even as strong as his had limits imposed by the body which contained it. That was a fact he either did not fully understand or somehow did not believe. His faith, the Colonel told himself, should be enough to sustain him through anything. Was. Should be. *Was*, he'd learned as a child from his teachers. But those lessons had been taught in comfortable classrooms in sight of the Wasatch Mountains, by teachers in clean white shirts and ties, holding their lesson books, speaking with confidence imparted by the history of their church and its members.

It's different here. Zacharias heard the little voice that said so, trying to ignore it, trying his best *not* to believe it, for believing it was a contradiction with his faith, and that contradiction was the single thing his mind could not allow. Joseph Smith had died for his faith, murdered in Illinois. Others had done the same. The history of Judaism and Christianity was replete with the names of martyrs—*heroes* to Robin Zacharias, because that was the word used by his professional community—who had sustained torture at Roman or other hands and had died with God's name on their lips.

But they didn't suffer as long as you, the voice pointed out. A few hours. The brief hellish minutes burning at the stake, a day or two, perhaps, nailed to the cross. That was one thing; you could see the end of it, and if you knew what lay beyond the end, then you could concentrate on that. But to see beyond the end, you had to know *where* the end was.

Robin Zacharias was alone. There were others here. He'd caught glimpses, but there was no communication. He'd tried the tap code, but no one ever answered. Wherever they were, they were too distant, or the building's arrangements didn't allow it, or perhaps his hearing was off. He could not share thoughts with anyone, and even prayers had limits to a mind as intelligent as his. He was afraid to pray for deliverance—a thought he was unable even to admit, for it would be an internal admission that his faith had somehow been shaken, and that was something he could not allow, but part of him knew that in *not* praying for deliverance, he was admitting something by omission; that if he prayed, and after a time deliverance didn't come, then his faith might start to die, and with that his soul. For Robin Zacharias, that was how despair began, not with a thought, but with the unwillingness to entreat his God for something that might not come.

He couldn't know the rest. His dietary deprivation, the isolation so especially painful to a man of his intelligence, and the gnawing fear of pain, for even faith could not take pain away, and all men know fear of that. Like carrying a heavy load, however strong a man might be, his strength was finite and gravity was not. Strength of body was easily understood, but in the pride and righteousness that came from his faith, he had failed to consider that the physical acted upon the psychological, just as surely as gravity but far more insidiously. He interpreted the crushing mental fatigue as a weakness assignable to something not supposed to break, and he faulted himself for nothing more than being human. Consultation with another Elder would have righted everything, but that wasn't possible, and in denying himself the escape hatch of merely admitting his human frailty, Zacharias forced himself further and further into a trap of his own creation, aided and abetted by people who wanted to destroy him, body and soul.

It was then that things became worse. The door to his cell opened. Two Vietnamese wearing khaki uniforms looked at him as though he were a stain on the air of their country. Zacharias knew what they were here for. He tried to meet them with courage. They took him, one man on each arm, and a third following behind with a rifle, to a larger room—but even before he passed through the doorway, the muzzle of the rifle stabbed hard into his back, right at the spot that still hurt, fully nine months after his painful ejection, and he gasped in pain. The Vietnamese didn't even show pleasure at his discomfort. They didn't ask questions. There wasn't even a plan to their abuse that he could recognize, just the physical attacks of five men operating all at once, and Zacharias knew that resistance was death, and while he wished for his captivity to end, to seek death in that way might actually be suicide, and he couldn't do that.

It didn't matter. In a brief span of seconds his ability to do anything at all was taken away, and he merely collapsed on the rough concrete floor, feeling the blows and kicks and pain add up like numbers on a ledger sheet, his muscles paralyzed by agony, unable to move any of his limbs more than an inch or two, wishing it would stop, knowing that it never would. Above it all he heard the cackling of their voices now, like jackals, devils tormenting him because he was one of the righteous and they'd gotten their hands on him anyway, and it went on, and on, and on—

A screaming voice blasted its way past his catatonia. One more desultory half-strength kick connected with his chest, and then he saw their boots draw back. His peripheral vision saw their faces cringe, all looking toward the door at the source of the noise. A final bellow and they hastily made their way out. The voice changed. It was a . . . *white* voice? How did he know that? Strong hands lifted him, sitting him up against the wall, and the face came into view. It was Grishanov.

"My God," the Russian said, his pale cheeks glowing red with anger. He turned and screamed something else in oddly accented Vietnamese. Instantly a canteen appeared, and he poured the contents over the American's face. Then he screamed something else and Zacharias heard the door close.

"Drink, Robin, drink this." He held a small metal flask to the American's lips, lifting it.

Zacharias took a swallow so quickly that the liquid was in his stomach before he noted the acidic taste of vodka. Shocked, he lifted his hand and tried to push it away.

"I can't," the American gasped, ". . . can't drink, can't . . ."

"Robin, it is medicine. This is not entertainment. Your religion has no rule against this. Please, my friend, you need this. It's the best I can do for you," Grishanov added in a voice that shuddered with frustration. "You must, Robin."

Maybe it is medicine, Zacharias thought. Some medicines used an alcohol base as a preservative, and the Church permitted that, didn't it? He couldn't remember, and in not knowing he took another swallow. Nor did he know that as the adrenaline that the beating had flooded into his system dissipated, the natural relaxation of his body would only be accentuated by the drink.

"Not too much, Robin." Grishanov removed the flask, then started tending to his injuries, straightening out his legs, using moistened cloth to clean up the man's face.

"Savages!" the Russian snarled. "Bloody stinking savages. I'll throttle Major Vinh for this, break his skinny little monkey neck." The Russian colonel sat down on the floor next to his American colleague and spoke from the heart. "Robin, we are enemies, but we are men also, and even war has rules. You serve your country. I serve mine. These . . . these people do not understand that without honor there is no true service, only barbarism." He held up the flask again. "Here. I cannot get anything else for the pain. I'm sorry, my friend, but I can't."

And Zacharias took another swallow, still numb, still disoriented, and even more confused than ever.

"Good man," Grishanov said. "I have never said this, but you are a courageous man, my friend, to resist these little animals as you have."

"Have to," Zacharias gasped.

"Of course you do," Grishanov said, wiping the man's face clean as tenderly as he might have done with one of his children. "I would, too." He paused. "God, to be flying again!"

"Yeah. Colonel, I wish—"

"Call me Kolya." Grishanov gestured. "You've known me long enough."

"Kolya?"

"My Christian name is Nikolay. Kolya is—nickname, you say?"

Zacharias let his head back against the wall, closing his eyes and remembering the sensations of flight. "Yes, Kolya, I would like to be flying again."

"Not too different, I imagine," Kolya said, sitting beside the man, wrapping a brotherly arm around his bruised and aching shoulders, knowing it was the first gesture of human warmth the man had experienced in almost a year. "My favorite is the MiG-17. Obsolete now, but, God, what a joy to fly. Just fingertips on the stick, and you—you just think it, just wish it in your mind, and the aircraft does what you want."

"The -86 was like that," Zacharias replied. "They're all gone, too."

The Russian chuckled. "Like your first love, yes? The first girl you saw as a child, the one who first made you think as a man thinks, yes? But the first airplane, that is better for one like us. Not so warm as a woman is, but much less confusing to handle." Robin tried to laugh, but choked. Grishanov offered him another swallow. "Easy, my friend. Tell me, what is your favorite?"

The American shrugged, feeling the warm glow in his belly. "I've flown nearly everything. I missed the F-94 and the -89, too. From what I hear, I didn't miss much there. The -104 was fun, like a sports car, but not much legs. No, the -86H is probably my favorite, just for handling."

"And the Thud?" Grishanov asked, using the nickname for the F-105 Thunderchief.

Robin coughed briefly. "You take the whole state of Utah to turn one in, darned if it isn't fast on the deck, though. I've had one a hundred twenty knots over the redline."

"Not really a fighter, they say. Really a bomb truck." Grishanov had assiduously studied American pilot's slang.

"That's all right. It will get you out of trouble in a hurry. You sure don't want to dogfight in one. The first pass better be a good one."

"But for bombing—one pilot to another, your bomb delivery in this wretched place is excellent."

"We try, Kolya, we surely do try," Zacharias said, his voice slurred. It amazed the Russian that the liquor had worked so quickly. The man had never had a drink in his life until twenty minutes earlier. How remarkable that a man would choose to live without drink.

"And the way you fight the rocket emplacements. You know, I've watched that. We are enemies, Robin," Kolya said again. "But we are also pilots. The courage and skill I have watched here, they are like nothing I have ever seen. You must be a professional gambler at home, yes?"

"Gamble?" Robin shook his head. "No, I can't do that."

"But what you did in your Thud . . ."

"Not gambling. Calculated risk. You plan, you know what you can do, and you stick to that, get a feel for what the other guy is thinking."

Grishanov made a mental note to refill his flask for the next one on his schedule. It had taken a few months, but he'd finally found something that worked. A pity that these little brown savages didn't have the wit to understand that in hurting a man you most often made his courage grow. For all their arrogance, which was considerable, they saw the world through a lens that was as diminutive as their stature and as narrow as their culture. They seemed unable to learn lessons. Grishanov sought out such lessons. Strangest of all, this one had been something learned from a fascist officer in the Luftwaffe. A pity also that the Vietnamese allowed only him and no others to perform these special interrogations. He'd soon write to Moscow about that. With the proper kind of pressure, they could make real use of this camp. How incongruously clever of the savages to establish this camp, and how disappointingly consistent that they'd failed to see its possibilities. How distasteful that he had to live in this hot, humid, insect-ridden country, surrounded by arrogant little people with arrogant little minds and the vicious dispositions of serpents. But the information he needed was here. As odious as his current work was, he'd discovered a phrase for it in a contemporary American novel of the type he read to polish up his already impressive language skills. A very American turn of phrase, too. What he was doing was "just business." That was a way of looking at the world he readily understood. A shame that the American next to him probably would not, Kolya thought, listening to every word of his rambling explanation of the life of a Weasel pilot.

The face in the mirror was becoming foreign, and that was good. It was strange how powerful habits were. He'd already filled the sink with hot water and had his hands lathered before his intellect kicked in and reminded him that he wasn't supposed to wash or shave. Kelly did brush his teeth. He couldn't stand the feel of film there, and for that part of the disguise he had his bottle of wine. *What foul stuff that was,* Kelly thought. *Sweet and heavy, strangely colored.* Kelly was not a wine connoisseur, but he did know that a decent table wine wasn't supposed to be the color of urine. He had to leave the bathroom. He couldn't stand to look in the mirror for long.

He fortified himself with a good meal, filling up with bland foods that would energize his body without making his stomach rumble. Then came the exercises. His ground-floor unit allowed him to run in place without the fear of disturbing a neighbor. It wasn't the same as real running, but it would suffice. Then came the push-ups. At long last his left shoulder was fully recovered, and the aches in his muscles were perfectly bilateral. Finally came the hand-to-hand exercises, which he practiced for general quickness in addition to the obvious utilitarian applications.

He'd left his apartment in daylight the day before, taking the risk of being seen in his disreputable state in order to visit a Goodwill store, where he'd found a bush jacket to go over his other clothing. It was so oversize and threadbare that they hadn't charged for it. Kelly had come to realize that disguising his size and physical conditioning was difficult, but that loose, shabby clothing did the trick. He'd also taken the opportunity to compare himself to the other patrons of the store. On inspection his disguise seemed to be effective enough. Though not the worst example of a street person, he certainly fit into the lower half, and the clerk who'd handed over the bush jacket for free had probably done so as much to get him out of the building as to express compassion for his state in life. And wasn't that an improvement? What would he have given in Vietnam to have been able to pass himself off as just another villager, and thus waited for the bad guys to come in?

He'd spent the previous night continuing his reconnaissance. No one had given him as much as a second look as he'd moved along the streets, just one more dirty, smelly drunk, not even worth mugging, which had ended his concerns about being spotted for what he really was. He'd spent another five hours in his perch, watching the streets from the second-story bay windows of the vacant house. Police patrols had turned out to be routine, and the bus noises far more regular than he'd initially appreciated.

Finished with his exercises, he disassembled his pistol and cleaned it, though it hadn't been used since his return flight from New Orleans. The same was done with the suppressor. He reassembled both, checking the match-up of the parts. He'd made one small change. Now there was a thin white painted line down the top of the silencer that served as a night-sight. Not good enough for distance shooting, but he wasn't planning any of that. Finished with the pistol, he loaded a round into the chamber and dropped the hammer carefully before slapping the clip into the bottom of the handgrip. He'd also acquired a Ka-Bar Marine combat knife in a surplus store, and while he'd watched the streets the night before, he'd worked the seven-inch Bowie-type blade across a whetstone. There was something that men feared about a knife even more than a bullet. That was foolish but useful. The pistol and knife went into his waistband side by side in the small of his back, well hidden by the loose bulk of the dark shirt and bush jacket. In one of the jacket pockets went a whiskey flask filled with tap water. Four Snickers went on the other side. Around his waist was a length of eight-gauge electrical wire.

In his pants pocket was a pair of Playtex rubber gloves. These were yellow, not a good color for invisibility, but he'd been unable to find anything else. They did cover his hands without giving away much in feel and dexterity, and he decided to take them along. He already had a pair of cotton work gloves in the car that he wore when driving. After buying the car he'd cleaned it inside and out, wiping every glass, metal, and plastic surface, hoping that he'd removed every trace of fingerprints. Kelly blessed every police show and movie he'd ever seen, and prayed that he was being para- noid *enough* about his every tactic.

What else? he asked himself. He wasn't carrying any ID. He had a few dollars in cash in a wallet also obtained at Goodwill. Kelly had thought about carrying more, but there was no point in it. Water. Food. Weapons. Rope- wire. He'd leave his binoculars home tonight. Their utility wasn't worth the bulk. Maybe he'd get a set of compact ones—make a note. He was ready. Kelly switched on the TV and watched the news to get a weather forecast— cloudy, chance of showers, low around seventy-five. He made and drank two cups of instant coffee for the caffeine, waiting for night to fall, which it presently did.

Leaving the apartment complex was, oddly enough, one of the most difficult parts of the exercise. Kelly looked out the windows, his interior lights already off, making sure that there wasn't anyone out there, before venturing out himself. Out the door of the building he stopped again, looking and listening before he walked directly to the Volkswagen, which he un- locked and entered. At once he put on the work gloves, and only after that did he close the car's door and start the engine. Two minutes after that he passed the place where he parked the Scout, wondering how lonely the car was now. Kelly had selected a single radio station, playing contemporary music, soft rock and folk, just to have the company of familiar noise as he drove south into the city.

Part of him was surprised at how tense it was, driving in. As soon as he got there he settled down, but the drive in, like the insertion flight on a Huey, was the time in which you contemplated the unknown, and he had to tell himself to be cool, to keep his face in an impassive mien while his hands sweated a little inside the gloves. He carefully obeyed every traffic law, observed all lights, and ignored the cars that sped past him. Amazing, he thought, how long twenty minutes could seem. This time he used a slightly different insertion route. He'd scouted the parking place the night before, two blocks from the objective—in his mind, the current tactical environment translated one block to a kilometer in the real jungle, a complementarity that made him smile to himself, briefly, as he pulled his car in behind someone's black 1957 Chevy. As before, he left the car quickly, ducking into an alley for the cover of darkness and the assumption of his physical disguise. Inside of twenty yards he was just one more shambling drunk.

"Hey, dude!" a young voice called. There were three of them, mid-to-late teens, sitting on a fence and drinking beer. Kelly edged to the other side of the alley to maximize his distance, but that wasn't to be. One of them hopped down off the fence and came towards him.

"Whatcha lookin' for, bum?" the boy inquired with all the unfeeling arrogance of a young tough. "Jesus, you sure do stink, man! Dint your mama teach ya to wash?"

Kelly didn't even turn as he cringed and kept moving. This wasn't part of the plan. Head down, turned slightly away from the lad who walked alongside him, keeping pace in a way calculated to torment the old bum, who switched his wine bottle to his other hand.

"I needs a drink, man," the youth said, reaching for the bottle.

Kelly didn't surrender it, because a street wino didn't do that. The youngster tripped him, shoving him against the fence to his left, but it ended there. He walked back to his friend, laughing, as the bum rose and continued on his way.

"And don' ya come back neither, man!" Kelly heard as he got to the end of the block. He had no plans to do so. He passed two more such knots of young people in the next ten minutes, neither of which deemed him worthy of any action beyond laughter. The back door of his perch was still ajar, and tonight, thankfully, the rats weren't present. Kelly paused inside, listening, and, hearing nothing, he stood erect, allowing himself to relax.

"Snake to Chicago," he whispered to himself, remembering his old call signs. "Insertion successful. At the observation point." Kelly went up the same rickety stairs for the third and last time, finding his accustomed place in the southeast corner, sat down, and looked out.

Archie and Jughead were also in their accustomed place, a block away, he saw at once, talking to a motorist. It was ten-twelve at night. Kelly allowed himself a sip of water and a candy bar as he leaned back, watching them for any changes in their usual pattern of activity, but there was none he could see in half an hour of observation. Big Bob was in his place, too, as was his lieutenant, whom Kelly now called Little Bob. Charlie Brown was also in business tonight, as was Dagwood, the former still working alone and the latter still teamed up with a lieutenant Kelly had not bothered to name. But the Wizard wasn't visible tonight. It turned out that he arrived late, just after eleven, along with his associate, whose assigned name was Toto, for he tended to scurry around like a little dog that belonged in the basket on the back of the Wicked Witch's bicycle. "And your little dog, too . . ." Kelly whispered to himself in amusement.

As expected, Sunday night was slower than the two preceding nights, but Arch and Jug seemed busier than the others. Perhaps it was because they had a slightly more upscale client base. Though all served both local and outside customers, Arch and Jug seemed more often to draw the larger cars whose cleanliness and polish made Kelly think they didn't belong in this part of town. That might have been an unwarranted assumption, but it was not important to the mission. The really important thing was something he had scoped out the previous night on his walk into the area and confirmed tonight as well. Now it was just a matter of waiting.

Kelly made himself comfortable, feeling his body relax now that all the decisions had been made. He stared down at the street, still intensely alert, watching, listening, noting everything that came and went as the minutes passed. At twelve-forty, a police radio car traveled one of the cross streets, doing nothing more than showing the flag. It would return a few minutes after two, probably. The city buses made their whirring diesel noises, and Kelly recognized the one-ten, with the brakes that needed work. Their thin screech must have annoyed every person who tried to sleep along its route. Traffic slowed perceptibly just after two. The dealers were smoking more now, talking more. Big Bob crossed the street to say something to the Wizard, and their relations seemed cordial enough, which surprised Kelly. He hadn't seen that before. Maybe the man just needed change for a hundred. The police cruiser made its scheduled pass. Kelly finished his third Snickers bar of the evening, collecting the wrappers. He checked the area. He'd left nothing. No surface he had touched was likely to retain a fingerprint. There was just too much dust and grit, and he'd been very careful not to touch a windowpane.

Okay.

Kelly made his way down the stairs and out the back door. He crossed the street into the continuation of the alley that paralleled the street, still keeping to the shadows, still moving in a shambling but now exceeding quiet gait.

The mystery of the first night had turned out to be a boon. Archie and Jughead had vanished from his sight in a span of two or three seconds. He hadn't looked away from them any longer than that. They hadn't driven away, and they hadn't had time to walk to the end of the block. Kelly had figured it out the previous night. These overlong blocks of row houses had not been built by fools. Halfway down, many of the continuous blocks had an arched passageway so that people could get to the alley more easily. It also made a fine escape route for Arch and Jug, and when conducting business they never strayed more than twenty feet from it. But they never really appeared to watch it either.

Kelly made sure of that, leaning against an outbuilding that might have been big enough to contain a Model-T Ford. Finding a pair of beer cans, he connected them with a piece of string and set them across the cement walk that led to the passage, making sure that no one could approach him from behind without making noise. Then he moved in, walking very lightly on his feet and reaching into his waistband for his silenced pistol. It was only thirty-five feet to cover, but tunnels transmitted sound better than telephones, and Kelly's eyes scanned the surface for anything on which he might trip or make noise. He avoided some newspaper and a patch of broken glass, arriving close to the other end of the passageway.

They looked different close-up, human almost. Archie was leaning back against the brown bricks of a wall, smoking a cigarette. Jughead was also smoking, sitting on someone's car fender, looking down the street, and every ten seconds the flaring of their cigarettes attacked and degraded their vision. Kelly could see them, but even ten feet away they couldn't see him. It didn't get much better.

"Don't move," he whispered, just for Archie. The man's head turned, more in annoyance than alarm, until he saw the pistol with the large cylinder screwed onto the end. His eyes flickered to his lieutenant, who was still facing the wrong way, humming some song or other, waiting for a customer who would never come. Kelly handled the notification.

"Hey!" Still a whisper, but enough to carry over the diminishing street sounds. Jughead turned and saw the gun aimed at his employer's head. He froze without being bidden. Archie had the gun and the money and most of the drugs. He also saw Kelly's hand wave him in, and not knowing what else to do, he approached.

"Business good tonight?" Kelly asked.

"Fair 'nuf," Archie responded quietly. "What you want?"

"Now what do you suppose?" Kelly asked with a smile.

"You a cop?" Jughead asked, rather stupidly, the other two thought.

"No, I'm not here to arrest anybody." He motioned with his hand. "In the tunnel, facedown, quick." Kelly let them go in ten feet or so, just enough to be lost to outside view, not so far that he didn't have some exterior light to see by. First he searched them for weapons. Archie had a rusty .32 revolver that went into a pocket. Kelly next took the electrical wire from around his waist and wrapped it tightly around both sets of hands. Then he rolled them over.

"You boys have been very cooperative."

"You better never come back here, man," Archie informed him, hardly realizing that he hadn't been robbed at all. Jug nodded and muttered. The response puzzled both of them.

"Actually, I need your help."

"What with?" Archie asked.

"Looking for a guy, name of Billy, drives a red Roadrunner."

"What? You dickin' my ass?" Archie asked in rather a disgusted voice.

"Answer the question, please," Kelly said reasonably.

"You get you fuckin' ass outa here," Archie suggested spitefully.

Kelly turned the gun slightly and fired two rounds into Jug's head. The body spasmed violently, and blood flew, but not on Kelly this time. Instead it showered across Archie's face, and Kelly could see the pusher's eyes open wide in horror and surprise, like little lights in the darkness. Archie had not expected that. Jughead hadn't seemed much of a conversationalist anyway, and the operation's clock was ticking.

"I said please, didn't I?"

"Sweet Jesus, man!" the voice rasped, knowing that to make any more noise would be death.

"Billy. Red Plymouth Roadrunner, loves to show it off. He's a distributor. I want to know where he hangs out," Kelly said quietly.

"If I tell you that—"

"You get a new supplier. Me," Kelly said. "And if you tell Billy that I'm out here, you'll get to see your friend again," he added, gesturing to the body whose warm bulk pressed limply against Archie's side. He had to offer the man hope, after all. Maybe even a little left-handed truth, Kelly thought: "Do you understand? Billy and his friends have been screwing around with the wrong people, and it's my job to straighten things out. Sorry about your friend, but I had to show you that I'm serious, like."

Archie's voice tried to calm itself, but didn't quite make it, though he reached for the hope he'd been offered. "Look, man, I can't—"

"I can always ask somebody else." Kelly paused significantly. "Do you understand what I just said?"

Archie did, or thought he did, and he talked freely until the time came for him to rejoin Jughead.

A quick search of Archie's pockets turned up a nice wad of cash and a collection of small drug envelopes which also found their way into his jacket pockets. Kelly stepped carefully over both bodies and made his way to the alley, looking back to make sure that he hadn't stepped in any blood. He'd discard the shoes in any case. Kelly untied the string from the cans and replaced them where he'd found them, before renewing his drunken gait, taking a roundabout path back to his car, repeating his carefully considered routine every step of the way. Thank God, he thought, driving north again, he'd be able to shower and shave tonight. But what the hell would he do with the drugs? That was a question that fate would answer.

The cars started arriving just after six, not so incongruous an hour for activity on a military base. Fifteen of them, clunkers, none less than three years old, and all of them had been totaled in auto accidents and sold for scrap. The only thing unusual about them was that though they were no longer drivable, they almost looked as though they were. The work detail was composed of Marines, supervised by a gunnery sergeant who had no idea what this was all about. But he didn't have to. The cars were worked into place, haphazardly, not in neat military rows, but more the way real people parked. The job took ninety minutes, and the work detail left. At eight in the morning another such detail arrived, this one with mannequins. They came in several sizes, and they were dressed in old clothes. The child-size ones went on the swings and in the sandbox. The adult ones were stood up, using the metal stands that came with them. And the second work party left, to return twice a day for the indefinite future and move the mannequins around in a random way prescribed by a set of instructions thought up and written down by some damned fool of an officer who didn't have anything better to do.

Kelly's notes had commented on the fact that one of the most debilitating and time-consuming aspects of Operation KINGPIN had been the daily necessity of setting up and striking down the mockup of their objective. He hadn't been the first to note it. If any Soviet reconnaissance satellites took note of this place, they would see an odd collection of buildings serving no readily identifiable purpose. They would also see a child's playground, complete with children, parents, and parked cars, all of which elements would move every day. That bit of information would counter the more obvious observation—that this recreational facility was half a mile off any paved road and invisible to the rest of the installation.

16
Exercises

R yan and Douglas stood back, letting the forensics people do their jobs. The discovery had happened just after five in the morning. On his routine patrol pattern, Officer Chuck Monroe had come down the street, and spotting an irregular shadow in this passage between houses, shone his car light down it. The dark shape might easily have been a drunk passed out and sleeping it off, but the white spotlight had reflected off the pool of red and bathed the arched bricks in a pink glow that looked wrong from the first instant. Monroe had parked his car and come in for a look, then made his call. The officer was leaning on the side of his car now, smoking a cigarette and going over the details of his discovery, which was to him less horrific and more routine than civilians understood. He hadn't even bothered to call an ambulance. These two men were clearly beyond any medical redemption.

"Bodies sure do bleed a lot," Douglas observed. It wasn't a statement of any significance, just words to fill the silence as the cameras flashed for one last roll of color film. It looked as if two full-size cans of red paint had been poured in one spot.

"Time of death?" Ryan asked the representative from the coroner's office.

"Not too long ago," the man said, lifting one hand. "No rigor yet. After midnight certainly, probably after two."

The cause of death didn't require a question. The holes in both men's foreheads answered that.

"Monroe?" Ryan called. The young officer came over. "What do you know about these two?"

"Both pushers. Older one on the right there is Maceo Donald, street name is Ju-Ju. The one on the left, I don't know, but he worked with Donald."

"Good eye spotting them, patrolman. Anything else?" Sergeant Douglas asked.

Monroe shook his head. "No, sir. Nothing at all. Pretty quiet night in the district, as a matter of fact. I came through this area maybe four times on my shift, and I didn't see anything out of the ordinary. The usual pushers doing the usual business." The implied criticism of the situation that everyone had to acknowledge as normal went unanswered. It was a Monday morning, after all, and that was bad enough for anyone.

"Finished," the senior photographer said. He and his partner, on the other side of the bodies, got out of the way.

Ryan was already looking around. There was a good deal of ambient light in the passageway, and the detective augmented that with a large flashlight, playing its beam over the edges of the walkway, his eyes looking for a coppery reflection.

"See any shell casing, Tom?" he asked Douglas, who was doing the same thing.

"Nope. They were shot from this direction, too, don't you think?"

"Bodies haven't been moved," the coroner said unnecessarily, adding, "Yes, definitely both shot from this side. Both were lying down when they were shot."

Douglas and Ryan took their time, examining every inch of the passageway three times, for thoroughness was their main professional weapon, and they had all the time in the world—or at least a few hours, which amounted to the same thing. A crime scene like this was one you prayed for. No grass to conceal evidence, no furniture, just a bare brick corridor not five feet wide, everything self-contained. That would be a time-saver.

"Nothing at all, Em," Douglas said, finishing his third sweep.

"Probably a revolver, then." It was a logical observation. Light .22 shell casings, ejected from an automatic, could fly incredible distances, and were so small that finding them could drive one to distraction. Rare was the criminal who recovered his brass, and to have recovered four little .22s in the dark—no, that wasn't very likely.

"Some robber with a cheap one, want to bet?" Douglas asked.

"Could be." Both men approached the bodies and squatted down close to them for the first time.

"No obvious powder marks," the sergeant said in some surprise.

"Any of these houses occupied?" Ryan asked Monroe.

"Not either one of these, sir," Monroe said, indicating both of those bordering the passageway. "Most of the ones on the other side of the street are, though."

"Four shots, early in the morning, you figure somebody might have heard?" *The brick tunnel ought to have focused the sound like the lens of a telescope,* Ryan thought, and the .22 had a loud, sharp bark. But how often had there been cases just like this one in which no one had heard a thing? Besides, the way this neighborhood was going, people divided into two classes: those who didn't look because they didn't care, and those who knew that looking merely increased the chance of catching a stray round.

"There's two officers knocking on doors now, Lieutenant. Nothing yet."

"Not bad shooting, Em." Douglas had his pencil out, pointing to the holes in the forehead of the unidentified victim. They were scarcely half an inch apart, just above the bridge of the nose. "No powder marks. The killer must have been standing . . . call it three, four feet, max." Douglas stood back at the feet of the bodies and extended his arm. It was a natural shot, extending your arm and aiming down.

"I don't think so. Maybe there's powder marks we can't see, Tom. That's why we have medical examiners." He meant that both men had dark complexions, and the light wasn't all that good. But if there was powder tattooing around the small entrance wounds, neither detective could see it. Douglas squatted back down to give the entrance wounds another look.

"Nice to know somebody appreciates us," the coroner's representative said, ten feet away, scribbling his own notes.

"Either way, Em, our shooter has a real steady hand." The pencil moved to the head of Maceo Donald. The two holes in his forehead, maybe a little higher on the forehead than the other man, were even closer together. "That's unusual."

Ryan shrugged and began his search of the bodies. Though the senior of the two, he preferred to do this himself while Douglas took the notes. He found no weapon on either man, and though both had wallets and ID, from which they identified the unknown as Charles Barker, age twenty, the amount of cash discovered wasn't nearly what men in their business would customarily have on their persons. Nor were there any drugs—

"Wait, here's something—three small glassine bags of white powdery substance," Ryan said in the language of his profession. "Pocket change, a dollar seventy-five; cigarette lighter, Zippo, brushed steel, the cheap one. Pack of Pall Malls from the shirt pocket—and another small glassine bag of white powdery substance."

"A drug ripoff," Douglas said, diagnosing the incident. It wasn't terribly professional but it was pretty obvious. "Monroe?"

"Yes, sir?" The young officer would never stop being a Marine. Nearly everything he said, Douglas noted, had "sir" attached to it.

"Our friends Barker and Donald—experienced pushers?"

"Ju-Ju's been around since I've been in the district, sir. I never heard of anybody messin' with him."

"No signs of a fight on the hands," Ryan said after turning them over. "Hands are tied up with . . . electrical wire, copper wire, white insulation, trademark on it, can't read it yet. No obvious signs of a struggle."

"Somebody got Ju-Ju!" It was Mark Charon, who had just arrived. "I had a case running on that fuck, too."

"Two exit wounds, back of Mr. Donald's head," Ryan went on, annoyed at the interruption. "I expect we'll find the bullets somewhere at the bottom of this lake," he added sourly.

"Forget ballistics," Douglas grunted. That wasn't unusual with the .22. First of all, the bullet was made of soft lead, and was so easily deformed that the striations imparted by the rifling of the gun barrel were most often impossible to identify. Second, the little .22 had a lot of penetrating power, more even than a .45, and often ended up splattering itself on some object beyond the victim. In this case the cement of the walkway.

"Well, tell me about him," Ryan ordered.

"Major street pusher, big clientele. Drives a nice red Caddy," Charon added. "Pretty smart one, too."

"Not anymore. His brain got homogenized about six hours ago."

"Rip?" Charon asked.

Douglas answered. "Looks that way. No gun, no drugs or money to speak of. Whoever did it knew their business. Looks real professional, Em. This wasn't some junkie who got lucky."

"I'd have to say that's the morning line, Tom," Ryan replied, standing up. "Probably a revolver, but those groups are awfully tight for a Saturday-night special. Mark, any word on an experienced robber working the street?"

"The Duo," Charon said. "But they use a shotgun."

"This is almost like a mob hit. Look 'em straight in the eye—whack." Douglas thought about his words. No, that wasn't quite right either, was it? Mob hits were almost never this elegant. Criminals were not proficient marksmen, and they used cheap weapons for the most part. He and Ryan had investigated a handful of gang-related murders, and typically the victim had either been shot in the back of the head at contact range, with all the obvious

forensic signs that attended such an event, or the damage was done so haphazardly that the victim was more likely to have a dozen widely scattered
holes in his anatomy. These two had been taken out by someone who knew
his business, and the collection of highly skilled Mafia soldiers was very
slim indeed. But who had ever said that homicide investigation was an exact
science? This crime scene was a mix of the routine and the unusual. A simple
robbery in that the drugs and money of the victims were missing, but an
unusually skillful killing in the fact that the shooter had been either very
lucky—twice—or an expert shot. And a mob hit was usually not disguised
as a robbery or anything else. A mob murder was most often a public statement.

"Mark, any noise on the street about a turf war?" Douglas asked.

"No, not really, nothing organized. A lot of stuff between pushers over
street corners, but that isn't news."

"You might want to ask around," Lieutenant Ryan suggested.

"No problem, Em. I'll have my people check that out."

We're not going to solve this one fast—maybe never, Ryan thought.
Well, he thought, *only on TV do you solve them in the first half hour—
between commercials.*

"Can I have 'em now?"

"All yours," Ryan told the man from the medical examiner's office.
His black station wagon was ready, and the day was warming up. Already
flies were buzzing around, drawn to the smell of blood. He headed off to his
own car, accompanied by Tom Douglas. Junior detectives would have the
rest of the routine work.

"Somebody that knows how to shoot—better than me even," Douglas
said as they drove back downtown. He'd tried out for the department's pistol
team once.

"Well, lots of people with that skill are around now, Tom. Maybe some
have found employment with our organized friends."

"Professional hit, then?"

"We'll call it skillful for now," Ryan suggested as an alternative.
"We'll let Mark do some of the scutwork on the intelligence side."

"That makes me feel warm all over." Douglas snorted.

Kelly arose at ten-thirty, feeling clean for the first time in several days.
He'd showered immediately on returning to his apartment, wondering if in
doing so he'd left rings on the sewers. Now he could shave, even, and that
compensated for the lack of sleep. Before breakfast—brunch—Kelly drove
half a mile to a local park and ran for thirty minutes, then drove back home

for another thoroughly wonderful shower and some food. Then there was work to do. All the clothing from the previous evening was in a brown paper grocery bag—slacks, shirt, underwear, socks, and shoes. It seemed a shame to part with the bush jacket, whose size and pockets had proven to be so useful. He'd have to get another, probably several. He felt certain that he hadn't been splattered with blood this time, but the dark colors made it difficult to be sure, and they probably *did* carry powder residue, and this was not the time to take any chances at all. Leftover food and coffee grounds went on top of the clothing, and found their way into the apartment complex's Dumpster. Kelly had considered taking them to a distant dumpsite, but that might cause more trouble than it solved. Someone might see him, and take note of what he did, and wonder why. Disposing of the four empty .22 cases was easy. He'd dumped them down a sewer while jogging. The noon news broadcast announced the discovery of two bodies, but no details. Maybe the newspaper would say more. There was one other thing.

"Hi, Sam."

"Hey, John. You in town?" Rosen asked from his office.

"Yeah. Do you mind if I come down for a few minutes? Say around two?"

"What can I do for you?" Rosen asked from behind his desk.

"Gloves," Kelly said, holding his hand up. "The kind you use, thin rubber. Do they cost much?"

Rosen almost asked what the gloves were for, but decided he didn't need to know. "Hell, they come in boxes of a hundred pair."

"I don't need that many."

The surgeon pulled open a drawer in his credenza and tossed over ten of the paper-and-plastic bags. "You look awfully respectable." And so Kelly did, dressed in a button-down white shirt and his blue CIA suit, as he'd taken to calling it. It was the first time Rosen had seen him in a tie.

"Don't knock it, doc." Kelly smiled. "Sometimes I have to be. I even have a new job, sort of."

"Doing what?"

"Sort of consulting." Kelly gestured. "I can't say about what, but it requires me to dress properly."

"Feeling okay?"

"Yes, sir, just fine. Jogging and everything. How are things with you?"

"The usual. More paperwork than surgery, but I have a whole department to supervise.'' Sam touched the pile of folders on his desk. The small talk was making him uneasy. It seemed that his friend was wearing a disguise, and though he knew Kelly was up to something, in *not* knowing exactly what it was, he managed to keep his conscience under control. ''Can you do me a favor?''

''Sure, doc.''

''Sandy's car broke down. I was going to run her home, but I've got a meeting that'll run till four. She gets off shift at three.''

''You're letting her work regular hours now?'' Kelly asked with a smile.

''Sometimes, when she's not teaching.''

''If it's okay with her, it's okay with me.''

It was only a twenty-minute wait that Kelly disposed of by going to the cafeteria for a light snack. Sandy O'Toole found him there, just after the three-o'clock change of shift.

''Like the food better now?'' she asked him.

''Even hospitals can't hurt a salad very much.'' He hadn't figured out the institutional fascination with Jell-O, however. ''I hear your car's broke.''

She nodded, and Kelly saw why Rosen had her working a more regular schedule. Sandy looked very tired, her fair skin sallow, with puffy dark patches under both eyes. ''Something with the starter—wiring. It's in the shop.''

Kelly stood. ''Well, my lady's carriage awaits.'' His remark elicited a smile, but it was one of politeness rather than amusement.

''I've never seen you so dressed up,'' she said on the way to the parking garage.

''Well, don't get too worked up about it. I can still roll in the mud with the best of 'em.'' And his jesting failed again.

''I didn't mean—''

''Relax, ma'am. You've had a long day at the office, and your driver has a crummy sense of humor.''

Nurse O'Toole stopped and turned. ''It's not your fault. Bad week. We had a child, auto accident. Doctor Rosen tried, but the damage was too great, and she faded out on my shift, day before yesterday. Sometimes I hate this work,'' Sandy concluded.

''I understand,'' Kelly said, holding the door open for her. ''Look, you want the short version? It's never the right person. It's never the right time. It never makes any sense.''

"That's a nice way of looking at things. Weren't you trying to cheer me up?" And that, perversely, made her smile, but it wasn't the kind of smile that Kelly wanted to see.

"We all try to fix the broken parts as best we can, Sandy. You fight your dragons. I fight mine," Kelly said without thinking.

"And how many dragons have you slain?"

"One or two," Kelly said distantly, trying to control his words. It surprised him how difficult that had become. Sandy was too easy to talk with.

"And what did it make better, John?"

"My father was a fireman. He died while I was over there. House fire, he went inside and found two kids, they were down from smoke. Dad got them out okay, but then he had a heart attack on the spot. They say he was dead before he hit the ground. That counted for something," Kelly said, remembering what Admiral Maxwell had said, in the sick bay of USS *Kitty Hawk,* that death should mean something, that his father's death had.

"You've killed people, haven't you?" Sandy asked.

"That's what happens in a war," Kelly agreed.

"What did that mean? What did it do?"

"If you want the big answer, I don't have it. But the ones I took out didn't ever hurt anybody else." PLASTIC FLOWER sure as hell didn't, he told himself. No more village chiefs and their families. Maybe someone else had taken the work over, but maybe not, too.

Sandy watched the traffic as he headed north on Broadway. "And the ones who killed Tim, did they think the same thing?"

"Maybe they did, but there's a difference." Kelly almost said that he'd never seen one of his people murder anyone, but he couldn't say *that* anymore, could he?

"But if everybody believes that, then where are we? It's not like diseases. You fight against things that hurt everybody. No politics and lying. We're not killing people. That's why I do this work, John."

"Sandy, thirty years ago there was a guy named Hitler who got his rocks off killing people like Sam and Sarah just because of what their goddamned names were. He had to be killed, and he was, too damned late, but he was." Wasn't that a simple enough lesson?

"We have problems enough right here," she pointed out. That was obvious from the sidewalks they passed, for Johns Hopkins was not in a comfortable neighborhood.

"I know that, remember?"

That statement deflated her. "I'm sorry, John."

"So am I." Kelly paused, searching for words. "There is a difference,

Sandy. There are good people. I suppose most people are decent. But there are bad people, too. You can't wish them away, and you can't wish them to be good, because most won't change, and somebody has to protect the one bunch from the other. That's what I did.''

''But how do you keep from turning into one of them?''

Kelly took his time considering that, regretting the fact that she was here at all. He didn't need to hear this, didn't want to have to examine his own conscience. Everything had been so clear the past couple of days. Once you decided that there was an enemy, then acting on that information was simply a matter of applying your training and experience. It wasn't something you had to *think* about. Looking at your conscience was hard, wasn't it?

''I've never had that problem,'' he said, finally, evading the issue. That was when he saw the difference. Sandy and her community fought against a *thing,* and fought bravely, risking their sanity in resisting the actions of forces whose root causes they could not directly address. Kelly and his fought against *people,* leaving the actions of their enemies to others, but able to seek them out and fight directly against their foe, even eliminating them if they were lucky. One side had absolute purity of purpose but lacked satisfaction. The other could attain the satisfaction of destroying the enemy, but only at the cost of becoming too much like what they struggled against. Warrior and healer, parallel wars, similarity of purpose, but so different in their actions. Diseases of the body, and diseases of humanity itself. Wasn't that an interesting way to look at it?

''Maybe it's like this: it's not what you fight against. It's what you fight for.''

''What are we fighting for in Vietnam?'' Sandy asked Kelly again, having asked herself that question no less than ten times per day since she'd received the unwelcome telegram. ''My husband died there and I don't still understand why.''

Kelly started to say something but stopped himself. Really there was no answer. Bad luck, bad decisions, bad timing at more than one level of activity created the random events that caused soldiers to die on a distant battlefield, and even if you were there, it didn't always make sense. Besides, she'd probably heard every justification more than once from the man whose life she mourned. Maybe looking for that kind of meaning was nothing more than an exercise in futility. Maybe it wasn't supposed to make sense. Even if that were true, how could you live without the pretense that it did, somehow? He was still pondering that one when he turned onto her street.

''Your house needs some paint,'' Kelly told her, glad that it did.

"I know. I can't afford painters and I don't have the time to do it myself."

"Sandy—a suggestion?"

"What's that?"

"Let yourself live. I'm sorry Tim's gone, but he is gone. I lost friends over there, too. You have to go on."

The fatigue in her face was painful to see. Her eyes examined him in a professional sort of way, revealing nothing of what she thought or what she felt inside, but the fact that she troubled herself to conceal herself from him told Kelly something.

Something's changed in you. I wonder what it is. I wonder why, Sandy thought. Something had resolved itself. He'd always been polite, almost funny in his overpowering gentility, but the sadness she'd seen, that had almost matched her own undying grief, was gone now, replaced with something she couldn't quite fathom. It was strange, because he had never troubled to hide himself from her, and she thought herself able to penetrate whatever disguises he might erect. On that she was wrong, or perhaps she didn't know the rules. She watched him get out, walk around the car, and open her door.

"Ma'am?" He gestured toward the house.

"Why are you so nice? Did Doctor Rosen . . . ?"

"He just said you needed a ride, Sandy, honest. Besides, you look awful tired." Kelly walked her to the door.

"I don't know why I like talking to you," she said, reaching the porch steps.

"I wasn't sure that you did. You do?"

"I think so," O'Toole replied, with an almost-smile. The smile died after a second. "John, it's too soon for me."

"Sandy, it's too soon for me, too. Is it too soon to be friends?"

She thought about that. "No, not too soon for that."

"Dinner sometime? I asked once, remember?"

"How often are you in town?"

"More now. I have a job—well, something I have to do in Washington."

"Doing what?"

"Nothing important." And Sandy caught the scent of a lie, but it probably wasn't one aimed at hurting her.

"Next week maybe?"

"I'll give you a call. I don't know any good places around here."

"I do."

"Get some rest," Kelly told her. He didn't attempt to kiss her, or even take her hand. Just a friendly, caring smile before he walked away. Sandy watched him drive off, still wondering what there was about the man that was different. She'd never forget the look on his face, there on the hospital bed, but whatever that had been, it wasn't something she needed to fear.

Kelly was swearing quietly at himself as he drove away, wearing the cotton work gloves now, and rubbing them across every surface in the car that he could reach. He couldn't risk many conversations like this one. What was it all about? How the hell was he supposed to know? It was easy in the field. You identified the enemy, or more often somebody told you what was going on and who he was and where he was—frequently the information was wrong, but at least it gave you a starting place. But mission briefs never told you, really, how it was going to change the world or bring the war to an end. That was stuff you read in the paper, information repeated by reporters who didn't care, taken down from briefers who didn't know or politicians who'd never troubled themselves to find out. "Infrastructure" and "cadre" were favorite words, but he'd hunted people, not infrastructure, whatever the hell that was supposed to be. Infrastructure was a *thing*, like what Sandy fought against. It wasn't a person who did evil things and could be hunted down like an offensive big-game animal. And how did that apply to what he was doing now? Kelly told himself that he had to control his thinking, stay to the easy stuff, just remember that he was hunting *people*, just as he had before. He wasn't going to change the whole world, just clean up one little corner.

"Does it still hurt, my friend?" Grishanov asked.

"I think I have some broken ribs."

Zacharias sat down in the chair, breathing slowly and in obvious pain. That worried the Russian. Such an injury could lead to pneumonia, and pneumonia could kill a man in this physical condition. The guards had been a little too enthusiastic in their assault on the man, and though it had been done at Grishanov's request, he hadn't wanted to do more than to inflict some pain. A dead prisoner would not tell him what he needed to know.

"I've spoken to Major Vinh. The little savage says he has no medicines to spare." Grishanov shrugged. "It might even be true. The pain, it is bad?"

"Every time I breathe," Zacharias replied, and he was clearly speaking the truth. His skin was even paler than usual.

"I have only one thing for pain, Robin," Kolya said apologetically, holding out his flask.

The American colonel shook his head, and even that appeared to hurt him. "I can't."

Grishanov spoke with the frustration of a man trying to reason with a friend. "Then you are a fool, Robin. Pain serves no one, not you, not me, not your God. Please, let me help you a little. Please?"

Can't do it, Zacharias told himself. To do so was to break his covenant. His body was a temple, and he had to keep it pure of such things as this. But the temple was broken. He feared internal bleeding most of all. Would his body be able to heal itself? It should, and under anything approaching normal circumstances, it would do so easily, but he knew that his physical condition was dreadful, his back still injured, and now his ribs. Pain was a companion now, and pain would make it harder for him to resist questions, and so he had to measure his religion against his duty to resist. Things were less clear now. Easing the pain might make it easier to heal, and easier to stick to his duty. So what was the right thing? What ought to have been an easy question was clouded, and his eyes looked at the metal container. There was relief there. Not much, but some, and some relief was what he needed if he were to control himself.

Grishanov unscrewed the cap. "Do you ski, Robin?"

Zacharias was surprised by the question. "Yes, I learned when I was a kid."

"Cross-country?"

The American shook his head. "No, downhill."

"The snow in the Wasatch Mountains, it is good for skiing?"

Robin smiled, remembering. "Very good, Kolya. It's dry snow. Powdery, almost like very fine sand."

"Ah, the best kind of all. Here." He handed the flask over.

Just this once, Zacharias thought. *Just for the pain.* He took a swallow. *Push the pain back a few steps, just so I can keep myself together.*

Grishanov watched him do it, saw his eyes water, hoping the man wouldn't cough and hurt himself more. It was good vodka, obtained from the embassy's storeroom in Hanoi, the one thing his country always had in good supply, and the one thing the embassy always had enough of. The best quality of paper vodka, Kolya's personal favorite, actually flavored with old paper, something this American was unlikely to note—and something he himself missed after the third or fourth drink, if the truth be known.

"You are a good skier, Robin?"

Zacharias felt the warmth in his belly as it spread out and allowed his body to relax. In that relaxation his pain lessened, and he felt a little stronger, and if this Russian wanted to talk skiing, well, that couldn't hurt much, could it?

"I ski the expert slopes," Robin said with satisfaction. "I started when I was a kid. I think I was five when Dad took me the first time."

"Your father—also a pilot?"

The American shook his head. "No, a lawyer."

"My father is a professor of history at Moscow State University. We have a dacha, and in the winter when I was little, I could ski in the woods. I love the silence. All you can hear is the—how you say, swish? Swish of the skis in the snow. Nothing else. Like a blanket on the earth, no noise, just silence."

"If you go up early, the mountains can be like that. You pick a day right after the snow ends, not much wind."

Kolya smiled. "Like flying, isn't it? Flying in a single-seat aircraft, a fair day with a few white clouds." He leaned forward with a crafty look. "Tell me, do you ever turn your radio off for a few minutes, just to be alone?"

"They let you do that?" Zacharias asked.

Grishanov chuckled, shaking his head. "No, but I do it anyway."

"Good for you," Robin said with a smile of his own, remembering what it was like. He thought of one particular afternoon, flying out of Mountain Home Air Force Base one February day in 1964.

"It is how God must feel, yes? All alone. You can ignore the noise of the engine. For me it just goes away after a few minutes. Is it the same for you?"

"Yeah, if your helmet fits right."

"That is the real reason I fly," Grishanov lied. "All the other rubbish, the paperwork, and the mechanical things, and the lectures, they are the price. To be up there, all alone, just like when I was a boy skiing in the woods—but better. You can see so far on a clear winter day." He handed Zacharias the flask again. "Do you suppose these little savages understand that?"

"Probably not." He wavered for a moment. Well, he'd already had one. Another couldn't hurt, could it? Zacharias took another swallow.

"What I do, Robin, I hold the stick just in my fingertips, like this." He demonstrated with the top of the flask. "I close my eyes for a moment, and when I open them, the world is different. Then I am not part of the world anymore. I am something else—an angel, perhaps," he said with good humor. "Then I possess the sky as I would like to possess a woman, but it is never quite the same. The best feelings are supposed to be alone, I think.''

This guy really understands, doesn't he? He really understands *flying.*
''You a poet or something?''

''I love poetry. I do not have the talent to make it, but that does not prevent me from reading it, and memorizing it, feeling what the poet tells me to feel,'' Grishanov said quietly, actually meaning what he said as he watched the American's eyes lose focus, becoming dreamy. ''We are much alike, my friend.''

''What's the story on Ju-Ju?'' Tucker asked.

''Looks like a ripoff. He got careless. One of yours, eh?'' Charon said.

''Yeah, he moved a lot for us.''

''Who did it?'' They were in the Main Branch of the Enoch Pratt Free Library, hidden in some rows, an ideal place, really. Hard to approach without being spotted, and impossible to bug. Even though a quiet place, there were just too many of the little alcoves.

''No telling, Henry. Ryan and Douglas were there, and it didn't look to me like they had much. Hey, you going to get that worked up over one pusher?''

''You know better than that, but it puts a little dent in things. Never had one of mine wasted before.''

''You know better than *that,* Henry.'' Charon flipped through some pages. ''It's a high-risk business. Somebody wanted a little cash, maybe some drugs, too, maybe break into the business quick? Look for a new pusher selling your stuff, maybe. Hell, as good as they were on the hit, maybe you could reach an understanding with 'em.''

''I have enough dealers. And making peace like that is bad for business. How they do 'em?''

''Very professional. Two in the head each. Douglas was talking like it was a mob hit.''

Tucker turned his head. ''Oh?''

Charon spoke calmly, his back to the man. ''Henry, this wasn't the outfit. Tony isn't going to do anything like that, is he?''

''Probably not.'' *But Eddie might.*

''I need something,'' Charon said next.

''What?''

''A dealer. What did you expect, a tip on the second at Pimlico?''

''Too many of 'em are mine now, remember?'' It had been all right— better than that, really—to use Charon to eliminate the major competition, but as Tucker had consolidated his control on the local trade, he was able to target fewer and fewer independent operators for judicial elimination. That was particularly true of the majors. He had systematically picked out people with whom he had no interest in working, and the few who were left might be useful allies rather than rivals, if he could only find a way to negotiate with them.

"If you want me to be able to protect you, Henry, then I have to be able to control investigations. For me to control the investigations, I have to land some big fish from time to time." Charon put the book back on the shelf. Why did he have to explain things like this to the man?

"When?"

"Beginning of the week, something tasty. I want to take down something that looks nice."

"I'll get back to you." Tucker replaced his book and walked away. Charon spent another few minutes, searching for the right book. He found it, along with the envelope that sat next to it. The police lieutenant didn't bother counting. He knew that the amount would be right.

Greer handled the introductions.

"Mr. Clark, this is General Martin Young, and this is Robert Ritter."

Kelly shook hands with both. The Marine was an aviator, like Maxwell and Podulski, both of whom were absent from this meeting. He hadn't a clue who Ritter was, but he was the one who spoke first.

"Nice analysis. Your language wasn't exactly bureaucratic, but you hit all the high points."

"Sir, it's not really all that hard to figure out. The ground assault ought to be fairly easy. You don't have first-line troops in a place like this, and those you have are looking in, not out. Figure two guys in each tower. The MGs are going to be set to point in, right? It takes a few seconds to move them. You can use the treeline to get close enough for M-79 range." Kelly moved his hands around the diagram. "Here's the barracks, only two doors, and I bet there's not forty guys in there."

"Come in here?" General Young tapped the southwest corner on the compound.

"Yes, sir." For an airedale, the Marine caught on pretty fast. "The trick's getting the initial strike team in close. You'll use weather for that, and this time of the year that shouldn't be real hard. Two gunships, just regular rockets and miniguns to hose these two buildings. Land the evac choppers here. It's all over in under five minutes from when the shooting starts. That's the land phase. I'll leave the rest to the fliers."

"So you say the real key is to get the assault element in close on the ground—"

"No, sir. If you want to do another Song Tay, you can duplicate the whole plan, crash the chopper in the compound, the whole nine yards—but I keep hearing you want it done small."

"Correct," Ritter said. "Has to be small. There's no way we can sell this as a major operation."

"Fewer assets, sir, and you have to use different tactics. The good news is that it's a small objective, not all that many people to get out, not many bad guys to get in the way."

"But no safety factor," General Young said, frowning.

"Not much of one," Kelly agreed. "Twenty-five people. Land them in this valley, they hump over this hill, get into place, do the towers, blow this gate. Then the gunships come in and hose these two buildings while the assault element hits this building here. The snakes orbit while the slicks do the pickup, and we all boogie the hell down the valley."

"Mr. Clark, you're an optimist," Greer observed, reminding Kelly of his cover name at the same time. If General Young found out that Kelly had been a mere chief, they'd never get his support, and Young had already stretched a long way for them, using up his whole year's construction budget to build the mockup in the woods of Quantico.

"It's all stuff I've done before, Admiral."

"Who's going to get the personnel?" Ritter asked.

"That's being taken care of," James Greer assured him.

Ritter sat back, looking at the photos and diagrams. He was putting his career on the line, as was Greer and everyone else. But the alternative to doing something was doing nothing. Doing nothing meant that at least one good man, and perhaps twenty more, would never come home again. That wasn't the real reason, though, Ritter admitted to himself. The real reason was that others had decided that the lives of those men didn't matter, and those others might make the same decision again. That kind of thinking would someday destroy his Agency. You couldn't recruit agents if the word got out that America didn't protect those who worked for her. Keeping faith was more than the right thing. It was also good business.

"Better to get things going before we break the story," he said. "It'll be easier to get a 'go-mission' if we've already got it ready to go. Make it look like a unique opportunity. That's the other big mistake they made with KINGPIN. It was too obviously aimed at getting a hunting license, and that was never in the cards. What we have here is a one-time rescue mission. I can take that to my friends in the NSC. That'll fly, probably, but we have to be ready to go when I do that.''

"Bob, does that mean you're on our side?'' Greer asked.

Ritter took a long moment before answering. "Yes, it does.''

"We need an additional safety factor,'' Young said, looking at the large-scale map, figuring how the helicopters would get in.

"Yes, sir,'' Kelly said. "Somebody has to go in early and eyeball things.'' They still had both photos of Robin Zacharias out, one of an Air Force colonel, standing upright, holding his cap under his arm, chest decorated with silver wings and ribbons, smiling confidently into the camera with his family arrayed around him; and the other of a bowed, bedraggled man, about to be butt-stroked from behind. *Hell,* he thought, *why not one more crusade?*

"I guess that's me.''

17
Complications

A rchie hadn't known much, but it turned out to be enough for Kelly's purposes. All he really needed now was a little more sleep.

Tracking someone in a car, he found, was harder than it appeared on TV, and harder than it had been in New Orleans the one time he'd attempted it. If you followed too closely you ran the risk of being spotted. If you held too far back, you might lose the guy. Traffic complicated everything. Trucks could obstruct your vision. Watching one car half a block away necessarily caused you to ignore cars closer to you, and those, he found, could do the damnedest things. For all that, he blessed Billy's red Roadrunner. It was easy to spot, with its bright color, and even though the driver liked to lay rubber on the street and corner, he still couldn't break all that many traffic laws without attracting the attention of the police, something he didn't want to do any more than Kelly did.

Kelly had sighted the car just after seven in the evening, close to the bar which Archie had identified. Whatever he was like, Kelly thought, he didn't know much about being covert, but the car told him that. The mud was gone, he saw at once. The car looked freshly washed and waxed, and from their previous encounter, he knew Billy to be a man who treasured the thing. It offered a few interesting possibilities which Kelly considered while he trailed him, never closer than half a block, getting a feel for how he moved. It was soon apparent that he stayed clear of the major thoroughfares as much as possible and knew the side streets as a weasel knew his den. That placed Kelly at a disadvantage. Balancing it was the fact that Kelly was driving a car nobody noticed. There were just too many used Beetles on the street for one more to attract notice.

After forty minutes the pattern became clear. The Roadrunner turned right quickly and came to a stop at the end of the block. Kelly weighed his options and kept going, slowly. As he approached he saw a girl get out, carrying a purse. She walked up to an old friend, the Wizard, several blocks from his usual hangout. Kelly didn't see a transfer of any kind—the two walked into a building and remained hidden for a minute or two until the girl came out—but he didn't have to. The event fitted what Pam had told him. Better yet, it identified the Wizard, Kelly told himself, turning left and approaching a red light. Now he knew two things he hadn't known before. In his rearview mirror he saw the Roadrunner cross the street. The girl headed the same way, disappearing from his view as the light changed. Kelly turned right and right again, spotting the Plymouth as it proceeded south with three people inside. He hadn't noticed the man—probably a man—before, crouching in back.

Darkness was falling rapidly, the good time of the day for John Kelly. He continued to follow the Roadrunner, leaving his lights off as long as he dared, and was rewarded by seeing it stop at a brownstone corner house, where all three occupants got out, having made their deliveries for the night to four pushers. He gave them a few minutes, parking his car a few blocks away and coming back on foot to observe, again disguised as a street drunk. The local architecture made it easier. All of the houses on the other side of the street had marble front steps, large, rectangular blocks of stone that made for good cover and concealment. It was just a matter of sitting on the sidewalk and leaning back against them, and he could not be seen from behind. Picking the right set of steps, close but not too close to a working street light, gave him a nice shadow in which to conceal himself, and besides, who paid any attention to a street bum anyway? Kelly adopted the same sort of drunken huddle he'd seen in others, occasionally lifting his bag-covered bottle for a simulated sip while he watched the corner brownstone for several hours.

Blood types O+, O−, and AB−, he remembered from the pathology report. The semen left inside Pam had been matched to those blood types, and he wondered what blood type Billy's was, as he sat there, fifty yards away from the house. The traffic moved on the street. People walked back and forth. Perhaps three people had given him a look, but nothing more than that as he feigned sleep, watching the house from the corner of his eye and listening to every sound for possible danger as the hours passed. A pusher was working the sidewalk perhaps twenty yards or so behind him, and he listened to the man's voice, for the first time hearing how he described his product and negotiated the price, listening also to the different voices of the customers. Kelly had always possessed unusually good hearing—it had saved his life more than once—and this, too, was valuable intelligence information for his mind to catalog and analyze as the hours passed. A stray dog came up to him, sniffing in a curious, friendly way, and Kelly didn't shoo it away. That would have been out of character—had it been a rat things might have been different, he thought—and maintaining his disguise was important.

What sort of neighborhood had this been? Kelly wondered. On his side the dwellings were fairly ordinary brick row-houses. The other side was a little different, the more substantial brownstones perhaps fifty percent wider. Maybe this street had been the border between ordinary working people and the more substantial members of the turn-of-the-century middle class. Maybe that brownstone had been the upscale home of a merchant or a sea captain. Maybe it had resonated to the sound of a piano on the weekends, from a daughter who'd studied at the Peabody Conservatory. But they'd all moved on to places where there was grass, and this house, too, was now vacant, a brown, three-story ghost of a different time. He was surprised at how wide the streets were, perhaps because when they'd been laid out the principal mode of transport had been horse-powered wagons. Kelly shook the thought off. It was not relevant, and his mind had to concentrate on what was.

Four hours, finally, had passed when the three came out again, the men in the lead, the girl following. Shorter than Pam, stockier. Kelly risked himself slightly by lifting his head to watch. He needed to get a good look at Billy, who he assumed to be the driver. Not a very impressive figure, really, perhaps five-nine, slim at one-fifty or so, something shiny at his wrist, a watch or bracelet; he moved with brisk economy—and arrogance. The other was taller and more substantial, but a subordinate, Kelly thought, from the way he moved and the way he followed. The girl, he saw, followed more docilely still, her head down. Her blouse, if that's what it was, wasn't fully buttoned, and she got into the car without raising her head to look around or do anything else that might proclaim interest in the world around her. The girl's movements were slow and uneven, probably from drugs, but that wasn't all of it. There was something else, something Kelly didn't quite catch about her that was disturbing nonetheless . . . a slackness, perhaps. Not laziness in her movement but something else. Kelly blinked hard when he remembered where he'd seen it before. At the *ville,* during PLASTIC FLOWER, the way the villagers had moved to assemble when they'd been summoned. Resigned, automatic motion, like living robots under the control of that major and his troops. They would have moved the same way to their deaths. And so she moved. And so would she.

So it was all true, then, Kelly thought. *They really did use girls as couriers . . . among other things.* The car started as he watched, and Billy's manner with the car matched the name to the driver. The car jerked a few feet to the corner, then turned left, accelerating with the squeal of tires across the intersection and out of Kelly's sight. *Billy, five-nine, slim, watch or bracelet, arrogant.* The positive identification was set in Kelly's brain, along with the face and the hair. He wouldn't forget it. The other male form was recorded as well, the one without a name—just a destiny far more immediate than its owner knew.

Kelly checked the watch in his pocket. One-forty. What had they been doing in there? Then he remembered other things that Pam had said. A little party, probably. That girl, whoever she was, probably also had O+, O−, or AB− fluid in her. But Kelly couldn't save the whole world, and the best way to save her had nothing at all to do with freeing her directly. He relaxed himself, just a little, waiting, because he didn't want his movement to appear to be linked with anything in case someone might have seen him, even be watching him now. There were lights in some of these houses, and so he lingered in his spot for another thirty minutes, enduring his thirst and some minor cramps before rising and shambling off to the corner. He'd been very careful tonight, very careful and very effective, and it was time for the second phase of the night's work. Time to continue his efforts at making a diversion.

Mainly he stuck to alleys, moving slowly, allowing his gait to wander left and right for several blocks in the undulating path of a snake—he smiled—before he went back to the streets, only pausing briefly to put on the pair of rubber surgical gloves. He passed a number of pushers and their lieutenants as time passed, looking for the right one. His path was what is called a quartering search, a series of ninety-degree turns centered actually on where his Volkswagen was parked. He had to be careful, as always, but he was the unknown hunter, and the prey animals had no idea what they were, deeming themselves to be predators themselves. They were entitled to their illusions.

It was almost three when Kelly selected him. A loner, as Kelly had taken to calling them. This one had no lieutenant, perhaps was a new one in this business, just learning the ropes. He wasn't that old, or didn't appear so from forty yards away, as he counted through his roll after the night's enterprise. There was a lump at his right hip, undoubtedly a handgun, but his head was down. He was somewhat alert. On hearing Kelly's approach the head came up and turned, giving him a quick once-over, but the head went back to its task, dismissing the approaching shape and counting the money as the distance closed.

Kelly had troubled himself to go to his boat earlier in the day, using the

Scout because he didn't want anyone at the yard to know that he had a different car, and retrieving something. As he approached Junior—every one had to have an assigned name, however briefly—Kelly shifted the wine bottle from his right hand to his left. The right hand then pulled the cotter pin from the tip of the bang stick that was inside his new bush jacket, held in cloth loops on the left side on the now unbuttoned garment. It was a simple metal rod, eighteen inches long, with a screw-on cylinder at the tip, and the cotter pin dangled from a short length of light chain. Kelly's right hand removed it from the loops, still holding it in place as he closed on Junior.

The pusher's head turned again in annoyance. Probably he had trouble counting, and now he was arranging the bills by denomination. Maybe Kelly's approach had disturbed his concentration, or maybe he was just dumb, which seemed the more likely explanation.

Kelly stumbled, falling to the sidewalk, his head lowered, making himself look all the more harmless. His eyes looked backwards as he rose. He saw no other pedestrians within more than a hundred yards, and the only automobile lights he noted were red, not white, all pointed or heading away. As his head came up, there was no one at all in his view except for Junior, who was finishing up the night's work, ready to go wherever home was for a nightcap or something else.

Ten feet now, and the pusher was ignoring him as he might ignore a stray dog, and Kelly knew the exhilaration that came the moment before it happened, that last moment of excited satisfaction when you just knew it was going to work, the enemy in the kill zone, unsuspecting that his time had come. The moment in which you could feel the blood in your veins, when you alone knew the silence was about to be violated, the wonderful satisfaction of knowing. Kelly's right hand came out a little as he took another step, still not headed all that close to the target, clearly walking past him, not towards him, and the criminal's eyes looked up again, just for a moment to make sure, no fear in his eyes, hardly even annoyance; not moving, of course, because people walked around *him*, not the reverse. Kelly was just an object to him, one of the things that occupied the street, of no more interest than an oil stain on the blacktop.

The Navy called it CPA, Closest Point of Approach, the nearest distance that a straight course took you to another ship or point of land. CPA here was three feet. When he was half a step away, Kelly's right hand pulled the bang stick from under his jacket. Then he pivoted on his left foot and drove off the right while his right arm extended almost as though to deliver a punch, all one hundred ninety-five pounds of his body mass behind the maneuver. The swollen tip of the bang stick struck the pusher just under the sternum, aimed sharply upward. When it did, the combined push of Kelly's arm and the inertial mass of the body pushed the chamber backwards, jamming the primer on the fixed firing pin, and the shotgun shell went off, its crimped green-plastic face actually in contact with Junior's shirt.

The sound was like that of dropping a cardboard box on a wooden floor. *Whump.* Nothing more than that, certainly not like a shot at all, because all the expanding gas from the powder followed the shot column into Junior's body. The light trap load—a low-brass shell with #8 birdshot, like that used for competition shooting, or perhaps an early-season dove hunt—would have only injured a man at more than fifteen yards, but in contact with his chest, it might as easily have been an elephant gun. The brutal power of the shot drove the air from his lungs in a surprisingly loud *whoosh,* forcing Junior's mouth open in a way that surprise might have done. And truly he was surprised. His eyes looked into Kelly's, and Junior was still alive, though his heart was already as destroyed as a toy balloon, and the bottom of his lungs torn to bits. Gratifyingly, there was no exit wound. The upward angle of the strike left all of the energy and shot inside the chest, and the power of the explosion served to keep his body erect for a second—no more than that, but for Junior and Kelly it seemed a moment that lasted for hours. Then the body just fell, straight down, like a collapsing building. There was an odd, deep sigh, from air and gun-gases forced out of the entrance wound by the fall, a foul odor of acrid smoke and blood and other things that stained the air, not unlike the ended life it represented. Junior's eyes were still open, still looking at Kelly, still focusing on his face and trying to say something, his mouth open and quivering until all movement stopped with the question un-asked and -answered. Kelly took the roll from Junior's still-firm hand and kept moving up the street, his eyes and ears searching for danger, and finding none. At the corner he angled to the gutter and swished the tip of the bang stick in some water to remove whatever blood might be there. Then he turned, heading west to his car, still moving slowly and unevenly. Forty minutes later he was home, richer by eight hundred forty dollars and poorer by one shotgun shell.

"And who's this one?" Ryan asked.

"Would you believe, Bandanna?" the uniformed officer answered. He was an experienced patrol officer, white, thirty-two years old. "Deals smack. Well, not anymore."

The eyes were still open, which was not terribly common in murder victims, but this one's death had been a surprise, and a very traumatic one at that, despite which the body was amazingly tidy. There was a three-quarter-inch entrance wound with a jet-black ring around it like a donut, perhaps an eighth of an inch in thickness. That was from powder, and the diameter of the hole was unmistakably that of a 12-gauge shotgun. Beyond the skin was just a hole, like into an empty box. All of the internal organs had either been immolated or simply pulled down by gravity. It was the first time in his life that Emmet Ryan had ever looked *into* a dead body this way, as though it were not a body at all, but a mannequin.

"Cause of death," the coroner observed with early-morning irony, "is the total vaporization of his heart. The only way we'll even be able to identify heart tissue is under a microscope. Steak tartare," the man added, shaking his head.

"An obvious contact wound. The guy must have jammed the muzzle right into him, then triggered it off."

"Jesus, he didn't even cough up any blood," Douglas said. The lack of an exit wound left no blood at all on the sidewalk, and from a distance Bandanna actually looked as though he were asleep—except for the wide and lifeless eyes.

"No diaphragm," the ME explained, pointing to the entrance *hole*. "That's between here and the heart. We'll probably find that the whole respiratory system is wiped out, too. You know, I've never seen anything this clean in my life." And the man had been working this job for sixteen years. "We need *lots* of pictures. This one will find its way into a textbook."

"How experienced was he?" Ryan asked the uniformed officer.

"Long enough to know better."

The detective lieutenant bent down, feeling around the left hip. "Still has a gun here."

"Somebody he knew?" Douglas wondered. "Somebody he let get real close, that's for damned sure."

"A shotgun's kinda hard to conceal. Hell, even a sawed-off is bulky. No warning at all?" Ryan stepped back for the ME to do his work.

"Hands are clean, no signs of a struggle. Whoever did this got real close without alarming our friend at all." Douglas paused. "Goddamn it, a shotgun's *noisy*. Nobody heard anything?"

"Time of death, call it two or three for now," the medical examiner estimated, for again there was no rigor.

"Streets are quiet then," Douglas went on. "And a shotgun makes a shitload of noise."

Ryan looked at the pants pockets. No bulge of a money roll, again. He looked around. There were perhaps fifteen people watching from behind the police line. Street entertainment was where you found it, and the interest on their faces was no less clinical and no more involved than that of the medical examiner.

"The Duo maybe?" Ryan asked nobody in particular.

"No, it wasn't," the ME said at once. "This was a single-barrel weapon. A double would have made a mark left or right of the entrance wound, and the powder distribution would have been different. Shotgun, this close, you only need one. Anyway, a single-barrel weapon."

"Amen," Douglas agreed. "Someone is doing the Lord's work. Three pushers down in a couple of days. Might put Mark Charon out of business if this keeps up."

"Tom," Ryan said, "not today." *One more folder,* he thought. *Another drug-pusher ripoff, done very efficiently—but not the same guy who'd taken Ju-Ju down. Different MO.*

Another shower, another shave, another jog in Chinquapin Park during which he could think. Now he had a place and a face to go along with the car. The mission was on profile, Kelly thought, turning right on Belvedere Avenue to cross the stream before jogging back the other way and completing his third lap. It was a pleasant park. Not much in the way of playground equipment, but that allowed kids to run and play free-form, which a number of them were doing, some under the semiwatchful eyes of a few neighborhood mothers, many with books to go along with the sleeping infants who would soon grow to enjoy the grass and open spaces. There was an undermanned pickup game of baseball. The ball evaded the glove of a nine-year-old and came close to his jogging path. Kelly bent down without breaking stride and tossed the ball to the kid, who caught it this time and yelled a thank-you. A younger child was playing with a Frisbee, not too well, and wandered in Kelly's way, causing a quick avoidance maneuver that occasioned an embarrassed look from her mother, to which Kelly responded with a friendly wave and smile.

This is how it's supposed to be, he told himself. Not very different from his own youth in Indianapolis. Dad's at work. Mom's with the kids because it was hard to be a good mom and have a job, especially when they were little; or at least, those mothers who had to work or chose to work could leave the kids with a trusted friend, sure that the little ones would be safe to play and enjoy their summer vacation in a green and open place, learning to play ball. And yet society had learned to accept the fact that it wasn't this way for many. This area was so different from his area of operations, and the privileges these kids enjoyed ought not to be privileges at all, for how could a child grow to proper adulthood without an environment like this?

Those were dangerous thoughts, Kelly told himself. The logical conclusion was to try to change the whole world, and that was beyond his capacity, he thought, finishing his three-mile run with the usual sweaty and good-tired feel, walking it off to cool down before he drove back to the apartment. The sounds drifted over of laughing children, the squeals, the angry shouts of *cheater!* for some perceived violation of rules not fully understood by either player, and disagreements over who was out or who was "it" in some other game. He got into his car, leaving the sounds and thought behind, because he was cheating, too, wasn't he? He was breaking the rules, important rules that he *did* fully understand, but doing so in pursuit of justice, or what he called justice in his own mind.

Vengeance? Kelly asked himself, crossing a street. *Vigilante* was the next word that came unbidden into his mind. That was a better word, Kelly thought. It came from *vigiles,* a Roman term for those who kept the watch, the *vigilia* during the night in the city streets, mainly watchmen for fire, if he remembered correctly from the Latin classes at St. Ignatius High School, but being Romans they'd probably carried swords, too. He wondered if the streets of Rome had been safe, safer than the streets of this city. Perhaps so—probably so. Roman justice had been . . . stern. Crucifixion would not have been a pleasant way to die, and for some crimes, like the murder of one's father, the penalty prescribed by law was to be bound in a cloth sack along with a dog and a rooster, and some other animal, then to be tossed in the Tiber—not to drown, but to be torn apart while drowning by animals crazed to get out of the sack. Perhaps he was the linear descendant of such times, of a *vigile,* Kelly told himself, keeping watch at night. It made him feel better than to believe that he was breaking the law. And "vigilantes" in American history books were very different from those portrayed in the press. Before the organization of real police departments, private citizens had patrolled the streets and kept the peace in a rough-and-ready way. As he was doing?

Well, no, not really, Kelly admitted to himself, parking the car. So what if it was vengeance? Ten minutes later another garbage bag filled with another set of discarded clothes found its way to the Dumpster, and Kelly enjoyed another shower before making a telephone call.

"Nurses' station, O'Toole."

"Sandy? It's John. Still getting out at three?"

"You do have good timing," she said, allowing herself a private smile at her stand-up desk. "The damn car is broke again." And taxicabs cost too much.

"Want me to look at it?" Kelly asked.

"I wish somebody could fix it."

"I make no promises," she heard him say. "But I come cheap."

"How cheap?" Sandy asked, knowing what the reply would be.

"Permit me to buy you dinner? You can pick the place, even."

"Yes, okay . . . but . . ."

"But it's still too soon for both of us. Yes, ma'am, I know that. Your virtue is not endangered—honest."

She had to laugh. It was just so incongruous that this big man could be so self-effacing. And yet she knew that she could trust him, and she was weary of cooking dinner for one, and being alone and alone and alone. Too soon or not, she needed company sometimes.

"Three-fifteen," she told him, "at the main entrance."

"I'll even wear my patient bracelet."

"Okay." Another laugh, surprising another nurse who passed by the station with a trayful of medications. "Okay, I said yes, didn't I?"

"Yes, ma'am. See you then," Kelly said with a chuckle, hanging up.

Some human contact would be nice, he told himself, heading out the door. First Kelly headed to a shoe store, where he purchased a pair of black high-tops, size eleven. Then he found four more shoe stores, where he did the same, trying not to get the same brand, but he ended up with one duplicate pair even so. The same problem attended the purchase of bush jackets. He could find only two brand names for that type of garment, and ended up getting a pair of duplicates, then to discover that they were exactly the same, different only in the name tag inside the neck. Planned diversity in disguise, he found, was harder than he'd expected it to be, but that didn't lessen the necessity of sticking to his plan. On getting back to his apartment—he was, perversely, thinking of it as "home" though he knew better—he stripped everything of tags and headed for the laundry room, where all the clothes went into the machine on a hot-hot cycle with plenty of Clorox bleach, along with the remaining dark-color clothes he'd picked up at yard sales. He was down to three clothing sets now, and realized he'd have to shop for more.

The thought evoked a frown. More yard sales, which he found tedious, especially now that he'd developed an operational routine. Like most men Kelly hated shopping, now all the more since his adventures were of necessity repetitive. His routine was also tiring him out, both from lack of sleep and the unremitting tension of his activity. None of it was routine, really. Everything was dangerous. Even though he was becoming accustomed to his mission, he would not become inured to the dangers, and the stress was there. That was partly good news in that he wasn't taking anything lightly, but stress could also wear at any man in little, hard-to-perceive ways such as the increased heart rate and blood pressure that resulted in fatigue. He was controlling it with exercise, Kelly thought, though sleep was becoming a problem. All in all it was not unlike working the weeds in 3rd SOG, but he was older now, and the lack of backup, the absence of companions to share the stress and ease the strain in the off-hours, was taking its toll. *Sleep,* he told himself, checking his watch. Kelly switched on the TV set in the bedroom, catching a noon news show.

"Another drug dealer was found dead in west Baltimore today," the reporter announced.

"I know," Kelly said back, fading out for his nap.

"Here's the story," a Marine colonel said at Camp Lejeune, North Carolina, while another was doing much the same thing at exactly the same time at Camp Pendleton, California. "We have a special job. We're selecting volunteers exclusively from Force Recon. We need fifteen people. It's dangerous. It's important. It's something you'll be proud of doing after it's over. The job will last two to three months. That's all I can say."

At Lejeune a collection of perhaps seventy-five men, all combat veterans, all members of The Corps' most exclusive unit, sat in their hard-backed chairs. Recon Marines, they'd all volunteered to become Marines first— there were no draftees here—then done so again to join the elite within the elite. There was a slightly disproportionate representation of minorities, but that was only a matter of interest to sociologists. These men were *Marines* first, last, always, as alike as their green suits could make them. Many bore scars on their bodies, because their job was more dangerous and demanding than that of ordinary infantrymen. They specialized in going out in small groups, to look and learn, or to kill with a very high degree of selectivity. Many of them were qualified snipers, able to place an aimed shot in a particular head at four hundred yards, or a chest at over a thousand, if the target had the good manners to stand still for the second or two needed for the bullet to cover the longer distance. They were the hunters. Few had nightmares from their duties, and none would ever fall victim to delayed-stress syndrome, because they deemed themselves to be predators, not prey, and lions know no such feelings.

But they were also men. More than half had wives and/or children who expected Daddy to come home from time to time; the rest had sweethearts and looked forward to settling down in the indeterminate future. All had served one thirteen-month tour of duty. Many had served two; a handful had actually served three, and none of this last group would volunteer. Some of them might have, perhaps most, had they only known the nature of the mission, because the call of duty was unusually strong in them, but duty takes many forms, and these men judged that they had served as much as any man should for one war. Now their job was to train their juniors, passing along the lessons that had enabled them to return home when others almost as good as they were had not; that was their institutional duty to The Corps, they all thought, as they sat quietly in their chairs and looked at the Colonel on the stage, wondering what *it* was, intensely curious but not curious enough to place their lives at risk again after having done so too often already. A few of them looked furtively left and right, reading the faces of the younger men, knowing from the expressions which ones would linger in the room and place their names in the hat. Many would regret not staying behind, knowing even now that not knowing what it was all about, and probably never finding out, would forever leave a blank spot on their consciences—but against that they weighed the faces of their wives and children and decided no, not this time.

After a few moments the men rose and filed out. Perhaps twenty-five or thirty stayed behind to register their names as volunteers. Their personnel jackets would be collected quickly and evaluated, and fifteen of their number would be selected in a process that appeared random but was not. Some special slots had to be filled with special skills, and in the nature of volunteering, some of the men rejected would actually be better and more proficient warriors than some of those accepted because their personal skills had been made redundant by another volunteer. Such was life in uniform, and the men all accepted it, each with feelings of regret and relief as they returned to their normal duties. By the end of the day, the men who were going were assembled and briefed on departure times and nothing more. A bus would be taking them, they noted. They couldn't be going very far. At least not yet.

Kelly awoke at two and got himself cleaned up. This afternoon's mission demanded that he look civilized, and so he wore a shirt and a tie and a jacket. His hair, still growing back from being shaved, needed a trim, but it was a little late for that. He selected a blue tie for his blue blazer and white shirt and walked out to where the Scout was parked, looking like the executive salesman he'd pretended to be, waving at the apartment manager on the way.

Luck smiled on Kelly. There was an opening on the traffic loop at the hospital's main entrance, and he walked in to see a large statue of Christ in the lobby, perhaps fifteen or twenty feet high, staring down at him with a benign expression more fitting to a hospital than to what Kelly had been doing only twelve hours earlier. He walked around it, his back to the statue's back because he didn't need that sort of question on his conscience—not now.

Sandy O'Toole appeared at three-twelve, and when he saw her come through the oak doors Kelly smiled until he saw the look on her face. A moment later he understood why. A surgeon was right behind her, a short, swarthy man in greens, walking as rapidly as his short legs permitted and talking loudly at her. Kelly hesitated, looking on with curiosity as Sandy stopped and turned, perhaps tired of running away or merely bending to the necessity of the moment. The doctor was of her height, perhaps a little less, speaking so rapidly that Kelly didn't catch all the words while Sandy looked in his eyes with a blank expression.

"The incident report is filed, doctor," she said during a brief pause in his tirade.

"You have no right to do that!" The eyes blazed angrily in his dark, pudgy face, causing Kelly to draw a little closer.

"Yes, I do, doctor. Your medication order was incorrect. I am the team leader, and I am *required* to report medication errors."

"I am *ordering* you to withdraw that report! Nurses do not give orders to doctors!" What followed was language that Kelly didn't like, especially in the presence of God's image. As he watched, the doctor's dark face grew darker, and he leaned into the nurse's space, his voice growing louder. For her part, Sandy didn't flinch, refusing to allow herself to be intimidated, which goaded the doctor further.

"Excuse me." Kelly intruded on the dispute, not too close, just to let everyone know that someone was here, and momentarily drawing an angry look from Sandra O'Toole. "I don't know what you two are arguing about, but if you're a doctor and the lady here is a nurse, maybe you two can disagree in a more professional way," he suggested in a quiet voice.

It was as though the physician hadn't heard a thing. Not since he was sixteen years old had anyone ignored Kelly so blatantly. He drew back, wanting Sandy to handle this herself, but the doctor's voice merely grew louder, switching now to a language he didn't understand, mixing English vituperation with Farsi. Through it all Sandy stood her ground, and Kelly was proud of her, though her face was growing wooden and her impassive mien had to be masking some real fear now. Her impassive resistance only goaded the doctor into raising his hand and then his voice even more. It was when he called her a "fucking cunt," doubtless something learned from a local citizen, that he stopped. The fist that he'd been waving an inch from

Sandy's nose had disappeared, encased, he saw with surprise, in the hairy forepaw of a very large man.

"Excuse me," Kelly said in his gentlest voice. "Is there somebody upstairs who knows how to fix a broken hand?" Kelly had wrapped his fingers around the surgeon's smaller, more delicate hand, and was pressing the fingers inward, just a little.

A security guard came through the door just then, drawn by the noise of the argument. The doctor's eyes went that way at once.

"He won't get here fast enough to help you, doctor. How many bones in the human hand, sir?" Kelly asked.

"Twenty-eight," the doctor replied automatically.

"Want to go for fifty-six?" Kelly tightened his pressure.

The doctor's eyes closed on Kelly's, and the smaller man saw a face whose expression was neither angry nor pleased, merely there, looking at him as though he were an object, whose polite voice was a mocking expression of superiority. Most of all, he knew that the man would do it.

"Apologize to the lady," Kelly said next.

"I do not abase myself before women!" the doctor hissed. A little more pressure on the hand caused his face to change. Only a little additional force, he knew, and things would begin to separate.

"You have very bad manners, sir. You only have a little time to learn better ones." Kelly smiled. "Now," he commanded. "Please."

"I'm sorry, Nurse O'Toole," the man said, without really meaning it, but the humiliation was still a bleeding gash on his character. Kelly released the hand. Then he lifted the doctor's name tag, and read it before staring again into his eyes.

"Doesn't that feel better, Doctor Khofan? Now, you won't ever yell at her again, at least not when she's right and you're wrong, will you? And you won't *ever* threaten her with bodily harm, will you?" Kelly didn't have to explain why that was a bad idea. The doctor was flexing his fingers to work off the pain. "We don't like that here, okay?"

"Yes, okay," the man said, wanting to run away.

Kelly took his hand again, shaking it with a smile, just enough pressure for a reminder. "I'm glad you understand, sir. I think you can go now."

And Dr. Khofan left, walking past the security guard without so much as a look. The guard did give one to Kelly, but let it go at that.

"Did you have to do that?" Sandy asked.

"What do you mean?" Kelly replied, turning his head around.

"I was handling it," she said, now moving to the door.

"Yes, you were. What's the story, anyway?" Kelly asked in a reasonable voice.

"He prescribed the wrong medication, elderly man with a neck problem, he's allergic to the med, and it's on the chart," she said, the words spilling out rapidly as Sandy's stress started bleeding off. "It could have really hurt Mr. Johnston. Not the first time with him, either. Doctor Rosen might get rid of him this time, and he wants to stay here. He likes pushing nurses around, too. We don't like that. But I was handling it!"

"Next time I'll let him break your nose, then." Kelly waved to the door. There wouldn't be a next time; he'd seen that in the little bastard's eyes.

"And then what?" Sandy asked.

"Then he'll stop being a surgeon for a while. Sandy, I don't like seeing people do things like that, okay? I don't like bullies, and I really don't like seeing them push women around."

"You really hurt people like that?"

Kelly opened the door for her. "No, not very often. Mainly they listen to my warnings. Look at it this way, if he hits you, you get hurt and he gets hurt. This way nobody gets hurt except for a few bent feelings, maybe, and nobody ever died from that."

Sandy didn't press the issue. Partly she was annoyed, feeling that she'd stood up well to the doctor, who wasn't all that good a surgeon and was far too careless on his post-op technique. He only did charity patients, and only those with simple problems, but that, she knew, was beside the point. Charity patients were *people,* and *people* merited the best care the profession could provide. He had frightened her. Sandy had been glad of the protection, but somehow felt cheated that she hadn't faced Khofan down herself. Her incident report would probably sink him once and for all, and the nurses on the unit would trade chuckles about it. Nurses in hospitals, like NCOs in any military unit, really ran things, after all, and it was a foolish doctor who crossed them.

But she'd learned something about Kelly this day. The look she'd seen and been unable to forget had not been an illusion. Holding Khofan's right hand, the look on John's face had been—well, no expression at all, not even amusement at his humiliation of the little worm, and that was vaguely frightening to her.

"So what's wrong with your car?" Kelly asked, pulling onto Broadway and heading north.

"If I knew that, it wouldn't be broke."

"Yeah, I guess that makes sense," Kelly allowed with a smile.

He's a changeling, Sandy told herself. He turns things on and off. With Khofan he was like a gangster or something. First he tried to calm things down with a reasonable word, but then he acted like he was going to inflict a permanent injury. Just like that. No emotion at all. Like squashing a bug. But if that's true, what *is* he? Was it temper? No, she told herself, probably not. He's too in control for that. A psychopath? That was a scary thought— but no, that wasn't possible either. Sam and Sarah wouldn't have a friend like that, and they're two very smart people.

What, then?

"Well, I brought my toolbox. I'm pretty good on diesels. Aside from our little friend, how was work?"

"A good day," Sandy said, glad again for the distraction. "We discharged one we were really worried about. Little black girl, three, fell out of her crib. Doctor Rosen did a wonderful job on her. In a month or two you'll never know she was hurt at all."

"Sam's a good troop," Kelly observed. "Not just a good doc—he's got class, too."

"So's Sarah." *Good troop, that's what Tim would have said.*

"Great lady." Kelly nodded, turning left onto North Avenue. "She did a lot for Pam," he said, this time reporting facts without the time for reflection. Then Sandy saw his face change again, freezing in place as though he'd heard the words from another's voice.

The pain won't ever go away, will it? Kelly asked himself. Again he saw her in his mind, and for a brief, cruel second, he told himself—lied, knowing it even as it happened—that she was beside him, sitting there on the right seat. But it wasn't Pam, never would be again. His hands tightened on the plastic of the steering wheel, the knuckles suddenly white as he commanded himself to set it aside. Such thoughts were like minefields. You wandered into them, innocent, expecting nothing, then found out too late that there was danger. *It would be better not to remember,* Kelly thought. *I'd really be better off that way.* But if without memories, good and bad, what was life, and if you forgot those who mattered to you, then what did you become? And if you didn't act on those memories, what value did life have?

Sandy saw it all on his face. A changeling, perhaps, but not always guarded. *You're not a psychopath. You feel pain and they don't—at least not from the death of a friend. What are you, then?*

18
Interference

"**D**o it again," he told her.

Thunk.

"Okay, I know what it is," Kelly said. He leaned over her Plymouth Satellite, jacket and tie off, sleeves rolled up. His hands were already dirty from half an hour's probing.

"Just like that?" Sandy got out of her car, taking the keys with her, which seemed odd, on reflection, since the damned car wouldn't start. *Why not leave them in and let some car thief go nuts?* she wondered.

"I got it down to one thing. It's the solenoid switch."

"What's that?" she asked, standing next to Kelly and looking at the oily-blue mystery that was an automobile engine.

"The little switch you put the key in isn't big enough for all the juice you need to turn the starter, so that switch controls a bigger one here." Kelly pointed with a wrench. "It activates an electromagnet that closes a bigger switch, and that one lets the electricity go to the starter motor. Follow me so far?"

"I think so." Which was almost true. "They told me I needed a new battery."

"I suppose somebody told you that mechanics love to—"

"Jerk women around 'cuz we're so dumb with cars?" Sandy noted with a grimace.

"Something like that. You're going to have to pay me something, though," Kelly told her, rummaging in his toolbox.

"What's that?"

"I'm going to be too dirty to take you out to dinner. We have to eat

here," he said, disappearing under the car, white shirt, worsted slacks and
all. A minute later he was back out, his hands dirty. "Try it now."

Sandy got back in and turned the key. The battery was down a little but
the engine caught almost at once.

"Leave it on to charge things up."

"What was it?"

"Loose wire. All I did was tighten it up some." Kelly looked at his
clothes and grimaced. So did Sandy. "You need to take it into the shop and
have a lock washer put on the nut. Then it shouldn't get loose again."

"You didn't have to—"

"You have to get to work tomorrow, right?" Kelly asked reasonably.
"Where can I wash up?"

Sandy led him into the house and pointed him towards a bathroom.
Kelly got the grime off his hands before rejoining her in the living room.

"Where'd you learn to fix cars?" she asked, handing him a glass of
wine.

"My dad was a shade-tree mechanic. He was a fireman, remember? He
had to learn all that stuff, and he liked it. I learned from him. Thanks." Kelly
toasted her with the glass. He wasn't a wine drinker, but it wasn't bad.

"Was?"

"He died while I was in Vietnam, heart attack on the job. Mom's gone,
too. Liver cancer, when I was in grade school," Kelly explained as evenly
as he could. The pain was distant now. "That was tough. Dad and I were
pretty close. He was a smoker, that's probably what killed him. I was sick
myself at the time, infection from a job I did. I couldn't get home or anything.
So I just stayed over there when I got better."

"I wondered why nobody came to visit you, but I didn't ask," Sandy
said, realizing how alone John Kelly was.

"I have a couple uncles and some cousins, but we don't see each other
much."

It was a little clearer now, Sandy thought. Losing his mother at a young
age, and in a particularly cruel and lingering way. He'd probably always
been a big kid, tough and proud, but helpless to change things. Every woman
in his life had been taken away by force of one kind or another: his mother,
his wife, and his lover. *How much rage he must feel,* she told herself. It
explained so much. When he'd seen Khofan threatening her, it was something he could protect her from. She still thought she could have handled it
herself, but now she understood a little better. It defused her lingering anger,
as did his manner. He didn't get too close to her, didn't undress her with his
eyes—Sandy particularly hated that, though, strangely, she allowed patients

to do it because she felt that it helped to perk them up. He acted like a *friend,* she realized, as one of Tim's fellow officers might have done, mixing familiarity with respect for her identity, seeing her as a person first, a woman after that. Sandra Manning O'Toole found herself liking it. As big and tough as he was, there was nothing to fear from this man. It seemed an odd observation with which to begin a relationship, if that was the thing happening.

Another *thunk* announced the arrival of the evening paper. Kelly got it and scanned the front page before dropping it on the coffee table. A front-page story on this slow summer news day was the discovery of another dead drug pusher. She saw Kelly looking at it, scanning the first couple of paragraphs.

Henry's increasing control of the local drug traffic virtually ensured that the newly dead dealer had been one of his distant minions. He'd known the dead man by his street name and only learned the real one, Lionel Hall, from the news article. They'd never actually met, but Bandanna had been mentioned to him as a clever chap, one worth keeping his eye on. Not clever enough, Tucker thought. The ladder to success in his business was steep, with slippery rungs, the selection process brutally Darwinian, and somehow Lionel Hall had not been equal to the demands of his new profession. A pity, but not a matter of great import. Henry rose from his chair and stretched. He'd slept late, having taken delivery two days earlier of fully fifteen kilograms of "material," as he was starting to call it. The boat trip to and from the packaging point had taken its toll—it was becoming a pain in the ass, Tucker thought, maintaining that elaborate cover. Those thoughts were dangerous, however, and he knew it. This time he'd merely watched his people do the work. And now two more knew more than they'd known before, but he was tired of doing such menial work himself. He had minions for that, little people who knew that they were little and knew they would prosper only so long as they followed orders exactly.

Women were better at that than men. Men had egos that they had to nurture within their own fertile minds, and the smaller the mind the greater the ego. Sooner or later one of his people would rebel, get a little too uppity. The hookers he used were so much more easily cowed, and then there was the fringe benefit of having them around. Tucker smiled.

Doris awoke about five, her head pounding with a barbiturate-induced hangover made worse still by the double shot of whiskey that someone had decided to give her. The pain told her that she would have to live another day, that the mixture of drugs and alcohol hadn't done the job she'd dared to hope for when she'd looked at the glass, hesitated, then gunned it down before the party. What had followed the whiskey and the drugs was only half remembered, and it blended into so many other such nights that she had trouble separating the new from the old.

They were more careful now. Pam had taught them that. She sat up, looking at the handcuff on her ankle, its other end locked in a chain that was in turn fastened to a fitting screwed into the wall. Had she thought about it, she might have tried ripping it out, which a healthy young woman might have accomplished with a few hours of determined effort. But escape was death, a particularly hard and lengthy death, and as much as she desired the escape from a life grown horrid beyond any nightmare, pain still frightened her. She stood, causing the chain to rattle. After a moment or two Rick came in.

"Hey, baby," the young man said with a smile that conveyed amusement rather than affection. He bent down, unlocked the cuffs, and pointed to the bathroom. "Shower. You need it."

"Where did you learn to cook Chinese?" Kelly asked.

"A nurse I worked with last year. Nancy Wu. She's teaching at the University of Virginia now. You like it?"

"You kidding me?" If the shortest distance to any man's heart is his stomach, then one of the better compliments a man can give a woman is to ask for seconds. He held himself to one glass of wine, but attacked the food as quickly as decent table manners allowed.

"It's not that good," Sandy said, blatantly fishing for a compliment.

"It's much better than what I fix for myself, but if you're thinking about writing a cookbook, you need somebody with better taste." He looked up. "I visited Taipei for a week once, and this is almost that good."

"What did you do there?"

"R and R, sort of a vacation from getting shot at." Kelly stopped it there. Not everything he and his friends had done was proper information to convey to a lady. Then he saw that he'd gone too far already.

"That's what Tim and—I already had it planned for us to meet in Hawaii, but—" Her voice stopped again.

Kelly wanted to reach out to her, take her hand across the table, just to comfort her, but he feared it might seem to be an advance.

"I know, Sandy. So what else did you learn to cook?"

"Quite a lot. Nancy stayed with me for a few months and made me do all the cooking. She's a wonderful teacher."

"I believe it." Kelly cleaned his plate. "What's your schedule like?"

"I usually get up quarter after five, leave here just after six. I like to be on the unit half an hour before shift change so I can check the status of the patients and get ready for the new arrivals from the OR. It's a busy unit. What about you?"

"Well, it depends on the job. When I'm shooting—"

"Shooting?" Sandy asked, surprised.

"Explosives. It's my specialty. You spend a lot of time planning it and setting it up. Usually there's a few engineers around to fuss and worry and tell me what not to do. They keep forgetting that it's a hell of a lot easier to blow something up than it is to build it. I do have one trademark, though."

"What's that?"

"On my underwater work, I shoot some blasting caps a few minutes before I do the real shoot." Kelly chuckled. "To scare the fish away."

She was puzzled for a second. "Oh—so they won't get hurt?"

"Right. It's a personal quirk."

It was just one more thing. He'd killed people in war, threatened a surgeon with permanent injury right in front of her and a security guard, but he went out of his way to protect *fish?*

"You're a strange one."

He had the good grace to nod. "I don't kill for the fun of it. I used to hunt, and I gave that up. I fish a little, but not with dynamite. Anyway, I set the caps a good ways from the real job—that's so it won't have any effect on the important part. The noise scares most of them away. Why waste a perfectly good game fish?" Kelly asked.

It was automatic. Doris was somewhat nearsighted, and the marks looked like dirt when her eyes were clouded by the falling water, but they weren't dirt and they didn't wash off. They never disappeared, merely migrating to different places at the vagaries of the men who inflicted them. She rubbed her hands over them, and the pain told her what they were, reminders of the more recent parties, and then the effort to wash herself became futile. She knew she'd never be clean again. The shower was only good for the smell, wasn't it? Even Rick had made that clear enough, and he was the nicest of them, Doris told herself, finding a fading brown mark that he had placed on her, not one so painful as the bruises that Billy seemed to like.

She stepped out to dry off. The shower was the only part of the room that was even vaguely tidy. Nobody ever bothered to clean the sink or toilet, and the mirror was cracked.

"Much better," Rick said, watching. His hand extended to give her a pill.

"Thanks." And so began another day, with a barbiturate to put distance between herself and reality, to make life, if not comfortable, not tolerable, then endurable. Barely. With a little help from her friends, who saw to it that she did endure the reality they made. Doris swallowed the pill with a handful of water, hoping that the effects would come fast. It made things easier, smoothing the sharp edges, putting a distance between herself and her self. It had once been a distance too great to see across, but no longer. She looked at Rick's smiling face as it swept over her.

"You know I love ya, baby," he said, reaching to fondle her.

A wan smile as she felt his hands. "Yes."

"Special party tonight, Dor. Henry's coming over."

Click. Kelly could almost hear the sound as he got out of the Volkswagen, four blocks from the corner brownstone, as he switched trains of thought. Entering the "treeline" was becoming routine. He'd established a comfort level that tonight's dinner had enhanced, his first with another human being in . . . five weeks, six? He returned to the matter at hand.

He settled into a spot on the other side of the cross street, again finding marble steps which generated a shadow, and waited for the Roadrunner to arrive. Every few minutes he'd lift the wine bottle—he had a new one now, with a red street wine instead of the white—for a simulated drink, while his eyes continuously swept left and right, even up and down to check second- and third-floor windows.

Some of the other cars were more familiar now. He spotted the black Karmann-Ghia which had played its part in Pam's death. The driver, he saw, was someone of his age, with a mustache, prowling the street looking for his connection. He wondered what the man's problem was that to assuage it he had to come from wherever his home might be to this place, risking his physical safety so that he might shorten his life with drugs. He was also leaving corruption and destruction in his wake with the money from the illicit traffic. Didn't he care about that? Didn't he see what drug money did to these neighborhoods?

But that was something Kelly was working very hard to ignore as well. There were still real people trying to eke out their lives here. Whether on welfare or subsisting on menial employment, real people lived here, in constant danger, perhaps hoping to escape to someplace where a real life was possible. They ignored the traffickers as best they could, and in their petty righteousness they ignored the street bums like Kelly, but he could not find it in himself to dislike them for that. In such an environment they, like he, had to concentrate on personal survival. Social conscience was a luxury that most people here could scarcely afford. You needed some rudimentary personal security of your own before you could take from its surplus and apply it to those more needy than yourself—and besides, how many were more needy than they were?

There were times when it was just a pleasure to be a man, Henry thought in the bathroom. Doris had her charms. Maria, the spindly, dumb one from Florida. Xantha, the one most drug-dependent, a cause for minor concern, and Roberta, and Paula. None were much beyond twenty, two still in their teens. All the same and all different. He patted some after-shave onto his face. He ought to have a real main-lady of his own, someone glamorous for other men to see and envy. But that was dangerous. To do that invited notice. No, this was just fine. He walked out of the room, refreshed and relaxed. Doris was still there, semiconscious now from the experience and the two-pill reward, looking at him with a smile that he decided was respectful enough. She'd made the proper noises at the proper times, done the things that he'd wanted done without being asked. He could mix his own drinks, after all, and the silence of solitude was one thing, while the silence of a dumb bitch in the house was something else, something tedious. Just to be pleasant he bent down, offering a finger to her lips, which she duly kissed, her eyes unfocused.

"Let her sleep it off," Henry told Billy on the way out.

"Right. I have a pickup tonight anyway," Billy reminded him.

"Oh?" Tucker had forgotten in the heat of the moment. Even Tucker was human.

"Little Man was short a thousand last night. I let it slide. It's the first time, and he said he just goofed on his count. The vig is an extra five yards. His idea."

Tucker nodded. It was the first time ever that Little Man had made that kind of mistake, and he had always shown proper respect, running a nice trade on his piece of sidewalk. "Make sure he knows that one mistake's the house limit."

"Yes, sir." Billy bobbed his head, showing proper respect himself.

"Don't let that word get out, either."

That was the problem. Actually several problems, Tucker thought. First, the street dealers were such small-timers, stupidly greedy, unable to see that a regular approach to their business made for stability, and stability was in everyone's interest. But street pushers were street pushers—criminals, after all—and he'd never change that. Every so often one would die from a rip or a turf fight. Some were even dumb enough to use their own stuff—Henry was as careful as he could be to avoid them, and had been mainly successful. Occasionally one would try to press the limits, claiming to be cash-short just to chisel a few hundred bucks when he had a street trade many times that. Such cases had a single remedy, and Henry had enforced that rule with sufficient frequency and brutality that it hadn't been necessary to repeat it for a long time. Little Man had probably spoken the truth. His willingness to pay the large penalty made it likely, also evidence of the fact that he valued his steady supply, which had grown in recent months as his trade increased. Still, for months to come he would have to be watched carefully.

What most annoyed Tucker was that he had to trouble himself with such trivialities as Little Man's accounting mistake. He knew it was just a case of growing pains, the natural transition process from small-time local supplier to major distributor. He'd have to learn to delegate his authority, letting Billy, for example, handle a higher level of responsibility. Was he ready? Good question, Henry told himself, leaving the building. He handed a ten to the youth who'd watched over his car, still considering the question. Billy had a good instinct for keeping the girls in line. A clever white boy from Kentucky's coal country, no criminal record. Ambitious. Team player. Maybe he was ready for a step up.

Finally, Kelly thought to himself. It was quarter after two when the Roadrunner appeared, after at least an hour's worrying that it might not appear at all. He settled back in the shadows, becoming a little more erect, and turned his head to give the man a good look. Billy and his sidekick. Laughing about something. The other one stumbled on the steps, maybe having had a drink too many or something. More to the point, when he fell there was a flutter of light little twirling rectangles that had to be banknotes.

That's where they count their money? Kelly wondered. *How interesting.* Both men bent down quickly to recover the cash, and Billy cuffed the other man on the shoulder, half playfully, saying something that Kelly couldn't make out from fifty yards off.

The buses passed every forty-five minutes at this time of night, and their route was several blocks away. The police patrol was highly predictable. The neighborhood routine was predictable as well. By eight the regular traffic was gone, and by nine-thirty the local citizens abandoned the streets entirely, barricading themselves behind triple-locked doors, thanking Providence that they had survived another day, already dreading the dangers of the next, and leaving the streets mainly to the illicit traffic. That traffic lingered until about two, Kelly had long since established, and on careful consideration he decided that he knew all that he needed to know. There were still random elements to be considered. There always were, but you could not predict the random, only prepare for it. Alternate evasion routes, constant vigilance, and weapons were the defense against it. Something was always left to chance, and however uncomfortable *that* was, Kelly had to accept it as a part of normal life—not that anything about his mission was normal.

He rose, tiredly, crossing the street and heading to the brownstone with his accustomed drunken gait. The door, he confirmed, wasn't locked. The brass plate behind the knob was askew, he saw as he took a single long look while he passed by. The image fixed itself in his mind, and as he moved he began planning his mission for the following night. He heard Billy's voice again, a laugh filtering through the upstairs windows, an oddly accented sound, decidedly unmusical. A voice he already loathed, and for which he had special plans. For the first time he was close to one of the men who had murdered Pam. Probably two of them. It didn't have the physical effect one might have expected. His body relaxed. He'd do this one right.

Be seeing you, guys, he promised in the silence of his thoughts. This was the next really big step forward, and he couldn't risk blowing it. Kelly headed up the block, his eyes fixed on the two Bobs, a quarter mile away, clearly visible due to their size and the perfectly straight, wide city street.

This was another test—he had to be sure of himself. He headed north, without crossing the street, because if he followed a straight path all the way to them, they might notice and be at least curious about it, if not really alert. His approach had to be invisible, and by changing his angle relative to his targets instead of holding constant, he allowed his stooped body to blend into the background of housefronts and parked cars. Just a head, a small dark shape, nothing dangerous. At one block's distance he crossed the street, taking the opportunity again to scan all four compass points. Turning left, he headed up the sidewalk. It was fully twelve or fifteen feet wide, punctuated by the marble steps, giving useful maneuvering room for his uneven, meandering walk. Kelly stopped, lifting the bag-wrapped bottle to his lips before moving on. Better yet, he thought, another demonstration of his harmless nature. He stopped again to urinate in the gutter.

"Shit!" a voice said, Big or Little, he didn't bother to check. The disgust in the word was enough, the sort of thing that made a man turn away from what he beheld. Besides, Kelly thought, he'd needed the relief.

Both men were larger than he. Big Bob, the dealer, was six-three. Little Bob, the lieutenant, was fully six-five, muscular, but already developing a pot from beer or starchy food. Both were quite formidable enough, Kelly decided, making a quick reevaluation of his tactics. Better to pass by and leave them be?

No.

But he did pass by first. Little Bob was looking across the street. Big Bob was leaning back against the building. Kelly drew an imaginary line between the two and counted three steps before turning left slowly so as not to alert them. He moved his right hand under the new-old bush jacket as he did so. As the right came out, the left covered it, wrapping around the handle of the Colt automatic in a two-hand grip and boxing posture later to be called the Weaver stance. His eyes went down, acquiring the white-painted line on the top of the suppressor as the gun came up. His arms extended full-length without locking the elbows, and the physical maneuver brought the sights in alignment with the first target, quickly but smoothly. The human eye is drawn to motion, particularly at night. Big Bob saw the move, knowing that something untoward was happening, but not sure what. His street-smart instincts made the correct analysis and screamed for action. Too late. *Gun,* he saw, starting to move his hand to a weapon of his own instead of dodging, which might have delayed his death.

Kelly's fingertip depressed the trigger twice, the first as the suppressor covered the target, the second right behind it, as soon as his wrist compensated for the .22's light recoil. Without shifting his feet he swiveled right, a mechanical turn that took the gun in an exact horizontal plane towards Little Bob, who had reacted already, seeing his boss starting to fall and reaching for his own weapon at his hip. Moving, but not fast enough. Kelly's first shot was not a good one, hitting low and doing little damage. But the second entered the temple, caroming off the thicker portions of the skull and racing around inside like a hamster in a cage. Little Bob fell on his face. Kelly lingered only long enough to be sure that both were dead, then turned and moved on.

Six, he thought, heading for the corner, his heart settling down from the rush of adrenaline, putting the gun back in its place next to the knife. It was two fifty-six as Kelly began his evasion drill.

Things hadn't started off well, the Recon Marine thought. The chartered bus had broken down once, and the ''shortcut'' the driver had selected to make up lost time had come to a halt behind a traffic tieup. The bus pulled into Quantico Marine Base just after three, following a jeep to its final destination. The Marines found an isolated barracks building already half occupied by snoring men and picked bunks for themselves so they could get some sleep. Whatever the interesting, exciting, dangerous mission was to be, the startup was just one more day in the Green Machine.

Her name was Virginia Charles, and her night wasn't going well either. A nurse's aide at St. Agnes Hospital, only a few miles out from her neighborhood, her shift had been extended by the late arrival of her relief worker and her own unwillingness to leave her part of the floor unattended. Though she'd worked the same shift at the hospital for eight years, she hadn't known that the bus schedule changed soon after her normal departure time, and having just missed one bus, she'd had to wait what seemed to be forever for the next. Now she was getting off, two hours past her normal bedtime, and having missed "The Tonight Show," which she watched religiously on weekdays. Forty, divorced from a man who had given her two children—one a soldier, thankfully in Germany not Vietnam, and the other still in high school—and little else. On her union job, which was somewhere between menial and professional, she'd managed to do well for both of her sons, ever worrying as mothers do about their companions and their chances.

She was tired when she got off the bus, asking herself again why she hadn't used some of the money she'd saved over the years to get herself a car. But a car demanded insurance, and she had a young son at home who would both increase the cost of driving and give her something else to worry about. Maybe in a few years when that one, too, entered the service, which was his only hope for the college education she wished for him but would never be able to afford on her own.

She walked quickly and alertly, a tense stiffness in her weary legs. How the neighborhood had changed. She'd lived within a three-block radius all her life, and she could remember a lively and *safe* street life with friendly neighbors. She could even remember being able to walk to the New Zion A.M.E. Church without a worry even on a rare Wednesday night off, which she had missed again due to her job. But she consoled herself with two hours of overtime which she could bank, and watched the streets for danger. It was only three blocks, she told herself. She walked fast, smoking a cigarette to stay alert, telling herself to be calm. She'd been mugged—the local term was actually "yoked"—twice in the previous year, both times by drug addicts needing money to support whatever habits they had, and the only good thing to come from that was the object lesson it had given to her sons. Nor had it cost her much in monetary terms. Virginia Charles never carried much more money than carfare and other change to get dinner at the hospital cafeteria. It was the assault on her dignity that hurt, but not quite as badly as her memories of better times in a neighborhood peopled by mostly law-abiding citizens. One more block to go, she told herself, turning a corner.

"Hey, mama, spare a dollar?" a voice said, already behind her. She'd seen the shadow and kept walking past it, not turning, not noticing, ignoring it in the hope that the same courtesy would be extended to her, but that sort of courtesy was becoming rare. She kept moving, lowering her head, telling herself to keep moving, that not too many street toughs would attack a woman from behind. A hand on her shoulder gave the lie to that assumption.

"Give me money, bitch," the voice said next, not even with anger, just a matter-of-fact command in an even tone that defined what the new rules of the street were.

"Ain't got enough to interest you, boy," Virginia Charles said, twisting her shoulders so that she could keep moving, still not looking back, for there was safety in movement. Then she heard a *click*.

"I'll cut you," the voice said, still calm, explaining the hard facts of life to the dumb bitch.

That sound frightened her. She stopped, whispering a quiet prayer, and opened her small purse. She turned slowly, still more angry than frightened. She might have screamed, and only a few years earlier it would have made a difference. Men would have heard it and looked, perhaps come out to chase the assailant away. She could see him now, just a boy, seventeen or eighteen, and his eyes had the lifeless amplification of some sort of drug, that plus the arrogant inhumanity of power. Okay, she thought, pay him off and go home. She reached into the purse and extracted a five-dollar bill.

"Five whole dollar?" The youth smirked. "I need more'n that, bitch. Come on, or I'll cut you."

It was the look in the eyes that really scared her, causing her to lose her composure for the first time, insisting, "It's all I have!"

"More, or you bleed."

Kelly turned the corner, only half a block from his car, just starting to relax. He hadn't heard anything until he made the turn, but there were two people, not twenty feet from the rusting Volkswagen, and a flare of reflected light told him that one was holding a knife.

His first thought was *Shit!* He'd already decided about this sort of thing. He couldn't save the whole world, and he wasn't going to try. Stopping one street crime might be fine for a TV show, but he was after bigger game. What he had not considered was an incident right next to his car.

He stopped cold, looking, and his brain started grinding as quickly as the renewed flood of adrenaline allowed. If anything serious happened here, the police would come right to this place, might be here for hours, and he'd left a couple of dead bodies less than a quarter mile behind him—not even that far, because it wasn't a straight line. This was not good, and he didn't have much time to make a decision. The boy had the woman by the arm, brandishing a knife, with his back to him. Twenty feet was an easy shot even in the dark, but not with a .22 that penetrated too much, and not with someone innocent or at least nonthreatening behind him. She was wearing some sort of uniform, older, maybe forty, Kelly saw, starting to move that way. That's when things changed again. The boy cut the woman's upper arm, the red clear in the glow of the streetlights.

Virginia Charles gasped when the knife sliced her arm, and yanked away, or tried to, dropping the five-dollar bill. The boy's other hand grabbed her throat to control her, and she could see in his eyes that he was deciding the next place for the knife to go. Then she saw movement, a man perhaps fifteen feet away, and in her pain and panic she tried to call for help. It wasn't much of a sound, but enough for the mugger to notice. Her eyes were fixed on something—what?

The youth turned to see a street wino ten feet away. What had been an instant and automatic alarm changed to a lazy smile.

Shit. This was not going well at all. Kelly's head was lowered, his eyes up and looking at the boy, sensing that the event was not really in his control.

"Maybe you got some money, too, pop?" he asked, intoxicated with power, and on a whim he took a step towards the man who had to have more money than this nursey bitch.

Kelly hadn't expected it, and it threw his timing off. He reached for his gun, but the silencer caught on his waistband, and the incoming mugger instinctively took his movement for the threatening act it had to be. He took another step, more quickly, extending his knife hand. There was no time now to bring the gun out. Kelly stopped, backing off a half step and coming up to an erect stance.

For all his aggressiveness, the mugger wasn't very skillful. His first lunge with the knife was clumsy, and he was surprised at how easily the wino batted it aside, then stepped inside its arc. A stiff, straight right to the solar plexus deflated his lungs, winding him but not stopping his movements entirely. The knife hand came back wildly as the mugger started folding up. Kelly grabbed the hand, twisting and extending the arm, then stepping over the body already headed to the pavement. An extended ripping/cracking sound announced the dislocation of the youth's shoulder, and Kelly continued the move, rendering the arm useless.

"Why don't you go home, ma'am" he told Virginia Charles quietly, turning his face away and hoping she hadn't seen it very well. She ought not to have done so, Kelly told himself; he'd moved with lightning speed.

The nurse's aide stooped down to recover the five-dollar bill from the sidewalk and left without a word. Kelly watched sideways, seeing her hold her right hand on the bleeding left arm as she tried not to stagger, probably in shock. He was grateful that she didn't need any help. She would call someone, sure as hell, at least an ambulance, and he really ought to have helped her deal with her wound, but the risks were piling up faster than his ability to deal with them. The would-be mugger was starting to moan now, the pain from his destroyed shoulder penetrating the protective fog of narcotics. And this one had definitely seen his face, close up.

Shit, Kelly told himself. Well, he'd attempted to hurt a woman, and he'd attacked Kelly with a knife, both of them, arguably, failed attempts at murder. Surely this wasn't his first such attempt. He'd picked the wrong game and, tonight, the wrong playground, and mistakes like that had a price. Kelly took the knife from his limp hand and shoved it hard into the base of his skull, leaving it there. Within a minute his Volkswagen was half a block away.

Seven, he told himself, turning east.

Shit.

19
Quantity of Mercy

It was becoming more routine than the morning coffee and Danish at his desk, Lieutenant Ryan told himself. Two pushers down, both with a pair of .22s in the head, but *not* robbed this time. No loose cartridge cases around, no evident sign of a struggle. One with his hand on his pistol grip, but the gun hadn't cleared his hip pocket. For all that, it was unusual. He'd at least seen danger and reacted to it, however ineffectively. Then had come the call from only a few blocks away, and he and Douglas had rolled to that one, leaving junior detectives to deal with this crime scene. The call had identified the new one as interesting.

"Whoa," Douglas said, getting out first. One did not often see a knife sticking in the back of a head, up in the air like a fence post. "They weren't kidding."

The average murder in this part of the city, or any part of any city for that matter, was some sort of domestic argument. People killed other family members, or close friends, over the most trivial disputes. The previous Thanksgiving a father had killed his son over a turkey leg. Ryan's personal "favorite" was a homicide over a crab cake—not so much a matter of amusement as hyperbole. In all such cases the contributing factors were usually alcohol and a bleak life that transformed ordinarily petty disputes into matters of great import. *I didn't mean it* was the phrase most often heard afterwards, followed by some variation of *why didn't he just back off a little?* The sadness of such events was like a slow-acting acid on Ryan's soul. The sameness of those murders was the worst part of all. Human life ought not to end like variations of a single theme. It was too precious for that, a lesson learned in the bocage country of Normandy and the snowy forests around

Bastogne when he'd been a young paratrooper in the 101st Airborne. The typical murderer claimed not to have meant it, and frequently copped to the crime immediately, as remorseful as he or she could be over the loss of a friend or loved one by his or her own hand, and so two lives were often destroyed by the crime. Those were crimes of passion and poor judgment, and that's what murder was, for the most part. But not this one.

"What the hell's the matter with the arm?" he asked the medical examiner. Aside from the needle tracks the arm was twisted around so much that he realized he was looking at the wrong side of it.

"The victim's shoulder appears to be dislocated. Make that wrecked," the ME added after a second's consideration. "We have bruising around the wrist from the force of the grip. Somebody held the arm with two hands and damned near tore the arm off, like taking a branch off a tree."

"Karate move?" Douglas asked.

"Something like that. That sure slowed him down some. You can see the cause of death."

"Lieutenant, over here," a uniformed sergeant called. "This is Virginia Charles, she lives a block over. She reported the crime."

"Are you okay, Miss Charles?" Ryan asked. A fireman-paramedic was checking the bandage she'd placed on her own arm, and her son, a senior at Dunbar High School, stood by her side, looking down at the murder victim without a trace of sympathy. Within four minutes Ryan had a goodly quantity of information.

"A bum, you say?"

"Wino—that's the bottle he dropped." She pointed. Douglas picked it up with the greatest care.

"Can you describe him?" Lieutenant Ryan asked.

The routine was so exactingly normal that they might have been at any Marine base from Lejeune to Okinawa. The daily-dozen exercises followed by a run, everyone in step, the senior NCO calling cadence. They took particular pleasure in passing formations of new second lieutenants in the Basic Officers Course, or even more wimpy examples of officer-wannabes doing their summer school at Quantico. Five miles, passing the five-hundred-yard KD range and various other teaching facilities, all of them named for dead Marines, approaching the FBI Academy, but turning back off the main road then, into the woods towards their training site. The morning routine merely reminded them that they were Marines, and the length of the run made them Recon Marines, for whom Olympic-class fitness was the norm. They were surprised to see a general officer waiting for them. Not to mention a sandbox and a swing set.

"Welcome to Quantico, Marines," Marty Young told them after they'd had a chance to cool down and been told to stand at ease. Off to the side, they saw two naval officers in sparkling undress whites, and a pair of civilians, watching and listening. Eyes narrowed collectively, and the mission was suddenly very interesting indeed.

"Just like looking at the photos," Cas observed quietly, looking around the training site; they knew what the lecture was about. "Why the playground stuff?"

"My idea," Greer said. "Ivan has satellites. The overhead schedules for the next six weeks are posted inside Building A. We don't know how good the cameras are, and so I'm going to assume that they're as good as ours, okay? You show the other guy what he wants to see or you make it easy for him to figure out. Any really harmless place has a parking lot." The drill was already determined. Every day the new arrivals would move the cars around randomly. Around ten every day they would take the mannequins from the cars and distribute them around the playground equipment. At two or three the cars would be moved again and the mannequins rearranged. They suspected correctly that the ritual would acquire a great deal of institutional humor.

"And after it's all over, it becomes a real playground?" Ritter asked, then answered his own question. "Hell, why not? Nice job, James."

"Thank you, Bob."

"It looks small this way," Admiral Maxwell said.

"The dimensions are accurate to within three inches. We cheated," Ritter said. "We have the Soviet manual for building places like this. Your General Young did a nice job."

"No glass in the windows on Building C," Casimir noted.

"Check the photos, Cas," Greer suggested. "There's a shortage of window glass over there. That building just has shutters, here and there. The callback"—he pointed to Building B—"has the bars. Just wood so that they can be removed later. We've just guessed at the inside arrangements, but we've had a few people released from the other side and we've modeled this place on the debriefs. It's not totally made up from thin air."

The Marines were already looking around, having learned a little of the mission. Much of the plan they already knew, and they were thinking about how to apply their lessons of real combat operations to this perverted playground, complete with child mannequins who would watch them train with blue doll eyes. M-79 grenades to blast the guard towers. Willie-pete through the barracks windows. Gunships to hose things down after that . . . the "wives" and "kids" would watch the rehearsal and tell no one.

The site had been carefully selected for its similarity with another place—the Marines hadn't needed to be told that; it had to be so—and a few eyes lingered on a hill half a mile from the site. You could see everything from there. After the welcoming speech, the men divided into predetermined units to draw their weapons. Instead of M16A1 rifles, they had the shorter CAR-15 carbines, shorter, handier, preferred for close work. Grenadiers had standard M-79 grenade launchers, whose sights had been painted with radioactive tritium to glow in the dark, and their bandoleers were heavy with practice rounds because weapons training would start immediately. They'd start in daylight for feel and proficiency, but almost immediately their training would switch exclusively to night work, which the General had left out. It was obvious in any case. This sort of job only happened at night. The men marched to the nearest weapons-firing range to familiarize themselves. Already set up were window frames, six of them. The grenadiers exchanged looks and fired off their first volley. One, to his shame, missed. The other five razzed him at once, after making sure that the white puffs from their training rounds had appeared behind the frames.

"All right, all right, I just have to warm up," the corporal said defensively, then placed five shots through the target in forty seconds. He was slow—it had been a mainly sleepless night.

"How strong do you have to be to do that, I wonder?" Ryan asked.

"Sure as hell isn't Wally Cox," the ME observed. "The knife severed the spinal cord just where it enters the medulla. Death was instantaneous."

"He already had the guy crippled. The shoulder as bad as it looks?" Douglas asked, stepping aside for the photographer to finish up.

"Worse, probably. We'll look at it, but I'll bet you the whole structure is destroyed. You don't repair an injury like this, not all the way. His pitching career was over even before the knife."

White, forty or older, long black hair, short, dirty. Ryan looked at his notes. "Go home, ma'am," he'd told Virginia Charles.

Ma'am.

"Our victim was still alive when she walked away." Douglas came over to his lieutenant. "Then he must have taken his knife away and gave it back. Em, in the past week we've seen four very expert murders and six very dead victims."

"Four different MOs. Two guys tied up, robbed, and executed, .22

revolver, no sign of a struggle. One guy with a shotgun in the guts, also robbed, no chance to defend himself. Two last night just shot, probably a .22 again, but not robbed, not tied up, and they were alerted before they were shot. Those were all pushers. But this guy's just a street hood. Not good enough, Tom.'' But the Lieutenant had started thinking about it. ''Have we ID'd this one yet?''

The uniformed sergeant answered. ''Junkie. He's got a rap sheet, six arrests for robbery, God knows what else.''

''It doesn't fit,'' Ryan said. ''It doesn't fit anything, and if you're talking about a really clever guy, why let somebody see him, why let her leave, why talk to her—hell, why take this guy out at all? What pattern does that fit?'' There was no pattern. Sure, the two pairs of drug dealers had been taken down with a .22, but the small-bore was the most commonly used weapon on the street, and while one pair had been robbed, the other had not; nor had the second pair been shot with the same deadly precision, though each *did* have two head wounds. The other murdered and robbed dealer had been done by a shotgun. ''Look, we have the murder weapon, and we have the wine bottle, and from one or both we'll get prints. Whoever this guy was, he sure as hell wasn't real careful.''

''A wino with a sense of justice, Em?'' Douglas prodded. ''Whoever took this punk down—''

''Yeah, yeah, I know. He wasn't Wally Cox.'' *But who and* what *the hell was he?*

Thank God for gloves, Kelly thought, looking at the bruises on his right hand. He'd let his anger get the better of him, and that wasn't smart! Looking back, reliving the incident, he realized that he'd been faced with a difficult situation. If he'd let the woman get killed or seriously injured, and just gotten into his car and driven off, first, he'd never really have been able to forgive himself, and second, if anyone had seen the car, he'd be a murder suspect. That extended thought evoked a snort of disgust. He *was* a murder suspect now. Well, somebody would be. On coming home, he'd looked in the mirror, wig and all. Whatever that woman had seen, it had not been John Kelly, not with a face shadowed by his heavy beard, smeared with dirt, under a long and filthy wig. His hunched-over posture made him appear several inches shorter than he was. And the light on the street had not been good. And she'd been even more interested in getting away than anything else. Even so. He'd somehow left his wine bottle behind. He remembered dropping it to parry the knife thrust, and then in the heat of the moment he'd not recovered it. *Dumb!* Kelly raged at himself.

What would the police know? The physical description would not be a good one. He'd worn a pair of surgical gloves, and though they allowed him to bruise his hands, they hadn't torn and he hadn't bled. Most important of all, he had never touched the wine bottle with ungloved hands. Of that he was certain because he'd decided from the beginning to be careful about it. The police would know a street bum had killed that punk, but there were lots of street bums, and he only needed one more night. It meant that he'd have to alter his operational pattern even so, and that tonight's mission was more dangerous than it ought to be, but his information on Billy was too good to pass up on, and the little bastard might be smart enough to change his own patterns. What if he used different houses to count his cash or only used one for a few nights? If that was true, any wait beyond a day or two might invalidate his whole reconnaissance effort, forcing him to start again with a new disguise—*if* he could select something equally effective, which was not immediately likely. Kelly told himself that he'd killed six people to get this far—the seventh was a mistake and didn't count . . . except maybe to that lady, whoever she was. He took a deep breath. If he'd watched her get hurt worse, or killed, how would he be able to look in a mirror? He had to tell himself that he'd made the best of a bad situation. Shit happens. It ran the risks up, but the only concern there was failure in the mission, not in danger to himself. It was time to set his thoughts aside. There were other responsibilities as well. Kelly lifted his phone and dialed.

"Greer."

"Clark," Kelly responded. At least that was still amusing.

"You're late," the Admiral told him. The call was supposed to have been before lunch, and Kelly's stomach churned a little at the rebuke. "No harm done, I just got back. We're going to need you soon. It's started."

That's fast, Kelly thought. *Damn.* "Okay, sir."

"I hope you're in shape. Dutch says you are," James Greer said more kindly.

"I think I can hold up, sir."

"Ever been to Quantico?"

"No, Admiral."

"Bring your boat. There's a marina there and it'll give us a place to chat. Sunday morning. Ten sharp. We'll be waiting, Mr. Clark."

"Aye aye." Kelly heard the phone click off.

Sunday morning. He hadn't expected that. It was going too fast, and it made his other mission all the more urgent. Since when had the government ever moved that quickly? Whatever the reason, it affected Kelly directly.

*   *   *

"I hate it, but it's the way we work," Grishanov said.

"You really are that tied to your ground radar?"

"Robin, there is even talk of having the missile firing done by the intercept-control officer from his booth on the ground." The disgust in his voice was manifest.

"But then you're just a driver!" Zacharias announced. "You have to trust your pilots."

I really should have this man speak to the general staff, Grishanov told himself with no small degree of disgust. *They won't listen to me. Perhaps they would listen to him.* His countrymen had vast respect for the ideas and practices of Americans, even as they planned to fight and defeat them.

"It is a combination of factors. The new fighter regiments will be deployed along the Chinese border, you see—"

"What do you mean?"

"You didn't know? We've fought the Chinese three times this year, at the Amur River and farther west."

"Oh, come on!" This was too incredible for the American to believe. "You're allies!"

Grishanov snorted. "Allies? Friends? From the outside, yes, perhaps it looks as though all socialists are the same. My friend, we have battled with the Chinese for centuries. Don't you read history? We supported Chiang over Mao for a long time—we trained his army for him. Mao hates us. We foolishly gave him nuclear reactors, and now they have nuclear arms, and do you suppose their missiles can reach my country or yours? They have Tu-16 bombers—Badgers you call them, yes? Can they reach America?"

Zacharias knew that answer. "No, of course not."

"They can reach Moscow, I promise you, and they carry half-megaton nuclear bombs, and for that reason the MiG-25 regiments are on the Chinese border. Along that axis we have no strategic depth. Robin, we've had real battles with these yellow bastards, division-size engagements! Last winter we crushed their attempt to take an island that belongs to us. They struck first, they killed a battalion of border guards and mutilated the dead—why do that, Robin, because of their red hair or because of their freckles?" Grishanov asked bitterly, quoting verbatim a wrathful article in *Red Star*. This was a very strange turn of events for the Russian. He was speaking the literal truth, and it was harder to convince Zacharias of this than any one of a number of clever lies he might have used. "We are not allies. We've even stopped shipping weapons to this country by train—the Chinese steal the consignments right off the rail carriages!"

"To use against you?"

"Against whom, then, the Indians? Tibet? Robin, these people are *different* from you and me. They don't see the world as we do. They're like the Hitlerites my father fought, they think they are better than other men—how you say?"

"Master race?" the American suggested helpfully.

"That is the word, yes. They believe it. We're animals to them, useful animals, yes, but they hate us, and they want what we have. They want our oil and our timber and our land."

"How come I've never been briefed on this?" Zacharias demanded.

"Shit," the Russian answered. "Is it any different in your country? When France pulled out of NATO, when they told your people to take your bases out, do you think any of us were told about it beforehand? I had a staff job then in Germany, and nobody troubled himself to tell me that anything was happening. Robin, the way you look to us is the same as how we look to you, a great colossus, but the internal politics in your country are as much a mystery to me as mine are to you. It can all be very confusing, but I tell you this, my friend, my new MiG regiment will be based between China and Moscow. I can bring a map and show you."

Zacharias leaned back against the wall, wincing again with the recurring pain from his back. It was just too much to believe.

"It hurts still, Robin?"

"Yeah."

"Here, my friend." Grishanov handed over his flask, and this time it was accepted without resistance. He watched Zacharias take a long pull before handing it back.

"So just how good is this new one?"

"The MiG-25? It's a *rocket*," Grishanov told him enthusiastically. "It probably turns even worse than your Thud, but for straight-line speed, you have no fighter close to it. Four missiles, no gun. The radar is the most powerful ever made for a fighter, and it cannot be jammed."

"Short range?" Zacharias asked.

"About forty kilometers." The Russian nodded. "We give away range for reliability. We tried to get both but failed."

"Hard for us, too," the American acknowledged with a grunt.

"You know, I do not expect a war between my country and yours. Truly I do not. We have little that you might wish to take away. What we have—resources, space, land—all these things you have. But the Chinese," he said, "they need these things, and they share a border with us. And we gave them the weapons that they will use against us, and there are so *many* of them! Little, evil people, like these here, but so many more."

"So what are you going to do about it?"

Grishanov shrugged. "I will command my regiment. I will plan to defend the Motherland against a nuclear attack from China. I just haven't decided how yet."

"It's not easy. It helps if you have space and time to play with, and the right people to play against."

"We have bomber people, but nothing like yours. You know, even without resistance, I doubt we could place as many as twenty bombers over your country. They're all based two thousand kilometers from where I will be. You know what that means? Nobody even to train against."

"You mean a red team?"

"We would call it a blue team, Robin. I hope you understand." Grishanov chuckled, then turned serious again. "But, yes. It will all be theoretical, or some fighters will pretend to be bombers, but their endurance is too short for a proper exercise."

"This is all on the level?"

"Robin, I will not ask you to trust me. That is too much. You know that and so do I. Ask yourself, do you really think your country will ever make war on my country?"

"Probably not," Zacharias admitted.

"Have I asked you about your war plans? Yes, certainly, they are most interesting theoretical exercises and I would probably find them fascinating war games, but have I asked about them?" His voice was that of a patient teacher.

"No, you haven't, Kolya, that's true."

"Robin, I am not worried about B-52s. I am worried about Chinese bombers. That is the war my country is preparing for." He looked down at the concrete floor, puffing on a cigarette and going on softly. "I remember when I was eleven. The Germans were within a hundred kilometers of Moscow. My father joined his transport regiment—they made it up from university teachers. Half of them never came back. My mother and I evacuated the city, east to some little village whose name I can't remember—it was so confusing then, so dark all the time—worrying about my father, a professor of history, driving a truck. We lost twenty million citizens to the Germans, Robin. Twenty million. People I knew. The fathers of friends—my wife's father died in the war. Two of my uncles died. When I went through the snow with my mother, I promised myself that someday I would defend my country, too, and so I am a fighter pilot. I do not invade. I do not attack. I defend. Do you understand this thing I tell you, Robin? My job is to protect my country so that other little boys will not have to run away from home in the middle of winter. Some of my classmates died, it was so cold. That is why I defend my country. The Germans wanted what we had, and now the Chinese want it, too.'' He waved towards the door of the cell. ''People like . . . like *that.*''

Even before Zacharias spoke, Kolya knew he had him. Months of work for this moment, Grishanov thought, like seducing a virgin, but much sadder. This man would never see his home again. The Vietnamese had every intention of killing these men when their utility ended. It was such a colossal waste of talent, and his antipathy to his supposed allies was every bit as real as he feigned it to be—it was no longer pretense. From the first moment he'd arrived in Hanoi, seeing first-hand their arrogant superiority, and their incredible cruelty—and their stupidity. He had just achieved more with kind words and not even a liter of vodka than what they and their torturers had failed to do with years of mindless venom. Instead of inflicting pain, he had shared it. Instead of abusing the man beside him, he had given kindness, respecting his virtues, assuaging his injuries as best he could, protecting him from more, and bitterly regretting that he'd necessarily been the agent of the most recent of them.

There was a downside, however. To achieve this breakthrough, he'd opened his soul, told true stories, dredged up his own childhood nightmares, reexamined his true reason for joining the profession he loved. Only possible, only thinkable, because he'd known that the man sitting next to him was doomed to a lonely, unknown death—already dead to his family and his country—and an unattended grave. This man was no fascist Hitlerite. He was an enemy, but a straightforward one who had probably done his utmost to spare harm to noncombatants because he, too, had a family. There was in him no illusion of racial superiority—not even hatred for the North Vietnamese, and that was the most remarkable thing of all, for he, Grishanov, was learning to hate them. Zacharias didn't deserve to die, Grishanov told himself, recognizing the greatest irony of all.

Kolya Grishanov and Robin Zacharias were now friends.

''How does this grab you?'' Douglas asked, setting it on Ryan's desk. The wine bottle was in a clear plastic bag, and the smooth, clear surface was uniformly coated with a fine yellow dust.

''No prints?'' Emmet looked it over in considerable surprise.

''Not even a smudge, Em. Zilch.'' The knife came down next. It was a simple switchblade, also dusted and bagged.

''Smudges here.''

''One partial thumbprint, matched with the victim. Nothing else we can use, but smudges, uniform smudges, the prints department says. Either he stabbed himself in the back of the neck or our suspect was wearing gloves.''

It was awfully warm this time of the year to wear gloves. Emmet Ryan leaned back, staring at the evidence items on his desk, then at Tom Douglas, sitting beside them. ''Okay, Tom, go on.''

''We've had four murder scenes, a total of six victims. No evidence left behind. Five of the victims—three incidents—are pushers, two different MOs. But in every case, no witnesses, roughly the same time of day, all within a five-block radius.''

''Craftsmanship.'' Lieutenant Ryan nodded. He closed his eyes, first mentally viewing the different crime scenes, then correlating the data. Rob, not rob, change MO. But the last one did have a witness. *Go home, ma'am.* Why was he polite? Ryan shook his head. ''Real life isn't Agatha Christie, Tom.''

''Our young lad, today, Em. Tell me about the method our friend used to dispatch him?''

''Knife there . . . I haven't seen anything like that in a long time. Strong son of a bitch. I did see one . . . back in '58 or '59.'' Ryan paused, collecting his thoughts. ''A plumber, I think, big, tough guy, found his wife in bed with somebody. He let the man leave, then he took a chisel, held her head up—''

''You have to be really pissed off to do it the hard way. Anger, right? Why do it that way?'' Douglas asked. ''You can cut a throat a lot easier, and the victim is just as dead.''

''A lot messier, too. Noisy . . .'' Ryan's voice trailed off as he thought it through. It was not appreciated that people with their throats cut made a great deal of noise. If you opened the windpipe there could be the most awful gurgling sound, and if not, people screamed their way to death. Then there was the blood, so much of it, flying like water from a cut hose, getting on your hands and clothes.

On the other hand, if you wanted to kill someone in a hurry, like turning off a light switch, and if you were strong and had him crippled already, the base of the skull, where the spinal cord joined the brain, was just the perfect spot: quick, quiet, and relatively clean.

''The two pushers were a couple blocks away, time of death almost identical. Our friend does them, walks over this way, turns a corner, and sees Mrs. Charles being hassled.''

Lieutenant Ryan shook his head. ''Why not just keep going? Cross the street, that's the smart move. Why get involved? A killer with morals?'' Ryan asked. That was where the theory broke down. ''And if the same guy is wasting pushers, what's the motive? Except for the two last night, it looks like robbery. Maybe with those two something spooked him off before he could collect the money and the drugs. A car going down the street, some noise? If we're dealing with a robber, then it doesn't connect with Mrs. Charles and her friend. Tom, it's just speculation.''

"Four separate incidents, no physical evidence, a guy wearing gloves—a street wino wearing gloves!''

"Not enough, Tom.''

"I'm going to have Western District start shaking them down anyway.''

Ryan nodded. That was fair enough.

It was midnight when he left his apartment. The area was so agreeably quiet on a weekday night. The old apartment complex was peopled with residents who minded their own business. Kelly had not so much as shaken a hand since the manager's. A few friendly nods, that was all. There were no children in the complex, just middle-aged people, almost all married couples sprinkled with a few widowed singles. Mainly white-collar workers, a surprising number of whom rode the bus to work downtown, watched TV at night, heading to bed around ten or eleven. Kelly moved out quietly, driving the VW down Loch Raven Boulevard, past churches and other apartment complexes, past the city's sports stadium as the neighborhoods evolved downward from middle- to working-class, and from working-class to subsistence, passing darkened office buildings downtown in his continuing routine. But tonight there was a difference.

Tonight would be his first major payoff. That meant risk, but it always did, Kelly told himself, flexing his hands on the plastic steering wheel. He didn't like the surgical gloves. The rubber held heat in, and though the sweat didn't affect his grip, the discomfort was annoying. The alternative was not acceptable, however, and he remembered not liking a lot of the things he'd done in Vietnam, like the leeches, a thought that generated a few chills. They were even worse than rats. At least rats didn't suck your blood.

Kelly took his time, driving around his objective almost randomly while he sized things up. It paid off. He saw a pair of police officers talking to a street bum, one of them close, the other two steps back, seemingly casual, but the distance between the two cops told him what he needed to know. One was covering the other. They saw the wino as someone potentially threatening.

Looking for you, Johnnie-boy, he told himself, turning the wheel and changing streets.

But the cops wouldn't change their whole operating routine, would they? Looking at and talking to winos would be an additional duty for the next few nights. There were other things that had higher priority: answering calls for holdup alarms in liquor stores, responding to family disputes, even traffic violations. No, hassling drunks would just be one more burden on men already overworked. It would be something with which to spice up their normal patrol patterns, and Kelly had troubled himself to learn what those patterns were. The additional danger was therefore somewhat predictable, and Kelly reasoned that he'd had his supply of bad luck for this mission. Just one more time and he'd switch patterns. To what he didn't know, but if things went right, what he should soon learn would provide the necessary information.

Thank you, he said to destiny, a block away from the corner brownstone. The Roadrunner was right there, and it was early still, a collection night; the girl wouldn't be there. He drove past it, continuing up the next block before turning right, then another block, and right again. He saw a police cruiser and checked the clock on the car. It was within five minutes of its normal schedule, and this one was a solo car. There wouldn't be another pass for about two hours, Kelly told himself, making a final right turn and heading towards the brownstone. He parked as close to it as he dared, then got out and walked away from the target house, heading back to the next block before dropping into his disguise.

There were two pushers on this block, both lone operators. They looked a little tense. Perhaps the word was getting out, Kelly thought with a suppressed smile. Some of their brethren were disappearing, and that had to be cause for concern. He kept well clear of both as he covered the block, inwardly amused that neither knew how close Death had passed them. How tenuous their lives were, and yet they didn't know. But that was a distraction, he told himself, turning yet again and heading to the objective. He paused at the corner, looking around. It was after one in the morning now, and things were settling down into the accustomed boredom that comes at the end of any working day, even the illegal kind. Activity on the street was diminishing, just as expected from all the reconnaissance he had done. There was nothing untoward on this street, and Kelly headed south past the rows of brownstones on one side of the street and brick row-houses on the other. It required all of his concentration to maintain his uneven, harmless gait. One of those who had hurt Pam was now within a hundred yards. Probably two of them. Kelly allowed his mind to see her face again, to hear her voice, to feel the curves of her body. He allowed his face to become a frozen mask of stone and his hands to ball into tight fists as his legs shambled down the wide sidewalk, but only for a few seconds. Then he cleared his mind and took five deep, slow breaths.

"Tactical," he murmured to himself, slowing his pace and watching the corner house, now only thirty yards away. Kelly took in a mouthful of wine and let it dribble down on his shirt again. *Snake to Chicago, objective in sight. Moving in now.*

The sentry, if that's what he was, betrayed himself. The streetlights revealed puffs of cigarette smoke coming out the door, telling Kelly exactly where the first target was. He switched the wine bottle to his left hand and flexed his right one, turning his wrist around to make sure his muscles were loose and ready. Approaching the wide steps, he slumped against them, coughing. Then he walked up towards the door, which he knew to be ajar, and fell against it. Kelly tumbled to the floor, finding himself at the feet of the man whom he'd seen accompany Billy. Along the way, the wine bottle broke, and Kelly ignored the man, whimpering over the broken glass and spreading stain of cheap California red.

"That's tough luck, partner," a voice said. It was surprisingly gentle. "You best move along now."

Kelly just continued his whimpering, down on all fours, weaving on them. He coughed a little more, turning his head to see the sentry's legs and shoes, confirming his identification.

"Come on, pop." Strong hands reached down. Both hands, lifting him. Kelly allowed his own arms to dangle, one going behind as the man started to turn him towards the door. He staggered, turning yet more, and now the sentry was supporting him almost fully. Weeks of training and preparation and careful reconnaissance came together in a single instant.

Kelly's left hand slapped against his face. The right drove the Ka-Bar through the ribs, and so alert were his senses that his fingertips could feel the heart, trying to beat, but only destroying itself on the razor-sharp, double-edged blade of the fighting knife. Kelly twisted the blade, leaving it in as the body shuddered. The dark eyes were wide and shocked, and the knees already buckling. Kelly let him down slowly, quietly, still holding the knife, but he had to allow himself a bit of satisfaction this time. He'd worked too hard for this moment to turn his emotions off completely.

"Remember Pam?" he whispered to the dying body in his hands, and for the question he received his satisfaction. There was recognition through the pain before the eyes rolled back.

Snake.

Kelly waited, counting to sixty before he withdrew the knife, which he wiped off on the victim's shirt. It was a good knife, and it didn't deserve to be stained with that kind of blood.

Kelly rested himself for a moment, breathing deeply. He'd gotten the right target, the subordinate. The principal objective was upstairs. Everything was going according to plan. He allowed himself exactly one minute to calm down and collect himself.

The stairs were creaky. Kelly attenuated that by keeping close to the wall, minimizing the displacement of the wooden treads, moving very slowly, eyes locked upwards because there was nothing below to concern him now. He had already replaced the knife in its scabbard. His .45/.22 was in his right hand now, suppressor screwed on, held low in his right hand as the left traced the cracked plaster wall.

Halfway up he started hearing sounds other than that of the blood coursing through his arteries. A slap, a whimper, a whine. Distant, animal sounds, followed by a cruel chuckle, barely audible even as he reached the landing and turned left towards their source. Breathing next, heavy, rapid and low.

Oh . . . shit! But he couldn't stop now.

"Please . . ." A despairing whisper that caused Kelly's knuckles to turn white around the pistol grip. He moved along the upstairs corridor slowly, again rubbing up against the wall. There was light coming from the master bedroom, only the illumination from streetlights through dirty windows, but with his eyes adjusted to darkness, he could see shadows on one wall.

"What's the matter, Dor?" a male voice asked as Kelly reached the doorframe. Very slowly he moved his head around the vertical barrier of painted wood.

There was a mattress in the room, and on the mattress a woman, kneeling, head down while a hand roughly squeezed her breast, then shook it. Kelly watched her mouth open in silent pain, remembering the photo that the detective had shown him. *You did that to Pam, too, didn't you . . . you little fuck!* Liquid dripped from the girl's face, and the face staring down at her was smiling when Kelly took a step into the room.

His voice was light, relaxed, almost comical. "This looks like fun. Can I play, too?"

Billy turned, looking at the shadow that had just spoken, and saw an extended arm with a big automatic. The face turned back to a pile of clothing and a carry bag of some sort. The rest of him was naked, and his left hand held a tool of some sort, but not a knife or a gun. Those tools were elsewhere, ten feet away, and his eyes could not bring them closer.

"Don't even think it, Billy," Kelly said in a conversational tone.

"Who the fuck—"

"On your face, spread-eagle, or I'll shoot that little dick of yours right off." Kelly altered his aim. It was amazing how much importance men placed on that organ, how easily a threat to it intimidated. Not even a serious threat, what with its size. The brain was much larger and easier to hit. "Down! Now!"

Billy did what he was told. Kelly pushed the girl back on the mattress and reached in his belt for the electrical wire. In a few seconds the hands were securely wrapped and knotted. The left hand still held a pair of pliers, which Kelly took and used to tighten the wire yet more, drawing a gasp from Billy.

Pliers?

Jesus.

The girl was staring at his face, eyes wide, breath heavy, but her movements were slow and her head was tilted. She was drugged to some extent. And she had seen his face, was looking at it now, memorizing it.

Why do you have to be here? This is out of the pattern. You're a complication. I ought to . . . ought to . . .

If you do that, John, then what the fuck are you?

Oh, shit!

Kelly's hands started shaking then. This was real danger. If he let her live, then someone would know who he was—a description, enough to start a proper manhunt, and that would—might—prevent him from accomplishing his goal. But the greater danger was to his soul. If he killed her, that was lost forever. Of that he was certain. Kelly closed his eyes and shook his head. Everything was supposed to have gone so smoothly.

Shit happens, Johnnie-boy.

"Get dressed," he told her, tossing some stuff in her direction. "Do it now, be quiet, and stay there."

"Who are you?" Billy asked, giving Kelly an outlet for his rage. The distributor felt something cold and round at the back of his head.

"You even breathe loud, and your brains go on this floor, got it?" The head nodded by way of an answer.

Now what the hell do I do? Kelly demanded of himself. He looked over at the girl, struggling to put panties on. The light caught her breasts and Kelly's stomach revolted at the marks he saw there. "Hurry up," he told her.

Damn damn damn. Kelly checked the wire on Billy's wrists and decided to do another loop at the elbows, hurting him badly, straining the shoulders, but ensuring that he wouldn't be doing any resisting. To make things worse, he lifted Billy by the arms to a standing position, which evoked a scream.

"Hurt a little, does it?" Kelly asked. Then he applied a gag and turned him to the door. "Walk." To the girl: "You, too."

Kelly conducted them down the steps. There was some broken glass, and Billy's feet danced around it, sustaining cuts. What surprised Kelly was the girl's reaction to the body at the bottom.

"Rick!" she gasped, then stooped down to touch the body.

It had a name, Kelly thought, lifting the girl. "Out the back."

He stopped them at the kitchen, leaving them alone for an instant and looking out the back door. He could see his car, and there was no activity in his view. There was danger in what came next, but danger had again become his companion. Kelly led them out. The girl was looking at Billy, and he at her, motioning with his eyes. Kelly was dumbfounded to see that she was reacting to his silent entreaties. He took her arm and moved her aside.

"Don't worry about him, miss." He pointed her to the car, maneuvering Billy by the upper arm.

A distant voice told him that if she tried to help Billy, then he would have an excuse to—

No, goddamn it!

Kelly unlocked the car, forcing Billy in, then the girl into the front seat, before moving fast to the left-side door. Before starting the car he leaned over the seat and wired up Billy's ankles and knees.

"Who are you?" the girl asked as the car started moving.

"A friend," Kelly said calmly. "I am not going to hurt you. If I wanted to do that, I could have left you with Rick, okay?"

Her reply was slow and uneven, but for all that, still amazing to Kelly. "Why did you have to kill him? He was nice to me."

What the hell? Kelly thought, looking over at her. Her face was scraped, her hair a mess. He turned his eyes back to the street. A police cruiser went past on a reciprocal heading, and despite a brief moment of panic on Kelly's part, it just kept going, disappearing as he turned north.

Think fast, boy.

Kelly could have done many things, but only one alternative was realistic. *Realistic?* he asked himself. *Oh, sure.*

One does not expect to hear doorbells at a quarter to three in the morning. Sandy first thought she had dreamed it, but her eyes had opened, and in the way of the mind, the sound played back to her as though she had actually awakened a second earlier. Even so, she must have dreamed it, the nurse told herself, shaking her head. She'd just started to close her eyes again when it repeated. Sandy rose, slipped on a robe, and went downstairs, too disoriented to be frightened. There was a shape on the porch. She turned on the lights as she opened the door.

"Turn that fucking light off!" A rasping voice that was nonetheless familiar. The command it carried caused her to flip the switch without so much as a thought.

"What are you doing here?" There was a girl at his side, looking thoroughly horrible.

"Call in sick. You're not going to work today. You're going to take care of her. Her name is Doris," Kelly said, speaking in the low commanding tone of a surgeon in the middle of a complex procedure.

"Wait a minute!" Sandy stood erect and her mind started racing. Kelly was wearing a woman's wig—well, too dirty for that. He was unshaven, had on awful clothes, but his eyes were burning with something. Rage was part of it, a fury at something, and the man's strong hands were shaking at his side.

"Remember about Pam?" he asked urgently.

"Well, yes, but—"

"This girl's in the same spot. I can't help her. Not now. I have to do something else."

"What are you doing, John?" Sandy asked, a different sort of urgency in her voice. And then, somehow, it was very clear. The TV news reports she'd been watching over dinner on the black-and-white set in the kitchen, the look she'd seen in his eyes in the hospital; the look she saw now, so close to the other, but different, the desperate compassion and the trust it demanded of her.

"Somebody's been beating the shit out of her, Sandy. She needs help."

"John," she whispered. "John . . . you're putting your life in my hands . . ."

Kelly actually laughed, after a fashion, a bleak snort that went beyond irony. "Yeah, well, you did okay the first time, didn't you?" He pushed Doris in the door and walked away, off to a car, without looking back.

"I'm going to be sick," the girl, Doris, said. Sandy hustled her to the first-floor bathroom and got her to the toilet in time. The young woman knelt there for a minute or two, emptying her belly into the white porcelain bowl. After another minute or so, she looked up. In the glare of incandescent lights off the white-tile walls, Sandra O'Toole saw the face of hell.

20

Depressurization

I t was after four when Kelly pulled into the marina. He backed the Scout to the transom of his boat and got out to open the cargo hatch after checking the darkness for spectators, of which, thankfully, there were none.

"Hop," he told Billy, and that he did. Kelly pushed him aboard, then directed him into the main salon. Once there, Kelly got some shackles, regular marine hardware, and fastened Billy's wrists to a deck fitting. Ten minutes more and he had cast off, heading out to the Bay, and finally Kelly allowed himself to relax. With the boat on autopilot, he loosed the wires on Billy's arms and legs.

Kelly was tired. Moving Billy from the back of the VW into the Scout had been harder than he'd expected, and at that he'd been lucky to miss the newspaper distributor, dumping his bundles on street corners for the paper boy to unwrap and deliver before six. He settled back into the control chair, drinking some coffee and stretching by way of reward to his body for its efforts.

Kelly had the lights turned way down so that he could navigate without being blinded by the internal glow of the salon. Off to port were a half-dozen cargo ships tied up at Dundalk Marine Terminal, but very little in his sight was moving. There was always something relaxing about the water at a time like this, the winds were calm, and the surface a gently undulating mirror that danced with lights on the shore. Red and green lights from buoys blinked on and off while telling ships to stay out of dangerous shallows. *Springer* passed by Fort Carroll, a low octagon of gray stone, built by First Lieutenant Robert E. Lee, U.S. Army Corps of Engineers; it had held twelve-inch rifles as recently as sixty years before. The orange fires of the Bethlehem Steel

Sparrow's Point Works glowed to the north. Tugboats were starting to move out of their basins to help various ships out of their berths, or to help bring new ones alongside, and their diesels growled across the flat surface in a distant, friendly way. Somehow that noise only emphasized the pre-dawn peace. The quiet was overwhelmingly comforting, just as things should be in preparation for the start of a new day.

"Who the fuck are you?" Billy asked, relieved of his gag and unable to bear the silence. His arms were still behind him, but his legs were free, and he sat up on the deck of the salon.

Kelly sipped his coffee, allowing his tired arms to relax and ignoring the noise behind him.

"I said, who the fuck are you!" Billy called more loudly.

It was going to be a warm one. The sky was clear. There were plenty of stars visible, with not even a hint of gathering clouds. No "Red Sky at Morning" to cause Kelly concern, but the outside temperature had dipped only to seventy-seven, and that boded ill for the coming day, with the hot August sun to beat down on things.

"Look, asshole, I want to know who the fuck you are!"

Kelly shifted a little in the wide control chair, taking another sip of his coffee. His compass course was one-two-one, keeping to the southern edge of the shipping channel, as was his custom. A brightly lit tug was coming in, probably from Norfolk, towing a pair of barges, but it was too dark to see what sort of cargo they bore. Kelly checked the lights and saw that they were properly displayed. That would please the Coast Guard, which wasn't always happy with the way the local tugs operated. Kelly wondered what sort of life it was, moving barges up and down the Bay. Had to be awfully dull doing the same thing, day in and day out, back and forth, north and south, at a steady six knots, seeing the same things all the time. It paid well, of course. A master and a mate, and an engineer, and a cook—they had to have a cook. Maybe a deckhand or two. Kelly wasn't sure about that. All taking down union wages, which were pretty decent.

"Hey, okay. I don't know what the problem is, but we can talk about it, okay?"

The maneuvering in close was probably pretty tricky, though. Especially in any kind of wind, the barges had to be unhandy things to bring alongside. But not today. Today it wouldn't be windy. Just hotter than hell. Kelly started his turn south as he passed Bodkin Point, and he could see the red lights blinking on the towers of the Bay Bridge at Annapolis. The first glow of dawn was decorating the eastern horizon. It was kind of sad, really. The last two hours before sunrise were the best time of the day, but some-

thing that few ever bothered to appreciate. Just one more case of people who
never knew what was going on around them. Kelly thought he saw something, but the glass windshield interfered with visibility, and so he left the
control station and went topside. There he lifted his marine 7 × 50s, and then
the microphone of his radio.

"Motor Yacht *Springer* calling Coast Guard forty-one-boat, over."

"This is Coast Guard, *Springer*. Portagee here. What are you doing up
so early, Kelly? Over."

"Carrying out my commerce on the sea, Oreza. What's your excuse?
Over."

"Looking out for feather merchants like you to rescue, getting some
training done, what do you think? Over."

"Glad to hear that, Coast Guard. You push those lever-things towards
the front of the boat—that's the pointy part, usually—and she goes faster.
And the pointy part goes the same way you turn the wheel—you know, left
to go left, right to go right. Over."

Kelly could hear the laughter over the FM circuit. "Roger, copy that,
Springer, I will pass that along to my crew. Thank you, sir, for the advice.
Over."

The crew on the forty-one-foot boat was howling after a long eight
hours of patrol, and doing very little. Oreza was letting a young seaman
handle the wheel, leaning on the wheelhouse bulkhead and sipping his own
coffee as he played with the radio mike.

"You know, *Springer,* I don't take that sort of guff off many guys.
Over."

"A good sailor respects his betters, Coast Guard. Hey, is it true your
boats have wheels on the bottom? Over."

"Ooooooo," observed a new apprentice.

"Ah, that's a negative, *Springer*. We take the training wheels off after
the Navy pukes leave the shipyard. We don't like it when you ladies get
seasick just from looking at them. Over!"

Kelly chuckled and altered course to port to stay well clear of the small
cutter. "Nice to know that our country's waterways are in such capable
hands, Coast Guard, 'specially with a weekend coming up."

"Careful, *Springer,* or I'll hit you for a safety inspection!"

"My federal tax money at work?"

"I hate to see it wasted."

"Well, Coast Guard, just wanted to make sure y'all were awake."

"Roger and thank you very much, sir. We were dozing a little. Nice to know we have real pros like you out here to keep us on our toes."

"Fair winds, Portagee."

"And to you, Kelly. Out." The radio frequency returned to the usual static.

And that took care of that, Kelly thought. It wouldn't do to have him come alongside for a chat. Not just now. Kelly secured the radio and went below. The eastern horizon was pink-orange now, another ten minutes or so until the sun made its appearance.

"What was that all about?" Billy asked.

Kelly poured himself another cup of coffee and checked the autopilot. It was warm enough now that he removed his shirt. The scars on his back from the shotgun blast could hardly have been more clear, even in the dim light of a breaking dawn. There was a remarkable long silence, punctuated by a deep intake of breath.

"You're . . ."

This time Kelly turned, looking down at the naked man chained to the deck. "That's right."

"I killed you," Billy objected. He'd never gotten the word. Henry hadn't passed it along, deeming it to be irrelevant to his operation.

"Think so?" Kelly asked, looking forward again. One of the diesels was running a little warmer than the other, and he made a note to check the cooling system after his other business was done. Otherwise the boat was behaving as docilely as ever, rocking gently on the almost invisible swells, moving along at a steady twenty knots, the bow pitched up at about fifteen degrees on an efficient planing angle. On the step, as Kelly called it. He stretched again, flexing muscles, letting Billy see the scars and what lay under them.

"So that's what it's about . . . she told us all about you before we snuffed her."

Kelly scanned the instrument panel, then checked the chart as he approached the Bay Bridge. Soon he'd cross over to the eastern side of the channel. He was now checking the boat's clock—he thought of it as a chronometer—at least once a minute.

"Pam was a great little fuck. Right up to the end," Billy said, taunting his captor, filling the silence with his own malignant words, finding a sort of courage there. "Not real smart, though. Not real smart."

Just past the Bay Bridge, Kelly disengaged the autopilot and turned the wheel ten degrees to port. There was no morning traffic to speak of, but he looked carefully anyway before initiating the maneuver. A pair of running lights just on the horizon announced the approach of a merchant ship, probably twelve thousand yards off. Kelly could have flipped on the radar to check, but in these weather conditions it just would have been a waste of electricity.

"Did she tell you about the passion marks?" Billy sneered. He didn't see Kelly's hands tighten on the wheel.

The marks about the breasts appear to have been made with an ordinary set of pliers, the pathology report had said. Kelly had it all memorized, every single word of the dry medical phraseology, as though engraved with a diamond stylus on a plate of steel. He wondered if the medics had felt the same way he did. Probably so. Their anger had probably manifested itself in the increased detachment of their dictated notes. Professionals were like that.

"She talked, you know, she told us everything. How you picked her up, how you partied. We taught her that, mister. You owe us for that! Before she ran, I bet she didn't tell you, she fucked us all, three, four times each. I guess she thought that was pretty smart, eh? I guess she never figured that we'd all get to fuck her some more."

O+, O−, AB−, Kelly thought. Blood type O was by far the most common of all, and so that meant there could well have been more than three of them. *And what blood type are you, Billy?*

"Just a whore. A pretty one, but just a fucking little whore. That's how she died, did you know? She died while she was fucking a guy. We strangled her, and her cute little ass was pumping hard, right up till the time her face turned purple. Funny to watch," Billy assured him with a leer that Kelly didn't have to see. "I had my fun with her—three times, man! I hurt her, I hurt her bad, you hear me?"

Kelly opened his mouth wide, breathing slowly and regularly, not allowing his muscles to tense up now. The morning wind had picked up some, letting the boat rock perhaps five degrees left and right of the vertical, and he allowed his body to ride with the rolls, commanding himself to accept the soothing motion of the sea.

"I don't know what the big deal is, I mean, she's just a dead whore. We should be able to cut a deal, like. You know how dumb you are? There was seventy grand back in the house, you dumb son of a bitch. Seventy grand!" Billy stopped, seeing it wasn't working. Still, an angry man made mistakes, and he'd rattled the guy before. He was sure of that, and so he continued.

"You know, the real shame, I guess, is she needed drugs. You know, if she just knew another place to score, we never woulda seen y'all. Then you fucked up, too, remember."

Yes, I remember.

"I mean, you really were dumb. Didn't you know about phones? Jesus, man. After our car got stuck, we called Burt and got his car, and just went cruisin', like, and there you were, easy as hell to spot in that jeep. You must've really been under her spell, man."

Phones? It was something that *simple that had killed Pam?* Kelly thought. His muscles went taut. *You fucking idiot, Kelly.* Then his shoulders went slack, just for a second, with the realization of how thoroughly he had failed her, and part of him recognized the emptiness of his efforts at revenge. But empty or not, it was something he would have. He sat up straighter in the control chair.

"I mean, shit, car easy to spot like that, how fuckin' dumb can a guy be?" Billy asked, having just seen real feedback from his taunts. Now perhaps he could start real negotiations. "I'm kinda surprised you're alive— hey, I mean, it wasn't anything personal. Maybe you didn't know the work she did for us. We couldn't let her loose with what she knew, right? I can make it up to you. Let's make a deal, okay?"

Kelly checked the autopilot and the surface. *Springer* was moving on a safe and steady course, and nothing in sight was on a converging path. He rose from his chair and moved to another, a few feet from Billy.

"She told you that we were in town to score some drugs? She told you that?" Kelly asked, his eyes level with Billy's.

"Yeah, that's right." Billy was relaxing. He was puzzled when Kelly started weeping in front of him. Perhaps here was a chance to get out of his predicament. "Geez, I'm sorry, man," Billy said in the wrong sort of voice. "I mean, it's just bad luck for you."

Bad luck for me? He closed his eyes, just a few inches from Billy's face. *Dear God, she was protecting me. Even after I failed her. She didn't even know if I was alive or not, but she lied to protect me.* It was more than he could bear, and Kelly simply lost control of himself for several minutes. But even that had a purpose. His eyes dried up after a time, and as he wiped his face, he also removed any human feelings he might have had for his guest.

Kelly stood and walked back to the control chair. He didn't want to look the little bastard in the face any longer. He might really lose control, and he couldn't risk that.

"Tom, I think you may be right after all," Ryan said.

According to his driver's license—already checked out: no arrest record, but a lengthy list of traffic violations—Richard Oliver Farmer was twenty-four and would grow no older. He had expired from a single knife thrust into the chest, through the pericardium, fully transiting the heart. The size of the knife wound—ordinarily such traumatic insults closed up until they became difficult for the layman to see—indicated that the assailant had twisted the blade as much as the space between the ribs allowed. It was a large wound, indicating a blade roughly two inches in width. More important, there was additional confirmation.

"Not real smart," the ME announced. Ryan and Douglas both nodding, looking. Mr. Farmer had been wearing a white cotton, button-down-collar shirt. There was a suit jacket, too, hanging on a doorknob. Whoever had killed him had wiped the knife on the shirt. Three wipes, it appeared, and one of them had left a permanent impression of the knife, marked in the blood of the victim, who had a revolver in his belt but hadn't had a chance to use it. Another victim of skill and surprise, but, in this case, less circumspection. The junior of the pair pointed to one of the stains with his pencil.

"You know what it is?" Douglas asked. It was rhetorical; he answered his own question immediately. "It's a Ka-Bar, standard-issue Marine combat knife. I own one myself."

"Nice edge on it, too," the ME told them. "Very clean cut, almost surgical in the way it went through the skin. He must have sliced the heart just about in half. A very accurate thrust, gentlemen, the knife came in perfectly horizontal so it didn't jam on the ribs. Most people think the heart's on the left. Our friend knew better. Only one penetration. He knew exactly what he was doing."

"One more, Em. Armed criminal. Our friend got in close and did him so fast—"

"Yeah, Tom, I believe you now." Ryan nodded and went upstairs to join the other detective team. In the front bedroom was a pile of men's clothes, a cloth satchel with a ton of cash in it, a gun, and a knife. A mattress with semen stains, some still moist. Also a lady's purse. So much evidence for the younger men to catalog. Blood types from the semen stains. Complete ID on all three—they assumed three—people who had been here. Even a car outside to run down. Finally something like a normal murder case. Latent Prints would be all over the place. The photographers had already shot a dozen rolls of film. But for Ryan and Douglas the matter was already settled in its curious way.

"You know that guy Farber over at Hopkins?"

"Yeah, Em, he worked the Gooding case with Frank Allen. I set the date up. He's real smart," Douglas allowed. "A little peculiar, but smart. I have to be in court this afternoon, remember?"

"Okay, I think I can handle it. I owe you a beer, Tom. You figured this one faster than I did."

"Well, thanks, maybe I can be a lieutenant, too, someday."

Ryan laughed, fishing out a cigarette as he walked down the stairs.

"You going to resist?" Kelly asked with a smile. He'd just come back into the salon after tying up to the quay.

"Why should I help you with anything?" Billy asked with what he thought to be defiance.

"Okay." Kelly drew the Ka-Bar and held it next to a particularly sensitive place. "We can start right now if you want."

The whole body shriveled, but one part more than the others. "Okay, okay!"

"Good. I want you to learn a little from this. I don't want you ever to hurt another girl again." Kelly loosed the shackles from the deck fitting, but his arms were still together, bolted in tight, as he stood Billy up.

"Fuck you, man! You're gonna kill me! And I ain't gonna tell you shit."

Kelly twisted him around to stare in his eyes. "I'm not going to kill you, Billy. You'll leave this island alive. I promise."

The confusion on his face was sufficiently amusing that Kelly actually smiled for a second. Then he shook his head. He told himself that he was treading a very narrow and hazardous path between two equally dangerous slopes, and to both extremes lay madness, of two different types but equally destructive. He had to detach himself from the reality of the moment, yet hold on to it. Kelly helped him down from the boat and walked him towards the machinery bunker.

"Thirsty?"

"I need to take a piss, too."

Kelly guided him onto some grass. "Go right ahead." Kelly waited. Billy didn't like being naked, not in front of another man, not in a subordinate position. Foolishly, he wasn't trying to talk to Kelly now, at least not in the right way. Coward that he was, he'd tried to build up his manhood earlier, trying to talk not so much to Kelly as himself as he'd recounted his part in ending Pam's life, creating for himself an illusion of power, when silence might—well, would probably not have saved him. It might have created doubts, though, especially if he'd been clever enough to spin a good yarn, but cowardice and stupidity were not strangers to each other, were they? Kelly let him stand untended while he dialed the combination lock. Turning on the interior lights, he pushed Billy inside.

It looked like—was in fact a steel cylinder, seventeen inches in diameter, sitting on its own legs with large caster-wheels at the bottom, just where he'd left it. The steel cover on the end was not in place, hanging down on its hinge.

"You going to get in that," Kelly told him.

"Fuck you, man!" Defiance again. Kelly used the butt end of the Ka-Bar to club him on the back of the neck. Billy fell to his knees.

"One way or another, you're getting in—bleeding or not bleeding, I really don't care." Which was a lie, but an effective one. Kelly lifted him by the neck and forced his head and shoulders into the opening. "Don't move."

It was so much easier than he'd expected. Kelly pulled a key off its place on the wall and unbolted the shackles on Billy's hands. He could feel his prisoner tense, thinking that he might have a chance, but Kelly was fast on the wrench—he only had to remove one bolt to free both hands, and a prod from the knife in the right place encouraged Billy not to back up, which was the necessary precursor to any kind of effective resistance. Billy was just too cowardly to accept pain as the price for a chance at escape. He trembled but didn't resist at all, for all his lavish and desperate thoughts.

"Inside!" A push helped, and when his feet were inside the rim, Kelly lifted the hatch and bolted it into place. Then he walked out, flipping the lights off. He needed something to eat and a nap. Billy could wait. The waiting would just make things easier.

"Hello?" Her voice sounded very worried.

"Hi, Sandy, it's John."

"John! What's going on?"

"How is she?"

"Doris, you mean? She's sleeping now," Sandy told him. "John, who—I mean, what's happened to her?"

Kelly squeezed the phone receiver in his hand. "Sandy, I want you to listen to me very carefully, okay? This is really important."

"Okay, go ahead." Sandy was in her kitchen, looking at a pot of coffee. Outside she could see neighborhood children playing a game of ball on a vacant field whose comforting normality now seemed to be very distant indeed.

"Number one, don't tell anybody that she's there. Sure as hell you don't tell the police."

"John, she's badly injured, she's hooked on pills, she probably has severe medical problems on top of that. I have to—"

"Sam and Sarah, then. Nobody else. Sandy, you got that? *Nobody else.*

Sandy . . .'' Kelly hesitated. It was too hard a thing to say, but he had to make it clear. ''Sandy, I have placed you in danger. The people who worked Doris over are the same ones—''

''I know, John. I kinda figured that one out.'' The nurse's expression was neutral, but she too had seen the photo of Pamela Starr Madden's body. ''John, she told me that you—killed somebody.''

''Yes, Sandy, I did.''

Sandra O'Toole wasn't surprised. She'd made the right guesses a few hours before, but hearing it from him—it was the way he'd just said it. Calm, matter-of-fact. *Yes, Sandy, I did.* Did you take the garbage out? Yes, Sandy, I did.

''Sandy, these are some very dangerous people. I could have left Doris behind—but I couldn't, could I? Jesus, Sandy, did you see what they—''

''Yes.'' It had been a long time since she'd worked the ER, and she'd almost forgotten the dreadful things that people did to one another.

''Sandy, I'm sorry that I—''

''John, it's done. I'll handle it, okay?''

Kelly stopped talking for a moment, taking strength from her voice. Perhaps that was the difference between them. His instinct was to lash out, to identify the people who did the evil things and to deal with them. *Seek out and destroy.* Her instinct was to protect in a different way, and it struck the former SEAL that her strength might well be the greater.

''I'll have to get her proper medical attention.'' Sandy thought about the young woman upstairs in the back bedroom. She'd helped her get cleaned off and been horrified at the marks on her body, the vicious physical abuse. But worst of all were her eyes, dead, absent of the defiant spark that she saw in patients even as they lost their fight for life. Despite years of work in the care of critically ill patients, she'd never realized that a person could be destroyed on purpose, through deliberate, sadistic malice. Now she might come to the attention of such people herself, Sandy knew, but greater than her fear for them was her loathing.

For Kelly those feelings were precisely inverted. ''Okay, Sandy, but please be careful. Promise me.''

''I will. I'm going to call Doctor Rosen.'' She paused for a moment. ''John?''

''Yes, Sandy?''

''What you're doing . . . it's *wrong*, John.'' She hated herself for saying that.

''I know,'' Kelly told her.

Sandy closed her eyes, still seeing the kids chasing a baseball outside, then seeing John, wherever he was, knowing the expression that had to be on his face. She knew she had to say the next part, too, and she took a deep breath: "But I don't care about that, not anymore. I understand, John."

"Thank you," Kelly whispered. "Are you okay?"

"I'll do fine."

"I'll be back as soon as I can. I don't know what we can do with her—"

"Let me worry about that. We'll take care of her. We'll come up with something."

"Okay, Sandy . . . Sandy?"

"What, John?"

"Thanks." The line clicked off.

You're welcome, she thought, hanging up. What a strange man. He was killing people, ending the lives of fellow human beings, doing it with an utter ruthlessness that she hadn't seen—had no desire to see—but which his voice proclaimed in its emotionless speech. But he'd taken the time and endangered himself to rescue Doris. She still didn't understand, Sandy told herself, dialing the phone again.

Dr. Sidney Farber looked exactly as Emmet Ryan expected: forty or so, small, bearded, Jewish, pipe-smoker. He didn't rise as the detective came in, merely motioning his guest to a chair with a wave of the hand. Ryan had messengered extracts from the case files to the psychiatrist before lunch, and clearly the doctor had read them. All of them were laid open on the desk, arrayed in two rows.

"I know your partner, Tom Douglas," Farber said, puffing on his pipe.

"Yes, sir. He said your work on the Gooding case was very helpful."

"A very sick man, Mr. Gooding. I hope he'll get the treatment he needs."

"How sick is this one?" Lieutenant Ryan asked.

Farber looked up. "He's as healthy as we are—rather healthier, physically speaking. But that's not the important part. What you just said. 'This one.' You're assuming one murderer for all these incidents. Tell me why." The psychiatrist leaned back in his chair.

"I didn't think so at first. Tom saw it before I did. It's the craftsmanship."

"Correct."

"Are we dealing with a psychopath?"

Farber shook his head. "No. The true psychopath is a person unable to

deal with life. He sees reality in a very individual and eccentric way, generally a way that is very different from the rest of us. In nearly all cases the
disorder is manifested in very open and easily recognized ways.''

''But Gooding—''

''Mr. Gooding is what we—there's a new term, 'organized psychopath.' ''

''Okay, fine, but he wasn't obvious to his neighbors.''

''That's true, but Mr. Gooding's disorder manifested itself in the gruesome way he killed his victims. But with these killings, there's no ritual
aspect to them. No mutilation. No sexual drive to them—that's usually indicated by cuts on the neck, as you know. No.'' Farber shook his head again.
''This fellow is all business. He's not getting any emotional release at all.
He's just killing people and he's doing it for a reason that is probably rational, at least to him.''

''Why, then?''

''Obviously it's not robbery. It's something else. He's a very angry
man, but I've met people like this before.''

''Where?'' Ryan asked. Farber pointed to the opposite wall. In an
oaken frame was a piece of red velvet on which were pinned a combat
infantryman's badge, jump wings, and a RANGER flash. The detective was
surprised enough to let it show.

''Pretty stupid, really,'' Farber explained with a deprecating gesture.
''Little Jewish boy wants to show how tough he is. Well''—Farber
smiled—''I guess I did.''

''I didn't like Europe all that much myself, but I didn't see the nice
parts.''

''What outfit?''

''Easy Company, Second of the Five-Oh-Sixth.''

''Airborne. One-Oh-One, right?''

''All the way, doc,'' the detective said, confirming that he too had once
been young and foolish, and remembering how skinny he'd been, leaping
out the cargo doors of C-47s. ''I jumped into Normandy and Eindhoven.''

''And Bastogne?''

Ryan nodded. ''That really wasn't fun, but at least we went in by
truck.''

''Well, that's what you're up against, Lieutenant Ryan.''

''Explain?''

''Here's the key to it.'' Farber held up the transcribed interview with
Mrs. Charles. ''The disguise. Has to be a disguise. It takes a strong arm to

slam a knife into the back of the skull. That wasn't any alcoholic. They have all sorts of physical problems.''

''But that one doesn't fit the pattern at all,'' Ryan objected.

''I think it does, but it's not obvious. Turn the clock back. You're in the Army, you're an elite member of an elite unit. You take the time to recon your objective, right?''

''Always,'' the detective confirmed.

''Apply that to a city. How do you do that? You camouflage yourself. So our friend decides to disguise himself as a wino. How many of those people on the street? Dirty, smelly, but pretty harmless except to one another. They're invisible and you just filter them out. Everyone does.''

''You still didn't—''

''But how does he get in and out? You think he takes a bus—a taxi?''

''Car.''

''A disguise is something you put on and take off.'' Farber held up the photo of the Charles murder scene. ''He makes his double-kill two blocks away, he clears the area, and comes here—why do you suppose?'' And there it was, right on the photo, a gap between two parked cars.

''Holy shit!'' The humiliation Ryan felt was noteworthy. ''What else did I miss, Doctor Farber?''

''Call me Sid. Not much else. This individual is very clever, changing his methods, and this is the only case where he displayed his anger. That's it, do you see? This is the only crime with rage in it—except maybe for the one this morning, but we'll set that aside for the moment. Here we see rage. First he cripples the victim, then he kills him in a particularly difficult way. Why?'' Farber paused for a few contemplative puffs. ''He was angry, but *why* was he angry? It had to have been an unplanned act. He wouldn't have planned something with Mrs. Charles there. For some reason he had to do something that he hadn't expected to do, and that made him angry. Also, he let her go—*knowing* that she saw him.''

''You still haven't told me—''

''He's a combat veteran. He's very, very fit. That means he's younger than we are, and highly trained. Ranger, Green Beret, somebody like that.''

''Why is he out there?''

''I don't know. You're going to have to ask him. But what you have is somebody who takes his time. He's watching his victims. He's picking the same time of day—when they're tired, when street traffic is low, to reduce the chance of being spotted. He's not robbing them. He may take the money, but that's not the same thing. Now tell me about this morning's kill,'' Farber commanded in a gentle but explicit way.

"You have the photo. There was a whole lot of cash in a bag upstairs. We haven't counted it yet, but at least fifty thousand dollars.''

"Drug money?''

"We think so.''

"There were other people there? He kidnapped them?''

"Two, we think. A man definitely, and probably a woman, too.''

Farber nodded and puffed away for a few seconds. "One of two things. Either that's the person he was after all along, or he's just one more step towards something else.''

"So all the pushers he killed were just camouflage.''

"The first two, the ones he wired up—''

"Interrogated them.'' Ryan grimaced. "We should have figured this out. They were the only ones who weren't killed in the open. He did it that way to have more time.''

"Hindsight is always easy,'' Farber pointed out. "Don't feel too bad. That one really did look like a robbery, and you had nothing else to go on. By the time you came here, there was a lot more information to look at.'' The psychiatrist leaned back and smiled at the ceiling. He loved playing detective. "Until this one''—he tapped the photos from the newest scene with his pipe—"you didn't really have much. This is the one that makes everything else clear. Your suspect knows weapons. He knows tactics. He's very patient. He stalks his victims like a hunter after a deer. He's changing his methodology to throw you off, but today he made a mistake. He showed a little rage this time, too, because he used a knife deliberately, and he showed the kind of training he had by cleaning the weapon right away.''

"But he's not crazy, you say.''

"No, I doubt he's disturbed in a clinical sense at all, but sure as hell he's motivated by something. People like this are highly disciplined, just like you and I were. Discipline shows in how he operates—but his anger also shows in *why* he operates. Something made this man start to do this.''

"'Ma'am.' ''

That one caught Farber short. "Exactly! Very good. Why didn't he eliminate her? That's the only witness we know about. He was polite to her. He let her go . . . interesting . . . but not enough to go on, really.''

"Except to say that he's not killing for fun.''

"Correct.'' Farber nodded. "Everything he does will have a purpose, and he has a lot of specialized training that he can apply to this mission. It is a *mission.* You have one really dangerous cat prowling the street.''

"He's after drug people. That's pretty clear," Ryan said. "The one—maybe two—he kidnapped . . ."

"If one is a woman, she'll survive. The man will not. From the condition of his body we'll be able to tell if he was the target."

"Rage?"

"That will be obvious. One other thing—if you have police looking for this guy, remember that he's better with weapons than almost anybody. He'll look harmless. He'll avoid a confrontation. He doesn't want to kill the wrong people, or he would have killed this Mrs. Charles."

"But if we corner him—"

"You don't want to do that."

"All comfy?" Kelly asked.

The recompression chamber was one of several hundred produced for a Navy contract requirement by the Dykstra Foundry and Tool Company, Inc., of Houston, Texas, or so the name plate said. Made of high-quality steel, it was designed to reproduce the pressure that came along with scuba diving. At one end was a triple-paned four-inch-square Plexiglas window. There was even a small air lock so that items could be passed in, like food or drink, and inside the chamber was a twenty-watt reading light in a protected fixture. Under the chamber itself was a powerful, gasoline-powered air compressor, which could be controlled from a fold-down seat, adjacent to which were two pressure gauges. One was labeled in concentric circles of millimeters and inches of mercury, pounds-per-square-inch, kilograms-per-square-centimeter, and "bar" or multiples of normal atmospheric pressure, which was 14.7 PSI. The other gauge showed equivalent water depth both in feet and meters. Each thirty-three feet of simulated depth raised the atmospheric pressure by 14.7 PSI, or one bar.

"Look, whatever you want to know, okay . . ." Kelly heard over the intercom.

"I thought you'd see things my way." He yanked the rope on the motor, starting the compressor. Kelly made sure that the simple spigot valve next to the pressure gauges was tightly shut. Then he opened the pressurization valve, venting air from the compressor to the chamber, and watched the needles rotate slowly clockwise.

"You know how to swim?" Kelly asked, watching his face.

Billy's head jerked with alarm. "What—look, please, don't drown me, okay?"

"That's not going to happen. So, can you swim?"

"Yeah, sure."

"Ever do any skin diving?" Kelly asked next.

"No, no, I haven't," replied a very confused drug distributor.

"Okay, well, you're going to learn what it's like. You should yawn and work your ears, like, to get used to the pressure," Kelly told him, watching the "depth" gauge pass thirty feet.

"Look, why don't you just ask your fucking questions, okay?"

Kelly switched the intercom off. There was just too much fear in the voice. Kelly didn't really like hurting people all that much, and he was worried about developing sympathy for Billy. He steadied the gauge at one hundred feet, closing off the pressurization valve but leaving the motor running. While Billy adjusted to the pressure, Kelly found a hose which he attached to the motor's exhaust pipe. This he extended outside to dump the carbon monoxide into the atmosphere. It would be a time-consuming process, just waiting for things to happen. Kelly was going on memory, and that was worrisome. There was a useful but rather rough instruction table on the side of the chamber, the bottom line of which commanded reference to a certain diving manual which Kelly did not have. He'd done very little deep diving of late, and the only one that had really concerned him had been a team effort, the oil rig down in the Gulf. Kelly spent an hour tidying things up around the machine shop, cultivating his memories and his rage before coming back to his fold-down seat.

"How are you feeling?"

"Look, okay, all right?" Rather a nervous voice, actually.

"Ready to answer some questions?"

"Anything, okay? Just let me outa here!"

"Okay, good." Kelly lifted a clipboard. "Have you ever been arrested, Billy?"

"No." A little pride in that one, Kelly noted. Good.

"Been in the service?"

"No." Such a stupid question.

"So you've never been in jail, never been fingerprinted, nothing like that?"

"Never." The head shook inside the window.

"How do I know you're telling the truth?"

"I am, man! I am!"

"Yeah, you probably are, but I have to make sure, okay?" Kelly reached with his left hand and twisted the spigot valve. Air hissed loudly out of the chamber while he watched the pressure gauges.

Billy didn't know what to expect, and it all came as a disagreeable surprise. In the preceding hour, he had been surrounded by four times the normal amount of air for the space he was in. His body had adapted to that. The air taken in through his lungs, also pressurized, had found its way into his bloodstream, and now his entire body was at 58.8 pounds per square inch of ambient pressure. Various gas bubbles, mainly nitrogen, were dissolved into his bloodstream, and when Kelly bled the air out of the chamber, those bubbles started to expand. Tissues around the bubbles resisted the force, but not well, and almost at once cell walls started first to stretch, and then, in some cases, to rupture. The pain started in his extremities, first as a dull but widespread ache and rapidly evolving into the most intense and unpleasant sensation Billy had ever experienced. It came in waves, timed exactly with the now-rapid beating of his heart. Kelly listened to the moan that turned into a scream, and the air pressure was only that of sixty feet. He twisted the release valve shut and re-engaged the pressurization one. In another two minutes the pressure was back to that of four bar. The restored pressure eased the pain almost completely, leaving behind the sort of ache associated with strenuous exercise. That was not something to which Billy was accustomed, and for him the pain was not the welcome sort that athletes know. More to the point, the wide and terrified eyes told Kelly that his guest was thoroughly cowed. They didn't look like human eyes now, and that was good.

Kelly switched on the intercom. "That's the penalty for a lie. I thought you should know. Now. Ever been arrested, Billy?"

"Jesus, man, no!"

"Never been in jail, fingerprinted—"

"No, man, like speeding tickets, I ain't never been busted."

"In the service?"

"No, I told you that!"

"Good, thank you." Kelly checked off the first group of questions. "Now let's talk about Henry and his organization." There was one other thing happening that Billy did not expect. Beginning at about three bar, the nitrogen gas that constituted the majority of what humans call air has a narcotic effect not unlike that of alcohol or barbiturates. As afraid as Billy was, there was also a whiplash feeling of euphoria, along with which came impaired judgment. It was just one more bonus effect from the interrogation technique that Kelly had selected mainly for the magnitude of the injury it could inflict.

"Left the money?" Tucker asked.

"More than fifty thousand. They were still counting when I left," Mark Charon said. They were back in the theater, the only two people in the balcony. But this time Henry wasn't eating any popcorn, the detective saw. It wasn't often that he saw Tucker agitated.

"I need to know what's going on. Tell me what you know."

"We've had a few pushers whacked in the past week or ten days—"

"Ju-Ju, Bandanna, two others I don't know. Yeah, I know that. You think they're connected?"

"It's all we got, Henry. Was it Billy who disappeared?"

"Yeah. Rick's dead. Knife?"

"Somebody cut his fuckin' heart out," Charon exaggerated. "One of your girls there, too?"

"Doris," Henry confirmed with a nod. "Left the money . . . why?"

"It could have been a robbery that went wrong somehow, but I don't know what would have screwed that up. Ju-Ju and Bandanna were both robbed—hell, maybe those cases are unrelated. Maybe what happened last night was, well, something else."

"Like what?"

"Like maybe a direct attack on your organization, Henry," Charon answered patiently. "Who do you know who would want to do that? You don't have to be a cop to understand motive, right?" Part of him—a large part, in fact—enjoyed having the upper hand on Tucker, however briefly. "How much does Billy know?"

"A lot—shit, I just started taking him to—" Tucker stopped.

"That's okay. I don't need to know and I don't want to know. But somebody else does, and you'd better think about that." A little late, Mark Charon was beginning to appreciate how closely his well-being was associated with that of Henry Tucker.

"Why not at least make it *look* like a robbery?" Tucker demanded, eyes locked unseeingly on the screen.

"Somebody's sending you a message, Henry. Not taking the money is a sign of contempt. Who do you know who doesn't need money?"

The screams were getting louder. Billy had just taken another excursion to sixty feet, staying there for a couple of minutes. It was useful to be able to watch his face. Kelly saw him claw at his ears when both tympanic membranes ruptured, not a second apart. Then his eyes and sinuses had been affected. It would be attacking his teeth, too, if he had any cavities—which he probably did, Kelly thought, but he didn't want to hurt him too much, not yet.

"Billy," he said, after restoring the pressure and eliminating most of the pain, "I'm not sure I believe that one."

"You motherfucker!" the person inside the chamber screamed at the microphone. "I fixed her, you know? I watched your little babydoll die with Henry's dick in her, slinging her cunt for him, and I seen you cry like a fucking baby about it, you fucking pussy!"

Kelly made sure his face was at the window when his hand opened the release valve again, bringing Billy back to eighty feet, just enough for a good taste. There would be bleeding in the major joints now, because the nitrogen bubbles tended to collect there for one reason or another, and the instinctive reaction of decompression sickness was to curl up in a ball, from which had come the original name for the malady, "the bends." But Billy couldn't fold up inside the chamber, much as he tried to. His central nervous system was being affected now, too, the gossamer fibers being squeezed, and the pain was multifaceted now, crushing aches in the joints and extremities, and searing, fiery threads throughout his body. Nerve spasms started as the tiny electrical fibers rebelled against what was happening to them, and his body jerked randomly as though being stung with electric shocks. The neurological involvement was a little disquieting this early on. That was enough for now. Kelly restored the pressure, watching the spasms slow down.

"Now, Billy, do you know how it was for Pam?" he asked, just to remind himself, really.

"Hurts." He was crying now. He'd gotten his arms up, and his hands were over his face, but for all that he couldn't conceal his agony.

"Billy," Kelly said patiently. "You see how it works? If I think you're lying, it hurts. If I don't like what you say, it hurts. You want me to hurt you some more?"

"Jesus—no, please!" The hands came away, and their eyes weren't so much as eighteen inches apart.

"Let's try to be a little bit more polite, okay?"

". . . sorry . . ."

"I'm sorry, too, Billy, but you have to do what I tell you, okay?" He got a nod. Kelly reached for a glass of water. He checked the interlocks on the pass-through system before opening the door and setting the glass inside. "Okay, if you open the door next to your head, you can have something to drink."

Billy did as he was told and was soon sipping water through a straw.

"Now let's get back to business, okay? Tell me more about Henry. Where does he live?"

"I don't know," he gasped.

"Wrong answer!" Kelly snarled.

"Please, no! I don't know, we meet at a place off Route 40, he doesn't let us know where—"

"You have to do better than that or the elevator goes back to the sixth floor. Ready?"

"*Nooooo!*" The scream was so loud that it came right through the inch-thick steel. "*Please, no! I don't know—I really don't.*"

"Billy, I don't have much reason to be nice to you," Kelly reminded him. "You killed Pam, remember? You tortured her to death. You got your rocks off using pliers on her. How many hours, Billy, how long did you and your friends work on her? Ten? Twelve? Hell, Billy, we've only been talking for seven hours. You're telling me you've worked for this guy for almost two years and you don't even know where he lives? I have trouble believing that. Going up," Kelly announced in a mechanical voice, reaching for the valve. All he had to do was crack it. The first hiss of pressurized air bore with it such terror that Billy was screaming before any real pain had a chance to start.

"*I DON'T FUCKING KNOOOOOOOOOWWW!*"

Damn! What if he doesn't?

Well, Kelly thought, *it doesn't hurt to be sure.* He brought him up just a little, just to eighty-five feet, enough to renew old pains without spreading the effects any further. Fear of pain was now as bad as the real thing, Kelly thought, and if he went too far, pain could become its own narcotic. No, this man was a coward who had often enjoyed inflicting pain and terror on others, and if he discovered that pain, however dreadful, could be survived, then he might actually find courage in himself. That was a risk Kelly was unwilling to run, however remote it might be. He closed the release valve again and brought the pressure back up, this time to one hundred ten feet, the better to attenuate the pain and increase the narcosis.

"My God," Sarah breathed. She hadn't seen the postmortem photos of Pam, and her only question on the matter had been discouraged by her husband, a warning which she'd heeded.

Doris was nude, and disturbingly passive. The best thing that could be said for her was that Sandy had helped her bathe. Sam had his bag open, passing over his stethoscope. Her heart rate was over ninety, strong enough but too rapid for a girl her age. Blood pressure was also elevated. Temperature was normal. Sandy moved in, drawing four 5-cc test tubes of blood which would be analyzed at the hospital lab.

"Who does this sort of thing?" Sarah whispered to herself. There were numerous marks on her breasts, a fading bruise to her right cheek, and other, more recent edemas on her abdomen and legs. Sam checked her eyes for pupillary response, which was positive—except for the total absence of re-action.

"The same people who killed Pam," the surgeon replied quietly.

"Pam?" Doris asked.

"You knew her? How?"

"The man who brought you here," Sandy said. "He's the one—"

"The one Billy killed?"

"Yes," Sam answered, then realized how foolish it might sound to an outside listener.

"I just know the phone number," Billy said, drunkenly now from the high partial-pressure of nitrogen gas, and his release from pain was helping him to be much more compliant.

"Give it to me," Kelly ordered. Billy did as he was told and Kelly wrote it down. He had two full pages of penciled notes now. Names, addresses, a few phone numbers. Seemingly very little, but far more than he'd had only twenty-four hours before.

"How do the drugs come in?"

Billy's head turned away from the window. "Don't know . . ."

"We have to do better than that." *Hissssssssssssss* . . .

Again Billy screamed, and this time Kelly let it happen, watching the depth-gauge needle rotate to seventy-five feet. Billy started gagging. His lung function was impaired now, and the choking coughs merely amplified the pain that now filled every cubic inch of his racked body. His whole body felt like a balloon, or more properly a collection of them, large and small, all trying to explode, all pressing on others, and he could feel that some were stronger and some weaker than others, and the weaker ones were those at the most important places inside him. His eyes were hurting now, seeming to expand beyond their sockets, and the way in which his paranasal sinuses were also expanding only made it worse, as though his face would detach from the rest of his skull; his hands flew there, desperately trying to hold it in place. The pain was beyond anything he had ever felt and beyond anything he had ever inflicted. His legs were bent as much as the steel cylinder allowed, and his kneecaps seemed to dig grooves into the steel, so hard they pressed against it. He was able to move his arms, and those twisted and turned about his chest, seeking relief, but only generating more pain as he struggled to hold his eyes in the sockets. He was unable even to scream now. Time stopped for Billy and became eternity. There was no light, no darkness, no sound or silence. All of reality was pain.

"... please ... please ..." the whisper carried over the speaker next to Kelly. He brought the pressure back up slowly, stopping this time at one hundred ten feet.

Billy's face was mottled now, like the rash from some horrible allergy. Some blood vessels had let go just below the surface of the skin, and a big one had ruptured on the surface of the left eye. Soon half of the "white" was red, closer to purple, really, making him look even more like the frightened, vicious animal he was.

"The last question was about how the drugs come in."

"I don't know," he whined.

Kelly spoke quietly into the microphone. "Billy, there's something you have to understand. Up until now what's happened to you, well, it hurts pretty bad, but I haven't really hurt you yet. I mean, not *really* hurt you."

Billy's eyes went wide. Had he been able to consider things in a dispassionate way, he would have remarked to himself that surely horror must stop *somewhere*, an observation that would have been both right and wrong.

"Everything that's happened so far, it's all things that doctors can fix, okay?" It wasn't much of a lie on Kelly's part, and what followed was no lie at all. "The next time we let the air out, Billy, then things will happen that nobody can fix. Blood vessels inside your eyeballs will break open, and you'll be blind. Other vessels inside your brain will let go, okay? They can't fix either one. You'll be blind and you'll be crazy. But the pain will never go away. The rest of your life, Billy, blind, crazy, and hurt. You're what? Twenty-five? You have lots more time to live. Forty years, maybe, blind, crazy, crippled. So it's a good idea to not lie to me, okay?

"Now—how do the drugs come in?"

No pity, Kelly told himself. He would have killed a dog or a cat or a deer in the condition he'd inflicted on this ... object. But Billy wasn't a dog or a cat or a deer. He was a human being, after a fashion. Worse than the pimp, worse than the pushers. Had the situation been reversed, Billy would not have felt what he was feeling. He was a person whose universe was very small indeed. It held only one person, himself, surrounded by *things* whose sole function was to be manipulated for his amusement or profit. Billy was one who enjoyed the infliction of pain, who enjoyed establishing dominance over *things* whose feelings were nothing of importance, even if they truly existed at all. Somehow he'd never learned that there were other human beings in his universe, *people* whose right to life and happiness was equal to his own; because of that he had run the unrecognized risk of offending another person whose very existence he had never really acknowledged. He was learning different now, perhaps, though it was a little late. Now he was learning that his future was indeed a lonely universe which he would share not with people, but with pain. Smart enough to see that future, Billy broke. It was obvious on his face. He started talking in a choked and uneven voice, but one which, finally, was completely truthful. It was only about ten years too late, Kelly estimated, looking up from his notes at the relief valve. That ought to have been a pity, and truly it was for many of those who had shared Billy's rather eccentric universe. Perhaps he'd just never figured it out, Kelly thought, that someone else might treat him the same way in which he treated so many others, smaller and weaker than himself. But that also was too late in coming. Too late for Billy, too late for Pam, and, in a way, too late for Kelly. The world was full of inequities and not replete with justice. It was that simple, wasn't it? Billy didn't know that justice might be out there waiting, and there simply hadn't been enough of it to warn him. And so he had gambled. And so he had lost. And so Kelly would save his pity for others.

"I don't know . . . I don't—"

"I warned you, didn't I?" Kelly opened the valve, bringing him all the way to fifty feet. The retinal blood vessels must have ruptured early. Kelly thought he saw a little red in the pupils, wide as their owner screamed even after his lungs were devoid of air. Knees and feet and elbows drummed against the steel. Kelly let it happen, waiting before he reapplied the air pressure.

"Tell me what you know, Billy, or it just gets worse. Talk fast."

His voice was that of confession now. The information was somewhat remarkable, but it had to be true. No person like this had the imagination to make it up. The final part of the interrogation lasted for three hours, only once letting the valve *hiss*, and then only for a second or two. Kelly left and revisited questions to see if the answers changed, but they didn't. In fact, the renewed question developed yet more information that connected some bits of data to others, formulating an overall picture that became clearer still, and by midnight he was sure that he'd emptied Billy's mind of all the useful data that it contained.

Kelly was almost captured by humanity when he set his pencils down. If Billy had shown Pam any mercy at all, perhaps he might have acted differently, for his own wounds were, just as Billy had said, only a business matter—more correctly, had been occasioned by his own stupidity, and he could not in good conscience harm a man for taking advantage of his own errors. But Billy had not stopped there. He had tortured a young woman whom Kelly had loved, and for that reason Billy was not a *man* at all, and did not merit Kelly's solicitude.

It didn't matter in any case. The damage had been done, and it progressed at its own speed as tissues torn loose by the barometric trauma wandered about blood vessels, closing them off one at a time. The worst manifestation of this was in Billy's brain. Soon his sightless eyes proclaimed the madness that they held, and though the final depressurization was a slow and gentle one, what came out of the chamber was not a man—but then, it never had been.

Kelly loosed the retaining bolts on the hatch. He was greeted with a foul stench that he ought to have expected but didn't. The buildup and release of pressure in Billy's intestinal tract and bladder had produced predictable effects. He'd have to hose it out later, Kelly thought, pulling Billy out and laying him on the concrete floor. He wondered if he had to chain him to something, but the body at his feet was useless to its owner now, the major joints nearly destroyed, the central nervous system good only to transmit pain. But Billy was still breathing, and that was just fine, Kelly thought, heading off to bed, glad it was over. With luck he would not have to do something like this again. With luck and good medical care, Billy would live for several weeks. If you could call it that.

21

Possibilities

elly was actually disturbed by how well he slept. It wasn't fitting, he worried, that he should have gotten ten hours of uninterrupted sleep after what he'd done to Billy. This was an odd time for his conscience to manifest itself, Kelly said to the face in the mirror as he shaved; also a little late. If a person went around injuring women and dealing drugs, then he should have considered the possible consequences. Kelly wiped his face off. He felt no elation at the pain he'd inflicted—he was sure of that. It had been a matter of gathering necessary information while meting out justice in a particularly fitting and appropriate way. Being able to classify his actions in familiar terms went a long way towards keeping his conscience under control.

He also had to go someplace. After dressing, Kelly got a plastic drop cloth. This went to the after well-deck of his cruiser. He was already packed, and his things went into the main salon.

It would be a trip of several hours, most of it boring and more than half in darkness. Heading south for Point Lookout, Kelly took the time to scan the collection of derelict "ships" near Bloodsworth Island. Built for the First World War, they were an exceedingly motley collection. Some made of timber, others of concrete—which seemed very odd indeed—all of them had survived the world's first organized submarine campaign, but had not been commercially viable even in the 1920s, when merchant sailors had come a lot cheaper than the tugboat crews who routinely plied the Chesapeake Bay. Kelly went to the flying bridge and while the autopilot handled his southerly course, he examined them through binoculars, because one of them probably held interest. He could discern no movement, however, and saw no boats in the morass that their final resting place had become. That was to be expected, he thought. It wouldn't be an ongoing industrial enterprise, though it was a clever hiding place for the activity in which Billy had so recently played a part. He altered course to the west. This matter would have to wait. Kelly made a conscious effort to change his thinking. He would soon be a team player, associated again with men like himself. A welcome change, he thought, during which he would have time to consider his tactics for the next phase of his operation.

The officers had merely been briefed on the incident with Mrs. Charles, but their alert level had been raised by follow-up information on the method by which her assailant had met his end. No additional cautionary words were needed. Two-man patrol cars handled most of them, though some solo cars driven by experienced—or overly confident—officers performed the same function in a way that would have grated on Ryan and Douglas had they seen it. One officer would approach while the other stood back, his hand resting casually on his service revolver. The lead officer would stand the wino up and frisk him, checking for weapons, and often finding knives, but no fire-arms—anyone in possession of one pawned it for money with which to buy alcohol or, in some cases, drugs. In the first night eleven such people were rousted and identified, with two arrests being made for what the officers deemed an improper attitude. But at the end of the shift, nothing of value had been turned up.

"Okay—I found something out," Charon said. His car sat in the park-ing lot outside a supermarket, next to a Cadillac.

"What's that?"

"They're looking for a guy disguised as a bum."

"You kidding me?" Tucker asked with some disgust.

"That's the word, Henry," the detective assured him. "They have orders to approach with caution."

"Shit," the distributor snorted.

"White, not too tall, forties. He's pretty strong, and he moves real good when he has to. They're going soft on the information that's out, but about the same time he interfered with a yoking, two more pushers turned up dead. I'm betting it's the same guy who's been taking pushers out."

Tucker shook his head. "Rick and Billy, too? It doesn't make any sense."

"Henry, whether it makes sense or not, that's what the word is, okay?

Now, you take this seriously. Whoever this guy is, he's a pro. You got that? A pro.''

"Tony and Eddie,'' Tucker said quietly.

"That's my best guess, Henry, but it's only a guess.'' Charon pulled out of his parking place.

But none of it made any real sense, Tucker told himself, driving out onto Edmondson Avenue. Why would Tony and Eddie try to do—what? What the hell was going on? They didn't know much about his operation, merely that it existed, and that he wanted it and his territory left alone while he evolved into their principal supplier. For them to harm his business without first suborning his method of importing the product was not logical. Suborning . . . he'd used the wrong word . . . but—

Suborned. What if Billy were still alive? What if Billy had cut a deal and Rick hadn't gone along with it—a possibility; Rick had been weaker but more reliable than Billy.

Billy kills Rick, takes Doris out and dumps her somewhere—Billy knows how to do that, doesn't he?—why? Billy has made contact with— who? Ambitious little bastard, Billy, Tucker thought. *Not all that smart, but ambitious and tough when he has to be.*

Possibilities. Billy makes contact with somebody. Who? What does Billy know? He knows where the product is processed, but not how it comes in . . . maybe the smell, the formaldehyde smell on the plastic bags. Henry had been careful about that before; when Tony and Eddie had helped him package the product in the start-up phase, Tucker had taken the trouble to rebag everything, just to be on the safe side. But not the last two shipments . . . *damn.* That was a mistake, wasn't it? Billy knew roughly where the processing was done, but could he find it on his own? Henry didn't think so. He didn't know much about boats and didn't even like them all that much, and navigating wasn't an easily acquired art.

Eddie and Tony know about boats, you idiot, Tucker reminded himself.

But *why* would they cross him now, just when things were blooming?

Whom else had he offended? Well, there was the New York crew, but he'd never even had direct contact with them. He'd invaded their market, though, taking advantage of a supply shortfall to establish an entry position. Might they be upset about that?

What about the Philadelphia crew? They had become the interface between himself and New York, and perhaps they were greedy. Perhaps they had found out about Billy.

Perhaps Eddie was making his move, betraying Tony and Henry at the same time.

Perhaps a lot of things. Whatever was happening, Henry still controlled the import pipeline. More to the point, he had to stand and defend what he had, his own territory, and his connections. Things were just starting to pay off big. Years of effort had been required to get to where he was now, Henry told himself, turning right towards his home. Starting over would entail dangers that, once run, were not easily repeated. A new city, setting up a new network. And Vietnam would be cooling off soon. The body count upon which he depended was declining. A problem now could wreck everything. If he could maintain his operation, his worst-case scenario was banking over ten million dollars—closer to twenty if he played the cards right—and leaving the business for good. That was not an unattractive option. Two years of high payoff to reach that spot. It might not be possible to start over from scratch. He had to stand and fight.

Stand and fight, boy. A plan began to form. He'd put the word out: he wanted Billy and he wanted him alive. He'd talk to Tony and sound him out on the chance that Eddie was playing a game of some sort, that Eddie was connected with rivals to the north. That was his starting point to gather information. Then he would act on it.

There's a likely spot, Kelly told himself. *Springer* was just crawling along, quietly. The trick was to find a place that was populated but not alert. Nothing unusual about that mission requirement, he smiled to himself. Toss in a bend in the river, and here was one. He checked the shoreline out carefully. It looked like a school, probably a boarding school, and there were no lights in the buildings. There was a town behind it, a small, sleepy one, just a few lights there, a car every couple of minutes, but those followed the main road, and nobody there could possibly see him. He let the boat proceed around a bend—better yet, a farm, probably tobacco from the look of it, an old one with a substantial house maybe six hundred yards off, the owners inside and enjoying their air conditioning, the glare from their lights and TV preventing them from seeing outside. He'd risk it here.

Kelly idled his motors and went forward to drop his lunch-hook, a small anchor. He moved quickly and quietly, lowering his small dinghy into the water and pulling it aft. Lifting Billy over the rail was easy enough, but putting the body in the dinghy defeated him. Kelly hurried into the after stateroom and returned with a life jacket which he put on Billy before tossing him over the side. It was easier this way. He tied the jacket off to the stern. Then he rowed as quickly as he could to the shore. It only took three or four minutes before the dinghy's bow touched the muddy banks. It was a school, Kelly saw. It probably had a summer program, and almost certainly had a maintenance staff which would show up in the morning. He stepped out of the dinghy and hauled Billy onto the bank before removing the life jacket.

"You stay here, now."

". . . stay . . ."

"That's right." Kelly pushed the dinghy back into the river. As he began rowing back, his aft-facing position forced him to look at Billy. He'd left him naked. No identification. He bore no distinguishing marks that Kelly had not created. Billy had said more than once that he'd never been fingerprinted. If true, then there was no way for police to identify him easily, probably not at all. And he couldn't live too long the way he was. The brain damage was more profound than Kelly had intended, and that indicated that other internal organs had to be severely damaged as well. But Kelly had shown some mercy after all. The crows probably wouldn't have a chance to pick at him. Just doctors. Soon Kelly had *Springer* moving back up the Potomac.

Two more hours and Kelly saw the marina at Quantico Marine Base. Tired, he made a careful approach, selecting a guest berth at the end of one of the piers.

"Who might you be?" a voice asked in the dark.

"The name's Clark," Kelly replied. "You should be expecting me."

"Oh, yeah. Nice boat," the man said, heading back to the small dock house. Within minutes a car came down the hill from officer-quarters.

"You're early," Marty Young said.

"Might as well get started, sir. Come aboard?"

"Thanks, Mr. Clark." He looked around the salon. "How did you get this baby? I suffer along with a little day-sailer."

"I don't know that I really should say, sir," Kelly replied. "Sorry." General Young accepted that with good grace.

"Dutch says you're going to be part of the op."

"Yes, sir."

"Sure you can hack it?" Young noticed the tattoo on Kelly's forearm and wondered what it denoted.

"I worked Phoenix for over a year, sir. What sort of people have signed on?"

"They're all Force Recon. We're training them pretty hard."

"Kick 'em loose around five-thirty?" Kelly asked.

"That's right. I'll have somebody pick you up." Young smiled. "We need to get you nice and fit, too."

Kelly just smiled. "Fair enough, General."

* * *

"So what's so damned important?" Piaggi asked, annoyed to be bothered at short notice on a weekend night.

"I think somebody's making a move on me. I want to know who."

"Oh?" And *that* made the meeting important, if poorly timed, Tony thought. "Tell me what's happened."

"Somebody's been taking pushers down on the west side," Tucker said.

"I read the papers," Piaggi assured him. He poured some wine into his guest's glass. It was important at times like these to make a show of normality. Tucker would never be part of the family to which Piaggi belonged, but for all that he was a valuable associate. "Why is that important, Henry?"

"The same guy took down two of my people. Rick and Billy."

"The same ones who—"

"That's right. One of my girls is missing, too." He lifted his glass and sipped, watching Piaggi's eyes.

"Rip?"

"Billy had about seventy thousand, cash. The cops found it, right there." Tucker filled in a few more details. "The police say it looks real professional, like."

"You have any other enemies on the street?" Tony inquired. It wasn't a terribly bright question—anyone in the business had enemies—but the skill factor was the important one.

"I've made sure the cops know about my major competitors."

Piaggi nodded. That was within normal business practice, but somewhat risky. He shrugged it off. Henry could be a real cowboy, a source of occasional worry to Tony and his colleagues. Henry was also very careful when he had to be, and the man seemed to understand how to mix the two traits.

"Somebody getting even?"

"None of them would walk away from that kind of cash."

"True," Piaggi conceded. "I got news for you, Henry. *I* don't leave that sort of bundle laying around."

Oh, really? Tucker wondered behind impassive eyes. "Tony, either the guy fucked up or he's trying to tell me something. He's killed like seven or eight people, real smart. He took Rick down with a knife. I don't think he fucked up, y'dig?" The odd thing was that both men thought that a knifing was something the other would do. Henry had the impression that knives were the weapon of Italians. Piaggi thought it the trademark of a black.

"What I hear, somebody is doing pushers with a pistol—a little one."

"One was a shotgun, right in the guts. The cops are rousting street bums, doing it real careful."

"I didn't hear that," Piaggi admitted. This man had some great sources, but then he lived closer to that part of town, and it was to be expected that his intelligence network would be speedier than Piaggi's.

"It sounds like a pro doing this," Tucker concluded. "Somebody really good, y'know?"

Piaggi nodded understanding while his mind was in a quandary. The existence of highly skilled Mafia assassins was for the most part a fiction created by TV and movies. The average organized-crime murder was not a skilled act, but rather something carried out by a man who mainly did other, real, money-generating activities. There was no special class of killers who waited patiently for telephone calls, made hits, then returned to their posh homes to await the next call. There *were* made members who were unusually good or experienced at killing, but that wasn't the same thing. One simply got a reputation as a person whom killing didn't affect—and that meant that the elimination would be done with a minimum of fuss, not a maximum of artistry. True sociopaths were rare, even in the Mafia, and bungled killings were the rule rather than the exception. And so "professional" to Henry meant something that existed only as a fiction, the TV image of a Mafia button man. But how the hell did Tony explain *that?*

"It isn't one of mine, Henry," he said after a moment's contemplation. That he didn't have *any* was another issue entirely, Piaggi told himself, watching the effect of his words on his associate. Henry had always assumed that Piaggi knew a good deal about killing. Piaggi *knew* that Tucker had more experience with that end of business than he ever wished to have, but that was just one more thing he would have to explain, and this clearly was not the time. For now, he watched Tucker's face, trying to read his thoughts as he finished his glass of Chianti.

How do I know he's telling the truth? The thought didn't require any special perception to read.

"You need some help, Henry?" Piaggi said, to break a very awkward silence.

"I don't think you're doing it. I think you're too smart," Tucker said, finishing his own glass.

"Glad to hear that." Tony smiled and refilled both glasses.

"What about Eddie?"

"What do you mean?"

"Is he ever going to get 'made'?" Tucker looked down, swirling the wine around the glass. One thing about Tony, he always set the right kind of atmosphere for a business discussion. It was one of the reasons they'd been drawn together. Tony was quiet, thoughtful, always polite, even when you asked a sensitive question.

"That's kind of touchy, Henry, and I really shouldn't talk that over with you. You can never be 'made.' You know that."

"No equal-opportunity in the outfit, eh? Well, that's okay. I know I'd never fit in real good. Just so's we can do business, Anthony." Tucker took the occasion to grin, breaking the tension somewhat and, he hoped, making it easier for Tony to answer the question. He got his wish.

"No," Piaggi said after a moment's contemplation. "Nobody thinks Eddie's got what it takes."

"Maybe he's lookin' for a way to prove differ'nt."

Piaggi shook his head. "I don't think so. Eddie's going to make a good living off this. He knows that."

"Who, then?" Tucker asked. "Who else knows enough? Who else would do a bunch of killings to cover up a move like this? Who else would make it look like a pro job?"

Eddie's not smart enough. Piaggi knew that, or thought he did.

"Henry, taking Eddie out would cause major problems." He paused. "But I'll check around."

"Thank you," Tucker said. He stood and left Tony alone with his wine.

Piaggi stayed at his table. Why did things have to be so complicated? Was Henry being truthful? Probably, he thought. He was Henry's only connection to the outfit, and severing that tie would be very bad for everyone. Tucker could become highly important but would never be an insider. On the other hand he was smart and he delivered. The outfit had lots of such people, inside-outsiders, associate members, whatever you might call them, whose value and status were proportional to their utility. Many of them actually wielded more power than some "made" members, but there was always a difference. In a real dispute, being made counted for much—in most cases, counted for *everything*.

That could explain matters. Was Eddie jealous of Henry's status? Did he crave becoming a real member so much that he might be willing to forfeit the benefits of the current business arrangement? It didn't make sense, Piaggi told himself. But what did?

"Ahoy the *Springer!*" a voice called. The Marine corporal was surprised to see the cabin door open immediately. He'd expected having to jolt this . . . civilian . . . from his cushy bed. Instead he saw a man come out in jungle boots and bush fatigues. They weren't Marine "utilities," but close enough to show the man was serious. He could see where some badges had been removed, where a name and something else would have gone, and that somehow made Mr. Clark look more serious still.

"This way, sir." The corporal gestured. Kelly followed without a word.

Sir didn't mean anything, Kelly knew. When in doubt, a Marine would call a lightpole "Sir." He followed the youngster to a car and they drove off, crossing the railroad tracks and climbing uphill while he wished for another few hours of sleep.

"You the General's driver?"

"Yes, sir." And that was the extent of their conversation.

There were about twenty-five of them, standing in the morning mist, stretching and chatting among themselves as the squad NCOs walked up and down the line, looking for bleary eyes or slack expressions. Heads turned when the General's car stopped and a man got out. They saw he wore the wrong sort of fatigues and wondered who the hell he was, especially since he had no rank insignia at all. He walked right up to the senior NCO.

"You Gunny Irvin?" Kelly asked.

Master Gunnery Sergeant Paul Irvin nodded politely as he sized the visitor up. "Correct, sir. Are you Mr. Clark?"

Kelly nodded. "Well, I'm trying to be, this early."

Both men traded a look. Paul Irvin was dark and serious-looking. Not as overtly threatening as Kelly had expected, he had the eyes of a careful, thoughtful man, which was to be expected for someone of his age and experience.

"What kinda shape you in?" Irvin asked.

"Only one way to find that out," "Clark" answered.

Irvin smiled broadly. "Good. I'll let you lead the run, sir. Our captain's away somewhere jerking off."

Oh, shit!

"Now let's get loosened up." Irvin walked back to the formation, calling it to attention. Kelly took a place on the right side of the second rank.

"Good morning, Marines!"

"*Recon!*" they bellowed back.

The daily dozen wasn't exactly fun, but Kelly didn't have to show off. He did watch Irvin, who was becoming more serious by the minute, doing his exercises like some sort of robot. Half an hour later they were indeed all loosened up, and Irvin brought them back to attention in preparation for the run.

"Gentlemen, I want to introduce a new member of our team. This is Mr. Clark. He'll be leading the run with me."

Kelly took his place, whispering, "I don't know where the hell we're going."

Irvin smiled in a nasty way. "No problem, sir. You can follow us in after you fall out."

"Lead off, jarhead," Kelly replied, one pro to another.

Forty minutes later, Kelly was still in the lead. Being there allowed him to set the pace, and that was the only good news. Not staggering was his other main concern, and that was becoming difficult, since when the body tires the fine-tuning controls go first.

"Left," Irvin said, pointing. Kelly couldn't know that he'd needed ten seconds to assemble the surplus air to speak. He'd also had the burden of singing the cadence, however. The new path, just a dirt trail, took them into the piney woods.

Buildings, oh Jesus, I hope that's the stopping place. Even his thoughts were gasps now. The path wound around a little, but there were cars there, and that had to be—what? He almost stopped in surprise, and on his own called, "Quick-time, march!" to slow the formation down.

Mannequins?

"Detail," Irvin called out, "*halt!* Stand at ease," he added.

Kelly coughed a few times, bending down slightly, blessing his runs in the park and around his island for allowing him to survive this morning.

"Slow," was all Irvin had to say at the moment.

"Good morning, Mr. Clark." It turned out that one of the cars was real, Kelly saw. James Greer and Marty Young waved him over.

"Good morning. I hope y'all slept well," Kelly told them.

"You volunteered, John," Greer pointed out.

"They're four minutes slow this morning," Young observed. "Not bad for a spook, though."

Kelly turned away in semidisgust. It took a minute or so for him to realize what this place was.

"Damn!"

"There's your hill." Young pointed.

"Trees are taller here," Kelly said, evaluating the distance.

"So's the hill. It's a wash."

"Tonight?" Kelly asked. It wasn't hard to catch the meaning of the General's words.

"Think you're up to it?"

"I suppose we need to know that. When's the mission going to go?"

Greer took that one. "You don't need to know that yet."

"How much warning will I have?"

The CIA official weighed that one before answering. "Three days before we move out. We'll be going over mission parameters in a few hours. For now, watch how these men are setting up." Greer and Young headed off to their car.

"Aye aye," Kelly replied to their backs. The Marines had coffee going. He got a cup and started blending in with the assault team.

"Not bad," Irvin said.

"Thanks. I always figured it's one of the most important things you need to know in this business."

"What's that?" Irvin asked.

"How to run away as far and fast as you can."

Irvin laughed and then came the first work detail of the day, something that let the men cool down and have a laugh of their own. They started moving the mannequins around. It had become a ritual, which woman went with which kids. They'd discovered that the models could be posed, and the Marines made great fun of that. Two had brought new outfits, both rather skimpy bikinis, which they ostentatiously put on two lounging lady-figures. Kelly watched with incredulous amazement, then realized that the swimsuit models had had their bodies—painted, in the interests of realism. *Jesus,* he thought, *and they say sailors are screwy!*

USS *Ogden* was a new ship, or nearly so, having emerged from the New York Naval Shipyard's building ways in 1964. Rather a strange-looking ship, she was 570 feet long, and her forward half had a fairly normal superstructure and eight guns to annoy attacking aircraft. The odd part was the after half, which was flat on top and hollow underneath. The flat part was good for landing helicopters, and directly under that was a well deck designed to be filled with water from which landing craft could operate. She and her eleven sister ships had been designed to support landing operations, to put Marines on the beach for the amphibious-assault missions that The Corps had invented in the 1920s and perfected in the 1940s. But the Pacific Fleet amphibious ships were without a mission now—the Marines *were* on the beach, generally brought in by chartered jetliners to conventional airports—and so some of the 'phibs were being outfitted for other missions. As *Ogden* was.

Cranes were lifting a series of trailer vans onto the flight deck. When secured in place, deck parties erected various radio antennas. Other such objects were being bolted into place on the superstructure. The activity was being done in the open—there is no convenient way of hiding a 17,000-ton warship—and it was clear that *Ogden,* like two more sister ships, was transforming herself into a platform for the gathering of electronic intelligence—ELINT. She sailed out of the San Diego Naval Base just as the sun began to set, without an escort and without the Marine battalion she was built to carry. Her Navy crew of thirty officers and four hundred ninety enlisted men settled into their routine watch bill, conducting training exercises and generally doing what most had chosen to do by enlisting in the Navy instead of risking a slot in the draft. By sunset she was well under the horizon, and her new mission had been communicated to various interested parties, not all of whom were friendly to the flag which she flew. With all those trailers aboard and a score of antennas looking like a forest of burnt trees to clutter up her flight deck—and no Marines embarked—she wouldn't be doing anyone direct harm. That was obvious to all who had seen her.

Twelve hours later, and two hundred miles at sea, bosun's mates assembled parties from the deck division and told some rather confused young men to unbolt all but one of the trailers—which were empty—and to strike down all of the antennas on the flight deck. Those on the superstructure would remain in place. The antennas went below first, into the capacious equipment-storage spaces. The empty trailers were wheeled after them, clearing the flight deck entirely.

At Subic Bay Naval Base, the commanding officer of USS *Newport News,* along with his executive officer and gunnery officer, looked over their missions for the coming month. His command was one of the last true cruisers in the world, with eight-inch guns like few others. They were semiautomatic, and loaded their powder charges not in loose bags but in brass cartridge cases different only in scale from the kind any deer hunter might jack into his Winchester .30-30. Able to reach almost twenty miles, *Newport News* could deliver a stunning volume of fire, as an NVA battalion had learned only two weeks earlier, much to its misfortune. Fifty rounds per gun tube per minute. The center gun of the number-two turret was damaged, and so the cruiser could be counted on to put only four *hundred* rounds per minute on target, but that was the equivalent of one hundred thousand-pound bombs. The cruiser's task for the next deployment, the Captain learned, was to go after selected triple-A batteries on the Vietnamese coast. That was fine with him, though the mission he really lusted for was to enter Haiphong harbor one night.

*   *   *

"Your lad seems to know his business—till now, anyway," General Young observed about quarter of two.

"It's a lot to ask him to do something like this the first night, Marty," Dutch Maxwell countered.

"Well, hell, Dutch, if he wants to play with my Marines . . ." That's how Young was. They were all "his" Marines. He'd flown with Foss off Guadalcanal, covered Chesty Puller's regiment in Korea, and was one of the men who'd perfected close-air support into the art form it now was.

They stood on the hilltop overlooking the site Young had recently erected. Fifteen of the Recon Marines were on the slopes, and their job was to detect and eliminate Clark as he climbed to his notional perch. Even General Young thought it an overly harsh test on Clark's first day with the team, but Jim Greer had made a very big deal of telling them how impressive the lad was, and spooks needed to be put in their place. Even Dutch Maxwell had agreed with that.

"What a crummy way to earn a living," said the admiral with seventeen hundred carrier landings under his belt.

"Lions and tigers and bears." Young chuckled. "Oh, my! I don't really expect him to make it here the first time. We have some fine people in this team, don't we, Irvin?"

"Yes, sir," the master gunnery sergeant agreed at once.

"So what do you think of Clark?" Young asked next.

"Seems like he knows a thing or two," Irvin allowed. "Pretty decent shape for a civilian—and I like his eyes."

"Oh?"

"You notice, sir? He's got cold eyes. He's been around the block." They spoke in low murmurs. Kelly was supposed to get here, but they didn't want their voices to make it too easy for him, nor to add any extraneous noise that might mask the sounds of the woods. "But not tonight. I told the people what would happen if this guy gets through the line on his first try."

"Don't you Marines know how to play fair?" Maxwell objected with an unseen smile. Irvin handled the answer.

"Sir, 'fair' means all my Marines get back home alive. Fuck the others, beg your pardon, sir."

"Funny thing, Sergeant, that's always been my definition of 'fair,' too." *This guy would have made one hell of a command master chief,* Maxwell thought to himself.

"Been following baseball, Marty?" The men relaxed. No way Clark would make it.

"I think the Orioles look pretty tough."

"Gentlemen, we're losing our concentration, like," Irvin suggested diplomatically.

"Quite right. Please excuse us," General Young replied. The two flag officers settled back into stillness, watching the illuminated hands of their watches turn to three o'clock, the operation's agreed stop-time. They didn't hear Irvin speak, or even breathe, for all that time. That took an hour. It was a comfortable one for the Marine general, but the Admiral just didn't like being in the woods, with all the bloodsucking bugs, and probably snakes, and all manner of unpleasant things not ordinarily found in the cockpit of a fighter aircraft. They listened to the whispering breezes in the pines, heard the flapping of bats and owls and perhaps some other night fliers, and little else. Finally it was 02:55. Marty Young stood and stretched, fishing in his pocket for a cigarette.

"Anybody got a smoke? I'm out, and I could sure use one," a voice murmured.

"Here you go, Marine," Young said, the gracious general. He held one out to the shadow and flicked his trusty Zippo. Then he jumped back a step. "Shit!"

"Personally, General, I think Pittsburgh looks pretty tough this year. The Orioles are a little weak in the pitching department." Kelly took one puff, without inhaling, and dropped it to the ground.

"How long have you been here?" Maxwell demanded.

" 'Lions and tigers and bears, oh, my!' " Kelly mimicked. "I 'killed' you around one-thirty, sir."

"You son of a bitch!" Irvin said. "You killed *me.*"

"And you were very polite about being quiet, too."

Maxwell turned on his flashlight. Mr. Clark—the Admiral had consciously decided to change the boy's name in his own mind—just stood there, a rubber knife in his hand, his face painted with green and black shadows, and for the first time since the Battle of Midway, his body shuddered with fear. The young face split into a grin as he pocketed his "knife."

"How the hell did you do that?" Dutch Maxwell demanded.

"Pretty well, I think, Admiral." Kelly chuckled, reaching down for Marty Young's canteen. "Sir, if I told, then everybody'd be able to, right?"

Irvin stood up from his place of repose and walked next to the civilian.

"Mr. Clark, sir, I think you'll do."

22
Titles

Grishanov was in the embassy. Hanoi was a strange city, a mixture of French-Imperial architecture, little yellow people and bomb craters. Traveling about a country at war was an unusual exercise, all the more so in an automobile daubed with camouflage paint. A passing American fighter-bomber coming back from a mission with an extra bomb or some unexpended 20-millimeter cannon rounds could easily use the car for practice, though they never seemed to do so. The luck of the draw made this a cloudy, stormy day, and air activity was at a minimum, allowing him to relax, but not to enjoy the ride. Too many bridges were down, too many roads cratered, and the trip lasted three times what ought to have been the norm. A helicopter trip would have been much faster, but would also have been madness. The Americans seemed to live under the fiction that an automobile might be civilian-owned—this in a country where a bicycle was a status symbol! Grishanov marveled—but a helicopter was an aircraft, and killing one was a *kill*. Now in Hanoi, he got the chance to sit in a concrete building where the electricity was a sometime thing—off at the moment— and air conditioning an absurd fantasy. The open windows and poorly fitting screens allowed insects freer reign than the people who worked and sweated here. For all that, it was worth the trip to be here in his country's embassy, where he could speak his native tongue and for a precious few hours stop being a semidiplomat.

"So?" his general asked.

"It goes well, but I must have more people. This is too much for one man to do alone."

"That is not possible." The General poured his guest a glass of mineral

355

water. The principal mineral present was salt. The Russians drank a lot of that here. "Nikolay Yevgeniyevich, they're being difficult again."

"Comrade General, I know that I am only a fighter pilot and not a political theorist. I know that our fraternal socialist allies are on the front line of the conflict between Marxism-Leninism and the reactionary Capitalist West. I know that this war of national liberation is a vital part of our struggle to liberate the world from oppression—"

"Yes, Kolya"—the General smiled slyly, allowing the man who was *not* a political theorist to dispense with further ideological incantations— "we know that all of this is true. Do go on. I have a busy day planned."

The Colonel nodded his appreciation. "These arrogant little bastards are not helping us. They are using us, they are using me, they are using *my* prisoners to blackmail us. And if this is Marxism-Leninism, then I'm a Trotskyite." It was a joke that few would have been able to make lightly, but Grishanov's father was a Central Committee member with impeccable political credentials.

"What are you learning, Comrade Colonel?" the General said, just to keep things on track.

"Colonel Zacharias is everything that we were told, and more. We are now planning how to defend the *Rodina* against the Chinese. He is the 'blue team' leader."

"What?" The General blinked. "Explain?"

"This man is a fighter pilot, but also an expert on defeating air defenses. Can you believe it, he's only flown bombers as a guest, but he's actually planned SAC missions and helped to write SAC doctrine for defense-avoidance and -suppression. So now he's doing that for me."

"Notes?"

Grishanov's face darkened. "Back at the camp. Our fraternal socialist comrades are 'studying' them. Comrade General, do you know how important this data is?"

The General was by profession a tank officer, not an aviator, but he was also one of the brighter stars rising in the Soviet firmament, here in Vietnam to study everything the Americans were doing. It was one of the premier jobs in his country's uniformed service.

"I would imagine that it's highly valuable."

Kolya leaned forward. "In another two months, perhaps six weeks, I will be able to reverse-plan SAC. I'll be able to think as they think. I will know not only what their current plans are, but I will also be able to duplicate their thinking into the future. Excuse me, I do not mean to inflate my importance," he said sincerely. "This American is giving me a graduate course in

American doctrine and philosophy. I've *seen* the intelligence estimates we get from KGB and GRU. At least half of it is wrong. That's only one man. Another one has told me about their carrier doctrine. Another about NATO war plans. It goes on, Comrade General."

"How do you do this, Nikolay Yevgeniyevich?" The General was new at this post, and had met Grishanov only once before, though his service reputation was better than excellent.

Kolya leaned back in his chair. "Kindness and sympathy."

"To our enemies?" the General asked sharply.

"Is it our mission to inflict pain on these men?" He gestured outside. "That's what *they* do, and what do they get for it? Mainly lies that sound good. My section in Moscow discounted nearly everything these little monkeys sent. I was told to come here to *get information.* That is what I am doing. I will take all the criticism I must in order to get information such as this, Comrade."

The General nodded. "So why are you here?"

"I need more people! It's too much for one man. What if I am killed—what if I get malaria or food poisoning—who will do my work? I can't interrogate all of these prisoners myself. Especially now that they are beginning to talk, I take more and more time with each, and I lose energy. I lose continuity. There are not enough hours in the day."

The General sighed. "I've tried. They offer you their best—"

Grishanov almost snarled in frustration. "Their best *what?* Best barbarians? That would destroy my work. I need *Russians.* Men, *kulturny* men! Pilots, experienced officers. I'm not interrogating private soldiers. These are real professional warriors. They are valuable to us because of what they know. They know much because they are intelligent, and because they are intelligent they will not respond well to crude methods. You know what I really need to support me? A good psychiatrist. And one more thing," he added, inwardly trembling at his boldness.

"Psychiatrist? That is not serious. And I doubt that we'll be able to get other men into the camp. Moscow is delaying shipments of antiaircraft rockets for 'technical reasons.' Our local allies are being difficult again, as I said, and the disagreement escalates." The General leaned back and wiped sweat from his brow. "What is this other thing?"

"Hope, Comrade General. I need hope." Colonel Nikolay Yevgeniyevich Grishanov gathered himself.

"Explain."

"Some of these men know their situation. Probably all suspect it. They are well briefed on what happens to prisoners here, and they know that their

status is unusual. Comrade General, the knowledge these men have is encyclopedic. Years of useful information.''

"You're building up to something.''

"We can't let them die,'' Grishanov said, immediately qualifying himself to lessen the impact of what he was saying. "Not all of them. Some we
must have. Some will serve us, but I must have something to offer to them.''

"Bring them back?''

"After the hell they've lived here—''

"They're *enemies,* Colonel! They all trained to kill *us!* Save your sympathy for your own countrymen!'' growled a man who'd fought in the snows
outside Moscow.

Grishanov stood his ground, as the General had once done. "They are
men, not unlike us, Comrade General. They have knowledge that is useful,
if only we have the intelligence to extract it. It is that simple. Is it too much
to ask that we treat them with kindness, that we give something in return for
learning how to save our country from possible destruction? We could torture them, as our 'fraternal socialist allies' have done, and get *nothing!* Does
that serve our country?'' It came down to that, and the General knew it. He
looked at the Colonel of Air Defense and his first expressed thought was the
obvious one.

"You wish to risk my career along with yours? My father is not a
Central Committeeman.'' *I could have used this man in my battalion. . . .*

"Your father was a soldier,'' Grishanov pointed out. "And like you, a
good one.'' It was a skillful play and both knew it, but what really mattered
was the logic and significance of what Grishanov was proposing, an intelligence coup that would stagger the professional spies of KGB and GRU.
There was only one possible reaction from a real soldier with a real sense of
mission.

General-Lieutenant Yuri Konstantinovich Rokossovskiy pulled a bottle of vodka from his desk. It was the Starka label, dark, not clear, the best
and most expensive. He poured two small glasses.

"I can't get you more men. Certainly I cannot get you a physician, not
even one in uniform, Kolya. But, yes, I will try to get you some hope.''

The third convulsion since her arrival at Sandy's house was a minor
one, but still troubling. Sarah had gotten her quieted down with as mild a shot
of barbiturate as she dared. The blood work was back, and Doris was a
veritable collection of problems. Two kinds of venereal disease, evidence of
another systemic infection, and possibly a borderline diabetic. She was al-

ready attacking the first three problems with a strong dose of antibiotics. The fourth would be handled with diet and reevaluated later. For Sarah the signs of physical abuse were like something from a nightmare about another continent and another generation, and it was the mental aftermath of that that was the most disquieting of all, even as Doris Brown closed her eyes and lapsed into sleep.

"Doctor, I—"

"Sandy, will you *please* call me Sarah? We're in your house, remember?"

Nurse O'Toole managed an embarrassed smile. "Okay, Sarah. I'm worried."

"So am I. I'm worried about her physical condition, I'm worried about her psychological condition. I'm worried about her 'friends'—"

"I'm worried about John," Sandy said discordantly. Doris was under control. She could see that. Sarah Rosen was a gifted clinician, but something of a worrier, as many good physicians were.

Sarah headed out of the room. There was coffee downstairs. She could smell it and was heading for it. Sandy came with her. "Yes, that, too. What a strange and interesting man."

"I don't throw my newspapers away. Every week, same time, I bundle them together for the garbage collection—and I've been checking the back issues."

Sarah poured two cups. She had very delicate movements, Sandy thought. "I know what I think. Tell me what you think," the pharmacologist said.

"I think he's killing people." It caused her physical pain to say that.

"I think you're right." Sarah Rosen sat down and rubbed her eyes. "You never met Pam. Prettier than Doris, willowy, sort of, probably from an inadequate diet. It was much easier to wean her off the drugs. Not as badly abused, physically anyway, but just as much emotional hurt. We never got the whole story. Sam says that John did. But that's not the important part." Sarah looked up, and the pain O'Toole saw there was real and deep. "We had her *saved,* Sandy, and then something happened, and then something—something changed in John."

Sandy turned to look out the window. It was quarter of seven in the morning. She could see people coming out in pajamas and bathrobes to get their morning papers and collect half-gallon bottles of milk. The early crowd was leaving for their cars, a process that in her neighborhood lasted until eight-thirty or so. She turned back. "No, nothing changed. It was always there. Something—I don't know, released it, let it out? Like opening the door of a cage. What sort of man—part of him's like Tim, but another part I just don't understand.''

"What about his family?''

"He doesn't have any. His mother and father are dead, no siblings. He was married—''

"Yes, I know about that, and then Pam.'' Sarah shook her head. "So lonely.''

"Part of me says he's a good man, but the other part . . .'' Sandy's voice trailed off.

"My maiden name was Rabinowicz,'' Sarah said, sipping her coffee. "My family comes from Poland. Papa left when I was too young to remember; mother died when I was nine, peritonitis. I was eighteen when the war started,'' she went on. For her generation "the war'' could mean only one thing. "We had lots of relatives in Poland. I remember writing to them. Then they all just disappeared. All gone—even now it's hard to believe it really happened.''

"I'm sorry, Sarah, I didn't know.''

"It's not the sort of thing you talk a lot about.'' Dr. Rosen shrugged. "People took something from me, though, and I couldn't do anything about it. My cousin Reva was a good pen pal. I suppose they killed her one way or another, but I never found out who or where. Back then I was too young to understand. I suppose I was more puzzled than anything else. Later, I got angry—but against whom? I didn't do anything. I couldn't. And there's this empty space where Reva was. I still have her picture, black-and-white of a girl with pigtails, twelve years old, I guess. She wanted to be a ballet dancer.'' Sarah looked up. "Kelly's got an empty place, too.''

"But revenge—''

"Yeah, revenge.'' The doctor's expression was bleak. "I know. We're supposed to think he's a bad person, aren't we? Call the police, even, turn him in for doing that.''

"I can't—I mean, yes, but I just—''

"Neither will I. Sandy, if he were a bad person, why did he bring Doris up here? He's risking his life two different ways.''

"But there's something very scary about him.''

"He could have just walked away from her,'' Sarah went on, not really hearing. "Maybe he's just the sort of person who thinks he has to fix everything himself. But now we have to help.''

That turned Sandy around, giving her a respite from her real thoughts. "What are we going to do with her?''

"We're going to get her well, as far as we can, and after that it'll be up to her. What else can we do?" Sarah asked, watching Sandy's face change again, returning to her real dilemma.

"But what about John?"

Sarah looked up. "I have never seen him do anything illegal. Have you?"

It was a weapons-training day. A solid cloud cover meant that no reconnaissance satellites, American or Soviet, could see what was happening here. Cardboard targets were set up around the compound, and the lifeless eyes of mannequins watched from the sandbox and swing set as the Marines emerged from the woods, passing through the simulated gate, firing low-powered rounds from their carbines. The targets were shredded in seconds. Two M-60 machine guns poured fire into the open door of the "barracks"— which would already have been wrecked by the two Huey Cobra gunships— while the snatch team raced into the "prison block." There, twenty-five more mannequins were in individual rooms. Each was weighted to about one hundred fifty pounds—nobody thought that the Americans at SENDER GREEN would weigh even that much—and every one was dragged out while the fire-support element covered the evacuation.

Kelly stood next to Captain Pete Albie, who, it had been assumed for the purpose of the exercise, was dead. He was the only officer on the team, an aberration that was compensated for by the presence of so many senior NCOs. As they watched, the mannequins were dragged to the simulated fuselages of the rescue helicopters. These were mounted on semitrailers, and had come in at dawn. Kelly clicked his stopwatch when the last man was aboard.

"Five seconds under nominal, Captain." Kelly held up the watch. "These boys are pretty good."

"Except we're not doing it in daylight, are we, Mr. Clark?" Albie, like Kelly, knew the nature of the mission. The Marines as yet did not—at least not officially—though by now they had to have a fairly good idea. He turned and smiled. "Okay, it's only the third run-through."

Both men went into the compound. The simulated targets were in feathery pieces, and their number was exactly double the worst-case estimate for the SENDER GREEN guard force. They replayed the assault in their minds, checking angles of fire. There were advantages and disadvantages to how the camp was set up. Following the rules in some nameless East Bloc manual, it didn't fit the local terrain. Most conveniently indeed, the best avenue of approach coincided with the main gate. In adhering to a standard that allowed for maximum security against a possible escape attempt of the prisoners, it also facilitated an assault from without—but they didn't expect that, did they?

Kelly ran over the assault plan in his mind. The insertion would put the Recon Marines on the ground one ridge away from SENDER GREEN. Thirty minutes for the Marines to approach the camp. M-79 grenades to eliminate the guard towers. Two Huey Cobra gunships—known with lethal elegance as "snakes" to the troops, and that appealed to him—would hose the barracks and provide heavy fire support—but the grenadiers on the team, he was sure, could take out the towers in a matter of five seconds, then pour willie-pete into the barracks and burn the guard force alive with deadly fountains of white flame, doing without the snakes entirely if they had to. Small and lean as this operation was, the size of the objective and the quality of the team made for unplanned safety factors. He thought of it as overkill, a term that didn't just apply to nuclear weapons. In combat operations, safety lay in not giving the other guy a chance, to be ready to kill him two, three, a dozen times over in as little time as possible. Combat wasn't supposed to be fair. To Kelly, things were looking very good indeed.

"What if they have mines?" Albie worried.

"On their own turf?" Kelly asked. "No sign of it from the photographs. The ground isn't disturbed. No warning signs to keep their people away."

"Their people would know, wouldn't they?"

"On one of the photos there's some goats grazing just outside the wire, remember?"

Albie nodded with some embarrassment. "Yeah, you're right. I remember that."

"Let's not borrow trouble," Kelly told him. He fell silent for a moment, realizing that he had been a mere E-7 chief petty officer, and now he was talking as an equal—more accurately as a superior—to an O-3 captain of Recon Marines. That ought to have been—what? Wrong? If so, then why was he doing so well at it, and why was the captain accepting his words? Why was he *Mr. Clark* to this experienced combat officer? "We're going to do it."

"I think you're right, Mr. Clark. And how do you get out?"

"As soon as the choppers come in, I break the Olympic record coming down that hill to the LZ. I call it a two-minute run."

"In the dark?" Albie asked.

Kelly laughed. "I run especially fast in the dark, Captain."

*   *   *

"Do you know how many Ka-Bar knives there are?"

From the tone of Douglas's question, Lieutenant Ryan knew the news had to be bad. "No, but I suppose I'm about to find out."

"Sunny's Surplus just took delivery of a thousand of the goddamn things a month ago. The Marines must have enough and so now the Boy Scouts can buy them for four ninety-five. Other places, too. I didn't know how many of the things were out there."

"Me, neither," Ryan admitted. The Ka-Bar was a very large and bulky weapon. Hoods carried smaller knives, especially switchblades, though guns were becoming increasingly common on the streets.

What neither man wanted to admit openly was that they were stymied again, despite what had appeared to be a wealth of physical evidence in the brownstone. Ryan looked down at the open file and about twenty forensic photographs. There had *almost* certainly been a woman there. The murder victim—probably a hood himself, but still officially a victim—had been identified immediately from the cards in his wallet, but the address on his driver's license had turned out to be a vacant building. His collection of traffic violations had been paid on time, with cash. Richard Farmer had brushed with the police, but nothing serious enough to have merited a detailed inquiry. Tracking his family down had turned up precisely nothing. His mother—the father was long dead—had thought him a salesman of some sort. But somebody had nearly carved his heart out with a fighting knife, so quickly and decisively that the gun on the body hadn't been touched. A full set of fingerprints from Farmer merely generated a new card. The central FBI register did not have a match. Neither did the local police, and though Farmer's prints would be compared with a wide selection of unknowns, Ryan and Douglas didn't expect much. The bedroom had provided three complete sets of Farmer's, all on window glass, and semen stains had matched his blood type—O. Another set of stains had been typed as AB, which could mean the killer or the supposed (not quite certain) missing owner of the Roadrunner. For all they knew the killer might have taken the time to have a quickie with the suspected female—unless homosexuality was involved, in which case the suspected female might not exist at all.

There were also a selection of partial prints, one of a girl (supposition, from their size), and one of a man (also supposition), but they were so partial that he didn't expect much in the way of results. Worst of all, by the time the latent-prints team had gotten to check out the car parked outside, the blazing August sun had heated the car up so much that what might have been something to match prints with the registered owner of the car, one William Peter Grayson, had merely been a collection of heat-distorted blobs. It wasn't widely appreciated that matching partial prints with less than ten points of identification was difficult at best.

A check of the FBI's new National Crime Information Computer had turned up nothing on Grayson or Farmer. Finally, Mark Charon's narcotics team had nothing on the names Farmer or Grayson. It wasn't so much a matter of being back to square one. It was just that square seventeen didn't lead them anywhere. But that was often the way of things in homicide investigation. Detective work was a combination of the ordinary and the remarkable, but more of the former than the latter. Forensic sciences could tell you much. They did have the imprint of a common-brand sneaker from tracks in the brownstone—brand new, a help. They did know the approximate stride of the killer, from which they had generated a height range of from five-ten to six-three, which, unfortunately, was taller than Virginia Charles had estimated—something they, however, discounted. They knew he was Caucasian. They knew he had to be strong. They knew that he was either very, very lucky or highly skilled with all manner of weapons. They knew that he probably had at least rudimentary skills in hand-to-hand combat—or, Ryan sighed to himself, had been lucky; after all, there had been only one such encounter, and that with an addict with heroin in his bloodstream. They knew he was disguising himself as a bum.

All of which amounted to not very much. More than half of male humanity fell into the estimated height range. Considerably more than half of the men in the Baltimore metropolitan area were white. There were millions of combat veterans in America, many from elite military units—and the fact of the matter was that infantry skills were infantry skills, and you didn't have to be a combat vet to know them, and his country had had a draft for over thirty years, Ryan told himself. There were perhaps as many as thirty thousand men within a twenty-mile radius who fit the description and skill-inventory of his unknown suspect. Was he in the drug business himself? Was he a robber? Was he, as Farber had suggested, a man on some sort of mission? Ryan leaned heavily to the latter model, but he could not afford to discount the other two. Psychiatrists, and detectives, had been wrong before. The most elegant theories could be shattered by a single inconvenient fact. *Damn.* No, he told himself, this one was exactly what Farber said he was. This wasn't a *criminal.* This was a *killer,* something else entirely.

"We just need the one thing," Douglas said quietly, knowing the look on his lieutenant's face.

"The one thing," Ryan repeated. It was a private bit of shorthand. *The one thing* to break a case could be a name, an address, the description or tag number of a car, a person who knew something. Always the same, though frequently different, it was for the detective the crucial piece in the jigsaw puzzle that made the picture clear, and for the suspect the brick which, taken from the wall, caused everything to fall apart. And it was out there. Ryan was sure of it. It had to be there, because this killer was a clever one, much too clever for his own good. A suspect like this who eliminated a single target could well go forever undetected, but this one was not satisfied with killing one person, was he? Motivated neither by passion nor by financial gain, he was committed to a *process,* every step of which involved complex dangers. That was what would do him in. The detective was sure of it. Clever as he was, those complexities would continue to mount one upon the other until something important fell loose from the pile. It might even have happened already, Ryan thought, correctly.

"Two weeks," Maxwell said.

"That fast?" James Greer leaned forward, resting his elbows on his knees. "Dutch, that's really fast."

"You think we should fiddle around?" Podulski asked.

"Damn it, Cas, I said it was fast. I didn't say it was wrong. Two weeks' more training, one week of travel and setup?" Greer asked, getting a nod. "What about weather?"

"The one thing we can't control," Maxwell admitted. "But weather works both ways. It makes flying difficult. It also messes up radar and gunnery."

"How in hell did you get all the pieces moving this early?" Greer asked with a mixture of disbelief and admiration.

"There are ways, James. Hell, we're admirals, aren't we? We give orders, and guess what? Ships actually move."

"So the window opens in twenty-one days?"

"Correct. Cas flies out tomorrow to *Constellation.* We start briefing the air-support guys. *Newport News* is already clued in—well, partway. They think they're going to sweep the coast for triple-A batteries. Our command ship is plodding across the big pond right now. They don't know anything either except to rendezvous with TF-77."

"I have a lot of briefing to do," Cas confirmed with a grin.

"Helicopter crews?"

"They've been training at Coronado. They come into Quantico tonight. Pretty standard stuff, really. The tactics are straightforward. What does your man 'Clark' say?"

"He's my man now?" Greer asked. "He tells me he's comfortable with how things are going. Did you enjoy being killed?"

"He told you?" Maxwell chuckled. "James, I knew the boy was good from what he did with Sonny, but it's different when you're there to see it—hell, to *not* see or hear it. He shut Marty Young up, and that's no small feat. Embarrassed a lot of Marines, too."

"Give me a timeline on getting mission approval," Greer said. It was serious now. He'd always thought the operation had merit, and watching it develop had been a lesson in many things that he'd need to know at CIA. Now he believed it possible. BOXWOOD GREEN might well succeed if allowed to go.

"You're sure Mr. Ritter won't waffle on us?"

"I don't think he will. He's one of us, really."

"Not until all the pieces are in place," Podulski said.

"He'll want to see a rehearsal," Greer warned. "Before you ask a guy to stick it on the line, he has to have confidence in the job."

"That's fair. We have a full-up live-fire rehearsal tomorrow night."

"We'll be there, Dutch," Greer promised.

The team was in an old barracks designed for at least sixty men, and there was plenty of room for everyone, enough that no one had a top bunk. Kelly had a private room set aside, one of those designed into the standard barracks for squad sergeants to sleep in. He'd decided not to live on his boat. One could not be part of the team and yet be totally separate from it.

They were enjoying their first night off since arriving at Quantico, and some kind soul had arranged for three cases of beer. That made for exactly three bottles each, since one of their number only drank Dr Pepper, and Master Gunnery Sergeant Irvin made sure that none of their number exceeded the limit.

"Mr. Clark," one of the grenadiers asked, "what's this all about?"

It wasn't fair, Kelly thought, to make them train without letting them know. They prepared for danger without knowing why, without knowing what purpose occasioned the risk of their lives and their future. It wasn't fair at all, but it wasn't unusual either. He looked straight in the man's eyes.

"I can't tell you, Corp. All I can say is, it's something you'll be mighty proud of. You have my word on that, Marine."

The corporal, at twenty-one the youngest and most junior man of the group, hadn't expected an answer, but he'd had to ask. He accepted the reply with a raise-can salute.

"I know that tattoo," a more senior man said.

Kelly smiled, finishing his second. "Oh, I got drunk one night, and I guess I got mistook for somebody else."

"All SEALs are good for is balancing a ball on their nose," a buck sergeant said, following it with a belch.

"Want me to demonstrate with one of yours?" Kelly asked quickly.

"Good one!" The sergeant tossed Kelly another beer.

"Mr. Clark?" Irvin gestured to the door. It was just as sticky-hot out there as inside, with a gentle breeze coming through the long-needled pines and the flapping of bats, invisibly chasing insects.

"What is it?" Kelly asked, taking a long pull.

"That's my question, Mr. Clark, sir," Irvin said lightly. Then his voice changed. "I know you."

"Oh?"

"Third Special Operations Group. My team backed you guys up on ERMINE COAT. You've come far for an E-6," Irvin observed.

"Don't spread it around, but I made chief before I left. Does anybody else know?"

Irvin chuckled. "No, I expect Captain Albie would sure as hell get his nose outa joint if he found out, and General Young might have a conniption. We'll just keep it 'tween us, Mr. Clark," Irvin said, establishing his position in oblique but uncertain terms.

"This wasn't my idea—being here, I mean. Admirals are easy to impress, I suppose."

"I'm not, Mr. Clark. You almost gave me a fucking heart attack with that rubber knife of yours. I don't remember your name, your real one, I mean, but you're the guy they called Snake, aren't you? You're the guy did PLASTIC FLOWER."

"That wasn't the smartest thing I ever did," Kelly pointed out.

"We were your backup on that, too. The goddamned chopper died— engine quit ten feet off the ground—*thump*. That's why we didn't make it. Nearest alternate was from First Cav. That's why it took so long."

Kelly turned. Irvin's face was as black as the night. "I didn't know."

The master gunnery sergeant shrugged in the darkness. "I seen the pictures of what happened. The skipper told us that you were a fool to break the rules like that. But that was our fault. We should have been there twenty minutes after your call. If'n we got there on time, maybe one or two of those little girls might have made it. Anyway, reason we didn't was a bad seal on the engine, just a little goddamn piece of rubber that cracked."

Kelly grunted. On such events the fates of nations turned. "Could have been worse—it could have let go at altitude and you woulda really been in the shitter."

"True. Miserable fuckin' reason for a child to die, isn't it?" Irvin paused, gazing into the darkness of the piney woods as men of his profession did, always looking and listening. "I understand why you did it. I wanted you to know. Probably woulda done the same myself. Maybe not as good as you, but sure as hell, I would have tried, and I wouldn't have let that mother-fucker live, orders or no orders."

"Thanks, Guns," Kelly said quietly, dropping back into Navyspeak.

"It's Song Tay, isn't it?" Irvin observed next, knowing that he'd get his answer now.

"Something close to that, yes. They should be telling you soon."

"You have to tell me more, Mr. Clark. I have Marines to worry about."

"The site is set up just right, perfect match. Hey, I'm going in, too, remember?"

"Keep talking," Irvin ordered gently.

"I helped plan the insertion. With the right people, we can do it. Those are good boys you have in there. I won't say it's easy or any dumb shit like that, but it's not all that hard. I've done harder. So have you. The training is going right. It looks pretty good to me, really."

"You sure it's worth it?"

That was a question with meaning so deep that few would have under-stood it. Irvin had done two combat tours, and though Kelly hadn't seen his official "salad bar" of decorations, he was clearly a man who had circled the block many times. Now Irvin was watching what might well be the destruc-tion of his Marine Corps. Men were dying for hills that were given back as soon as they were taken and the casualties cleared, then to return in six months to repeat the exercise. There was just something in the professional soldier that hated repetition. Although training was just that—they had "as-saulted" the site numerous times—the reality of war was supposed to be one battle for one place. In that way a man could tell what progress was. Before looking forward to a new objective, you could look back to see how far you had come and measure your chance for success by what you had learned before. But the third time you watched men die for the same piece of ground, then you knew. You just knew how things were going to end. Their country was still sending men to that place, asking them to risk their lives for dirt already watered in American blood. The truth was that Irvin would not have voluntarily gone back for a third combat tour. It wasn't a question of courage or dedication or love of country. It was that he knew his life was too valuable to be risked for nothing. Sworn to defend his country, he had a right to ask for something in return—a real mission to fight for, not an abstraction, something *real*. And yet Irvin felt guilt, felt that he had broken faith, had betrayed the motto of The Corps, *Semper Fidelis:* Always Faithful. The guilt had compelled him to volunteer for one last mission despite his doubts and questions. Like a man whose beloved wife has slept with another man, Irvin could not stop loving, could not stop caring, and he would accept to himself the guilt unacknowledged by those who had earned it.

"Guns, I can't tell you this, but I will anyway. The place we're hitting, it's a prison camp, like you think, okay?"

Irvin nodded. "More to it. There has to be."

"It's not a regular camp. The men there, they're all dead, Guns." Kelly crushed the beer can. "I've seen the photos. One guy we identified for sure, Air Force colonel, the NVA said he was killed, and so we think these guys, they'll never come home unless we go get 'em. I don't want to go back either, man. I'm scared, okay? Oh, yeah, I'm good, I'm real good at this stuff. Good training, maybe I have a knack for it." Kelly shrugged, not wanting to say the next part.

"Yeah. But you can only do it so long." Irvin handed over another beer.

"I thought three was the limit."

"I'm a Methodist, not supposed to drink at all." Irvin chuckled. "People like us, Mr. Clark."

"Dumb sunzabitches, aren't we? There's Russians in the camp, probably interrogating our people. They're all high-rank, and we think they're all officially dead. They're probably being grilled real hard for what they know, because of who they are. We know they're there, and if we don't do anything . . . what's that make us?" Kelly stopped himself, suddenly needing to go further, to *tell* what else he was doing, because he had found someone who might truly understand, and for all his obsession with avenging Pam his soul was becoming heavy with its burden.

"Thank you, Mr. Clark. That's a fuckin' mission," Master Gunnery Sergeant Paul Irvin told the pine trees and the bats. "So you're first in and last out?"

"I've worked alone before."

23

Altruism

"Where am I?" Doris Brown asked in a barely understandable voice.

"Well, you're in my house," Sandy answered. She sat in the corner of the guest bedroom, switching off the reading light and setting down the paperback she'd been reading for the past few hours.

"How did I get here?"

"A friend brought you here. I'm a nurse. The doctor is downstairs fixing breakfast. How are you feeling?"

"Terrible." Her eyes closed. "My head . . ."

"That's normal, but I know it's bad." Sandy stood and came over, touching the girl's forehead. No fever, which was good news. Next she felt for a pulse. Strong, regular, though still a touch fast. From the way her eyes were screwed shut, Sandy guessed that the extended barbiturate hangover must have been awful, but that too was normal. The girl smelled from sweating and vomiting. They'd tried to keep her clean, but that had been a losing battle, if a not terribly important one compared to the rest. Until now, perhaps. Doris's skin was sallow and slack, as though the person inside had shrunk. She must have lost ten or fifteen pounds since arriving, and while that wasn't an entirely bad thing, she was so weak that she'd not yet noticed the restraints holding her hands, feet, and waist in place.

"How long?"

"Almost a week." Sandy took a sponge and wiped her face. "You gave us quite a scare." Which was an understatement. No less than seven convulsions, the second of which had almost panicked both nurse and physician, but number seven—a mild one—was eighteen hours behind them now, and the patient's vital signs were stabilized. With luck that phase of her recovery was behind them. Sandy let Doris have some water.

"Thank you," Doris said in a very small voice. "Where's Billy and Rick?"

"I don't know who they are," Sandy replied. It was technically correct. She'd read the articles in the local papers, always stopping short of reading any names. Nurse O'Toole was telling herself that she didn't really know anything. It was a useful internal defense against feelings so mixed that even had she taken the time to figure things out, she knew she would have only confused herself all the more. It was not a time for bare facts. Sarah had convinced her of that. It was a time for riding with the shape of events, not the substance. "Are they the ones who hurt you?"

Doris was nude except for the restraints and the oversized diapers used on patients unable to manage their bodily functions. It was easier to treat her that way. The horrid marks on her breasts and torso were fading now. What had been ugly, discrete marks of blue and black and purple and red were fading to poorly defined areas of yellow-brown as her body struggled to heal itself. She was young, Sandy told herself, and while not yet healthy, she could become so. Enough to heal, perhaps, inside and outside. Already her systemic infections were responding to the massive doses of antibiotics. The fever was gone, and her body could now turn to the more mundane repair tasks.

Doris turned her head and opened her eyes. "Why are you doing this for me?"

That answer was an easy one: "I'm a nurse, Miss Brown. It's my job to take care of sick people."

"Billy and Rick," she said next, remembering again. Memory for Doris was a variable and spotty thing, mainly the recollection of pain.

"They're not here," O'Toole assured her. She paused before going on, and to her surprise found satisfaction in the words: "I don't think they'll be bothering you again." There was almost comprehension in the patient's eyes, Sandy thought. Almost. And that was encouraging.

"I have to go. Please—" She started to move and then noticed the restraints.

"Okay, wait a minute." Sandy removed the straps. "You think you can stand today?"

". . . try," she groaned. Doris rose perhaps thirty degrees before her body betrayed her. Sandy got her sitting up, but the girl couldn't quite make her head sit straight on her neck. Standing her up was even harder, but it wasn't that far to the bathroom, and the dignity of making it there was worth the pain and the effort for her patient. Sandy sat her down there, holding her hand. She took the time to dampen a washcloth and do her face.

"That's a step forward," Sarah Rosen observed from the door. Sandy turned and smiled by way of communicating the patient's condition. They put a robe on her before bringing her back to the bedroom. Sandy changed the linen first, while Sarah got a cup of tea into the patient.

"You're looking much better today, Doris," the physician said, watching her drink.

"I feel awful."

"That's okay, Doris. You have to feel awful before you can start to feel better. Yesterday you weren't feeling much of anything. Think you can try some toast?"

"So hungry."

"Another good sign," Sandy noted. The look in her eyes was so bad that both doctor and nurse could *feel* the skull-rending headache which today would be treated only with an ice pack. They'd spent a week leaching the drugs from her system, and this wasn't the time for adding new ones. "Lean your head back."

Doris did that, resting her head on the back of the overstuffed chair Sandy had once bought at a garage sale. Her eyes were closed and her limbs so weak that her arms merely rested on the fabric while Sarah handled the individual slices of dry toast. The nurse took a brush and started working on her patient's hair. It was filthy and needed washing, but just getting it straightened out would help, she thought. Medical patients put an amazing amount of stock in their physical appearance, and however odd or illogical it might seem to be, it was real, and therefore something which Sandy recognized as important. She was a little surprised by Doris's shudder a minute or so after she started.

"Am I alive?" The alarm in the question was startling.

"Very much so," Sarah answered, almost smiling at the exaggeration. She checked her blood pressure. "One twenty-two over seventy-eight."

"Excellent!" Sandy noted. It was the best reading all week.

"Pam . . ."

"What's that?" Sarah asked.

It took Doris a moment to go on, still wondering if this were life or death, and if the latter, what part of eternity she had found. "Hair . . . when she was dead . . . brushed her hair."

Dear God, Sarah thought. Sam had related that one part of the postmortem report to her, morosely sipping a highball at their home in Green Spring

Valley. He hadn't gone further than that. It hadn't been necessary. The photo on the front page of the paper had been quite sufficient. Dr. Rosen touched her patient's face as gently as she could.

"Doris, who killed Pam?" She thought that she could ask this without increasing the patient's pain. She was wrong.

"Rick and Billy and Burt and Henry . . . killed her . . . watching . . ." The girl started crying, and the racking sobs only magnified the shuddering waves of pain in her head. Sarah held back on the toast. Nausea might soon follow.

"They made you watch?"

"Yes . . ." Doris's voice was like one from the grave.

"Let's not think about that now." Sarah's body shuddered with the kind of chill she associated with death itself as she stroked the girl's cheek.

"There!" Sandy said brightly, hoping to distract her. "That's much better."

"Tired."

"Okay, let's get you back to bed, dear." Both women helped her up. Sandy left the robe on her, setting an ice bag on her forehead. Doris faded off into sleep almost at once.

"Breakfast is on," Sarah told the nurse. "Leave the restraints off for now."

"Brushed her hair? What?" Sandy asked, heading down the stairs.

"I didn't read the report—"

"I saw the photo, Sarah—what they did to her—Pam, her name was, right?" Sandy was almost too tired to remember things herself.

"Yes. She was my patient, too," Dr. Rosen confirmed. "Sam said it was pretty bad. The odd thing, somebody brushed her hair out after she was dead, he told me that. I guess it was Doris who did it."

"Oh." Sandy opened the refrigerator and got milk for the morning coffee. "I see."

"I don't," Dr. Rosen said angrily. "I don't *see* how people can do that. Another few months and Doris would have died. As it was, any closer—"

"I'm surprised you didn't admit her under a Jane Doe," Sandy observed.

"After what happened to Pam, taking a chance like that—and it would have meant—"

O'Toole nodded. "Yes, it would have meant endangering John. That's what I understand."

"Hmph?"

"They killed her friend and made her watch . . . the things they did to her . . . To them *she* was just a *thing!* . . . Billy and Rick,'' Sandy said aloud, not quite realizing it.

"Burt and Henry," Sarah corrected. "I don't think the other two will be hurting anybody anymore." The two women shared a look, their eyes meeting across the breakfast table, their thoughts identical, though both were distantly shocked at the very idea of holding them, much less understanding them.

"Good."

"Well, we've shaken down every bum west of Charles Street," Douglas told his lieutenant. "We've had one cop cut—not seriously, but the wino is in for a long drying-out period at Jessup. A bunch have been puked on," he added with a smirk, "but we still don't know crap. He's not out there, Em. Nothing new in a week."

And it was true. The word had gotten out to the street, surprisingly slow but inevitable. Street pushers were being careful to the point of paranoia. That might or might not explain the fact that not a single one had lost his life in over a week.

"He's still out there, Tom."

"Maybe so, but he's not doing anything."

"In which case everything he did was to get Farmer and Grayson," Ryan noted with a look at the sergeant.

"You don't believe that."

"No, I don't, and don't ask me why, because I don't know why."

"Well, it would help if Charon could tell us something. He's been pretty good taking people down. Remember that bust he did with the Coast Guard?"

Ryan nodded. "That was a good one, but he's slowed down lately."

"So have we, Em," Sergeant Douglas pointed out. "The only thing we really know about this guy is that he's strong, he wears new sneaks, and he's white. We don't know age, weight, size, motive, what kind of car he drives."

"Motive. We know he's pissed about something. We know he's very good at killing. We know he's ruthless enough to kill people just to cover his own activities . . . and he's patient." Ryan leaned back. "Patient enough to take time off?"

Tom Douglas had a more troubling idea. "Smart enough to change tactics."

That was a disturbing thought. Ryan considered it. What if he'd seen the shakedowns? What if he'd decided that you could only do one thing so long, and then you had to do something else? What if he'd developed information from William Grayson, and that information was now taking him in other directions—out of town, even? What if they'd never know, never close these cases? That would be a professional insult to Ryan, who hated leaving cases open, but he had to consider it. Despite dozens of field interviews, they had not turned up so much as a single witness except for Virginia Charles, and she'd been sufficiently traumatized that her information was scarcely believable—and contradicted the one really useful piece of forensic evidence they had. The suspect had to be taller than she had said, had to be younger, and sure as hell was as strong as an NFL linebacker. He wasn't a wino, but had chosen to camouflage himself as one. You just didn't *see* people like that. How did you describe a stray dog?

"The Invisible Man," Ryan said quietly, finally giving the case a name. "He should have killed Mrs. Charles. You know what we've got here?"

Douglas snorted. "Somebody I don't want to meet alone."

"Three groups to take Moscow out?"

"Sure, why not?" Zacharias replied. "It's your political leadership, isn't it? It's a huge communications center, and even if you get the Politburo out, they'll still get most of your military and political command and control—"

"We have ways to get our important people out," Grishanov objected out of professional and national pride.

"Sure." Robin almost laughed, Grishanov saw. Part of him was insulted, but on reflection he was pleased with himself that the American colonel felt that much at ease now. "Kolya, we have things like that, too. We have a real ritzy shelter set up in West Virginia for Congress and all that. The 1st Helicopter Squadron is at Andrews, and their mission is to get VIPs the heck out of Dodge—but guess what? The durned helicopters can't hop all the way to the shelter and back without refueling on the return leg. Nobody thought about that when they selected the shelter, because *that* was a political decision. Guess what else? We've never tested the evacuation system. Have you tested yours?"

Grishanov sat down next to Zacharias, on the floor, his back against the dirty concrete wall. Nikolay Yevgeniyevich just looked down and shook his head, having learned yet more from the American. "You see? You see why I say we'll never fight a war? We're *alike!* No, Robin, we've never tested it, we've never tried to evacuate Moscow since I was a child in the snow. Our big shelter is at Zhiguli. It's a big stone—not a mountain, like a big—bubble? I don't know the word, a huge circle of stone from the center of the earth.''

''Monolith? Like Stone Mountain in Georgia?''

Grishanov nodded. There was no harm in giving secrets to this man, was there? ''The geologists say it is immensely strong, and we tunneled into it back in the late 1950s. I've been there twice. I helped supervise the air-defense office when they were building it. We expect—this is the truth, Robin—we expect to get our people there by *train.*''

''It won't matter. We know about it. If you know where it is, you can take it out, just a matter of how many bombs you put there.'' The American had a hundred grams of vodka in him. ''Probably the Chinese do, too. But they'll go for Moscow anyway, especially if it's a surprise attack.''

''Three groups?''

''That's how I'd do it.'' Robin's feet straddled an air-navigation chart of the southeastern Soviet Union. ''Three vectors, from these three bases, three aircraft each, two to carry the bombs, one a protective jammer. Jammer takes the lead. Bring in all three groups on line, like, spaced wide like this.'' He traced likely courses on the map. ''Start your penetration descent here, take 'em right into these valleys, and by the time they hit the plains—''

''Steppes,'' Kolya corrected.

''They're through your first line of defense, okay? They're smoking in low, like three hundred feet. Maybe they don't even jam at first. Maybe you have one special group, even. The guys you really train.''

''What do you mean, Robin?''

''You have night flights into Moscow, airliners, I mean?''

''Of course.''

''Well, what say you take a Badger, and you leave the strobes on, okay, and maybe you have little glow lights down the fuselage that you can turn on and off—you know, like windows? Hey, I'm an airliner.''

''You mean?''

''It's something we looked at once. There's a squadron with the light kits still at . . . Pease, I think. That used to be the job—the B-47s based in England. If we ever decided like you guys were going to go after us, from intelligence or something, okay? You gotta have a plan for everything. That was one of ours. We called it JUMPSHOT. Probably in the dead files now, that was one of LeMay's specials. Moscow, Leningrad, Kiev—and Zhiguli. Three birds targeted there, two weapons each. Decap your whole political and military command structure. Hey look, I'm an airliner!''

It would work, Grishanov thought with an eerie chill. The right time of year, the right time of day . . . the bomber comes in on a regularly scheduled airliner route. Even in a crisis, the very illusion of something normal would be like a touchstone while people looked for the unusual. Maybe an air-defense squadron would put an aircraft up, a young pilot standing night alert while the senior men slept. He'd close to a thousand meters or so, but at night . . . at night your mind saw what the brain told it to see. Lights on the fuselage, well, of course it's an airliner. What bomber would be lit up? That was one op-plan the KGB had never tumbled to. How many more gifts would Zacharias give him?

"Anyway, if I was John Chinaman, that's one option. If they don't have much imagination, and go with a straight attack, over this terrain, yeah, they can do that. Probably one group is diversionary. They have a real target, too, but short of Moscow. They fly in high, off vector. About this far out"—he swept a hand across the map—"they make a radical turn and hit something, you can decide what's important, lots of good targets there. Chances are your fighters keep after them, right?"

"*Da.*" They'd think the inbound bombers were turning away for a secondary target.

"The other two groups loop around from another direction, and they smoke in low. One of 'em's gonna make it, too. We've played it out a million times, Kolya. We know your radars, we know your bases, we know your airplanes, we know how you train. You're not that hard to beat. And the Chinese, they studied with you, right? You taught them. They know your doctrine and everything."

It was how he said it. No guile at all. And this was a man who had penetrated the North Vietnamese air defenses over eighty times. Eighty times.

"So how do I—"

"Defend against it?" Robin shrugged, bending down to examine the chart again. "I need better maps, but first thing, you examine the passes one at a time. You remember that a bomber isn't a fighter. He can't maneuver all that great, especially low. Most of what he's doing is keeping the airplane from crunching into the ground, right? I don't know about you, but that makes me nervous. He's going to pick a valley he can maneuver in. Especially at night. You put your fighters there. You put ground radars there. You don't need big sexy ones. That's just a bell-ringer. Then you plan to catch him when he comes out."

"Move the defenses back? I can't do that!"

"You put your defenses where they can work, Kolya, not to follow a dotted line on a piece of paper. Or do you like eating Chinese all that much?

That's always been a weakness with you people. By the way, it also shortens your lines, right? You save money and assets. Next thing, you remember that the other guy, he knows how pilots think, too—a kill is a kill, right? Maybe there's decoy groups designed to draw your people out, okay? We have scads of radar lures we plan to use. You have to allow for that. You *control* your people. They stay in their sectors unless you have a really good reason to move them. . . ."

Colonel Grishanov had studied his profession for more than twenty years, had studied Luftwaffe documents not merely related to prisoner interrogation, but also classified studies of how the Kammhuber Line had been set up. This was incredible, almost enough to make him take a drink himself. But not quite, he told himself. This wasn't a briefing document in the making, wasn't a learned White Paper for delivery at the Voroshilov Academy. This was a learned book, highly classified, but a *book*: *Origin and Evolution of American Bomber Doctrine*. From such a book he could go on to marshal's stars, all because of his American friend.

"Let's all stay back here," Marty Young said. "They're shooting all live stuff."

"Makes sense to me," Dutch said. "I'm used to having things go off a couple hundred yards behind me."

"And four hundred knots of delta-V," Greer added for him.

"A lot safer that way, James," Maxwell pointed out.

They stood behind an earthen berm, the official military term for a pile of dirt, two hundred yards from the camp. It made watching difficult, but two of the five had aviator's eyes, and they knew where to look.

"How long have they been moving in?"

"About an hour. Any time now," Young breathed.

"I can't hear a thing," Admiral Maxwell whispered.

It was hard enough to see the site. The buildings were visible only because of their straight lines, something which nature abhors for one reason or another. Further concentration revealed the dark rectangles of windows. The guard towers, erected only that day, were hard to spot as well.

"There's a few tricks we play," Marty Young noted. "Everybody gets vitamin-A supplements for night vision. Maybe a few percentage points of improvement in night vision. You play every card in the deck, right?"

All they heard was the wind whispering through the treetops. There was a surreal element to being in the woods like this. Maxwell and Young were accustomed to the hum of an aircraft engine and the faint glow of instrument lights that their eyes scanned automatically between outward sweeps for hostile aircraft, and the gentle floating sensation of an aircraft moving through the night sky. Being rooted to the land gave the feeling of motion that didn't exist as they waited to see something they had never experienced.

"There!"

"Bad news if you saw him move," Maxwell observed.

"Sir, SENDER GREEN doesn't have a parking lot with white cars on it," the voice pointed out. The fleeting shadow had been silhouetted against it, and only Kelly had seen it in any case.

"I guess that's right, Mr. Clark."

The radio sitting on the berm had been transmitting only the noise of static. That changed now, with four long dashes. They were answered at intervals by one, then two, then three, then four dots.

"Teams in place," Kelly whispered. "Hold your ears. The senior grenadier takes the first shot when he's ready, and that's the kickoff."

"Shit," Greer sneered. He soon regretted it.

The first thing they heard was a distant mutter of twin-bladed helicopter rotors. Designed to make heads turn, and even though every man at the berm knew the plan in intimate detail, it still worked, which pleased Kelly no end. He'd drawn up much of the plan, after all. All heads turned but his.

Kelly thought he might have caught a glimpse of the tritium-painted M-79 sights of one grenadier, but it might as easily have been the blink of a lonely lightning bug. He saw the muted flash of a single launch, and not a second later the blinding white-red-black flash of a fragmentation grenade against the floor of one of the towers. The sudden, sharp bark made the men at his side jump, but Kelly wasn't paying attention to that. The tower where men and guns would have been disintegrated. The echo had not yet dispersed through the theater of pines when the other three were similarly destroyed. Five seconds later the gunships came skimming in over the treetops, not fifty feet separating their rotors as miniguns ripped into the barracks building, two long neon fingers reaching in. The grenadiers were already pumping white-phosphorus rounds into the windows, and any semblance of night vision was lost in an instant.

"Jesus!" The way that the spreading fountains of burning phosphorus were concealed inside the building made the spectacle only more horrid, while the miniguns concentrated on the exits.

"Yeah," Kelly said, loudly to make himself heard. "Anybody inside is a crispy critter. The smart ones who try to run come right into the mini fire. Slick."

The fire element of the Marine assault force continued to pour fire into the barracks and admin buildings while the snatch team raced to the prison block. Now the rescue choppers came in, behind the AH-1 Huey Cobras, landing noisily close to the main gate. The fire element split, with half deploying around the choppers while the other half continued to hose the barracks. One of the gunships began circling the area now, like an anxious sheepdog on the prowl for wolves.

The first Marines appeared, dragging the simulated prisoners in relays. Kelly could see Irvin checking and doing a count at the gate. There were shouts now, men calling off numbers and names, and the roar of the big Sikorsky choppers almost covered it all. The last Marines in were the fire-support teams, and then the rescue choppers increased power and lifted off into the darkness.

"That was fast," Ritter breathed as the sound faded. A moment later two fire engines appeared to extinguish the blazes left behind by the various explosive devices.

"That was fifteen seconds under nominal," Kelly said, holding up his watch.

"What if something goes wrong, Mr. Clark?" Ritter asked.

Kelly's face lit up in a wicked grin. "Some things did, sir. Four of the team were 'killed' coming in. I assume maybe a broke leg or two—"

"Wait a minute, you mean there's a chance—"

"Let me explain, sir?" Kelly said. "From the photos there is no reason to believe there are any people between the LZ and the objective. No farming on those hills, okay? For tonight's exercise, I eliminated four people at random. Call all of them broken legs. The people had to be carried into the objective and carried out, in case you didn't notice. Backups on everything. Sir, I *expect* a clean mission, but I messed it up some tonight just to check."

Ritter nodded, impressed. "I expected everything to be run by the book for this rehearsal."

"In combat things go wrong, sir. I allowed for that. Every man is cross-trained for at least one alternate job." Kelly rubbed his nose. He'd been nervous, too. "What you just saw was a successful simulated mission despite greater-than-expected complications. This one's going to work, sir."

"Mr. Clark, you sold me." The CIA field officer turned to the others. "What about medical support, that sort of thing?"

"When *Ogden* forms up with Task Force 77, we cross-deck medical personnel over to her," Maxwell said. "Cas is on his way there now to brief the people in. CTF-77 is one of my people, and he'll play ball. *Ogden*'s a pretty large boat. We'll have everything we need to care for them, medics, intel guys to debrief, the works. She sails them right to Subic Bay. We hop them out of Clark ASAP. From the time the rescue choppers get off, we'll have them in California in . . . four and a half days.''

''Okay, this part of the mission looks fine. What about the rest?''

Maxwell handled the answer: ''*Constellation*'s whole air group will be in support. *Enterprise* will be farther up north working the Haiphong area. That should get the attention of their air-defense net and their high command. *Newport News* will be trolling the coast shooting up triple-A sites for the next few weeks. It's to be done randomly, and this area will be the fifth. She lays ten miles out and lobs in heavy fire. The big antiaircraft belt is within the range of her guns. Between the cruiser and the air group, we can blast a corridor for the helos to get in and out. Essentially we'll be doing so much that they oughtn't to notice this mission until it's already over.''

Ritter nodded. He'd read through the plan, and had only wished to hear it from Maxwell—more to the point, to hear how he expressed himself. The Admiral was calm and confident, more so than Ritter had expected.

''It's still very risky,'' he said after a moment.

''It is that,'' Marty Young agreed.

''What's the risk to our country if the people in that camp tell everything they know?'' Maxwell asked.

Kelly wanted to step back from this part of the discussion. Danger to country was something beyond his purview. His reality was at the small-unit level—or, more recently, even lower than that—and though his country's health and welfare started at that lowest common denominator, the big stuff required a perspective he didn't have. But there was no gracious way for him to withdraw, and so he stayed and listened and learned.

''You want an honest answer?'' Ritter asked. ''I'll give you one— none.''

Maxwell took it with surprising calm that concealed outrage. ''Son, you want to explain that?''

''Admiral, it's a matter of perspective. The Russians want to know a lot about us, and we want to know a lot about them. Okay, so this Zachary guy can tell them about SAC War Plans, and the other notional people there can tell them other things. So—we change our plans. It's the strategic stuff you're worried about, right? First, those plans change on a monthly basis. Second, do you ever think we'll implement them?''

''We might have to someday.''

Ritter fished out a cigarette. ''Admiral, do you *want* us to implement those plans?''

Maxwell stood a little straighter. ''Mr. Ritter, I flew my F6F over

Nagasaki just after the war ended. I've seen what those things do, and that was just a little one.'' Which was all the answer anyone needed.

"And they feel the same way. How does that grab you, Admiral?'' Ritter just shook his head. "They're not crazy either. They're even more afraid of us than we are of them. What they learn from those prisoners might scare them enough to sober them up, even. It works that way, believe it or not.''

"Then why are you supporting—*are* you supporting us?''

"Of course I am.'' *What a stupid question,* his tone said, enraging Marty Young.

"But why then?'' Maxwell asked.

"Those are our people. We sent them. We have to get them back. Isn't that reason enough? But don't tell me about vital national-security interests. You can sell that to the White House staff, even on The Hill, but not to me. Either you keep faith with your people or you don't,'' said the field spook who had risked his career to rescue a foreigner whom he hadn't even liked very much. "If you don't, if you fall into that habit, then you're not worth saving or protecting, and then people stop helping you, and *then* you're in real trouble.''

"I'm not sure I approve of you, Mr. Ritter,'' General Young said.

"An operation like this one will have the effect of saving our people. The Russians will respect that. It shows them we're serious about things. That will make my job easier, running agents behind the curtain. That means we'll be able to recruit more agents and get more information. That way I gather information that you want, okay? The game goes on until someday we find a new game.'' That was all the agenda he needed. Ritter turned to Greer. "When do you want me to brief the White House?''

"I'll let you know. Bob, this is important—you are backing us?''

"Yes, sir,'' replied the Texan. For reasons that the others didn't understand, didn't trust, but had to accept.

"So? What's the beef?''

"Look, Eddie,'' Tony said patiently. "Our friend's got a problem. Somebody took down two of his people.''

"Who?'' Morello asked. He was not in a particularly good mood. He'd just learned, again, that he was not a candidate to be accepted as a full member of the outfit. After all he'd done. Morello felt betrayed. Incredibly, Tony was siding with a black man instead of blood—they were distant cousins after all—and now the bastard was coming to him for help, of course.

"We don't know. His contacts, my contacts, we got nothin'.''

"Well, ain't that just too fuckin' bad?" Eddie segued into his own agenda. "Tony, he came to *me*, remember? Through Angelo, and maybe Angelo tried to set us up, and we took care of that, remember? You wouldn't have this setup except for me, so now what's happening? I get shut out and he gets closer in—so what gives, Tony, you gonna get *him* made?"

"Back off, Eddie."

"How come you didn't stand up for me?" Morello demanded.

"I can't make it happen, Eddie. I'm sorry, but I can't." Piaggi hadn't expected this conversation to go well, but neither had he expected it to go this badly, this quickly. Sure, Eddie was disappointed. Sure, he had expected to be taken in. But the dumb fuck was getting a good living out of it, and what was it about? Being inside or making a living? Henry could see that. Why couldn't Eddie? Then Eddie took it one step further.

"I set this deal up for you. Now, you got a little-bitty problem, and who you come to—me! You *owe* me, Tony." The implications of the words were clear for Piaggi. It was quite simple from Eddie's point of view. Tony's position in the outfit was growing in importance. With Henry as a potential—a very real—major supplier, Tony would have more than a position. He would have influence. He'd still have to show respect and obeisance to those over him, but the command structure of the outfit was admirably flexible, and Henry's double-blind methods meant that whoever was his pipeline into the outfit had real security. Security of place in his organization was a rare and treasured thing. Piaggi's mistake was in not taking the thought one step further. He looked inward instead of outward. All he saw was that Eddie could replace him, become the intermediary, and then become a made man, adding status to his comfortable living. All Piaggi had to do was die, obligingly, at the right time. Henry was a businessman. He'd make the accommodation. Piaggi knew that. So did Eddie.

"Don't you see what he's doing? He's using you, man." The odd part was that while Morello was beginning to understand that Tucker was manipulating both of them, Piaggi, the target of that manipulation, did not. As a result, Eddie's correct observation was singularly ill-timed.

"I've thought about that," Piaggi lied. "What's in it for him? A linkup with Philadelphia, New York?"

"Maybe. Maybe he thinks he can do it. Those people are getting awful big for their pants, man."

"We'll sweat that one out later, and I don't see him doing that. What we want to know is, who's taking his people down? You catch anything about somebody from out of town?" *Put him on the spot*, Piaggi thought. *Make him commit.* Tony's eyes bored in across the table at a man too angry to notice or care what the other man was thinking.

"I haven't heard shit about that."

"Put feelers out," Tony ordered, and it was an order. Morello had to follow it, had to check around.

"What if he was taking out some people from inside, reliability problems, like? You think he's loyal to anybody?"

"No. But I don't think he's offing his own people, either." Tony rose with a final order. "Check around."

"Sure," Eddie snorted, left alone at his table.

24

Hellos

"People, that went very well," Captain Albie announced, finishing his critique of the exercise. There had been various minor deficiencies on the approach march, but nothing serious, and even his sharp eye had failed to notice anything of consequence on the simulated assault phase. Marksmanship especially had been almost inhumanly accurate, and his men had sufficient confidence in one another that they were now running within mere feet of fire streams in order to get to their assigned places. The Cobra crews were in the back of the room, going over their own performance. The pilots and gunners were treated with great respect by the men they supported, as were the Navy flight crews of the rescue birds. The normal us-them antipathy found among disparate units was down to the level of friendly joshing, so closely had the men trained and dedicated themselves. That antipathy was about to disappear entirely.

"Gentlemen," Albie concluded, "you're about to learn what this little picnic outing is all about."

"Ten-*hut!*" Irvin called.

Vice Admiral Winslow Holland Maxwell walked up the center of the room, accompanied by Major General Martin Young. Both flag officers were in their best undress uniforms. Maxwell's whites positively glistened in the incandescent lights of the building, and Young's Marine khakis were starched so stiff that they might well have been made of plywood. A Marine lieutenant carried a briefing board that nearly dragged on the floor. This he set on an easel as Maxwell took his place behind the lectern. From his place on the corner of the stage, Master Gunnery Sergeant Irvin watched the young faces in the audience, reminding himself that he had to pretend surprise at the announcement.

"Take your seats, Marines," Maxwell began pleasantly, waiting for them to do so. "First of all, I want to tell you for myself how proud I am to be associated with you. We've watched your training closely. You came here without knowing why, and you've worked as hard as any people I have ever seen. Here's what it's all about." The Lieutenant flipped the cover off the briefing board, exposing an aerial photograph.

"Gentlemen, this mission is called BOXWOOD GREEN. Your objective is to rescue twenty men, fellow Americans who are now in the hands of the enemy."

John Kelly was standing next to Irvin, and he, too, was watching faces instead of the Admiral. Most were younger than his, but not by much. Their eyes were locked on the reconnaissance photographs—an exotic dancer would not have drawn the sort of focus that was aimed at the blowups from the Buffalo Hunter drone. The faces were initially devoid of emotion. They were like young, fit, handsome statues, scarcely breathing, sitting at attention while the Admiral spoke to them.

"This man here is Colonel Robin Zacharias, U.S. Air Force," Maxwell went on, using a yard-long wooden pointer. "You can see what the Vietnamese did to him just for looking at the asset that snapped the picture." The pointer traced over to the camp guard about to strike the American from behind. "Just for looking up."

Eyes narrowed at that, all of them, Kelly saw. It was a quiet, determined kind of anger, highly disciplined, but that was the deadliest kind of all, Kelly thought, suppressing a smile that only he would have understood. And so it was for the young Marines in the audience. It wasn't a time for smiles. Each of the people in the room knew about the dangers. Each had survived a minimum of thirteen months of combat operations. Each had seen friends die in the most terrible and noisy way that the blackest of nightmares could create. But there was more to life than fear. Perhaps it was a quest. A sense of duty that few could articulate but which all of them felt. A vision of the world that men shared without actually seeing. Every man in the room had seen death in all its dreadful majesty, knowing that all life came to an end. But all knew there was more to life than the avoidance of death. Life had to have a purpose, and one such purpose was the service of others. While no man in the room would willingly give his life away, every one of them would run the risk, trusting to God or luck or fate in the knowledge that each of the others would do the same. The men in these pictures were unknown to the

Marines, but they were comrades—more than friends—to whom loyalty was owed. And so they would risk their lives for them.

"I don't have to tell you how dangerous the mission is," the Admiral concluded. "The fact of the matter is, you know those dangers better than I do, but these people are Americans, and they have the right to expect us to come for them."

"Fuckin' A, *sir!*" a voice called from the floor, surprising the rest of the Marines.

Maxwell almost lost it then. *It's all true,* he told himself. *It really does matter. Mistakes and all, we're still what we are.*

"Thank you, Dutch," Marty Young said, walking to center stage. "Okay, Marines, now you know. You volunteered to be here. You have to volunteer again to deploy. Some of you have families, sweethearts. We won't make you go. Some of you might have second thoughts," he went on, examining the faces, and seeing the insult he had caused them, not by accident. "You have today to think it over. Dismissed."

The Marines got to their feet, to the accompaniment of the grating sound of chairs scraping on the tile floor, and when all were at attention, their voices boomed as one:

"RECON!"

It was clear to those who saw the faces. They could no more shrink from this mission than they could deny their manhood. There were smiles now. Most of the Marines traded remarks with their friends, and it wasn't glory they saw before their eyes. It was purpose, and perhaps the look to be seen in the eyes of the men whose lives they would redeem. *We're Americans and we're here to take you home.*

"Well, Mr. Clark, your admiral makes a pretty good speech. I wish we recorded it."

"You're old enough to know better, Guns. It's going to be a dicey one."

Irvin smiled in a surprisingly playful way. "Yeah, I know. But if you think it's a crock, why the hell are you going in alone?"

"Somebody asked me to." Kelly shook his head and went off to join the Admiral with a request of his own.

She made it all the way down the steps, holding on to the banister, her head still hurting, but not so badly this morning, following the smell of the coffee to the sound of conversation.

Sandy's face broke into a smile. "Well, good morning!"

"Hi," Doris said, still pale and weak, but she smiled back as she walked through the doorway, still holding on. "I'm real hungry."

"I hope you like eggs." Sandy helped her to a chair and got her a glass of orange juice.

"I'll eat the shells," Doris replied, showing her first sign of humor.

"You can start with these, and don't worry about the shells," Sarah Rosen told her, shoveling the beginnings of a normal breakfast from the frying pan onto a plate.

She had turned the corner. Doris's movements were painfully slow, and her coordination was that of a small child, but the improvement from only twenty-four hours before was miraculous. Blood drawn the day before showed still more favorable signs. The massive doses of antibiotics had obliterated her infections, and the lingering signs of barbiturates were almost completely gone—the remnants were from the palliative doses Sarah had prescribed and injected, which would not be repeated. But the most encouraging sign of all was how she ate. Awkwardness and all, she unfolded her napkin and sat it in the lap of the terrycloth robe. She didn't shovel the food in. Instead she consumed her first real breakfast in months in as dignified a manner as her condition and hunger allowed. Doris was turning back into a person.

But they still didn't know anything about her except her name—Doris Brown. Sandy got a cup of coffee for herself and sat down at the table.

"Where are you from?" she asked in as innocent a voice as she could manage.

"Pittsburgh." A place as distant to her house guest as the back end of the moon.

"Family?"

"Just my father. Mom died in '65, breast cancer," Doris said slowly, then unconsciously felt inside her robe. For the first time she could remember, her breasts didn't hurt from Billy's attention. Sandy saw the movement and guessed what it meant.

"Nobody else?" the nurse asked evenly.

"My brother . . . Vietnam."

"I'm sorry, Doris."

"It's okay—"

"Sandy's my name, remember?"

"I'm Sarah," Dr. Rosen added, replacing the empty plate with a full one.

"Thank you, Sarah." This smile was somewhat wan, but Doris Brown was reacting to the world around her now, an event far more important than the casual observer might have guessed. *Small steps,* Sarah told herself. *They don't have to be big steps. They just have to head in the right direction.* Doctor and nurse shared a look.

There was nothing like it. It was too hard to explain to someone who hadn't been there and done it. She and Sandy had reached into the grave and pulled this girl back from grasping earth. Three more months, Sarah had estimated, maybe not that long, and her body would have been so weakened that the most trivial outside influence would have ended her life in a matter of hours. But not now. Now this girl would live, and the two medics shared without words the feeling that God must have known when He had breathed life into Adam. They had defeated Death, redeeming the gift that only God could give. For this reason both had entered their shared profession, and moments like this one pushed back the rage and sorrow and grief for those patients whom they couldn't save.

"Don't eat too fast, Doris. When you don't eat for a while, your stomach actually shrinks down some," Sarah told her, returning to form as a medical doctor. There was no sense in warning her about problems and pain sure to develop in her gastrointestinal tract. Nothing would stop it, and getting nourishment into her superseded other considerations at the moment.

"Okay. I'm getting a little full."

"Then relax a little. Tell us about your father."

"I ran away," Doris replied at once. "Right after David . . . after the telegram, and Daddy . . . he had some trouble, and he blamed me."

Raymond Brown was a foreman in the Number Three Basic Oxygen Furnace Shed of the Jones and Laughlin Steel Company, and that was all he was, now. His house was on Dunleavy Street, halfway up one of the steep hills of his city, one of many detached frame dwellings built around the turn of the century, with wood clapboard siding that he had to paint every two or three years, depending on the severity of the winter winds that swept down the Monongahela Valley. He worked the night shift because his house was especially empty at night. Nevermore to hear the sounds of his wife, nevermore to take his son to Little League or play catch in the sloped sanctity of his tiny backyard, nevermore to worry about his daughter's dates on weekends.

He'd tried, done everything a man could do, after it was too late, which was so often the way of things. It had just been too much. His wife, discovering a lump, still a pretty young woman in her thirty-seventh year, his best and closest friend. He'd supported her as best he could after the surgery, but then came another lump, another surgery, medical treatment, and the downhill slide, always having to be strong for her until the end. It would have been a crushing burden for any man, and then followed by another. His only son, David, drafted, sent to Vietnam, and killed two weeks later in some nameless valley. The support of his fellow workers, the way they had come to Davey's funeral, hadn't stopped him from crawling inside a bottle, desperately trying to cling to what he had left, but too tightly. Doris had borne her own grief, something Raymond hadn't fully understood or appreciated, and when she'd come home late, her clothing not quite right, the cruel and hateful things he'd said. He could remember every word, the hollow sound as the front door had slammed.

Only a day later he'd come to his senses, driving with tears in his eyes to the police station, abasing himself before men whose understanding and sympathy he never quite recognized, desperate again to get his little girl back, to beg from her the forgiveness that he could never give himself. But Doris had vanished. The police had done what they could, and that wasn't much. And so for two years he'd lived inside a bottle, until two fellow workers had taken him aside and talked as friends do once they have gathered the courage to invade the privacy of another man's life. His minister was a regular guest in the lonely house now. He was drying out—Raymond Brown still drank, but no longer to excess, and he was working to cut it down to zero. Man that he was, he had to face his loneliness that way, had to deal with it as best he could. He knew that solitary dignity was of little value. It was an empty thing to cling to, but it was all he had. Prayer also helped, some, and in the repeated words he often found sleep, though not the dreams of the family which had once shared the house with him. He was tossing and turning in his bed, sweating from the heat, when the phone rang.

"Hello?"

"Hello, is this Raymond Brown?"

"Yeah, who's this?" he asked with closed eyes.

"My name is Sarah Rosen. I'm a doctor in Baltimore, I work at Johns Hopkins Hospital."

"Yes?" The tone of her voice opened his eyes. He stared at the ceiling, the blank white place that so closely matched the emptiness of his life. And there was sudden fear. Why would a doctor from Baltimore call him? His mind was spinning off towards a named dread when the voice went on quickly.

"I have somebody here who wants to talk to you, Mr. Brown."

"Huh?" He next heard muffled noises that might have been static from a bad line, but was not.

*   *   *

"I can't."

"You have nothing to lose, dear," Sarah said, handing over the phone. "He's your father. Trust him."

Doris took it, holding it in both hands close to her face, and her voice was a whisper.

"Daddy?"

From hundreds of miles away, the whispered word came through as clearly as a church bell. He had to breathe three times before answering, and that came out as a sob.

"Dor?"

"Yes—Daddy, I'm sorry."

"Are you okay, baby?"

"Yes, Daddy, I'm fine." And incongruous as the statement was, it was not a lie.

"Where are you?"

"Wait a minute." Then the voice changed. "Mr. Brown, this is Doctor Rosen again."

"She's there?"

"Yes, Mr. Brown, she is. We've been treating her for a week. She's a sick girl, but she's going to be okay. Do you understand? She's going to be okay."

He was grasping his chest. Brown's heart was a steel fist, and his breathing came in painful gasps that a doctor might have taken for something they were not.

"She's okay?" he asked anxiously.

"She's going to be fine," Sarah assured him. "There's no doubt of that, Mr. Brown. Please believe me, okay?"

"Oh, sweet Jesus! Where, where are you?"

"Mr. Brown, you can't see her just yet. We will bring her to you just as soon as she's fully recovered. I worried about calling you before we could get you together, but—but we just couldn't *not* call you. I hope you understand."

Sarah had to wait two minutes before she heard anything she could understand, but the sounds that came over the line touched her heart. In reaching into one grave, she had extracted two lives.

"She's really okay?"

"She's had a bad time, Mr. Brown, but I promise you she will recover fully. I'm a good doc, okay? I wouldn't say that unless it were true."

"Please, please let me talk to her again. Please!"

Sarah handed the phone over, and soon four people were weeping. Nurse and physician were the luckiest, sharing a hug and savoring their victory over the cruelties of the world.

Bob Ritter pulled his car into a slot in West Executive Drive, the closed-off former street that lay between the White House and the Executive Office Building. He walked towards the latter, perhaps the ugliest building in Washington—no mean accomplishment—which had once held much of the executive branch of government, the State, War, and Navy departments. It also held the Indian Treaty Room, designed for the purpose of overawing primitive visitors with the splendor of Victorian gingerbread architecture and the majesty of the government which had constructed this giant tipi. The wide corridors rang with the sound of his footsteps on marble as he searched for the right room. He found it on the second floor, the room of Roger MacKenzie, Special Assistant to the President for National Security Affairs. "Special," perversely, made him a second-line official. The National Security *Advisor* had a corner office in the West Wing of the White House. Those who reported to him had offices elsewhere, and though distance from the Seat of Power defined influence, it didn't define arrogance of position. MacKenzie had to have a staff of his own in order to remind himself of his importance, real or illusory. Not really a bad man, and actually a fairly bright one, Ritter thought, MacKenzie was nonetheless jealous of his position, and in another age he would have been the clerk who advised the chancellor who advised the King. Except today the clerk had to have an executive secretary.

"Hi, Bob. How are things at Langley?" MacKenzie asked in front of his secretarial staff, just to be sure they would know that he was meeting with an up-and-coming CIA official, and was therefore still very important indeed to have such guests calling on him.

"The usual." Ritter smiled back. *Let's get on with it.*

"Trouble with traffic?" he asked, letting Ritter know that he was almost, if not quite, late for the appointment.

"There's a little problem on the GW." Ritter gestured with his head towards MacKenzie's private office. His host nodded.

"Wally, we need someone to take notes."

"Coming, sir." His executive assistant rose from his desk in the secretarial area and brought a pad.

"Bob Ritter, this is Wally Hicks. I don't think you've met."

"How do you do, sir?" Hicks extended his hand. Ritter took it, seeing yet one more eager White House aide. New England accent, bright-looking, polite, which was about all he was entitled to expect of such people. A minute later they were sitting in MacKenzie's office, the inner and outer doors closed in the cast-iron frames that gave the Executive Office Building the structural integrity of a warship. Hicks hurried himself about to get coffee for everyone, like a page at some medieval court, which was the way of things in the world's most powerful democracy.

"So what brings you in, Bob?" MacKenzie asked from behind his desk. Hicks flipped open his note pad and began his struggle to take down every word.

"Roger, a rather unique opportunity has presented itself over in Vietnam." Eyes opened wider and ears perked up.

"What might that be?"

"We've identified a special prison camp southwest of Haiphong," Ritter began, quickly outlining what they knew and what they suspected.

MacKenzie listened intently. Pompous though he might have been, the recently arrived investment banker was also a former aviator himself. He'd flown B-24s in the Second World War, including the dramatic but failed mission to Ploesti. A patriot with flaws, Ritter told himself. He would try to make use of the former while ignoring the latter.

"Let me see your imagery," he said after a few minutes, using the proper buzzword instead of the more pedestrian "pictures."

Ritter took the photo folder from his briefcase and set it on the desk. MacKenzie opened it and took a magnifying glass from a drawer. "We know who this guy is?"

"There's a better photo in the back," Ritter answered helpfully.

MacKenzie compared the official family photo with the one from the camp, then with the enhanced blowup.

"Very close. Not definitive but close. Who is he?"

"Colonel Robin Zacharias. Air Force. He spent quite some time at Offutt Air Force Base, SAC War Plans. He knows everything, Roger."

MacKenzie looked up and whistled, which, he thought, was what he was supposed to do in such circumstances. "And this guy's no Vietnamese . . ."

"He's a colonel in the Soviet Air Force, name unknown, but it isn't hard to figure what he's there for. Here's the real punchline." Ritter handed over a copy of the wire-service report on Zacharias's death.

"Damn."

"Yeah, all of a sudden it gets real clear, doesn't it?"

"This sort of thing could wreck the peace talks," MacKenzie thought aloud.

Walter Hicks couldn't say anything. It wasn't his place to speak in such circumstances. He was like a necessary appliance—an animated tape machine—and the only real reason he was in the room at all was so his boss would have a record of the conversation. Wreck the peace talks he scribbled down, taking the time to underline it, and though nobody else noticed, his fingers went white around the pencil.

"Roger, the men we believe to be in this camp know an awful lot, enough to seriously compromise our national security. I mean *seriously,*" Ritter said calmly. "Zacharias knows our nuclear war plans, he helped write SIOP. This is very serious business." Merely in speaking *sy-op,* merely by invoking the unholy name of the "Single Integrated Operations Plan," Ritter had knowingly raised the stakes of the conversation. The CIA field officer amazed himself at the skillful delivery of the lie. The White House pukes might not grasp the idea of getting people out because they were *people.* But they had their hot issues, and nuclear war-plans were the unholy of unholies in this and many other temples of government power.

"You have my attention, Bob."

"Mr. Hicks, right?" Ritter asked, turning his head.

"Yes, sir."

"Could you please excuse us?"

The junior assistant looked to his boss, his neutral face imploring MacKenzie to let him stay in the room, but that was not to be.

"Wally, I think we'll carry on for the moment in executive session," the special assistant to the President said, easing the impact of the dismissal with a friendly smile—and a wave towards the door.

"Yes, sir." Hicks stood and walked out the door, closing it quietly.

Fuck, he raged to himself, sitting back down at his desk. How could he advise his boss he didn't hear what came next? Robert Ritter, Hicks thought. The guy who'd nearly destroyed sensitive negotiations at a particularly sensitive moment by violating orders and bringing some goddamned *spy* out of Budapest. The information he'd brought *had* somehow changed the U.S. negotiating position, and *that* had set the treaty back three months because America had decided to chisel something else out of the Soviets, who had been reasonable *as hell* to concede the matters already agreed to. That fact had saved Ritter's career—and probably encouraged him in that idiotically romantic view that individual people were more important than world peace, when peace itself was the only thing that mattered.

And Ritter knew how to jerk Roger around, didn't he? All that war-plans stuff was pure horseshit. Roger had his office walls covered with photos from The Old Days, when he'd flown his goddamned airplane all over hell and gone, pretending that he was personally winning the war against Hitler, just one more fucking war that good diplomacy would have prevented if only people had focused on the real issues as he and Peter hoped someday to do. This thing wasn't about war plans or SIOP or any of the other uniformed bullshit that people in this section of the White House Staff played with every goddamned day. It was about *people,* for Christ's sake. Uniformed people. Dumbass soldiers, people with big shoulders and little minds who did nothing more useful than kill, as though that made anything in the world better. And besides, Hicks fumed, they took their chances, didn't they? If they wanted to drop bombs on a peaceful and friendly people like the Vietnamese, well, they should have thought ahead of time that those people might not like it very much. Most important of all, if they were dumb enough to gamble their *lives,* then they implicitly accepted the possibility of losing them, and so why then should people like Wally Hicks give a flying fuck about them when the dice came up wrong? They probably loved the action. It undoubtedly attracted the sort of women who thought that big dicks came along with small brains, who liked "men" who dragged their knuckles on the ground like well-dressed apes.

This could wreck the peace talks. Even MacKenzie thought that.

All those kids from his generation, dead. And now they might risk not ending the war because of *fifteen* or *twenty* professional *killers* who probably liked what they did. It just made no sense. *What if they gave a war and nobody came?* was one of his generation's favored aphorisms, though he knew it to be a fantasy. Because people like that *one* guy—Zacharias— would always seduce people into following them because little people who lacked Hicks's understanding and perspective wouldn't be able to see that it was just all a waste of energy. That was the most amazing part of all. Wasn't it *clear* that war was just plain *awful?* How smart did you have to be to understand *that?*

Hicks saw the door open. MacKenzie and Ritter came out.

"Wally, we're going across the street for a few minutes. Could you tell my eleven o'clock that I'll be back as soon as I can?"

"Yes, sir."

Wasn't that typical? Ritter's seduction was complete. He had MacKenzie sold enough that Roger would make the pitch to the National Security Advisor. And they would probably raise pure fucking hell at the peace table, and maybe set things back three months or more, unless somebody saw through the ruse. Hicks lifted his phone and dialed a number.

"Senator Donaldson's office."

"Hi, I was trying to get Peter Henderson."

"I'm sorry, he and the Senator are in Europe right now. They'll get back next week."

"Oh, that's right. Thanks." Hicks hung up. *Damn*. He was so upset that he'd forgotten.

Some things have to be done very carefully. Peter Henderson didn't even know that his code name was CASSIUS. It had been assigned to him by an analyst in the U.S.-Canada Institute whose love of Shakespeare's plays was as genuine as that of any Oxford don. The photo in the file, along with the one-page profile of the agent, had made him think of the self-serving "patriot" in *The Tragedy of Julius Caesar*. Brutus would not have been right. Henderson, the analyst had judged, did not have sufficient quality of character.

His senator was in Europe on a "fact-finding" tour, mainly having to do with NATO, though they would stop in on the peace talks at Paris just to get some TV tape that might be shown on Connecticut TV stations in the fall. In fact, the "tour" was mainly a shopping trip punctuated by a brief every other day. Henderson, enjoying his first such trip as the Senator's expert on national-security issues, had to be there for the briefs, but the rest of the time was his, and he had made his own arrangements. At the moment he was touring the White Tower, the famous centerpiece of Her Majesty's Tower of London, now approaching its nine hundredth year of guardianship on the River Thames.

"Warm day for London," another tourist said.

"I wonder if they get thunderstorms here," the American replied casually, examining Henry VIII's immense suit of armor.

"They do," the man replied, "but not as severe as those in Washington."

Henderson looked for an exit and headed towards it. A moment later he was strolling around Tower Green with his new companion.

"Your English is excellent."

"Thank you, Peter. I am George."

"Hi, George." Henderson smiled without looking at his new friend. It really was like James Bond, and doing it here—not just in London, but in the historical seat of Britain's royal family—well, that was just delicious.

George was his real name—actually Georgiy, which was the Russian equivalent—and he rarely went into the field anymore. Though he'd been a highly effective field officer for KGB, his analytical ability was such that he'd been called back to Moscow five years earlier, promoted to lieutenant colonel and placed in charge of a whole section. Now a full colonel, George looked forward to general's stars. The reason he'd come to London, via Helsinki and Brussels, was that he'd wanted to eyeball CASSIUS himself— and get a little shopping done for his own family. Only three men of his age in KGB shared his rank, and his young and pretty wife liked to wear Western clothes. Where else to shop for them but London? George didn't speak French or Italian.

"This is the only time we will meet, Peter."

"Should I be honored?"

"If you wish." George was unusually good-natured for a Russian, though that was part of his cover. He smiled at the American. "Your senator has access to many things."

"Yes, he does," Henderson agreed, enjoying the courtship ritual. He didn't have to add, *and so do I.*

"Such information is useful to us. Your government, especially with your new president—honestly, he frightens us."

"He frightens me," Henderson admitted.

"But at the same time there is hope," George went on, speaking in a reasonable and judicious voice. "He is also a realist. His proposal for *détente* is seen by my government as a sign that we can reach a broad international understanding. Because of that we wish to examine the possibility that his proposal for discussions is genuine. Unfortunately we have problems of our own."

"Such as?"

"Your president, perhaps he means well. I say that sincerely, Peter," George added. "But he is highly . . . competitive. If he knows too much about us, he will press us too hard in some areas, and that might prevent us from reaching the accommodation that we all desire. You have adverse political elements in your government. So do we—leftovers from the Stalin era. The key to negotiations such as those which may soon begin is that both sides must be reasonable. We need your help to control the unreasonable elements on our side."

Henderson was surprised by that. The Russians could be so open, like Americans. "How can I do that?"

"Some things we cannot allow to be leaked. If they are, it will poison our chances for *détente.* If we know too much about you, or you know too much about us, well, the game becomes skewed. One side or the other seeks too much advantage, and then there can be no understanding, only domination, which neither side will accept. Do you see?"

"Yes, that makes sense."

"What I am asking, Peter, is that you let us know from time to time certain special things that you have learned about us. I won't even tell you what, exactly. I think you are intelligent enough to see for yourself. We will trust you on that. The time for war is behind us. The coming peace, if it does come, will depend on people like you and me. There must be trust between our nations. That trust begins between two people. There is no other way. I wish there were, but that is how peace must begin.''

''Peace—that would be nice,'' Henderson allowed. ''First we have to get our damned war ended.''

''We are working towards that end, as you know. We're—well, not pressuring, but we are *encouraging* our friends to take a more moderate line. Enough young men have died. It is time to put an end to it, an end that both sides will find acceptable.''

''That's good to hear, George.''

''So can you help us?''

They'd walked all around Tower Green, now facing the chapel. There was a chopping block there. Henderson didn't know if it had actually been used or not. Around it was a low chain fence, and standing on it at the moment was a raven, one of those kept on Tower grounds for the mixed reasons of tradition and superstition. Off to their right a Yeoman Warder was conducting a bunch of tourists around.

''I've been helping you, George.'' Which was true. Henderson had been nibbling at the hook for nearly two years. What the KGB colonel had to do now was to sweeten the bait, then see if Henderson would swallow the hook down.

''Yes, Peter, I know that, but now we are asking for a little more, some very sensitive information. The decision is yours, my friend. It is easy to wage war. Waging peace can be far more dangerous. No one will ever know the part you played. The important people of ministerial rank will reach their agreements and shake hands across the table. Cameras will record the events for history, and people like you and me, our names will never find their way into the history books. But it will matter, my friend. People like us will set the stage for the ministers. I cannot force you in this, Peter. You must decide if you wish to help us on your own account. You will also decide what it is that we need to know. You're a bright young man, and your generation in America has learned the lessons that must be learned. If you wish, I will let you decide over time—''

Henderson turned, making his decision. ''No. You're right. Somebody has to help make the peace, and dithering around won't change that. I'll help you, George.''

''There is danger involved. You know that,'' George warned. It was a struggle not to react, but now that Henderson was indeed swallowing the hook, he had to set it firmly.

"I'll take my chances. It's worth it."

Ahhh.

"People like you need to be protected. You will be contacted when you get home." George paused. "Peter, I am a father. I have a daughter who is six and a son who is two. Because of your work, and mine, they will grow up in a much better world—a peaceful world. For them, Peter, I thank you. I must go now."

"See you, George," Henderson said. It caused George to turn and smile one last time.

"No, Peter, you will not." George walked down the stone steps towards Traitor's Gate. It required all of his considerable self-control not to laugh aloud at the mixture of what he had just accomplished and the thundering irony of the portcullised stone arch before his eyes. Five minutes later he stepped into a black London taxi and directed the driver to head towards Harrods Department Store in Knightsbridge.

Cassius, he thought. No, that wasn't right. Casca, perhaps. But it was too late to change it now, and besides, who would have seen the humor in it? Glazov reached in his pocket for his shopping list.

25

Departures

One demonstration, however perfect, wasn't enough, of course. For each of the next four nights, they did it all again, and twice more in daylight, just so that positioning was clear to everyone. The snatch team would be racing into the prison block only ten feet away from the stream of fire from an M-60 machine gun—the physical layout of the camp demanded it, much to everyone's discomfort—and that was the most dangerous technical issue of the actual assault. But by the end of the week, the BOXWOOD GREEN team was as perfectly trained as men could be. They knew it, and the flag officers knew it. Training didn't exactly slack off, but it did stabilize, lest the men become overtrained and dulled by the routine. What followed was the final phase of the preparation. While training, men would stop the action and make small suggestions to one another. Good ideas were bumped immediately to a senior NCO or to Captain Albie and more often than not incorporated in the plan. This was the intellectual part of it, and it was important that every member of the team felt as though he had a chance to affect things to some greater or lesser degree. From that came confidence, not the bravado so often associated with elite troops, but the deeper and far more significant professional judgment that considered and adjusted and readjusted until things were just right—and then *stopped*.

Remarkably, their off-duty hours were more relaxed now. They knew about the mission, and the high-spirited horseplay common to young men was muted. They watched TV in the open bay, read books or magazines, waiting for the word in the knowledge that halfway across the world other men were waiting, too, and in the quiet of twenty-five individual human minds, questions were being asked. Would things go right or wrong? If the former, what elation would they feel? If the latter—well, they all had long since decided that win or lose, this wasn't the sort of thing you walked away from. There were husbands to be restored to their wives, fathers to their children, men to their country. Each knew that if death was to be risked, then this was the time and the purpose for it.

At Sergeant Irvin's behest, chaplains came to the group. Consciences were cleared. A few wills were drafted—just in case, the embarrassed Marines told the visiting officers—and all the while the Marines focused more and more on the mission, their minds casting aside extraneous concerns and concentrating on something identified only by a code name selected at random from separate lists of words. Every man walked over to the training site, checking placement and angles, usually with his most immediate teammate, practicing their run-in approach or the paths they'd take once the shooting started. Every one began his own personal exercise regime, running a mile or two on his own in addition to the regular morning and afternoon efforts, both to work off tension and to be just a little bit more certain that he'd be ready for it. A trained observer could see it from their look: serious but not tense, focused but not obsessive, confident but not cocky. Other Marines at Quantico kept their distance when they saw the team, wondering why the special place and the odd schedule, why the Cobras on the flight line, why the Navy rescue pilots in the Q, but one look at the team in the piney woods was all the warning they needed to mute the questions and keep their distance. Something special was happening.

· "Thanks, Roger," Bob Ritter said in the sanctity of his office in Langley. He switched buttons on his phone and dialed another in-house number. "James? Bob. It's a go. Start pushing buttons."

"Thank you, James." Dutch Maxwell turned in his swivel chair and looked at the side panel affixed to his wall, blue aluminum from his F6F Hellcat fighter, with its even rows of red-and-white painted flags, each denoting a victim of his skill. It was his personal touchstone to his profession. "Yeoman Grafton," he called.

"Yes, sir?" a petty officer appeared in his doorway.

"Make signal to Admiral Podulski on *Constellation:* 'Olive Green.' "

"Aye aye, sir."

"Have my car come around, then call Anacostia. I need a helo in about fifteen minutes."

"Yes, Admiral."

Vice Admiral Winslow Holland Maxwell, USN, rose from his desk and headed out the side door into the E-Ring corridor. His first stop was at the office in the Air Force's section of the building.

"Gary, we're going to need that transport we talked about."

"You got it, Dutch," the General replied, asking no questions.

"Let my office know the details. I'm heading out now, but I'll be calling in every hour."

"Yes, sir."

Maxwell's car was waiting at the River entrance, a master chief aviation bosun's mate at the wheel. "Where to, sir?"

"Anacostia, Master Chief, the helo pad."

"Aye." The senior chief dropped the car into gear and headed for the river. He didn't know what it was all about, but he knew it was about something. The Old Man had a spring in his step like the chief's daughter heading out for a date.

Kelly was working on his woodcraft, again, as he'd been doing for several weeks. He'd picked his weapons load-out in the fervent hope that he would not need to fire a single shot. The primary weapon was a CAR-15 carbine version of the M-16 assault rifle. A silenced 9mm automatic went into a shoulder holster, but his real weapon was a radio, and he would be carrying two of those, just to be sure, plus food and water and a map—and extra batteries. It came out to a twenty-three-pound load, not counting his special gear for the insertion. The weight wasn't excessive, and he found that he could move through the trees and over the hills without noticing it. Kelly moved quickly for a man of his size, and silently. The latter was a matter of where he walked more than anything else, where he placed his feet, how he twisted and turned to pass between trees and bushes, watching both his path and the area around him with equal urgency.

Overtraining, he told himself. *You should take it easier now.* He stood erect and headed down the hill, surrendering to his instincts. He found the Marines training in small groups, miming the use of their weapons while Captain Albie consulted with the four helicopter crews. Kelly was just approaching the site's LZ when a blue Navy helo landed and Admiral Maxwell emerged. Kelly, by chance, was the first one there. He knew the purpose and the message of the visit before anyone had a chance to speak.

"We're going?"

"Tonight," Maxwell confirmed with a nod.

Despite the expectation and enthusiasm, Kelly felt the usual chill. It wasn't practice anymore. His life was on the line again. The lives of others would depend on him. He would have to get the job done. *Well,* he told himself, *I know how to do that.* Kelly waited by the chopper while Maxwell went over to Captain Albie. General Young's staff car pulled up so that he could deliver the news as well. Salutes were exchanged as Kelly watched. Albie got the word, and his back went a little straighter. The Recon Marines gathered around, and their reaction was surprisingly sober and matter-of-fact. Looks were exchanged, rather dubious ones, but they soon changed to simple, determined nods. The mission was GO. The message delivered, Maxwell came back to the helicopter.

"I guess you want that quick liberty."

"You said you'd do it, sir."

The Admiral clapped the younger man on the shoulder and pointed to the helo. Inside, they put on headsets while the flight crew spooled up the engine.

"How soon, sir?"

"You be back here by midnight." The pilot looked back at them from the right seat. Maxwell motioned for him to stay on the ground.

"Aye aye, sir." Kelly removed the headset and jumped out of the helicopter, going to join General Young.

"Dutch told me," Young said, the disapproval clear in his voice. You just didn't do things this way. "What do you need?"

"Back to the boat to change, then run me up to Baltimore, okay? I'll drive back myself."

"Look, Clark—"

"General, I helped plan this mission. I'm first in and I'm last out." Young wanted to swear but didn't. Instead he pointed to his driver, then to Kelly.

Fifteen minutes later, Kelly was in another life. Since leaving *Springer* tied up at the guest slip, the world had stopped, and he'd moved backwards in time. Now he was in forward motion for a brief period. A quick look determined that the dockmaster was keeping an eye on things. He raced through a shower and changed into civilian clothes, heading back to the General's staff car.

"Baltimore, Corporal. Matter of fact, I'll make it easy on you. Just drop me off at the airport. I'll catch a cab the rest of the way."

"You got it, sir," the driver told a man already fading into sleep.

"So what's the story, Mr. MacKenzie?" Hicks asked.

"They approved it," the special assistant replied, signing a few papers and initialing a few others for various official archives where future historians would record his name as a minor player in the great events of his time.

"Can you say what?"

What the hell, MacKenzie thought. Hicks had a clearance, and it was a chance to display something of his importance to the lad. In two minutes he covered the high points of BOXWOOD GREEN.

"Sir, that's an invasion," Hicks pointed out as evenly as he could manage, despite the chill on his skin and the sudden knot in his stomach.

"I suppose they might think so, but I don't. They've invaded three sovereign countries, as I recall."

More urgently: "But the peace talks—you said yourself."

"Oh, screw the peace talks! Damn it, Wally, we have *people* over there, and what they know is vital to our national security. Besides"—he smiled—"I helped sell it to Henry." *And if this one comes off . . .*

"But—"

MacKenzie looked up. Didn't this kid get it? "But *what,* Wally?"

"It's dangerous."

"War is that way, in case nobody ever told you."

"Sir, I'm supposed to be able to talk here, right?" Hicks asked pointedly.

"Of course you are, Wally. So talk."

"The peace talks are at a delicate stage now—"

"Peace talks are always delicate, aren't they? Go on," MacKenzie ordered, rather enjoying his pedagogic discourse. Maybe this kid would learn something for a change.

"Sir, we've lost too many people already. We've killed a *million* of them. And for what? What have we gained? What has anybody gained?" His voice was almost a plea.

That wasn't exactly new, and MacKenzie was tired of responding to it. "If you're asking me to defend how we got stuck with this mess, Wally, you're wasting your time. It's been a mess since the beginning, but that wasn't the work of *this* Administration, was it? We got elected with the mandate to get us the hell out of there."

"Yes, sir," Hicks agreed, as he had to. "That's exactly my point. Doing this might harm our chances to bring it to an end. I think it's a mistake, sir."

"Okay." MacKenzie relaxed, giving a tolerant eye to his aide. "That point of view may—I'll be generous, *does* have merit. What about the people, Wally?"

"They took their chances. They lost," Hicks answered with the coldness of youth.

"You know, that sort of detachment may have its use, but one difference between us is that I've been there and you haven't. You've never been in uniform, Wally. That's a shame. You might have learned something from it.''

Hicks was genuinely taken aback by the irrelevancy. ''I don't know what that might be, sir. It would only have interfered with my studies.''

''Life isn't a book, son,'' MacKenzie said, using a word that he'd intended to be warm, but which merely sounded patronizing to his aide. ''Real people bleed. Real people have feelings. Real people have dreams, and families. They have real lives. What you would have learned, Wally, is that they may not be *like* you, but they're still real people, and if you work in this government of the people, you must take note of that.''

''Yes, sir.'' What else could he say? There was no way he'd win this argument. Damn, he really needed someone to talk to about this.

''John!'' Not a word in two weeks. She'd feared that something had happened to him, but now she had to face the contradictory thought that he was indeed alive, and perhaps doing things best considered in the abstract.

''Hello, Sandy.'' Kelly smiled, dressed decently again, in a tie and blue blazer. It was so obviously a disguise, and so different from the way she'd last seen the man, that even his appearance was disturbing.

''Where have you been?'' Sandy asked, waving him in, not wanting the neighbors to know.

''Off doing something,'' Kelly dodged.

''Doing what?'' The immediacy of her tone demanded a substantive response.

''Nothing illegal, I promise,'' was the best he could do.

''You're sure?'' A very awkward moment developed out of thin air. Kelly just stood there, right inside the door, suddenly oscillating between anger and guilt, wondering why he'd come here, why he'd asked Admiral Maxwell for a very special favor, and not really knowing the answer now.

''John!'' Sarah called down the stairs, saving both from their thoughts.

''Hey, doc,'' Kelly called, and both were glad for the distraction.

''Have we got a surprise for you!''

''What?''

Dr. Rosen came down the stairs, looking as frumpy as ever despite her smile. ''You look different.''

''I've been exercising pretty regularly,'' Kelly explained.

''What brings you here?'' Sarah asked.

''I'm going to be going somewhere, and I wanted to stop over before I left.''

''Where to?''

"I can't say." The answer chilled the room.

"John," Sandy said. "We know."

"Okay." Kelly nodded. "I figured you would. How is she?"

"She's doing fine, thanks to you," Sarah answered.

"John, we need to talk, okay?" Sandy insisted. Dr. Rosen bent to her wishes and went back upstairs while nurse and former patient drifted into the kitchen.

"John, what exactly have you been doing?"

"Lately? I can't say, Sandy. I'm sorry, but I can't."

"I mean—I mean everything. What have you been up to?"

"You're better off not knowing, Sandy."

"Billy and Rick?" Nurse O'Toole said, putting it on the table.

Kelly motioned his head to the second floor. "You've seen what they did to her? They won't be doing that anymore."

"John, you can't do things like that! The police—"

"—are infiltrated," Kelly told her. "The organization has compromised somebody, probably someone very high up. Because of that I can't trust the police, and neither can you, Sandy," he concluded as reasonably as he could.

"But there are others, John. There are others who—" His statement finally penetrated. "How do you know that?"

"I asked Billy some questions." Kelly paused, and her face gave him yet more guilt. "Sandy, do you really think somebody is going to go out of his way to investigate the death of a prostitute? That's what it is to them. Do you think anybody really cares about them? I asked you before, remember? You said that nobody even has a program to help them. You care. That's why I brought her here. But do the cops? No. Maybe I could scratch up information to burn the drug ring. I'm not sure, it's not what I've been trained for, but that's what I've been doing. If you want to turn me in, well, I can't stop you. I won't hurt you—"

"I know that!" Sandy almost screamed. "John, you can't do this," she added more calmly.

"Why not?" Kelly asked. "They kill people. They do horrible things, and nobody's doing anything about it. What about the victims, Sandy? Who speaks for them?"

"The law does!"

"And when the law doesn't work, then what? Do we just let them die? Die like that? Remember the picture of Pam?"

"Yes," Sandy replied, losing the argument, knowing it, wishing it were otherwise.

"They took hours on her, Sandy. Your—houseguest—watched. They *made her watch.*"

"She told me. She's told us everything. She and Pam were friends. After—after Pam died, she's the one who brushed Pam's hair out, John."

The reaction surprised her. It was immediately clear that Kelly's pain was behind a door, and some words could bring it out in the open with a sudden speed that punished him badly. He turned away for a moment and took a deep breath before turning back. "She's okay?"

"We're going to take her home in a few days. Sarah and I will drive her there."

"Thanks for telling me that. Thank you for taking care of her."

It was the dichotomy that unsettled her so badly. He could talk about inflicting death on people so calmly, like Sam Rosen in a discussion of a tricky surgical procedure—and like the surgeon, Kelly cared about the people he—saved? Avenged? Was that the same thing? He thought so.

"Sandy, it's like this: They killed Pam. They raped and tortured and killed her—as an *example,* so they could use other girls the same way. I'm going to get every one of them, and if I die in the process, that's the chance I'm going to take. I'm sorry if you don't like me for that."

She took a deep breath. There was nothing more to be said.

"You said you're going away."

"Yes. If things work out I should be back in about two weeks."

"Will it be dangerous?"

"Not if I do it right." Kelly knew she would see through that one.

"Doing what?"

"A rescue mission. That's as far as I can go, and please don't repeat that to anyone. I'm leaving tonight. I've been off training for it, down at a military base."

It was Sandy's turn to look away, back towards the kitchen door. He wasn't giving her a chance. There were too many contradictions. He'd saved a girl who would otherwise have certainly died, but he'd killed to do it. He loved a girl who was dead. He was willing to kill others because of that love, to risk everything for it. He'd trusted her and Sarah and Sam. Was he a bad man or a good one? The mixture of facts and ideas was impossible to reconcile. Seeing what had happened to Doris, working so hard now to get her well, hearing her voice—and her father's—it had all made sense to her at the time. It was always easy to consider things dispassionately, when they were at a distance. But not now, faced with the man who had done it all, who explained himself calmly and directly, not lying, not concealing, just telling the truth, and trusting her, again, to understand.

"Vietnam?" she asked after a few moments, temporizing, trying to add more substance to a very muddled collection of thoughts.

"That's right." Kelly paused. He had to explain it, just a little, to help her understand. "There are some people over there who won't get back unless we do something, and I am part of it."

"But why do *you* have to go?"

"Why me? It has to be somebody, and I'm the one they asked. Why do *you* do the things you do, Sandy? I asked that before, remember?"

"Damn you, John! I've started to *care* about you," she blurted out.

The pain returned to his face one more time. "Don't. You might get hurt again, and I wouldn't want that." Which was exactly the wrong thing for him to say. "People who get attached to me get hurt, Sandy."

Sarah came in just then, leading Doris into the kitchen, for the moment saving both of them from themselves. The girl was transformed. Her eyes were animated now. Sandy had trimmed her hair and found decent clothes for her. She was still weak, but moving under her own power now. Her soft brown eyes fixed on Kelly.

"You're him," she said quietly.

"I guess I am. How are you?"

She smiled. "I'm going home soon. Daddy—Daddy wants me back."

"I'm sure he does, ma'am," Kelly said. She was so different from the victim he'd seen only a few weeks before. Maybe it did all mean something.

The same thought came into Sandy's mind just then. Doris was the innocent one, the real victim of forces that had descended on her, and but for Kelly, she would be dead. Nothing else could have saved her. Other deaths had been necessary, but—but *what?*

"So maybe it was Eddie," Piaggi said. "I told him to sniff around and he says he doesn't have anything."

"And nothing's happened since you talked to him. Everything's back to normal, like," Henry replied, telling Anthony Piaggi what he already knew and following with a conclusion that he had also considered. "What if he was just trying to shake things up a little? What if he just wanted to be more important, Tony?"

"Possible."

Which led to the next question: "How much you want to bet that if Eddie takes a little trip, nothing else happens?"

"You think he's making a move?"

"You got anything else that makes sense?"

"Anything happens to Eddie, there could be trouble. I don't think I can—"

"Let me handle it? I have a way that'll work just fine."

"Tell me about it," Piaggi said. Two minutes later he nodded approval.

"Why did you come here?" Sandy asked while she and Kelly cleaned up the dinner table. Sarah took Doris back upstairs for more rest.

"I wanted to see how she was doing." But that was a lie, and not an especially good one.

"It's lonely, isn't it?" Kelly took a long time to answer.

"Yeah." She'd forced him to face something. Being alone was not the sort of life he wanted to have, but fate and his own nature had forced it on him. Every time he'd reached out, something terrible had happened. Vengeance against those who had made his life into what it now was did make for a purpose, but it wasn't enough to fill the void they'd created. And now it was clear that what he was doing, all of it, was merely distancing him from someone else. How did life get so complicated as this?

"I can't say it's okay, John. I wish I could. Saving Doris was a fine thing, but not through killing people. There is supposed to be another way—"

"—and if there isn't, then what?"

"Let me finish?" Sandy asked quietly.

"Sorry."

She touched his hand. "Please be careful."

"I usually am, Sandy. Honest."

"What you're doing, what you're going off to, it's not—"

He smiled. "No, it's a real job. Official stuff and everything."

"Two weeks?"

"If it goes according to plan, yes."

"Will it?"

"Sometimes it actually does."

Her hand squeezed his. "John, please, think it over. Please? Try to find another way. Let it go. Let it stop. You saved Doris. That's a wonderful thing. Maybe with what you've learned you can save the others without— without any more killing?"

"I'll try." He couldn't say no to that, not with the warmth of her hand on his, and Kelly's trap was that his word, once given, could not be taken back. "Anyway, I have other things to worry about now." Which was true.

"How will I know, John—I mean—"

"About me?" He was surprised she would even want to know.

"John, you can't just leave me not knowing."

Kelly thought for a moment, pulled a pen from his coat, and wrote down a phone number. "This goes to a guy—an admiral named James Greer. He'll know, Sandy."

"Please be careful." Her grip and her eyes were desperate now.

"I will. I promise. I'm good at this, okay?"

So was Tim. She didn't have to say it. Her eyes did, and Kelly understood how cruel it could be to leave anyone behind.

"I have to go now, Sandy."

"Just make sure you come back."

"I will. Promise." But the words sounded empty, even to him. Kelly wanted to kiss her but couldn't. He moved away from the table, feeling her hand still on his. She was a tall woman, and very strong and brave, but she'd been hurt badly before, and it frightened Kelly that he might bring yet more pain to her life. "See you in a couple weeks. Say goodbye to Sarah and Doris for me, okay?"

"Yes." She followed him towards the front door. "John, when you get back, let it stop."

"I'll think about it," he said without turning, because he was afraid to look at her again. "I will."

Kelly opened the door. It was dark outside now, and he'd have to hustle to get to Quantico on time. He could hear her behind him, hear her breathing. Two women in his life, one taken by an accident, one by murder, and now perhaps a third whom he was driving away all by himself.

"John?" She hadn't let go of his hand, and he had to turn back despite his fear.

"Yes, Sandy?"

"Come back."

He touched her face again, and kissed her hand, and drew away. She watched him walk to the Volkswagen and drive off.

Even now, she thought. *Even now he's trying to protect me.*

Is it enough? Can I stop now? But what was "enough"?

"Think it through," he said aloud. "What do you know that others can use?"

It was quite a lot, really. Billy had told him much, perhaps a sufficient amount. The drugs were processed on one of those wrecked ships. He had Henry's name, and Burt's. He knew a senior narcotics officer was in Henry's employ. Could the police take that and spin it into a case firm enough to put them all behind bars for drug trafficking and murder? Might Henry get a death sentence? And if the answer to every question was yes, was that good enough?

As much as Sandy's misgivings, his association with the Marines had brought the same questions to the front of his mind. What would they think if they knew that they were associating with a murderer? Would they see it that way or would they be sympathetic to his point of view?

"The bags stink," Billy had said. "Like dead bodies, like the stuff they use."

What the hell did that mean? Kelly wondered, going through town one last time. He saw police cars operating. They couldn't all be driven by corrupt cops, could they?

"Shit," Kelly snarled at the traffic. "Clear your mind, sailor. There's a job waiting, a real job."

But that had said it all. BOXWOOD GREEN was a *real* job, and the realization came as clear and bright as the headlights of approaching cars. If someone like Sandy didn't understand—it was one thing to do it alone, just with your own thoughts and rage and loneliness, but when others saw and knew, even people who liked you, and knew exactly what it was all about. . . . When even they asked you to stop. . . .

Where was right? Where was wrong? Where was the line between them? It was easy on the highway. Some crew painted the lines, and you had to stay in the proper lane, but in real life it wasn't so clear.

Forty minutes later he was on I-495, the Washington Beltway. What was more important, killing Henry or getting those other women out of there?

Another forty and he was across the river into Virginia. Seeing Doris— what a dumb name—alive, after the first time when she'd been almost as dead as Rick. The more he thought about it, the better that seemed.

BOXWOOD GREEN wasn't about killing the enemy. It was about rescuing people.

He turned south on Interstate 95, and a final forty-five or so delivered him to Quantico. It was eleven-thirty when he drove into the training site.

"Glad you made it," Marty Young observed sourly. He was dressed in utilities for once instead of his khaki shirt.

Kelly looked hard into the General's eyes. "Sir, I've had a bad enough night. Be a pal and stow it, all right?"

Young took it like the man he was. "Mr. Clark, you sound like you're ready."

"That isn't what it's about, sir. Those guys in SENDER GREEN are ready."

"Fair enough, tough guy."

"Can I leave the car here?"

"With all these clunkers?"

Kelly paused, but the decision came quickly enough. "I think it's served its purpose. Junk it with the rest of 'em."

"Come on, the bus is down the hill a ways."

Kelly collected his personal gear and carried them to the staff car. The same corporal was driving as he sat in the back with the Marine aviator who wouldn't be going.

"What do you think, Clark?"

"Sir, I think we have a really good chance."

"You know, I wish just once, just one goddamned time, we could say, yeah, this one's going to work."

"Was it ever that way for you?" Kelly asked.

"No," Young admitted. "But you don't stop wishing."

"How was England, Peter?"

"Pretty nice. It rained in Paris, though. Brussels was pretty decent, my first time there," Henderson said.

Their apartments were only two blocks apart, comfortable places in Georgetown built during the late thirties to accommodate the influx of bureaucrats serving a growing government. Built of solid cinder-arch construction, they were more structurally sound than more recent buildings. Hicks had a two-bedroom unit, which compensated for the smallish living-dining room.

"So what's happening that you wanted to tell me about?" the Senate aide asked, still recovering from jet lag.

"We're invading the North again," the White House aide answered.

"What? Hey, I was at the peace talks, okay? I observed some of the chitchat. Things are moving along. The other side just caved in on a big one."

"Well, you can kiss that goodbye for a while," Hicks said morosely. On the coffee table was a plastic bag of marijuana, and he started putting a smoke together.

"You should lay off that shit, Wally."

"Doesn't give me a hangover like beer does. Shit, Peter, what's the difference?"

"The difference is your fucking security clearance!" Henderson said pointedly.

"Like that matters? Peter, they don't listen. You talk and talk and talk to them, and they just don't listen.'' Hicks lit up and took a long pull. ''I'm going to leave soon anyway. Dad wants me to come and join the family business. Maybe after I make a few mill', maybe then somebody'll listen once in a while.''

''You shouldn't let it get to you, Wally. It takes time. Everything takes time. You think we can fix things overnight?''

''I don't think we can fix things at all! You know what this all is? It's like Sophocles. We have our fatal flaw, and they have their fatal flaw, and when the fucking *deus* comes *ex* the fucking *machina,* the *deus* is going to be a cloud of ICBMs, and it's all going to be over, Peter. Just like we thought a few years ago up in New Hampshire.'' It wasn't Hicks's first smoke of the evening, Henderson realized. Intoxication always made his friend morose.

''Wally, tell me what the problem is.''

''There's supposedly this camp . . .'' Hicks began, his eyes down, not looking at his friend at all now as he related what he knew.

''That is bad news.''

''They *think* there's a bunch of people there, but it's just supposition. We only know about one. What if we're fucking over the peace talks for *one guy,* Peter?''

''Put that damned thing out,'' Henderson said, sipping his beer. He just didn't like the smell of the stuff.

''No.'' Wally took another big hit.

''When is it going?''

''Not sure. Roger didn't say exactly.''

''Wally, you have to stay with it. We need people like you in the system. Sometimes they will listen.''

Hicks looked up. ''When will that be, do you think?''

''What if this mission fails? What if it turns out that you're right? Roger will listen to you then, and Henry listens to Roger, doesn't he?''

''Well, yeah, sometimes.''

What a remarkable chance this was, Henderson thought.

The chartered bus drove to Andrews Air Force Base, duplicating, Kelly saw, more than half of his drive. There was a new C-141 on the ramp, painted white on the top and gray on the bottom, its strobe lights already rotating. The Marines got out of the bus, finding Maxwell and Greer waiting for them.

''Good luck,'' Greer said to each man.

''Good hunting,'' was what Dutch Maxwell told them.

Built to hold more than double their number, the Lockheed Starlifter was outfitted for litter patients, with a total of eighty beds bolted to the side of the aircraft and room for twenty or so attendants. That gave every Marine a place to lie down and sleep, plus room for all the prisoners they expected to rescue. The time of night made it easy for everyone, and the Starlifter started turning engines as soon as the cargo hatch was shut.

"Jesus, I hope this works," Maxwell said, watching the aircraft taxi into the darkness.

"You've trained them well, Admiral," Bob Ritter observed. "When do we go out?"

"Three days, Bob," James Greer answered. "Got your calendar clear?"

"For this? You bet."

26

Transit

A new aircraft, the Starlifter was also a disappointingly slow one. Its cruising speed was a mere 478 miles per hour, and their first stop was Elmendorf Air Force base in Alaska, 3,350 miles and eight hours away. It never ceased to amaze Kelly that the shortest distance to any place on Earth was a curve, but that was because he was used to flat maps, and the world was a sphere. The great-circle route from Washington to Danang would actually have taken them over Siberia, and that, the navigator said, just wouldn't do. By the time of their arrival at Elmendorf, the Marines were up and rested. They departed the aircraft to look at snow on not-so-distant mountains, having only a few hours before left a place where heat and humidity were in a daily race for 100. But here in Alaska they found mosquitoes sufficiently large that a few might have carried one of their number off. Most took the opportunity to jog a couple of miles, to the amusement of the Air Force personnel, who typically had little contact with Marines. Servicing the C-141 took a programmed time of two and a quarter hours. After refueling and one minor instrument replacement, the Marines were just as happy to reboard the aircraft for the second leg of the journey, for Yakoda, in Japan. Three hours after that, Kelly walked onto the flight deck, growing bored with the noise and confinement.

"What's that over there?" he asked. In the distant haze was a brown-green line that denoted somebody's coast.

"Russia. They have us on radar right now."

"Oh, that's nice," Kelly observed.

"It's a small world, sir, and they own a big hunk of it."

"You talk to them—air-traffic control, like?"

"No." The navigator laughed. "They're not real neighborly. We talk on HF to Tokyo for this leg, and after Yakoda, we're controlled through Manila. Is the ride smooth enough?"

"No beefs so far. Gets long, though."

"It does that," the navigator acknowledged, turning back to his instruments.

Kelly walked back into the cargo area. The C-141 was noisy, a constant high-frequency whine from the engines and the air through which they were passing. The Air Force didn't waste any money, as airlines did, on sound insulation. Every Marine was wearing earplugs, which made conversation difficult, and after a time didn't really block the noise anyway. The worst part of air travel was the boredom, Kelly thought, made worse by the sound-induced isolation. You could only sleep so much. Some of the men were honing knives which they would never really use, but it gave you something to do, and a warrior had to have a knife for some reason. Others were doing push-ups on the metal cargo deck of the aircraft. The Air Force crewmen watched impassively, not wanting to laugh, wondering what this obviously select group of Marines was up to, but unable to ask. It was for them just one more mystery as their aircraft slid down the Siberian coast. They were used to it, but to a man they wished the Marines well on whatever their job was.

The problem was the first thing on his mind when his eyes opened. *What do I do about this?* Henderson asked himself crossly.

It wasn't what he wanted to do, but what he would be able to do. He'd delivered information before. At first unknowingly, through contacts in the peace movement, he'd—well, not so much given over information as had joined in rambling discussions which over time had become more and more pointed until finally one of his friends had asked something just a little too directed to be a random inquiry. A friendly question she'd asked, and at a very friendly moment, but the look in her eyes was a little too interested in the reply and not enough interested in him, a situation which had immediately reversed when he'd answered the question. A spoonful of sugar, he'd told himself later, rather vexed with himself that he'd fallen prey to such an obvious and old-fashioned—well, not an error, really. He liked her, believed as she did in the way the world should be, and if anything he was annoyed that she'd felt it necessary to manipulate his body in order to get something that reason and intellect would have elicited quite readily from his mind . . . well, probably.

She was gone now, gone somewhere. Henderson didn't know where, though he was sure that he'd never see her again. Which was sad, really.

She'd been a great lay. One thing had led to another in a seemingly gradual and natural series of steps ending with his brief conversation at H.M. Tower of London, and now—now he had something the other side really needed. It was just that he didn't have anyone to tell it to. Did the Russians really know what they had there at that damned-fool camp southwest of Haiphong? It was information which, if used properly, would make them feel far more comfortable about *détente,* would allow them to back off a little, in turn allowing America to back off a little. That was how it had to start. It was a shame Wally didn't grasp that it had to start as little things, that you couldn't change the world all at once. Peter knew that he had to get that message across. He couldn't have Wally leave government service now, to become just one more goddamned financial puke, as though the world didn't have enough of them already. He was valuable where he was. Wally just liked to talk too much. It went along with his emotional instability. And his drug use, Henderson thought, looking in the mirror as he shaved.

Breakfast was accompanied by a morning paper. There it was again, on the first page as it was almost every day. Some medium-sized battle for some hill that had been exchanged a dozen or more times, X number of Americans and Y number of Vietnamese, all dead. The implications for the peace talks of some air raid or other, another boring and predictable editorial. Plans for a demonstration. *One, Two, Three, Four. We don't want your fucking war.* As though something so puerile as that really meant anything. In a way, he knew, it did. It did put pressure on political figures, did catch media attention. There was a mass of politicians who wanted the war to end, as Henderson did, but not yet a critical mass. His own senator, Robert Donaldson, was still on the fence. He was called a reasonable and thoughtful man, but Henderson merely found him indecisive, always considering everything about an issue and then most often going with the crowd as though he hadn't thought anything at all on his own. There had to be a better way, and Henderson was working on that, advising his senator carefully, shading things just a little bit, taking his time to become trusted so that he could learn things that Donaldson wasn't supposed to tell anyone—but that was the problem with secrets. You just *had to* let others know, he thought on the way out the door.

Henderson rode the bus to work. Parking on The Hill was such a pain in the rump, and the bus went nearly from door to door. He found a seat in the back where he could finish reading the paper. Two blocks later he felt the bus stop, and immediately thereafter a man sat down next to him.

"How was London?" the man asked in a conversational voice, barely over the noise of the bus's diesel. Henderson looked over briefly. It wasn't someone he'd met before. Were they *that* efficient?

"I met someone there," Peter said cautiously.

"I have a friend in London. His name is George." Not a trace of an accent, and now that contact was established, the man was reading the sports page of the *Washington Post*. "I don't think the Senators will make it this year. Do you?"

"George said he had a . . . friend in town."

The man smiled at the box score. "My name is Marvin; you can call me that."

"How do we . . . how do I . . . ?"

"What are you doing for dinner tonight?" Marvin asked.

"Nothing much. Want to come over—"

"No, Peter, that is not smart. Do you know a place called Alberto's?"

"Wisconsin Avenue, yeah."

"Seven-thirty," Marvin said. He rose and got off at the next stop.

The final leg started at Yakoda Air Force Base. After another programmed two-and-a-quarter-hour service wait, the Starlifter rotated off the runway, clawing its way back into the sky. That was when things started to get real for everyone. The Marines made a concerted effort to sleep now. It was the only way to deal with the tension that grew in inverse proportion to the distance from their final destination. Things were different now. It wasn't just a training exercise, and their demeanor was adapting itself to a new reality. On a different sort of flight, a commercial airliner, perhaps, where conversation might have been possible, they'd trade jokes, stories of amorous conquests, talk about home and family and plans for the future, but the noise of the C-141 denied them that, and so they traded brave smiles that hung under guarded eyes, each man alone with his thoughts and fears, needing to share them and deflect them, but unable to in the noisy cargo compartment of the Starlifter. That was why many of them exercised, just to work off the stress, to tire themselves enough for the oblivion of sleep. Kelly watched it, having seen and done it himself, alone with his own thoughts even more complex than theirs.

It's about rescue, Kelly told himself. What had started the whole adventure was saving Pam, and the fact of her death was his fault. Then he had killed, to get even, telling himself it was for her memory and for his love, but was that really true? What good things came from death? He'd *tortured* a man, and now he had to admit to himself that he'd taken satisfaction for Billy's pain. If Sandy had learned that, then what? What would she think of him? It was suddenly important to consider what she thought about him. She who worked so hard to save that girl, who nurtured and protected, following through on his more simple act of rescue, what would she think of someone who'd torn Billy's body apart one cell at a time? He could not, after all, stop all the evil in the world. He could not win the war to which he was now returning, and as skilled as this team of Recon Marines was, they would not win the war either. They were going for something else. Their purpose was rescue, for while there could be little real satisfaction in the taking of life, saving life was ever something to recall with the deepest pride. That was his mission now, and must be his mission on returning. There were four other girls in the control of the ring. He'd get them clear, somehow . . . and maybe he could somehow let the cops know what Henry was up to, and then they could deal with him. Somehow. How exactly he wasn't sure. But at least then he could do something that memory would not try to wash away.

And all he had to do was survive this mission. Kelly grunted to himself. No big deal, right?

Tough guy, he told himself with bravado that rang false even within the confines of his own skull. *I can do this. I've done it before.* Strange, he thought, how the mind doesn't always remember the scary parts until it was too late. Maybe it was proximity. Maybe it was easier to consider dangers that were half a world away, but then when you started getting closer, things changed. . . .

"Toughest part, Mr. Clark," Irvin said loudly, sitting down beside him after doing his hundred push-ups.

"Ain't it the truth?" Kelly half-shouted back.

"Something you oughta remember, squid—you got inside and took me out that night, right?" Irvin grinned. "And I'm pretty damned good."

"They ought not to be all that alert, their home turf an' all," Kelly observed after a moment.

"Probably not, anyway, not as alert as we were that night. Hell, we knew you were coming in. You kinda expect home troops, like, go home to the ol' lady every night, thinking about havin' a piece after dinner. Not like us, man."

"Not many like us," Kelly agreed. He grinned. "Not many dumb as we are."

Irvin slapped him on the shoulder. "You got that right, Clark." The master gunnery sergeant moved off to encourage the next man, which was his way of dealing with it.

Thanks, Guns, Kelly thought, leaning back and forcing himself back into sleep.

*   *   *

Alberto's was a place waiting to be fully discovered. A small and rather typical mom-and-pop Italian place where the veal was especially good. In fact, everything was good, and the couple who ran it waited patiently for the *Post*'s food critic to wander in, bringing prosperity with him. Until then they subsisted on the college crowd from nearby Georgetown University and a healthy local trade of neighborhood diners without which no restaurant could really survive. The only disappointing note was the music, schmaltzy tapes of Italian opera that oozed out of substandard speakers. The mom and pop in question would have to work on that, he thought.

Henderson found a booth in the back. The waiter, probably an illegal Mexican who comically tried to mask his accent as Italian, lit the candle on the table with a match and went off for the gin-and-tonic the new customer wanted.

Marvin arrived a few minutes later, dressed casually and carrying the evening paper, which he sat on the table. He was of Henderson's age, totally nondescript, not tall or short, portly or thin, his hair a neutral brown and of medium length, wearing glasses that might or might not have held prescription lenses. He wore a blue short-sleeve shirt without a tie, and looked like just another local resident who didn't feel like doing his own dinner tonight.

"The Senators lost again," he said when the waiter arrived with Henderson's drink. "The house red for me," Marvin told the Mexican.

"*Sí,*" the waiter said and moved off.

Marvin had to be an illegal, Peter thought, appraising the man. As a staffer for a member of the Select Committee on Intelligence, Henderson had been briefed in by serious members of the FBI's Intelligence Division. "Legal" KGB officers had diplomatic covers, and if caught could only be PNG'd—declared persona non grata—and sent home. So they were secure from serious mishandling on the part of the American government, which was the good news; the bad news was that they were also more easily tracked, since their residences and automobiles were known. Illegals were just that, Soviet intelligence officers who came into the country with false papers and who if caught would end up in federal prison until the next exchange, which could take years. Those facts explained Marvin's superb English. Any mistake he made would have serious consequences. That made his relaxed demeanor all the more remarkable.

"Baseball fan, eh?"

"I learned the game long ago. I was a pretty good shortstop, but I never learned to hit a curve ball." The man grinned. Henderson smiled back. He'd seen satellite imagery of the very place where Marvin had learned his trade, that interesting little city northwest of Moscow.

"How will it work?"

"I like that. Good. Let's get down to business. We won't be doing this very often. You know why."

Another smile. "Yeah, they say that winters at Leavenworth are a motherfucker."

"Not a laughing matter, Peter," the KGB officer said. "This is a very serious business." *Please, not another bloody cowboy,* Marvin thought to himself.

"I know. Sorry," Henderson apologized. "I'm new to this."

"First of all, we need to set up a way of contacting me. Your apartment has curtains on the front windows. When they are all the way open, or all the way closed, there is nothing to concern us. When there is, leave them halfway closed. I will check your windows twice a week, on Tuesday and Friday mornings, about nine. Is that acceptable?"

"Yes, Marvin."

"For starters, Peter, we'll use a simple transfer method. I will park my car on a street close to your home. It's a dark-blue Plymouth Satellite with license number HVR-309. Repeat that back to me. Don't ever write it down."

"HVR-309."

"Put your messages in this." He passed something under the table. It was small and metallic. "Don't get it too close to your watch. There's a powerful magnet in it. When you walk past my car, you can bend down to pick up a piece of litter, or rest your foot on the bumper and tie your shoe. Just stick the container on the inside surface of the bumper. The magnet will hold it in place."

It seemed very sophisticated to Henderson, though everything he'd just heard was kindergarten-level spycraft. This was good for the summer. Winter weather would require something else. The dinner menu arrived, and both men selected veal.

"I have something now if you're interested," Henderson told the KGB officer. *Might as well let them know how important I am.*

Marvin, whose real name was Ivan Alekseyevich Yegorov, had a real job, and everything that went along with it. Employed by the Aetna Casualty and Surety Company as a loss-control representative, he'd been through company training on Farmington Avenue in Hartford, Connecticut, before returning to the Washington regional office, and his job was to identify safety hazards at the many clients of the company, known in the trade as "risks." Selected mainly for its mobility—the post even came with a company car—the job carried with it the unexpected bonus of visiting the offices of various government contractors whose employees were not always as careful covering up the papers on their desks as they ought to have been. His immediate boss was delighted with Marvin's performance. His new man was highly observant and downright superb at documenting his business affairs. He'd already turned down promotion and transfer to Detroit—*sorry, boss, but I just like the Washington area too much*—which didn't bother his supervisor at all. A guy with his skills, holding a fairly low-paying job, just made his part of the office look all the better. For Marvin, the job meant being out of the office four days out of five, which allowed him to meet people whenever and wherever he wished, along with a free car—Aetna even paid gas and maintenance—and a life so comfortable that had he believed in God he might have thought himself dead and in heaven. A genuine love for baseball took him to RFK Stadium, where the anonymity of the crowd was as perfect a place for brush-passes and other meets as the *KGB Field Operations Manual* dared to hope for. All in all, Captain Yegorov was a man on the way up, comfortable with his cover and his surroundings, doing his duty for his country. He'd even managed to arrive in America just in time to catch the sexual revolution. All he really missed was the vodka, something Americans did poorly.

Isn't this interesting? Marvin asked himself in his Chevy Chase apartment. It was downright hilarious that he had learned about a high-level Russian intelligence operation from an American, and here was a chance to hurt his country's Main Enemy through surrogates—if they could get things moving in time. He would also be able to inform his control officers of something the Soviet Air Force cretins had running that had significant implications for the Soviet Union's defense. They'd probably try to take that operation over. You couldn't trust pilots—it had to be a PVO Strany officer doing the questioning, he was sure—with something as important as national defense. He made his notes, photographed them, and rewound the film into the tiny cassette. His first appointment tomorrow was an early call at a local contractor. From there he would stop off to have breakfast at a Howard Johnson's, where he'd make his transfer. The cassette would be in Moscow in two days, maybe three, by diplomatic pouch.

Captain Yegorov ended his work for the evening just in time to catch the end of the Senators game—despite a ninth-inning homer by Frank Howard they fell short again, losing to Cleveland 5–3. Wasn't this something, he thought, sipping at his beer. Henderson was a plum all by himself, and nobody had bothered to tell him—probably hadn't known—that he had his own source within the White House Office of National Security Affairs. Wasn't that a kick in the ass?

Mission stress and all, it was a relief when the C-141 thumped down at Danang. They'd been in transit for a total of twenty-three noisy and mind-numbing hours, and that was quite long enough, they all thought, until reality struck them hard and fast. Scarcely had the cargo hatch opened when the smell hit them. It was what all veterans of this place came to think of as the Smell of Vietnam. The contents of various latrines were dumped into barrels and burned with diesel fuel.

"Smell o' home!" one Marine joked, badly, evoking isolated barks of semiamusement.

"Saddle up!" Irvin shouted as the engine noise died. It took a little time. Reactions were slowed by fatigue and stiffness. Many shook their heads to clear off the dizziness induced by the earplugs, along with yawns and stretches which psychologists would have called typical nonverbal expressions of unease.

The flight crew came aft just as the Marines left. Captain Albie went to them, thanking them for the ride, which had been smooth, if long. The Air Force crew looked forward to several days of enforced crew-rest after the marathon stint, not yet knowing that they would hold in this area until the team was ready to fly home, perhaps catching a few cargo hops back and forth to Clark. Then Albie led his men off the aircraft. Two trucks were waiting, and they drove to a different part of the air base, where two aircraft waited. These were Navy C-2A Greyhounds. With a few desultory moans, the Marines selected seats for the next part of their journey, a one-hour hop to USS *Constellation*. Once there, they boarded a pair of CH-46 Sea Knight helicopters for a transfer to USS *Ogden*, where, disoriented and exhausted by travel, they were led to capacious and empty troop quarters—and bunks. Kelly watched them file off, wondering what came next for him.

"How was the trip?" He turned to see Admiral Podulski, dressed in wrinkled khakis and far too cheerful for the moment.

"Aviators gotta be crazy," Kelly bitched.

"Does get kinda long. Follow me," the Admiral ordered, leading him into the superstructure. Kelly looked around first. *Constellation* was on the eastern horizon, and he could see aircraft flying off one end while others circled to land on the other. Two cruisers were in close attendance, and destroyers ringed the formation. It was part of the Navy which Kelly had rarely seen, the Big Blue Team at work, commanding the ocean. "What's that?" he asked, pointing.

"Russian fishing trawler, AGI." Podulski waved Kelly through a watertight door.

"Oh, that's just great!"

"Don't worry. We can deal with that," the Admiral assured him.

Inside the superstructure, the two men headed up a series of ladders, finding flag quarters, or what passed for them at the moment. Admiral Podulski had taken over the Captain's in-port cabin for the duration of the mission, relegating *Ogden*'s CO to his smaller accommodations nearer the bridge. There was a comfortable sitting room, and the ship's captain was there.

"Welcome aboard!" Captain Ted Franks said in greeting. "You're Clark?"

"Yes, sir."

Franks was a fifty-year-old pro who'd been in amphibious ships since 1944. *Ogden* was his fifth and would be his last command. Short, pudgy, and losing his hair, he still had the look of a warrior on a face that was by turns good-natured and deadly serious. At the moment, it was the former. He waved Kelly to a chair next to a table in the center of which was a bottle of Jack Daniel's.

"That ain't legal," Kelly observed at once.

"Not for me," Captain Franks agreed. "Aviator rations."

"I arranged for them," Casimir Podulski explained. "Brought 'em over from *Connie*. You need something to steady down after all that time with the Air Scouts."

"Sir, I never argue with admirals." Kelly dropped two ice cubes into a tumbler and covered them with alcohol.

"My XO is talking with Captain Albie and his people. They're all getting entertained, too," Franks added, meaning that every man had two miniatures on his assigned bunk. "Mr. Clark, our ship is yours. Anything we have, you got it."

"Well, Cap'n, you surely know how to say hello." Kelly sipped at his drink, and the first touch of the booze made his body remember how wrung-out he was. "So when do we start?"

"Four days. You need two to recover from the trip," the Admiral said. "The submarine will be with us two days after that. The Marines go in Friday morning, depending on weather."

"Okay." There was nothing else he could say.

"Only the XO and I know anything yet. Try not to spread things around. We've got a pretty good crew. The intel team is aboard and working. The medical team gets here tomorrow.''

"Recon?"

Podulski handled that one. "We'll have photos of the camp later today, from a Vigilante working off *Connie*. Then another set twelve hours before you move out. We have Buffalo Hunter shots, five days old. The camp is still there, still guarded, same as before.''

"Items?'' Kelly asked, using the code word for prisoners.

"We've only got three shots of Americans in the compound.'' Podulski shrugged. "They don't make a camera yet that can see through a tile roof.''

"Right.'' Kelly's face said it all.

"I'm worried about that, too,'' Cas admitted.

Kelly turned. "Captain, you have an exercise place, something like that?''

"Weight room, aft of the crew's mess. Like I said, it's yours if you want it.''

He finished off his drink. "Well, I think I need to get some rack time.''

"You'll mess with the Marines. You'll like the food here,'' Captain Franks promised.

"Fair enough.''

"I saw two men not wearing their hard-hats,'' Marvin Wilson said to the boss.

"I'll talk to them.''

"Aside from that, thanks a lot for your cooperation.'' He'd made a total of eleven safety recommendations, and the owner of the cement company had adopted every one, hoping for a reduction in his insurance rates. Marvin took off his white hard-hat and wiped the sweat from his brow. It was going to be a hot one. The summer climate was not all that much unlike Moscow, but more humid. At least the winters were milder.

"You know, if they made these things with little holes in them for ventilation, they'd be a lot more comfortable to wear.''

"I've said that myself,'' Captain Yegorov agreed, heading off to his car. Fifteen minutes later he pulled into a Howard Johnson's. The blue Plymouth took a spot along the west side of the building, and as he got out, a patron inside finished off his coffee and left his spot at the counter, along with a quarter tip to thrill the waitress. The restaurant had a double set of doors to save on the air-conditioning bill, and when the two men met there, just the two of them, moving, with the glass of the doors interfering with anyone who might be observing them, the film was passed. Yegorov/Wilson continued inside, and a "legal" KGB major named Ishchenko went his way. Relieved of his burden for the day, Marvin Wilson sat at the counter and ordered orange juice to start. There were so many good things to eat in America.

"I'm eating too much." It was probably true, but it didn't stop Doris from attacking the pile of hotcakes.

Sarah didn't understand the Americans' love for emaciation. "You lost plenty in the last two weeks. It won't hurt you to put a little back," Sarah Rosen told her graduating patient.

Sarah's Buick was parked outside, and today would see them in Pittsburgh. Sandy had worked on Doris's hair a little more, and made one more trip to get clothes that befitted the day, a beige silk blouse and a burgundy skirt that ended just above the knee. The prodigal son could return home in rags, but the daughter had to arrive with some pride.

"I don't know what to say," Doris Brown told them, standing to collect the dishes.

"You just keep getting better," Sarah replied. They went out to the car, and Doris got in the back. If nothing else, Kelly had taught them caution. Dr. Sarah Rosen headed out quickly, turning north on Loch Raven, getting on the Baltimore Beltway and heading west to Interstate 70. The posted limit on the new highway was seventy miles per hour, and Sarah exceeded it, pushing her heavy Buick northwest toward the Catoctin Mountains, every mile between them and the city an additional safety factor, and by the time they passed Hagerstown she relaxed and started enjoying the ride. What were the chances, after all, of being spotted in a moving car?

It was a surprisingly quiet ride. They'd talked themselves out in the previous few days as Doris had returned to a condition approximating normality. She still needed drug counseling, and seriously needed psychiatric help, but Sarah had already taken care of that with a colleague at the University of Pittsburgh's excellent medical school, a sixtyish woman who knew not to report things to the local police, assured that that part of the matter was already in hand. In the silence of the car Sandy and Sarah could feel the tension build. It was something they'd talked about. Doris was returning to a home and a father she'd left for a life that had nearly become a death. For many months the principal component of her new life would be guilt, part earned, part not. On the whole she was a very lucky young lady, something Doris had yet to grasp. She was, first of all, alive. With her confidence and self-esteem restored she might in two or three years be able to continue her life on a course so normal that no one would ever suspect her past or notice the fading scars. Restored health would change this girl, returning her not only to her father but also to the world of real people.

Perhaps she might even become stronger, Sarah hoped, if the psychiatrist brought her along slowly and carefully. Dr. Michelle Bryant had a stellar reputation, a correct one, she hoped. For Dr. Rosen, still racing west slightly over the legal limit, this was one of the hard parts of medicine. She had to let the patient go with the job not yet complete. Her clinical work with drug abusers had prepared her for it, but those jobs, like this one, were never really finished. It was just that there came a time when you had to let go, hoping and trusting that the patient could do the rest. Perhaps sending your daughter off to be married was like this, Sarah thought. It could have been so much worse in so many ways. Over the phone her father seemed a decent man, and Sarah Rosen didn't need a specialization in psychiatry to know that more than anything else, Doris needed a relationship with an honorable and loving man so that she could, one day, develop another such relationship that would last her lifetime. That was now the job of others, but it didn't stop Sarah from worrying about her patient. Every doctor can be a Jewish mother, and in her case it was difficult to avoid.

The hills were steep in Pittsburgh. Doris directed them along the Monongahela River and up the right street, suddenly tense while Sandy checked the numbers on the houses. And there it was. Sarah pulled the red Buick into a parking place and everyone took a deep breath.

"You okay?" she asked Doris, getting a frightened nod in response.

"He's your father, honey. He loves you."

There was nothing remarkable about Raymond Brown, Sarah saw a moment later. He must have been waiting at the door for hours, and he, too, was nervous, coming down the cracked concrete steps, holding the rail as he did so with a trembling hand. He opened the car door, helping Sandy out with awkward gallantry. Then he reached inside, and though he was trying to be brave and impassive, when his fingers touched Doris's, the man burst into tears. Doris tripped coming out of the car, and her father kept her from falling, and clutched her to his chest.

"Oh, Daddy!"

Sandy O'Toole turned away, not put off by the emotion of the moment, but wanting them to have it alone, and the look she gave Dr. Rosen was its own culminating moment for people of their profession. Both medics bit their lips and examined the other's moist eyes.

"Let's get you inside, baby," Ray Brown said, taking his little girl up the steps, needing to have her in his house and under his protection. The other two women followed without being bidden.

The living room was surprisingly dark. A day-sleeper, Mr. Brown had added dark shades to his home and had forgotten to raise them this day. It was a cluttered room of braided rugs and overstuffed '40s furniture, small mahogany tables with lacelike doilies. There were framed photos everywhere. A dead wife. A dead son. And a lost daughter—four of those. In the dark security of the house, father clutched daughter again.

"Honey," he said, recounting words that he'd been practicing for days. "The things I said, I was wrong, I was so damned wrong!"

"It's okay, Daddy. Thank you for . . . for letting me—"

"Dor, you're my little girl." Nothing more had to be said. That hug lasted over a minute, and then she had to draw back with a giggle.

"I have to go."

"The bathroom's in the same place," her father said, wiping his own eyes. Doris moved off, finding the stairs and going up. Raymond Brown turned his attention to his guests.

"I, uh, I have lunch ready." He paused awkwardly. This wasn't a time for good manners or considered words. "I don't know what I'm supposed to say."

"That's okay." Sarah smiled her benign doctor's smile, the sort that told him that everything was all right, even though it wasn't, really. "But we need to talk. This is Sandy O'Toole, by the way. Sandy's a nurse, and she's more responsible for your daughter's recovery than I am."

"Hi," Sandy said, and handshakes were exchanged all around.

"Doris still needs a lot of help, Mr. Brown," Dr. Rosen said. "She's been through a really terrible time. Can we talk a little bit?"

"Yes, ma'am. Please, sit down. Can I get you anything?" he asked urgently.

"I've set your daughter up with a doctor at Pitt. Her name's Michelle Bryant. She's a psychiatrist—"

"You mean Doris is . . . sick?"

Sarah shook her head. "No, not really. But she's been through a very bad time, and good medical attention will help her recover a lot faster. Do you understand?"

"Doc, I will do *anything* you tell me, okay? I've got all the medical insurance I need through the company."

"Don't worry about that. Michelle will handle this as a matter of professional courtesy. You have to go there with Doris. Now, it is very important that you understand, she's been through a really horrible experience. Terrible things. She's going to get better—she's going to recover fully, but you have to do your part. Michelle can explain all that better than I can. What I'm telling you, Mr. Brown, is this: no matter what awful things you learn, please—"

"Doc," he interrupted softly, "that's my little girl. She's all I have, and I'm not going to . . . foul up and lose her again. I'd rather die."

"Mr. Brown, that is exactly what we needed to hear."

Kelly awoke at one in the morning, local time. The big slug of whiskey he'd downed along the way had blessedly not resulted in a hangover. In fact, he felt unusually rested. The gentle rocking of the ship had soothed his body during the day/night, and lying in the darkness of his officers' accommodations he heard the gentle creaks of steel compressing and expanding as USS *Ogden* turned to port. He made his way to the shower, using cold water to wake himself up. In ten minutes he was dressed and presentable. It was time to explore the ship.

Warships never sleep. Though most work details were synchronized to daylight hours, the unbending watch cycle of the Navy meant that men were always moving about. No less than a hundred of the ship's crew were always at their duty stations, and many others were circulating about the dimly lit passageways on their way to minor maintenance tasks. Others were lounging in the mess spaces, catching up on reading or letter-writing.

He was dressed in striped fatigues. There was a name tag that said *Clark,* but no badges of rank. In the eyes of the crew that made "Mr. Clark" a civilian, and already they were whispering that he was a CIA guy—to the natural accompaniment of James Bond jokes that evaporated on the sight of him. The sailors stood aside in the passageways as he wandered around, greeting him with respectful nods that he acknowledged, bemused to have officer status. Though only the Captain and Executive Officer knew what this mission was all about, the sailors weren't dumb. You didn't send a ship all the way from 'Dago just to support a short platoon of Marines unless there was one hell of a good reason, and the bad-ass bunch that had come aboard looked like the sort to make John Wayne take a respectful step back.

Kelly found the flight deck. Three sailors were walking there, too. *Connie* was still on the horizon, still operating aircraft whose strobes blinked away against the stars. In a few minutes his eyes adapted to the darkness. There were destroyers present, a few thousand yards out. Aloft on *Ogden,* radar antennas turned to the hum of electric motors, but the dominating sound was the continuous broomlike swish of steel hull parting water.

"Jesus, it's pretty," he said, mainly to himself.

Kelly headed back into the superstructure and wandered forward and upwards until he found the Combat Information Center. Captain Franks was there, sleepless, as many captains tended to be.

"Feeling better?" the CO asked.

"Yes, sir." Kelly looked down at the plot, counting the ships in this formation, designated TF-77.1. Lots of radars were up and running, because North Vietnam had an air force and might someday try to do something really dumb.

"Which one's the AGI?"

"This is our Russian friend." Franks tapped the main display. "Doing the same thing we are. The Elint guys we have embarked are having a fine old time," the Captain went on. "Normally they go out on little ships. We're like the *Queen Mary* for them."

"Pretty big," Kelly agreed. "Seems real empty, too."

"Yep. Well, no scuffles to worry about, 'tween my kids and the Marine kids, I mean. You need to look at some charts? I have the whole package under lock in my cabin."

"Sounds like a good idea, Cap'n. Maybe some coffee, too?"

Franks' at-sea cabin was comfortable enough. A steward brought coffee and breakfast. Kelly unfolded the chart, again examining the river he'd be taking up.

"Nice and deep," Franks observed.

"As far as I need it to be," Kelly agreed, munching on some toast. "The objective's right here."

"Better you than me, my friend." Franks pulled a pair of dividers out of his pocket and walked off the distance.

"How long you been in this business?"

"Gator navy?" Franks laughed. "Well, they kicked my ass out of Annapolis in two and a half years. I wanted destroyers, so they gave me a first-flight LST. XO as a jaygee, would you believe? First landing was Peli-leu. I had my own command for Okinawa. Then Inchon, Wonsan, Lebanon. I've scraped off a lot of paint on a lot of beaches. You think . . . ?" he asked, looking up.

"We're not here to fail, Captain." Kelly had every twist of the river committed to memory, yet he continued to look at the chart, an exact copy of the one he'd studied at Quantico, looking for something new, finding nothing. He continued to stare at it anyway.

''You're going in alone? Long swim, Mr. Clark,'' Franks observed.

''I'll have some help, and I don't have to swim back, do I?''

''I suppose not. Sure will be nice to get those guys out.''

''Yes, sir.''

27

Insertion

Phase One of Operation BOXWOOD GREEN began just before dawn. The carrier USS *Constellation* reversed her southerly course at the transmission of a single code word. Two cruisers and six destroyers matched her turn to port, and the handles on nine different sets of engine-room enunciators were pushed down to the FULL setting. All of the various ships' boilers were fully on line already, and as the warships heeled to starboard, they also started accelerating. The maneuver caught the Russian AGI crew by surprise. They'd expected *Connie* to turn the other way, into the wind to commence flight operations, but unknown to them the carrier was standing down this morning and racing northeast. The intelligence-gathering trawler also altered course, increasing power on her own in the vain hope of soon catching up with the carrier task force. That left *Ogden* with two Adams-class missile-destroyer escorts, a sensible precaution after what had so recently happened to USS *Pueblo* off the Korean coast.

Captain Franks watched the Russian ship disappear an hour later. Two more hours passed, just to be sure. At eight that morning a pair of AH-1 Huey Cobras completed their lonely overwater flight from the Marine air base at Danang, landing on *Ogden*'s ample flight deck. The Russians might have wondered about the presence of two attack helicopters on the ship which, their intelligence reports confidently told them, was on an electronic-intelligence mission not unlike their own. Maintenance men already aboard immediately wheeled the "snakes" to a sheltered spot and began a complete maintenance check which would verify the condition of every component. Members of *Ogden*'s crew lit up their own machine shop, and skilled chief machinist's mates offered everything they had to the new arrivals. They were still not briefed on the mission, but it was clear now that something most unusual indeed was under way. The time for questioning was over. Whatever the hell it was, every resource of their ship was made available even before officers troubled themselves to relay that order to their various divisions. Cobra gunships meant action, and every man aboard knew they were a hell of a lot closer to North Vietnam than South. Speculation was running wild, but not that wild. They had a spook team aboard, then Marines, now gunships, and more helicopters would land this afternoon. The Navy medical corpsmen aboard were told to open up the ship's hospital spaces for new arrivals.

"We're going to raid the fuckers," a bosun's mate third observed to his chief.

"Don't spread that one around," the twenty-eight-year veteran growled back.

"Who the fuck am I gonna tell, Boats? Hey, man, I'm for it, okay?"

What is my Navy coming to? the veteran of Leyte Gulf asked himself.

"You, you, you," the junior man called, pointing to some new seamen. "Let's do a FOD walkdown." That started a detailed examination of the flight deck, searching for any object that might get sucked into an engine intake. He turned back to the bosun. "With your permission, Boats."

"Carry on." *College boys,* the senior chief thought, *avoiding the draft.*

"And if I see anybody smoking out here, I'll tear him a new asshole!" the salty third-class told the new kids.

But the real action was in officers' country.

"A lot of routine stuff," the intelligence officer told his visitors.

"We've been working on their phone systems lately," Podulski explained. "It makes them use radios more."

"Clever," Kelly noted. "Traffic from the objective?"

"Some, and one last night was in Russian."

"That's the indicator we want!" the Admiral said at once. There was only one reason for a Russian to be at SENDER GREEN. "I hope we get that son of a bitch!"

"Sir," Albie promised with a smile, "if he's there, he's got."

Demeanors had changed again. Rested now, and close to the objective, thoughts turned away from abstract dread and back into focus on the hard facts of the matter. Confidence had returned—leavened with caution and concern, but they *had* trained for this. They were now thinking of the things that would go right.

The latest set of photos had come aboard, taken by an RA-5 Vigilante that had screamed low over no less than three SAM sites to cover its interest in a minor and secret place. Kelly lifted the blowups.

"Still people in the towers."

"Guarding something," Albie agreed.

"No changes I see," Kelly went on. "Only one car. No trucks . . . nothing much in the immediate area. Gentlemen, it looks pretty normal to me."

"*Connie* will hold position forty miles off seaward. The medics cross-deck today. The command team arrives tomorrow, and the next day—" Franks looked across the table.

"I go swimming," Kelly said.

The film cassette sat, undeveloped, in a safe in the office of a section chief of the KGB's Washington Station, in turn part of the Soviet Embassy, just a few blocks up 16th Street from the White House. Once the palatial home of George Mortimer Pullman—it had been purchased by the government of Nikolay II—it contained both the second-oldest elevator and the largest espionage operation in the city. The volume of material generated by over a hundred trained field officers meant that not all the information that came in through the door was processed locally, and Captain Yegorov was sufficiently junior that his section chief didn't deem his information worthy of inspection. The cassette finally went into a small manila envelope which was sealed with wax, then found its way into the awkward canvas bag of a diplomatic courier who boarded a flight to Paris, flying first class courtesy of Air France. At Orly, eight hours later, the courier walked to catch an Aeroflot jet to Moscow, which developed into three and a half hours of pleasant conversation with a KGB security officer who was his official escort for this part of the journey. In addition to his official duties, the courier did quite well for himself by purchasing various consumer goods on his regular trips west. The current item of choice was pantyhose, two pairs of which went to the KGB escort.

Upon arriving in Moscow and walking past customs control, the waiting car took him into the city, where the first stop was not the Foreign Ministry, but KGB Headquarters at #2 Dzerzhinskiy Square. More than half the contents of the diplomatic pouch were handed over there, which included most of the flat pantyhose packages. Two more hours allowed the courier to find his family flat, a bottle of vodka, and some needed sleep.

The cassette landed on the desk of a KGB major. The identification chit told him which of his field force had originated it, and the desk officer filled out a form of his own, then called a subordinate to convey it to the photo lab for development. The lab, while large, was also quite busy today, and he'd have to wait a day, perhaps two, his lieutenant told him on returning. The Major nodded. Yegorov was a new though promising field officer, and was starting to develop an agent with interesting legislative connections, but it was expected that it would be a while before CASSIUS turned over anything of great importance.

Raymond Brown left the University of Pittsburgh Medical School struggling not to quiver with anger after their first visit to Dr. Bryant. It had actually gone quite well. Doris had explained many of the events of the preceding three years with a forthright if brittle voice, and throughout he'd held her hand to lend support, both physical and moral. Raymond Brown actually blamed himself for everything that had happened to his daughter. If only he'd controlled his temper that Friday night so long before—but he hadn't. It was done. He couldn't change things. He'd been a different person then. Now he was older and wiser, and so he controlled his rage on the walk to the car. This process was about the future, not the past. The psychiatrist had been very clear about that. He was determined to follow her guidance on everything.

Father and daughter had dinner at a quiet family restaurant—he'd never learned to cook well—and talked about the neighborhood, which of Doris's childhood friends were doing what, in a gentle exercise at catching up on things. Raymond kept his voice low, telling himself to smile a lot and let Doris do most of the talking. Every so often her voice would slow, and the hurt look would reappear. That was his cue to change the subject, to say something nice about her appearance, maybe relate a story from the shop. Most of all he had to be strong and steady for her. Over the ninety minutes of their first session with the doctor, he'd learned that the things he'd feared for three years had indeed come to pass, and somehow he knew that other things as yet unspoken were even worse. He would have to tap on undiscovered resources to keep his anger in, but his little girl needed him to be a—a *rock,* he told himself. A great big rock that she could hold on to, as solid as the hills on which his city was built. She needed other things, too. She needed to rediscover God. The doctor had agreed with him about it, and Ray Brown was going to take care of it, with the help of his pastor, he promised himself, staring into his little girl's eyes.

It was good to be back at work. Sandy was running her floor again, her two-week absence written off by Sam Rosen as a special-duty assignment, which his status as a department chairman guaranteed would pass without question. The post-op patients were the usual collection of major and minor cases. Sandy's team organized and managed their care. Two of her fellow nurses asked a few questions about her absence. She answered merely by saying she'd done a special research project for Dr. Rosen, and that was enough, especially with a full and busy patient load. The other members of the nursing team saw that she was somewhat distracted. There was a distant look in her eyes from time to time, her thoughts elsewhere, dwelling on something. They didn't know what. Perhaps a man, they all hoped, glad to have the team leader back. Sandy was better at handling the surgeons than anyone else on the service, and with Professor Rosen backing her up, it made for a comfortable routine.

"So, you replace Billy and Rick yet?" Morello asked.

"That'll take a while, Eddie," Henry replied. "This is going to mess up our deliveries."

"Aw, crap! You got that too complicated anyway."

"Back off, Eddie," Tony Piaggi said. "Henry has a good routine set up. It's safe and it works—"

"And it's too complicated. Who's gonna take care of Philadelphia now?" Morello demanded.

"We're working on that," Tony answered.

"All you're doing is dropping the stuff off and collecting the money, for Crissake! They're not going to rip anybody off, we're dealing with *business* people, remember?" *Not street niggers,* he had the good sense not to add. That part of the message got across anyway. *No offense, Henry.*

Piaggi refilled the wineglasses. It was a gesture Morello found both patronizing and irritating.

"Look," Morello said, leaning forward. "I helped set up this deal, remember? You might not even be starting with Philly yet if it wasn't for me."

"What are you saying, Eddie?"

"I'll make your damn delivery while Henry gets his shit back together. How hard is it? Shit, you got broads doing it for you!" *Show a little panache,* Morello thought, *show them I have what it takes.* Hell, at least he'd show the guys in Philly, and maybe they could do for him what Tony wouldn't do. Yeah.

"Sure you want to take the chance, Eddie?" Henry asked with an inward smile. This wop was so easy to predict.

"Fuck, yeah."

"Okay," Tony said with a display of being impressed. "You make the call and set it up." Henry was right, Piaggi told himself. It had been Eddie all along, making his own move. How foolish. How easily dealt with.

"Still nothing," Emmet Ryan said, summarizing the Invisible Man Case. "All this evidence—and nothing."

"Only thing that makes sense, Em, is somebody was making a move." Murders didn't just start and stop. There had to be a reason. The reason might be hard, even impossible to discover in many cases, but an organized and careful series of murders was a different story. It came down to two possibilities. One was that someone had launched a series of killings to cover the real target. That target had to be William Grayson, who had dropped from the face of the earth, probably never to return alive, and whose body might someday be discovered—or not. Somebody very angry about something, very careful, and very skilled, and that somebody—the Invisible Man—had taken it to that point and stopped there.

How likely was that? Ryan asked himself. The answer was impossible to evaluate, but somehow the start-stop sequence seemed far too arbitrary. Far too much buildup for a single, seemingly inconsequential target. Whatever Grayson had been, he hadn't been the boss of anyone's organization, and if the murders had been a planned sequence, his death simply was not a logical stopping place. At least, Ryan frowned, that was what his instincts told him. He'd learned to trust those undefined inner feelings, as all cops do. And yet the killings *had* stopped. Three more pushers had died in the last few weeks; he and Douglas had visited every crime scene only to find that they'd been two quite ordinary robberies gone bad, with the third a turf fight that one had lost and another won. The Invisible Man was gone, or at least inactive, and that fact blew away the theory which had to him seemed the most sensible explanation for the killings, leaving only something far less satisfying.

The other possibility did make more sense, after a fashion. Someone had made a move on a drug ring as yet undiscovered by Mark Charon and his squad, eliminating pushers, doubtless encouraging them to switch allegiance to a new supplier. Under that construction, William Grayson had been somewhat more important in the great scheme of things—and perhaps there was another murder or two, as yet undiscovered, which had eliminated the command leadership of this notional ring. One more leap of imagination told Ryan that the ring taken down by the Invisible Man was the same he and Douglas had been chasing after, lo these many months. It all tied together in a very neat theoretical bundle.

But murders rarely did that. Real murder wasn't like a TV cop show. You never figured it all out. When you knew who, you might never really learn why, at least not in a way that really satisfied, and the problem with applying elegant theories to the real-life fact of death was that people didn't fit theories terribly well. Moreover, even if that model for the events of the past month were correct, it had to mean that a highly organized, ruthless, and deadly-efficient individual was now operating a criminal enterprise in Ryan's city, which wasn't exactly good news.

"Tom, I just don't buy it."

"Well, if he's your commando, why did he stop?" Douglas asked.

"Do I remember right? Aren't you the guy who came up with that idea?"

"Yeah, so?"

"So you're not helping your lieutenant very much, Sergeant."

"We have a nice weekend to think about it. Personally, I'm going to cut the grass and catch the double-header on Sunday, and pretend I'm just a regular citizen. Our friend is gone, Em. I don't know where, but he might as well be on the other side of the world. Best guess, somebody from out of town who came here on a job, and he did the job, and now he's gone."

"Wait a minute!" That was a new theory entirely, a contract assassin right out of the movies, and those people simply did not exist. But Douglas just headed out of the office, ending the chance for a discussion that might have demonstrated that each of the detectives was half wrong and half right.

Weapons practice started under the watchful eyes of the command team, plus whatever sailors could find an excuse to come aft. The Marines told themselves that the two newly arrived admirals and the new CIA puke had to be as jet-lagged as they'd been upon arrival, not knowing that Maxwell, Greer, and Ritter had flown a VIP transport most of the way, taking the Pacific in easier hops, with drinks and comfortable seats.

Trash was tossed over the side, with the ship moving at a stately five knots. The Marines perforated the various blocks of wood and paper sacks in an exercise that was more a matter of entertainment for the crew than real training value. Kelly took his turn, controlling his CAR-15 with two- and three-round bursts, and hitting the target. When it was over the men safed their weapons and headed back to their quarters. A chief stopped Kelly as he was reentering the superstructure.

"You're the guy going in alone?"

"You're not supposed to know that."

The chief machinist's mate just chuckled. "Follow me, sir." They headed forward, diverting from the Marine detail and finding themselves in *Ogden*'s impressive machine shop. It had to be impressive, as it was designed not merely to service the ship herself, but also the needs of whatever mobile equipment might be embarked. On one of the worktables, Kelly saw the sea sled he'd be using to head up the river.

"We've had this aboard since San Diego, sir. Our chief electrician and I been playing with it. We've stripped it down, cleaned everything, checked the batteries—they're good ones, by the way. It's got new seals, so it oughta keep the water out. We even tested it in the well deck. The guarantee says five hours. Deacon and I worked on it. It's good for seven," the chief said with quiet pride. "I figured that might come in handy."

"It will, Chief. Thank you."

"Now let's see this gun." Kelly handed it over after a moment's hesitation, and the chief started taking it apart. In fifteen seconds it was field-stripped, but the chief didn't stop there.

"Hold on!" Kelly snapped as the front-sight assembly came off.

"It's too noisy, sir. You *are* going in alone, right?"

"Yes, I am."

The machinist didn't even look up. "You want me to quiet this baby down or do you like to advertise?"

"You can't do that with a rifle."

"Says who? How far you figure you have to shoot?"

"Not more than a hundred yards, probably not that much. Hell, I don't even want to have to use it—"

" 'Cuz it's noisy, right?" The chief smiled. "You want to watch me, sir? You're gonna learn something."

The chief walked the barrel over to a drill press. The proper bit was already in place, and under the watchful eyes of Kelly and two petty officers he drilled a series of holes in the forward six inches of the hollow steel rod.

"Now, you can't silence a supersonic bullet all the way, but what you can do is trap all the gas, and that'll surely help."

"Even for a high-power cartridge?"

"Gonzo, you all set up?"

"Yeah, Chief," a second-class named Gonzales replied. The rifle barrel went onto a lathe, which cut a shallow but lengthy series of threads.

"I already got this made up." The chief held up a can-type suppressor, fully three inches in diameter and fourteen inches long. It screwed nicely onto the end of the barrel. A gap in the can allowed reattachment of the front sights, which also locked the suppressor fully in place.

"How long did you work on this?"

"Three days, sir. When I looked over the arms we embarked, it wasn't hard to figure what you might need, and I had the spare time. So I played around some."

"But how the hell did you know I was going—"

"We're exchanging signals with a sub. How hard is all that to figure out?"

"How did you know that?" Kelly demanded, knowing the answer even so.

"Ever know a ship that had secrets? Captain's got a yeoman. Yeomen talk," the machinist explained, completing the reassembly process. "It makes the weapon about six inches longer, I hope you don't mind."

Kelly shouldered the carbine. The balance was actually improved somewhat. He preferred a muzzle-heavy weapon since it made for better control.

"Very nice." He had to try it out, of course. Kelly and the chief headed aft. Along the way the machinist got a discarded wooden box. On the fantail, Kelly slapped a full magazine into the carbine. The chief tossed the wood into the water and stepped back. Kelly shouldered the weapon and squeezed off his first round.

Pop. A moment later came the sound of the bullet hitting the wood, actually somewhat louder than the report of the cartridge. He'd also distinctly heard the working of the bolt mechanism. This chief machinist's mate had done for a high-powered rifle what Kelly himself had done for a .22 pistol. The master craftsman smiled benignly.

"The only hard part's making sure there's enough gas to work the bolt. Try it full auto, sir."

Kelly did that, rippling off six rounds. It still sounded like gunfire, but the actual noise generated was reduced by at least ninety-five percent, and that meant that no one could hear it beyond a couple hundred yards—as opposed to over a thousand for a normal rifle.

"*Good* job, Chief."

"Whatever you're up to, sir, you be careful, hear?" the chief suggested, walking off without another word.

"You bet," Kelly told the water. He hefted the weapon a little more, and emptied the magazine at the wood before it grew too far off. The bullets converted the wooden box into splinters to the accompaniment of small white fountains of seawater.

You're ready, John.

*   *   *

So was the weather, he learned a few minutes later. Perhaps the world's most sophisticated weather-prediction service operated to support air operations over Vietnam—not that the pilots really appreciated or acknowledged it. The senior meteorologist had come across from *Constellation* with the admirals. He moved his hands across a chart of isobars and the latest satellite photo.

"The showers start tomorrow, and we can expect rain on and off for the next four days. Some heavy stuff. It'll go on until this slow-moving low-pressure area slides up north into China," the chief petty officer told them.

All of the officers were there. The four flight crews assigned to the mission evaluated this news soberly. Flying a helicopter in heavy weather wasn't exactly fun, and no aviator liked the idea of reduced visibility. But falling rain would also muffle the noise of the aircraft, and reduced visibility worked both ways. The main hazard that concerned them was light antiaircraft guns. Those were optically aimed, and anything that hindered the ability of the crews to hear and see their aircraft made for safety.

"Max winds?" a Cobra pilot asked.

"At worst, gusts to thirty-five or forty knots. It will be a little bumpy aloft, sir."

"Our main search radar is pretty good for weather surveillance. We can steer you around the worst of it," Captain Franks offered. The pilots nodded.

"Mr. Clark?" Admiral Greer asked.

"Rain sounds good to me. The only way they can spot me on the inbound leg is the bubbles I leave on the surface of the river. Rain'll break that up. It means I can move in daylight if I have to." Kelly paused, knowing that to go on would merely make the final commitment. "*Skate* ready for me?"

"Whenever we say so," Maxwell answered.

"Then it's 'go-mission' on my end, sir." Kelly could feel his skin go cold. It seemed to contract around his entire body, making him seem smaller somehow. But he'd said it anyway.

Eyes turned to Captain Albie, USMC. A vice admiral, two rear admirals, and an up-and-coming CIA field officer now depended on this young Marine to make the final decision. He would take the main force in. His was the ultimate operational responsibility. It seemed very strange indeed to the young captain that seven stars needed him to say "go," but twenty-five Marines and perhaps twenty others had their lives riding on his judgment. It was his mission to lead, and it had to be exactly right the first time. He looked over at Kelly and smiled.

"Mr. Clark, sir, you be real careful. I think it's time for your swim. This mission is 'go.' "

There was no exultation. In fact, every man around the chart table looked down at the maps, trying to convert the two-dimensional ink on paper into three-dimensional reality. Then the eyes came up, almost simultaneously, and each pair read all the others. Maxwell spoke first to one of the helicopter crews.

"I guess you'd better get your helo warmed up." Maxwell turned. "Captain Franks, would you signal *Skate?*" Two crisp *aye aye, sirs* answered him, and the men stood erect, stepping back from the chart and their decision.

It was a little late for the sober pause, Kelly told himself. He put his fear aside as best he could and started focusing his mind on twenty men. It seemed so strange to risk his life for people he hadn't met, but then, risk of life wasn't supposed to be rational. His father had spent a lifetime doing it, and had lost his life in the successful rescue of two children. *If I can take pride in my dad,* he told himself, *then I can honor him best in this way.*

You can do it, man. You know how. He could feel the determination begin to take over. All the decisions were made. He was committed to action now. Kelly's face took a hard set. Dangers were no longer things to be feared, but to be dealt with. To be overcome.

Maxwell saw it. He'd seen the same thing in ready rooms on carriers, fellow pilots going through the mental preparations necessary before you tossed the dice, and the Admiral remembered how it had been for him, the way the muscles tense, how your eyesight suddenly becomes very sharp. First in, last out, just as his mission had often been, flying his F6F Hellcat to eliminate fighters and then cover the attack aircraft all the way home. *My second son,* was what Dutch suddenly told himself, *as brave as Sonny and just as smart.* But he'd never sent Sonny into danger personally, and Dutch was far older than he'd been at Okinawa. Somehow danger assigned to others was larger and more horrid than that which you assumed for yourself. But it had to be this way, and Maxwell knew that Kelly trusted him, as he in his time had trusted Pete Mitscher. That burden was a heavy one, all the more because he had to see the face he was sending into enemy territory, alone. Kelly caught the look from Maxwell, and his face changed into a knowing grin.

"Don't sweat it, sir." He walked out of the compartment to pack up his gear.

"You know, Dutch"—Admiral Podulski lit up a cigarette—"we

could have used that lad, back a few years. I think he would have fit in just fine." It was far more than a "few" years, but Maxwell knew the truth of the statement. They'd been young warriors once, and now was the time of the new generation.

"Cas, I just hope he's careful."

"He will be. Just like we were."

The sea sled was wheeled out to the flight deck by the men who had prepared it. The helicopter was up and running now, its five-bladed rotor turning in the pre-dawn darkness as Kelly walked through the watertight door. He took a deep breath before striding out. He'd never had an audience like this before. Irvin was there, along with three of the other senior Marine NCOs, and Albie, and the flag officers, and the Ritter guy, seeing him off like he was goddamned Miss America or something. But it was the two Navy chiefs who came up to him.

"Batteries are fully charged. Your gear's in the container. It's watertight, so no problems there, sir. The rifle is loaded and chambered in case you need it in a hurry, safety on. New batteries for all the radios, and two sets of spares. If there's anything else to do, I don't know what it is," the chief machinist's mate shouted over the sound of the helicopter engines.

"Sounds good to me!" Kelly shouted back.

"Kick ass, Mr. Clark!"

"See you in a few—and thanks!" Kelly shook hands with the two chiefs, then went to see Captain Franks. For comic effect he stood at attention and saluted. "Permission to leave the ship, sir."

Captain Franks returned it. "Permission granted, sir."

Then Kelly looked at all the rest. *First in, last out.* A half smile and a nod were sufficient gestures for the moment, and at this moment they took their courage from him.

The big Sikorsky rescue chopper lifted off a few feet. A crewman attached the sled to the bottom of the helo, and then it headed aft, out of the burble turbulence of *Ogden*'s superstructure, flying off into the darkness without strobes and disappearing in a matter of seconds.

USS *Skate* was an old-fashioned submarine, modified and developed from the first nuclear boat, USS *Nautilus*. Her hull was shaped almost like that of a real ship rather than a whale, which made her relatively slow underwater, but her twin screws made for greater maneuverability, especially in shallow water. For years *Skate* had drawn the duty of inshore intelligence ship, creeping close to the Vietnamese coast and raising whip antennas to snoop on radar and other electronic emissions. She'd also put more than one swimmer on the beach. That included Kelly, several years before, though there was not a single member of that crew still aboard to remember his face. He saw her on the surface, a black shape darker than the water that glistened with the waning quarter moon soon to be hidden by clouds. The helicopter pilot first of all set the sled on *Skate*'s foredeck, where the sub's crew secured it in place. Then Kelly and his personal gear were lowered by hoist. A minute later he was in the sub's control room.

"Welcome aboard," Commander Silvio Esteves said, anticipating his first swimmer mission. He was not yet through his first year in command.

"Thank you, sir. How long to the beach?"

"Six hours, more until we scope things out for you. Coffee? Food?"

"How about a bed, sir?"

"Spare bunk in the XO's cabin. We'll see you're not disturbed." Which was a better deal than that accorded the technicians aboard from the National Security Agency.

Kelly headed forward to the last real rest he'd have for the next three days—if things went according to plan. He was asleep before the submarine dived back under the waters of the South China Sea.

"This is interesting," the Major said. He dropped the translation on the desk of his immediate superior, another major, but this one was on the Lieutenant Colonel's list.

"I've heard about this place. GRU is running the operation—trying to, I mean. Our fraternal socialist allies are not cooperating very well. So the Americans know about it at last, eh?"

"Keep reading, Yuriy Petravich," the junior man suggested.

"Indeed!" He looked up. "Who exactly is this CASSIUS fellow?" Yuriy had seen the name before, attached to a large quantity of minor information that had come through various sources within the American left.

"Glazov did the final recruitment only a short time ago." The Major explained on for a minute or so.

"Well, I'll take it to him, then. I'm surprised Georgiy Borissovich isn't running the case personally."

"I think he will now, Yuriy."

They knew something bad was about to happen. North Vietnam had a multitude of search radars arrayed along its coast. Their main purpose was to provide raid warning for incoming strikes from the aircraft carriers the Americans had sailing on what they called Yankee Station, and the North

Vietnamese called something else. Frequently the search radars were jammed, but not this badly. This time the jammer was so powerful as to turn the Russian-made screen into a circular mass of pure white. The operators leaned in more closely, looking for particularly bright dots that might denote real targets amid the jamming noise.

"Ship!" a voice called into the operations center. "Ship on the horizon." It was yet another case where the human eye outperformed radar.

If they were dumb enough to put their radars and guns on hilltops, that wasn't his lookout. The master chief firecontrolman was in "Spot 1," the forward fire-director tower that made the most graceful part of his ship's profile. His eyes were glued to the eyepieces of the long-base rangefinders, designed in the late 1930s and still as fine a piece of optical gear as America had ever produced. His hand turned a small wheel, which operated not unlike the focusing mechanism of a camera, bringing a split-image together. His focus was on the radar antenna, whose metal framework, not protected now with camouflage netting, made a nearly perfect aiming reference.

"Mark!"

The firecontrolman 2/c next to him keyed the microphone, reading the numbers off the dial. "Range One-Five-Two-Five-Zero."

In central fire-control, a hundred feet below Spot 1, mechanical computers accepted the data, telling the cruiser's eight guns how much to elevate. What happened next was simple enough. Already loaded, the guns rotated with their turrets, coming up to the proper angle of elevation calculated a generation earlier by scores of young women—now grandmothers—on mechanical calculators. On the computer, the cruiser's speed and course were already set, and since they were firing at a stationary target, it was assigned an identical but reversed velocity vector. In this way the guns would automatically remain locked on target.

"Commence firing," the gunnery officer commanded. A young sailor closed the firing keys, and USS *Newport News* shook with the first salvo of the day.

"Okay, on azimuth, we're short by . . . three hundred . . ." the master chief said quietly, watching the fountains of dirt in the twenty-power rangefinders.

"Up three hundred!" the talker relayed, and the next salvo thundered off fifteen seconds later. He didn't know that the first salvo had inadvertently immolated the command bunker for the radar complex. The second salvo arced through the air. "This one does it," the master chief whispered.

It did. Three of the eight rounds landed within fifty yards of the radar antenna and shredded it.

"On target," he said over his own microphone, waiting for the dust to clear. "Target destroyed."

"Beats an airplane any day," the Captain said, observing from the bridge. He'd been a young gunnery officer on USS *Mississippi* twenty-five years earlier, and had learned shore-bombardment against live targets in the Western Pacific, as had his treasured master chief in Spot 1. This was sure to be the last hurrah for the Navy's real gunships, and the Captain was determined that it would be a loud one.

A moment later some splashes appeared a thousand yards off. These would be from 130mm long guns the NVA used to annoy the Navy. He would engage them before concentrating on triple-A sites.

"Counterbattery!" the skipper called to central fire-control.

"Aye, sir, we're on it." A minute later *Newport News* shifted fire, her rapid-fire guns searching for and finding the six 130s that really should have known better.

It was a diversion, the Captain knew. It had to be. Something was happening somewhere else. He didn't know what, but it had to be something good to allow him and his cruiser on the gunline north of the DMZ. Not that he minded, the CO said to himself, feeling his ship shudder yet again. Thirty seconds later a rapidly expanding orange cloud announced the demise of that gun battery.

"I got secondaries," the CO announced. The bridge crew hooted briefly, then settled back down to work.

"There you are." Captain Mason stepped back from the periscope.

"Pretty close." Kelly needed only one look to see that Esteves was a cowboy. *Skate* was scraping off barnacles. The periscope was barely above water, the water lapping at the lower half of the lens. "I suppose that'll do."

"Good rainstorm topside," Esteves said.

" 'Good' is right." Kelly finished off his coffee, the real Navy sort with salt thrown in. "I'm going to use it."

"Right now?"

"Yes, sir." Kelly nodded curtly. "Unless you plan to go in closer," he added with a challenging grin.

"Unfortunately, we don't have any wheels on the bottom or I might just try." Esteves gestured him forward. "What's this one about? I usually know."

"Sir, I can't say. Tell you this, though: if it works, you'll find out."
That would have to do, and Esteves understood.

"Then you better get ready."

As warm as the waters were, Kelly still had to worry about the cold. Eight hours in water with only a small temperature differential could sap the energy from his body like a short-circuited battery. He worked his way into a green-and-black neoprene wet suit, adding double the normal amount of weight belts. Alone in the executive officer's stateroom, he had his last sober pause, beseeching God to help not himself, but the men whom he was trying to rescue. It seemed a strange thing to pray, Kelly thought, after what he'd done so recently yet so far away, and he took the time to ask forgiveness for anything wrong he might have done, still wondering if he had transgressed or not. It was a time for that sort of reflection, but only briefly. He had to look forward now. Maybe God would help him to rescue Colonel Zacharias, but he had to do his part, too. Kelly's last thought before leaving the stateroom was of the photo of a lonely American about to be clubbed from behind by some little NVA fuck. It was time to put an end to that, he told himself, opening the door.

"Escape trunk's this way," Esteves said.

Kelly climbed up the ladder, watched by Esteves and perhaps six or seven other men of *Skate*.

"Make sure we find out," the Captain said, levering the hatch shut himself.

"I'll sure as hell try," Kelly replied, just as the metal fitting locked into place. There was an aqualung waiting for him. The gauge read full, Kelly saw, checking it again himself. He lifted the waterproof phone.

"Clark here. In the trunk, ready to go."

"Sonar reports nothing except heavy rain on the surface. Visual search is negative. *Vaya con dios,* Señor Clark."

"*Gracias,*" Kelly chuckled his reply. He replaced the phone and opened the flooding valve. Water entered the bottom of the compartment, the air pressure changing suddenly in the cramped space.

Kelly checked his watch. It was eight-sixteen when he cracked the hatch and pulled himself to the submerged foredeck of USS *Skate*. He used a light to illuminate the sea sled. It was tied down at four points, but before loosing it he clipped a safety line to his belt. It wouldn't do to have the thing motor off without him. The depth gauge read forty-nine feet. The submarine *was* in dangerously shallow water, and the sooner he got away the sooner her crew would be safe again. Unclipping the sled, he flipped the power switch, and two shrouded propellers started turning slowly. Good. Kelly pulled the knife from his belt and banged it twice on the deck, then adjusted the flippers on the sled and headed off, on a compass course of three-zero-eight.

There was now no turning back, Kelly told himself. But for him there rarely was.

28

First In

I t was just as well that he couldn't smell the water. At least not at first. Few things can be as unnerving or disorienting as swimming underwater at night. Fortunately the people who'd designed the sled were divers themselves, and knew that. The sled was slightly longer than Kelly was tall. It was, in fact, a modified torpedo with attachments allowing a man to steer it and control its speed, essentially making it a minisubmarine, though in appearance it was more like an aircraft drawn by a child. The "wings"—actually referred to as flippers—were controlled by hand. There was a depth gauge and an up/down-angle indicator, along with a battery-strength gauge and the vital magnetic compass. The electric motor and batteries had originally been designed to drive the shape through the water at high speed for over ten thousand yards. At lower speeds it could go much farther. In this case, it had five-to-six-hour endurance at five knots—more if the craftsmen aboard *Ogden* were right.

It was strangely like flying over in the C-141. The whirring of the twin props couldn't be heard any great distance, but Kelly was a mere six feet from them; the steady high-speed whine was already making him grimace inside his diving mask. Part of that was all the coffee he'd drunk. He had to stay nervously alert, and he had enough caffeine in him to enliven a corpse. So many things to worry about. There was boat traffic on the river. Whether ferrying triple-A ammo from one bank of the river to another or perhaps the Vietnamese version of a teenybopper crossing to see his girlfriend, there were small boats here. Running into one could be lethal in one of several ways, differing only in immediacy, not the final outcome. Perversely, visibility was almost nil, and so Kelly had to assume that he'd have no more than two or three seconds to avoid something. He held to the middle of the channel as best he could. Every thirty minutes he'd slow down and ease his head above the surface for a position fix. There was no activity at all he could see. This country didn't have much in the way of electrical power stations anymore, and without lights by which to read or perhaps power radios, life for the ordinary people was as primitive as it was brutish for their enemies. It was all vaguely sad. Kelly didn't think that the Vietnamese people were any more innately warlike than any other, but there was a war here, and their behavior, as he had seen, fell short of exemplary. He took his fix and headed down again, careful not to go deeper than ten feet. He'd heard of a case of a diver who'd died while making an overly rapid ascent after being pressurized for a few hours at *fifteen* feet, and he had no desire at all to relive it himself.

Time crept by. Every so often the overhead clouds would thin out, and the light of the quarter moon would give definition to the raindrops on the surface of the river, fragile black circles expanding and disappearing on the ghostly blue screen ten feet above his head. Then the clouds would thicken again, and all he'd see was a dark gray roof, and the sound of the falling drops would compete with the infernal whirring of the props. Another danger was hallucination. Kelly had an active mind, and he was now in an environment devoid of input. Worse, his body was being lulled. He was in a nearly weightless state, rather like it must have been in the womb, and the sheer comfort of the experience was dangerous. His mind might react by dreaming, and he couldn't have that. Kelly developed a routine, sweeping his eyes over the rudimentary instruments, playing little games, like trying to hold his craft exactly level without using the angle indicator—but that proved impossible. What pilots called vertigo happened even more quickly here than in the air, and he found that he couldn't manage it for more than fifteen or twenty seconds before he started to tilt and go deeper. Every so often he'd do a complete roll, just for the difference of it, but mainly he cycled his eyes to the water and back to the instruments, repeating the process again and again, until that also became dangerously monotonous. Only two hours into the passage, Kelly had to tell himself to concentrate—but he couldn't concentrate on just one thing, or even two. Comfortable as he was, every human being within a five-mile radius would wish nothing better than to end his life. Those people lived here, knew the land and the river, knew the sounds and the sights. And theirs was a country at war, where the unusual meant the dangerous, and the enemy. Kelly didn't know if the government paid bounty for dead or live Americans, but something like that must have been operating. People worked harder for a reward, especially one that coincided with patriotism. Kelly wondered how it had all happened. Not that it mattered.

These people were enemies. Nothing would soon change that. Certainly not in the next three days, which was as far as the future went for Kelly. If there were to be anything beyond it, he had to pretend that there was not.

His next programmed halt was at a meandering horseshoe bend. Kelly slowed the sled and lifted his head carefully. Noise on the north bank, perhaps three hundred yards. It carried across the water. Male voices speaking in the language whose lilts had somehow always sounded poetic to him— but quickly turned ugly when the content was anger. Like the people, he supposed, listening for perhaps ten seconds. He took the sled back down, watching the course change on the compass as he followed the sweeping bend. What a strange intimacy that had been, if only for a few seconds. What were they talking about? Politics? Boring subject in a Communist country. Farming, perhaps? Talk of the war? Perhaps, for the voices were subdued. America was killing enough of this country's young men that they had reason to hate us, Kelly thought, and the loss of a son could be little different here than at home. They might talk to others about their pride for the little boy gone off to be a soldier—fried in napalm, dismembered by a machine gun, or turned to vapor by a bomb; the stories had to come back one way or another, even as lies, which amounted to the same thing—but in every case it must have been a child who'd taken a first step and said "daddy" in his native tongue. But some of the same children had grown up to follow PLASTIC FLOWER, and he did not regret killing them. The talk he'd heard sounded human enough, even if he couldn't understand it, and then came the casual question, What made them different?

They are *different, asshole! Let the politicians worry about why.* Asking those kinds of questions distracted him from the fact that there were twenty people like Kelly up the river. He swore in his mind and concentrated again on driving the sled.

Few things distracted Pastor Charles Meyer from the preparation of his weekly sermons. It was perhaps the most important part of his ministry, telling people what they needed to hear in a clear, concise manner, because his flock saw him only once a week unless something went wrong—and when something went badly wrong they needed the foundation of faith already in place if his special attention and counsel were to be truly effective. Meyer had been a minister for thirty years, all of his adult life, and the natural eloquence that was one of his true gifts had been polished by years of practice to the point where he could choose a Scripture passage and develop it into a finely focused lesson in morality. The Reverend Meyer was not a stern man. His message of faith was that of mercy and love. He was quick to smile and to joke, and though his sermons were of necessity a serious business, for salvation was the most serious of human goals, it was his task, he thought, to emphasize God's true nature. Love. Mercy. Charity. Redemption. His entire life, Meyer thought, was dedicated to helping people return after a bout of forgetfulness, to embrace despite rejection. A task as important as that was worth a diversion of his time.

"Welcome back, Doris," Meyer said as he entered Ray Brown's house. A man of medium height, his thick head of gray hair gave him a stately and learned appearance. He took both her hands in his, smiling warmly. "Our prayers are answered."

For all his pleasant and supportive demeanor, this would be an awk-ward meeting for all three participants. Doris had erred, probably rather badly, he thought. Meyer recognized that, trying not to dwell on it in a punitive way. The really important thing was that the prodigal had returned, and if Jesus had spent His time on earth for any reason, that parable con-tained it all in just a few verses. All of Christianity in a single story. No matter how grave one's misdeeds might be, there would always be a wel-come for those with the courage to return.

Father and daughter sat together on the old blue sofa, with Meyer to their left in an armchair. Three cups of tea were on the low table. Tea was the proper drink for a moment like this.

"I'm surprised how good you look, Doris." He smiled, concealing his desperate desire to put the girl at ease.

"Thank you, Pastor."

"It's been hard, hasn't it?"

Her voice became brittle. "Yes."

"Doris, we all make mistakes. God made us imperfect. You have to accept that, and you have to try to do better all the time. We don't always succeed—but you *did* succeed. You're back now. The bad things are behind you, and with a little work you can leave them behind you forever."

"I will," she said with determination. "I really will. I've seen . . . and done . . . such awful things. . . ."

Meyer was a difficult man to shock. Clergymen were in the profession of listening to stories about the reality of hell, because sinners could not accept forgiveness until they were able to forgive themselves, a task which always required a sympathetic ear and a calm voice of love and reason. But what he heard now did shock him. He tried to freeze his body into place. Above all he tried to remember that what he heard was indeed *behind* his afflicted parishio-ner as over the course of twenty minutes he learned of things that even he had never dreamed of, things from another time, since his service as a young Army chaplain in Europe. There was a devil in creation, something for which his Faith had prepared him, but the face of Lucifer was not for unprotected eyes of men—certainly not for the eyes of a young girl whom an angry father had mistakenly driven away at a young and vulnerable age.

It only got worse. Prostitution was frightening enough. What damage it did to young women could last a lifetime, and he was grateful to learn that Doris was seeing Dr. Bryant, a wonderfully gifted physician to whom he'd referred two of his flock. For several minutes he shared Doris's pain and shame while her father bravely held her hand, fighting back his own tears.

Then it turned to drugs, first the use of them, then the transfer of them to other, evil men. She was honest through it all, trembling, with tears dripping from her eyes, facing a past to make the strongest of hearts quail. Next came the recounting of sexual abuse, and, finally, the worst part of all.

It became very real to Pastor Meyer. Doris seemed to remember it all—as well she might. It would take all of Dr. Bryant's skills to drive this horror into the past. She told the story in the manner of a motion picture, seemingly leaving nothing out. That was a healthy thing, to put it all in the open in this way. Healthy for Doris. Even healthy for her father. But Charles Meyer necessarily became the recipient of the horror that others were attempting to cast away. Lives had been lost. Innocent lives—victims' lives, two girls not unlike the one before him, murdered in a way worthy of . . . damnation, the pastor told himself in a voice of sadness mixed with rage.

"The kindness you showed to Pam, my dear, that is one of the most courageous things I've ever heard," the pastor said quietly, after it was all over, moved nearly to tears himself. "That was God, Doris. That was God acting through your hands and showing you the goodness of your character."

"You think so?" she asked, bursting then into uncontrolled tears.

He had to move then, and he did, kneeling in front of father and daughter, taking their hands in his. "God visited you, and saved you, Doris. Your father and I prayed for this moment. You've come back, and you won't ever do things like that again." Pastor Meyer couldn't know what he hadn't been told, the things that Doris had deliberately left out. He knew that a Baltimore physician and nurse had restored his parishioner to physical health. He didn't know how Doris had come to that point, and Meyer assumed that she'd escaped, as the girl Pam had almost done. Nor did he know that Dr. Bryant had been warned to keep all of this information close. That might not have mattered in any case. There were other girls still in the control of this Billy person and his friend Rick. As he had dedicated his life to denying souls to Lucifer, so also he had a duty to deny their bodies to him. He had to be careful. A conversation like this one was privileged in the ultimate sense.

He would counsel Doris to speak with the police, though he could never force her to do so. But as a citizen, as a man of God, he had to do *something* to help those other girls. Exactly what, he wasn't sure. He'd ask his son about that, a young sergeant with the Pittsburgh city police force.

There. Kelly's head was above the water only enough to expose his eyes. He reached up with his hands to pull the rubber hood off his head, allowing his ears better access to the sounds of the area. There was all manner of noise. Insects, the flapping of bats, and loudest of all the rain that was sprinkling lightly at the moment. To his north was darkness that his acclimated eyes began to break into shapes. There was "his" hilltop, a mile away past another, lower hill. He knew from the aerial photographs that there were no habitations between where he was and where he had to go. There was a road only a hundred yards away, and at the moment it was totally vacant. So quiet it was that any mechanical sound would surely have reached him. There was none. It was time.

Kelly steered the sled close to the bank. He selected a place with overhanging trees for the additional concealment. His first physical contact with the soil of North Vietnam had an electric feel to it. That soon passed. Kelly stripped off the wet suit, stuffing it in the waterproof container on the now surfaced sled. He quickly donned his camouflage fatigues. The jungle boots had soles copied from the NVA's in case anyone spotted tracks that looked out of the ordinary. Next he did his camouflage makeup, dark green on forehead and cheekbones and jaw, with lighter colors under his eyes and in the hollow of his cheeks. Shouldering his gear, he flipped the power switch on the sled. It motored off towards the middle of the river, its flotation chambers vented now, sinking it to the bottom. Kelly made an effort not to watch it hum away. It was bad luck, he remembered, to watch the helicopter fly away from the LZ. It showed lack of purpose. Kelly turned to the land, listening again for traffic on the road. Hearing none, he climbed the bank and crossed the gravel path immediately, disappearing at once into the thick foliage, moving slowly and deliberately up the first hill.

People cut wood here for cooking fires. That was disturbing—might people be out cutting tomorrow?—but helpful, too, as it allowed him to make his way more quickly and more quietly. He walked in a tense crouch, careful where he placed his feet, his eyes and ears sweeping around constantly as he moved. His carbine was in his hands. His thumb felt the selector switch, in the "safe" position. A round was chambered. He'd already checked that. The Navy chief had prepared the weapon properly and would understand that

Kelly had needed to verify it visually, but if there was any one thing Kelly did not wish to do, it was to fire a single round from his CAR-15.

Climbing the first hill took half an hour. Kelly stopped there, finding a clear spot from which to look and listen. It was approaching three in the morning, local time. The only people awake were those who had to be, and they wouldn't like it very much. The human body was linked to a day/night cycle, and at this time of the morning bodily functions ebbed.

Nothing.

Kelly moved on, going down the hill. At the bottom was a small stream that fed into the river. He took the opportunity to fill one of his canteens, dropping in a purification tablet as he did so. Again he listened, since sound followed nicely down valleys and over streams. Still nothing. He looked up at "his" hill, a gray mass under the cloudy sky. The rain was picking up as Kelly started his climb. Fewer trees had been cut here, which made sense, as the road didn't come all that close. This area was a little steep for proper farming, and with good bottomland so close by, he felt he could depend on a minimum of visitors. Probably that's why SENDER GREEN had been placed here, he told himself. There was nothing around to attract serious attention. That would cut both ways.

Halfway up, his eyes got their first look at the prison camp. It was an open space amidst forest. He didn't know if the area had started off as a meadow or if the trees had been cut for one reason or another. A branch of the river road came straight in from the other side of "his" hill. Kelly saw a flare of light from one of the guard towers—someone with a cigarette, no doubt. Didn't people ever learn? It could take hours to get your night vision really working, and just that much could ruin it. Kelly looked away, concentrating on the remainder of his climb, moving around bushes, seeking open spots where his uniform wouldn't rub against branches and leaves, making deadly noise. It almost came as a surprise when he reached the top.

He sat down for a moment, making himself totally still, looking and listening some more before he began his examination of the camp. He found a very good spot, perhaps twenty feet below the crest. The far side of the hill was steep, and a casual climber would make noise. In this place he wouldn't be skylined to an observer below. His place was within the shroud of bushes to break up whatever outline he might present. This was his place on his hill. He reached in his vest and pulled out one of his radios.

"SNAKE calling CRICKET, over."

"SNAKE, this is CRICKET, reading you five by five," one of the communicators replied inside the commo van parked on *Ogden*'s deck.

"In place, beginning surveillance. Over."

"Copy that. Out." He looked up at Admiral Maxwell. Phase Two of BOXWOOD GREEN was now complete.

Phase Three began at once. Kelly took the marine 7 × 50 binoculars from their case and began examining the camp. There were guards in all four towers, two of them smoking. That had to mean their officer was asleep. The NVA had adamantine discipline and punished transgressions harshly— death was not an uncommon price for even a minor offense. There was a single automobile present, parked as expected near the building which had to house the officers at this compound. There were no lights at all, and no sounds. Kelly rubbed the rain from his eyes and checked the focus on both eyepieces before he commenced his survey. In a strange way it was like being back at Quantico Marine Base. The similarity of angle and perspective was uncanny. There seemed to be some minor differences in the buildings, but it could be the dark causing that, or perhaps a slight change in color. No, he realized. It was the courtyard, parade ground—whatever he was supposed to call it. There was no grass there. The surface was flat and bare, just the red clay of this region. The different color and lack of texture gave the buildings a subtly different setting. Different roofing materials, but the same slope. It *was* like being at Quantico, and with luck the battle would be as successful as the drills. Kelly settled in, allowing himself a sip of water. It had the distilled tastelessness of what they made on the submarine, clean and foreign, as he was in this alien place.

At quarter to four he saw some lights in the barracks, flickering yellow, like candles. Guard change, perhaps. The two soldiers in the tower nearest him were stretching, chatting to each other casually. Kelly could barely make out the murmur of conversation but not the words or cadence. They were bored. This would be that sort of duty. They might grouse about it, but not that badly. The alternative would be a stroll down the Ho Chi Minh Trail through Laos, and, patriotic though they might have been, only a fool would relish that thought. Here they kept watch on twenty or so men, locked in individual cells, perhaps chained to walls or otherwise hobbled, with as much chance of escaping the camp as Kelly had of walking on water—and even if they succeeded in that most impossible of feats, what would they be? Six-foot-tall white men in a land of small yellow people, none of whom would lift a hand on their behalf. Alcatraz Federal Prison could be no more secure than this. So the guards had three squares a day and quiet boring duty that would dull their senses.

Good news, Kelly told himself. *Stay bored, guys.*

The barracks doors opened. Eight men came out. No NCO in charge of the detail. That was interesting, surprisingly casual for the NVA. They broke into pairs, each heading for a tower. In each case the relief crew climbed up before the duty crew came down, which was to be expected. A few remarks were exchanged, and the soldiers going off duty climbed down. Two lit up before heading back in the barracks, speaking to each other at the entrance. It was all in all a comfortable and grossly normal routine conducted by men who'd been doing the same thing for months.

Wait. Two of them limped, Kelly realized. *Veterans.* That was good news and bad news. People with combat experience were simply different. The time would come for action, and they'd react well, probably. Even without recent training, instincts would kick in, and they'd try to fight back effectively even without leadership—but as veterans they'd also be softer, disdainful of their duty, however cushy it might be, lacking the awkward eagerness of fresh young troops. As with all swords, that one cut in two directions. In either case, the plan of attack allowed for it. Kill people without warning, and their training was a moot point, which made it a hell of a lot safer.

Anyway, that was one wrong assumption. Troops on POW-guard duty were usually second-raters. These at least were combat troops, even if they had sustained wounds that relegated them to backup service. Any other mistakes? Kelly wondered. He couldn't see any yet.

His first substantive radio message was a single code group which he tapped out using Morse Code.

"EASY SPOT, sir." The communications technicians tapped out an acknowledgment.

"Good news?" Captain Franks asked.

"It means everything is as expected, no major news," Admiral Podulski replied. Maxwell was catching a nap. Cas wouldn't sleep until the mission was concluded. "Our friend Clark even delivered it exactly on time."

Colonel Glazov didn't like working on weekends any more than his Western counterparts, even less so when it was because his administrative assistant had made a mistake and set this report on the wrong pile. At least the boy had admitted it, and called his boss at home to report his error. He couldn't very well do much more than chide the oversight, at the same time he had to praise the lad's honesty and sense of duty. He drove his personal car into Moscow from his dacha, found a parking place in the rear of the building, and submitted himself to the tiresome security-clearance procedures before taking the elevator up. Then came the necessity of unlocking his office and sending for the right documents from Central Files, which also took longer than usual on this weekend day. All in all, just getting to the point at which he could examine the damned thing required two hours from the unwelcome phone call that had started the process. The Colonel signed for the documents and watched the file clerk depart.

"Bloody hell," the Colonel said in English, finally alone in his fourth-floor office. CASSIUS had a friend in the White House National Security Office? No wonder some of his information had been so good—good enough to force Georgiy Borissovich to fly to London to consummate the recruitment. The senior KGB officer now had to chide himself. CASSIUS had kept that bit of information up his sleeve, perhaps in the knowledge that he'd rattle his ultimate control officer. The case officer, Captain Yegorov, had taken it in stride—as well he might—and described the first-contact meeting in exquisite detail.

"Boxwood Green," Glazov said. Just a code name for the operation, selected for no particular reason, as the Americans did. The next question was whether or not to forward the data to the Vietnamese. That would be a political decision, and one to be made quickly. The Colonel lifted the phone and dialed his most immediate superior, who was also at home and instantly in a foul humor.

Sunrise was an equivocal thing. The color of the clouds changed from the gray of slate to the gray of smoke as somewhere aloft the sun made its presence known, though that would not be the case here until the low-pressure area had passed north into China—or so the weather briefing had declared. Kelly checked his watch, making his mental notes at every point. The guard force was forty-four men, plus four officers—and maybe a cook or two. All except the eight on tower duty formed up just after dawn for calisthenics. Many had trouble doing their morning exercises, and one of the officers, a senior lieuten-ant from his shoulder boards, hobbled around with a cane—probably a bad arm, too, from the way he used it. *What got you?* Kelly wondered. A crippled and foul-tempered NCO walked the lines of soldiers, swearing at them in a way that showed long months of practice. Through his binoculars Kelly watched the expressions that trailed behind the little bastard's back. It gave the NVA guards a human quality that he didn't welcome.

Morning exercise lasted half an hour. When it ended, the soldiers headed off for morning chow, falling out in a decidedly casual and unmili-tary way. The tower guards spent most of their time looking in, as expected, most often leaning on their elbows. Their weapons were probably not cham-bered, a sensible safety precaution that would count against them either this night or the next, depending on weather. Kelly made another check of his surroundings. It would not do for him to fix too closely on the objective. He wouldn't move about now, not even in the gray daylight that had come with the morning, but he could turn his head to look and listen. Catching the patterns of bird calls, getting used to it so that a change would register at once. He had a green cloth across the muzzle of his weapon, a floppy hat to break up the outline of his head within and behind the bush, and facial camouflage paint, all of which conspired to make him invisible, part of this warm, humid environment that—*I mean,* why *do people fight for the damned place?* he wondered. Already he could feel bugs on his skin. The worst of them were put off by the unscented repellent he'd spread around. But not all, and the feel of things crawling on him combined with the knowledge that he couldn't make any rapid moves. There were no small risks in a place like this. He'd forgotten so much. Training was good and valuable, but it never quite made it all the way to full preparation. There was no substitute for the actual dangers involved, the slightly increased heart rate that could tire you out even when you lay still. You never quite forgot it, but you never really remembered it all, either.

Food, nourishment, strength. He reached into a pocket, moving his hand slowly and withdrawing a pair of food bars. Nothing he'd eat by choice in any other place, but it was vital now. He tore off the plastic wrappers with his teeth and chewed them up slowly. The strength they imparted to his body was probably as much psychological as real, but both factors had their uses, as his body had to deal with both fatigue and stress.

At eight, the guard cycle changed again. Those relieved from the towers went in for chow. Two men took posts at the gate, bored before they got there, looking out at the road for traffic that would probably never come to this backwater camp. Some work details formed, and the jobs they performed were as clearly useless to Kelly as to those who carried them out in a stoic, unhurried way.

Colonel Grishanov arose just after eight. He'd been up late the night before, and though he'd planned to arise earlier, he'd just learned to his displeasure that his mechanical alarm clock had finally given up the ghost, corroded to death by the miserable climate. Eight-ten, he saw, looking at his aviator's watch. *Damn.* No morning run. It would soon be too hot for that, and besides, it looked like it would be raining all day. He brewed his own pot of tea over a small army-type cook stove. No morning paper to read—again. No news of the football scores. No review of a new ballet production. Nothing at all in this miserable place to distract him. Important as his duty was, he needed distraction as much as any man did. Not even decent plumbing. He was used to all of that, but it didn't help. God, to be able to go home, to hear people speaking his native language again, to be in a cultured place where there was something to talk about. Grishanov frowned in the shaving mirror. Months more to go, and he was grumbling like a private soldier, a damned recruit. He was supposed to know better.

His uniform needed pressing. The humidity here attacked the cotton fibers, making his usually crisp blouse look like pajamas, and he was already on his third set of shoes, Grishanov thought, sipping now at his tea and going over notes from the previous night's interrogations. All work and no play ... and he was already late. He tried to light a cigarette, but the humidity had also rendered his matches useless. Well, he had the cookstove for that. Where had he left his lighter ... ?

There were compensations, if you could call them that. The Vietnamese soldiers treated him with respect, almost awe—except for the camp commander, Major Vinh, worthless bastard that he was. Courtesy to a fellow socialist ally demanded that Grishanov be given an orderly, in this case a small, ignorant peasant boy with only one eye who was able to make the bed and carry out the slops bowl every morning. The Colonel was able to walk out in the knowledge that his room would be somewhat tidy when he returned. And he had his work. Important, professionally stimulating. But he would have killed for his morning *Sovietskiy Sport*.

"Good morning, Ivan," Kelly whispered to himself. He didn't even need the binoculars for that. The size was so different—the man was over six feet—and the uniform far neater than that worn by the NVA. The glasses showed Kelly the man's face, pale and florid, with a narrowed-eye expression to contemplate the day. He made a gesture to a small private who'd been waiting outside the door of the officers' quarters. *Orderly,* Kelly thought. A visiting Russian colonel would like his comforts, wouldn't he? Definitely a pilot from the wings over the blouse pocket, plenty of ribbons. *Only one?* Kelly wondered. *Only one Russian officer to help torture the prisoners? Odd when you think about it.* But that meant only one extraneous person to have to kill, and for all his lack of political sophistication, Kelly knew that killing Russians wouldn't do anyone much good. He watched the Russian walk across the parade ground. Then the senior visible Vietnamese officer, a major, went towards him. Another limper, Kelly saw. The little Major saluted the tall Colonel.

*   *   *

"Good morning, Comrade Colonel."

"Good morning, Major Vinh." *Little bastard can't even learn to salute properly. Perhaps he simply cannot make a proper gesture to his betters.* "The rations for the prisoners?"

"They will have to be satisfied with what they have," the smaller man replied in badly accented and phrased Russian.

"Major, it is important that you understand me," Grishanov said, stepping closer so that he could look more sharply down at the Vietnamese. "I need the information they have. I cannot get it if they are too sick to speak."

"*Tovarisch,* we have problems enough feeding our own people. You ask us to waste good food on murderers?" The Vietnamese soldier responded quietly, using a tone that both conveyed his contempt for the foreigner and at the same time seemed respectful to his soldiers, who would not have understood exactly what this was all about. After all, they thought that the Russians were fast allies.

"*Your* people do not have what my country needs, Major. And if *my* country gets what she needs, then *your* country might get more of what *it* needs."

"I have my orders. If you are experiencing difficulty in questioning the Americans, then I am prepared to help." *Arrogant dog.* It was a suffix that didn't need to be spoken, and Vinh knew how to stick his needle into a sensitive place.

"Thank you, Major. That will not be necessary." Grishanov made a salute himself, even sloppier than that given him by this annoying little man. It would be good to watch him die, the Russian thought, walking off to the prison block. His first "appointment" with the day was with an American naval aviator who was just about ready to crack.

Casual enough, Kelly thought from several hundred yards away. *Those two must get along fairly well.* His scrutiny of the camp was relaxed now. His greatest fear was that the guard force might send out security patrols, as a line unit in hostile country would surely have done. But they were not in hostile territory, and this was not really a line unit. His next radio message to *Ogden* confirmed that everything was within acceptable risk limits.

Sergeant Peter Meyer smoked. His father didn't approve, but accepted his son's weakness so long as he did it outside, as they were now, on the back porch of the parsonage after Sunday evening dinner.

"It's Doris Brown, right?" Peter asked. At twenty-six he was one of his department's youngest sergeants, and like most of the current class of police officers a Vietnam veteran. He was within six credit hours of completing his night-school degree and was considering making an application to the FBI Academy. Word that the wayward girl had returned was now circulating through the neighborhood. "I remember her. She had a reputation as a hot number a few years back."

"Peter, you know I can't say. This is a pastoral matter. I will counsel the person to speak to you when the time is right, but—"

"Pop, I understand the law on that, okay? You have to understand, we're talking two homicides here. Two dead people, plus the drug business." He flipped the butt of his Salem into the grass. "That's pretty heavy stuff, Pop."

"Even worse than that," his father reported more quietly still. "They don't just kill the girls. Torture, sexual abuse. It's pretty horrible. The person is seeing a doctor about it. I know I have to do something, but I can't—"

"Yeah, I know you can't. Okay, I can call the people in Baltimore and fill them in on what you've told me. I really ought to hold off until we can give them something they can really use, but, well, like you say, we have to do something. I'll call down first thing tomorrow morning."

"Will it put her—the person—in danger?" the Reverend Meyer asked, vexed with himself for the slip.

"Shouldn't," Peter judged. "If she's gotten herself away—I mean, they ought not to know where she is, and if they did, they might have got her already."

"How can people do things like that?"

Peter lit up another. His father was just too good a man to understand. Not that he did either. "Pop, I see it all the time, and I have trouble believing it, too. The important part's getting the bastards."

"Yes, I suppose it is."

The KGB *rezident* in Hanoi had General-Major rank, and his job was mainly that of spying on his country's putative allies. What were their real objectives? Was their supposed estrangement with China real or a sham? Would they cooperate with the Soviet Union when and if the war came to a successful conclusion? Might they allow the Soviet Navy use of a base after the Americans left? Was their political determination really as solid as they said it was? Those were all questions whose answers he thought he had, but orders from Moscow and his own skepticism about everyone and everything compelled him to keep asking. He employed agents within the CPVN, the country's Foreign Ministry, and elsewhere, Vietnamese whose willingness to give information to an ally would probably have meant death—though to be politic about it, the deaths would be disguised "suicides" or "accidents" because it was in neither country's interest to have a formal breach. Lip-service was even more important in a socialist country than a capitalist one, the General knew, because symbols were far easier to produce than reality.

The enciphered dispatch on his desk was interesting, all the more so since it did not give him direct guidance on what to do about it. How like the Moscow bureaucrats! Always quick to meddle in matters that he was able to handle himself, now they didn't know what to do—but they were afraid to do nothing. So they stuck him with it.

He knew about the camp, of course. Though a military-intelligence operation, he had people in the office of the attaché who reported to him as well. The KGB watched everyone, after all; that was their job. Colonel Grishanov was using irregular methods, but he was reporting good results, better than the General's own office got from these little savages. Now the Colonel had come up with the boldest idea of all. Instead of letting the Vietnamese kill the prisoners in due course, bring them home to Mother Russia. It was brilliant in its way, and the KGB general was trying to decide if he'd endorse the idea to Moscow, where this decision would surely be kicked up to ministerial, or perhaps even Politburo level. On the whole, he thought that the idea had real merit . . . and that decided matters.

As entertaining as it might be for the Americans to rescue their people with this BOXWOOD GREEN operation, as much as it might show the Vietnamese again that they should cooperate more closely with the Soviet Union, that they really were a *client* state, it would also mean that the knowledge locked in those American minds would be lost to his country, and it was knowledge they must have.

How long, he wondered, could he let this one wait? The Americans moved quickly, but not that quickly. The mission had been approved at White House level only a week or so earlier. All bureaucracies were alike, after all. In Moscow it would take forever. Operation KINGPIN had gone on forever, else it would have succeeded. Only the good luck of a low-level agent in the Southern United States had allowed them to warn Hanoi, and then almost too late—but now they had real forewarning.

Politics. You just couldn't separate that from intelligence operations. Before, they'd all but accused him of delaying matters—he shouldn't give them that excuse again. Even client states need to be treated as comrades. The General lifted his phone to make a luncheon date. He'd bring his contact over to the embassy, just to be sure that he had some decent food to eat.

29

Last Out

There was a vicarious exhilaration in watching them. The twenty-five Marines worked out, finishing with a single-file run that looped around the helicopters parked on the deck. Sailors looked on quietly. The word was out now. The sea sled had been seen by too many, and like professional intelligence officers, sailors at their mess tables assembled the few facts and garnished them with speculation. The Marines were going into the North. After what, nobody knew, but everyone wondered. Maybe to trash a missile site and bring back some important piece of hardware. Maybe to take down a bridge, but most likely the target was human. The Vietnamese party bosses, perhaps.

"Prisoners," a bosun's mate third-class said, finishing his hamburger, called a "slider" in the Navy. "It's gotta be," he added, motioning his head to the newly arrived medical corpsmen who ate at their own isolated table. "Six corpsmen, four doctors, awful lot of talent, guys. What d'ya suppose they're here for?"

"Jesus," another sailor observed, sipping at his milk. "You're right, man."

"Feather in our cap if it comes off," noted another.

"Dirty weather tonight," a quartermaster put in. "The fleet-weather chief was smiling about it—and I seen him puke his guts out last night. I guess he can't handle anything smaller'n a carrier." USS *Ogden* did have an odd ride, which resulted from her configuration, and running broadside-to the gusting westerly winds had only worsened it. It was always entertaining to see a chief petty officer lose his lunch—dinner in this case—and a man was unlikely to be *happy* about weather conditions that made him ill. There

471

had to be a reason for it. The conclusion was obvious, and the sort of thing to make a security officer despair.

"Jesus, I hope they make it."

"Let's get the flight deck fodded again," the junior bosun suggested. Heads nodded at once. A work gang was quickly assembled. Within an hour there would be not so much as a matchstick on the black no-skid surface.

"Good bunch of kids, Captain," Dutch Maxwell observed, watching the walkdown from the starboard wing of the bridge. Every so often a man would bend down and pick up something, a "foreign object" that might destroy an engine, a result called *FOD*, for "foreign-object damage." Whatever might go wrong tonight, the men were promising with their actions, it wouldn't be the fault of their ship.

"Lots of college kids," Franks replied, proudly watching his men. "Sometimes I think the deck division's as smart as my wardroom." Which was an entirely forgivable hyperbole. He wanted to say something else, the same thing that everyone was thinking: *What do you suppose the chances are?* He didn't voice the thought. It would be the worst kind of bad luck. Even thinking it loudly might harm the mission, but hard as he tried he couldn't stop his mind from forming the words.

In their quarters, the Marines were assembled around a sand-table model of the objective. They'd already gone over the mission once and were doing so again. The process would be repeated once more before lunch, and many times after it, as a whole group and as individual teams. Each man could see everything with his eyes closed, thinking back to the training site at Quantico, reliving the live-fire exercises.

"Captain Albie, sir?" A yeoman came into the compartment. He handed over a clipboard. "Message from Mr. Snake."

The Captain of Marines grinned. "Thanks, sailor. You read it?"

The yeoman actually blushed. "Beg pardon, sir. Yes, I did. Everything's cool." He hesitated for the moment before adding a dispatch of his own. "Sir, my department says good luck. Kick some ass, sir."

"You know, skipper," Sergeant Irvin said as the yeoman left the space, "I may never be able to punch out a swabbie again."

Albie read the dispatch. "People, our friend is in place. He counts forty-four guards, four officers, one Russian. Normal duty routine, nothing unusual is happening there." The young captain looked up. "That's it, Marines. We're going in tonight."

One of the younger Marines reached in his pocket and pulled out a large rubber band. He broke it, marked two eyes on it with his pen, and dropped it atop what they now called Snake Hill. "That dude," he said to his team-mates, "is one cool motherfucker."

"Y'all remember now," Irvin warned loudly. "You fire-support guys remember, he's gonna be pounding down that hill soon as we show up. It wouldn't do to shoot his ass."

"No prob', Gunny," the fire-team leader said.

"Marines, let's get some chow. I want you people to rest up this after-noon. Eat your veggies. We want our eyes to work in the dark. Weapons stripped and cleaned for inspection at seventeen-hun'rd," Albie told them. "Y'all know what this is all about. Let's stay real cool and we'll get it done." It was his time to meet again with the chopper crews for a final look at the insertion and extraction plans.

"Aye aye, sir," Irvin said for the men.

"Hello, Robin."

"Hi, Kolya," Zacharias said weakly.

"I'm still working on better food."

"Would be nice," the American acknowledged.

"Try this." Grishanov handed over some black bread his wife had sent him. The climate had already started to put mold on it, which Kolya had trimmed off with a knife. The American wolfed it down anyway. A sip from the Russian's flask helped.

"I'll turn you into a Russian," the Soviet Air Force colonel said with an unguarded chuckle. "Vodka and good bread go together. I would like to show you my country." Just to plant the seed of the idea, in a friendly way, as one man talks to another.

"I have a family, Kolya. God willing—"

"Yes, Robin, God willing." Or North Vietnam willing, or the Soviet Union willing. Or someone. Somehow he'd save this man, and the others. So many were friends now. He knew so much about them, their marriages, good and bad, their children, their hopes and dreams. These Americans were so strange, so open. "Also, God willing, if the Chinese decide to bomb Mos-cow, I have a plan now to stop them." He unfolded the map and set it on the floor. It was the result of all his talks with his American colleague, every-thing he had learned and analyzed formulated on a single sheet of paper. Grishanov was quite proud of it, not the least because it was the clear presen-tation of a highly sophisticated operational concept.

Zacharias ran his fingers over it, reading the notations in English, which looked incongruous on a map whose legend was in Cyrillic. He smiled his approval. A bright guy, Kolya, a good student in his way. The way he layered his assets, the way he had his aircraft patrolling back rather than forward. He understood defense in depth now. SAM traps at the ends of the most likely mountain passes, positioned for maximum surprise. Kolya was thinking like a bomber pilot now instead of a fighter jock. That was the first step in understanding how it was done. If every Russian PVO commander understood how to do this, then SAC would have one miserable time . . .

Dear God.

Robin's hands stopped moving.

This wasn't about the ChiComs at all.

Zacharias looked up, and his face revealed his thought even before he found the strength to speak.

"How many Badgers do the Chinese have?"

"Now? Twenty-five. They are trying to build more."

"You can expand on everything I've told you."

"We'll have to, as they build up their force, Robin. I've told you that," Grishanov said quickly and quietly, but it was too late, he saw, at least in one respect.

"I've told you everything," the American said, looking down at the map. Then his eyes closed and his shoulders shook. Grishanov embraced him to ease the pain he saw.

"Robin, you've told me how to protect the children of my country. I have not lied to you. My father *did* leave his university to fight the Germans. I *did* have to evacuate Moscow as a child. I *did* lose friends that winter in the snow—little boys and little girls, Robin, children who froze to death. It *did* happen. I *did* see it."

"And I did betray my country," Zacharias whispered. The realization had come with the speed and violence of a falling bomb. How could he have been so blind, so stupid? Robin leaned back, feeling a sudden pain in his chest, and in that moment he prayed it was a heart attack, for the first time in his life wishing for death. But it wasn't. It was just a contraction of his stomach and the release of a large quantity of acid, just the perfect thing, really, to eat away at his stomach as his mind ate away the defenses of his soul. He'd broken faith with his country and his God. He was damned.

"My friend—"

"You *used* me!" Robin hissed, trying to pull away.

"Robin, you must listen to me." Grishanov wouldn't let go. "I love my country, Robin, as you love yours. I have sworn an oath to defend her. I have never lied to you about that, and now it is time for you to learn other things."

Robin had to understand. Kolya had to make it clear to Zacharias, as Robin had made so many things clear to Kolya.

"Like what?"

"Robin, you are a dead man. The Vietnamese have reported you dead to your country. You will never be allowed to return home. That is why you are not in the prison—Hoa Lo, the Hilton, your people call it, yes?" It seared Kolya's soul when Robin looked at him, the accusation there was almost more than he could bear. When he spoke again, his voice was the one doing the pleading.

"What you are thinking is wrong. I have *begged* my superiors to let me save your life. I swear this on the lives of my children: *I will not let you die.* You cannot go back to America. I will make for you a new home. You will be able to *fly* again, Robin! You will have a new life. I can do no more than that. If I could restore you to your Ellen and your children, I would do it. I am not a monster, Robin, I am a man, like you. I have a country, like you. I have a family, like you. In the name of your God, man, put yourself in my place. What would you have done in my place? What would you feel in my place?" There was no reply beyond a sob of shame and despair.

"Would you have me let them torture you? I can do that. Six men in this camp have died, did you know that? Six men died before I came here. *I put a stop to it!* Only one has died since my arrival—only one, and I wept for him, Robin, did you know that! I would gladly kill Major Vinh, the little fascist. *I have saved you!* I've done everything in my power, and I have begged for more. I give you my own food, Robin, things that my Marina sends to me!"

"And I've told you how to kill American pilots—"

"Only if they attack my country can I hurt them. Only if they try to kill my people, Robin! Only then! Do you wish them to kill my family?"

"It's not like that!"

"Yes, it is. Don't you see? This is not a game, Robin. We are in the business of death, you and I, and to save lives one must also take them."

Perhaps he'd see it in time, Grishanov hoped. He was a bright man, a rational man. Once he had time to examine the facts, he would see that life was better than death, and perhaps they could again be friends. For the moment, Kolya told himself, I have saved the man's life. *Even if the American curses me for that, he will have to breathe air to speak his curse.* Colonel Grishanov would bear that burden with pride. He'd gotten his information and saved a life in the process, as was entirely proper for an air-defense pilot of PVO Strany who'd sworn his life's real oath as a frightened and disoriented boy on his way from Moscow to Gorkiy.

*   *   *

The Russian came out of the prison block in time for dinner, Kelly saw. He had a notebook in his hands, doubtless full of the information he'd sweated out of the prisoners.

"We're going to get your sorry red ass," Kelly whispered to himself. "They're gonna put three willie-petes through that window, pal, and cook you up for dinner—along with all your fucking notes. Yeah."

He could feel it now. It was, again, the private pleasure of knowing what would be, the godlike satisfaction of seeing the future. He took a sip from his canteen. He couldn't afford to dehydrate. Patience came hard now. Within his sight was a building with twenty lonely, frightened, and badly hurt Americans, and though he'd never met any of them, and though he only knew one by name, his was a worthy quest. For the rest, he tried to find the Latin from his high school: *Morituri non cognant,* perhaps. Those who are about to die—just don't know. Which was just fine with Kelly.

"Homicide."

"Hi, I'm trying to get Lieutenant Frank Allen."

"You got him," Allen replied. He'd been at his desk just five minutes this Monday morning. "Who's this?"

"Sergeant Pete Meyer, Pittsburgh," the voice replied. "Captain Dooley referred me to you, sir."

"I haven't talked to Mike in a while. Is he still a Pirates fan?"

"Every night, Lieutenant. I try to catch some of the games myself."

"You want a line on the Series, Sarge?" Allen asked with a grin. Cop fellowship.

"Bucs in five. Roberto's real tough this year." Clemente was having a career year.

"Oh, yeah? Well, so are Brooks and Frank." The Robinsons weren't doing so badly either. "What can I do for you?"

"Lieutenant, I have some information for you. Two homicides, both victims female, in their late teens, early twenties."

"Back up, please." Allen got a clean sheet of paper. "Who's your source?"

"I can't reveal that yet. It's privileged. I'm working on changing that, but it might take a while. Can I go on?"

"Very well. Names of victims?"

"The recent one was named Pamela Madden—very recent, only a few weeks ago."

Lieutenant Allen's eyes went wide. "Jesus—the fountain murder. And the other one?"

"Her name was Helen, sometime last fall. Both murders were ugly, Lieutenant, torture and sexual abuse."

Allen hunched forward with the phone very close to his ear. "You telling me you have a witness to both killings?"

"That is correct, sir, I believe we do. I got two likely perps for you, too. Two white males, one named Billy and the other named Rick. No descriptions, but I can work on that, too."

"Okay, they're not my cases. It's being handled downtown—Lieutenant Ryan and Sergeant Douglas. I know both names—both victims, I mean. These are high-profile cases, Sarge. How solid is your information?"

"I believe it to be very solid. I have one possible indicator for you. Victim number two, Pamela Madden—her hair was brushed out after she was killed."

In every major criminal case, several important pieces of evidence were always left out of press accounts in order to screen out the usual collection of nuts who called in to confess to something—anything that struck their twisted fancies. This thing with the hair was sufficiently protected that even Lieutenant Allen didn't know about it.

"What else do you have?"

"The murders were drug-related. Both girls were mules."

"Bingo!" Allan exclaimed quietly. "Is your source in jail or what?"

"I'm pushing the edge here, but—okay, I'll level with you. My dad's a preacher. He's counseling the girl. Lieutenant, this is really off-the-record stuff, okay?"

"I understand. What do you want me to do?"

"Could you please forward the info to the investigating officers? They can contact me through the station." Sergeant Meyer gave over his number. "I'm a watch supervisor here, and I have to roll out now to deliver a lecture at the academy. I'll be back about four."

"Very well, Sergeant. I'll pass that along. Thanks a lot for the input. You'll be hearing from Em and Tom. Depend on it." *Jesus, we'll give Pittsburgh the fuckin' Series to bag these bastards.* Allen switched buttons on his phone.

"Hey, Frank," Lieutenant Ryan said. When he set his coffee cup down, it appeared like slow-motion. That stopped when he picked up a pen. "Keep talking. I'm writing this down."

Sergeant Douglas was late this morning because of an accident on I-83.

He came in with his usual coffee and danish to see his boss scribbling furiously.

"Brushed out the hair? He said that?" Ryan asked. Douglas leaned across the desk, and the look in Ryan's eyes was like that of a hunter who just heard the first rustle in the leaves. "Okay, what names did he—" The detective's hand balled into a fist. A long breath. "Okay, Frank, where is this guy? Thanks. 'Bye."

"Break?"

"Pittsburgh," Ryan said.

"Huh?"

"Call from a police sergeant in Pittsburgh, a possible witness in the murders of Pamela Madden and Helen Waters."

"No shit?"

"This is the one who brushed her hair, Tom. And guess what other names came along with it?"

"Richard Farmer and William Grayson?"

"Rick and Billy. Close enough? Possible mule for a drug ring. Wait . . .." Ryan leaned back, staring at the yellowed ceiling. "There was a girl there when Farmer was killed—we think there was," he corrected himself. "It's the connection, Tom. Pamela Madden, Helen Waters, Farmer, Grayson, they're all related . . . and that means—"

"The pushers, too. All connected somehow. What connects them, Em? We know they were all—probably all—in the drug business."

"Two different MOs, Tom. The girls were slaughtered like—no, you don't even do that to cattle. All the rest, though, all of them were taken down by the Invisible Man. Man on a mission! That's what Farber said, a man on a mission."

"Revenge," Douglas said, pacing Ryan's analysis on his own. "If one of those girls was close to me—Jesus, Em, who could blame him?"

There was only one person connected with either murder who'd been close with a victim, and he was known to the police department, wasn't he? Ryan grabbed his phone and called back to Lieutenant Allen.

"Frank, what was the name of that guy who worked the Gooding case, the Navy guy?"

"Kelly, John Kelly, he found the gun off Fort McHenry, then downtown contracted him to train our divers, remember? Oh! Pamela Madden! Jesus!" Allen exclaimed when the connection became clear.

"Tell me about him, Frank."

"Hell of a nice guy. Quiet, kinda sad—lost his wife, auto accident or something."

"Veteran, right?"

"Frogman, underwater demolitions. That's how he earns his living, blowing things up. Underwater stuff, like."

"Keep going."

"Physically he's pretty tough, takes care of himself." Allen paused. "I saw him dive, there's some marks on him, scars, I mean. He's seen combat and caught some fire. I got his address and all if you want."

"I have it in my case file, Frank. Thanks, buddy." Ryan hung up. "He's our guy. He's the Invisible Man."

"Kelly?"

"I have to be in court this morning—damn it!" Ryan swore.

"Nice to see you again," Dr. Farber said. Monday was an easy day for him. He'd seen his last patient of the day and was heading out for after-lunch tennis with his sons. The cops had barely caught him heading out of his office.

"What do you know about UDT guys?" Ryan asked, walking out into the corridor with him.

"Frogmen, you mean? Navy?"

"That's right. Tough, are they?"

Farber grinned around his pipe. "They're the first guys on the beach, ahead of the Marines. What do you think?" He paused. Something clicked in his mind. "There's something even better now."

"What do you mean?" the detective lieutenant asked.

"Well, I still do a little work for the Pentagon. Hopkins does a lot of things for the government. Applied Physics Lab, lots of special things. You know my background." He paused. "Sometimes I do psychological testing, consulting—what combat does to people. This is classified material, right? There's a new special-operations group. It's a spin-off of UDT. They call them SEALs now, for Sea Air Land—they're commandos, real serious folks, and their existence is not widely known. Not just tough. Smart. They're trained to think, to plan ahead. Not just muscle. Brains, too."

"Tattoo," Douglas said, remembering. "He has a tattoo of a seal on his arm."

"Doc, what if one of these SEAL guys had a girl who was brutally murdered?" It was the most obvious of questions, but he had to ask it.

"That's the mission you were looking for," Farber said, heading out the door, unwilling to reveal anything else, even for a murder investigation.

"That's our boy. Except for one thing," Ryan said quietly to the closed door.

"Yeah. No evidence. Just one hell of a motive."

* * *

Nightfall. It had been a dreary day for everyone at SENDER GREEN except for Kelly. The parade ground was mush, with fetid puddles, large and small. The soldiers had spent most of the day trying to keep dry. Those in the towers had adjusted their position to the shifting winds. Weather like this did things to people. Most humans didn't like being wet. It made them irritable and dull of mind, all the more so if their duty was also boring, as it was here. In North Vietnam, weather like this meant fewer air attacks, yet another reason for the men down below to relax. The increasing heat of the day had energized the clouds, adding moisture to them which the clouds just as quickly gave back to the ground.

What a shitty day, all the guards would be saying to one another over their dinner. All would nod and concentrate on their meals, looking down, not up, looking inward, not outward. The woods would be damp. It was far quieter to walk on wet leaves than dry ones. No dry twigs to snap. The humid air would muffle sound, not transmit it. It was, in a word, perfect.

Kelly took the opportunity of the darkness to move around some, stiff from the inactivity. He sat up under his bush, brushing off his skin and eating more of his ration concentrates. He drained down a full canteen, then stretched his arms and legs. He could see the LZ, and had already selected his path to it, hoping the Marines wouldn't be trigger-happy when he ran down towards them. At twenty-one hundred he made his final radio transmission.

Light Green, the technician wrote on his pad. *Activity Normal.*

"That's it. That's the last thing we need." Maxwell looked at the others. Everyone nodded.

"Operation BOXWOOD GREEN, Phase Four, commences at twenty-two hundred. Captain Franks, make signal to *Newport News.*"

"Aye aye, sir."

On *Ogden,* flight crews dressed in their fire-protective suits, then walked aft to preflight their aircraft. They found sailors wiping all the windows. In the troop spaces, the Marines were donning their striped utilities. Weapons were clean. Magazines were full with fresh ammo just taken from airtight containers. The individual grunts paired off, each man applying camouflage paint to his counterpart. No smiles or joking now. They were as serious as actors on opening night, and the delicacy of the makeup work gave a strange counterpoint to the nature of the evening's performance. Except for one of their number.

"Easy on the eye shadow, sir," Irvin told a somewhat jumpy Captain

Albie, who had the usual commander's jitters and needed a sergeant to steady him down.

In the squadron ready room aboard USS *Constellation,* a diminutive and young squadron commander named Joshua Painter led the briefing. He had eight F-4 Phantoms loaded for bear.

"We're covering a special operation tonight. Our targets are SAM sites south of Haiphong," he went on, not knowing what it was all about, hoping that it was worth the risk to the fifteen officers who would fly with him tonight, and that was just his squadron. Ten A-6 Intruders were also flying Iron Hand, and most of the rest of *Connie*'s air wing would trail their coats up the coast, throwing as much electronic noise into the air as they could. He hoped it was all as important as Admiral Podulski had said. Playing games with SAM sites wasn't exactly fun.

Newport News was twenty-five miles off the coast now, approaching a point that would put her exactly between *Ogden* and the beach. Her radars were off, and the shore stations probably didn't know quite where she was. After the last few days the NVA were getting a little more circumspect about using their coastal surveillance systems. The Captain was sitting in his bridge chair. He checked his watch and opened a sealed manila envelope, reading quickly through the action orders he'd had in his safe for two weeks.

"Hmm," he said to himself. Then: "Mr. Shoeman, have engineering bring boilers one and four fully on line. I want full power available as soon as possible. We're doing some more surfing tonight. My compliments to the XO, gunnery officer, and his chiefs. I want them in my at-sea cabin at once."

"Aye, sir." The officer of the deck made the necessary notifications. With all four of her boilers on line, *Newport News* could make thirty-four knots, the quicker to close the beach, and the quicker to depart from it.

"Surf City, here we come!" the petty officer at the wheel sang out loud as soon as the Captain was off the bridge. It was the official ship's joke— because the Captain liked it—actually made up several months before by a seaman first-class. It meant going inshore, right into the surf, for some shooting. "Goin' to Surf City, where it's two-to-one!"

"Mark your head, Baker," the OOD called to end the chorus.

"Steady on one-eight-five, Mr. Shoeman." His body moved to the beat. *Surf City, here we come!*

"Gentlemen, in case you're wondering what we've done to deserve the fun of the past few days, this is it," the Captain said in his cabin just off the bridge. He explained on for several minutes. On his desk was a map of the coastal area, with every triple-A battery marked from data on aerial and satellite photographs. His gunnery department looked things over. There were plenty of hilltops for good radar references.

"Oh, yeah!" the master chief firecontrolman breathed. "Sir, everything? Five-inchers, too?"

The skipper nodded. "Chief Skelley, if we bring any ammo back to Subic, I'm going to be very disappointed with you."

"Sir, I propose we use number-three five-inch mount for star shell and shoot visually as much as we can."

It was an exercise in geometry, really. The gunnery experts—that included the commanding officer—leaned across the map and decided quickly how it would be done. Already briefed on the mission, the only change was that they had expected to do it in daylight.

"There won't be anybody left alive to fire on those helos, sir."

The growler phone on the CO's desk rang. He grabbed it. "Captain speaking."

"All four boilers are now on line, sir. Full-speed bell is thirty, flank is thirty-three."

"Nice to know the ChEng is all awake. Very well. Sound General Quarters." He hung up the phone as the ship's gong started sounding. "Gentlemen, we have some Marines to protect," he said confidently. His cruiser's gunnery department was as fine as *Mississippi*'s had ever been. Two minutes later he was back on the bridge.

"Mr. Shoeman, I have the conn."

"Captain has the conn," the OOD agreed.

"Right-standard rudder, come to new course two-six-five."

"Right-standard rudder, aye, come to new course two-six-five, aye." Petty Officer Sam Baker rotated the wheel. "Sir, my rudder is right-standard."

"Very well," the Captain acknowledged, adding, "Surf City, here we come!"

"Aye aye, sir!" the helmsman hooted back. The skipper was really with it for an old fart.

It was the time for nerves now. *What could go wrong?* Kelly asked himself atop his hill. Lots of things. The helicopters might collide in midair. They might come right over an unknown flak site and be blotted from the sky. Some little widget or seal could let go, crashing them to the ground.

What if the local National Guard was having a training exercise tonight? Something was always left to chance. He'd seen missions go wrong for any number of dumb and unpredictable reasons. But not tonight, he promised himself. Not with all this preparation. The helo crews had trained intensively for three weeks, as had the Marines. The birds had been lovingly maintained. The sailors on *Ogden* had invented helpful things to do. You could never eliminate risk, but preparation and training could attenuate it. Kelly made sure his weapon was in proper shape and stayed in a tight sitting position. This wasn't sitting in a corner house in west Baltimore. This was real. This would enable him to put it all behind. His attempt to save Pam had ended in failure due to his error, but perhaps it had had a purpose after all. He'd made no mistakes for this mission. Nobody had. He wasn't rescuing one person. He was rescuing twenty. He checked the illuminated dial of his watch. The sweep hand was moving so slowly now. Kelly closed his eyes, hoping that when he opened them it would move more quickly. It didn't. He knew better. The former Chief of SEALs commanded himself to take a deep breath and continue the mission. For him that meant laying the carbine across his lap and concentrating on his binoculars. His reconnaissance had to continue right to the moment the first M-79 grenades were fired at the guard towers. The Marines were counting on him.

Well, maybe this would show the guys from Philly how important he was. *Henry's operation breaks down and I handle things. Eddie Morello is important,* he thought, stoking the fires of his own ego as he drove up Route 40 towards Aberdeen.

Idiot can't run his own operation, can't get dependable people. I told Tony he was too smart for his own good, too clever, not really a serious businessman—Oh, no, he's serious. He's more serious than you are, Eddie. Henry is going be the first nigger to get "made." You watch. Tony is going to do it. Can't do it for you. Your own cousin can't do it for you, after you connected him with Henry. Goddamned deal wouldn't be made except for me. I made the deal but I can't get made.

"Fuck!" he snarled at a red light. *Somebody starts taking Henry's operation apart and they ask me to check it out. Like Henry can't figure things out himself. Probably can't, not as smart as he thinks he is. So then what—he gets between me and Tony.*

That was it, wasn't it? Eddie thought. *Henry wanted to separate me from Piaggi—just like he got them to take Angelo out. Angelo was his first connection. Angelo introduced him to me . . . I introduced him to*

Tony . . . Tony and I handle the connection with Philly and New York . . . Angelo and me were a pair of connections . . . Angelo was the weak one . . . and Angelo gets whacked . . .

Tony and I are another pair of connections . . .

He only needs one, doesn't he? Just one connection to the rest of the outfit.

Separating me from Tony . . .

Fuck.

Morello fished in his pocket for a cigarette and punched the lighter on his Cadillac convertible. The top was down. Eddie liked the sun and the wind. It was almost like being out on his fishing boat. It also gave him fine visibility. That it made him somewhat easier to spot and trail hadn't occurred to him. Next to him, on the floor, was a leather attaché case. Inside that were six kilos of pure stuff. Philadelphia, they'd told him, was real short, and would handle the cutting themselves. Big cash deal. The identical case that was now southbound would be filled with nothing smaller than twenties. Two guys. Nothing to worry about. They were pros, and this was a long-term business relationship. He didn't have to worry about a rip, but he had his snubby anyway, concealed under his loose shirt, just at his belt buckle, the most useful, most uncomfortable place.

He had to think this one through, Morello told himself urgently. He might just have it all figured out. Henry was manipulating them. *Henry* was *manipulating* the outfit. A jig was trying to outthink them.

And succeeding. Probably he whacked his own people. The fuck liked to shit all over women—especially white ones. That figured, Morello thought. They were all like that. Thought he was pretty smart, probably. Well, he *was* pretty smart. But not smart enough. Not anymore. It wouldn't be hard to explain all of this to Tony. Eddie was sure of that. Make the transfer and drive back. Dinner with Tony. Be calm and reasonable. Tony likes that. Like he went to Harvard or something. Like a damned lawyer. Then we work on Henry, and we take over his operation. It was business. His people would play. They weren't in it because they loved him. They were in it for the money. Everybody was. And then he and Tony could take the operation over, and *then* Eddie Morello would be a made man.

Yeah. He had it all figured out now. Morello checked the time. He was right on as he pulled into the half-empty parking lot of a diner. The old-fashioned kind, made from a railroad car—the Pennsylvania Railroad was close by. He remembered his first meal out of the house with his father, in a place just like this, watching the trains go past. The memory made him smile as he finished the cigarette and flipped it onto the blacktop.

The other car pulled in. It was a blue Oldsmobile, as he'd been led to expect. The two guys got out. One carried an attaché case and walked towards him. Eddie didn't know him, but he was well-dressed, respectable, like a businessman should be, in a nice tan suit. Like a lawyer. Morello smiled to himself, not looking too obviously in his direction while the backup man stayed at the car, watching, just to be on the safe side. Yeah, serious people. And soon they'd know that Eddie Morello was a serious man, too, he thought, with his hand in his lap, six inches from his hidden revolver.

"Got the stuff?"

"Got the money?" Morello asked in return.

"You made a mistake, Eddie," the man said without warning as he opened the briefcase.

"What do you mean?" Morello asked, suddenly alert, about ten seconds and a lifetime too late.

"I mean, it's goodbye, Eddie," he added quietly.

The look in the eyes said it all. Morello immediately went for his weapon, but it only helped the other man.

"Police, freeze!" the man shouted just before the first round burst through the opened top of the case.

Eddie got his gun out, just, and managed to fire one round into the floor of his car, but the cop was only three feet away and couldn't possibly miss. The backup officer was already running in, surprised that Lieutenant Charon hadn't been able to get the drop on the guy. As he watched, the attaché case fell aside and the detective extended his arm, nearly placing his service revolver on the man's chest and firing straight into his heart.

It was all so clear to Morello now, but only for a second or two. Henry had done it all. He'd made himself, that was it. And Morello knew that his only purpose in life had been to get Henry and Tony together. It didn't seem like much, not now.

"Backup!" Charon screamed over the dying man. He reached down to seize Eddie's revolver. Within a minute two State Police cars screeched into the parking lot.

"Damned fool," Charon told his partner five minutes later, shaking as he did so, as men do after killing. "He just went for the gun—like I didn't have the drop on him."

"I saw it all," the junior detective said, thinking that he had.

"Well, it's just what you said, sir," the State Police sergeant said. He opened the case from the floor of the Olds. It was filled with bags of heroin. "Some bust."

"Yeah," Charon growled. "Except dead the dumb fuck can't tell any-body anything." Which was exactly true. Remarkable, he thought, succeeding in his struggle not to smile at the mad humor of the moment. He'd just committed the perfect murder, under the eyes of other police officers. Now Henry's organization was safe.

Almost time now. The guard had changed. *Last time for that.* The rain continued to fall steadily. *Good.* The soldiers in the towers were huddling to stay dry. The dreary day had bored them even more than normal, and bored men were less alert. All the lights were out now. Not even candles in the barracks. Kelly made a slow, careful sweep with his binoculars. There was a human shape in the window of the officers' quarters, a man looking out at the weather—the Russian, wasn't it? *Oh, so that's your bedroom? Great: The first shot from grenadier number three—Corporal Mendez, wasn't it?— is programmed for that opening. Fried Russian.*

Let's get this one on. I need a shower. God, you suppose they have any more of that Jack Daniel's left? Regs were regs, but some things were special.

The tension was building. It wasn't the danger factor. Kelly deemed himself to be in no danger at all. The scary part had been the insertion. Now it was up to the airedales, then the Marines. His part was almost done, Kelly thought.

"Commence firing," the Captain ordered.

Newport News had switched her radars on only a few moments earlier. The navigator was in central fire-control, helping the gunnery department to plot the cruiser's exact position by radar fixes on known landmarks. That was being overly careful, but tonight's mission called for it. Now navigation and fire-control radars were helping everyone compute their position to a whisker.

The first rounds off were from the portside five-inch mount. The sharp bark of noise from the twin 5"/38s was very hard on the ears, but along with it came something oddly beautiful. With each shot the guns generated a ring of yellow fire. It was some empirical peculiarity of the weapon that did it. Like a yellow snake chasing its tail, undulating for its few milliseconds of life. Then it vanished. Six thousand yards downrange, the first pair of star shells ignited, and it was the same metallic yellow that had a few seconds earlier decorated the gun mount. The wet, green landscape of North Vietnam turned orange under the light.

"Looks like a fifty-seven-mike-mike mount. I can see the crew, even." The rangefinder in Spot-1 was already trained into the proper bearing. The light just made it easier. Master Chief Skelley dialed in the range with remarkable delicacy. It was transmitted at once to "central." Ten seconds after that, eight guns thundered. Another fifteen, and the triple-A site vanished in a cloud of dust and fire.

"On target with the first salvo. Target Alfa is destroyed." The master chief took his command from below to shift bearings to the next. Like the Captain he would soon retire. Maybe they could open a gun store.

It was like distant thunder, but not right somehow. The surprising part was the absence of reaction below. Through the binoculars he could see heads turn. Maybe some remarks were exchanged. Nothing more than that. It was a country at war, after all, and unpleasant noises were normal here, especially the kind that sounded like distant thunder. Clearly too far away to be a matter of concern. You couldn't even see any flashes through the weather. Kelly had expected an officer or two to come out and look around. He would have done that in their place—probably. But they didn't.

Ninety minutes and counting.

The Marines were lightly loaded as they filed aft. Quite a few sailors were there to watch them. Albie and Irvin counted them off as they headed out onto the flight deck, directing them to their choppers.

The last sailors in line were Maxwell and Podulski. Both were wearing their oldest and most disreputable khakis, shirts and pants they'd worn in command at sea, things associated with good memories and good luck. Even admirals were superstitious. For the first time the Marines saw that the pale Admiral—that's how they thought of him—had the Medal of Honor. The ribbon caught many glances, and quite a few nods of respect that his tense face acknowledged.

"All ready, Captain?" Maxwell asked.

"Yes, sir," Albie replied calmly over his nervousness. Showtime. "See you in about three hours."

"Good hunting." Maxwell stood ramrod-straight and saluted the younger man.

"They look pretty impressive," Ritter said. He, too, was wearing khakis, just to fit in with the ship's wardroom. "Oh, Jesus, I hope this works."

"Yeah," James Greer breathed as the ship turned to align herself with the wind. Deck crewmen with lighted wands went to both troop carriers to guide their takeoffs, and then, one by one, the big Sikorskys lifted off, steadying themselves in the burble and turning west towards land and the mission. "It's in their hands now."

"Good kids, James," Podulski said.

"That Clark guy is pretty impressive, too. Smart," Ritter observed. "What's he do in real life?"

"I gather he's sort of at odds at the moment. Why?"

"We always have room for a guy who can think on his feet. The boy's smart," Ritter repeated as all headed back to CIC. On the flight deck, the Cobra crews were doing their final preflight checks. They'd get off in forty-five minutes.

"SNAKE, this is CRICKET. Time check is nominal. Acknowledge."

"Yes!" Kelly said aloud—but not too loud. He tapped three long dashes on his radio, getting two back. *Ogden* had just announced that the mission was now running and copied his acknowledgment. "Two hours to freedom, guys," he told the prisoners in the camp below. That the event would be less liberating for the other people in the camp was not a matter of grave concern.

Kelly ate his last ration bar, sliding all the wrappers and trash into the thigh pockets of his fatigues. He moved from his hiding place. It was dark now, and he could afford to. Reaching back in, he tried to erase the marks of his presence. A mission like this might be tried again, after all, and why let the other side know anything about how it had happened? The tension finally reached the point that he had to urinate. It was almost funny, and made him feel like a little kid, though he'd drunk half a gallon of water that day.

Thirty minutes' flying time to the first LZ, thirty more for the approach. When they crest the far hill, I go into live contact with them to control the final approach.

Let's get it on.

"Shifting fire right. Target Hotel in sight," Skelley reported. "Range . . . nine-two-five-zero." The guns thundered once more. One of the hundred-millimeter gun mounts was actually firing at them, now. The crew had watched *Newport News* immolate the rest of their antiaircraft battalion and, unable to desert their guns, they were trying, at least, to fire back and wound the monster that was hovering off their coastline.

"There's the helos," the XO said at his post in CIC. The blips on the main radar display crossed the coast right over where Targets Alfa and Bravo had been. He lifted the phone.

"Captain here."

"XO here, sir. The helos are feet-dry, going right up the corridor we made them."

"Very well. Prepare to stand-down the fire mission. We'll be HIFR-ing those helos in thirty minutes. Keep a very sharp eye on that radar, X."

"Aye, sir."

"Jesus," a radar operator observed. "What's going on here?"

"First we shoot their ass," his neighbor opined, "then we invade their ass."

Only minutes now until the Marines were on the ground. The rain remained steady though the wind had died down.

Kelly was in the open now. It was safe. He wasn't skylined. There was ample flora behind him. All of his clothing and exposed skin was colored to blend in. His eyes were sweeping everywhere, searching for danger, for something unusual, finding nothing. It was muddy as hell. The wet and the red clay of these miserable hills was part of him now, through the fabric of his uniform, into every pore.

Ten minutes out from the LZ. The distant thunder from the coast continued sporadically, and its very continuance made it less of a danger. It sounded even more like thunder now, and only Kelly knew that it was the eight-inch guns of a ship of war. He sat back, resting his elbows on his knees, sweeping the glasses over the camp. Still no lights. Still no movement. Death was racing towards them and they didn't know. He was concentrating so much with his eyes that he almost neglected his ears.

It was hard to pick it out through the rain: a distant rumble, low and tenuous, but it didn't fade. It grew in intensity. Kelly lifted his head from the eyepieces, turning, his mouth open, trying to figure it out.

Motors.

Truck motors. Well, okay, there was a road not too far away—no, the main road is too far . . . other direction.

A supply truck maybe. Delivering food and mail.

More than one.

Kelly moved to the top of the hill, leaning against a tree, looking down to where this spur of a dirt road reached out to the one that traced the north bank of the river. Movement. He put the glasses on it.

Truck . . . two . . . three . . . four . . . oh, my God . . .

They had lights on—just slits, the headlights taped over. That meant military trucks. The lights of the second gave some illumination to the first. People in the back, lined on both sides.

Soldiers.

Wait, Johnnie-boy, don't panic. Take your time . . . maybe . . .

They turned around the base of Snake Hill. A guard in one of the towers shouted something, The call was relayed. Lights came on in the officers' quarters. Somebody came out, probably the Major, not dressed, shouting a question.

The first truck stopped at the gate. A man got out and roared for somebody to open it. The other truck stopped behind it. Soldiers dismounted. Kelly counted . . . ten . . . twenty . . . thirty . . . more . . . but it wasn't the number. It was what they started to do.

He had to look away. What more would fate take away from him? Why not just take his life and be done with it? But it wasn't just his life that fate was interested in. It never was. He was responsible, as always, for more than that. Kelly reached for his radio and flipped it on.

"CRICKET, this is SNAKE, over."

Nothing.

"CRICKET, this is SNAKE, over."

"What gives?" Podulski asked.

Maxwell took the microphone. "SNAKE, this is CRICKET ACTUAL, what is your message, over?"

"Abort abort abort—acknowledge," was what they all heard.

"Say again SNAKE. Say again."

"Abort the mission," Kelly said, too loudly for his own safety. "Abort abort abort. Acknowledge immediately."

It took a few seconds. "We copy your order to abort. Acknowledged. Mission aborted. Stand by."

"Roger, standing by."

"What is it?" Major Vinh asked.

"We have information that the Americans may try to raid your camp," the Captain replied, looking back at his men. They were deploying skillfully, half heading for trees, the other half taking positions inside the perimeter, digging in as soon as they picked their places. "Comrade Major, I am ordered to take charge of the defense until more units arrive. You are ordered to take your Russian guest to Hanoi for safety."

"But—"

"The orders come from General Giap himself, Comrade Major."

Which settled matters very quickly indeed. Vinh went back to his quarters to dress. His camp sergeant went to awaken his driver.

Kelly could do nothing more than watch. Forty-five, maybe more. It was hard to count them as they moved. Teams digging machine gun pits. Patrol elements in the woods. That was an immediate danger to him, but he waited even so. He had to be sure that he'd done the right thing, that he hadn't panicked, hadn't been a sudden coward.

Twenty-five against fifty, with surprise and a plan, not hard. Twenty-five against a hundred, without surprise . . . hopeless. He'd done the right thing. There was no reason to add twenty-five more bodies to the ledger sheet that they kept in Washington. His conscience didn't have room for that kind of mistake or for those kinds of lives.

"Helos coming back, sir, same way they went in," the radar operator told the XO.

"Too fast," the XO said.

"Goddamn it, Dutch! Now what—"

"The mission's aborted, Cas," Maxwell said, staring down at the chart table.

"But *why?*"

"Because Mr. Clark said so," Ritter answered. "He's the eyes. He makes the call. You don't need anybody to tell you that, Admiral. We still have a man in there, gentlemen. Let's not forget that."

"We have *twenty* men in there."

"That's true, sir, but only one of them is coming out tonight." *And then only if we're lucky.*

Maxwell looked up to Captain Franks. "Let's move in towards the beach, fast as you can."

"Yes, sir."

"Hanoi? Why?"

"Because we have orders." Vinh was looking over the dispatch the Captain had delivered. "Well, the Americans wanted to come here, eh? I hope they do. This will be no Song Tay for them!"

The idea of an infantry action didn't exactly thrill Colonel Grishanov, and a trip to Hanoi, even an unannounced one, also meant a trip to the embassy. "Let me pack, Major."

"Be quick about it!" the little man snapped back, wondering if his trip to Hanoi was for some manner of transgression.

It could be worse. Grishanov now had all his notes together and slid them into a backpack. All of his work, now that Vinh had so kindly released it back to him. He'd drop it off with General Rokossovskiy, and with that in official hands, he could make his case for keeping these Americans alive. It was an ill wind, he thought, remembering the English aphorism.

He could hear them coming. Far off, moving without a great deal of skill, probably tired, but coming.

"CRICKET, this is SNAKE, over."

"We read you, SNAKE."

"I'm moving. There are people on my hill, coming my way. I will head west. Can you send a helo for me?"

"Affirmative. Be careful, son." It was Maxwell's voice, still concerned.

"Moving now. Out." Kelly pocketed the radio and headed to the crest. He took a moment to look, comparing what he saw now with what he'd seen before.

I run especially fast in the dark, he'd told the Marines. Time now to prove it. With one last listen to the approaching NVA, Kelly picked a thin spot in the foliage and headed down the hill.

30

Travel Agents

I t was obvious to everyone that things were wrong. The two rescue helos touched down on *Ogden* not an hour after they'd left. One was wheeled aside at once. The other, flown by the senior pilot, was refueled. Captain Albie was out almost the second it landed, sprinting to the superstructure, where the command team was waiting for him. He could feel that *Ogden* and her escorts were racing into the beach. His dejected Marines trailed out as well, silent, looking down at the flight deck as they cleared their weapons.

"What happened?" Albie asked.

"Clark waved it off. All we know is that he's moved off his hill; he said other people were there. We're going to try to get him out. Where do you think he'll go?" Maxwell asked.

"He'll look for a place the helo can get him. Let's see the map."

Had he had the time to reflect, Kelly might have considered how quickly things could go from good to bad. But he didn't. Survival was an all-encompassing game, and at the moment it was also the only game in town. Certainly it wasn't a boring one, and with luck not overly demanding. There weren't all that many troops for the purpose of securing the camp against an assault, not enough—yet—to conduct real defensive patrols. If they were worried about another Song Tay–type mission, they'd keep their firepower in close. They'd put observation teams on hilltops, probably nothing more than that at least for the moment. The top of Snake Hill was now five hundred meters in his wake. Kelly slowed his descent, catching his breath—he was more winded from fear than effort, though the two traded off heavily against each other. He found a secondary crest and rested on the far side of it. Standing still now, he could hear talk behind him—talk, not movement. Okay, good, he'd guessed right on the tactical situation. Probably more troops would be arriving in due course, but he'd be long gone by then.

If they can get that helo in.

Pleasant thought.

I've been in tighter spots than this, Defiance proclaimed.

When? Pessimism inquired delicately.

The only thing that made sense at the moment was to put as much distance as possible between himself and the NVA. Next came the necessity of finding something approximating an LZ so that he could get the hell out of this place. It wasn't a time to panic, but he couldn't dally either. Come daylight there would be more troops here, and if their commander was a competent one, he'd want to know if there might be an enemy reconnaissance element on his turf. Failure to get out before dawn would materially degrade Kelly's chances of ever escaping this country. Move. Find a good spot. Call the helo. Get the hell out of here. He had four hours until dawn. The helo was about thirty minutes away. Make it two or three hours to find a spot and make the call. That didn't seem overly difficult. He knew the area around SENDER GREEN from the recon photos. Kelly took a few minutes to look around, orienting himself. The quickest way to a clear spot was that way, across a twist in the road. It was a gamble but a good one. He rearranged his load, moving his spare magazines within easier reach. More than anything else, Kelly feared capture, to be at the mercy of men like PLASTIC FLOWER, to be unable to fight back, to lose control of his life. A quiet little voice in the back of his mind told him that death was preferred to that. Fighting back, even against impossible odds, wasn't suicide. Okay. That was decided. He started moving.

"Call him?" Maxwell asked.

"No, not now." Captain Albie shook his head. "He'll call us. Mr. Clark is busy right now. We leave him be." Irvin came into the Combat Information Center.

"Clark?" the master gunnery sergeant asked.

"On the run," Albie told him.

"Want me and some people on Rescue One, riding shotgun?" That they would try to get Clark out was not a question. Marines have an institutional loathing of leaving people behind.

"My job, Irvin," Albie said.

"Better you run the rescue, sir," Irvin said reasonably. "Anybody can shoot a rifle."

Maxwell, Podulski, and Greer stayed out of the conversation, watching and listening to two professionals who knew what they were about. The Marine commander bent to the wisdom of his most senior NCO.

"Take what you need." Albie turned to Maxwell. "Sir, I want Rescue One up now."

The Assistant Chief of Naval Operations (Air) handed over the headset to a Marine officer only twenty-eight years old; with it came tactical command of the busted mission. With it went the end of Dutch Maxwell's career.

It was less fearful to be moving. Movement gave Kelly the feeling that he had control of his life. It was an illusion, and intellectually he knew it, but his body took the message that way, which made things better. He got to the bottom of the hill, into thicker growth. There. Right across the road was an open space, a meadow or something, maybe a floodplain area from the river. That would do just fine. Nothing fancy. He grabbed his radio.

"SNAKE to CRICKET, over."

"This is CRICKET. We read you, and we are standing by."

The message came in gasps, spoken one short breath at a time: "West of my hill, past the road, about two miles west of objective, open field. I'm close. Send the helo. I can mark with strobe."

Albie looked at the map, then the aerial photos. Okay, that looked easy enough. He stabbed a finger on the map, and the air-control petty officer relayed the information at once. Albie waited for the confirmation before transmitting back to Clark.

"Roger, copy. Rescue One is moving in now, two-zero minutes away."

"Copy that." Albie could hear the relief in Clark's voice through the static. "I'll be ready. Out."

Thank you, God.

Kelly took his time now, moving slowly and quietly towards the road. His second sojourn into North Vietnam wouldn't end up being as long as the first. He didn't have to swim out this time, and with all the shots he'd gotten before coming in, maybe this time he wouldn't be getting sick from the water in that goddamned river. He didn't so much relax as lose some of his tension. As though on cue, the rain picked up, dampening noise and reducing visibility. More good news. Maybe God or fate or the Great Pumpkin hadn't decided to curse him after all. He stopped again, ten meters short of the road, and looked around. Nothing. He gave himself a few minutes to relax and let the stress bleed off. There was no sense in hurrying across just to be in open ground. Open ground was dangerous for a man alone in enemy territory. His hands were tight on his carbine, the infantryman's teddy bear, as he forced himself to breathe deeply and slowly in order to bring his heart rate down. When he felt approximately normal again, he allowed himself to approach the road.

Miserable roads, Grishanov thought, *even worse than those in Russia.* The car was something French, oddly enough. More remarkably, it ran fairly well, or would have done so, except for the driver. Major Vinh ought to have driven it himself. As an officer he probably knew how, but status-conscious fool that he was, he had to let his orderly do it, and this little lump of a peasant probably didn't know how to drive anything more complicated than an ox. The car was swerving in the mud. The driver was having trouble seeing in the rain as well. Grishanov closed his eyes in the rear seat, clutching his backpack. No sense watching. It might just scare him to watch. It was like flying in bad weather, he thought, something no pilot relished—even less so when someone else was in control.

He waited, looking before crossing, listening for the sound of a truck's engine, which was the greatest danger to him. Nothing. Okay, about five minutes on the helo now. Kelly stood erect, reaching back with his left hand for the marker-strobe. As he crossed the road, he kept looking to his left, the route that additional troop trucks would take to approach the now entirely secure prison camp. *Damn!*

Rarely had concentration ever worked against John Kelly, but it did this time. The sound of the approaching car, swishing through the muddy surface of the road, was a little too close to the environmental noises, and by the time he recognized the difference it was too late. When the car came around the bend, he was right in the middle of the road, standing there like a deer in the headlights, and surely the driver must see him. What followed was automatic.

Kelly brought his carbine up and fired a short burst into the driver's area. The car didn't swerve for a moment, and he laid a second burst into the front-passenger seat. The car changed directions then, slamming directly into a tree. The entire sequence could not have taken three seconds, and Kelly's heart started beating again after a dreadfully long hiatus. He ran to the car. Whom had he killed?

The driver had come through the windshield, two rounds in his brain. Kelly wrenched open the passenger door. The person there was—the Major!

Also hit in the head. The shots weren't quite centered, and though the man's skull was opened on the right side, his body was still quivering. Kelly yanked him out of the vehicle and had knelt down to search him before he heard a groan from the inside. He lunged inside, finding another man—Russian!—on the floor in the rear. Kelly pulled him out, too. The man had a backpack clutched in his hands.

The routine came as automatically as the shot. Kelly clubbed the Russian to full unconsciousness with his buttstock, then quickly turned back to rifle the Major's uniform for intelligence material. He stuffed all documents and papers into his pockets. The Vietnamese was looking at him, one of his eyes still functioning.

"Life's a bitch, ain't it?" Kelly said coldly as the eyes lost their animation.

"What the hell do I do with you?" Kelly asked, turning to the Russian body. "You're the guy who's been hassling our guys, aren't you?" He knelt there, opening the backpack and finding whole sheaves of paper, which answered his question for him—something the Soviet colonel was singularly unable to do.

Think fast, John—the helo isn't very far out now.

"I got the strobe!" the copilot said.

"Coming in hot." The pilot was driving his Sikorsky as hard as the engines would allow. Two hundred yards short of the clearing he pulled back sharply on the cyclic, and the forty-five-degree nose-up attitude stopped forward motion quickly—perfectly in fact, as he leveled out within feet of the blinking infrared strobe light. The rescue helicopter came to a steady hover two feet over the deck, buffeted by the winds. The Navy commander was fighting all manner of forces to hold his aircraft steady, and was slow to respond to something his eyes had told him. He had seen the rotor wash knock his intended survivor down, but—

"Did I see *two* people out there?" he asked over the intercom.

"Go go go!" another voice said over the IC circuit. "Pax aboard now, go!"

"Getting the hell outa Dodge City, now!" The pilot pulled collective for altitude, kicked rudder pedal, and dropped his nose, heading back to the river as the helicopter accelerated. *Wasn't there just supposed to be one person?* He set it aside. He had to fly now, and it was thirty twisty miles to the water and safety.

"Who the fuck is this?" Irvin asked.

"Hitchhiker," Kelly answered over the din of the engines. He shook his head. Explanations would be lengthy and would have to wait. Irvin understood, offering him a canteen. Kelly drained it. That's when the shaking started. In front of the helicopter crew and five Marines, Kelly shivered like a man in the Arctic, huddling and clutching himself, holding his weapon close until Irvin took it away and cleared it. It had been fired, the master gunnery sergeant saw. Later he'd find out why and at what. The door gunners scanned the river valley while their aircraft screamed out, barely a hundred feet over the meandering surface. The ride proved uneventful, far different from what they had expected, as was the case with this whole night. What had gone wrong? they all wanted to know. The answer was in the man they'd just picked up. But who the hell was the other one, and wasn't that a Russian uniform? Two Marines sat over him. One of them tied his hands up. A third secured the pack's flap in place with the straps.

"Rescue One, feet-wet. We have SNAKE aboard, over."

"Rescue One, this is CRICKET, roger, copy that. Standing by. Out." Albie looked up. "Well, that's it."

Podulski took it the hardest of all. BOXWOOD GREEN had been his idea from the start. Had it been successful, it might have changed everything. It might have opened the door for CERTAIN CORNET, might have changed the course of the war—and his son's death would not have been for nothing. He looked up at the others. He almost asked if they might still try it again, but he knew better. Washout. It was a bitter concept and an even more bitter reality for one who had served his adopted country for nearly thirty years.

"Tough day?" Frank Allen asked.

Lieutenant Mark Charon was surprisingly chipper for a man who'd been through a fatal shooting and the almost-as-rigorous interrogation that had followed it.

"The damned fool. Didn't have to happen that way," Charon said. "I guess he didn't like the idea of life on Falls Road," the narcotics-division lieutenant added, referring to the Maryland State Penitentiary. Located in downtown Baltimore, the building was so grim that its inmates referred to it as Frankenstein's Castle.

Allen didn't have to tell him much. The procedures for the incident were straightforward. Charon would go on administrative leave for ten working days while the Department made sure that the shooting had not been contrary to official policy guidelines for the use of "deadly force." It was essentially a two-week vacation with pay, except that Charon might have to face additional interviews. Not likely in this case, as several police officers had observed the whole thing, one from a mere twenty feet away.

"I've got the case, Mark," Allen told him. "I've been over the preliminaries. Looks like you'll come out okay on this. Anything you might have done to spook him?"

Charon shook his head. "No, I didn't shout or anything until he went for his piece. I tried to ease him into it, y'know, calm him down, like? But he just jumped the wrong way. Eddie Morello died of the dumbs," the Lieutenant observed, impassively enjoying the fact that was telling the exact truth.

"Well, I'm not gonna cry over the death of a doper. Good day all around, Mark."

"How's that, Frank?" Charon sat down and stole a cigarette.

"Got a call from Pittsburgh today. Seems there may be a witness for the Fountain Murder that Em and Tom are handling."

"No shit? That's good news. What do we have?"

"Somebody, probably a girl from how the guy was talking, who saw Madden and Waters get it. Sounds like she's talking to her minister about it and he's trying to coax her into opening up."

"Great," Charon observed, concealing his inward chill as well as he'd hid his elation at his first contract murder. One more thing to clean up. With luck that would be the end of it.

The helicopter flared and made a soft landing on USS *Ogden*. As soon as it was down, people came back out on the flight deck. Deck crewmen secured the aircraft in place with chains while they approached. The Marines came out first, relieved to be safe, but also bitterly disappointed at the way the night had turned out. The timing was nearly perfect, they knew. This was their programmed time to return to the ship, with their rescued comrades, and they'd looked forward to this moment as a sports team might anticipate the joys of a winning locker room. But not now. They'd lost and they still didn't know why.

Irvin and another Marine climbed out, holding a body, which really surprised the assembled flag officers as Kelly alighted next. The helicopter pilot's eyes grew wide as he watched. There had been two bodies in the meadow. But mainly he was relieved at achieving another semisuccessful rescue mission into North Vietnam.

"What the hell?" Maxwell asked as the ship commenced a turn to the east.

"Uh, guys, let's get this guy inside and isolated right now!" Ritter said.

"He's unconscious, sir."

"Then get a medic, too," Ritter ordered.

They picked one of *Ogden*'s many empty troop-berthing spaces for the debrief. Kelly was allowed to wash his face, but nothing else. A medical corpsman checked out the Russian, pronouncing him dazed but healthy, both pupils equal and reactive, no concussion. A pair of Marines stood guard over him.

"Four trucks," Kelly said. "They just drove right in. A reinforced platoon—weapons platoon, probably, they showed up while the assault team was inbound, started digging in right away—about fifty of 'em. I had to blow it off."

Greer and Ritter traded a look. *No coincidence.*

Kelly looked at Maxwell. "God, I'm sorry, sir." He paused. "It would not have been possible to execute the mission. I had to leave the hill because they were putting listening posts out. I mean, even if we were able to deal with that—"

"We had gunships, remember?" Podulski growled.

"Back off, Cas," James Greer warned.

Kelly looked long at the Admiral before responding to the accusation. "Admiral, the chances of success were exactly zero. You guys gave me the job of eyeballing the objective so that we could do it on the cheap, right? With more assets, maybe we could have done it—the Song Tay team could have done it. It would have been messy, but they had enough firepower to bring it off, coming right into the objective like they did." He shook his head again. "Not this way."

"You're sure?" Maxwell asked.

Kelly nodded. "Yes, sir. Sure as hell."

"Thank you, Mr. Clark," Captain Albie said quietly, knowing the truth of what he'd just heard. Kelly just sat there, still tensed from the night's events.

"Okay," Ritter said after a moment. "What about our guest, Mr. Clark?"

"I fucked up," Kelly admitted, explaining how the car had gotten so close. He reached into his pockets. "I killed the driver and the camp commander—I think that's what he was. He had all this on him." Kelly reached into his pockets and handed over the documents. "Lots of papers on the Russian. I figured it wasn't smart to leave him there. I figured—I thought maybe he might be useful to us."

"These papers are in Russian," Irvin announced.

"Give me some," Ritter ordered. "My Russian's pretty good."

"We need somebody who can read Vietnamese, too."

"I have one of those," Albie said. "Irvin, get Sergeant Chalmers in here."

"Aye aye, sir."

Ritter and Greer moved to a corner table "Lord," the field officer observed, flipping through the written notes. "This guy's gotten a lot . . . Rokossovskiy? He's in Hanoi? Here's a summary sheet."

Staff Sergeant Chalmers, an intelligence specialist, started reading through the papers taken from Major Vinh. Everyone else waited for the spooks to get through the papers.

"Where am I?" Grishanov asked in Russian. He tried to reach for his blindfold, but his hands couldn't move.

"How are you feeling?" a voice answered in the same language.

"Car smashed into something." The voice stopped. "Where am I?"

"You're aboard USS *Ogden,* Colonel," Ritter told him in English.

The body strapped in the bunk went rigid, and the prisoner immediately said, in Russian, that he didn't speak English.

"Then why are some of your notes in English?" Ritter asked reasonably.

"I am a Soviet officer. You have no right—"

"We have as much right as you had to interrogate American prisoners of war, and to conspire to kill them, Comrade Colonel."

"What do you mean?"

"Your friend Major Vinh is dead, but we have his dispatches. I guess you were finished talking to our people, right? And the NVA were trying to figure the most convenient way to eliminate them. Are you telling me you didn't know that?"

The oath Ritter heard was a particularly vile one, but the voice held genuine surprise that was interesting. This man was too injured to dissimulate well. He looked up at Greer.

"I've got some more reading to do. You want to keep this guy company?"

The one good thing that happened to Kelly that night was that Captain Franks hadn't tossed the aviator rations over the side after all. Finished with his debrief, he found his cabin and downed three stiff ones. With the release from the tension of the night, physical exhaustion assaulted the young man. The three drinks knocked him out, and he collapsed into his bunk without so much as a cleansing shower.

It was decided that *Ogden* would continue as planned, steaming at twenty knots back towards Subic Bay. The big amphibious ship became a quiet place. The crew, pumped up for an important and dramatic mission, became subdued with its failure. Watches were changed, the ship continued to function as before, but the mess rooms' only noise was that of the metal trays and utensils. No jokes, no stories. The additional medical personnel took it the hardest of all. With no one to treat and nothing to do, they just wandered about. Before noon the helicopters departed, the Cobras for Danang and the rescue birds back to their carrier. The signal-intelligence people switched over to more regular duties, searching the airways for radio messages, finding a new mission to replace the old.

Kelly didn't awaken until 1800 hours. After showering, he headed below to find the Marines. He owed them an explanation, he thought. Somebody did. They were in the same space. The sand-table model was still there as well.

"I was right up here," he said, finding the rubber band with two eyes on it.

"How many bad guys?"

"Four trucks, they came in this road, stopped here," Kelly explained. "They were digging in crew-served weapons here and here. They sent people up my hill. I saw another team heading this way right before I moved."

"Jesus," a squad leader noted. "Right on our approach route."

"Yeah," Kelly confirmed. "Anyway, that's why."

"How'd they know to send in the reinforcements?" a corporal asked.

"Not my department."

"Thanks, Snake," the squad leader said, looking from the model that would soon be tossed over the side. "Tough call, wasn't it?"

Kelly nodded. "I'm sorry, pal. Jesus God, I'm sorry."

"Mr. Clark, I got a baby due in two months. 'Cept for you, well . . ." The Marine extended his hand across the model.

"Thank you, sir." Kelly took it.

"Mr. Clark, sir?" A sailor stuck his head into the compartment. "The admirals are looking for you. Up in officer country, sir."

"Doctor Rosen," Sam said, lifting the phone.

"Hi, doctor. This is Sergeant Douglas."

"What can I do for you?"

"We're trying to track down your friend Kelly. He isn't answering his phone. Do you have any idea where he is?"

"I haven't seen him in a long time," the surgeon said guardedly.

"You know anybody who has?"

"I'll check around. What's the story?" Sam added, asking what he knew might be a highly inconvenient question, wondering what sort of answer he might get.

"I, uh, can't say, sir. I hope you understand."

"Ummhmm. Yeah, okay, I'll ask."

"Feeling better?" Ritter asked first.

"Some," Kelly allowed. "What's the story on the Russian?"

"Clark, you just might have done something useful." Ritter gestured to a table with no fewer than ten piles of documents on them.

"They're planning to kill the prisoners," Greer said.

"Who? The Russians?" Kelly asked.

"The Vietnamese. The Russians want them alive. This guy you picked up is trying to take them home," Ritter said, lifting a sheet of paper. "Here's his draft of the letter justifying it."

"Is that good or bad?"

The outside noises were different, Zacharias thought. More of them, too. Shouts with purpose to them, though he didn't know what purpose. For the first day in a month, Grishanov hadn't visited him, even for a few minutes. The loneliness he felt became even more acute, and his only company was the realization that he'd given to the Soviet Union a graduate-level course in continental air-defense. He hadn't meant to do it. He hadn't even known what he was doing. That was no consolation, however. The Russian had played him for a fool, and Colonel Robin Zacharias, USAF, had just given it all up, outsmarted by some kindness and fellowship from an atheist . . . and drink. Stupidity and sin, such a likely combination of human weaknesses, and he'd done it all.

He didn't even have tears for his shame. He was beyond that, sitting on the floor of his cell, staring at the rough, dirty concrete between his bare feet. He'd broken faith with his God and his country, Zacharias told himself, as his evening meal was pushed through the slot at the bottom of his door. Thin, bodiless pumpkin soup and maggoty rice. He made no move towards it.

Grishanov knew he was a dead man. They wouldn't give him back. They couldn't even admit that they had him. He'd disappear, as other Russians in Vietnam had disappeared, some at SAM sites, some doing other things for those ungrateful little bastards. Why were they feeding him so well? It had to be a large ship, but it was also his first time at sea. Even the decent food was hard to get down, but he swore not to disgrace himself by succumbing to motion sickness mixed with fear. He was a fighter pilot, a good one who had faced death before, mainly at the controls of a malfunctioning aircraft. He remembered wondering at the time what they'd tell his Marina. He wondered now. A letter? What? Would his family be looked after by his fellow officers in PVO Strany? Would the pension be sufficient?

"Are you kidding me?"

"Mr. Clark, the world can be a very complicated place. Why did you think the Russians like them?"

"They give them weapons and training, don't they?"

Ritter stubbed out his Winston. "We give those things to people all over the world. They're not all nice folks, but we have to work with them. It's the same for the Russians, maybe less so, but still pretty much the same. Anyway, this Grishanov guy was going to a considerable effort to keep our people alive." Ritter held up another sheet. "Here's a request for better food—for a *doctor*, even."

"So what do we do with him?" Admiral Podulski asked.

"That, gentlemen, is our department," Ritter said, looking at Greer, who nodded.

"Wait a minute," Kelly objected. "He was pumping them for information."

"So?" Ritter asked. "That was his job."

"We're getting away from the real issue here," Maxwell said.

James Greer poured some coffee for himself. "I know. We have to move fast."

"And finally . . ." Ritter tapped a translation of the Vietnamese message. "We know that somebody burned the mission. We're going to track that bastard down."

Kelly was still too drugged from sleep to follow it all, much less see far enough into the future to realize how he had assumed his place in the center of the affair.

"Where's John?"

Sandy O'Toole looked up from her paperwork. It was close to the end of her shift, and Professor Rosen's question brought to the fore a worry that she'd managed to suppress for over a week.

"Out of the country. Why?"

"I got a call today from the police. They're looking for him."

Oh, God. "Why?"

"He didn't say." Rosen looked around. They were alone at the nurses' station. "Sandy, I know he's been doing things—I mean, I think I know, but I haven't—"

"I haven't heard from him, either. What are we supposed to do?"

Rosen grimaced and looked away before replying. "As good citizens, we're supposed to cooperate with the police—but we're not doing that, are we? No idea where he is?"

"He told me, but I'm not supposed to—he's doing something with the government... over in ..." She couldn't finish, couldn't bring herself to say the word. "He gave a number I can call. I haven't used it."

"I would," Sam told her, and left.

It wasn't right. He was off doing something scary and important, only to come back to a police investigation. It seemed to Nurse O'Toole that the unfairness of life had gotten as bad as it could. She was wrong.

"Pittsburgh?"

"That's what he said," Henry confirmed.

"It's cute, by the way, having him as your man on the inside. Very professional," Piaggi said with respect.

"He said we need to take care of it quick, like. She hasn't said much yet."

"She saw it all?" Piaggi didn't have to add that he didn't think that very professional at all. "Henry, keeping people in line is one thing. Making them into witnesses is another."

"Tony, I'm going to take care of that, but we need to handle this problem right quick, y'dig?" It seemed to Henry Tucker that he was in the stretch run, and over the finish line were both safety and prosperity. That five more people had to die to get him across that line was a small matter after the race he'd already run.

"Go on."

"The family name is Brown. Her name is Doris. Her father's name is Raymond."

"You sure of this?"

"The girls talk to each other. I got the street name and everything. You got connections. I need you to use 'em fast."

Piaggi copied down the information. "Okay. Our Philly connections can handle it. It's not going to be cheap, Henry."

"I didn't expect it would be."

* * *

The flight deck looked very empty. All four of the aircraft briefly assigned to *Ogden* were gone now, and the deck reassumed its former status as the ship's unofficial town square. The stars were the same as before, now that the ship was again under clear skies, and a sliver of a waning moon was high in the sky in these early hours. No sailors were out now, however. Those awake at this hour were on duty, but for Kelly and the Marines the day/night cycle was askew, and the gray steel walls of their spaces were too confining for the thoughts they had. The ship's wake was a curious luminescent green from the photoplankton stirred up by the ship's screws, and left a long trail showing where she'd been. Half a dozen men stood well aft, staring at it without words.

"It could have been a hell of a lot worse, you know." Kelly turned. It was Irvin. It had to be.

"Could have been a hell of a lot better, too, Guns."

"Wasn't no accident, them showing up like that, was it?"

"I don't think I'm supposed to say. Is that a good enough answer?"

"Yes, sir. And Lord Jesus said, 'Father, forgive them, for they know not what they do.' "

"And what if they do know?"

Irvin grunted. "I think you know what my vote is. Whoever it was, they could have killed all of us."

"You know, Guns, just once, *just one time,* I'd like to finish something the right way," Kelly said.

"Yeah." Irvin took a second before going on, and going back. "Why the hell would anybody do something like that?"

A shape loomed close. It was *Newport News,* a lovely silhouette only two thousand yards off, and visible in a spectral way despite the absence of lights. She, too, was heading back, the last of the Navy's big-gun cruisers, creature of a bygone age, returning home after the same failure that Kelly and Irvin knew.

"Seven-one-three-one," the female voice said.

"Hello, I'm trying to get Admiral James Greer," Sandy told the secretary.

"He's not in."

"Can you tell me when he'll be back?"

"Sorry, no, I don't know."

"But it's important."

"Could you tell me who's calling, please?"

"What is this place?"

"This is Admiral Greer's office."

"No, I mean, is it the Pentagon?"

"Don't you know?"

Sandy didn't know, and that question led her off in a direction she didn't understand. "Please, I need your help."

"Who's calling, please?"

"Please, I need to know where you are!"

"I can't tell you that," the secretary responded, feeling herself to be one of the fortress walls that protected U.S. National Security.

"Is this the Pentagon?"

Well, she could tell her that. "No, it isn't."

What then? Sandy wondered. She took a deep breath. "A friend of mine gave me this number to call. He's with Admiral Greer. He said I could call here to find out if he's okay."

"I don't understand."

"Look, I *know* he went to Vietnam!"

"Miss, I cannot discuss where Admiral Greer is." *Who violated security!* She'd have to make a report on this.

"It's not about him, it's about John!" *Calm down. You're not helping anyone this way.*

"John who?" the secretary asked.

Deep breath. Swallow. "Please get a message to Admiral Greer. This is Sandy. It's about John. He will understand. Okay? He will understand. This is most important." She gave her home and work numbers.

"Thank you. I will do what I can." The line went dead.

Sandy wanted to scream, and nearly did so. So the Admiral had gone, too. Okay, he'd be close to where John is. The secretary would get the message through. She would have to. People like that, if you said *most important,* didn't have the imagination not to do it. Settle down. Anyway, where he was, the police couldn't get him either. But for the rest of the day, and into the next, the second hand on her watch seemed to stand still.

USS *Ogden* pulled into Subic Bay Naval Station in the early afternoon. Coming alongside seemed to take forever in the moist tropical heat. Finally lines were tossed and a brow advanced to the ship's side. A civilian sprinted up first even before it was properly secured. Soon thereafter the Marines filed off to a bus which would take them to Cubi Point. The deck division watched them walk off. A few hands were shaken as everyone tried to leave at least one good memory from the experience, but "good try" just didn't make it, and "good luck" seemed blasphemous. Their C-141 was waiting there for the flight stateside. Mr. Clark, they saw, wasn't with them.

"John, it seems you have a lady friend who's worried about you," Greer said, handing the message over. It was the friendliest of the dispatches that the junior CIA officer had brought up from Manila. Kelly scanned it while three admirals reviewed the others.

"Do I have time to call her, sir? She's worried about me."

"You left her my office number?" Greer was slighted vexed.

"Her husband was killed with the First Cav, sir. She worries," Kelly explained.

"Okay." Greer put his own troubles aside for the moment. "I'll have Barbara tell her you're safe."

The rest of the messages were less welcome. Admirals Maxwell and Podulski were being summoned back to Washington soonest to report on the failure of Boxwood Green. Ritter and Greer had similar orders, though they also had an ace in the hole. Their KC-135 was waiting at Clark Air Force Base. A puddle jumper would hop over the mountains. The best news at the moment was their disrupted sleep cycle. The flight back to the American East Coast would bring them back in just the right way.

Colonel Grishanov came into the sunlight along with the admirals. He was wearing clothing borrowed from Captain Franks—they were of approximately the same size—and escorted by Maxwell and Podulski. Kolya was under no illusions of his chance to escape anywhere, not on an American naval base located on the soil of an American ally. Ritter was talking to him quietly, in Russian, as all six men walked down to the waiting cars. Ten minutes later, they climbed into an Air Force C-12 twin-prop Beechcraft. Half an hour later that aircraft taxied right alongside the larger Boeing jet, which got off less than an hour after they'd left *Ogden*. Kelly found himself a nice wide seat and strapped himself in, asleep before the windowless transport started rolling. The next stop, they'd told him, was Hickam in Hawaii, and he didn't plan to be awake for any of that.

31

Home Is the Hunter

The flight wasn't as restful for the others. Greer had managed to get a couple of messages taken care of before the takeoff, but he and Ritter were the busiest. Their aircraft—the Air Force had lent it to them for the mission, no questions asked—was a semi-VIP bird belonging to Andrews Air Force Base, and was often used for Congressional junkets. That meant an ample supply of liquor, and while they drank straight coffee, their Russian guest's cups were laced with brandy, a little at first, then in increasing doses that his decaffeinated brew didn't begin to attenuate.

Ritter handled most of the interrogation. His first task was to explain to Grishanov that they had no plans to kill him. Yes, they were CIA. Yes, Ritter was a field officer—a spy, if you like—with ample experience behind the Iron Curtain—excuse me, working as a slinking spy in the peace-loving Socialist East Bloc—but that was his job, as Kolya—do you mind if I call you Kolya?—had *his* job. Now, please, Colonel, can you give us the names of our men? (That was already listed in Grishanov's voluminous notes.) Your friends, you say? Yes, we are very grateful indeed for your efforts to keep them alive. They all have families, you know, just like you do. More coffee, Colonel? Yes, it is good coffee, isn't it? Of *course* you'll go home to your family. What do you think we are, barbarians? Grishanov had the good manners not to answer that one

Damn, Greer thought, *but Bob is good at this sort of thing.* It wasn't about courage or patriotism. It was about humanity. Grishanov was a tough hombre, probably a hell of a good airplane-driver—what a shame they couldn't let Maxwell or especially Podulski in on this!—but he was at bottom a man, and the quality of his character worked against him. He didn't want the American prisoners to die. That plus the stress of capture, plus the whiplash surprise of the cordial treatment, plus a lot of good brandy, all conspired to loosen his tongue. It helped a lot more that Ritter didn't even approach matters of grave concern to the Soviet state. *Hell, Colonel, I know you're not going to give up any secrets—so why ask?*

"Your man killed Vinh, did he?" the Russian asked halfway across the Pacific.

"Yes, he did. It was an accident and—" The Russian cut Ritter off with a wave.

"Good. He was *nekulturny,* a vicious little fascist bastard. He wants to kill those men, murder them," Kolya added with the aid of six brandies.

"Well, Colonel, we're hoping to find a way to prevent that."

"Neurosurgery West," the nurse said.

"Trying to get Sandra O'Toole."

"Hold on, please. Sandy?" The nurse on desk duty held the phone up. The nursing-team leader took it.

"This is O'Toole."

"Miss O'Toole, this is Barbara—we spoke earlier. Admiral Greer's office?"

"Yes!"

"Admiral Greer told me to let you know—John is okay and he's now on his way home."

Sandy's head spun around, to look in a direction where there were no eyes to see the sudden tears of relief. A mixed blessing perhaps, but a blessing still. "Can you tell me when?"

"Sometime tomorrow, that's all I know."

"Thank you."

"Surely." The line went immediately dead.

Well, that's something—maybe a lot. She wondered what would happen when he got here, but at least he was coming back alive. More than Tim had managed to do.

The hard landing at Hickam—the pilot was tired—startled Kelly into wakefulness. An Air Force sergeant gave him a friendly shake to make sure as the aircraft taxied to a remote part of the base for refueling and servicing. Kelly took the time to get out and walk around. The climate was warm here, but not the oppressive heat of Vietnam. It was American soil, and things were different here. . . .

Sure they are.

Just once, just one time . . . he remembered saying. *Yes, I'm going to get those other girls out just like I got Doris out. It shouldn't be all that hard. I'll get Burt next and we'll talk. I'll even let the bastard go when I'm done, probably. I can't save the whole world, but . . . by Jesus, I'll save some of it!*

He found a phone in the Distinguished Visitors lounge and placed a call.

"Hello?" the groggy voice said, five thousand miles away.

"Hi, Sandy. It's John!" he said with a smile. Even if those aviators weren't coming home just yet—well, he was, and he was grateful for that.

"John! Where are you?"

"Would you believe Hawaii?"

"You're okay?"

"A little tired, but, yes. No holes or anything," he reported with a smile. Just the sound of her voice had brightened his day. But not for long.

"John, there's a problem."

The sergeant at the reception desk saw the DV's face change. Then he turned back into the phone booth and became less interesting.

"Okay. It must be Doris," Kelly said. "I mean, only you and the docs know about me, and—"

"It wasn't us," Sandy assured him.

"Okay. Please call Doris and . . . be careful, but—"

"Warn her off?"

"Can you do that?"

"Yes!"

Kelly tried to relax a little, almost succeeding. "I'll be back in about . . . oh, nine or ten hours. Will you be at work?"

"I have the day off."

"Okay, Sandy. See you soon. 'Bye."

"John!" she called urgently.

"What?"

"I want . . . I mean . . ." her voice stopped.

Kelly smiled again. "We can talk about that when I get there, honey." Maybe he wasn't just going home. Maybe he was going home *to* something. Kelly made a quick inventory of everything he'd done. He still had his converted pistol and other weapons on the boat, but everything he'd worn on every job: shoes, socks, outer clothing, even underwear, were now in whatever trash dump. He'd left behind no evidence that he knew of. The police might be interested in talking to him, fine. He did *not* have to talk to them.

That was one of the nice things about the Constitution, Kelly thought as he walked back to the aircraft and trotted up the stairs.

One flight crew found the beds just aft of the flight deck while the relief crew started engines. Kelly sat with the CIA officers. The Russian, he saw, was snoring loudly and blissfully.

Ritter chuckled. "He's going to have one hell of a hangover."

"What'd you get into him?"

"Started off with good brandy. Ended up with California stuff. Brandy really messes me up the next day," Ritter said tiredly as the KC-135 started rolling. He was drinking a martini now that his prisoner was no longer able to answer questions.

"So what's the story?" Kelly asked.

Ritter explained what he knew. The camp had indeed been established as a bargaining chip for use with the Russians, but it seemed that the Vietnamese had used that particular chip in a rather inefficient way and were now thinking about eliminating it along with the prisoners.

"You mean because of the raid?" *Oh, God!*

"Correct. But settle down, Clark. We got us a Russian, and that's a bargaining chip too. Mr. Clark," Ritter said with a tight smile, "I like your style."

"What do you mean?"

"Bringing that Russian in, you showed commendable initiative. And the way you blew the mission off, that showed good judgment."

"Look, I didn't—I mean, I couldn't—"

"You didn't screw up. Somebody else might have. You made a quick decision, and it was the right decision. Interested in serving your country?" Ritter asked with an alcohol-aided smile of his own.

Sandy awoke at six-thirty, which was late for her. She got her morning paper, started the coffee, and decided to stick to toast for breakfast, watching the kitchen-wall clock and wondering how early she might call Pittsburgh.

The lead story on the front page was the drug shooting. A police officer had gotten himself in a gunfight with a drug dealer. Well, good, she thought. Six kilograms of "pure" heroin, the news piece said—that was a lot. She wondered if this was the same bunch that . . . no, the leader of that group was black, at least Doris had said so. Anyway, another druggie had left the face of the planet. Another look at the clock. Still too early for a civilized call. She went into the living room to switch on the TV. It was already a hot, lazy day. She'd been up late the night before and had difficulty getting back to sleep after John's call. She tried to watch the "Today Show" and didn't quite notice that her eyes were growing heavy. . . .

It was after ten when her eyes opened back up. Angry with herself, she shook her head clear and went back to the kitchen. Doris's number was pinned next to the phone. She called, and heard the phone ring . . . four—six—ten times, without an answer. Damn. Out shopping? Off to see Dr. Bryant? She'd try again in an hour. In the meantime she'd try to figure out exactly what she would say. Might this be a crime? Was she obstructing justice? How deeply was she involved in this business? The thought came as an unpleasant surprise. But she was involved. She'd helped rescue this girl from a dangerous life, and she couldn't stop now. She'd just tell Doris not to hurt the people who had helped her, to be very, very careful. Please.

Reverend Meyer came late. He'd been held up by a phone call at the parsonage and was in a profession where one couldn't say that he had to leave for an appointment. As he parked, he noticed a flower-delivery truck heading up the hill. It turned right, disappearing from view as he took the parking place it had occupied a few doors up from the Brown house. He was a little worried as he locked his car. He had to persuade Doris to speak with his son. Peter had assured him that they'd be extremely careful. Yes, Pop, we can protect her. Now all he had to do was to get that message across to a frightened young woman and a father whose love had survived the most rigorous of tests. Well, he'd handled more delicate problems than this, the minister told himself. Like shortstopping a few divorces. Negotiating treaties between nations could not be harder than saving a rocky marriage.

Even so, the way up to the front porch seemed awfully steep, Meyer thought, holding the rail as he climbed up the chipped and worn concrete steps. There were a few buckets of paint on the porch. Perhaps Raymond was going to do his house now that it contained a family again. A good sign, Pastor Meyer thought as he pushed the button. He could hear the doorbell's two-tone chime. Raymond's white Ford was parked right here. He knew they were home . . . but no one came to the door. Well, maybe someone was dressing or in the bathroom, as often happened to everyone's embarrassment. He waited another minute or so, frowning as he pushed the button again. He was slow to note that the door wasn't quite closed all the way. *You are a minister,* he told himself, *not a burglar.* With a small degree of uneasiness, he pushed it open and stuck his head inside.

"Hello? Raymond? . . . Doris?" he called, loudly enough to be heard anywhere in the house. The TV was on, some mindless game show playing on the living-room set. "Hellooooo!"

This was odd. He stepped inside, somewhat embarrassed with himself for doing so, wondering what the problem was. There was a cigarette burning in an ashtray here, almost down to the filter, and the vertical trail of smoke was a clear warning that something was amiss. An ordinary citizen possessed of his intelligence would have withdrawn then, but Reverend Meyer was not ordinary. He saw a box of flowers on the rug, opened, long-stem roses inside. Roses were not made to lie on the floor. He remembered his military service just then, how unpleasant it had been, but how uplifting to attend the needs of men in the face of death—he wondered why that thought had sprung so clearly into his mind; its sudden relevance started his heart racing. Meyer walked through the living room, quiet now, listening. He found the kitchen empty too, a pot of water coming to boil on the stove, cups and tea bags on the kitchen table. The basement door was open as well, the light on. He couldn't stop now. He opened the door all the way and started down. He was halfway to the bottom when he saw their legs.

Father and daughter were facedown on the bare concrete floor, and the blood from their head wounds had pooled together on the uneven surface. The horror was immediate and overwhelming. His mouth dropped open with a sudden intake of breath as he looked down at two parishioners whose funeral he would officiate in two days' time. They were holding hands, he saw, father and daughter. They'd died together, but the consolation that this tragically afflicted family was now united with their God could not stop a scream of fury at those who had been in this home only ten minutes earlier. Meyer recovered after a few seconds, continued down the stairs and knelt, reaching down to touch the intertwined hands and entreating God to have mercy on their souls. Of that he had confidence. Perhaps she'd lost her life, but not her soul, Meyer would say over the bodies, and her father had reclaimed his daughter's love. He'd let his parishioners know that both had been saved, Meyer promised himself. Then it was time to call his son.

The stolen flower truck was left in a supermarket parking lot. Two men got out and walked into the store, just to be careful, and out the back door, where their car was parked. They drove southeast onto the Pennsylvania Turnpike for the three-hour trip back to Philadelphia. Maybe longer, the driver thought. They didn't want a state cop to stop them. Both men were ten thousand dollars richer. They didn't know the story. They had no need to know.

*   *   *

"Hello?"

"Mr. Brown?"

"No. Who's this?"

"This is Sandy. Is Mr. Brown there?"

"How do you know the Brown family?"

"Who is this?" Sandy asked, looking out her kitchen window with alarm.

"This is Sergeant Peter Meyer, Pittsburgh Police Department. Now, who are you?"

"I'm the one who drove Doris back—what's the matter?"

"Your name, please?"

"Are they okay?"

"They appear to have been murdered," Meyer replied in a harshly patient way. "Now, I need to know your name and—"

Sandy brought her finger down on the switch, cutting the circuit before she could hear more. To hear more might force her to answer questions. Her legs were shaking, but there was a chair close by. Her eyes were wide. It wasn't possible, she told herself. How could anyone know where she was? Surely she hadn't called the people who—no, not possible, the nurse thought.

"Why?" she whispered the question aloud. "Why, why, why?" *She couldn't hurt anyone—yes, she could . . . but how did they find out?*

They have the police infiltrated. She remembered the words from John's mouth. He was right, wasn't he?

But that was a side issue.

"Damn it, we saved her!" Sandy told the kitchen. Sandy could remember every minute of that nearly sleepless first week, and then the progress, the elation, the purest and best kind of professional satisfaction for a job well done, the joy of seeing the look in her dad's face. Gone. A waste of her time.

No.

Not a waste of time. That was her task in life, to make sick people well. She'd done that. She was proud of that. It was not wasted time. It was stolen time. Stolen time, two stolen lives. She started crying and had to go to the downstairs bathroom, grabbing tissue to wipe her eyes. Then she looked in the mirror, seeing eyes that she'd never beheld before. And seeing that, she truly understood.

Disease was a dragon that she fought forty hours or more per week. A skilled nurse and teacher who worked well with the surgeons on her unit, Sandra O'Toole fought those dragons in her way, with professionalism and kindness and intelligence, more often winning than losing. And every year things got better. Progress was never fast enough, but it was real and could be measured, and perhaps she'd live long enough to see the last dragon on her unit die once and for all.

But there was more than one kind of dragon, wasn't there? Some couldn't be killed with kindness and medications and skilled nursing care. She'd defeated one, but another had killed Doris anyway. *That* dragon needed the sword, in the hands of a warrior. The sword was a tool, wasn't it? A necessary tool, if you wanted to slay that particular dragon. Perhaps it was one she could never use herself, but necessary nonetheless. Someone had to hold that sword. John wasn't a bad man at all, just realistic.

She fought her dragons. He fought his. *It was the same fight.* She'd been wrong to judge him. Now she understood, seeing in her eyes the same emotion that she'd beheld months earlier in his, as her rage passed, but not very far, and the determination set in.

"Well, everybody lucked out," Hicks said, handing over a beer.

"How so, Wally?" Peter Henderson asked.

"The mission was a washout. It aborted just in time. Didn't even get anyone hurt in the process, thank God. Everyone's flying home right now."

"Good news, Wally!" Henderson said, meaning it. He didn't want to kill anybody either. He just wanted the damned war to end, the same as Wally did. It was a shame about the men in that camp, but some things couldn't be helped. "What happened exactly?"

"Nobody knows yet. You want me to find out?"

Peter nodded. "Carefully. It's something the Intelligence Committee ought to know about, when the Agency fucks up like that. I can get the information to them. But you have to be careful."

"No problem. I'm learning how to stroke Roger." Hicks lit up his first joint of the evening, annoying his guest.

"You could lose your clearance that way, you know?"

"Well, gee, then I'll have to join Dad and make a few mill' on The Street, eh?"

"Wally, do you want to change the system or do you want to let other people keep it the same?"

Hicks nodded. "Yeah, I suppose."

The following winds had allowed the KC-135 to make the hop in from Hawaii without a refueling stop, and the landing was a gentle one. Remarkably, Kelly's sleep cycle was about right now. It was five in the afternoon, and in another six or seven hours he'd be ready for more sleep.

"Can I get a day or two off?"

"We'll want you back to Quantico for an extended debrief," Ritter told him, stiff and sore from the extended flight.

"Fine, just so I'm not in custody or anything. I could use a lift up to Baltimore."

"I'll see what I can do," Greer said as the plane came to a halt.

Two security officers from the Agency were the first up the mobile stairs, even before the oversized cargo hatch swung up. Ritter woke the Russian up.

"Welcome to Washington."

"Take me to my embassy?" he asked hopefully. Ritter almost laughed.

"Not quite yet. We'll find you a nice, comfortable place, though."

Grishanov was too groggy to object, rubbing his head and needing something for the pain. He went with the security officers, down the steps to their waiting car. It left at once for a safe house near Winchester, Virginia.

"Thanks for the try, John," Admiral Maxwell said, taking the younger man's hand.

"I'm sorry for what I said before," Cas said, doing the same. "You were right." They, too, had a car waiting. Kelly watched them enter it from the hatch.

"So what happens to them?" he asked Greer.

James shrugged, leading Kelly out and down the stairs. Noise from other aircraft made his voice hard to hear. "Dutch was in line for a fleet, and maybe the CNO's job. I don't suppose that'll happen now. The operation—well, it was his baby, and it didn't get born. That'll finish him."

"That's not fair," Kelly said loudly. Greer turned.

"No, it isn't, but that's the way things are." Greer, too, had a ride waiting. He directed his driver to head to the wing-headquarters building, where he arranged a car to take Kelly to Baltimore. "Get some rest and call me when you're ready. Bob was serious about what he said. Think it over."

"Yes, sir," Kelly replied, heading to the blue Air Force sedan.

It was amazing, Kelly thought, the way life was. Within five minutes the sergeant drove onto an interstate highway. Scarcely twenty-four hours earlier he'd been on a ship approaching Subic Bay. Thirty-six hours prior to that he'd been on the soil of an enemy country—and now here he was in the backseat of a government Chevy, and the only dangers to which he was exposed came from other drivers. At least for a little while. All the familiar things, the highway exit signs painted that pleasant shade of green, traveling in the last half of the local rush hour. Everything about him proclaimed the normality of life, when three days earlier everything had been alien and hostile. Most amazing of all, he'd adjusted to it.

The driver didn't speak a word except to inquire about directions, though he must have wondered who the man was that had arrived on a special flight. Perhaps he had many such jobs, Kelly mused as the car pulled off Loch Raven Boulevard, enough that he'd stopped wondering about things he'd never be told.

"Thanks for the lift," Kelly told him.

"Yes, sir, you're welcome." The car pulled away and Kelly walked to his apartment, amused that he'd taken his keys all the way to Vietnam and back. Did the keys know how far they had come? Five minutes later he was in the shower, the quintessentially American experience, changing from one reality into another. Another five and he was dressed in slacks and a short-sleeve shirt, and headed out the door to his Scout, parked a block away. Another ten and he'd parked the car within sight of Sandy's bungalow. The walk from his Scout to her door was yet another transition. He'd come home to something, Kelly told himself. For the first time.

"John!" He hadn't expected the hug. Even less so the tears in her eyes.

"It's okay, Sandy. I'm fine. No holes or scratches or anything." He was slow to grasp the desperation of her hold on him, pleasant as it was. But then the face against his chest started sobbing, and he knew that this event was not for him at all. "What's wrong?"

"They killed Doris."

Time stopped again. It seemed to split into many pieces. Kelly closed his eyes, in pain at first, and in that instant he was back on his hilltop over-looking SENDER GREEN, watching the NVA troops arrive; he was in his hospital bed looking at a photograph; he was outside some nameless village listening to the screams of children. He'd come home, all right, but to the same thing he'd left. No, he realized, to the thing that he had never left, which followed him everywhere he went. He'd never get away from it be-cause he'd never really finished it, not even once. *Not even once.*

And yet there was a new element as well, this woman holding him and feeling the same blazing pain that sliced through his chest.

"What happened, Sandy?"

"We got her well, John. We took her home, and then I called today like you told me to, and a policeman answered. Doris and her father, too, both murdered."

"Okay." He moved her to the sofa. He wanted at first to let her calm down, not to hold her too close, but that didn't work. She clung to him, letting out the feelings that she'd closeted off, along with worry for his safety, and he held Sandy's head to his shoulder for several minutes. "Sam and Sarah?"

"I haven't told them yet." Her face came up, and she looked across the room, her gaze unfocused. Then the nurse in her came out, as it had to. "How are you?"

"A little frazzled from all the traveling," he said, just to put words after her question. Then he had to tell the truth. "It was a washout. The mission didn't work. They're still there."

"I don't understand."

"We were trying to get some people out of North Vietnam, prisoners— but something went wrong. Failed again," he added quietly.

"Was it dangerous?"

Kelly managed a grunt. "Yeah, Sandy, you might say that, but I came out okay."

Sandy set that one aside. "Doris said there were others, other girls, they still have 'em."

"Yeah. Billy said the same thing. I'm going to try and get them out." Kelly noticed she didn't react to his mention of Billy's name.

"It won't matter—getting them out, unless . . ."

"I know." The thing that kept following him around, Kelly thought. There was only one way to make it stop. Running couldn't distance him from it. He had to turn and face it.

"Well, Henry, that little job was taken care of this morning," Piaggi told him. "Nice and clean."

"They didn't leave—"

"Henry, they were two pros, okay? They did the job and now they're back home, couple hundred miles away. They didn't leave anything behind except for the two bodies." The phone report had been very clear on that. It had been an easy job, since neither target had expected anything.

"Then that's that," Tucker observed with satisfaction. He reached into his pocket and pulled out a fat envelope. He handed it to Piaggi, who had fronted the money himself, good partner that he was.

"With Eddie out of the way, and with that leak plugged, things ought to go back to normal." *Best twenty grand I ever spent,* Henry thought.

"Henry, the other girls?" Piaggi pointed out. "You've got a real business now. People inside like them are dangerous. Take care of it, okay?" He pocketed the envelope and left the table.

*   *   *

''Twenty-two's, back of the head, both of 'em,'' the Pittsburgh detective reported over the phone. ''We've dusted the whole house—nothing. The flower box—nothing. The truck—nothing. The truck was stolen sometime last night—this morning, whatever. The florist has eight of them. Hell, we recovered it before the all-points was on the air. It was wise guys, had to be. Too smooth, too clean for local talent. No word on the street. They're probably out of town already. Two people saw the truck. One woman saw two guys walking to the door. She figured it was a flower delivery, and besides she was across the street half a block away. No description, nothing. She doesn't even remember what color they were.''

Ryan and Douglas were listening on the same line, and their eyes met every few seconds. They knew it all from the tone of the man's voice. The sort of case that policemen hate and fear. No immediately apparent motive, no witnesses, no usable evidence. Nowhere to start and nowhere to go. The routine was as predictable as it was futile. They'd pump the neighbors for information, but it was a working-class neighborhood, and few had been at home at the time. People noticed mainly the unusual, and a flower truck wasn't unusual enough to attract the inquiring look that developed into a physical description. Committing the perfect murder wasn't really all that demanding, a secret known within the fraternity of detectives and belied by a whole body of literature that made them into superhuman beings they never claimed to be, even among themselves in a cop bar. Someday the case might be broken. One of the killers might be caught for something else and cop to this one in order to get a deal. Less likely, someone would talk about it, bragging in front of an informant who'd pass it along to someone else, but in either case it would take time and the trail, cold as it already was, would grow colder still. It was the most frustrating part of the business of police work. Truly innocent people had died, and there was no one to speak for them, to avenge their deaths, and other cases would come up, and the cops would set this one aside for something fresher, and from time to time someone would reopen the file and look things over, then put it back in the *Unsolved* drawer, where it would grow thicker only because of the forms that announced that there was still nothing new on the case.

It was even worse for Ryan and Douglas. Yet again there had been a possible link that might open up two of their *Unsolved* files. Everyone would care about Raymond and Doris Brown. They'd had friends and neighbors, evidently a good minister. They'd be missed, and people would think *what a shame it was* ... But the files on Ryan's desk were for people about whom no one but police officers cared, and somehow that only made it worse because someone should mourn for the dead, not just cops who were paid to do so. Worse still, it was yet another MO in a string of homicides that were somehow linked, but not in a way that made any sense. This was not their Invisible Man. Yes, the weapon had been a .22, but he'd had a chance to kill the innocent twice. He'd spared Virginia Charles, and he had somehow gone dangerously far out of his way to spare Doris Brown. He had saved her from Farmer and Grayson, probably, and someone else. . . .

"Detective," Ryan asked, "what was the condition of Doris's body?"

"What do you mean?"

It seemed an absurd question even as his mind formed it, but the man on the other end of the line would understand. "What was her physical condition?"

"The autopsy is tomorrow, Lieutenant. She was neatly dressed, all cleaned up, hair was nice, she looked pretty decent." *Except for the two holes in the back of her head,* the man didn't have to add.

Douglas read his lieutenant's mind and nodded. *Somebody took the time to get her well.* That was a starting place.

"I'd appreciate it if you could send me anything that might be useful. It'll work both ways," Ryan assured him.

"Some guy went way out of his way to murder them. We don't see many like this. I don't like it very much," the detective added. It was a puerile conclusion, but Ryan fully understood. How else did you say it, after all?

It was called a safe house, and it was indeed safe. Located on a hundred rolling acres in the Virginia hills, there was on the estate a stately house and a twelve-stall stable half-occupied with hunter-jumpers. The title for the house showed a name, but that person owned another place nearby and leased this one to the Central Intelligence Agency—actually to a shadow corporation that existed only as a piece of paper and a post-office box— because he'd served his time in OSS, and besides, the money was right. Nothing unusual from the outside, but a more careful inspection might show that the doors and doorframes were steel, the windows unusually thick and strong, and sealed. It was as secure from outside assault and from an internal attempt at escape as a maximum-security prison, just a lot more pleasant to behold.

Grishanov found clothing to wear, and shaving things that worked but with which he couldn't harm himself. The bathroom mirror was steel, and the cup in the holder was paper. The couple that managed the house spoke passable Russian and were just as pleasant as they could be, already briefed on the nature of their new guest—they were more accustomed to defectors, though all their visitors were "protected" by a team of four security guards inside who came when they had "company," and two more who lived full-time in the caretaker's house close to the stables.

Not unusually, their guest was out of synch with local time, and his disorientation and unease made him talkative. They were surprised that their orders were to limit their conversations to the mundane. The lady of the house fixed breakfast, always the best meal for the jet-lagged, while her husband launched a discussion of Pushkin, delighted to find that like many Russians, Grishanov was a serious devotee of poetry. The security guard leaned against the doorframe, just to keep an eye on things.

"The things I have to do, Sandy—"

"John, I understand," she told him quietly. Both were surprised at how strong her voice was, how determined. "I didn't before, but I do now."

"When I was over there"—was it only three days before?—"I thought about you. I need to thank you," he told her.

"What for?"

Kelly looked down at the kitchen table. "Hard to explain. It's scary, the things I do. It helps when you have somebody to think about. Excuse me—I don't mean—" Kelly stopped. He did, actually, mean that. The mind wanders when alone, and his had wandered.

Sandy took his hand and smiled in a gentle way. "I used to be afraid of you."

"Why?" he asked with considerable surprise.

"Because of the things you do."

"I'd never hurt you," he said without looking up, yet more miserable now that she had felt the need to fear him.

"I know that now."

Despite her words, Kelly felt a need to explain himself. He wanted her to understand, not realizing that she already did. How to do it? Yes, he killed people, but only for a reason. How had he come to be what he was? Training was part of it, the rigorous months spent at Coronado, the time and effort spent to inculcate automatic responses, more deadly still, to learn patience. Along with that had somehow come a new way of seeing things—and then, actually seeing them and seeing the reasons why killing sometimes had to be. Along with the reasons had come a code, a modification, really, of what he'd learned from his father. His actions had to have a purpose, usually assigned by others, but his mind was agile enough to make its own decisions, to fit his code into a different context, to apply it with care—but to apply it.

A product of many things, he sometimes surprised himself with what he was. Someone had to try, and he most often was best suited to—

"You love too much, John," she said. "You're like me."

Those words brought his head up.

"We lose patients on my floor, we lose them all the time—and I *hate* it! I hate being there when life goes away. I *hate* watching the family cry and knowing that we couldn't stop it from happening. We all do our best. Professor Rosen is a wonderful surgeon, but we don't always win, and I hate it when we lose. And with Doris—we won that one, John, and somebody took her away anyway. And that wasn't disease or some damned auto accident. Somebody meant to do it. She was one of *mine,* and somebody killed her and her father. So I do understand, okay? I really do."

Jesus, she really does . . . better than me.

"Everybody connected with Pam and Doris, you're all in danger now."

Sandy nodded. "You're probably right. She told us things about Henry. I know what kind of person he is. I'll tell you everything she told us."

"You do understand what I'm going to do with that information?"

"Yes, John, I do. Please be careful." She paused and told him why he had to be. "I want you back."

32

Home Is the Prey

The one bit of usable information to come out of Pittsburgh was a name. *Sandy.* Sandy had driven Doris Brown back home to her father. Just one word, not even a proper name, but cases routinely broke on less than that. It was like pulling on a string. Sometimes all you got was a broken piece of thread, sometimes you got something that just didn't stop until everything unraveled into a tangled mess in your hands. Somebody named Sandy, a female voice, young. She'd hung up before saying anything, though it hardly seemed likely that she'd had anything at all to do with the murders. One might return to the scene of the crime—it really did happen—but not via telephone.

How did it fit in? Ryan leaned back in his chair, staring at the ceiling while his trained mind examined everything he knew.

The most likely supposition was that Doris Brown, deceased, had been directly connected with the same criminal enterprise that had killed Pamela Madden and Helen Waters, and that had also included as active members Richard Farmer and William Grayson. John Terrence Kelly, former UDT sailor, and perhaps a former Navy SEAL, had somehow happened upon and rescued Pamela Madden. He'd called Frank Allen about it several weeks later, telling him not very much. Something had gone badly wrong—short version, he'd been an ass—and Pamela Madden had died as a result. The photos of the body were something Ryan would never fully put from his mind. Kelly had been badly shot. A former commando whose girlfriend had been brutally murdered, Ryan reminded himself. Five pushers eliminated as though James Bond had appeared on the streets of Baltimore. One extraneous killing in which the murderer had intervened in a street robbery for reasons unknown. Richard Farmer—''Rick''?—eliminated with a knife, the second possible show of rage (and the first one didn't count, Ryan reminded himself). William Grayson, probably kidnapped and killed. Doris Brown, probably rescued at the same time, cleaned up over a period of weeks and returned to her home. That meant some sort of medical care, didn't it? Probably. *Maybe,* he corrected himself. The Invisible Man . . . could he have done that himself? Doris was the girl who'd brushed out Pamela Madden's hair. There was a connection.

Back up.

Kelly had rescued the Madden girl, but he'd had help getting her straightened out. Professor Sam Rosen and his wife, another physician. So Kelly finds Doris Brown—whom would he take her to? *That* was a starting place! Ryan lifted his phone.

"Hello."

"Doc, it's Lieutenant Ryan."

"I didn't know I gave you my direct line," Farber said. "What's up?"

"Do you know Sam Rosen?"

"Professor Rosen? Sure. He runs a department, hell of a good cutter, world-class. I don't see him very often, but if you ever need a head worked on, he's the man."

"And his wife?" Ryan could hear the man sucking on his pipe.

"I know her quite well. Sarah. She's a pharmacologist, research fellow across the street, also works with our drug-abuse unit. I help out with that group, too, and we—''

"Thank you." Ryan cut him off. "One more name. Sandy."

"Sandy who?"

"That's all I have," Lieutenant Ryan admitted. He could imagine Farber now, leaning away from his desk in the high-backed leather chair with his contemplative look.

"Let me make sure I understand things, okay? Are you asking me to check up on two colleagues as part of a criminal investigation?"

Ryan weighed the merits of lying. This guy was a psychiatrist. His job was looking around in people's minds. He was good at it.

"Yes, doctor, I am," the detective admitted after a pause long enough for the psychiatrist to make an accurate guess as to its cause.

"You're going to have to explain yourself," Farber announced evenly. "Sam and I aren't exactly close, but he is not a person who would *ever* hurt another human being. And Sarah is a damned angel with these messed-up kids we see in here. She's setting aside some important research work to do that, stuff she could make a big reputation with.'' Then Farber realized that she'd been away an awful lot in the past couple of weeks.

"Doctor, I'm just trying to develop some information, okay? I have no reason whatever to believe that either one of them is implicated in any illegal act.'' His words were too formal, and he knew it. Perhaps another tack. It was even honest, maybe. "If my speculation is correct, there may be some danger to them that they don't know about.''

"Give me a few minutes.'' Farber broke the connection.

"Not bad, Em,'' Douglas said.

It was bottom-fishing, Ryan thought, but, hell, he'd tried just about everything else. It seemed an awfully long five minutes before the phone rang again.

"Ryan.''

"Farber. No docs on neuro by that name. One nurse, though, Sandra O'Toole. She's a team leader on the service. I don't know her myself. Sam thinks highly of her, or so I just found out from his secretary. She was working something special for him, recently. He had to fiddle the pay records.'' Farber had already made his own connection. Sarah had been absent from her clinical work at the same time. He'd let the police develop that themselves. He'd gone far enough—too far. These were colleagues, after all, and this wasn't a game.

"When was that?'' Ryan asked casually.

"Two or three weeks ago, lasted ten working days.''

"Thank you, doctor. I'll be back to you.''

"Connection,'' Douglas observed after the circuit was broken. "How much you want to bet that she knows Kelly, too?''

The question was more hopeful than substantive, of course. Sandra was a common-enough name. Still, they'd been on this case, this endless series of deaths, for more than six months, and after all that time spent with no evidence and no connections at all, it looked like the morning star. The problem was that it was evening now, and time to go home for dinner with his wife and children. Jack would be returning to Boston College in another week or so, Ryan thought, and he missed time with his son.

There was no easy way to get things organized. Sandy had to drive him to Quantico. It was her first time on a Marine base, but only briefly, as Kelly guided her to the marina. Already, he thought. You get home for once with your body in tune with the local day/night cycle, and already he had to break it. Sandy was not yet back on I-95 when he pulled away from the dock, heading out for the middle of the river, advancing his throttles to max-cruise as soon as he could.

The lady had brains to go with her guts, Kelly told himself, sipping his first beer in a very long time. He supposed it was normal that a clinical nurse would have a good memory. Henry, it seemed, had been a talker at certain moments, one of them being when he had a girl under his direct control. A boastful man, Kelly thought, the best sort. He still didn't have an address to go along with the phone number, but he had a new name, Tony P-something—Peegee, something like that. White, Italian, drove a blue Lincoln, along with a decent physical description. Mafia, probably, either in it or a wannabe. Somebody else named Eddie—but Sandy had matched that name with a guy who had been killed by a police officer; it had made the front page of the local paper. Kelly took it one step further: what if that cop was the man Henry had inside? It struck him as odd that a senior officer like a lieutenant would be involved in a shooting. Speculation, he told himself, but worth checking out—he wasn't sure yet exactly how. He had all night for it, and a smooth body of water to reflect his thoughts as it did the stars. Soon he passed the spot where he'd left Billy. At least someone had collected the body.

The ground was settling over the grave in a place that some still called Potter's Field, a tradition dating back to someone named Judas. The doctors at the community hospital that had treated the man were still going over the pathology report from the Medical College of Virginia. Baro-Trauma. There were fewer than ten severe cases of this condition in the whole country in a year, and all of those in coastal regions. It was no disgrace that they hadn't made the diagnosis—and, the report went on, there was no difference it could have made. The precise cause of death had been a fragment of *bone marrow* that had somehow found its way into a cerebral artery, occluding it and causing a massive, fatal stroke. Damage to other organs had been so extensive that it would only have been a matter of a few more weeks in any case. The bone-marrow blockage was evidence of a very large pressurization imbalance, 3-Bar, probably more. Even now police were inquiring about divers in the Potomac, which could be very deep in some places. There was still hope that someone would eventually claim the body, whose location was recorded in the county administrator's office. But not much.

"What do you mean, you don't know?" General Rokossovskiy demanded. "He's my man! Did you misplace him?"

"Comrade General," Giap replied sharply, "I have told you everything I know!"

"And you say an American did it?"

"You have seen the intelligence information as well as I have."

"That man has information that the Soviet Union requires. I find it hard to believe that the Americans planned a raid whose only result was the abduction of the one Soviet officer in the area. I would suggest, Comrade General, that you make a more serious effort."

"We are at war!"

"Yes, I am aware of that," Rokossovskiy observed dryly. "Why do you think I am here?"

Giap could have sworn at the taller man who stood before his desk. He was the commander of his country's armed forces, after all, and a general of no mean abilities himself. The Vietnamese general swallowed his pride with difficulty. He also needed the weapons that only the Russians could provide, and so he had to abase himself before him for the sake of his country. Of one thing he was certain. The camp wasn't worth the trouble it had caused him.

The strange part was that the routine had become relatively benign. Kolya wasn't here. That was certain. Zacharias was sufficiently disoriented that he had difficulty determining the passage of days, but for four sleeps now he hadn't heard the Russian's voice even outside the door. By the same token, no one had come in to abuse him. He'd eaten and sat and thought in solitude. To his surprise it had made things better instead of worse. His time with Kolya had become an addiction more dangerous than his dalliance with alcohol, Robin saw now. It was loneliness that was his real enemy, not pain, not fear. From a family and a religious community that fostered fellowship, he'd entered a profession that lived on the same, and being denied it his mind had fed on itself. Then add a little pain and fear, and what did you have? It was something far more easily seen from without than from within. Doubtless it had been apparent to Kolya. *Like you,* he'd said so often, *like you.* So, Zacharias told himself, that's how he did his job. Cleverly, too, the Colonel admitted to himself. Though not a man accustomed to failure and mistakes, he was not immune to them. He'd almost killed himself with a youthful error at Luke Air Force Base while learning to fly fighters, and five years later, the time he'd wondered what the inside of a thunderstorm was really like and nearly ended up hitting the ground in the manner of a thunderbolt. And now he'd made another.

Zacharias didn't know the reason for his respite from the interrogations. Perhaps Kolya was off reporting on what he'd learned. Whatever the reason, he had been granted the chance to reflect. *You've sinned,* Robin told himself. *You've been very foolish. But you won't do that again.* The determination was weak, and Zacharias knew he'd have to work to strengthen it. Fortunately, he now had the time for reflection. If it was not a real deliverance, it was something. Suddenly he was shocked into full concentration, as if he were flying a combat mission. *My God,* he thought, *that word. I was afraid to pray for deliverance . . . and yet . . .* His guards would have been surprised to see the wistful smile on his face, especially had they known that he was starting to pray again. Prayer, they'd all been taught, was a farce. But that was their misfortune, Robin thought, and might yet be his salvation.

He couldn't make the call from his office. It just wouldn't do. Nor did he wish to do so from his home. The call would cross a river and a state line, and he knew that for security reasons there were special provisions for telephone calls made in the D.C. area. They were all recorded on computer tape, the only place in America where that was true. Even so, there was a procedure for what he had to do. You were supposed to have official sanction for it. You had to discuss it with your section head, then with the chief of the directorate, and it could well go all the way to the "front office" on the seventh floor. Ritter didn't want to wait that long, not with lives at stake. He took the day off, not unreasonably claiming that he needed the time to recover from all the travel. So he decided to drive into town, and picked the Smithsonian's Museum of Natural History. He walked past the elephant in the lobby and consulted the YOU ARE HERE plate on the wall to find the public telephones, into one of which he dropped a dime and called 347-1347. It was almost an institutional joke. That number connected him to a telephone that rang on the desk of the KGB *rezident,* the chief of station for Washington, D.C. They knew, and knew that people interested knew they knew. The espionage business could be so baroque, Ritter told himself.

"Yes?" a voice said. It was the first time Ritter had done this, a whole new collection of sensations—his own nervousness, the evenness of the voice at the other end, the excitement of the moment. What he had to say, however, was programmed in such a way that outsiders could not interfere with official business:

"This is Charles. There is a matter of concern to you. I propose a brief meeting and discussion. I'll be at the National Zoo in an hour, at the enclosure for the white tigers."

"How will I know you?" the voice asked.

"I'll be carrying a copy of *Newsweek* in my left hand."

"One hour," the voice grumbled. He probably had an important meeting this morning, Ritter thought. Wasn't that too bad? The CIA field officer left the museum for his car. On the right seat was a copy of *Newsweek* he'd purchased at a drugstore on the way into town.

Tactics, Kelly thought, turning to port, finally rounding Point Lookout. There was a wide selection. He still had his safe house in Baltimore with a false name on everything. The police might be interested in talking to him, but they hadn't made contact with him yet. He'd try to keep it that way. The enemy didn't know who he was. That was his starting place. The fundamental issue was the three-way balance among what he knew, what he didn't know, and how he might use the first to affect the second. The third element, the *how,* was tactics. He could prepare for what he did not yet know. He could not yet act upon it, but he actually knew what he would do. Getting to that point simply required a strategic approach to the problem. It was frustrating, though. Four young women awaited his action. An as yet undetermined number of people awaited death.

They were driven by fear, Kelly knew. They'd been afraid of Pam, and afraid of Doris. Afraid enough to kill. He wondered if the death of Edward Morello had been a further manifestation. Certainly they had killed for their safety, and now they probably did feel safe. That was good; if fear was their driving force, then they had more of it now that they felt it a thing of their past.

The worrisome part was the time element. There was a clock on this. The police were sniffing at him. While he thought there was nothing they could possibly have to use against him, he still couldn't feel good about it. The other worry was the safety—he snorted—of those four young women. There was no such thing as a good *long* operation. Well, he'd have to be patient on one thing, and with luck, just the one.

He hadn't been to the zoo in years. Ritter thought he'd have to bring his kids here again now that they were old enough to appreciate things a little more. He took the time to look at the bear pit—there was just something interesting about bears. Kids thought of them as large, animated versions of the stuffed toys they clutched at night. Not Ritter. They were the image of the enemy, large and strong, far less clumsy and far more intelligent than they appeared. A good thing to remember, he told himself, heading over to the tiger cage. He rolled the *Newsweek* in his left hand, watching the large cats and waiting. He didn't bother checking his watch.

"Hello, Charles," a voice said beside him.

"Hello, Sergey."

"I do not know you," the *rezident* observed.

"This conversation is unofficial," Ritter explained.

"Aren't they all?" Sergey noted. He started walking. Any single place could be bugged, but not a whole zoo. For that matter, his contact could be wearing a wire, though that would not have been in accordance with the rules, such as they were. He and Ritter walked down the gentle paved slope to the next animal exhibit, with the *rezident*'s security guard in close attendance.

"I just returned from Vietnam," the CIA officer said.

"Warmer there than here."

"Not at sea. It's rather pleasant out there."

"The purpose of your cruise?" the *rezident* asked.

"A visit, an unplanned one."

"I believe it failed," the Russian said, not tauntingly, just letting "Charles" know that he knew what was going on.

"Not completely. We brought someone home with us."

"Who might that be?"

"His name is Nikolay." Ritter handed over Grishanov's paybook. "It would be an embarrassment to your government if it were to be revealed that a Soviet officer was interrogating American POWs."

"Not a great embarrassment," Sergey replied, flipping briefly through the paybook before pocketing it.

"Well, actually it would be. You see, the people he's been interrogating have been reported as being dead by your little friends."

"I don't understand." He was telling the truth, and Ritter had to explain for a few minutes. "I did not know any of that," Sergey said after hearing the facts of the matter.

"It's true, I assure you. You will be able to verify it through your own means." And he would, of course. Ritter knew that, and Sergey knew that he knew.

"And where is our colonel?"

"In a safe place. He's enjoying better hospitality than our people are."

"Colonel Grishanov hasn't dropped bombs on anyone," the Russian pointed out.

"That is true, but he did take part in a process that will end with the death of American prisoners, and we have hard evidence that they are alive. As I said earlier, a potential embarrassment for your government."

Sergey Voloshin was a highly astute political observer and didn't need this young CIA officer to tell him that. He could also see where this discussion was headed.

"What do you propose?"

"It would be helpful if your government could persuade Hanoi to restore these men to life, as it were. That is, to take them to the same prison where the other prisoners are, and make the proper notifications so that their families will know they are alive after all. In return for that, Colonel Grishanov will be returned unharmed, and uninterrogated."

"I will forward that proposal to Moscow." With a favorable endorsement, his tone said clearly.

"Please be quick. We have reason to believe that the Vietnamese may be contemplating something drastic to relieve themselves of the potential embarrassment. That would be a very serious complication," Ritter warned.

"Yes, I suppose it would be." He paused. "Your assurance that Colonel Grishanov is alive and well?"

"I can have you to him in . . . oh, about forty minutes if you wish. Do you think I would lie about something as important as this?"

"No, I do not. But some questions must be asked."

"Yes, Sergey Ivan'ch, I know that. We have no wish to harm your colonel. He seems to have behaved rather honorably in his treatment of our people. He was also a very effective interrogator. I have his notes." Ritter added, "The offer to meet with him is open if you wish to make use of it."

Voloshin thought about it, seeing the trap. Such an offer, if taken, would have to be reciprocated, because that's the way things were. To call Ritter's hand on this would commit his own government to something, and Voloshin didn't want to do that without guidance. Besides, it would be madness for CIA to lie in a case like this. Those prisoners could always be made to disappear. Only the goodwill of the Soviet Union could save them, and only the continuance of that goodwill would keep them healthy.

"I will take you at your word, Mister—"

"Ritter, Bob Ritter."

"Ah! Budapest."

Ritter grinned rather sheepishly. Well, after all he'd done to get his agent out, it was clear that he'd never go back into the field again, at least not in any place that mattered—which for Ritter started at the River Elbe. The Russian poked him in the chest.

"You did well getting your man out. I commend you on your loyalty to your agent." Most of all Voloshin respected him for the risk he'd taken, something not possible in the KGB.

"Thank you, General. And thank you for responding to my proposal. When can I call you?"

"I'll need two days . . . shall I call you?"

"Forty-eight hours from now. I'll make the call."

"Very well. Good day." They shook hands like the professionals they were. Voloshin walked back to his driver/bodyguard and headed back to the car. Their walk had ended up at the enclosure for the Kodiak bear, large, brown, and powerful. Had that been an accident? Ritter wondered.

On the walk back to his car he realized that the whole thing had been an accident of sorts. On the strength of this play, Ritter would become a section chief. Failed rescue mission or not, he'd just negotiated an important concession with the Russians, and it had all happened because of the presence of mind of a man younger than himself, scared and on the run, who'd taken the time to think. He wanted people like that in the Agency, and now he had the clout to bring him in. Kelly had demurred and temporized on the flight back from Hawaii. Okay, so he'd need a little convincing. He'd have to work with Jim Greer on that, but Ritter decided on the spot that his next mission was to bring Kelly in from the cold, or the heat, or whatever you called it.

"How well do you know Mrs. O'Toole?" Ryan asked.

"Her husband's dead," the neighbor said. "He went to Vietnam right after they bought the house, and then he was killed. Such a nice young man, too. She's not in any trouble, is she?"

The detective shook his head. "No, not at all. I've only heard good things about her."

"It's been awful busy over there," the elderly lady went on. She was the perfect person to talk to, about sixty-five, a widow with nothing to do who compensated for the empty space in her life by keeping track of everyone else's. With a little reassurance that she wasn't hurting anyone, she'd relate everything she knew.

"What do you mean?"

"I think she had a houseguest a while back. She sure was shopping a lot more than usual. She's such a nice, pretty girl. It's so sad about her husband. She really ought to start dating again. I'd like to tell her, but I don't want her to think I'm nosy. Anyway, she was shopping a lot, and somebody else came almost every day, stayed overnight a lot, even."

"Who was that?" Ryan asked, sipping his iced tea.

"A woman, short like me, but heavier, messy hair. She drove a big car, a red Buick, I think, and it had a sticker-thing on the windshield. Oh! That's right!"

"What's that?" Ryan asked.

"I was out with my roses when the girl came out, that's when I saw the sticker-thing."

"Girl?" Ryan asked innocently.

"That's who she was shopping for!" the elderly lady said, pleased with herself for the sudden discovery. "She bought clothes for her, I bet. I remember the Hecht Company bags."

"Can you tell me what the girl looked like?"

"Young, like nineteen or twenty, dark hair. Kinda pale, like she was sick. They drove away, when was that . . . ? Oh, I remember. It's the day my new roses came from the nursery. The eleventh. The truck came very early because I don't like the heat, and I was out there working when they came out. I waved at Sandy. She's such a nice girl. I don't talk to her very much, but when I do she always has a kind word. She's a nurse, you know, she works at Johns Hopkins, and—"

Ryan finished off his tea without letting his satisfaction show. Doris Brown had returned home to Pittsburgh on the afternoon of the eleventh. Sarah Rosen drove a Buick, and it undoubtedly had a parking sticker in the window. Sam Rosen, Sarah Rosen, Sandra O'Toole. They had treated Miss Brown. Two of them had also treated Miss Madden. They had also treated Mr. Kelly. After months of frustration, Lieutenant Emmet Ryan had a case.

"There she is now," the lady said, startling him out of his private thoughts. Ryan turned and looked to see an attractive young lady, on the tall side, carrying a bag of groceries.

"I wonder who that man was?"

"What man?"

"He was there last night. Maybe she has a boyfriend after all. Tall, like you, dark hair—big."

"How do you mean?"

"Like a football player, you know, big. He must be nice, though. I saw her hug him. That was just last night."

Thank God, Ryan thought, *for people who don't watch TV.*

For his long gun, Kelly had selected a bolt-action .22, a Savage Model 54, the lightweight version of that company's Anschutz match weapon. It was expensive enough at a hundred fifty dollars with tax. Almost as costly were the Leupold scope and mounts. The rifle was almost too good for its purpose, which was the hunting of small game, and had a particularly fine walnut stock. It was a shame that he'd have to scar it up. It would have been more of a shame to waste the lesson from that chief machinist's mate, however.

*   *   *

The one bad thing about the demise of Eddie Morello was that sweetening the deal had required the loss of a large quantity of pure, uncut heroin, a six-kilogram donation to the police evidence locker. That had to be made up. Philadelphia was hungry for more, and his New York connections were showing increasing interest now that they'd had their first taste. He'd do one last batch on the ship. Now he could change over again. Tony was setting up a secure lab that was easier to reach, more in keeping with the burgeoning success he was enjoying, but until that was ready, one more time the old way. He wouldn't make the trip himself.

"How soon?" Burt asked.

"Tonight."

"Fair enough, boss. Who goes with me?"

"Phil and Mike." The two new ones were from Tony's organization, young, bright, ambitious. They didn't know Henry yet, and would not be part of his local distribution network, but they could handle out-of-town deliveries and were willing to do the menial work that was part of this business, mixing and packaging. They saw it, not inaccurately, as a rite of passage, a starting place from which their status and responsibility would grow. Tony guaranteed their reliability. Henry accepted that. He and Tony were bound now, bound in business, bound in blood. He'd accept Tony's counsel now that he trusted him. He'd rebuild his distribution network, removing the need for his female couriers, and with the removal of the need for them, so would end the reason for their lives. It was too bad, but with three defections, it was plain that they were becoming dangerous. A useful part of his operation in the growth phase, perhaps, but now a liability.

But one thing at a time.

"How much?" Burt asked.

"Enough to keep you busy for a while." Henry waved to the beer coolers. There wasn't room for much beer in them now, but that was as it should be. Burt carried them out to his car, not casual, but not tense. Businesslike, the way things should be. Perhaps Burt would become his principal lieutenant. He was loyal, respectful, tough when he had to be, far more dependable than Billy or Rick, and a brother. It was funny, really. Billy and Rick had been necessary at the beginning since the major distributors were always white, and he'd taken them on as tokens. Well, fate had settled that. Now the white boys were coming to him, weren't they?

"Take Xantha with you."

"Boss, we're going to be busy," Burt objected.

"You can leave her there when you're done." Perhaps one at a time was the best way to do it.

* * *

Patience never came easy. It was a virtue he'd learned, after a fashion, but only from necessity. Activity helped. He set the gun barrel in the vise, damaging the finish even before he started to do anything substantive. Setting the milling machine on high-speed, rotating the control wheel, he started drilling a series of holes at regular intervals in the outermost six inches of the barrel. An hour later he had a steel can–body affixed over it, and the telescopic sight attached. The rifle, as modified, proved to be quite accurate, Kelly thought.

"Tough one, Dad?"

"Eleven months' worth, Jack," Emmet admitted over dinner. He was home on time for once, to his wife's pleasure—almost.

"That awful one?" his wife asked.

"Not over dinner, honey, okay?" he replied, answering the question. Emmet did his best to keep that part of his life out of the house. He looked over at his son and decided to comment on a decision his son recently made. "Marines, eh?"

"Well, Dad, it pays for the last two years of school, doesn't it?" It was like his son to worry about things like that, about the cost of education for his sister, still in high school and away at camp for the moment. And like his father, Jack craved a little adventure before settling down to whatever place life would find for him.

"My son, a jarhead," Emmet grumbled good-naturedly. He also worried. Vietnam wasn't over, might not be over when his son graduated, and like most fathers of his generation, he wondered why the hell he'd had to risk his life fighting Germans—so that his son might have to do the same, fighting people he'd never even heard about at his son's age.

"What falls out of the sky, pop?" Jack asked with a college-boy grin, repeating something Marines like to say.

Such talk worried Catherine Burke Ryan, who remembered seeing Emmet off, remembered praying all day in St. Elizabeth Church on June 6, 1944, and many days thereafter despite the regular letters and assurances. She remembered the waiting. She knew this kind of talk worried Emmet too, though not quite in the same way.

What falls out of the sky? Trouble! the detective almost told his son, for the Airborne, too, were a proud group, but the thought stopped before it got to his lips.

Kelly. We tried calling him. We had the Coast Guard look at that island he lives on. The boat wasn't there. The boat wasn't anywhere. Where was he? He was back now, though, if the little old lady was right. What if he was away? But now he's back. The killings just plain stopped after the Farmer–Grayson–Brown incident. The marina had remembered seeing the boat about that time, but he'd left in the middle of the night—*that night*—and just vanished. Connection. Where had the boat been? Where was it now? What falls out of the sky? Trouble. That's exactly what had happened before. It just dropped out of the sky. Started and stopped.

His wife and son saw it again. Chewing on his food, his eyes focused on infinity, unable to turn his mind off as it churned his information over and over. Kelly's not really all that different from what I used to be, Ryan thought. One-Oh-One, the Screaming Eagles of the 101st Infantry Division (Airborne), who still swaggered in their baggy pants. Emmet had started off as a buck private, ended up with a late-war battlefield commission to the rank he still held, lieutenant. He remembered the pride of being something very special, the sense of invincibility that strangely came arm in arm with the terror of jumping out of an aircraft, being the first on enemy territory, in the dark, carrying light weapons only. The hardest men with the hardest mission. Mission. He'd been like that once. But no one had ever killed his lady . . . what might have happened, back in 1946, perhaps, if someone had done that to Catherine?

Nothing good.

He'd saved Doris Brown. He'd given her over to people he trusted. He'd seen one of them last night. He knows she's dead. He saved Pamela Madden, she died, and he was in the hospital, and a few weeks after he got out people started dying in a very expert way. A few weeks . . . to get in shape. Then the killings just stopped and Kelly was nowhere to be found.

What if he's just been away?

He's back now.

Something's going to happen.

It wasn't a thing he could take to court. The only physical evidence they had was the imprint of a shoe sole—a common brand of sneaker, of course, hundreds sold every day. Zilch. They had motive. But how many murders happened every year, and how many people followed up on it? They had opportunity. Could he account for his time in front of a jury? No one could. How, the detective thought, do you explain this to a judge—no, some judges would understand, but no jury would, not after a brand-new law-school graduate had explained a few things to them.

The case was solved, Ryan thought. He *knew*. But he had nothing for it but the knowledge that something was going to happen.

*   *   *

"Who's that, you suppose?" Mike asked.

"Some fisherman, looks like," Burt observed from the driver's seat. He kept *Henry's Eighth* well clear of the white cabin cruiser. Sunset was close. They were almost too late to navigate the tangled waters into their laboratory, which looked very different at night. Burt gave the white boat a look. The guy with the fishing rod waved, a gesture he returned as he turned to port—left, as he thought of it. There was a big night ahead. Xantha wouldn't be much help. Well, maybe a little, when they broke for meals. A shame, really. Not really a bad girl, just dumb, badly spaced out. Maybe that's how they'd do it, just give her a nice taste of real good stuff before they broke out the netting and the cement blocks. They were sitting right in the open, right in the boat, and she didn't have a clue what they were for. Well, that wasn't his lookout.

Burt shook his head. There were more important things to consider. How would Mike and Phil feel about working under him? He'd have to be polite about it, of course. They'd understand. With the money involved, they ought to. He relaxed in his chair, sipping his beer and looking for the red marker buoy.

"Lookee, lookee," Kelly breathed. It wasn't hard, really. Billy had told him all he needed to know. They had a place in there. They came in the Bay side, by boat, usually at night, and usually left the following morning. Turned in at the red lighted buoy. Hard as hell to find, almost impossible in the dark. Well, probably was if you didn't know the water. Kelly did. He reeled in the unbaited hook and lifted his binoculars. Size and color were right. *Henry's Eighth* was the name. Check. He settled back, watching it move south, then turn east at the red buoy. Kelly marked his chart. Twelve hours at least. That should be plenty of time. The problem with so secure a place is that it depended absolutely on secrecy which, once blown, became a fatal liability. People never learned. One way in, one way out. Another clever way to commit suicide. He'd wait for sunset. While waiting, Kelly got out a can of spray paint and put green stripes on his dinghy. The inside he painted black.

33

Poisoned Charm

I t usually took all night, Billy had told him. That gave Kelly time to eat, relax, and prepare. He moved *Springer* in close to the cluttered ground he would be hunting tonight and set his anchors. The meal he prepared was only sandwiches, but it was better than he'd had atop "his" hill less than a week before. *God, a week ago I was on* Ogden, *getting ready,* he thought with a rueful shake of the head. How could life be so mad as this?

His small dinghy, now camouflaged, went into the water after midnight. He'd attached a small electric trolling motor to the transom, and hoped he had enough battery power to get in and out. It couldn't be too far. The chart showed that the area was not a large one, and the place they used had to be in the middle for maximum isolation. With darkened face and hands he moved into the maze of derelicts, steering the dinghy with his left hand while his eyes and ears searched for something that didn't belong. The sky helped. There was no moon, and the starlight was just enough to show him the grass and reeds that had grown in this tidal wetland that had been created when the hulks had been left there, silting up this part of the Bay and making a place that birds loved in the fall season.

It was like before. The low hum of the trolling motor was so much like that of the sled he'd used, moving him along at perhaps two knots, conserving power, guided this time by stars. The marsh grass grew to perhaps six or seven feet above the water, and it wasn't hard to see why they didn't navigate their way in by night. It truly was a maze if you didn't know how. But Kelly did. He watched the stars, knowing which to follow and which to ignore as their position rotated in the arching sky. It was a matter of comfort, really. They were from the city, were not seamen as he was, and as secure as they felt in their chosen place to prepare their illicit product, they weren't at ease here in this place of wild things and uncertain paths. *Won't you come into my parlor,* Kelly told himself. He was more listening than looking now. A gentle breeze rustled through the tall grass, following the widest channel here among the silted bars; twisty as it was, it had to be the one they'd followed. The fifty-year-old hulks around him looked like ghosts of another age, as indeed they were, relics of a war that had been won, cast-offs of a much simpler time, some of them sitting at odd angles, forgotten toys of the huge child their country had been, a child now grown into a troubled adult.

A voice. Kelly stopped his motor, drifting for a few seconds, pivoting his head around to get a fix on it. He'd guessed right on the channel. It looped around to the right just ahead there, and the noise had come from the right as well. Carefully now, slowly, he came around the bend. There were three of the derelicts. Perhaps they'd been towed in together. The tugboat skippers had probably tried to leave them in a perfect line as a personal conceit. The westernmost one was sitting at a slight angle, and listed seven or eight degrees to port, resting on a shifting bottom. The profile was an old one, with a low superstructure whose tall steel funnel had long since rusted away. But there was a light where the bridge ought to be. Music, he thought, some contemporary rock from a station that tried to keep truckers awake at night.

Kelly waited a few minutes, letting his eyes gather a fuller picture in the darkness, selecting his route of approach. He'd come in fine on the bow so that the body of the ship would screen him from view. He could hear more than one voice now. A sudden rolling laugh from a joke, perhaps. He paused again, searching the ship's outline for a bump, something that didn't belong, a sentry. Nothing.

They'd been clever selecting this place. It was as unlikely a spot as one might imagine, ignored even by local fishermen, but you had to have a lookout because no place was ever quite that secure . . . there was the boat. Okay. Kelly crept up at half a knot now, sticking close to the side of the old ship until he got to their boat. He tied his painter off to the nearest cleat. A rope ladder led up to the derelict's weather deck. Kelly took a deep breath and started climbing.

The work was every bit as menial and boring as Burt had told them it would be, Phil thought. Mixing the milk sugar in was the easy part, sifting it into large stainless-steel bowls like flour for a cake, making sure it was all evenly distributed. He remembered helping his mother with baking when he'd been a small child, watching her and learning things that a kid forgot as soon as he discovered baseball. They came back now, the rattling sound of

the sifter, the way the powders came together. It was actually rather a pleasant excursion back to a time when he hadn't even had to wake up and go to
school. But that was the easy part. Then came the tedious job of doling out
precisely measured portions into the little plastic envelopes which had to be
stapled shut, and piled, and counted, and bagged. He shared an exasperated
look with Mike, who felt the same way he did. Burt probably felt the same
way, but didn't let it show, and he had been nice enough to bring entertainment along. They had a radio playing, and for breaks they had this Xantha
girl, half-blasted on pills, but . . . compliant, they'd all found out at their
midnight break. They'd gotten her nice and tired, anyway. She was sleeping
in the corner. There would be another break at four, allowing each of them
enough time to recover. It was hard staying awake, and Phil was worried
about all this powder, some of it dust in the air. Was he breathing it in? Might
he get high on the stuff? If he had to do this again, he promised himself some
sort of mask. He might like the idea of making money off selling the shit, but
he had no desire at all to use it. Well, Tony and Henry were setting up a
proper lab. Travel wouldn't be such a pain in the ass. That was something.

Another batch done. Phil was a little faster than the others, wanting to
get it done. He walked over to the cooler and lifted the next one-kilo bag. He
smelled it, as he had the others. Foul, chemical smell, like the chemicals used
in the biology lab at his high school, formaldehyde, something like that. He
slit open the bag with a penknife, dumping the contents into the first mixing
bowl at arm's length, then adding a premeasured quantity of sugar and stirring with a spoon by the light of one of the Coleman lamps.

''Hello.''

There had been no warning at all. Suddenly there was someone else
there at the door, holding a pistol. He was dressed in military clothes, striped
fatigues, and his face was painted green and black.

There wasn't any need for silence. His prey had seen to that. Kelly had
reconverted his Colt back to .45 caliber, and he knew that the hole in the front
of the automatic would seem large enough to park a car to the others in the
room. He pointed with his left hand. ''That way. On the deck, facedown,
hands at the back of the neck, one at a time, you first,'' he said to the one at
the mixing bowl.

''Who the hell are you?'' the black one asked.

''You must be Burt. Don't do anything dumb.''

''How you know my name?'' Burt demanded as Phil took his place on
the deck.

Kelly pointed at the other white one, directing him next to his friend.

"I know lots of things," Kelly said, moving towards Burt now. Then he saw the sleeping girl in the corner. "Who's she?"

"Look, asshole!" The .45 went level with his face, an arm's length away.

"What was that?" Kelly asked in a conversational voice. "Down on the deck, now." Burt complied at once. The girl, he saw, was sleeping. He'd let that continue for the moment. His first task was to search them for weapons. Two had small handguns. One had a useless little knife.

"Hey, who are you? Maybe we can talk," Burt suggested.

"We're going to do that. Tell me about the drugs," Kelly started off.

It was ten in the morning in Moscow when Voloshin's dispatch emerged from the decoding department. A senior member of the KGB's First Chief Directorate, he had a pipeline into any number of senior officers, one of whom was an academician in Service I, an American specialist who was advising the senior KGB leadership and the Foreign Ministry on this new development that the American media called *détente*. This man, who didn't hold a paramilitary rank within the KGB hierarchy, was probably the best person to get fast action, though an information copy of the dispatch had also gone to the Deputy Chairman with oversight duties for Voloshin's Directorate. Typically, the message was short and to the point. The Academician was appalled. The reduction of tension between the two superpowers, in the midst of a shooting war for one of them, was little short of miraculous, and coming as it did in parallel with the American approach to China, it could well signal a new era in relations. So he had said to the Politburo in a lengthy briefing only two weeks earlier. The public revelation that a Soviet officer had been involved in something like this—it was madness. What cretin at GRU had thought this one up? Assuming it really was true, which was something he had to check. For that he called the Deputy Chairman.

"Yevgeniy Leonidovich? I have an urgent dispatch from Washington."

"As do I, Vanya. Your recommendations?"

"If the American claims are true, I urge immediate action. Public knowledge of such idiocy could be ruinous. Could you confirm that this is indeed under way?"

"*Da.* And then . . . Foreign Ministry?"

"I agree. The military would take too long. Will they listen?"

"Our fraternal socialist allies? They'll listen to a shipment of rockets. They've been screaming for them for weeks," the Deputy Chairman replied.

How typical, the Academician thought, *in order to save American lives*

*we will send weapons to take more of them, and the Americans will under-
stand.* Such madness. If there was ever an illustration as to why *détente* was
necessary, this was it. How could two great countries manage their affairs
when both were involved, directly or not, in the affairs of minor countries?
Such a worthless distraction from important matters.

"I urge speed, Yevgeniy Leonidovich," the Academician repeated.
Though far outranked by the Deputy Chairman, they'd been classmates,
years earlier, and their careers had crossed many times.

"I agree completely, Vanya. I'll be back to you this afternoon."

It was a miracle, Zacharias thought, looking around. He hadn't seen the
outside of his cell in months, and just to smell the air, warm and humid as it
was, seemed a gift from God, but that wasn't it. He counted the others,
eighteen other men in the single line, men like himself, all within the same
five-year age bracket, and in the fading light of dusk he saw faces. There was
the one he'd seen so long before, a Navy guy by the look of him. They
exchanged a look and thin smiles as all the men did what Robin was doing.
If only the guards would let them talk, but the first attempt had earned one
of their number a slap. Even so, for the moment just seeing their faces was
enough. To *not* be alone any longer, to know that there were others here, just
that was enough. Such a small thing. Such a large one. Robin stood as tall as
his injured back allowed, squaring his shoulders while that little officer was
saying something to his people, who were also lined up. He hadn't picked up
enough Vietnamese to understand the rapid speech.

"This is the enemy," the Captain was telling his men. He'd be taking
his unit south soon, and after all the lectures and battle practice, here was an
unexpected opportunity for them to get a real look. They weren't so tough,
these Americans, he told them. See, they're not so tall and forbidding, are
they? They bend and break and bleed—very easily, too! And these are the
elite of them, the ones who drop bombs on our country and kill our people.
These are the men you'll be fighting. Do you fear them now? And if the
Americans are foolish enough to try to rescue these dogs, we'll get early
practice in the art of killing them. With those rousing words, he dismissed his
troops, sending them off to their night guard posts.

He could do this, the Captain thought. It wouldn't matter soon. He'd
heard a rumor through his regimental commander that as soon as the political leadership got their thumbs out, this camp would be closed down in a
very final way, and his men would indeed get a little practice before they had
to walk down Uncle Ho's trail, where they would have the chance to kill
armed Americans next. Until then he had them as trophies to show his men,

to lessen their dread of the great unknown of combat, and to focus their rage, for these *were* the men who'd bombed their beautiful country into a wasteland. He'd select recruits who had trained especially hard and well . . . nineteen of them, so as to give them a taste of killing. They'd need it. The captain of infantry wondered how many of them he'd be bringing home.

Kelly stopped off for fuel at the Cambridge town dock before heading back north. He had it all now—well, he had enough now, Kelly told himself. Full bunkers, and a mind full of useful data, and for the first time he'd hurt the bastards. Two weeks, maybe three weeks of their product. That would shake things loose. He might have collected it himself and perhaps used it as bait, but no, he couldn't do that. He wouldn't have it around him, especially now that he suspected he knew how it might come in. Somewhere on the East Coast, was all that Burt actually knew. Whoever this Henry Tucker was, he was on the clever side of paranoid, and compartmentalized his operation in a way that Kelly might have admired under other circumstances. But it was Asian heroin, and the bags it arrived in smelled of death, and they came in on the East Coast. How many things from Asia that smelled of death came to the Eastern United States? Kelly could think of only one, and the fact that he'd known men whose bodies had been processed at Pope Air Force Base only fueled his anger and his determination to see this one thing through. He brought *Springer* north, past the brick tower of Sharp's Island Light, heading back into a city that held danger from more than one direction.

One last time.

There were few places in Eastern America as sleepy as Somerset County. An area of large and widely separated farms, the whole county had but one high school. There was a single major highway, allowing people to transit the area quickly and without stopping. Traffic to Ocean City, the state's beach resort, bypassed the area, and the nearest interstate was on the far side of the Bay. It was also an area with a crime rate so low as to be nearly invisible except for those who took note of a single-digit increase in one category of misbehavior or another. One lone murder could be headline news for weeks in the local papers, and rarely was burglary a problem in an area where a homeowner was likely to greet a nocturnal intruder with a 12-gauge and a question. About the only problem was the way people drove, and for that they had the State Police, cruising the roads in their off-yellow cars. To compensate for boredom the cars on the Eastern Shore of Maryland had unusually large engines with which to chase down speeders who all too often visited the local liquor stores beforehand in their effort to make a dull if comfortable area somewhat more lively.

Trooper First Class Ben Freeland was on his regular patrol routine. Every so often something real would happen, and he figured it was his job to know the area, every inch of it, every farm and crossroads, so that if he ever did get a really major call he'd know the quickest way to it. Four years out of the Academy at Pikesville, the Somerset native was thinking about advancement to corporal when he spotted a pedestrian on Postbox Road near a hamlet with the unlikely name of Dames Quarter. That was unusual. Everybody rode down here. Even kids started using bikes from an early age, often starting to drive well under age, which was another of the graver violations he dealt with on a monthly basis. He spotted her from a mile away—the land was very flat—and took no special note until he'd cut that distance by three quarters. She—definitely a female now—was walking unevenly. Another hundred yards of approach told him that she wasn't dressed like a local. That was odd. You didn't get here except by car. She was also walking in zigzags, even the length of her stride changing from one step to another, and that meant possible public intoxication—a *huge* local infraction, the trooper grinned to himself—and *that* meant he ought to pull over and give her a look. He eased the big Ford over to the gravel, bringing it to a smooth and safe stop fifty feet from her, and got out as he'd been taught, putting his uniform Stetson on and adjusting his pistol belt.

"Hello," he said pleasantly. "Where you heading, ma'am?"

She stopped after a moment, looking at him with eyes that belonged on another planet. "Who're you?"

The trooper leaned in close. There was no alcohol on her breath. Drugs were not much of a problem here yet, Freeland knew. That may have just changed.

"What's your name?" he asked in a more commanding tone.

"Xantha, with a ex," she answered, smiling.

"Where are you from, Xantha?"

"Aroun'."

"Around where?"

" 'Lanta."

"You're a long way from Atlanta."

"I *know* that!" Then she laughed. "He dint know I had more." Which, she thought, was quite a joke, and a secret worth confiding. "Keeps them in my brassiere."

"What's that now?"

"My pills. Keep them in my brassiere, and he dint know."

"Can I see them?" Freeland asked, wondering a lot of things and knowing that he had a real arrest to make this day.

She laughed as she reached in. "You step back, now."

Freeland did so. There was no sense alerting her to anything, though his right hand was now on his gunbelt just in front of his service revolver. As he watched, Xantha reached inside her mostly unbuttoned blouse and came out with a handful of red capsules. So that was that. He opened the trunk of his car and reached inside the evidence kit he carried to get an envelope.

"Why don't you put them in here so you don't lose any?"

"Okay!" What a helpful fellow this policeman was.

"Can I offer you a ride, ma'am?"

"Sure. Tired a' walkin'."

"Well, why don't you just come right along?" Policy required that he handcuff such a person, and as he helped her into the back of the car, he did. She didn't seem to mind a bit.

"Where we goin'?"

"Well, Xantha, I think you need a place to lie down and get some rest. So I think I'll find you one, okay?" He already had a dead-bang case of drug possession, Freeland knew, as he pulled back onto the road.

"Burt and the other two restin', too, 'cept they ain't gonna wake up."

"What's that, Xantha?"

"He killed their ass, bang bang bang." She mimed with her hand. Freeland saw it in the mirror, nearly going off the road as he did so.

"Who's that?"

"He a white boy, dint get his name, dint see his face neither, but he killed their ass, bang bang bang."

Holy shit.

"Where?"

"On the boat." Didn't everybody know that?

"What boat?"

"The one out on the water, fool!" That was pretty funny, too.

"You shittin' me, girl?"

"An' you know the funny thing, he left all the drugs right there, too, the white boy did. 'Cept'n he was *green.*"

Freeland didn't have much idea what this was all about, but he intended to find out just as fast as he could. For starters he lit up his rotating lights and pushed the car just as fast as the big 427 V-8 would allow, heading for the State Police Barracks "V" in Westover. He ought to have radioed ahead, but it wouldn't really have accomplished much except to convince his captain that he was the one on drugs.

"Yacht *Springer,* take a look to your port quarter."

Kelly lifted his mike. "Anybody I know?" he asked without looking.

"Where the H have you been, Kelly?" Oreza asked.

"Business trip. What do you care?"

"Missed ya," was the answer. "Slow down some."

"Is it important? I have to get someplace, Portagee."

"Hey, Kelly, one seaman to another, back down, okay?"

Had he not known the man . . . no, he had to play along regardless of who it was. Kelly cut his throttles, allowing the cutter to pull alongside in a few minutes. Next he'd be asked to stop for a boarding, which Oreza had every legal right to do, and trying to evade would solve nothing. Without being so bidden, Kelly idled his engines and was soon laying to. Without asking permission, the cutter eased alongside and Oreza hopped aboard.

"Hey, Chief," the man said by way of a greeting.

"What gives?"

"I was down your sandbar twice in the last couple of weeks looking to share a beer with you, but you weren't home."

"Well, I wouldn't want to make you unfit for duty."

"Kinda lonely out here with nobody to harass." Suddenly it was clear that both men were uneasy, but neither one knew why the other was. "Where the hell were you?"

"I had to go out of the country. Business," Kelly answered. It was clear that he'd go no further than that.

"Fair enough. Be around for a while?"

"I plan to be, yeah."

"Okay, maybe I'll stop by next week and you can tell me some lies about being a Navy chief."

"Navy chiefs don't have to lie. You need some pointers on seamanship?"

"In a pig's ass! Maybe I ought to give you a safety inspection right now!"

"I thought this was a friendly visit," Kelly observed, and both men became even more uncomfortable. Oreza tried to cover it with a smile.

"Okay, I'll go easy on you." But that didn't work. "Catch you next week, Chief."

They shook hands, but something had changed. Oreza waved for the forty-one-footer to come back in, and he jumped aboard like the pro he was. The cutter pulled away without a further word.

Well, that makes sense. Kelly advanced his throttles anyway.

Oreza watched *Springer* continue north, wondering what the hell was going on. *Out of the country,* he'd said. For sure his boat hadn't been anywhere on the Chesapeake—but where, then? Why were the cops so interested in the guy? Kelly a killer? Well, he'd gotten that Navy Cross for something. UDT guy, that much Oreza knew. Beyond that, just a good guy to have a beer with, and a serious seaman in his way. It sure got complicated when you stopped doing search-and-rescue and started doing all that other cop stuff, the quartermaster told himself, heading southwest for Thomas Point. He had a phone call to make.

"So what happened?"

"Roger, they knew we were coming," Ritter answered with a steady look.

"How, Bob?" MacKenzie asked.

"We don't know yet."

"Leak?"

Ritter reached into his pocket and extracted a photocopy of a document and handed it across. The original was written in Vietnamese. Under the text of the photocopy was the handwritten translation. In the printed English were the words "green bush."

"They knew the name?"

"That's a security breakdown on their side, Roger, but, yes, it appears that they did. I suppose they planned to use that information for any of the Marines they might have captured. That sort of thing is good for breaking people down in a hurry. But we got lucky."

"I know. Nobody got hurt."

Ritter nodded. "We put a guy on the ground in early. Navy SEAL, very good at what he does. Anyway, he was watching things when the NVA reinforcements came in. He's the guy who blew the mission off. Then he just walked off the hill." It was always far more dramatic to understate things, especially for someone who'd smelled gunsmoke in his time.

That, MacKenzie thought, was worth a whistle. "Must be rather a cool customer."

"Better than that," Ritter said quietly. "On the way out he bagged the Russian who was talking to our people, and the camp commander. We have them in Winchester. Alive," Ritter added with a smile.

"That's how you got the dispatch? I figured SigInt," MacKenzie said, meaning signals intelligence. "How'd he manage that?"

"As you said, a cool customer." Ritter smiled. "That's the good news."

"I'm not sure I want to hear the bad news."

"We have an indicator that the other side might want to eliminate the camp and everyone in it."

"Jesus . . . Henry is over in Paris right now," MacKenzie said.

"Wrong approach. If he brings this up, even in one of the informal sessions, they'll just deny, and it might spook them so much that they'll try to make sure they can deny it." It was well known that the real work at such conferences was done during the breaks, not when people had to address the issues formally over the conference table, the very shape of which had taken so much time.

"True. What then?"

"We're working through the Russians. We have a pipeline for that. I initiated the contact myself."

"Let me know how it turns out?"

"You bet."

"Thanks for letting me talk to you," Lieutenant Ryan said.

"What's this all about?" Sam Rosen asked. They were in his office—not a large one, and the room was crowded with four people in it. Sarah and Sandy were there, too.

"It's about your former patient—John Kelly." That news didn't come as much of a surprise, Ryan saw. "I need to talk to him."

"What's stopping you?" Sam asked.

"I don't know where he is. I was kind of hoping you folks might."

"About what?" Sarah asked.

"About a series of killings," Ryan answered at once, in the hope of shocking them.

"Killing who?" This question came from the nurse.

"Doris Brown, for one, and several others."

"John didn't hurt her—" Sandy said before Sarah Rosen was able to touch her hand.

"Then you know who Doris Brown is," the detective observed, just a little too quickly.

"John and I have become . . . friends," Sandy said. "He's been out of the country for the past couple of weeks. He couldn't have killed anybody."

Ouch, Ryan thought. That was both good and bad news. He'd overplayed his hand on Doris Brown, though the nurse's reaction to the accusation had resulted in a little too much emotional response. He'd also just had a speculation confirmed as fact, however. "Out of the country? Where? How do you know?"

"I don't think I'm supposed to say where. I'm not supposed to know that."

"What do you mean by that?" the cop asked in surprise.

"I don't think I'm supposed to say, sorry." The way she answered the question showed sincerity rather than evasion.

What the hell did that *mean?* There was no answering that one, and Ryan decided to go on. "Someone named Sandy called the Brown house in Pittsburgh. It was you, wasn't it?"

"Officer," Sarah said, "I'm not sure I understand why you're asking all these questions."

"I'm trying to develop some information, and I want you to tell your friend that he needs to talk with me."

"This is a criminal investigation?"

"Yes, it is."

"And you're asking us questions," Sarah observed. "My brother is a lawyer. Should I ask him to come here? You seem to be asking us what we know about some murders. You're making me nervous. I have a question— are any of us under suspicion of anything?"

"No, but your friend is." If there was anything Ryan didn't need now, it was to have an attorney present.

"Wait a minute," Sam said. "If you think John might have done something wrong, and you want us to find him for you, you're saying that you think we know where he is, right? Doesn't that make us possible . . . helpers, accessories is the word, isn't it?"

Are you? Ryan would have liked to ask. He decided on, "Did I say that?"

"I've never had questions like this before, and they make me nervous," the surgeon told his wife. "Call your brother."

"Look, I have no reason to believe that any of you has done anything wrong. I *do* have reason to believe that your friend has. What I'm telling you is this: you'll be doing him a favor by telling him to call me."

"Who's he supposed to have killed?" Sam pressed.

"Some people who deal drugs."

"You know what I do?" Sarah asked sharply. "What I spend most of my time on here, you know what it is?"

"Yes, ma'am, I do. You work a lot with addicts."

"If John's really doing that, maybe I ought to buy him a gun!''

"Hurts when you lose one, doesn't it?'' Ryan asked quietly, setting her up.

"You bet it does. We're not in this business to lose patients.''

"How did it feel to lose Doris Brown?'' She didn't reply, but only because her intelligence stopped her mouth from reacting as it wanted to. "He brought her to you for help, didn't he? And you and Mrs. O'Toole here worked very hard to clean her up. You think I'm condemning you for that? But before he dropped her off with you, he killed two people. I *know* it. They were probably two of the people who murdered Pamela Madden, and those were his real targets. Your friend Kelly is a very tough guy, but he's not as smart as he thinks he is. If he comes in now, it's one thing. If he makes us catch him, it's something else. You tell him that. You'll be doing him a favor, okay? You'll be doing yourselves a favor, too. I don't think you've broken the law to this point. Do anything for him now except what I've told you, and you might be. I don't usually warn people this way,'' Ryan told them sternly. "You people aren't criminals. I know that. The thing you did for the Brown girl was admirable, and I'm sorry it worked out the way it did. But Kelly is out there killing people, and that's *wrong,* okay? I'm telling you that just in case you might have forgotten something along the way. I don't like druggies either. Pamela Madden, the girl on the fountain, that's *my* case. I *want* those people in a cage; I want to watch them walk into the gas chamber. That's *my* job, to see that justice happens. Not his, mine. Do you understand?''

"Yes, I think we do,'' Sam Rosen answered, thinking about the surgical gloves he'd given Kelly. It was different now. Back then he'd been distant from things—emotionally close to the terrible parts, yet far away from what his friend was doing, approving it as though reading a news article on a ballgame. It was different now, but he was involved. "Tell me, how close are you to getting the people who killed Pam?''

"We know a few things,'' Ryan answered without realizing that with his answer, he'd blown it after coming so close.

Oreza was back at his desk, the part of his work that he hated, and one reason he worried about striking for chief, which would entail having his own office, and becoming part of "management'' instead of just being a boat-driver. Mr. English was on leave, and his second-in-command, a chief, was off seeing to something or other, leaving him as senior man present—but it was his job anyway. The petty officer searched on his desk for the card and dialed the number.

"Homicide."

"Lieutenant Ryan, please."

"He's not here."

"Sergeant Douglas?"

"He's in court today."

"Okay, I'll call back." Oreza hung up. He looked at the clock. Pushing four in the afternoon—he'd been at the station since midnight. He pulled open a drawer and started filling out the forms accounting for the fuel he'd burned up today, making the Chesapeake Bay safe for drunks who owned boats. Then he planned to get home, get dinner, and get some sleep.

The problem was making sense out of what she said. A physician was called in from his office across the street, and diagnosed her problem as barbiturate intoxication, which wasn't exactly news, and then went on to say that they'd just have to wait for the stuff to work its way out of her system, for which two opinions he charged the county twenty dollars. Talking to her for several hours had only made her at turns amused and annoyed, but her story hadn't changed, either. Three people dead, *bang bang bang*. It was less funny to her now. She'd started remembering what Burt was like, and that talk was quite foul.

"If this girl was any higher she'd be up on the moon with the astronauts," the Captain thought.

"Three dead people on a boat somewhere," Trooper Freeland repeated. "Names and everything."

"You believe it?"

"Story stays the same, doesn't it?"

"Yeah." The Captain looked up. "You like to fish out there. What's it sound like to you, Ben?"

"Like around Bloodsworth Island."

"We'll hold her overnight on public drunkenness . . . we have her dead-bang on possession, right?"

"Cap'n, all I had to do was ask. She *handed* the stuff to me."

"Okay, process her all the way through."

"And then, sir?"

"Like helicopter rides?"

He picked a different marina this time. It turned out to be pretty easy, with so many boats always out fishing or partying, and this one had plenty of guest slips for transient boats which in the summer season plied up and down the coast, stopping off on the way for food and fuel and rest much as motorists did. The dockmaster watched him move in expertly to his third-largest guest slip, which didn't always happen with the owners of the larger cruisers. He was more surprised to see the youth of the owner.

"How long you plan to be here?" the man asked, helping with the lines.

"Couple of days. Is that okay?"

"Sure."

"Mind if I pay cash?"

"We honor cash," the dockmaster assured him.

Kelly peeled off the bills and announced that he'd be sleeping aboard this night. He didn't say what would be happening the next day.

34
Stalking

"We missed something, Em," Douglas announced at eight-ten in the morning.

"What was it this time?" Ryan asked. Missing something wasn't exactly a new happening in their business.

"How they knew she was in Pittsburgh. I called that Sergeant Meyer, had 'em check the long-distance charges on the house phone. None, not a single outgoing call for the last month."

The detective lieutenant stubbed out his cigarette. "You have to assume that our friend Henry knew where she was from. He had two girls get loose from him, he probably took the time to ask where they were from. You're right," Ryan said after a second's thought. "He probably assumed she was dead."

"Who knew she was there?"

"The people who took her there. They sure as hell didn't tell anyone."

"Kelly?"

"Found out yesterday over at Hopkins, he was out of the country."

"Oh, really? Where?"

"The nurse, O'Toole, she says she knows but she isn't allowed to say, whatever the hell that means." He paused. "Back to Pittsburgh."

"The story is, Sergeant Meyer's dad is a preacher. He was counseling the girl and told his son a little of what he knew. Okay. The sergeant goes up the chain to his captain. The Captain knows Frank Allen, and the sarge calls him for advice on who's running the case. Frank refers him to us. Meyer didn't talk to anybody else." Douglas lit up one of his own. "So how did the info get to our friends?"

This was entirely normal, but not particularly comfortable. Now both men thought that they had a breaking case. This was happening, it *was* breaking open. Not unusually, things were now happening too fast for the analytical process that was necessary to make sense of it all.

"As we've thought all along, they have somebody inside."

"Frank?" Douglas asked. "He's never been connected with any of the cases. He doesn't even have access to the information that our friends would need." Which was true. The Helen Waters case had started in the Western District with one of Allen's junior detectives, but the Chief had turned it over to Ryan and Douglas almost immediately because of the degree of violence involved. "I suppose you could call this progress, Em. Now we're sure. There has to be a leak inside the Department."

"What other good news do we have?"

The State Police only had three helicopters, all Bell Jet Rangers, and were still learning how to make use of them. Getting one was not the most trivial of exercises, but the Captain running Barracks "V" was a senior man who ran a quiet county—this was less a matter of his competence than of the nature of his area, but police hierarchies tend to place stock in results, however obtained. The helicopter arrived on the barracks helicopter pad at a quarter to nine. Captain Ernest Joy and Trooper 1/c Freeland were waiting. Neither had taken a helicopter ride before, and both were a little nervous when they saw how small the aircraft was. They always look smaller close up, and smaller still on the inside. Mainly used for Medevac missions, the aircraft had a pilot and a paramedic, both of whom were gun-toting State Police officers in sporty flight suits that went well, they thought, with their shoulder holsters and aviator shades. The standard safety lecture took a total of ninety seconds, delivered so quickly as to be incomprehensible. The ground-pounders strapped in, and the helicopter spooled up. The pilot decided against jazzing up the ride. The senior man was a captain, after all, and cleaning vomit out of the back was a drag.

"Where to?" he asked over the intercom.

"Bloodsworth Island," Captain Joy told him.

"Roger that," the pilot replied as he thought an aviator ought, turning southeast and lowering the nose. It didn't take long.

The world looks different from above, and the first time people go up in helicopters the reaction is always the same. The takeoff, rather like jerking aloft in an amusement-park cable-car ride, is initially startling, but then the fascination begins. The world transformed itself before the eyes of both officers, and it was as though it all suddenly made sense. They could see the

roads and the farms all laid out like a map. Freeland grasped it first. Knowing
his territory as he did, he instantly saw that his mental picture of it was
flawed; his idea of how things really were was not quite right. He was only
a thousand feet above it, a linear distance his car traversed in seconds, but
this perspective was new, and he immediately started learning from it.

"That's where I found her," he told the Captain over the intercom.

"Long way from where we're going. You think she walked that far?"

"No, sir." But it wasn't that far from the water, was it? Perhaps two
miles away, they saw the old dock of a farm up for sale, and that was less than
five miles from where they were heading, scarcely two minutes' flying time.
The Chesapeake Bay was a wide blue band now, under the morning haze. To
the northwest was the large expanse of Patuxent River Naval Air Test Center, and they could both see aircraft flying there—a matter of concern to the
pilot, who kept a wary eye out for low-flying aircraft. The Navy jocks liked
to smoke in low.

"Straight ahead," he said. The paramedic pointed so that the passengers would know where straight-ahead was.

"Sure looks different from up here," Freeland said, a boy's wonder in
his voice. "I fish around there. From the surface it just looks like marshes."

But it didn't now. From a thousand feet it looked like islands at first,
connected by silt and grass, but islands for all that. As they got closer, the
islands took on regular shapes, lozengelike at first, and then with the fine
lines of ships, grown over, surrounded by grass and reeds.

"Jeez, there's a bunch of 'em," the pilot observed. He'd rarely flown
down here, and then mostly at night with accident cases.

"World War One," the Captain said. "My father said they're leftovers
from the war, the ones the Germans didn't get."

"What exactly are we looking for?"

"Not sure, maybe a boat. We picked up a druggie yesterday," the
Captain explained. "Said there was a lab in there, and three dead people."

"No shit? A drug lab in *there?*"

"That's what the lady said," Freeland confirmed, learning something
else. As forbidding as it looked from the surface, there *were* channels in here.
Probably a hell of a good place to go crabbing. From the deck of his fishing
boat, it looked like one massive island, but not from up here. Wasn't that
interesting?

"Got a flash down this way." The paramedic pointed the pilot over to
the right. "Off glass or something."

"Let's check it out." The stick went right and down a little as he
brought the Jet Ranger down. "Yeah, I got a boat by those three."

"Check it out," the paramedic ordered with a grin.

"You got it." It would be a chance to do some real flying. A former Huey driver from the 1st Air Cav, he loved being able to play with his aircraft. Anyone could fly straight and level, after all. He circled the place first, checking winds, then lowered his collective a little, easing the chopper down to about two hundred feet.

"Call it an eighteen-footer," Freeland said, and they could see the white nylon line that held it fast to the remains of the ship.

"Lower," the Captain commanded. In a few seconds they were fifty feet over the deck of the derelict. The boat was empty. There was a beer cooler, and some other stuff piled up in the back, but nothing else. The aircraft jerked as a couple of birds flew out of the ruined superstructure of the ship. The pilot instinctively maneuvered to avoid them. One crow sucked into his engine intake could make them a permanent part of this man-made swamp.

"Whoever owns that boat sure isn't real interested in us," he said over the intercom. In the back, Freeland mimed three shots with his hand. The Captain nodded.

"I think you may be right, Ben." To the pilot: "Can you mark the exact position on a map?"

"Right." He considered the possibility of going into a low hover and dropping them off on the deck. Simple enough if they had been back in the Cav, it looked too dangerous for this situation. The paramedic pulled out a chart and made the appropriate notations. "Seen what you need?"

"Yeah, head back."

Twenty minutes later, Captain Joy was on the phone.

"Coast Guard, Thomas Point."

"This is Captain Joy, State Police. We need a little help." He explained on for a few minutes.

"Take about ninety minutes," Warrant Officer English told him.

"That'd be fine."

Kelly called a Yellow Cab, which picked him up at the marina entrance. His first stop of the day was a rather disreputable business establishment called Kolonel Klunker, where he rented a 1959 Volkswagen, prepaying it for a month, with no mileage charge.

"Thank you, Mr. Aiello," the man said to a smiling Kelly, who was using the ID from a man who no longer needed it. He drove the car back to the marina and started unloading the things he needed. Nobody paid much attention, and in fifteen minutes the Beetle was gone.

Kelly took the opportunity to drive through the area he'd be hunting, checking traffic patterns. It was agreeably vacant, a part of the city he'd never visited before, off a bleak industrial thoroughfare called O'Donnell Street, a place where nobody lived and few would want to. The air was laden with the smells of various chemicals, few of them pleasant. Not as busy as it once had been, many of the buildings in the district looked unused. More to the point, there was much open ground here, many buildings separated from one another by flat areas of bare dirt which trucks used for a convenient place to reverse direction. No kids playing sandlot ball, not a single house in sight, and because of that, not a single police car to be seen. Rather a clever ploy on the part of his enemies, Kelly thought, at least from one perspective. The place he was interested in was a single freestanding building with a half-destroyed sign over the entrance. The back of it was just a blank wall. There were only three doors, and though they were on two different walls, all could be observed from a single point, and to Kelly's rear was another vacant building, a tall concrete structure with plenty of broken windows. His initial reconnaissance complete, Kelly headed north.

Oreza was heading south. He'd already been partway there, conducting a routine patrol and wondering why the hell the Coast Guard didn't start up a ministation farther down on the Eastern Shore, or maybe by Cove Point Light, where there was an existing station for the guys who spent their waking hours, if any, making sure the light bulb at the top of the tower worked. That wasn't especially demanding duty to Oreza's mind, though it was probably all right for the kid who ran the place. His wife had just delivered twins, after all, and the Coast Guard was a family-oriented branch of the military.

He was letting one of his junior seamen do the driving, enjoying the morning, standing outside the cramped wheelhouse, drinking some of his home-brewed coffee.

"Radio," one of the crewmen said.

Oreza went inside and took the microphone. "Four-One Alfa here."

"Four-One Alfa, this is English at Thomas Base. Your pickup is at a dock at Dame's Choice. You'll see cop cars there. Got an ETA?"

"Call it twenty or twenty-five, Mr. E."

"Roger that. Out."

"Come left," Oreza said, looking at his chart. The water looked plenty deep. "One-six-five."

"One-six-five, aye."

*   *   *

Xantha was more or less sober, though weak. Her dark skin had a gray pallor to it, and she complained of a splitting headache that analgesics had scarcely touched. She was aware that she was under arrest now, and that her rap sheet had arrived on teletype. She was also canny enough to have requested the presence of a lawyer. Strangely, this had not bothered the police very much.

"My client," the attorney said, "is willing to cooperate." The agreement had taken all of ten minutes to strike. If she was telling the truth, and if she was not involved in a major felony, the possession charge against her would be dropped, subject to her enrollment in a treatment program. It was as good a deal as anyone had offered Xantha Matthews in some years. It was immediately apparent why this was true.

"They was gonna kill me!" she said, remembering it all now that she was outside the influence of the barbiturates, and now that her attorney gave her permission to speak.

"Who's 'they'?" Captain Joy asked.

"They dead. He killed 'em, the white boy, shot 'em dead. An' he left the drugs, whole shitload of 'em."

"Tell us about the white man," Joy asked, with a look to Freeland that ought to have been disbelieving but was not.

"Big dude, like him"—she pointed to Freeland—"but he face all green like a leaf. He blindfold me af'er he took me down, then he put me on that pier an' tol' me to catch a bus or somethin'."

"How do you know he was white?"

"Wrists was white. Hands was green, but not up here, like," she said, indicating on her own arms. "He wear green clothes with stripes on 'em, like a soldier, carry a big .45. I was asleep when he shoot, that wake me up, see? Make me get dress, take me away, drop me off, he boat just go away."

"What kind of boat?"

"Big white one, tall, like, big, like thirty feet lon'."

"Xantha, how do you know they were going to kill you?"

"White boy say so, he show me the things in the boat, the little one."

"What do you mean?"

"Fishnet shit, like, and cement blocks. He say they tell him they do it before."

The lawyer decided it was his turn to speak. "Gentlemen, my client has information about what may be a major criminal operation. She may require protection, and in return for her assistance, we would like to have state funding for her treatment."

"Counselor," Joy replied quietly, "if this is what it sounds like, I'll fund it out of my own budget. May I suggest, sir, that we keep her in our lockup for the time being? For her own safety, the need for which seems quite apparent, sir.'' The State Police captain had been negotiating with lawyers for years, and had started sounding like one, Freeland thought.

"The food here is fo' shit!" Xantha said, her eyes closed in pain.

"We'll take care of that, too," Joy promised her.

"I think she needs some medical help," the lawyer noted. "How can she get it here?"

"Doctor Paige will be here right after lunch to see her. Counselor, your client is in no condition to look after herself now. All charges against her are dropped pending verification of her story. You'll get everything you want, in return for her cooperation. I can't do any more than that."

"My client agrees to your conditions and suggestions," the lawyer said without consulting her. The county would even pay his fee. Besides, he felt as though he might be doing the world a good deed. It was quite a change from getting drunk drivers off.

"There's a shower that way. Why not get her cleaned up? You may also wish to get her some decent things to wear. Give us the bill."

"A pleasure doing business with you, Captain Joy," he said as the barracks commander left for Freeland's car.

"Ben, you really fell into something. You handled her real nice. I won't forget. Now show me how fast this beast goes."

"You got it, Cap'n." Freeland engaged the lights before passing seventy. They made it to the dock just as the Coast Guard turned out of the main channel.

The man wore lieutenant's bars—though he called himself a captain—and Oreza saluted him as he came aboard. Both police officers were given life jackets to wear because Coast Guard regulations required them on small boats, and then Joy showed him the chart.

"Think you can get in there?"

"No, but our launch can. What gives?"

"A possible triple homicide, possible drug involvement. We overflew the area this morning. There's a fishing boat right here."

Oreza nodded as impassively as possible and took the wheel himself, pushing the throttles to the stops. It was a bare five miles to the graveyard—that was how Oreza thought of it—and he plotted his approach as carefully as possible.

"No closer? The tide's in," Freeland said.

"That's the problem. Place like this, you go it at low water so's in case you beach you can float off. From here on we use the launch.'' Wheels were turning in his mind while his crewmen got the fourteen-foot launch deployed. Months earlier, that stormy night with Lieutenant Charon from Baltimore, a possible drug deal that he'd expected to take place somewhere on the Bay. *Some real serious guys,* he'd told Portagee. Oreza already wondered if there might be a connection.

They motored in, powered by a ten-horse outboard. The quartermaster took note of the tidal flow, following what appeared to be a channel that meandered generally in the direction indicated by their marked-up chart. It was quiet in here, and Oreza remembered his tour of duty for Operation MARKET TIME, the Coast Guard's effort to assist the Navy in Vietnam. He'd spent time with the brown-water guys, running Swift boats manufactured right in Annapolis by the Trumpy Yard. It was so similar, the tall grass that could, and often did, conceal people with guns. He wondered if they might be facing something similar soon. The cops were fingering their revolvers, and Oreza asked himself, too late, why he hadn't brought a Colt with him. Not that he knew how to use it. His next thought was that this would have been a good place to have Kelly with him. He wasn't quite sure what the story was on Kelly, but he suspected the man was one of the SEALs, with whom he'd worked briefly in the Mekong Delta. Sure as hell he'd gotten that Navy Cross for something, and the tattoo on his arm wasn't there by accident.

"Well, damn," Oreza breathed. "Looks like a Starcraft sixteen . . . no, more like eighteen." He lifted his portable radio. "Four-One Alpha, this is Oreza."

"Reading you, Portagee."

"We got the boat, right where they said. Stand by."

"Roger."

Suddenly things got very tense indeed. The two cops exchanged a look, wondering why they hadn't brought more people out. Oreza eased his launch right up to the Starcraft. The cops got aboard gingerly.

Freeland pointed to the back. Joy nodded. There were six cement blocks and a rolled-up section of nylon netting. Xantha hadn't lied about that. There was also a rope ladder going up. Joy went first, his revolver in his right hand. Oreza just watched as Freeland followed. Once they got to the deck, the men wrapped both hands around their handguns and headed for the superstructure, disappearing from view for what seemed like an hour, but in reality was only four minutes. Some birds scattered aloft. When Joy came back, his revolver wasn't visible.

"We have three bodies up here, and a hell of a large quantity of what looks like heroin. Call your boat, have them tell my barracks that we need crime lab. Sailor, you just started running a ferry service.''

''Sir, fish-and-game has better boats for this. Want me to call them to support you?''

''Good idea. You might want to circle around this area some. The water looks pretty clear, and she told us that they've dumped some bodies here-abouts. See the stuff in the fishing boat?'' Oreza looked, noticing the fishnet and blocks for the first time.

Jesus. ''That's how you do it. Okay, I'll motor around.'' Which he did, after making his radio call.

''Hi, Sandy.''

''John! Where are you?''

''My place in town.''

''There was a policeman in to see us yesterday. They're looking for you.''

''Oh?'' Kelly's eyes narrowed as he chewed on his sandwich.

''He said you should come in and talk to him, that it's better if you do it right away.''

''That's nice of him,'' Kelly observed with a chuckle.

''What are you going to do?''

''You don't want to know, Sandy.''

''You sure?''

''Yes, I'm sure.''

''Please, John, please think it through.''

''I have, Sandy. Honest. It'll be okay. Thanks for the information.''

''Something wrong?'' another nurse asked after she hung up.

''No,'' Sandy replied, and her friend knew it was a lie.

Hmm. Kelly finished off his Coke. That confirmed his suspicion about Oreza's little visit. So things were getting complicated now, but they'd been pretty complicated the week before, too. He headed off to the bedroom, almost there when there came a knock at the door. That startled him rather badly, but he had to answer it. He'd opened windows to air the apartment out, and it was plain that someone was here. He took a deep breath and opened the door.

''Wondered where you were, Mr. Murphy,'' the manager said, much to Kelly's relief.

''Well, two weeks of work in the Midwest and a week's vacation down in Florida,'' he lied with a relaxed smile.

"You didn't get much of a tan."

An embarrassed grin. "Spent a lot of my time inside." The manager thought that was pretty good.

"Good for you, well, just wanted to see if everything was okay."

"No problems here," Kelly assured the man, closing the door before he could ask anything else. He needed a nap. It seemed that all of his work was at night. It was like being on the other side of the world, Kelly told himself, lying down on his lumpy bed.

It was a hot day at the zoo. Better to have met in the panda enclosure. It was crowded with people who wanted to gawk at this wonderful goodwill gift from the People's Republic of China—Chinese Communists to Ritter. The place was air conditioned and comfortable, but intelligence officers usually were uncomfortable in places like that, and so today he was strolling by the remarkably large area that contained the Galapagos tortoises, or turtles—Ritter didn't know the difference, if there was one. Why they needed so large an area, he didn't know either. Certainly it seemed expansive for a creature that moved at roughly the speed of a glacier.

"Hello, Bob." "Charles" was now an unnecessary subterfuge, though Voloshin had initiated the call—right to Ritter's desk, to show how clever he was. It worked both ways in the intelligence business. In the case of a call initiated by the Russians, the code name was "Bill."

"Hello, Sergey." Ritter pointed to the reptiles. "Kind of reminds you of the way our governments work, doesn't it?"

"Not my part of it." The Russian sipped at his soft drink. "Nor yours."

"Okay, what's the word from Moscow?"

"You forgot to tell me something."

"What's that?"

"That you have a Vietnamese officer also."

"Why should that concern you?" Ritter asked lightly, clearly concealing his annoyance that Voloshin knew this, as his interlocutor could see.

"It is a complication. Moscow doesn't know yet."

"Then don't tell them," Ritter suggested. "It is, as you say, a complication. I assure you that your allies don't know."

"How can that be?" the Russian demanded.

"Sergey, do you reveal methods?" Ritter replied, ending that phase of the discussion. This part of the game had to be played very carefully indeed, and for more than one reason. "Look, General, you don't like the little bastards any more than we do, right?"

"They are our fraternal socialist allies."

"Yes, and we have bulwarks of democracy all over Latin America, too. Did you come here for a quick course in political philosophy?"

"The nice thing about enemies is that you know where they stand. This is not always true of friends," Voloshin admitted. That also explained the comfort level of his government with the current American president. A bastard, perhaps, but a known bastard. And, no, Voloshin admitted—to himself—he had little use for the Vietnamese. The real action was in Europe. Always had been. Always would be. That was where the course of history had been set for centuries, and nothing was going to change that.

"Call it an unconfirmed report, check up on it, maybe? Delay? Please, General, the stakes here are too high for that. If anything happens to those men, I promise you, we *will* produce your officer. The Pentagon knows, Sergey, and they want those men back, and they don't care a rat-fuck about *détente.*" The profanity showed what Ritter really thought.

"Do you? Does your Directorate?"

"It sure will make life a lot more predictable. Where were you in '62, Sergey?" Ritter asked—knowing and wondering what he'd say.

"In Bonn, as you know, watching your forces go on alert because Nikita Sergeyevich decided to play his foolish game." Which had been contrary to KGB and Foreign Ministry advice, as both men knew.

"We're never going to be friends, but even enemies can agree to rules for the game. Isn't that what this is about?"

A judicious man, Voloshin thought, which pleased him. It made for predictable behavior, and that above all things was what the Russians wanted of the Americans. "You are persuasive, Bob. You assure me that our allies do not know their man is missing?"

"Positive. My offer for you to meet your man is still open," he added.

"Without reciprocal rights?" Voloshin tried.

"For that I need permission from upstairs. I can try if you ask me to, but that also would be something of a complication." He dumped his empty drink cup in a bin.

"I ask." Voloshin wanted that made clear.

"Very well. I'll call you. And in return?"

"In return I will consider your request." Voloshin walked off without another word.

Gotcha! Ritter thought, heading towards where his car was parked. He'd played a careful but inventive game. There were three possible leaks on Boxwood Green. He'd visited each of them. To one he'd said that they actually had gotten a prisoner out, who had died of wounds. To another, that the Russian was badly wounded and might not survive. But Ritter had saved his best piece of bait for the most likely leak. Now he knew. That narrowed it to four suspects. Roger MacKenzie, that prep-school-reject aide, and two secretaries. This was really an FBI job, but he didn't want any additional complications, and an espionage investigation of the Office of the President of the United States was about as complicated as things could be. Back in his car, he decided to meet with a friend in the Directorate of Science and Technology. Ritter had a great deal of respect for Voloshin. A clever man, a very careful, methodical man, he'd run agents all over Western Europe before being assigned to the Washington *rezidentura.* He'd keep his word, and to make sure he didn't get into any trouble about it, he'd play everything strictly by the exacting rules of his parent agency. Ritter was gambling big on that. Pull this one off in addition to the other coup in the works, and how much higher might he rise? Better yet, he'd be earning his way up, not some fair-haired political payoff, but the son of a Texas Ranger who'd waited tables to get his degree at Baylor. Something Sergey would have appreciated, in good Marxist-Leninist fashion, Ritter told himself; pulling onto Connecticut Avenue. Working-class kid makes good.

It was an unusual way to gather information, something he'd never done before, and pleasant enough that he might even get used to it. He sat at a corner booth in Mama Maria's, working slowly through his second course—thank you, no wine, I'm driving. Dressed in his CIA suit, well-groomed and sporting a new businesslike haircut, he enjoyed the looks of a few unattached women, and a waitress who positively doted on him, especially with his good manners. The excellence of the food explained the crowded room, and the crowding explained why it was a convenient place for Tony Piaggi and Henry Tucker to meet here. Mike Aiello had been very forthcoming about that. Mama Maria's was, in fact, owned by the Piaggi family, now in its third generation of providing food and other, less legal, services to the local community, dating back to Prohibition. The owner was a bon vivant, greeting favored customers, guiding them to their places with Old World hospitality. Snappy dresser, too, Kelly saw, recording his face and build, gestures and mannerisms, as he ate through his calamari. A black man came in, dressed in a nicely cut suit. He looked like he knew the place, smiling at the hostess and waiting a few seconds for his reward, and Kelly's.

Piaggi looked up and headed to the front, stopping only briefly to shake hands with someone on the way. He did the same with the black man, then led him back past Kelly's table, and up the back stairs to where the private rooms were. No particular notice was taken. There were other black couples in the restaurant, treated the same as everyone else. But those others did honest work, Kelly was sure. He turned his thoughts away from the distraction. *So that's Henry Tucker. That's the one who killed Pam.* He didn't look like a monster. Monsters rarely did. To Kelly he looked like a target, and his particulars went into Kelly's memory, alongside Tony Piaggi's. He was surprised when he looked down and saw that the fork in his hands was bent.

"What's the problem?" Piaggi asked upstairs. He poured each of them a glass of Chianti, good host that he was, but as soon as the door had closed, Henry's face started telling him something.

"They haven't come back."

"Phil, Mike, and Burt?"

"Yes!" Henry snarled, meaning, *no.*

"Okay, settle down. How much stuff did they have?"

"Twenty kees of pure, man. This was supposed to take care of me and Philly, and New York for a while."

"Lot of stuff, Henry." Tony nodded. "Maybe it just took them a while, okay?"

"Shoulda been back by now."

"Look, Phil and Mike are new, probably clumsy, like Eddie and me were out first time—hell, Henry, that was only five kees, remember?"

"I allowed for that," he said, wondering if he'd really be right about that or not.

"Henry," Tony said, sipping his wine and trying to appear calm and reasonable, "look, okay? Why are you getting excited? We've taken care of all the problems, right?"

"Something's wrong, man."

"What?"

"I don't know."

"Want to get a boat and go down there to see?"

Tucker shook his head. "Takes too long."

"The meet with the other guys isn't for three days. Be cool. They're probably on their way here now."

Piaggi thought he understood Tucker's sudden case of the shakes. Now it was big-time. Twenty kilograms of pure translated into a huge quantity of street drugs, and selling it already diluted and packaged made for sufficient convenience to their customers that they were for the first time paying top dollar. This was the really big score that Tucker had been working towards for several years. Just assembling all the cash to pay for it was a major undertaking. It was an understandable case of nerves.

"Tony, what if it wasn't Eddie at all?"

Exasperation: "You're the one who said it had to be, remember?"

Tucker couldn't pursue that. He'd merely wanted an excuse to eliminate the man as an unnecessary complication. His anxiety was partly what Tony thought it was, but something else, too. The things that had happened earlier in the summer, the things that had just started for no reason, then stopped with no reason—he had told himself that they were Eddie Morello's doing. He'd managed to convince himself of that, but only because he had wanted to believe it. Somewhere else the little voice that had brought him this far had told him otherwise, and now the voice was back, and there was no Eddie to be the focus for his anxiety and anger. A streetwise man who'd gotten this far through the complex equation of brain and guts and instinct, he trusted that last quality most. Now it was telling him things that he didn't understand, couldn't reason out. Tony was right. It could just be a matter of clumsiness in the processing. That was one reason they were setting their lab up in east Baltimore. They could afford that now, with experience behind them and a viable front business setting up in the coming week. So he drank his wine and settled down, the rich, red alcohol soothing his abraded instincts.

"Give 'em until tomorrow."

"So how was it?" the man at the wheel asked. An hour north of Bloodsworth Island, he figured he'd waited long enough to ask the silent petty officer who stood beside him. After all, they just stood by and waited.

"They fed a guy to the fuckin' crabs!" Oreza told them. "They took like two square yards of net and weighted it down with blocks, and just sunk his ass—practically nothing left but the damned bones!" The police lab people were still discussing how to recover the body, for all he knew. Oreza was certain it was a sight he'd take years to forget, the skull just lying there, the bones still dressed, moving because of the water currents . . . or maybe some crabs inside. He hadn't cared to look that closely.

"Heavy shit, man," the helmsman agreed.

"You know who it is?"

"What d'ya mean, Portagee?"

"Back in May, when we had that Charon guy aboard—the day-sailer with the candystripe main, that's who it was, I'll bet ya."

"Oh, yeah. You could be right on that one, boss."

They'd let him see it all, just as a courtesy that in retrospect he would as soon have done without, but which at the time had been impossible to avoid. He could not have chickened out in front of cops, since he, too, was a cop of sorts. And so he'd climbed up the ladder after reporting on the body he'd found only fifty yards from the derelict, and seen three more, all lying facedown on the deck of what had probably been the freighter's wardroom, all dead, all shot in the back of the neck, the wounds having been picked at by birds. He'd almost lost control of himself at that realization. The birds had been sensible enough not to pick at the drugs, however.

"I'm talking twenty kilograms—forty-some pounds of the shit—that's what the cops said, anyway. Like, millions of bucks," Oreza related.

"Always said I was in the wrong business."

"Jesus, the cops look like they all had hard-ons, 'specially that captain. They'll probably be there all night, way it sounded."

"Hey, Wally?"

The tape was disappointingly scratchy. That was due to the old phone lines, the technician explained. Nothing he could do about that. The switch box in the building dated back to when Alexander Graham Bell was doing hearing aids.

"Yeah, what is it?" the somewhat uneven voice replied.

"The deal with the Vietnamese officer they got. You sure about that?"

"That's what Roger told me." *Bingo!* Ritter thought.

"Where they have him?"

"I guess out at Winchester with the Russian."

"You're sure?"

"Damned right. It surprised me, too."

"I wanted to check up on that before—well, you know."

"Sure thing, man." With that the line went dead.

"Who is he?" Greer asked.

"Walter Hicks. All the best schools, James—Andover and Brown. Father's a big-time investment banker who pulled a few well-tuned political strings, and look where little Wally ends up." Ritter tightened his hand into a fist. "You want to know why those people are still in SENDER GREEN? That's it, my friend."

"So what are you going to do about it?"

"I don't know." *But it won't be legal.* The tape wasn't. The tap had been set up without a court order.

"Think it over carefully, Bob," Greer warned. "I was there, too, remember?"

"What if Sergey can't get it done fast enough? Then this little *fuck* gets away with ending the lives of twenty men!"

"I don't like that very much either."

"I don't like it at all!"

"Treason is still a capital crime, Bob."

Ritter looked up. "It's supposed to be."

Another long day. Oreza found himself envying the first-class who was tending Cove Point Light. At least he had his family with him all the time. Here Oreza was with the brightest little girl in kindergarten and he hardly ever saw her. Maybe he'd take that teaching job at New London after all, Portagee thought, just so that he could have a family life for a year or two. It meant hanging out with children who would someday be officers, but at least they'd learn seamanship the right way.

Mainly he was lonely with his thoughts. His crew was bedding down now in the bunkroom that he should have gone to, but the images haunted him. The crabman, and the three bird-feeders would deny him sleep for hours unless he got it off his conscience . . . and he had an excuse, didn't he? Oreza rummaged around his desk, finding the card.

"Hello?"

"Lieutenant Charon? This is Quartermaster First Class Oreza, down at Thomas Point."

"It's kinda late, you know," Charon pointed out. He'd been caught on his way to bed.

"Remember back in May, looking for that sailboat?"

"Yeah, why?"

"I think maybe we found your man, sir." Oreza thought he could hear eyeballs click.

"Tell me about it?"

Portagee did, leaving nothing out, and he could feel the horror leaving him, almost as though he were transmitting it over the phone wire. He didn't know that was precisely what he was doing.

"Who's the captain running the case for the troopers?"

"Name's Joy, sir. Somerset County. Know him?"

"No, I don't."

"Oh, yeah, something else," Oreza remembered.

"Yeah?" Charon was taking lots of notes.

"You know a Lieutenant Ryan?"

"Yeah, he works downtown, too."

"He wanted me to check up a guy for him, fellow named Kelly. Oh, yeah! You've seen him, remember?"

"What do you mean?"

"The night we were out after the day-sailer, the guy in the cruiser we saw just before dawn. Lives on an island, not far from Bloodsworth. Anyway, this Ryan guy wanted me to find him for him, okay? He's back, sir, probably up in Baltimore right now. I tried calling, sir, but he was out, and I've been running my ass off all day. Could you pass that one along, please?''

''Sure,'' Charon replied, and his brain was working very quickly indeed now.

35

Rite of Passage

Mark Charon found himself in rather a difficult position. That he was a corrupted cop did not make him a stupid one. In fact, his was a careful and thoroughly analytical mind, and while he made mistakes, he was not blind to them. That was precisely the case as he lay alone in bed, hanging up the phone after his conversation with the Coast Guard. The first order of business was that Henry would not be pleased to learn that his lab was gone, and three of his people with it. Worse still, it sounded as though a vast quantity of drugs had been lost, and even Henry's supply was finite. Worst of all, the person or persons who had accomplished that feat was unknown, at large, and doing—what?

He knew who Kelly was. He'd even reconstructed matters to the rather stunning coincidence that Kelly had been the one who'd picked Pam Madden off the street quite by accident the day Angelo Vorano had been eliminated, and that she'd actually been aboard his boat, not twenty feet from the Coast Guard cutter after that stormy and vomitous night. Now Em Ryan and Tom Douglas wanted to know about him, and had taken the extraordinary step of having the Coast Guard check up on him. Why? A follow-up interview with an out-of-town witness was something for the telephone more often than not. Em and Tom were working the Fountain Case, along with all the other ones that had started a few weeks later. "Rich beach bum" was what he'd told Henry, but the department's number-one homicide team was interested in him, and he'd been directly involved with one of the defectors from Henry's organization, and he had a boat, and he lived not too far from the processing lab that Henry was still foolish enough to use. That was a singularly long and unlikely string of coincidences made all the more troubling by the realization that Charon was no longer a policeman investigating a crime, but rather a criminal himself who was *part* of the crimes being checked out.

That realization struck surprisingly hard at the Lieutenant lying in his bed. Somehow he didn't think of himself in those terms. Charon actually had believed himself above it all, watching, taking an occasional part, but not *being* part of what unfolded below him. After all, he had the longest string of successes in the history of the narcotics unit, capped off with his personal elimination of Eddie Morello, perhaps the most artful action of his professional life—doubly so in that he had eliminated a genuine dealer by premeditated murder in front of no less than six other officers, then had it pronounced a clean shooting on the spot, which had given him a paid vacation in addition to what Henry had paid him for the event. Somehow it had seemed like a particularly entertaining game, and one not too far distanced from the job the citizens of his city paid him to do. Men live by their illusions, and Charon was no different from the rest. It wasn't so much that he'd told himself what he'd been doing was all right as that he'd simply allowed himself to concentrate on the breaks that Henry had been feeding him, thus taking off the street every supplier who'd threatened the man's market standing. Able to control which of his detectives investigated what, he'd actually been able to give the entire local market to the one supplier about whom he had no real information in his files. That had enabled Henry to expand his own operation, attracting the attention of Tony Piaggi and his own East Coast connections. Soon, and he'd told Henry this, he would be forced to allow his people to nibble at the edges of the operation. Henry had understood, doubtless after counseling from Piaggi, who was sophisticated enough to grasp the finer points of the game.

But someone had tossed a match into this highly volatile mixture. The information he had led only in one direction, but not far enough. So he had to get more, didn't he? Charon thought for a moment and lifted his phone. He needed three calls to get the right number.

"State Police."

"Trying to get Captain Joy. This is Lieutenant Charon, Baltimore City Police."

"You're in luck, sir. He just got back in. Please hold." The next voice that came on was a tired one.

"Captain Joy."

"Hello, this is Lieutenant Charon, Mark Charon, City Police. I work narcotics. I hear you just took down something big."

"You might say that." Charon could hear the man settling into his chair with a combination of satisfaction and fatigue.

"Could you give me a quick sketch? I may have some information on this one myself."

"Who told you about this anyway?"

"That Coast Guard sailor who drove you around—Oreza. I've worked with him on a couple cases. Remember the big marijuana bust, the Talbot County farm?"

"Was that you? I thought the Coasties took credit for that."

"I had to let them, to protect my informant. Look, you can call them if you want to confirm that. I'll give you the phone number, the boss of the station is Paul English."

"Okay, Charon, you sold me."

"Back in May I spent a day and a night out with them looking for a guy who just disappeared on us. We never found him, never found his boat. Oreza says—"

"The crabman," Joy breathed. "Somebody got dumped in the water, looks like he's been there a while. Anything you can tell me about him?"

"His name is probably Angelo Vorano. Lived here in town, small-time dealer who was looking to make it into the bigs." Charon gave a description.

"Height's about right. We'll have to check dental records for a positive ID, though. Okay, that ought to help, Lieutenant. What do you need from me?"

"What can you tell me?" Charon took several minutes of notes. "What are you doing with Xantha?"

"Holding her as a material witness, with her lawyer's approval by the way. We want to take care of this girl. Looks like we're dealing with some pretty nasty folks here."

"I believe it," Charon replied. "Okay, let me see what I can shake loose for you at this end."

"Thanks for the assist."

"Jesus," Charon said after hanging up. *White boy . . . big white boat.* Burt and the two people Tony had evidently seconded to the operation, back of the head, .45s. Execution-style killings were not yet the vogue in the drug business, and the sheer coldness of it gave Charon a chill. But it wasn't so much coldness as efficiency, was it? Like the pushers. Like the case Tom and Em were working, and they wanted to see about this Kelly guy, and he was a white guy with a big white boat who lived not far from the lab. That was too much of a coincidence.

About the only good news was that he could call Henry in safety. He knew every drug-related wiretap in the area, and not one was targeted on Tucker's operation.

"Yeah?"

"Burt and his friends are dead," Charon announced.

"What's that?" said a voice that was fully waking up.

"You heard me. The State Police in Somerset have them bagged. Angelo, too, what's left of him. The lab is gone, Henry. The drugs are gone, and they have Xantha in custody." There was actually some satisfaction in this. Charon was still enough of a cop that the demise of a criminal operation was not yet a matter of grief for him.

"What the fuck is going on?" a shrill voice inquired.

"I think I can tell you that, too. We need to meet."

Kelly took another look at his perch, just driving by in his rented Beetle, before heading back to his apartment. He was tired, though sated from the fine dinner. His afternoon nap had been enough to keep him going after a long day, but mainly the reason was to work off the anger, which driving often did for him. He'd seen the man now. The one who had finished the process of killing Pamela, with a shoestring. It would have been so easy to take care of him there. Kelly had never killed anyone barehanded, but he knew how. A lot of skilled people had spent a lot of time at Coronado, California, teaching him the finer points until whenever he looked at any person his mind applied something like a sheet of graph paper, this place for this move, that place for that one—and seeing he'd known that, yes, it was all worth it. It was worth the danger, and it was worth the consequences . . . but that didn't mean that he had to embrace them, as risk of life didn't mean throwing it away. That was the other side of it.

But he could see the end now, and he had to start planning beyond the end. He had to be even more careful. Okay, so the cops knew who he was, but he was certain that they had nothing. Even if the girl, Xantha, someday decided to talk to the cops, she'd never seen his face—the camouflage paint took care of that. About the only danger was that she'd seen the registration number on his boat as he'd backed away from that dock, but that didn't seem to be much of a worry. Without physical evidence they had nothing they could use in front of a court of law. So they knew he disliked some people— fine. So they might even know what his training was—fine. The game he played was in accordance with one set of rules. The game they played had another. On balance, the rules worked in his favor, not theirs.

He looked out the car window, measuring angle and distance, making a preliminary plan and working in several variations. They'd picked a spot where there were few police patrols and lots of open ground. No one could approach them easily without being seen . . . probably so that they could destroy whatever they had in there if it became necessary. It was a logical approach to their tactical problem, except for one thing. They hadn't considered a different set of tactical rules.

Not my problem, Kelly thought, heading back to his apartment.

"God almighty . . ." Roger MacKenzie was pale and suddenly nauseous. They were standing on the breakfast porch of his house in northwest Washington. His wife and daughter were shopping in New York for the fall season. Ritter had arrived unannounced at six-fifteen, fully dressed and grim, a discordant note for the cool, pleasant morning breezes. "I've known his father for thirty years."

Ritter sipped his orange juice, though the acid in it didn't exactly do his stomach any good either. This was treason of the worst sort. Hicks had *known* what he did would hurt fellow citizens, one of whom he knew by name. Ritter had already made his mind up on the matter, but Roger had to have his time to rattle on.

"We went through Randolph together, we were in the same Bomb Group," MacKenzie was saying. Ritter decided to let him get it all out, even though it would take a little time. "We've done deals together . . ." the man finished, looking down at his untouched breakfast.

"I can't fault you for taking him into your office, Roger, but the boy's guilty of espionage."

"What do you want to do?"

"It's a criminal offense, Roger," Ritter pointed out.

"I'm going to be leaving soon. They want me on the reelection team, running the whole Northeast."

"This early?"

"Jeff Hicks will be running the campaign in Massachusetts, Bob. I'll be working directly with him." MacKenzie looked across the table, speaking in barely connected bursts. "Bob, an espionage investigation in our office—it could ruin things. If what we did—if your operation became public—I mean, the way it happened and what went wrong—"

"I'm sorry about that, Roger, but this little bastard betrayed his country."

"I could pull his security clearance, kick him out—"

"Not good enough," Ritter said coldly. "People may die because of him. He is *not* going to walk away from it."

"We could order you to—"

"To obstruct justice, Roger?" Ritter observed. "Because that's what it is. That's a felony."

"Your tap was illegal."

"National-security investigation—there's a war going on, remember?—slightly different rules, and besides, all that has to happen is let him hear it and he'll split open." Ritter was sure of that.

"And run the risk of bringing down the President? Now? At this time? Do you think that'll do the country any good? What about our relations with the Russians? This is a *crucial* time, Bob." *But then, it always is, isn't it?* Ritter wanted to add, but didn't.

"Well, I'm coming to you for guidance," Ritter said, and then he got it, after a fashion.

"We can't afford an investigation that leads to a public trial. That is politically unacceptable." MacKenzie hoped that would be enough.

Ritter nodded and stood. The drive back to his office at Langley was not all that comfortable. Though it was satisfying to have a free hand, Ritter was now faced with something that, however desirable, he did not want to become a habit. The first order of business was to pull the wiretap. In one big hurry.

After everything that had happened, it was the newspaper that broke things loose. The four-column head, below the fold, announced a drug-related triple murder in sleepy Somerset County. Ryan devoured the story, never getting to the sports page that usually occupied fifteen minutes of his morning routine.

It's got to be him, the Lieutenant thought. *Who else would leave "a large quantity" of drugs behind, along with three bodies?* He left the house forty minutes early that morning, surprising his wife.

"Mrs. O'Toole?" Sandy had just finished her first set of morning rounds, and was checking off some forms when the phone rang.

"Yes?"

"This is James Greer. You've spoken to my secretary, Barbara, I believe."

"Yes, I have. Can I help you?"

"I hate to bother you, but we're trying to track John down. He's not at home."

"Yes, I think he's in town, but I don't know where exactly."

"If you hear from him, could you please ask him to call me? He has my number. Please forgive me for asking this," the man said politely.

"I'll be glad to." *And what's that about?* she wondered.

It was getting to her. The police were after John, and she'd told him, and he hadn't seemed to care. Now somebody else was trying to get hold of him. Why? Then she saw a copy of the morning paper sitting on the table in the lounge area. The brother of one of her patients was reading something or other, but right there on the lower-right side of the front page was the headline: DRUG MURDER IN SOMERSET.

"Everybody's interested in that guy," Frank Allen observed.

"What do you mean?" Charon had come into Western District on the pretense of checking up on the administrative investigation of the Morello shooting. He'd talked Allen into allowing him to review the statements of the other officers and three civilian witnesses. Since he'd graciously waived his right to counsel, and since the shooting looked squeaky clean, Allen hadn't seen any harm in the matter, so long as it was done in front of him.

"I mean, right after the call from Pittsburgh, that Brown girl who got whacked, Em called here about him. Now you. How come?"

"His name came up. We're not sure why, and it's just a quick check. What can you tell me about him?"

"Hey, Mark, you're on vacation, remember?" Allen pointed out.

"You're telling me I won't be back to work soon? I'm supposed to turn my brain off, Frank? Did I miss the article in the paper that says the crooks are taking a few weeks off?"

Allen had to concede the point. "All this attention, now I'm starting to think there might be something wrong with the guy. I suppose I have some information on him—yeah, that's right, I forgot. Wait a minute." Allen walked away from his desk toward the file room, and Charon pretended to read the statements for several minutes until he came back. A thin manila folder landed in his lap. "Here."

It was part of Kelly's service record, but not very much, Charon saw as he paged through it. It included his dive-qualification records, his instructor's rating, and a photograph, along with some other gingerbread stuff. Charon looked up. "Lives on an island? That's what I heard."

"Yeah, I asked him about that. Funny story. Anyway, why are you interested?"

"Just a name that came up, probably nothing, but I wanted to check it out. I keep hearing rumbles of a bunch that works out on the water."

"I really ought to send that down to Em and Tom. I forgot I had it."
Better yet. "I'm heading that way. Want me to drop it off?"

"Would you?"

"Sure." Charon tucked it under his arm. His first stop was a branch of the Pratt Library, where he made photocopies of the documents for ten cents each. Then he hit a photo shop. His badge enabled him to have five blowups of the small ID photo made in less than ten minutes. Those he left in the car when he parked at headquarters, but he only went inside long enough to have an officer run the file up to homicide. He could have just kept the information to himself, but on reflection it seemed the more intelligent choice to act like a normal cop doing a normal task.

"So what happened?" Greer asked behind the closed door of his office.

"Roger says an investigation would have adverse political consequences," Ritter answered.

"Well, isn't that just too goddamned bad?"

"Then he said to handle it," Ritter added. *Not in so many words, but that's what he meant.* There was no sense in confusing the issue.

"Meaning what?"

"What do you think, James?"

"Where did this come from?" Ryan asked when the file landed on his desk.

"Detective handed it to me downstairs, sir," the young officer answered. "I don't know the guy, but he said it was for your desk."

"Okay." Ryan waved him off and flipped it open, for the first time seeing a photograph of John Terrence Kelly. He'd joined the Navy two weeks after his eighteenth birthday, and stayed in . . . six years, honorably discharged as a chief petty officer. It was immediately apparent that the file had been heavily edited. That was to be expected, as the Department had mainly been interested in his qualifications as a diver. There was his graduation date from UDT School, and his later qualification as an instructor that the Department had been interested in. The three rating sheets in the folder were all 4.0, the highest Navy grade, and there was a flowery letter of recommendation from a three-star admiral which the Department had taken at face value. The Admiral had thoughtfully tucked in a list of his decorations, the more to impress the Baltimore City Police: Navy Cross, Silver Star, Bronze Star with Combat "V" and two clusters in lieu of repeat awards of the same decoration. Purple Heart with two clusters in lieu of—

Jesus, this guy's everything I thought, isn't he?

Ryan set the folder down, seeing that it was part of the Gooding Murder file. That meant Frank Allen—again. He called him.

"Thanks for the info on Kelly. What brought it up?"

"Mark Charon was over," Allen told him. "I'm doing the follow-up on his shoot, and he brought the name up, says it came up in one of his cases. Sorry, pal, I forgot I had this. He said he'd drop it off. He's not the sort of guy I'd figure for being drugged up, y'know, but . . ." His voice went on past the point of Ryan's current interest.

This is going too fast now, too damned fast.

Charon. He keeps appearing, doesn't he?

"Frank, I got a tough one for you. When that Sergeant Meyer called in from Pittsburgh, anybody else you mention that to?"

"What do you mean, Em?" Allen asked, annoyance beginning to form in his mind at the suggestion.

"I'm not saying you called the papers, Frank."

"That was the day Charon popped the dealer, wasn't it?" Allen thought back. "I might have said something to him . . . only other person I talked with that day, come to think of it."

"Okay, thanks, Frank." Ryan looked up the number of Barracks "V" of the State Police.

"Captain Joy," said a very weary voice. The barracks commander would have taken a bed in his own jail if he'd had to, but by tradition a State Police barracks was just that, and he'd found a comfortable bed for his four and a half hours of sleep. Joy was already wishing that Somerset County would go back to normal, though he well might make major's rank from this episode.

"Lieutenant Ryan, City Police homicide."

"You big-city boys sure are interested in us now," Joy commented wryly. "What do you want to know?"

"What do you mean?"

"I mean I was on my way to bed last night when another one of your people called down here, Lieutenant Chair—something like that, I didn't write it down. Said he could ID one of the bodies . . . I *did* write that down somewhere. Sorry, I'm turning into a zombie."

"Could you fill me in? I'll take the short version." It turned out that the short version was plenty. "The woman is in custody?"

"You bet she is."

"Captain, you keep her that way until I say different, okay? Excuse me, *please* keep her that way. She may be a material witness in a multiple homicide."

"Yeah, I know that, remember?"

"I mean up here, too, sir. Two bad ones, I have nine months invested in this."

"She isn't going anywhere for a while," Joy promised. "We have a lot of talking to do with her ourselves, and her lawyer's playing ball."

"Nothing more on the shooter?"

"Just what I said: male Caucasian, six foot or so, and he painted himself green, the girl says." Joy hadn't included that in his initial recounting.

"What?"

"She said his face and hands were green, like camouflage stuff, I suppose. There is one more thing," Joy added. "He's a right good shot. The three people he whacked, one shot each, all in the X-ring—like, perfect."

Ryan flipped the folder back open. At the bottom of Kelly's list of awards: Distinguished Rifleman, Master Pistol.

"I'll be back to you, Captain. Sounds like you've handled this one awfully well for a guy who doesn't get many homicides."

"I'd just as soon stick to speeders," Joy confirmed, hanging up.

"You're in early," Douglas observed, coming in late. "See the paper?"

"Our friend's back, and he got on the scoreboard again." Ryan handed the photo across.

"He looks older now," the sergeant said.

"Three Purple Hearts'll do that." Ryan filled Douglas in. "Want to drive down to Somerset and interview this girl?"

"You think . . . ?"

"Yes, I think we have our witness. I think we have our leaker, too." Ryan explained that one quietly.

He had just called to hear the sound of her voice. So close to his goal, he was allowing himself to look beyond it. It wasn't terribly professional, but for all his professionalism, Kelly remained human.

"John, where are you?" The urgency in her voice was even greater than the day before.

"I have a place," was all he was willing to say.

"I have a message for you. James Greer, he said you should call him."

"Okay." Kelly grimaced—he was supposed to have done that the day before.

"Was that you in the paper?"

"What do you mean?"

"I mean," she whispered, "three dead people on the Eastern Shore!"

"I'll get back to you," he said almost as fast as the chill hit him.

Kelly didn't have the paper delivered to his apartment for the obvious reason, but now he needed one. There was a dispenser at the corner, he remembered. He only needed one look.

What does she know about me?

It was too late for recrimination. He'd faced the same problem with her as with Doris. She'd been asleep when he'd done the job, and the pistol shots had awakened her. He'd blindfolded her, dumped her, explained to her that Burt had planned to kill her, given her enough cash to catch a Greyhound to somewhere. Even with the drugs, she'd been shocked and scared. But the cops had her already. How the hell had that happened?

Screw the how, son, they have her.

Just that fast the world had changed for him.

Okay, so now what do you do? It was that thought which occupied his mind for the walk back to his apartment.

For starters, he had to get rid of the .45, but he'd already decided to do that. Even if he had left no evidence at all behind, it was a link. When this mission was over, it was *over*. But now he needed help, and where else to get it but from the people for whom he had killed?

"Admiral Greer, please? This is Mr. Clark."

"Hold, please," Kelly heard, then: "You were supposed to call in yesterday, remember?"

"I can be there in two hours, sir."

"I'll be waiting."

"Where's Cas?" Maxwell asked, annoyed enough to use his nickname. The chief who ran his office understood.

"I already called his home, sir. No answer."

"That's funny." Which it wasn't, but the chief understood that, too.

"Want me to have somebody at Bolling check it out, Admiral?"

"Good idea." Maxwell nodded and returned to his office.

Ten minutes later a sergeant of the Air Force's Security Police drove from his guard shack to the collection of semidetached dwellings used by senior officers on Pentagon duty. The sign on the yard said Rear Admiral C. P. Podulski, USN, and showed a pair of aviator wings. The sergeant was only twenty-three and didn't interact with flag officers any more than he had to, but he had orders to see if there was any trouble here. The morning paper was sitting on the step. There were two automobiles in the carport, one of which had a Pentagon pass on the windshield, and he knew that the Admiral and his wife lived alone. Summoning his courage, the sergeant knocked on the door, firmly but not too noisily. No luck. Next he tried the bell. No luck. *Now what?* the young NCO wondered. The whole base *was* government property, and he had the right under regulations to enter any house on the post, and he had orders, and his lieutenant would probably back him up. He opened the door. There was no sound. He looked around the first floor, finding nothing that hadn't been there since the previous evening. He called a few times with no result, and then decided that he had to go upstairs. This he did, with one hand on his white leather holster . . .

Admiral Maxwell was there twenty minutes later.

"Heart attack," the Air Force doctor said. "Probably in his sleep."

That wasn't true of his wife, who lay next to him. She had been such a pretty woman, Dutch Maxwell remembered, and devastated by the loss of their son. The half-filled glass of water sat on a handkerchief so as not to harm the wooden night table. She'd even replaced the top of the pill container before she'd lain back down beside her husband. Dutch looked over to the wooden valet. His undress white shirt was there, ready for another day's service to his adopted country, the Wings of Gold over the collection of ribbons, the topmost of which was pale blue, with five white stars. They'd had a meeting planned to talk about retirement. Somehow Dutch wasn't surprised.

"God have mercy," Dutch said, seeing the only friendly casualties of Operation BOXWOOD GREEN.

What do I say? Kelly asked himself, driving through the gate. The guard eyeballed him pretty hard despite his pass, perhaps wondering how badly the Agency paid its field personnel. He did get to park his wreck in the visitors' lot, better placement than people on the payroll, which seemed slightly odd. Walking into the lobby, Kelly was met by a security officer and led upstairs. It seemed more ominous now, walking the drab and ordinary corridors peopled with anonymous people, but only because this building was about to become a confessional of sorts for a soul who had not quite decided if he were a sinner or not. He hadn't visited Ritter's office before. It was on the fourth floor and surprisingly small. Kelly had thought the man important—and though he actually was, his office as yet was not.

"Hello, John," Admiral Greer said, still reeling from the news he'd received a half hour before from Dutch Maxwell. Greer pointed him to a seat, and the door was closed. Ritter was smoking, to Kelly's annoyance.

"Glad to be back home, Mr. Clark?" the field officer asked. There was a copy of the *Washington Post* on his desk, and Kelly was surprised to see that the Somerset County story had made the first page there, too.

"Yes, sir, I guess you can say that." Both of the older men caught the ambivalence. "Why did you want me to come in?"

"I told you on the airplane. It may turn out that your action bringing that Russian out might save our people yet. We need people who can think on their feet. You can. I'm offering you a job in my part of the house."

"Doing what?"

"Whatever we tell you to do," Ritter answered. He already had something in mind.

"I don't even have a college degree."

Ritter pulled a thick folder from his desk. "I had this brought in from St. Louis." Kelly recognized the forms. It was his complete Navy personnel-records package. "You really should have taken the college scholarship. Your intelligence scores are even higher than I thought, and it shows you have language skills that are better than mine. James and I can waive the degree requirements."

"A Navy Cross goes a long way, John," Greer explained. "What you did, helping to plan BOXWOOD GREEN and then later in the field, that sort of thing goes a long way, too."

Kelly's instinct battled against his reason. The problem was, he wasn't sure which part of him was in favor of what. Then he decided that he had to tell the truth to somebody.

"There's a problem, gentlemen."

"What's that?" Ritter asked.

Kelly reached across the desk and tapped the article on the front page of the paper. "You might want to read that."

"I did. So? Somebody did the world a favor," the officer said lightly. Then he caught the look in Kelly's eyes, and his voice became instantly wary. "Keep talking, Mr. Clark."

"That's me, sir."

"What are you talking about, John?" Greer asked.

"The file's out, sir," the records clerk said over the phone.

"What do you mean?" Ryan objected. "I have some copies from it right here."

"Could you hold for a moment? I'll put my supervisor on." The phone went on hold, something that the detective cordially hated.

Ryan looked out his window with a grimace. He'd called the military's central records–storage facility, located in St. Louis. Every piece of paper relating to every man or woman who had ever served in uniform was there, in a secure and carefully guarded complex, the nature of which was a curiosity, but a useful one, to the detective, who'd more than once gotten data from the facility.

"This is Irma Rohrerbach," a voice said after some electronic chirping. The detective had the instant mental image of an overweight Caucasian female sitting at a desk cluttered with work that could have been done a week earlier.

"I'm Lieutenant Emmet Ryan, Baltimore City Police. I need information from a personnel file you have—"

"Sir, it's not here. My clerk just showed me the notes."

"What do you mean? You're not allowed to check files out that way. I know."

"Sir, that is not true. There *are* certain cases. This is one of them. The file was taken out and will be returned, but I do not know when."

"Who has it?"

"I'm not allowed to say, sir." The tone of the bureaucrat's voice showed her intensity of interest, too. The file was gone, and until it came back it was no longer part of the known universe as far as she was concerned.

"I can get a court order, you know." That usually worked on people, few of whom enjoyed the attention of a note from somebody's bench.

"Yes, you can. Is there any other way I can help you, sir?" She was also used to being blustered at. The call was from Baltimore, after all, and a letter from some judge eight hundred miles away seemed a distant and trivial thing. "Do you have our mailing address, sir?"

Actually, he couldn't. He still didn't quite have enough to take to a judge. Matters like this were handled more as a matter of courtesy than as actual orders.

"Thank you, I'll get back."

"Have a good day." The well-wish was in fact the bland dismissal of one more forgettable irrelevance in the day of a file clerk.

Out of the country. Why? For whom? What the hell's so different about this case? Ryan knew that it had many differences. He wondered if he'd ever have them all figured out.

"That's what they did to her," Kelly told them. It was the first time he'd actually said it all out loud, and in recounting the details of the pathology report it was as though he were listening to the voice of another person. "Because of her background the cops never really assigned much of a priority to the case. I got two more girls out. One they killed. The other one, well . . ." He waved at the newspaper.

"Why did you just turn her loose?"

"Was I supposed to murder her, Mr. Ritter? That's what they were planning to do," Kelly said, still looking down. "She was more or less sober when I let her go. I didn't have the time to do anything else. I miscalculated."

"How many?"

"Twelve, sir," he answered, knowing that Ritter wanted the total number of kills.

"Good Lord," Ritter observed. He actually wanted to smile. There was talk, actually, of getting CIA involved in antidrug operations. He opposed that policy—it wasn't important enough to divert the time of people who should be protecting their country against genuine national-security threats. But he couldn't smile. This was far too serious for that. "The article says twenty kilograms of the stuff. Is that true?"

"Probably." Kelly shrugged. "I didn't weigh it. There's one other thing. I think I know how the drugs come in. The bags smell like—embalming fluid. It's Asian heroin."

"Yes?" Ritter asked.

"Don't you see? Asian stuff. Embalming fluid. Comes in somewhere on the East Coast. Isn't it obvious? They're using the bodies of our KIAs to bring the fucking stuff in."

All this, and analytical ability too?

Ritter's phone rang. It was the intercom line.

"I said no calls," the field spook growled.

"It's 'Bill,' sir. He says it's important."

The timing was just perfect, the Captain thought. The prisoners were brought out in the darkness. There was no electricity, again, and the only illumination came from battery-powered flashlights and a few torches that his senior sergeant had cobbled together. Every prisoner had his feet hobbled; in each case the hands and elbows were bound behind their backs. They all walked slightly bent forward. It wasn't just to control them. Humiliation was important, too, and every man had in close attendance a conscript to chivvy him along, right to the center of the compound. His men were entitled to this, the Captain thought. They'd trained hard, were about to begin their long march south to complete the business of liberating and reuniting their country. The Americans were disoriented, clearly frightened at this break in their daily routine. Things had gone easy for them in the past week. Perhaps his earlier assembly of the group had been a mistake. It might have fostered some semblance of solidarity among them, but the object lesson to his troops was more than worth that. His men would soon be killing Americans in larger groups than this, the Captain was sure, but they had to start somewhere. He shouted a command.

As one man, the twenty selected soldiers took their rifles and butt-stroked their individual charges in the abdomen. One American managed to remain standing after the first blow, but not after the second.

Zacharias was surprised. It was the first direct attack on his person since Kolya had stopped that one, months before. The impact drove the air from him. His back already hurt from the lingering effect of his ejection and the deliberately awkward way they'd made him walk, and the impact of the steel buttplate of the AK-47 had taken control of his weakened and abused body away from him at once. He fell to his side, his body touching that of another prisoner, trying to draw his legs in and cover up. Then the kicks started. He couldn't even protect his face with his arms bound painfully behind him, and his eyes saw the face of the enemy. Just a boy, maybe seventeen, almost girlish in appearance, and the look on his face was that of a doll, the same empty eyes, the same absence of expression. No fury, not even baring his teeth, just kicking him as a child might kick at a ball, because it was something to do. He couldn't hate the boy, but he could despise him for his cruelty, and even after the first kick broke his nose he kept watching. Robin Zacharias had seen the depths of despair, had faced the fact that he'd broken on the inside and given up things that he knew. But he'd also had the time to understand it. He wasn't a coward any more than he was a hero, Robin told himself through the pain, just a man. He'd bear the pain as the physical penalty for his earlier mistake, and he would continue to ask his God for strength. Colonel Zacharias kept his now-blackened eyes on the face of the child tormenting him. *I will survive this. I've survived worse, and even if I die I'm still a better man than you will ever be,* his face told the diminutive soldier. *I've survived loneliness, and that's worse than this, kid.* He didn't pray for deliverance now. It had come from within, after all, and if death came, then he could face it as he had faced his weakness and his failings.

Another shouted command from their officer and they backed off. In Robin's case there was one last, final kick. He was bleeding, one eye almost shut, and his chest was racked with pain and coughs, but he was still alive, still an American, and he had survived one more trial. He looked over at the Captain commanding the detail. There was fury in his face, unlike that of the soldier who'd taken a few steps back. Robin wondered why.

"Stand them up!" the Captain screamed. Two of the Americans were unconscious, it turned out, and required two men each to lift them. It was the best he could do for his men. Better to kill them, but the order in his pocket prohibited that, and his army didn't tolerate the violation of orders.

Robin was now looking in the eyes of the boy who'd attacked him. Close, not six inches away. There was no emotion there, but he kept staring, and there was no emotion in his own eyes either. It was a small and very private test of wills. Not a word was spoken, though both men were breathing irregularly, one from exertion, the other from pain.

Care to try it again someday? Man to man. Think you can hack that, sonny? Do you feel shame for what you did? Was it worth it? Are you more of a man now, kid? I don't think so, and you might cover it up as best you can, but we both know who won this round, don't we? The soldier stepped to Robin's side, his eyes having revealed nothing, but the grip on the American's arm was very tight, the better to keep him under control, and Robin took that as his victory. The kid was still afraid of him, despite everything. He was one of those who roamed the sky—hated, perhaps, but feared too. Abuse was the weapon of the coward, after all, and those who applied it knew the fact as well as those who had to accept it.

Zacharias almost stumbled. His posture made it hard to look up, and he didn't see the truck until he was only a few feet away. It was a beat-up Russian vehicle, with fence wire over the top, both to prevent escape and to let people see the cargo. They were going somewhere. Robin had no real idea where he was and could hardly speculate on where he might go. Nothing could be worse than this place had been—and yet he'd survived it somehow, Robin told himself as the truck rumbled away. The camp faded into the darkness, and with it the worst trial of his life. The Colonel bowed his head and whispered a prayer of thanksgiving, and then, for the first time in months, a prayer for deliverance, whatever form it might take.

"That was your doing, Mr. Clark," Ritter said after a long, deliberate look at the phone he'd just replaced.

"I didn't exactly plan it that way, sir."

"No, you didn't, but instead of killing that Russian officer you brought him back." Ritter looked over at Admiral Greer. Kelly didn't see the nod that announced the change in his life.

"I wish Cas could have known."

"So what do they know?"

"They have Xantha, alive, in Somerset County jail. How much does she know?" Charon asked. Tony Piaggi was here, too. It was the first time the two had met. They were using the about-to-be-activated lab in east Baltimore. It would be safe for Charon to come here just one time, the narcotics officer thought.

"This is trouble," Piaggi observed. It seemed facile to the others until he went on. "But we can handle it. First order of business, though, is to worry about making our delivery to my friends."

"We've lost *twenty kees,* man," Tucker pointed out bleakly. He knew fear now. It was clear that there was something out there worthy of his fear.

"You have more?"

"Yeah, I have ten at my place."

"You keep it at home?" Piaggi asked. "Jesus, Henry!"

"The bitch doesn't know where I live."

"She knows your name, Henry. We can do a lot with just a name," Charon told him. "Why the hell do you think I've kept my people away from your people?"

"We've got to rebuild the whole organization," Piaggi said calmly. "We can do that, okay? We have to move, but moving's easy. Henry, your stuff comes in somewhere else, right? You move it in to here, and we move it out of here. So moving your operation is not a big deal."

"I lose my local—"

"Fuck local, Henry! I'm going to take over distribution for the whole East Coast. Will you think, for Christ's sake? You lose maybe twenty-five percent of what you figured you were going to take in. We can make that up in two weeks. Stop thinking small-time."

"Then it's a matter of covering your tracks," Charon went on, interested by Piaggi's vision of the future. "Xantha is just one person, an addict. When they picked her up she was wasted on pills. Not much of a witness unless they have something else to use, and if you move to another area, you ought to be okay."

"The other ones have to go. Fast," Piaggi urged.

"With Burt gone, I'm out of muscle. I can get some people I know—"

"No way, Henry! You want to bring new people in now? Let me call Philly. We have two people on retainer, remember?" Piaggi got a nod, settling that issue. "Next, we have to keep my friends happy. We need twenty kees' worth of stuff, processed and ready to go, and we need it right fast."

"I only have ten," Tucker noted.

"I know where there's some more, and so do you. Isn't that right, Lieutenant Charon?" That question shook the cop badly enough that he forgot to tell them something else that concerned him.

36

Dangerous Drugs

It was a time for introspection. He'd never done anything like this before at the behest of others, except for Vietnam, which was a different set of circumstances altogether. It had required a trip back to Baltimore, which was now as dangerous a thing as any he'd ever done. He had a new set of ID, but they were for a man known to be dead, if anyone took the time to check them out. He remembered almost fondly the time when the city had been divided into two zones—one relatively small and dangerous, and the other far larger and safe. That was changed. Now it was all dangerous. The police had his name. They might soon have his face, which would mean that every police car—there seemed an awful lot of them now—would have people in it who might spot him, just like that. Worse still, he couldn't defend himself against them, he could not allow himself to kill a police officer.

And now this . . . Things had become very confused today. Not even twenty-four hours earlier he'd seen his ultimate target, but now he wondered if it would ever be finished.

Maybe it would have been better if he had never begun, just accepted Pam's death and gone on, waiting patiently for the police to break the case. But no, they would never have broken it, would never have devoted the time and manpower to the death of a whore. Kelly's hands squeezed the wheel. And her murder would never have been truly avenged.

Could I have lived the rest of my life with that?

He remembered high school English classes, as he drove south, now on the Baltimore-Washington Parkway. Aristotle's rules of tragedy. The hero had to have a tragic flaw, had to drive himself to his fate. Kelly's flaw . . . he loved too much, cared too much, invested too much in the things and the people who touched his life. He could not turn away. Though it might save his life, to turn away would inevitably poison it. And so he had to take his chances and see things through.

He hoped Ritter understood it, understood why he was doing what he had been asked to do. He simply could not turn away. Not from Pam. Not from the men of BOXWOOD GREEN. He shook his head. But he wished they'd asked someone else.

The parkway became a city street, New York Avenue. The sun was long since down. Fall was approaching, the change of seasons from the moist heat of mid-Atlantic summer. Football season would soon begin, and baseball end, and the turning of the years went on.

Peter was right, Hicks thought. He had to stay in. His father was taking his own step into the system, after a fashion, becoming the most important of political creatures, a fund-raiser and campaign coordinator. The President would be reelected and Hicks would accumulate his own power. Then he could *really* influence events. Blowing the whistle on that raid was the best thing he had ever done. Yeah, yeah, it was all coming together, he thought, lighting up his third joint of the night. He heard the phone ring.

"How's it going?" It was Peter.

"Okay, man. How's with you?"

"Got a few minutes? I want to go over something with you." Henderson nearly swore to himself—he could tell Wally was stoned again.

"Half an hour?"

"See you then."

Not a minute later, there was a knock on the door. Hicks stubbed out his smoke and went to answer it. Too soon for Peter. Could it be a cop? Fortunately, it wasn't.

"You're Walter Hicks?"

"Yeah, who are you?" The man was about his age, if somewhat less polished-looking.

"John Clark." He looked nervously up and down the corridor. "I need to talk to you for a few minutes, if that's okay."

"What about?"

"BOXWOOD GREEN."

"What do you mean?"

"There's some things you need to know," Clark told him. He was working for the Agency now, so Clark was his name. It made it easier, somehow.

"Come on in. I only have a few minutes, though."

"That's all I need. I don't want to stay too long."

Clark accepted the waved invitation to enter and immediately smelled the acrid odor of burning rope. Hicks waved him to a chair opposite his.

"Can I get you anything?"

"No, thanks, I'm fine," he answered, careful where he put his hands. "I was there."

"What do you mean?"

"I was at SENDER GREEN, just last week."

"You were on the team?" Hicks asked, intensely curious and not seeing the danger that had walked into his apartment.

"That's right. I'm the guy who brought the Russian out," his visitor said calmly.

"You *kidnapped* a Soviet *citizen?* Why the fuck did you do that?"

"Why I did it is not important now, Mr. Hicks. One of the documents I took off his body is. It was an order to make preparations to kill all of our POWs."

"That's too bad," Hicks said with a perfunctory shake of the head. *Oh—your dog died? That's too bad.*

"Doesn't that mean anything to you?" Clark asked.

"Yes, it does, but people take chances. Wait a minute." Hicks's eyes went blank for a moment, and Kelly could see that he was trying to identify something he'd missed. "I thought we had the camp commander, too, didn't we?"

"No, I killed him myself. That bit of information was given to your boss so that we could identify the name of the guy who leaked the mission." Clark leaned forward. "That was you, Mr. Hicks. I was there. We had it wired. Those prisoners ought to be with their families right now—all twenty of them."

Hicks brushed it aside. "I didn't *want* them to die. Look, like I said, people take chances. Don't you understand, it just wasn't worth it. So what are you going to do, arrest me? For what? You think I'm dumb? That was a black operation. You can't reveal it or *you* run the risk of fucking up the talks, and the White House will never let you do that."

"That's correct. I'm here to kill you."

"What?" Hicks almost laughed.

"You betrayed your country. You betrayed twenty men."

"Look, that was a matter of conscience."

"So's this, Mr. Hicks." Clark reached into his pocket and pulled out a plastic bag. In it were drugs he'd taken off the body of his old friend Archie, and a spoon, and a glass hypodermic needle. He tossed the bag into his lap.

"I won't do it."

"Fair enough." From behind his back came his Ka-Bar knife. "I've done people this way, too. There are twenty men over there who ought to be home. You've stolen their life from them. Your choice, Mr. Hicks."

His face was very pale now, his eyes wide.

"Come on, you wouldn't really—"

"The camp commander was an enemy of my country. So are you. You got one minute."

Hicks looked at the knife that Clark was turning in his hand, and knew that he had no chance at all. He'd never seen eyes like those across the coffee table from him, but he knew what they held.

Kelly thought about the previous week as he sat there, remembering sitting in the mud generated by falling rain, only a few hundred yards from twenty men who ought now to be free. It became slightly easier for him, though he hoped never to have to obey such orders again.

Hicks looked around the room, hoping to see something that might change the moment. The clock on the mantel seemed to freeze as he considered what was happening. He'd faced the prospect of death in a theoretical way at Andover in 1962, and subsequently lived his life in accordance with the same theoretical picture. The world had been an equation for Walter Hicks, something to be managed and adjusted. He saw now, knowing it was too late, that he was merely one more variable in it, not the guy with the chalk looking at the blackboard. He considered jumping from the chair, but his visitor was already leaning forward, extending the knife a few inches, and his eyes fixed on the thin silvery line on the parkerized blade. It looked so sharp that he had trouble drawing breath. He looked at the clock again. The second hand had moved, after all.

Peter Henderson took his time. It was a weekday night, and Washington went to bed early. All the bureaucrats and aides and special-assistants-to rose early and had to have their rest so that they'd be alert in the management of their country's affairs. It made for empty sidewalks in Georgetown, where the roots of trees heaved up the concrete slabs of sidewalk. He saw two elderly folk walking their little dog, but only one other, on Wally's block. Just a man about his age, fifty yards away, getting into a car whose lawn-mower sound marked it as a Beetle, probably an older one. Damned ugly things lasted forever if you wanted them to. A few seconds later he knocked on Wally's door. It wasn't fully closed. Wally was sloppy about some things. He'd never make it as a spy. Henderson pushed the door open, ready to reprove his friend, until he saw him there, sitting in the chair.

Hicks had his left sleeve rolled up. His right hand had caught on his collar, as though to help himself breathe, but the real reason was on the inside of his left elbow. Peter didn't approach the body. For a moment, he didn't do anything. Then he knew he had to get out of here.

He removed a handkerchief and wiped the doorknob, closed the door, and walked away, trying to keep his stomach under control.

Damn you, Wally! Henderson raged. *I needed you. And to die like this— from a drug overdose.* The finality of death was as clear to him as it was unexpected. But there remained his beliefs, Henderson thought as he walked home. At least those hadn't died. He would see to that.

The trip took all night. Every time the truck hit a bump, bones and muscles screamed their protest. Three of the men were hurt worse than he was, two of them unconscious on the floor, and there wasn't a thing he could do for them with his hands and legs bound up. Yet there was satisfaction of a sort. Every destroyed bridge they had to drive around was a victory for them. Someone was fighting back; someone was hurting these bastards. A few men whispered things that the guard at the back of the truck didn't hear over the engine noise. Robin wondered where they were going. The cloudy sky denied him the reference of stars, but with dawn came an indication of where east was, and it was plain that they were heading northwest. Their true destination was too much to hope for, Robin told himself, but then he decided that hope really was something without limit.

Kelly was relieved it was over. There was no satisfaction in the death of Walter Hicks. He'd been a traitor and coward, but there ought to have been a better way. He was glad that Hicks had decided to take his own life, for he wasn't at all sure that he could have killed him with a knife—or any other way. But Hicks had deserved his fate, of that one thing he had no doubts. *But don't we all,* Kelly thought.

Kelly packed his clothing into the suitcase, which was large enough to contain it all, and carried it out to the rented car, and with that his residence in the apartment ended. It was after midnight when he drove south again, into the center of the danger zone, ready to act one last time.

Things had settled down for Chuck Monroe. He still responded to break-ins and all manner of other crimes, but the slaughter of pushers in his district had ended. Part of him thought it was too bad, and he admitted as much to other patrolmen over lunch—in his case, the mercifully unnamed three-in-the-morning meal.

Monroe drove his radio car in his almost-regular patrol pattern, still looking for things out of the ordinary. He noted that two new people had taken Ju-Ju's place. He'd have to learn their street names, maybe have an informant check them out. Maybe the narcs from downtown could start making a few things happen out here. Someone had, however briefly, Monroe admitted, heading west towards the edge of his patrol area. Whoever the hell it was. A street bum. That made him smile in the darkness. The informal name applied to the case seemed so appropriate. The Invisible Man. Amazing that the papers hadn't picked that one up. A dull night made for such thoughts. He was thankful for it. People had stayed up late to watch the Orioles sock it to the Yankees. He had learned that you could often track street crime by sports teams and their activities. The O's were in a pennant race and were looking to go all the way on the strength of Frank Robinson's bat and Brooks Robinson's glove. Even hoods liked baseball, Monroe thought, perplexed by the incongruity but accepting it for the fact it was. It made for a boring night, and he didn't mind. It gave him a chance to cruise and observe and learn, and to think. He knew all the regulars on the street now, and was now learning to spot what was different, to eyeball it as a seasoned cop could, to decide what to check out and what to let slide. In learning that he would come to prevent some crimes, not merely respond to them. It was a skill that could not come too quickly, Monroe thought to himself.

The very western border of his area was a north-south street. One side was his, the other that of another officer. He was about to turn onto it when he saw another street bum. Somehow the person looked familiar, though he was not one Monroe had shaken down several weeks earlier. Tired of sitting in his car, and bored with not having had anything more than a single traffic citation tonight, he pulled over.

"Yo, hold up there, sport." The figure kept moving, slowly, unevenly. Maybe a public-drunkenness arrest in the making, more likely a street person whose brain was permanently impaired by long nights of guzzling the cheap stuff. Monroe slid his baton into the ring holder and walked quickly to catch up. It was only a fifty-foot walk, but it was like the poor old bastard was deaf or something, he didn't even hear the click of his leather heels on the sidewalk. His hand came down on the bum's shoulder. "I said hold up, now."

Physical contact changed everything. This shoulder was firm and strong—and tense. Monroe simply wasn't ready for it, too tired, too bored, too comfortable, too sure of what he'd seen, and though his brain immediately shouted *the Invisible Man,* his body was not ready for action. That wasn't true of the bum. Almost before his hand came down, he saw the world rotate wildly from low-right to high-left, showing him a sky and then the sidewalk and then the sky again, but this time his view of the stars was interrupted by a pistol.

"Why couldn't you have just stayed in your fuckin' car?" the man asked angrily.

"Who—"

"Quiet!" The pistol against his forehead ensured that, almost. It was the surgical gloves that gave him away and forced the officer to speak.

"Jesus." It was a respectful whisper. "You're him."

"Yes, I am. Now, what the hell do I do about you?" Kelly asked.

"I ain't gonna beg." The man's name was Monroe, Kelly saw from the name tag. He didn't seem like the sort for begging.

"You don't have to. Roll over—now!" The policeman did so, with a little help. Kelly pulled the cuffs off his belt and secured them to both wrists. "Relax, Officer Monroe."

"What do you mean?" The man kept his voice even, earning his captor's admiration.

"I mean I'm not going to kill any cops." Kelly stood him up and started walking him back to the car.

"This doesn't change anything, sport," Monroe told him, careful to keep his voice low.

"Tell me about it. Where do you keep your keys?"

"Right side pocket."

"Thank you." Kelly took them as he put the officer in the backseat of the car. There was a screen there to keep arrested passengers from annoying the driver. He quickly started the patrol car and parked it in an alley. "Your hands okay, not too tight on the cuffs?"

"Yeah, I'm just fuckin' fine back here." The cop was shaking now, mainly rage, Kelly figured. That was understandable.

"Settle down. I don't want you to get hurt. I'll lock the car. Keys'll be in a sewer somewhere."

"Am I supposed to thank you or something?" Monroe said.

"I didn't ask for that, did I?" Kelly had an overwhelming urge to apologize for embarrassing the man. "You made it easy for me. Next time be more careful, Officer Monroe."

His own release of tension almost evoked a laugh as he walked away quickly to the rear. *Thank God,* he thought, heading west again, but not for everything. They're still rousting drunks. He'd hoped that they'd gotten bored with it in the past month. One more complication. Kelly kept to the shadows and alleys as much as possible.

It was a storefront, just as Billy had told him and Burt had confirmed, an out-of-business store with vacant houses to the left and right. Such talkative people, under the proper circumstances. Kelly looked at it from across the street. Despite the vacant ground level, there was a light on upstairs. The front door, he could see, was secured with a large brass lock. The back one, too, probably. Well, he could do this one the hard way . . . or the other hard way. There was a clock ticking. Those cops had to have a regular reporting system. Even if not, sooner or later Monroe would be sent a call to get somebody's kitten out of a tree, and real quick his sergeant would start wondering where the hell he was, and then the cops would be all over the place, looking for a missing man. They'd look carefully and hard. That was a possibility Kelly didn't want to contemplate, and one which waiting would not improve.

He crossed the street briskly, for the first time breaking his cover in public, such as it was, weighing risks and finding the balance evenly set on madness. But then, the whole enterprise had been mad from the start, hadn't it? First he did his best to check out the street level for people. Finding none, Kelly took the Ka-Bar from his sheath and started attacking the caulking around the full-length glass pane in the old wooden door. Perhaps burglars just weren't patient, he thought, or maybe just dumb—or smarter than he was being at the moment, Kelly told himself, using both hands to strip the caulking away. It took six endless minutes, all of it under a streetlight not ten feet away, before he was able to lower the glass, cutting himself twice in the process. Kelly swore quietly, looking at the deep cut on his left hand. Then he stepped sideways through the opening and headed for the back of the building. Some mom-and-pop store, he thought, abandoned or something, probably because the neighborhood itself was dying. Well, it could have been worse. The floor was dusty but uncluttered. There were stairs in the back. Kelly could hear noise upstairs, and he went up, his .45 leading the way.

"It's been a nice party, honey, but it's over now," a male voice said. Kelly heard the rough humor in it, followed by a female whimper.

"Please . . . you don't mean you're . . ."

"Sorry, honey, but that's just the way things are," another voice said. "I'll do the front."

Kelly eased down the corridor. Again the floor was unobstructed, just dirty. The wooden floor was old, but had been recent—

—It creaked—

"What's that?"

Kelly froze for the briefest moment, but there was neither time nor a place to hide, and he darted the last fifteen feet, then dived in low and rolled to unmask his pistol.

There were two men, both in their twenties, just shapes, really, as his mind filtered out the irrelevancies and concentrated on what mattered now: size, distance, movement. One was reaching for a gun as Kelly rolled, and even got his gun out of his belt and coming around before two rounds entered his chest and another his head. Kelly brought his weapon around even before the body fell.

"Jesus Christ! Okay! Okay!" A small chrome revolver dropped to the floor. There was a loud scream from the front of the building, which Kelly ignored as he got back to his feet, his automatic locked on the second man as though connected by a steel rod.

"They're gonna kill us." It was a surprisingly mousy voice, frightened but slow from whatever she was using.

"How many?" Kelly snapped at her.

"Just these two, they're going to—"

"I don't think so," Kelly told her, standing. "Which one are you?"

"Paula." He was covering his target.

"Where are Maria and Roberta?"

"They're in the front room," Paula told him, still too disoriented to wonder how he knew the names. The other man spoke for her.

"Passed out, pal, okay?" *Let's talk,* the man's eyes tried to say.

"Who are you?" There was just something about a .45 that made people talk, Kelly thought, not knowing what his eyes looked like behind the sights.

"Frank Molinari." An accent, and the realization that Kelly wasn't a policeman.

"Where from, Frank?—You stay put!" Kelly told Paula with a pointed left hand. He kept the gun level, eyes sweeping around, ears searching for a danger sound.

"Philly. Hey, man, we can talk, okay?" He was shaking, eyes flickering down to the gun he'd just dropped, wondering what the hell was happening.

Why was somebody from Philadelphia doing Henry's dirty work? Kelly's mind raced. Two of the men at the lab had sounded the same way. Tony Piaggi. Sure, the mob connection, and Philadelphia. . . .

"Ever been to Pittsburgh, Frank?" Somehow the question just popped out.

Molinari took his best guess. It was not a good one. "How did you know that? Who you working for?"

"Killed Doris and her father, right?"

"It was a job, man, ever do a job?"

Kelly gave him the only possible answer, and there was another scream from the front as he brought the gun back in close to his chest. Time to think. The clock was still ticking. Kelly walked over and yanked Paula to her feet.

"That hurts!"

"Come on, let's get your friends."

Maria was wearing only panties and was too stoned to do any looking. Roberta was conscious and afraid. He didn't want to look at them, not now. He didn't have time. Kelly got them together and forced them down the stairs, then outside. None had shoes, and the combination of drugs and the grit and glass on the sidewalk made them walk in a crippled fashion, whimpering and crying on their way east. Kelly pushed at them, growled at them, making them move faster, fearing nothing more grave than a passing car, because that was enough to wreck everything he'd done. Speed was vital, and it took ten minutes as endless as his race down the hill from SENDER GREEN, but the police car was still there where he'd left it. Kelly unlocked the front and told the women to get in. He'd lied about the keys.

"What the fuck!" Monroe objected. Kelly handed the keys to Paula, who seemed the best able to drive. At least she was able to hold her head up. The other two huddled on the right side, careful to keep their legs away from the radio.

"Officer Monroe, these ladies will be driving you to your station. I have instructions for you. You ready to listen?"

"I got a choice, asshole?"

"You want to play power games or do you want some good information?" Kelly asked as reasonably as he could. Two pairs of sober eyes lingered in a long moment of contact. Monroe swallowed hard on his pride and nodded.

"Go ahead."

"Sergeant Tom Douglas is the man you want to talk to—nobody else, just him. These ladies are in some really deep shit. They can help you break some major cases. Nobody but him—that's important, okay?" *You fuck that up and we'll meet again,* Kelly's eyes told him.

Monroe caught all the messages and nodded his head. "Yeah."

"Paula, you drive, don't stop for anything, no matter what he says, you got that?" The girl nodded. She'd seen him kill two men. "Get moving!"

She really was too intoxicated to drive, but it was the best he could do.

The police car crept away, scraping a telephone pole halfway down the alley. Then it turned the corner and was gone. Kelly took a deep breath, turning back to where his own auto was. He hadn't saved Pam. He hadn't saved Doris. But he had saved these three, and Xantha, at a peril to his life that had at turns been both unintentional and necessary. It was almost enough.

But not quite.

The two-truck convoy had to take a route even more circuitous than planned, and they didn't arrive at the destination until after noon. That was Hoa Lo Prison. The name meant "place of cooking fires," and its reputation was well known to the Americans. When the trucks had pulled into the courtyard and the gates were secure, the men were let down. Again, each man was given an individual guard who took him inside. They were allowed a drink of water and nothing more before assignment to individual cells that were scattered around, and presently Robin Zacharias found his. It wasn't much of a change, really. He found a nice piece of floor and sat down, tired from the journey, resting his head against the wall. It took several minutes before he heard the tapping.

Shave and a haircut, six-bits.
Shave and a haircut, six-bits.

His eyes opened. He had to think. The POWs used a communications code as simple as it was old, a graphic alphabet.

A	B	C	D	E
F	G	H	I	J
L	M	N	O	P
Q	R	S	T	U
V	W	X	Y	Z

tap-tap-tap-tap-tap pause tap-tap

5/2, Robin thought, the novelty of the moment fighting through fatigue. *Letter W. Okay, I can do this.*

2/3, 3/4, 4/2, 4/5

tap-tap-tap-tap-tap-tap . . . Robin broke that off for his reply.

4/2, 3/4, 1/2, 2/4, 3/3, 5/5, 1/1, 1/3

tap-tap-tap-tap-tap-tap

1/1, 3/1, 5/2, 1/1, 3/1, 3/1

Al Wallace? Al? He's alive?

tap-tap-tap-tap-tap-tap

HOW U? he asked his friend of fifteen years.

MAKIN IT came the reply, then an addition for his fellow Utahan.

1/3, 3/4, 3/2, 1/5, 1/3, 3/4, 3/2, 1/5, 5/4 1/5

Come, come, ye saints . . .

Robin gasped, not hearing the taps, hearing the Choir, hearing the music, hearing what it meant.

tap-tap-tap-tap-tap-tap

1/1, 3/1, 3/1 2/4, 4/3, 5/2, 1/5, 3/1, 3/1, 1/1, 3/1, 3/1 2/4, 4/3, 5/2, 1/5, 3/1, 3/1

Robin Zacharias closed his eyes and gave thanks to his God for the second time in a day and the second time in over a year. He'd been foolish, after all, to think that deliverance might not come. This seemed a strange place for it, and stranger circumstances, but there was a fellow Mormon in the next cell, and his body shuddered as his mind heard that most beloved of hymns, whose final line was not a lie at all, but an affirmation.

All is well, all is well.

Monroe didn't know why this girl, Paula, didn't listen to him. He tried reason, he tried a bellowed order, but she kept driving, albeit following his directions, creeping along the early-morning streets at all of ten miles per hour, and, at that, staying in her lane only rarely and with difficulty. It took forty minutes. She lost her way twice, mistaking right for left, and once stopped the car entirely when another of the women vomited out the window. Slowly Monroe came to realize what was happening. It was a combination of things that did it, but mainly that he had the time to dope it out.

"What did he do?" Maria asked.

"Th–th–they were going to kill us, just like the others, but he shot *them!*"

Jesus, Monroe thought. That cinched it.

"Paula?"

"Yes?"

"Did you ever know somebody named Pamela Madden?"

Her head went up and down slowly as she concentrated on the road once more. The station was in sight now.

"Dear God," the policeman breathed. "Paula, turn right into the parking lot, okay? Pull around the back . . . that's a good girl . . . you can stop right here, okay." The car jerked to a halt and Paula started crying piteously. There was nothing for him to do but wait a minute or two until she got over the worst of it, and Monroe's fear was now for them, not himself. "Okay, now, I want you to let me out."

She opened her door and then the rear one. The cop needed help getting to his feet, and she did it for him on instinct.

"The car keys, there's a handcuff key on it, can you unlock me, miss?" It took her three tries before his hands were free. "Thank you."

"This better be good!" Tom Douglas growled. The phone cord came across his wife's face, waking her up, too.

"Sergeant, this is Chuck Monroe, Western District. I have three witnesses to the Fountain Murder." He paused. "I think I have two more bodies for the Invisible Man, too. He told me I should only talk to you."

"Huh?" The detective's face twisted in the darkness. "Who did?"

"The Invisible Man. You want to come down here, sir? It's a long one," Monroe said.

"Don't talk to anybody else. Not anybody, you got that?"

"He told me that, too, sir."

"What is it, honey?" Beverly Douglas asked, as awake as her detective husband now.

It was eight months now since the death of a sad, petite girl named Helen Waters. Then Pamela Madden. Then Doris Brown. He was going to get the bastards now, Douglas told himself, incorrectly.

"What are you doing here?" Sandy asked the figure standing next to her car, the one he had fixed.

"Saying goodbye for a while," Kelly told her quietly.

"What do you mean?"

"I'm going to have to go away. I don't know for how long."

"Where to?"

"I can't really say."

"Vietnam again?"

"Maybe. I'm not sure. Honest."

It just wasn't the time for this, as though it ever was, Sandy thought. It was early, and she had to be at work at six-thirty, and though she wasn't running late, there simply weren't the minutes she needed for what had to be said.

"Will you be back?"

"If you want, yes."

"I do, John."

"Thank you. Sandy . . . I got four out," he told her.

"Four?"

"Four girls, like Pam and Doris. One's over on the Eastern Shore, the other three are here in town at a police station. Make sure somebody takes care of them, okay?"

"Yes."

"No matter what you hear, I'll be back. Please believe that."

"John!"

"No time, Sandy. I'll be back," he promised her, walking away.

Neither Ryan nor Douglas wore a tie. Both sipped at coffee from Styrofoam cups while the lab boys did their job again.

"Two in the body," one of them was saying, "one in the head—always leaves the target dead. *This* is a professional job."

"The real kind," Ryan breathed to his partner. It was a .45. It had to be. Nothing else made that kind of mess—and besides, there were six brass cartridge cases on the hardwood floor, each circled in chalk for the photographers.

The three women were in a cell in Western District, with a uniformed officer in constant attendance. He and Douglas had spoken to them briefly, long enough to know that they had their witnesses against one Henry Tucker, murderer. Name, physical description, nothing else, but infinitely more than they'd had only hours before. They'd first check their own files for the name, then the FBI's national register of felons, then the street. They'd check motor-vehicle records for a license in that name. The procedure was entirely straightforward, and with a name they'd get him, maybe soon, maybe not. But then there was this other little matter before them.

"Both of them from out of town?" Ryan asked.

"Philadelphia. Francis Molinari and Albert d'Andino," Douglas confirmed, reading the names off their driver's licenses. "How much you want to bet . . . ?"

"No bet, Tom." He turned, holding up a photograph. "Monroe, this face look familiar?"

The patrol officer took the small ID photo from Ryan's hand and looked at it in the poor light of the upstairs apartment. He shook his head. "Not really, sir."

"What do you mean? You were face-to-face with the guy."

"Longer hair, smudges on his face, mainly when we were up close I saw the front end of a Colt. Too fast, too dark."

* * *

It was tricky and dangerous, which wasn't unusual. There were four automobiles parked out front, and he couldn't afford to make any noise—but it was the safest course of action as well, with those four cars parked in front. He was standing on the marginal space provided by a sill of a bricked-up window, reaching for the telephone cable. Kelly hoped nobody was using the phone as he clipped into the wires, quickly attaching leads of his own. With that done, he dropped down and started walking north along the back of the building, trailing out his own supply of commo wire, just letting it lie on the ground. He turned the corner, letting the spool dangle from his left hand like a lunch pail, crossing the little-used street, moving casually like a person who belonged here. Another hundred yards and he turned again, entering the deserted building and climbing to his perch. Once there he returned to his rented car and got out the rest of what he needed, including his trusty whiskey flask, filled with tap water, and a supply of Snickers bars. Ready, he settled down to his task.

The rifle wasn't properly sighted in. Mad as it seemed, the most sensible course of action was to use the building as his target. He shouldered the weapon in a sitting position and searched the wall for a likely spot. There, an off-color brick. Kelly controlled his breathing, with the scope dialed to its highest magnification, and squeezed gently.

It was strange firing this rifle. The .22 rimfire is a small, inherently quiet round, and with the elaborate suppressor he'd constructed on it, for the first time in his life he heard the music-note *pingggggggg* of the striker hitting the firing pin, along with the muted *pop* of the discharge. The novelty of it almost distracted Kelly from hearing the far louder *swat* of the impact of the round on the target. The bullet created a puff of dust, two inches left and one inch high of his point of aim. Kelly clicked in the adjustment on the Leupold scope and fired again. Perfect. Kelly worked the bolt and then fed three rounds into the magazine, dialing the scope back to low power.

"Did you hear something?" Piaggi asked tiredly.

"What's that?" Tucker looked up from his task. More than twelve hours now, doing the scut-work that he'd thought to be behind him forever. Not even halfway done, despite the two "soldiers" that were down from Philadelphia. Tony didn't like it either.

"Like something falling," Tony said, shaking his head and getting back to it. The only good thing that could be said about this was that it would earn him respect when he related the tale to his associates up and down the coast. A serious man, Anthony Piaggi. When everything went to shit, he'd done the work himself. He makes his deliveries and meets his obligations. You can depend on Tony. It was a rep worth earning, even if this was the price. It was a resolute thought that persisted for perhaps thirty seconds.

Tony slit open another bag, noting the evil, chemical smell on it, not quite recognizing it for what it was. The fine white powder went into the bowl. Next he dumped in the milk sugar. He mixed the two elements with spoons, stirring it slowly. He was sure there must be a machine for this operation, but it was probably too large, like what they used at commercial bakeries. Mainly his mind was protesting that this was work for little people, hirelings. Still, he had to make that delivery, and there was no one else to help out.

"What'd you say?" Henry asked tiredly.

"Forget it." Piaggi concentrated on his task. Where the hell were Albert and Frank? They were supposed to be here a couple hours ago. Thought they were special because they whacked people, like that stuff really mattered.

"Hey, Lieutenant." The sergeant who ran the central evidence storage room was a former traffic officer whose three-wheel bike had run afoul of a careless driver. That had cost him one leg and relegated him to administrative duty, which suited the sergeant, who had his desk and his donuts and his paper in addition to clerkish duties that absorbed maybe three hours of real work per eight-hour shift. It was called retirement-in-place.

"How's the family, Harry?"

"Fine, thanks. What can I do for you?"

"I need to check the numbers on the drugs I brought in last week," Charon told him. "I think there might be a mixup on the tags. Anyway"—he shrugged—"I have to check it out."

"Okay, just give me a minute and I'll—"

"Read your paper, Harry. I know where to go," Charon told him with a pat on the shoulder. Official policy was that nobody wandered around in this room without an official escort, but Charon was a lieutenant, and Harry was short one leg, and his prosthesis was giving him trouble, as it usually did.

"That was a nice shoot, Mark," the sergeant told his back. *What the hell,* he thought, *Mark whacked the guy who'd been carrying the stuff.*

Charon looked and listened for any other person who might be here, but there was none. They'd pay him big-time for this. Talk about moving their operation, eh? Leave him out in the cold, back to chasing pushers . . . well, not entirely a bad thing. He had a lot of money banked away, enough to keep his former wife happy and educate the three kids he'd given her, plus a little for him. He'd probably even get a promotion soon because of the work he'd done, taking down several drug distributors . . . there.

The ten kilos he had taken from Eddie Morello's car were in a labeled cardboard box, sitting on the third shelf, right where they were supposed to be. He took the box down and looked to be sure. Each of the ten one-kilo bags had to be opened, tested, and resealed. The lab technician who'd done it had just initialed the tags, and his initials were easy to fake. Charon reached into his shirt and pants, pulling out plastic bags of Four-X sugar, which was of the same color and consistency as the heroin. Only his office would ever touch this evidence, and he could control that. In a month he'd send a memo recommending destruction of the evidence, since the case on it was closed. His captain would approve. He'd dump it down the drain with several other people watching, and the plastic bags would be burned, and nobody would ever know. It certainly seemed simple enough. Within three minutes he was walking away from the evidence racks.

"Numbers check out?"

"Yeah, Harry, thanks," Charon said, waving on the way out.

"Somebody get the fuckin' phone," Piaggi growled. Who the hell would be calling here, anyway? It was one of the Philly guys who walked over, taking the time to light a cigarette.

"Yeah?" The man turned. "Henry, it's for you."

"What the hell?" Tucker walked over.

"Hi, Henry," Kelly said. He'd wired a field phone into the building's telephone line, cutting it off from the outside world. He sat there, next to the canvas-covered instrument, having rung the other end just by turning the crank. It seemed rather primitive, but it was something familiar and comfortable to him, and it worked.

"Who's this?"

"The name's Kelly, John Kelly," he told him.

"So who's John Kelly?"

"Four of you killed Pam. You're the only one left, Henry," the voice said. "I got the rest. Now it's your turn." Tucker turned and looked around the room as though he expected to find the voice there. Was this some kind of sick joke that they were playing on him?

"How—how'd you get this number? Where are you?"

"Close enough, Henry," Kelly told him. "You nice and comfy in there with your friends?"

"Look, I don't know who you are—"

"I told you who I am. You're in there with Tony Piaggi. I saw you at his restaurant the other night. How was your dinner, by the way? Mine was just great," the voice taunted.

Tucker stood straight up, his hand tight on the phone. "So what the fuck are you gonna do, boy?"

"I ain't gonna kiss you on both cheeks, *boy*. I got Rick, and I got Billy, and I got Burt, and now I'm going to get you. Do me a favor, put Mr. Piaggi on the line," the voice suggested.

"Tony, you better come here," Tucker said.

"What is it, Henry?" Piaggi tripped on his chair getting up. *So damned tired from all this. Those bastards in Philly better have the cash all ready.* Henry handed him the phone.

"Who's this?"

"Those two guys on the boat, the ones you gave to Henry? I got 'em. I got the other two this morning, too."

"What the fuck is this?"

"You figure it out." The line went dead. Piaggi looked over at his partner, and since he couldn't get an answer from the phone, he'd get one from Tucker.

"Henry, what the hell is this?"

Okay, let's see what that stirred up. Kelly allowed himself a sip of water and a Snickers. He was on the third story of the building. Some sort of warehouse, he thought, massively constructed of reinforced concrete, a good place to be when The Bomb went off. The tactical problem was an interesting one. He couldn't just burst inside. Even if he'd had a machine gun—he didn't—four against one was long odds, especially when you didn't know what was inside the door, especially when stealth was something you couldn't count on as an ally, and so he'd try another approach. He'd never done anything like this before, but from his perch he could cover every door of the building. The windows in the back were bricked up. The only ways out were under his sight, and at just over a hundred yards, he hoped that they'd try it. Kelly shouldered the rifle, but kept his head up, sweeping left and right in an even, patient way.

* * *

"It's him," Henry said quietly so the others couldn't hear.

"Who?"

"The guy who did all those pushers, the guy who got Billy and the rest, the guy who did the ship. It's *him.*"

"Well, who the fuck is *him,* Henry?"

"I don't know, goddamn it!" The voice was higher now, and the other two heads looked up. Tucker got more control of himself. "He says he wants us to come out."

"Oh, that's just great—what are we up against? Wait a minute." Piaggi lifted the phone but got no dial tone. "What the hell?"

Kelly heard the buzz and lifted his handset. "Yeah, what is it?"

"Who the fuck are you?"

"It's Tony, right? Why did you have to kill Doris, Tony? She wasn't any danger to you. Now I have to do you, too."

"*I* didn't—"

"You know what I mean, but thanks for bringing those two down here. I wanted to tie that loose end up, but I didn't expect to have the chance. They're in the morgue by now, I suppose."

"Trying to scare me?" the man demanded over the scratchy phone line.

"No, just trying to kill you," Kelly told him.

"Fuck!" Piaggi slammed the phone down.

"He says he saw us at the restaurant, man. He says he was right there." It was clear to the other two that something was amiss. They were looking up now, mainly curious, but wary as they saw their two superiors in an agitated state. What the hell was this all about?

"How could he know—oh," Piaggi said, his voice trailing off to a quieter tone. "Yeah, they knew me, didn't they . . . ? Jesus."

There was only one window with clear glass. The others had glass bricks, the four-inch-square blocks favored for letting light in without being easily broken by vandals. They also prevented anyone from seeing out. The one window with clear glass had a crank, allowing the panes to open upward at an angle. This office had probably been set up by some asshole of a manager who didn't want his secretaries looking out the windows. Well, the bastard had gotten his wish. Piaggi cranked the window open—tried to, the three moving panes had only gone forty degrees before the mechanism froze.

* * *

Kelly saw it move and wondered if he should announce his presence in a more direct way. Better not to, he thought, better to be patient. Waiting grows hard on those who don't know what's happening.

The remarkable thing was that it was ten o'clock in the morning now, a clean, sunny late-summer day. There was truck traffic on O'Donnell Street, only half a block away, and some private autos as well, driving past, going about their business. Perhaps their drivers saw the tall abandoned building Kelly was in, wondering, as he was, what it had been constructed for; seeing the four automobiles parked at the former trucking building, wondering if that business was starting up again; but if they did, it wasn't worth anything more than a passing thought for people who had work to do. The drama was being played in plain sight, and only the players knew.

"I don't see shit," Piaggi said, squatting down to look out the windows. "There's nobody around."

This is the guy who did the pushers, Tucker was telling himself as he stood away from the window. *Five or six of 'em. Killed Rick with a fuckin' knife . . .*

Tony had picked the building. It was to be an ostensible part of a small interstate trucking concern whose owners were connected and very careful players. Just perfect, he'd thought, so close to major highways, quiet part of town, little police activity, just an anonymous building doing anonymous work. Perfect, Henry had thought on seeing it.

Oh, yeah, just perfect . . .

"Let me look." It wasn't time to back off. Henry Tucker didn't think of himself as a coward. He'd fought and killed, himself, and not just women. He'd spent years establishing himself, and the first part of the process hadn't been without bloodshed. Besides, he couldn't appear to be weak now, not in front of Tony and two "soldiers." "Nothin'," he agreed.

"Let's try something." Piaggi walked to the phone and lifted it. There wasn't a dial tone, just a buzz. . . .

Kelly looked at the field phone, listening to the noise it made. He'd let it be for the moment, let them do the waiting now. Though the tactical situation was of his design, still his options were limited. Talk, don't talk. Shoot, don't shoot. Move, don't move. With only three basic choices to be made, he had to select his actions carefully to achieve the desired effect. This battle was not a physical one. Like most battles, it was a thing of the mind.

It was getting warm. The last hot days before the leaves started turning.

Already eighty degrees, maybe going past ninety, one last time. He wiped perspiration from his face, watching the building, listening to the buzz, letting them sweat from something other than the heat of the day.

"Shit," Piaggi snarled, slamming the phone down. "You two!"

"Yeah?" It was the taller one, Bobby.

"Take a walk around the building—"

"No!" Henry said, thinking. "What if he's right outside? You can't see shit out that window. He could be standing right next to the door. You want to risk that?"

"What do you mean?" Piaggi asked.

Tucker was pacing now, breathing a little faster than usual, commanding himself to think. *How would I do it?* "I mean, the bastard cuts the phone line, makes his call, spooks us, and then he just waits for us right outside, like."

"What do you know about this guy?"

"I know he killed five pushers, and four of my people—"

"And four of mine if he ain't lyin'—"

"So we gotta outthink him, okay? How would you handle it?"

Piaggi thought that one over. He'd never killed. It had just never worked out that way. He was more the brains side of the business. He had roughed people up in his time, however, had delivered some fearful beatings, and that was close enough, wasn't it? *How would I do this?* Henry's idea made sense. You just stay out of sight, like around a corner, in an alley, in the shadows, and then you let them look the other way. The nearest door, the one they'd used, swung to the left, and you could tell that from the outside from where the hinges were. It also had the virtue of being closest to the cars, and since that was their only means of escape, that's the one he'd expect them to use.

Yeah.

Piaggi looked over to his partner. Henry was looking up. The acoustical panels had been removed from the drop ceiling. Right there, in the flat roof, was an access door. It was locked shut with a simple manual latch to keep burglars out. It would open easily, maybe even quietly, to the flat tar-and-gravel roof, and a guy could get up there, and walk to the edge, and look down, and whack whoever was waiting there next to the front door.

Yeah.

"Bobby, Fred, come here," Piaggi ordered. He filled them in on the tactical situation. By this time they'd guessed that something was gravely wrong, but it wasn't cops—that was the worst thing that could go wrong, they thought, and the assurance that it wasn't cops actually relieved both of them. Both had handguns. Both were smart, and Fred had killed once, taking care of a small family problem in riverside Philadelphia. The two of them slid a desk under the access door. Fred was eager to show that he was a serious guy, and so gain favor with Tony, who also looked like a serious guy. He stood on the desk. It wasn't quite enough. They put a chair atop the desk, which allowed him to open the door and look out on the roof.

Aha! Kelly saw the man standing there—actually only his head and chest were visible. The rifle came up, and the crosshairs found the face. He almost took the shot. What stopped him was the way the man had his hands on the door coaming, the way he was looking around, scanning the flat roof before he moved farther. He wanted to get up there. *Well, I guess I'll let him,* Kelly thought as a tractor-trailer rumbled past, fifty yards away. The man lifted himself up on the roof. Through his telescopic sight, Kelly could see a revolver in his hand. The man stood erect, looking all the way around, and then moved very slowly towards the front of the building. It wasn't bad tactics, really. Always a good thing to do your reconnaissance first . . . *oh, that's what they're thinking,* he thought. Too bad.

Fred had removed his shoes. The small pea-size gravel hurt his feet, and so did the heat radiating from the sticky black tar under the stones, but he had to be quiet—and besides, he was a tough customer, as someone had once learned on the bank of the Delaware River. His hands flexed familiarly on the grip of his short-barreled Smith. If the bastard was there, he'd shoot straight down. Tony and Henry would pull the body in, and they'd pour water to wash the blood away, and get back to business, because this was an important delivery. Halfway there. Fred was very concentrated now. He approached the parapeted edge with his feet in the lead, his body leaning back until his stockinged toes got all the way to the low wall of bricks that extended above the roofline. Then, quickly, he leaned forward, gun aimed downwards at—nothing. Fred looked up and down the front of the building.

"Shit!" He turned, and called, "There's nobody here!"

"What?" Bobby's head came up in the opening to look, but Fred was now checking the cars out for someone crouching there.

Kelly told himself that patience was almost always rewarded. That thought had enabled him to fight off the buck fever that always came when you had a target in your sights. As soon as his peripheral vision caught movement at the opening, he brought the gun left. A face, white, twenties, dark eyes, looking at the other one, a pistol in his right hand. Just a target now. *Take him first.* Kelly centered the crosshairs in the bridge of the nose and squeezed gently.

Smack. Fred's head turned when he heard a sound that was both wet and hard, but when he did, there was nothing there. He'd heard nothing else but that wet, sharp sound, but now there was also a clatter, as though Bobby's chair had slipped off the desk and he'd fallen to the floor. Nothing else, but for no apparent reason the skin at the back of his neck turned to ice. He backed away from the edge of the roof, looking all around at the flat, rectangular horizon just as fast as his head could turn. Nothing.

The gun was new, and the bolt still a little stiff as he drove the second round home. Kelly brought it back to the right. Two for the price of one. The head was turning rapidly now. He could see the fear there. He knew there was danger but not where or what kind. Then the man started moving back to the opening. He couldn't allow that. Kelly applied about six inches of lead and squeezed again. *Pingggggg.*

Smack. The sound of the impact was far louder than the muted *pop* of the shot. Kelly ejected the spent cartridge and slammed in another as a car approached on O'Donnell Street.

Tucker was still looking at Bobby's face when his head jerked upwards, hearing the thud of what had to be another body, rattling the steel-bar joists of the roof. ''Oh, my God . . .''

37

Trial by Ordeal

"You're looking much better than the last time, Colonel," Ritter said pleasantly in Russian. The security officer rose and walked out of the living room, giving the two men privacy. Ritter was carrying an attaché case, which he set on the coffee table. "Feeding you well?"

"I have no complaints," Grishanov said warily. "When can I go home?"

"This evening, probably. We're waiting for something." Ritter opened the case. This made Kolya uneasy, but he didn't allow it to show. For all he knew there might be a pistol in there. Comfortable as his imprisonment had been, friendly as his conversations with the residents in this place were, he was on enemy soil, under the control of enemies. It made him think of another man in a distant place under very different circumstances. The differences ate at his conscience and shamed him for his fear.

"What is that?"

"Confirmation that our people are in Hoa Lo Prison."

The Russian lowered his head and whispered something Ritter didn't catch. Grishanov looked up. "I am glad to hear that."

"You know, I believe you. Your letters back and forth to Rokossovskiy make that clear." Ritter poured himself some tea from the pot on the table, filling up Kolya's cup also.

"You have treated me correctly." Grishanov didn't know what else to say, and the silence was heavy in him.

"We have a lot of experience being friendly to Soviet guests," Ritter assured him. "You're not the first to stay here. Do you ride?"

"No, I've never been on a horse."

"Ummhmm." The attaché case was quite full with papers, Kolya saw, wondering what they were. Ritter took out two large cards and an ink pad. "Could I have your hands, please?"

"I don't understand."

"Nothing to worry about." Ritter took his left hand and inked the fingertips, rolling them one at a time in the appropriate boxes on one card, then the other. The procedure was duplicated with the right hand. "There, that didn't hurt, did it? You can wash your hands now, better to do it before the ink dries." Ritter slid one of the cards into the file, substituting it for the one removed. The other just went on top. He closed the case, then carried the old card to the fireplace, where he ignited it with his cigarette lighter. It burned fast, joining the ash pile from the fires that the custodians liked to have every other night. Grishanov came back with clean hands.

"I still don't understand."

"It's really nothing that need concern you. You just helped me out on something, that's all. What say we have lunch? Then we can meet with a countryman of yours. Please be at ease, Comrade Colonel," Ritter said as reassuringly as he could. "If your side sticks to the bargain, you'll be on your way home in about eight hours. Fair enough?"

Mark Charon was uncomfortable coming here again, safe though the location might be this early into its use. Well, this wouldn't take long. He pulled his unmarked Ford to the front of the building, got out, and walked to the front door. It was locked. He had to knock. Tony Piaggi yanked it open, a gun in his hand.

"What's this?" Charon demanded in alarm.

"What's this?" Kelly asked himself quietly. He hadn't expected the car to come right up to the building, and had been loading two more rounds into the clip when the man pulled in and got out. The rifle was so stiff that he had trouble getting the clip back in, and by the time he had it up, the figure was moving too rapidly for a shot. Damn. Of course, he didn't know who it was. He twisted the scope to max-power and examined the car. Cheap body . . . an extra radio antenna . . . police car? Reflected light prevented him from seeing the interior. Damn. He'd made a small mistake. He'd expected a down-time after dropping the two on the roof. *Never take anything for granted, dummy!* The slight error made him grimace.

*   *   *

"What the hell is going on?" Charon snapped at them. Then he saw the body on the floor, a small hole slightly above and to the left of the open right eye.

"It's him! He's out there!" Tucker said.

"Who?"

"The one who got Billy and Rick and Burt—"

"Kelly!" Charon exclaimed, turning around to look at the closed door.

"You know his name?" Tucker asked.

"Ryan and Douglas are after him—they want him for a string of killings."

Piaggi grunted. "The string is longer by two. Bobby here, and Fred on the roof." He stooped by the window again. *He's got to be right across the road there . . .*

Charon had his gun out now, for no apparent reason. Somehow the bags of heroin seemed unusually heavy now, and he set his service revolver down and unloaded them from his clothing onto the table with the rest of them, along with the mixing bowl, and the envelopes, and the stapler. That activity ended his current ability to do anything but look at the other two. That was when the phone rang. Tucker got it.

"Having fun, you cocksucker?"

"Did you have fun with Pam?" Kelly asked coldly. "So," he asked more pleasantly, "who's your friend? Is that the cop you have on the payroll?"

"You think you know it all, don't you?"

"No, not all. I don't know why a man would get his rocks off killing girls, Henry. You want to tell me that?" Kelly asked.

"Fuck you, man!"

"You want to come on out and try? You swing that way too, sweetie-pie?" Kelly hoped Tucker didn't break the phone, the way he slammed it down. He just didn't understand the game, and that was good. If you didn't know the rules, you couldn't fight back effectively. There was an edge of fatigue on his voice, and Tony's also. The one on the roof hadn't had his shirt buttoned; it was rumpled, Kelly saw, examining the body through his sight. The trousers had creases inside the knees, as though the man had been sitting up all night. Had he merely been a slob? That didn't seem likely. The shoes he'd left by the opening were quite shiny. Probably up all night, Kelly judged after a few seconds' reflection. *They're tired, and they're scared, and they don't know the game. Fine.* He had his water and his candy bars, and all day.

* * *

"If you knew that bastard's name, how come you—goddamn it!" Tucker swore. "You told me he's just a rich beach bum, I *said* I could take him out in the hospital, remember, but *no! . . .* you said leave him fuckin' be!"

"Settle down, Henry," Piaggi said as calmly as he could manage. *This is one very serious boy we have out there. He's done six of my people. Six! Jesus. This is not the time to panic.*

"We have to think this one through, okay?" Tony rubbed the heavy stubble on his face, collecting himself, thinking it through. "He's got a rifle and he's in that big white building across the street."

"You wanna just walk over there and get him, Tony?" Tucker pointed to Bobby's head. "Look what he did here!"

"Ever hear of nightfall, Henry? There's one light out there, right over the door." Piaggi walked over to the fuse box, checked the label inside the door, and unscrewed the proper fuse. "There, the light don't work anymore. We can wait for night and make our move. He can't get us all. If we move fast enough, he might not get any."

"What about the stuff?"

"We can leave one guy here to guard it. We get muscle in here to go after that bastard, and we finish business, okay?" It was a viable plan, Piaggi thought. The other guy didn't hold all the cards. He couldn't shoot through the walls. They had water, coffee, and time on their side.

The three stories were as close to word-for-word identical as anything he might have hoped for under the circumstances. They'd interviewed them separately, as soon as they'd recovered enough from their pills to speak, and their agitated state only made things better. Names, the place it had happened, how this Tucker bastard was dealing his heroin out-of-town now, something Billy had said about the way the bags stank—confirmed by the "lab" busted on the Eastern Shore. They now had a driver's license number and possible address on Tucker. The address might be bogus—not an unlikely situation—but they also had a car make, from which they'd gotten a tag number. He had it all, or at least was close enough that he could treat the investigation as something with an end to it. It was a time for him to stand back and let things happen. The all-points was just now going on the air. At the next series of squad-room briefings, the name Henry Tucker, and his car, and his tag number would be made known to the patrol officers who were the real eyes of the police force. They could get very lucky, very fast, bring him in, arraign him, indict him, try him, and put his ass away forever even if the Supreme Court had the bad grace to deny him the end his life had earned. Ryan was going to bag that inhuman bastard.

And yet.

And yet Ryan knew he was one step behind someone else. The Invisible Man was using a .45 now—not his silencer; he had changed tactics, was going for quick, sure kills . . . didn't care about noise anymore . . . and he'd talked to others before killing them, and probably knew even more than he did. That dangerous cat Farber had described to him was out on the street, hunting in the light now, probably, and Ryan didn't know where.

John T. Kelly, Chief Boatswain's Mate, U.S. Navy SEALs. Where the hell are you? If I were you . . . where would I be? Where would I go?

"Still there?" Kelly asked when Piaggi lifted the phone.

"Yeah, man, we're having a late lunch. Wanna come over and join us?"

"I had calamari at your place the other night. Not bad. Your mother cook it up?" Kelly inquired softly, wondering about the reply he'd get.

"That's right," Tony replied pleasantly. "Old family recipe, my great-grandmother brought it over from the Old Country, y'know?"

"You know, you surprise me."

"How's that, Mr. Kelly?" the man asked politely, his voice more relaxed now. He was wondering what effect it would have on the other end of the phone line.

"I expected you to try and cut a deal. Your people did, but I wasn't buying," Kelly told him, allowing irritation to show in his voice.

"Like I said, come on over and we can talk over lunch." The line clicked off.

Excellent.

"There, that ought to give the fucker something to think about." Piaggi poured himself another cup of coffee. The brew was old and thick and rancid now, but it was so heavily laced with caffeine that his hands remained still only with concerted effort. But he was fully awake and alert, Piaggi told himself. He looked at the other two, smiling and nodding confidently.

"Sad about Cas," the Superintendent observed to his friend.

Maxwell nodded. "What can I say, Will? He wasn't exactly a good candidate for retirement, was he? Family gone, here and there both. This was his life, and it was coming to an end one way or another." Neither man wanted to discuss what his wife had done. Perhaps after a year or so they might see the poetic symmetry in the loss of two friends, but not now.

"I hear you put your papers in, too, Dutch." The Superintendent of the United States Naval Academy didn't quite understand it. Talk was about that Dutch was a sure thing for a fleet command in the spring. The talk had died only days before, and he didn't know why.

"That's right." Maxwell couldn't say why. The orders—couched as a "suggestion"—had come from the White House, through the CNO. "Long enough, Will. Time for some new blood. Us World War Two guys . . . well, time to make room, I guess."

"Sonny doing okay?"

"I'm a grandfather."

"Good for them!" At least there was some good news in the room when Admiral Greer entered it, wearing his uniform for once.

"James!"

"Nice principal's office," Greer observed. "Hiya, Dutch."

"So, to what do I owe all this high-level attention?"

"Will, we're going to steal one of your sailboats. You have something nice and comfortable that two admirals can handle?"

"Wide selection. You want one of the twenty-sixes?"

"That's about right."

"Well, I'll call the Seamanship Department and have them chop one loose for you." It made sense, the Admiral thought. They'd both been close with Cas, and when you said goodbye to a sailor, you did it at sea. He placed his call, and they took their leave.

"Run outa ideas?" Piaggi asked. His voice showed defiant confidence now. The momentum had passed across the street, the man thought. Why not reinforce that?

"I don't see that you have any to speak of. You bastards afraid of the sunlight. I'll give you some!" Kelly snarled. "Watch."

He set the phone down and lifted the rifle, taking aim at the window.

Pop.

Crash.

"You dumb fuck!" Tony said into the phone, even though he knew it to be disconnected. "You see? He knows he can't get us. He knows time's on our side."

Two panes were shattered, then the shooting stopped again. The phone rang. Tony let it ring a while before he answered.

"Missed, you jerk!"

"I don't see you going anywhere, asshole!" The shout was loud enough that Tucker and Charon heard the buzz from ten feet away.

"I think it's time for you to start runnin', Mr. Kelly. Who knows, maybe we won't catch you. Maybe the cops will. They're after you too, I hear."

"You're still the ones in the trap, remember."

"You say so, man." Piaggi hung up on him again, showing who had the upper hand.

"And how are you, Colonel?" Voloshin asked.

"It has been an interesting trip." Ritter and Grishanov were sitting on the steps of the Lincoln Memorial, just two tourists tired after a hot day, joined by a third friend, under the watchful eyes of a security guard ten yards away.

"And your Vietnamese friend?"

"What?" Kolya asked in some surprise. "What friend?"

Ritter grinned. "That was just a little ploy on my part. We had to identify the leak, you see."

"I thought that was your doing," the KGB general observed sourly. It was such an obvious trap and he'd fallen right into it. Almost. Fortune had smiled on him, and probably Ritter didn't know that.

"The game goes on, Sergey. Will you weep for a traitor?"

"For a traitor, no. For a believer in the cause of a peaceful world, yes. You are very clever, Bob. You have done well." *Perhaps not,* Voloshin thought, *perhaps not as far into the trap as you believe, my young American friend. You moved too fast. You managed to kill this Hicks boy, but not* CASSIUS. *Impetuous, my young friend. You miscalculated and you really don't know it, do you?*

Time for business. "What about our people?"

"As agreed, they are with the others. Rokossovskiy confirms. Do you accept my word, Mr. Ritter?"

"Yes, I will. Very well, there's a PanAm flight from Dulles to Paris tonight at eight-fifteen. I'll deliver him there if you wish to see him off. You can have him met at Orly."

"Agreed." Voloshin walked away.

"Why did he leave me?" Grishanov asked, more surprised than alarmed.

"Colonel, that's because he believes my word, just like I believe his."
Ritter stood. "We have a few hours to kill—"

"Kill?"

"Excuse me, that's an idiom. We have a few hours of private time.
Would you like to walk around Washington? There's a moon rock in the
Smithsonian. People love to touch it for some reason."

Five-thirty. The sun was in his eyes now. Kelly had to wipe his face
more often. Watching the partly broken window, he saw nothing except an
occasional shadow. He wondered if they were resting. That wouldn't do. He
lifted the field phone and turned the crank. They made him wait again.

"Who's calling?" Tony asked. He was the formidable one, Kelly
thought, almost as formidable as he thought he was. It was a shame, really.

"Your restaurant do carry-out?"

"Getting hungry, are we?" Pause. "Maybe you want to make a deal
with us."

"Come on outside and we can talk about it," Kelly replied. The reply
was a *click*.

Just about right, Kelly thought, watching the shadows move across the
floor. He drank the last of his water and ate his last candy bar, looking around
the area again for any changes. He'd long since decided what to do. In a way,
they'd decided that for him. There was again a clock running, ticking down
to a zero-time that was flexible but finite. He could walk away from this if
he had to, but—no, he really couldn't. He checked his watch. It was going to
be dangerous, and the passage of time would not change it any more than it
already had. They'd been awake for twenty-four hours, probably longer.
He'd given them fear and let them get comfortable with it. They thought they
held a good playing hand now, just as he'd dared to hope they would.

Kelly slid backwards on the cement floor, leaving his gear behind. He'd
need it no longer no matter how this turned out. Standing, he brushed off his
clothes and checked his Colt automatic. One in the chamber, seven in the
magazine. He stretched a little, and then he knew that he could delay no
longer. He headed down the stairs, pulling out the keys to the VW. It started
despite his sudden fear that it might not. He let the engine warm up while
watching traffic on the north-south street in front of him. He darted across,
incurring the noisy wrath of a southbound driver, but fitting neatly into the
rush-hour traffic.

"See anything?"

Charon had been the one to suggest that the angles precluded Kelly from seeing all the way into their building. He might try to come across after all, they thought, but two of them could each cover one side of the white building. And they knew he was still there. They were getting to him. He hadn't thought it all the way through, Tony pronounced. He was pretty smart, but not that smart, and when it was dark, and when there were shadows, they'd make their move. It would work. A dinky little .22 wouldn't penetrate a car body if they could make it that far, and if they surprised him, they could—

"Just traffic on the other side."

"Don't get too close to the window, man."

"Fuckin' A," Henry said. "What about the delivery?"

"We got a saying in the family, man, better late than never, y'dig?"

Charon was the most uncomfortable of the three. Perhaps it was just the proximity to the drugs. Evil stuff. *A little late to think about that.* Could there be a way out of this?

The money for his delivery was right there, next to the desk. He had a gun.

To die like a criminal? He watched them there, left and right of the window. They were the criminals. He hadn't done anything to offend this Kelly. Well, nothing that he knew about. It was Henry who'd killed the girl, and Tony who'd set the other one up. Charon was just a crooked cop. This was a *personal* matter for Kelly. Not a hard thing to understand. Killing Pam that way had been brutal and foolish. He'd told Henry that. He could come out of this a hero, couldn't he? Got a tip, walked right into it. Crazy shoot-out. He could even help Kelly. And he'd never, ever get mixed up with anything like this again. Bank the money, get the promotion, and take down Henry's organization from what he knew. They'd never bust him back after that, would they? All he had to do was to get on the phone and *reason* with the man. Except for one little thing.

Kelly turned left, proceeded west one block, then left again, heading south towards O'Donnell Street. His hands were sweating now. There were three of them, and he'd have to be very, very good. But he *was* good, and he had to finish the job, even if the job might finish him. He stopped the car a block away, getting out, locking it, and walking the rest of the way to the building. The other businesses here were closed down now—he'd counted three, up and operating throughout the day, totally unaware of what was happening . . . in one case just across the street.

Well, you planned that one right, didn't you?

Yeah, Johnnie-boy, but that was the easy part.

Thanks. He stood right there at the corner of the building, looking in all directions. Better from the other side... he walked to the corner with the phone and electrical service, using the same half-windowsill he'd used before, reaching for the parapet and doing his best to avoid the electrical wires.

Okay, now you just have to walk across the roof without making any noise.

On tar and gravel?

There was one alternative he hadn't considered. Kelly stood on the parapet. It was at least eight inches wide, he told himself. It was also quiet as he walked the flat brick tightrope towards the opening in the roof, wondering if they might be using the phone.

Charon had to make his move soon. He stood, looking at the others, and stretched rather theatrically before heading in their direction. His coat was off, his tie loose, and his five-shot Smith was at his right hip. Just shoot the bastards and then talk to this Kelly character on the phone. Why not? They were *hoods,* weren't they? Why should he die for what they did?

"What are you doing, Mark?" Henry asked, not seeing the danger, too focused on the window. *Good.*

"Tired of sittin'." Charon pulled the handkerchief from his right hip pocket and wiped his face with it as he measured angles and distance, then back to the phone, where his only safety lay. He was sure of that. It was his only chance to get out of this.

Piaggi just didn't like the look in his eyes. "Why not just sit back down and relax, okay? It's going to get busy soon."

Why is he looking at the phone? Why is he looking at us?

"Back off, Tony, okay?" Charon said in a challenging voice, reaching back to replace the handkerchief. He didn't know that his eyes had given him away. His hand had barely touched the revolver when Tony aimed and fired one shot into his chest.

"Real smart guy, huh?" Tony said to the dying man. Then he noticed that the oblong rectangle of light from the roof door had a shadow in it. Piaggi was still looking at the shadow when it disappeared, replaced by a blur barely caught by his peripheral vision. Henry was looking at Charon's body.

The shot startled him—the obvious thought was that it had been aimed at himself—but he was committed, and jumped into the square hole. It was like a parachute jump, *keep your feet together, knees bent, back straight, roll when you hit.*

He hit hard. It was a tile-over-concrete floor, but his legs took the worst of it. Kelly rolled at once, straightening his arm. The nearest one was Piaggi. Kelly brought the gun up, leveling the sights with his chest and firing twice, changing aim then and hitting the man under the chin.

Shift targets.

Kelly rolled again, trained to do so by some NVA he'd met. There he was. Time stopped in that moment. Henry had his own gun out and aimed, and their eyes met and for what seemed the longest time they simply looked, hunter and hunter, hunter and prey. Then Kelly remembered, first, what the sight picture was for. His finger depressed the trigger, delivering a finely aimed shot into Tucker's chest. The Colt jumped in his hand, and his brain was running so fast now that he saw the slide dash backwards, ejecting the empty brass case, then dashing forward to feed another just as the tension in his wrist brought the gun back down, and that round, too, went into the man's chest. Tucker was off-balance from turning. Either he slipped on the floor or the impact of the two slugs destroyed his balance, dropping him to the floor.

Mission accomplished, Kelly told himself. At least he'd gotten one job done after all the failures of this bleak summer. He got to his feet and walked to Henry Tucker, kicking the gun from his hand. He wanted to say something to the face that was still alive, but Kelly was out of words. Maybe Pam would rest easier now, but probably not. It didn't work that way, did it? The dead were gone and didn't know or care what they'd left behind. Probably. Kelly didn't know how that worked, though he'd wondered about it often enough. If the dead still lived on the surface of this earth, then it was in the minds of those who remembered them, and for that memory he'd killed Henry Tucker and all the others. Perhaps Pam would not rest any more easily. But he would. Kelly saw that Tucker had departed this life while he'd been thinking, examining his thoughts and his conscience. No, there was no remorse for this man, none for the others. Kelly safed his pistol and looked around the room. Three dead men, and the best thing that could be said was that he wasn't one of them. He walked to the door, and out of it. His car was a block away, and he still had an appointment to keep, and one more life to end.

Mission accomplished.

The boat was where he'd left it. Kelly parked his car, an hour later, taking out the suitcase. He locked the car with the keys inside, for that too was something he'd never need again. The drive through town and into the marina had been blissfully empty of thought, mechanical action only, maneuvering the car, stopping for some lights, proceeding through others, heading for the sea, or the Bay, one of the few places where he felt he belonged. He hefted the suitcase, walked out the dock to *Springer,* and hopped aboard. Everything looked okay, and in ten minutes he'd be away from everything he'd come to associate with the city. Kelly slid open the door to the main salon and stopped dead when he first smelled smoke, then heard a voice.

"John Kelly, right?"

"Who might you be?"

"Emmet Ryan? You've met my partner, Tom Douglas."

"What can I do for you?" Kelly set his suitcase down on the deck, remembering the Colt automatic at the small of his back, inside the unbuttoned bush jacket.

"You can tell me why you've killed so many people," Ryan suggested.

"If you think I've done it, then you know why."

"True. I'm looking for Henry Tucker at the moment."

"He's not here, is he?"

"Maybe you could help me, then?"

"Corner of O'Donnell and Mermen might be a good place to look. He's not going anywhere," Kelly told the detective.

"What am I supposed to do about you?"

"The three girls this morning, are they—"

"They're safe. We'll look after them. You and your friends did nicely with Pam Madden and Doris Brown. Not your fault it didn't work out. Well, maybe a little." The officer paused. "I have to take you in, you know."

"What for?"

"For murder, Mr. Kelly."

"No." Kelly shook his head. "It's only murder when innocent people die."

Ryan's eyes narrowed. He saw only the outline of the man, really, with the yellowing sky behind him. But he'd heard what he said, and part of him wanted to agree with it.

"The law doesn't say that."

"I'm not asking you to forgive me. I won't be any more trouble to you, and I'm not going to any jail."

"I can't let you go." But his weapon wasn't out, Kelly saw. What did that mean?

"I gave you that Officer Monroe back."

"Thank you for that," Ryan acknowledged.

"I don't just kill people. I've been trained to do it, but there has to be a reason somewhere. I had a good enough reason."

"Maybe. Just what do you think you accomplished?" Ryan asked. "This drug problem isn't going away."

"Henry Tucker won't kill any more girls. I accomplished that. I never expected to do any more, but I took that drug operation down." Kelly paused. There was something else this man needed to know. "There's a cop at that building. I think he was dirty. Tucker and Piaggi shot him. Maybe he can come out of this a hero. There's a load of stuff there. It won't look too bad for your department that way." *And thank God I didn't have to kill a cop—even a bad one.* "I'll give you one more. I know how Tucker was getting his stuff in." Kelly elaborated briefly.

"I can't just let you go," the detective said again, though part of him wished it were otherwise. But that couldn't be, and he would not have made it so, for his life had rules, too.

"Can you give me an hour? I know you'll keep looking. One hour. It'll make things better for everybody."

The request caught Ryan by surprise. It was against everything he stood for—but then, so were the monsters the man had killed. *We owe him something . . . would I have cleared those cases without him? Who would have spoken for the dead . . . and besides, what could the guy do—where could he go? . . . Ryan, have you gone nuts?* Yes, maybe he had . . .

"You've got your hour. After that I can recommend you to a good lawyer. Who knows, a good one might just get you off."

Ryan rose and headed for the side door without looking back. He stopped at the door just for a second.

"You spared when you could have killed, Mr. Kelly. That's why. Your hour starts now."

Kelly didn't watch him leave. He hit his engine controls, warming up the diesels. One hour should just about do it. He scrambled out on the deck, slipping his lines, leaving them attached to the dock piles, and by the time he got back inside the salon, the diesels were ready for turning. They caught at once, and he pivoted the boat, heading out into the harbor. As soon as he was out of the yacht basin he firewalled both throttles, bringing *Springer* to her top speed of twenty-two knots. With the channel empty, Kelly set his autopilot and rushed to make the necessary preparations. He cut the corner at Bodkin Point. He had to. He knew who they'd send after him.

"Coast Guard, Thomas Point."

"This is the Baltimore City Police."

Ensign Tomlinson took the call. A new graduate of the Coast Guard Academy at New London, he was here for seasoning, and though he ranked the Chief Warrant Officer who ran the station, both the boy and the man understood what this was all about. Only twenty-two, young enough that his gold officer's bars still had the original shine, it was time to turn him loose on a mission, Paul English thought, but only because Portagee would really be running things. Forty-One-Bravo, the second of the station's big patrol craft, was warmed up and ready. The young ensign sprinted out, as though they might leave without him, much to the amusement of CWO English. Five seconds after the lad had snapped on his life vest, Forty-One-Bravo rumbled away from the dock, turning north short of the Thomas Point Light.

The man sure didn't give me any slack, Kelly thought, seeing the cutter closing from starboard. Well, he'd asked for an hour, and an hour he'd received. Kelly almost flipped on his radio for a parting salute, but that wouldn't have been right, and more was the pity. One of his diesels was running hot, and that was also a pity, though it wouldn't be running hot much longer.

It was a kind of race now, and there was a complication, a large French freighter standing out to sea, right where Kelly needed to be, and he would soon be caught between her and the Coast Guard.

"Well, here we are," Ritter said, dismissing the security guard who'd followed them like a shadow all afternoon. He pulled a ticket from his pocket. "First class. The booze is free, Colonel." They'd been able to skip passport control on the strength of an earlier phone call.

"Thank you for your hospitality."

Ritter chuckled. "Yeah, the U.S. government's flown you three quarters of the way around the world. I guess Aeroflot can handle the rest." Ritter paused and went on formally. "Your behavior to our prisoners was as correct as circumstances allowed. Thank you for that."

"It is my wish that they get home safely. They are not bad men."

"Neither are you." Ritter led him to the gate, where a large transfer vehicle waited to take him out to a brand-new Boeing 747. "Come back sometime. I'll show you more of Washington." Ritter watched him board and turned to Voloshin.

"A good man, Sergey. Will this injure his career?"

"With what he has in his head? I think not."

"Fine with me," Ritter said, walking away.

They were too closely matched. The other boat had a slight advantage, since it was in the lead, and able to choose, while the cutter needed her half-knot speed advantage to draw closer so painfully slowly. It was a question of skill, really, and that, too, was down to whiskers of difference from one to the other. Oreza watched the other man slide his boat across the wake of the freighter, surfing it, really, sliding her onto the front of the ship-generated wave and riding it to port, gaining perhaps half a knot's momentary advantage. Oreza had to admire it. He couldn't do anything else. The man really was sailing his boat downhill as though in a joke against the laws of wind and wave. But there was nothing funny about this, was there? Not with his men standing around the wheelhouse carrying loaded guns. Not with what he had to do to a friend.

"For Christ's sake," Oreza snarled, easing the wheel to starboard a little. "Be careful with those goddamned guns!" The other crewmen in the wheelhouse snapped the covers down on their holsters and ceased fingering their weapons.

"He's a dangerous man," the man behind Oreza said.

"No, he isn't, not to us!"

"What about all the people he—"

"Maybe the bastards had it comin'!" A little more throttle and Oreza slid back to port. He was at the point of scanning the waves for smooth spots, moving the forty-one-foot patrol boat a few feet left and right to make use of the surface chop and so gain a few precious yards in his pursuit, just as the other was doing. No America's Cup race off of Newport had ever been as exciting as this, and inwardly Oreza raged at the other man that the purpose of the race should be so perverse.

"Maybe you should let—"

Oreza didn't turn his head. "Mr. Tomlinson, you think anybody else can conn the boat better'n me?"

"No, Petty Officer Oreza," the Ensign said formally. Oreza snorted at the windowglass. "Maybe call a helicopter from the Navy?" Tomlinson asked lamely.

"What for, sir? Where you think he's goin', Cuba, maybe? I have double his bunkerage and half a knot more speed, and he's only three hundred yards ahead. Do the math, sir. We're alongside in twenty minutes any way you cut it, no matter how good he is." *Treat the man with respect,* Oreza didn't say.

"But he's dangerous," Ensign Tomlinson repeated.

"I'll take my chances. There . . ." Oreza started his slide to port now, riding through the freighter's wake, using the energy generated by the ship to gain speed. *Interesting, this is how a dolphin does it . . . that got me a whole knot's worth and my hull's better at this than his is . . .* Contrary to everything he should have felt, Manuel Oreza smiled. He'd just learned something new about boat-handling, courtesy of a friend he was trying to arrest for murder.

For murdering people who needed killing, he reminded himself, wondering what the lawyers would do about that.

No, he had to treat him with respect, let him run his race as best he could, take his shot at freedom, doomed though he might be. To do less would demean the man, and, Oreza admitted, demean himself. When all else failed there was still honor. It was perhaps the last law of the sea, and Oreza, like his quarry, was a man of the sea.

It was devilishly close. Portagee was just too damned good at driving his boat, and for that reason all the harder to risk what he'd planned. Kelly did everything he knew how. Planing *Springer* diagonally across the ship's wake was the cleverest thing he'd ever done afloat, but that damned Coastie matched it, deep hull and all. Both his engines were redlined now, and both were running hot, and this damned freighter was going just a little too fast for things. *Why couldn't Ryan have waited another ten friggin' minutes?* Kelly wondered. The control for the pyro charge was next to him. Five seconds after he hit that, the fuel tanks would blow, but that wasn't worth a damn with a Coast Guard cutter two hundred goddamned yards back.

Now what?

"We just gained twenty yards," Oreza noted with both satisfaction and sorrow.

He wasn't even looking back, the petty officer saw. He knew. He had to know. *God, you're good,* the Quartermaster First Class tried to say with his mind, regretting all the needling he'd inflicted upon the man, but he had to know that it had only been banter, one seaman to another. And in running the race this way he, too, was doing honor to Oreza. He'd have weapons there, and he could have turned and fired to distract and annoy his pursuers. But he didn't, and Portagee Oreza knew why. It would have violated the rules of a race such as this. He'd run the race as best he could, and when the time came he'd accept defeat, and there would be both pride and sadness for both men to share, but each would still have the respect of the other.

"Going to be dark soon," Tomlinson said, ruining the petty officer's reverie. The boy just didn't understand, but he was only a brand-new ensign. Perhaps he'd learn someday. They mostly did, and Oreza hoped that Tomlinson would learn from today's lesson.

"Not soon enough, sir."

Oreza scanned the rest of the horizon briefly. The French-flagged freighter occupied perhaps a third of what he could see of the water's surface. It was a towering hull, riding high on the surface and gleaming from a recent painting. Her crew knew nothing of what was going on. A new ship, the petty officer's brain noted, and her bulbous bow made for a nice set of bow waves that the other boat was using to surf along.

The quickest and simplest solution was to pull the cutter up behind him on the starboard side of the freighter, then duck across the bow, and *then* blow the boat up . . . but . . . there was another way, a better way . . .

"Now!" Oreza turned the wheel perhaps ten degrees, sliding to port and gaining fully fifty yards seemingly in an instant. Then he reversed his rudder, leaped over another five-foot roller, and prepared to repeat the maneuver. One of the younger seamen hooted in sudden exhilaration.

"You see, Mr. Tomlinson? We have a better hull form for this sort of thing than he does. He can beat us by a whisker in flat seas, but not in chop. This is what we're made for." Two minutes had halved the distance between the boats.

"You sure you want this race to end, Oreza?" Ensign Tomlinson asked.

Not so dumb after all, is he? Well, he was an officer, and they were supposed to be smart once in a while.

"All races end, sir. There's always a winner and always a loser," Oreza pointed out, hoping that his friend would understand that, too. Portagee reached in his shirt pocket for a cigarette and lit it with his left hand while his right—just the fingertips, really—worked the wheel, making tiny adjustments as demanded by the part of his brain that read and reacted to every ripple on the surface. He'd told Tomlinson twenty minutes. He'd been pessimistic. Sooner than that, he was sure.

Oreza scanned the surface again. A lot of boats out, mostly heading in, not one of them recognizing the race for what it was. The cutter didn't have her police lights blinking. Oreza didn't like the things: they were an insult to his profession. When a cutter of the United States Coast Guard pulled alongside, you shouldn't need police lights, he thought. Besides, this race was a private thing, seen and understood only by professionals, the way things ought to be, because spectators always degraded things, distracted the players from the game.

He was amidships on the freighter now, and Portagee had swallowed the bait . . . as he had to, Kelly thought. Damn but that guy was good. Another mile and he'd be alongside, reducing Kelly's options to precisely zero, but he did have his plan now, seeing the ship's bulbous bow, partly exposed. A crewman was looking down from the bridge, as on that first day with Pam, and his stomach became hollow for a moment, remembering. So long ago, so many things in between. Had he done right or wrong? Who would judge? Kelly shook his head. He'd let God do that. Kelly looked back for the first time in this race, measuring distance, and it was damnably close.

The forty-one boat was squatting back on her stern, pitched up perhaps fifteen degrees, her deep-displacement hull cutting through the choppy wake. She rocked left and right through a twenty-degree arc, her big down-rated marine diesels roaring in their special feline way. And it was all in Oreza's hands, throttles and wheels at his skilled fingertips while his eyes scanned and measured. His prey was doing exactly the same, milking every single turn from his own engines, using his skill and experience. But his assets added up short of Portagee's, and while that was too bad, that's how things were.

Just then Oreza saw the man's face, looking back for the first time.

It's time, my friend. Come on, now, let's end this honorably. Maybe you'll get lucky and you'll get out after a while and we can be friends again.

"Come on, cut power and turn to starboard," Oreza said, hardly knowing he spoke, and each man of his crew was thinking exactly the same thing, glad to know that they and their skipper were reading things the same way. It had been only a half-hour race, but it was the sort of sea story they would remember for their whole careers.

The man's head turned again. Oreza was barely half a ship-length back now. He could easily read the name on the transom, and there was no sense stringing it out to the last foot. That would spoil the race. It would show a meanness of spirit that didn't belong on the sea. That was something done by yachtsmen, not professionals.

Then Kelly did something unexpected. Oreza saw it first, and his eyes measured the distance once, then twice, and a third time, and in every case the answer came up wrong, and he reached for his radio quickly.

"Don't try it!" the petty officer shouted onto the "guard" frequency.

"What?" Tomlinson asked quickly.

Don't do it! Oreza's mind shouted, suddenly alone in a tiny world, reading the other's mind and revolting at the thought it held. This was no way for things to end. There was no honor in this.

Kelly eased his rudder right to catch the bow wave, his eyes watching the foaming forefoot of the freighter. When the moment was right, he put the rudder over. The radio squawked. It was Portagee's voice, and Kelly smiled hearing it. What a good guy he was. Life would be so lonely without men such as he.

Springer lurched to starboard from the force of the radical turn, then even more from the small hill of water raised by the freighter's bow. Kelly held on to the wheel with his left hand and reached with his right for the air tank around which he'd strung six weight belts. *Jesus,* he thought instantly as *Springer* went over ninety degrees, *I didn't check the depth. What if the water's not deep enough—oh, God . . . oh, Pam. . . .*

The boat turned sharply to port. Oreza watched from only a hundred yards away, but the distance might as well have been a thousand miles for all the good it did, and his mind saw it before reality caught up: already heeling hard to the right from the turn, the cruiser rode up high on the curling bow-wave of the freighter and, crosswise to it, rolled completely over, her white hull instantly disappearing in the foaming forefoot of the cargo ship . . .

It was no way for a seaman to die.

Forty-One-Bravo backed down hard, rocking violently with the passage of the ship's wake as she came to a stop. The freighter stopped at once, too, but it took fully two miles, and by that time Oreza and his cutter were poking through the wreckage. Searchlights came on in the gathering darkness, and the eyes of the coastguardsmen were grim.

"Coast Guard Forty-One, Coast Guard Forty-One, this is U.S. Navy sailboat on your port beam, can we render assistance, over?"

"We could use some extra eyes, Navy. Who's aboard?"

"Couple of admirals, the one talking's an aviator, if that helps."

"Join in, sir."

He was still alive. It was as much a surprise to Kelly as it would have been to Oreza. The water here was deep enough that he and the air tank had plummeted seventy feet to the bottom. He fought to strap the tank to his chest in the violent turbulence of the passing ship overhead. Then he fought to swim clear of the descending engines and heavy gear from what had seconds earlier been an expensive cruiser. Only after two or three minutes did he accept the fact that he'd survived this trial by ordeal. Looking back, he wondered just how crazy he'd been to risk this, but for once he'd felt the need to entrust his life to judgment superior to his own, prepared to take the consequences either way. And the judgment had spared him. Kelly could see the Coast Guard hull over to the east . . . and to the west the deeper shape of a sailboat, pray God the right one. Kelly disengaged four of the weight belts from the tank and swam towards it, awkwardly because he had it on backwards.

His head broke the surface behind the sailboat as it lay to, close enough to read the name. He went down again. It took another minute to come up on the west side of the twenty-six-footer.

"Hello?"

"Jesus—is that you?" Maxwell called.

"I think so." *Well, not exactly.* His hand reached up.

The doyen of naval aviation reached over the side, hauled the bruised and sore body aboard, and directed him below.

"Forty-One, this is Navy to your west now . . . this doesn't look real good, fella."

"I'm afraid you're right, Navy. You can break off if you want. I think we'll stay a while," Oreza said. It had been good of them to quarter the surface for three hours, a good assist from a couple of flag officers. They even handled their sailboat halfway decent. At another time he'd have taken the thought further and made a joke about Navy seamanship. But not now. Oreza and Forty-One-Bravo would continue their search all night, finding only wreckage.

It made the papers in a big way, but not in any way that made sense. Detective Lieutenant Mark Charon, following up a lead on his own time— on administrative leave following a shooting, no less—had stumbled into a drug lab and in the ensuing gun battle had lost his life in the line of duty while ending those of two major traffickers. The coincidental escape of three young women resulted in the identification of one of the deceased traffickers as a particularly brutal murderer, which perhaps explained Charon's heroic zeal, and closed a number of cases in a fashion that the police reporters found overly convenient. On page six was a squib story about a boating accident.

Three days later, a file clerk from St. Louis called Lieutenant Ryan to say that the Kelly file was back but she couldn't say from where. Ryan thanked her for her effort. He'd closed that case along with the rest, and didn't even try the FBI records center for Kelly's card, and thus made unnecessary Bob Ritter's substitution of the prints of someone unlikely ever to visit America again.

The only loose end, which troubled Ritter greatly, was a single telephone call. But even criminals got one phone call, and Ritter didn't want to cross Clark on something like that. Five months later, Sandra O'Toole resigned her position at Johns Hopkins and moved to the Virginia tidewater, where she took over a whole floor of the area's teaching hospital on the strength of a glowing recommendation from Professor Samuel Rosen.

February 12, 1973

"We are honored to have the opportunity to serve our country under difficult circumstances," Captain Jeremiah Denton said, ending a thirty-four-word statement that rang across the ramp at Clark Air Force Base with "God bless America."

"How about that," the commentator said, sharing the experience as he was paid to do. "Right there behind Captain Denton is Colonel Robin Zacharias, of the Air Force. He's one of the fifty-three prisoners about whom we had no information until very recently, along with . . ."

John Clark didn't listen to the rest. He looked at the TV that sat on his wife's dresser in the bedroom, at the face of a man half a world away, to whom he'd been much closer in body, closer still in spirit not so long before. He saw the man embrace his wife after what had to be five years of separation. He saw a woman who'd grown old with worry, but now was young with love for the husband she'd thought dead. Kelly wept with them, seeing the man's face for the first time as a thing of animation, seeing the joy that really could replace pain, no matter how vast. He squeezed Sandy's hand so hard that he almost hurt it until she rested his on her belly to feel the movement of their soon-to-be firstborn. The phone rang then, and Kelly was angry for the invasion of the moment until he heard the voice.

"I hope you're proud of yourself, John," Dutch Maxwell said. "We're getting all twenty back. I wanted to make sure you knew that. It wouldn't have happened without you."

"Thank you, sir." Clark hung up. There was nothing else to be said.

"Who was that?" Sandy asked, holding his hand in place.

"A friend," Clark said, wiping his eyes as he turned to kiss his wife. "From another life."